MONUMENTS OF GRASS

~

BOOK FOUR – NEW FRANCE

MONUMENTS OF GRASS

An American Romance

~

BOOK FOUR – NEW FRANCE

1900

* * *

BRENDAN FRAIN

A catalogue record for this
book is available from the
National Library of Australia

For Sat,
Upon my soul

Introduction

I N 1867 SEVERAL SELF-GOVERNING British colonies in North America including Quebec, Ontario, New Brunswick and Nova Scotia united to form a federal union that became the Dominion of Canada. At the time, Quebec was steeped in a conservative Catholicism which was one badge of its distinctive identity within Confederation, the French language being the other. Catholic religious institutions operated hospitals, charities, orphanages and schools and the church was an all-pervasive presence in the daily lives of Quebecers, providing a sense of shared destiny.

"For over a century, French Canadian nationalism was generally linked to conservative causes and to the perpetuation of a traditional society. For the clerical and professional elite, fidelity to language, culture and religion implied respect for the acceptance of the established social order in which the Roman Catholic Church dominated, agriculture was lauded as society's material and moral foundation, parish and family were the basic social institutions, commercial and industrial pursuits were disdained, and foreign influences were shunned."[1]

The determination to maintain Quebec's distinctive society was demonstrated by French-Canadian opposition to the Boer War in South Africa—supported by English Canada—and, again, during the First World War and the conscription crisis.

Language and religion

Maintaining the French language and the Catholic faith in a sea of Protestant English-speakers is a recurrent theme in the history of French-speaking Canada. While the power and influence of the Catholic Church has waned since the so-called 'Quiet Revolution' of the sixties, the Catholic church was still a dominating influence on French-Canadian lives at the turn of the 20th century. But as the status of Catholicism diminished, the importance of linguistic identity increased, especially in the area of education.

In 1890 the government of Manitoba—constitutionally a bilingual province—revoked the status of French as an official language. It went further and created a system of non-denominational schools with English as the language of instruction and restricted public funding to these schools. Catholic schools, pre-dominantly French speaking, would now have to rely on private funding.

In 1912 Ontario introduced Regulation 17, limiting French instruction to the first two years of primary school. It took years of French-Canadian resistance and acts of civil disobedience before Regulation 17 was scrapped in 1927. But the attempts to limit French language education and Catholic instruction in schools entrenched a feeling of Anglophone oppression among Quebecers and increased the emotive appeal of French-Canadian nationalism.

The fictional region of New France is subject to all of the above tensions while, in addition, fiercely protective of its semiautonomous status within Quebec and Canada as a whole.

1. French Canadian Nationalism | The Canadian Encyclopaedia

Contents

NEW FRANCE

There is no remembrance of former things,
neither shall there be remembrance of things
that shall come after.

—ECCLESIASTES 1:11

Ab Initio

GRIPPING THE RIFLE, HUGO Gagnon followed an elk path through the undergrowth. Circling away from his companions, he stepped silently through the snowy brush, vigilant for the snorting grunt of a deer. Reaching a small clearing he took up position behind a fallen tree and settled down to wait. He had barely assumed position when he heard a cracking sound in the bushes on the far side of the clearing. The branches of a hemlock rustled, and he glimpsed a mottled, indistinct form through the dense foliage. Expecting a deer, he was astounded to glimpse a bear moving through the foliage, rooting among the ferns for berries or pinecones.

Trembling at this rare opportunity to impress his comrades, he levelled the Winchester as the bear ambled through the brush towards the clearing. As he waited for the bear to advance into the open, something gave him pause. He released his finger from the trigger, confused by the nature of the beast before him. Surely, the creature was not travelling on its hind legs! He strained to see past the screening foliage his nerves on edge. The bear emerged from the shadows into a pool of brilliant sunlight and Hugo gasped in horror. 'Mother of God!' He crossed himself, his blood turning to ice.

The apparition before him stood tall as a man, its carriage unnaturally upright as it stood suspended in the shafting sunlight. The torso was protected by a dense layer of brown fur while the savage head was framed by a bristling black mane. The strange hybrid appeared to be testing the air, suspiciously turning its head this way and the other as if scenting the hidden danger. The hairs on the back of Hugo's neck stood up as he realised the creature was communing with itself in a strange, other-worldly voice.

He backed up through the trees, his fearful gaze never once straying from the spectre before him. A twig cracked loudly beneath his feet, and he froze in horror as the beast whirled and gave a baleful stare in his direction. For a long moment, hunter and prey stared at each other. And then the creature emitted a trembling, low-pitched wail and took a step forward—in threat or supplication the Frenchman could not tell.

'Christ and all the saints protect me!' With shaking hands Hugo aimed the rifle and fired. The beast gave a fearsome cry and vanished. Hastily reloading, Hugo fired into the air while loudly calling upon his companions for help.

'Hugo!' Calling out his name, his companions rushed through the trees to his aid. They found him sat in the shelter of a thicket, his face pale with fright.

'It's the Painted One!' He pointed shakily to where the creature had disappeared.

Exchanging glances, his companions assisted him to his feet. They were dressed alike in hooded capotes, fur-lined gloves, leather boots and woollen toques. They listened with disbelieving faces as Hugo gasped out what he had seen.

'Only you, Hugo Gagnon, could hunt for deer and find the devil!' Denis Vachon's voice left no doubt as to his exasperation at this interruption to the hunt.

'You didn't see it! The beast was unnatural.'

'Then where is it?' Claude Charbonneau searched the surrounding trees, his eyes alert for movement. 'If it truly was the devil then where the devil did it go?' He grinned at his own joke.

'It was there a moment ago.' Still badly shaken by the encounter, Hugo pulled off his gloves and blew on his fingers. 'I must have hit it because the creature gave out an unearthly wail, like a soul in torment.'

Martin Cloutier cursed, his breath spurting into the air. 'I'm freezing my balls! Let's find this beast, whatever it is.'

Venturing forward, the party came to the edge of a ravine. Claude Charbonneau peered at the dense brush below. 'I don't see it. Your devil seems to have vanished.'

'There!' Martin Cloutier pointed to a patch of blood in the snow. Close by, something lay half-concealed in a thick growth of maidenhair ferns. The companions strained to make out the dark shape amidst the fronds.

'By the Holy Cross!' Charbonneau stared, nonplussed. 'What is it?'

'It's a bear, what else?'

'It doesn't look like a bear.'

They peered, struggling to identify the beast.

'It's a wood … thing of some kind,' Cloutier speculated, recalling Indian legends of a sinister two-legged creature that stalked the deep woods. Leaning forward, he pointed to the elongated limbs. 'Witness the unnatural shape,' he said, as further evidence for the claim.

'It looks almost human,' Vachon admitted, his earlier scepticism giving way to doubt.

'It may be the fruit of some sinful miscegenation,' suggested Charbonneau, having read of such things in *The Catholic Chronicles*. His companions hastily signed to ward off evil spirits.

'We should go down and see, to make sure,' said Cloutier. The suggestion drew an exchange of looks.

'Hugo, you shot it, it's your responsibility.'

'Me? Why don't you go.'

Vachon grunted, his scepticism returning. 'We'll all go—unless you don't have the balls?'

'Then lead the way!'

After a moment's hesitation, Vachon began to descend the steep slope, the others following.

'Careful, it's slippery!'

Reaching the bottom, they advanced cautiously, ready to fire should the creature leap up as they approached. It lay half-concealed in the ferns, its brown fur sprinkled with snow. Something abnormal about its appearance prickled the hairs on the back of Charbonneau's neck.

'Be careful! It has snares!' warned Hugo as Vachon gingerly poked the insensible beast with his rifle barrel.

'By the Cross, it's a man!' Vachon directed a shocked look at Hugo. 'You shot a man!'

'He's right.' confirmed Cloutier, bending to see. 'That's a buffalo coat he's wearing. My grandfather had one just like it.'

'What the fuck is going on?' Emerging from the trees, Serge Villeneuve elbowed his way past the companions.

'Hugo shot someone!'

'I swear to God, I thought it was a bear!'

Villeneuve knelt beside the prostrate figure and brushed aside the ferns. 'He's breathing.' He peered closely at the bloodied scalp. 'But I don't like his chances, whoever he is. The poor prick looks fucked.' He looked up at Hugo. 'Finally, you hit something!'

'He looked like a bear—in that coat!'

'What in God's name was he doing in the woods?'

'From the looks of him, I'd say he was lost, or starving.'

'I don't recognise him.' Charbonneau bent to scrutinise the ravaged features.

'He may be a bandit,' suggested Cloutier, 'and dangerous.'

Villeneuve snorted, gesturing at the comatose stranger. 'Here be your dangerous bandit!'

'What should we do with him?'

'Do?' Villeneuve frowned. 'We get him to the hospital. What in Christ's name do you think?'

Charbonneau glanced at Hugo. 'There'll be questions.'

'Are you mad! We can't leave him here.'

'What's that?' Vachon edged the ferns aside with his foot to reveal a stained, canvas haversack.

'Open it! It may contain gold.' urged Charbonneau.

'Remember, we all found him,' Cloutier thought it prudent to remark.

Vachon rummaged inside the haversack. 'It's a Bible!' He muttered in astonishment as he withdrew the volume. 'It's soaked. He must have dropped it in the snow.' He pried open the sodden pages. 'Mother of God!'

'What is it?'

'The Holy Scriptures—in English.'

'What's an Englishman doing here—and carrying a Bible?'

Mystified, the companions looked at each other. 'It may not be his own,' Charbonneau pointed out.

'Then why else would he carry it through these infernal woods?'

Charbonneau pondered this. 'Perhaps he found it,' he speculated.

The companions stared, intrigued, at the wounded man.

'Is he Catholic?' asked Hugo, his guilt compounded.

'How the devil should I know?'

'If he's English, then he's most likely Protestant,' suggested Cloutier.

'Give it here!' Taking the book, Villeneuve examined the inside cover. 'There must be a name,' he said, turning the water-soaked flyleaves. 'Hugo, you're the only one of us that speaks English, you look.' He handed the Bible to Hugo.

Hugo turned the wet pages, careful lest they tear. 'There's nothing— wait!' His eyes fixed on a coloured plate. 'It's a marriage record. I can't make out the date. The ink's all blotted.' He peered closely. 'There's a date! 1838. Or perhaps '28.' He held the page closer to his eyes. 'Ab … Abb … Abe! Abe … Wheeler. Abe is short for "Abraham" among the English,' he explained.

'1838? What good does that do?'

'At least we have his name—his family name. What did you say it was?'

'Wheeler. Abraham Wheeler.'

'That must be the fellow's grandfather,' suggested Claude.

'How do you know it's his grandfather?'

'Well, it can't be him. Does he look 62-years old?'

'There's money!' Hugo tugged a wad of soiled banknotes from between the pages. 'American dollars.'

'How much?' Charbonneau stepped forward to look. 'We should split it equally,' he said.

'Why on earth would we do that?' With a frown at his companion, Hugo put the notes in the pocket of his capote. 'I'll keep them for him until he recovers.'

'*If* he recovers.' Disgruntled, Charbonneau stepped back. 'Besides, the money may be stolen.'

Villeneuve looked down at the prostrate figure. 'Well, Monsieur, who-ever you are, we'd better get you to the hospital. Denis, Hugo. Go back and fetch the wagon. Be quick!'

THEY LIFTED THE INSENSIBLE stranger onto the wagon bed and set off on the trek back to town. Serge Villeneuve and Martin Cloutier shared the bench seat while Hugo, Claude Charbonneau and Denis Vachon sat in the back alongside the wounded man. The wagon struck a rut, and the stranger uttered an agonised groan.

'Hurry up, Serge! Can't you make those donkeys go faster?'

'He looks feverish. I doubt he'll make it.'

'Don't say that!'

Denis frowned at Hugo. 'Why not? It would make things easier for you.'

'It was an accident,' objected Claude. 'There can be no blame attached to Hugo.'

Denis shrugged. 'Tell our friend that.'

'He looks dead already.' Claude leaned over the wounded man, 'and he's white as a ghost. He's not long for this world if you ask me. I doubt he'll live to see the hospital—or anyplace else.'

'Saint Raphael, protect him.' Hugo fished inside his shirt and withdrew a crucifix from around his neck. He pressed it between his fingers, closing his eyes in prayer.

'He needs a doctor, not a saint. Mother of God!' Denis drew back in fright as the man suddenly convulsed, coughing up blood. 'Serge! He's not going to last to the hospital.'

Villeneuve turned in the seat, taking in the convulsive figure and the blood bubbling from his mouth. 'I've an idea,' he said. 'The midwife lives close by. We'll take him there.'

'The Indian?' Claude looked nonplussed at the suggestion.

'She knows medicine. She set my brother's arm when he fell out of the tree.'

The others exchanged glances.

'She's no better than a fishwife!'

'Madame Beaulieu swears by her,' insisted Villeneuve. 'She claims she saved her daughter's baby from the fever when the doctors had given up on her. What do you say, Hugo? It's up to you.'

Hugo twisted the crucifix, his face anguished. 'I don't know! What is best?'

'He won't live to get to the hospital. And the midwife's cabin is not far.'

'And there'll be no questions asked,' added Denis.

'Well?' Villeneuve waited for an answer.

'Alright. But hurry, for God's sake!'

'Hi-yup!' cried Villeneuve and snapped the whip.

A SHORT TIME LATER, Villeneuve reined to a halt. They were stopped in a clearing before a small cabin, smoke wisping from its chimney. Climbing down, Villeneuve mounted the porch steps and banged on the door. 'Midwife! Open up! We have a wounded man with us!'

He turned to look at the others as they lifted the stricken man out of the wagon and began to carry him up the steps. 'Hurry!' He banged on the door again.

'Hold your balls! Who knocks my door down!' The door opened a crack and an annoyed face peered out. 'Who are you?'

'Midwife, it's me, Serge Villeneuve. You set my brother's arm when he broke it. Do you remember?'

The door opened further. 'Who's that?' The voice was suspicious as the unseen figure took in the wounded man.

'He's a stranger. We found him in the woods. He's been shot. Can you help?'

The door opened and a short, remarkably fat woman dressed in a calico blouse and thick wool skirt emerged. Her skin was the colour of varnished walnut. Grumbling at the intrusion, she bent to squint at the wounded man. 'He looks fucked.'

'He's still alive. Can you help?'

She sniffed. 'Who'll pay me?'

'I will! My name is Hugo Gagnon, Madame. I will guarantee payment for his treatment.'

The woman deliberated a moment longer. 'Bring him in.' She gripped Hugo by the sleeve. 'Payment in advance,' she said. 'I'm not your Jesus that can work miracles.'

They laid the wounded man down on the plank floor in front of a roaring fire. The cabin was cluttered with bric-a-brac. A strong, earthy smell of herbs and lotions filled the air. A faded, decorative deerskin was tacked above the hearth.

The midwife grimaced as she bent to examine the wounded man. 'Who shot him?' she asked.

'We found him like that,' said Villeneuve with a warning glance at Hugo. 'The authorities will have to be informed.'

'Why? He's a stranger,' objected Claude. 'He has no family here.'

'He's English,' volunteered Denis.

'Then pay me extra for my trouble.'

'Anything! But for God's sake help him.'

'Leave him with me. But I make no promises. I cannot raise the dead! Help me take that coat off him.'

'It made him look like a bear!' insisted Hugo as they divested the stranger of his coat.

The midwife fetched a bearskin and used it to cover the insensible man.

'Come on boys.' Villeneuve made for the door. 'We'll check on him tomorrow. Hugo?'

'Here.' Hugo pressed a five-dollar bill into the midwife's hand. 'I'll come back tomorrow and settle up if more is required.' He took one last look at where the stranger lay unmoving, his face drawn and bloodless in the firelight. 'God be with you, Monsieur!'

'WELL, THAT'S THAT. WE did our best.' Denis announced as they resumed their journey back to town. 'Our conscience is clear.'

'Clear? We shot him!'

'*You* shot him!'

'You were with me!'

'Close by,' corrected Denis, 'close by.'

'Christ's blood!' Serge turned in the seat. 'You quarrel like a bunch of old women!'

'The poor bastard is in God's hands now. You did all that you could, Hugo,' offered Claude.

'I could have not shot him!'

'For God's sake! It was an accident.'

'I wonder who he is?' said Denis.

The woods thinned out as they followed a wagon track. Villeneuve hailed a man hauling some cut logs on a sledge, his breath puffing in the cold air. The sky was grey with cloud, a biting wind making them huddle into their capotes.

Before long the stone walls surrounding the town came into view. The track led to an arched entrance way flanked by flagpoles set above the open gates. The fleur-de-lis fluttered from one pole, a white and green flag from the other.

The dirt road turned to pavers as they passed beneath the arch and followed the road where it led into the town. The two-horse team snorted, their hot breaths rising like steam, their hooves clopping on the stone. The road passed by a military barracks. On the ramparts two soldiers clad in heavy wool coats looked down as the wagon clattered past.

They came to the outer environs of the town, the wagon slowing as it creaked past the church of Sainte-Chappelle with its distinctive bell tower. In spite of the weather, the streets were busy, pedestrians bundled up against the cold as they went about their affairs.

Hugo sighed, his thoughts in turmoil as the fate of the dying man—for so he thought of him—pressed heavily upon his conscience. 'What time is it?' he asked. The others, absorbed in their own thoughts, made no answer. They passed a bakery on rue Saint-Denis and the smell of fresh pastries came to his nose. Josette would love a religieuse, he thought distractedly, the taste of crème pâtisserie filling his mouth.

Behind them, the bells of Sainte-Chappelle rang out. He counted the peals. Three o' clock. The number struck him as significant, mystical even, given the circumstances. 'They are just bells, Hugo,' he imagined Josette saying. Perhaps, he told himself, and perhaps not.

'Let me off here.' Denis stood up, holding onto the side of the wagon.

'Me, too.' Hugo balanced himself, looping the rifle across his shoulder.

The wagon halted to allow himself and Denis to scramble over the side.

Villeneuve turned and pressed a finger to his lips. 'Keep what happened between us. If the stranger dies, there'll be an investigation. Remember, we just happened across him in the woods. Not a word of who fired the shot. We say we found him like that. Hugo keep your conscience on a leash, understood?'

Hugo nodded as Villeneuve started the wagon forward again.

'So long!' Martin Cloutier called out, touching a finger to his wool toque.

'Don't fret about the Englishman, Hugo.' Denis's voice was sympathetic as the wagon creaked off. 'I'm sure the midwife will patch him up. And if not …' He shrugged. 'The authorities will write it off as a hunting accident—as it was. They happen every year. 'What a day! Remember, say nothing to Josette, do you hear? Save your conscience for Père Boudreau and the confessional.'

The two companions shook hands and parted ways.

Hugo crossed the road to rue de l'Èglise, his thoughts consumed by the shooting. *Why did he have to emerge from the trees just there—right in front of me? Did he not think that coat would make him a target?* Torn between blame and self-exculpation, he made his way up the steep street, careful not to slip on the ice-slicked cobbles. He stepped into the road to pass a pair of men unloading a goods wagon. *The trees were so thick, who could see anything? And that coat!*

He reached the *Couvent des Ursulines* at the top of the hill. A procession of nuns clad in wimples and flowing black tunics exited the stone walls, wool coats over their vestments. He stood aside and bowed his head as the sisters began their descent of the cobbled street. To his surprise, Bishop Drolet himself strolled along behind the sisters, his arm linked with Bernard Benoit with whom he was deeply engaged in conversation.

'Good day to you, Monseigneur, and to you, Monsieur Benoit.'

The prelate looked up, startled. 'Gracious, Monsieur Gagnon!' He lifted his hand in reflexive blessing as he passed. The merchant nodded peremptorily and continued the conversation, holding the bishop lightly by the elbow as if to steer him down the winding street.

Two blocks further on, Hugo turned into rue Henri Brisson, heartily relieved to see his own front door further along the street.

HE SANK INTO THE upholstered chair, still severely shaken by the incident. Josette poured a glass of brandy as he blurted out the entire, tragic affair while protesting his complete innocence in the matter.

'He wore a buffalo coat! The same colour as a bear. Imagine! It could have been anyone—Serge, Denis, Claude, or Martin who shot him. It just happened to be my bad luck.' He gulped the brandy, his hand trembling as he held the glass.

Josette, a handsome young woman with a head of rich, chestnut-coloured hair sat down in the other chair. She wore a beige blouse with a long grey skirt and a wool shawl around her shoulders, 'It was an accident, as you say,' she said, in a practical voice. 'There is no blame to anyone. Where is the Englishman now?'

'At the midwife's. You know the one—that fat Indian who sells herbs and god-knows-what concoctions to the gullible. What?' he said in response to her surprised look.

'Should you not have taken him to the hospital?'

'He was at death's door! Who knows, he may be dead already.' Hugo shuddered at the thought and poured himself another brandy.

'I am just surprised you chose to take him there. They say she incants to pagan idols in the woods.'

'I don't give a fig what they say!' In his agitation he spilled the brandy. 'Forgive me sweetness,' he said, his voice contrite. 'I am out of my wits with this disaster.'

'Did she not ask questions—the midwife?'

'Yes! How much could I pay! No,' he conceded with a sigh, 'I do her an injustice. At least she was willing to take him in. It would have been easier to send us on our way. Serge told her we found the Englishman like that.'

'So, no one's to blame, then?'

'But I fired the shot! His death, if he dies, is upon me.' Hugo groaned with guilt.

Josette stood up and pulled the shawl around her shoulders. 'If he's a stranger then no one will ask too many questions. They'll assume it was a hunting accident, as it was. You'll feel better once you eat something.'

Only partly reassured by his wife's unfussed practicality, Hugo sat down to a bowl of vegetable soup and a slice of bread and butter. After a second slice of bread, he was sufficiently calmed to think of the way ahead.

'Tomorrow I'll go and visit him.'

Josette arched an eyebrow. 'Why?'

'My dear, I am responsible for his condition. In addition, the midwife doesn't speak English. I must be there to interpret when he wakes up—if he wakes up.'

'Leave him be. You have done your Catholic duty. He is no one to you.'

No one to me! The words haunted him as he lay in bed tossing and turning, tormented by his conscience. *We are bound by that shot. What if he should die—or is already dead?* Possessed by that fear, he woke repeatedly throughout the night, once startled by the sound of a fretful moan before realising it was coming from his own mouth.

A New World Samaritan

THE FOLLOWING DAY, STILL tormented by guilt at the Englishman's fate, he finished work early at Government House, leaving a pile of books on the desk. 'You're off, sir?' The junior archivist looked up in surprise as Hugo put on his coat.

'Yes, I have an appointment. Put these away when you have the time.'

He took an omnibus to the military barracks and from there walked through the stone arch and onto the dirt road that led into the woods. Leaving the road behind he followed the wagon track where it wound into the trees. He walked more than a mile through the snow and brush, muttering at his wet feet. 'I should have brought boots, or oilskins to cover my shoes!' Angry with himself at the omission, he glanced up at the leaden sky, hoping it wouldn't snow.

The air was hushed within the trees, sudden avalanches of powder falling from the branches. He trudged on, doing his best to ignore his cold feet and dreading what he might find at the midwife's cabin. *If he is dead then that would solve a lot of problems*, he told himself, recalling the words of Denis Vachon. Immediately, his overwrought conscience kicked in. *But if he is dead then I am guilty of murder!* He shivered, not from cold, and crossed himself.

He found the midwife sitting at the table mixing a compound in a bowl. The Englishman was lying near the fire where they had left him. He was moaning and muttering, his face glistening with sweat as he trembled feverishly beneath the bear skin. A cloth bandage was wound around his head.

Suddenly he gave an agonized cry and made as if to sit up before collapsing back onto the makeshift bed.

Hugo shivered in fright. 'What is wrong with him? Is he dying?' He glanced at the midwife, who seemed unfazed by the groans and delirious mutterings.

'The poor fool is off of his head with fever. I dug the bullet out of his skull, but it was broken.' She indicated the projectile where it sat on the table. Hugo peered, unwilling to pick it up. The tip was missing. 'Where is the rest of it?'

'Inside his head I expect.'

'Inside his head!' His eyes widened in horror.

She clucked her tongue. 'Where else?'

'God forgive me!' he groaned and slumped in the chair.

The midwife regarded him, a shrewd look on her face. 'Ah!' she said.

Hugo shook his head, too wretched to deny the truth.

The wounded man muttered again, his limbs twitching in delirium.

'What's he saying?' Hugo got up and leaned over to listen. The man seemed to be addressing someone, talking feverishly to the air.

'It is the fever, or perhaps he talks to ghosts.'

'Ghosts?' Hugo clutched the crucifix beneath his shirt.

'If he is a bear then he has the power.' The midwife stuck a finger in the potion to taste it.

'Why on earth do you call him that—a bear?'

'He looked like a bear when you brought him in.'

'He did, didn't he!' Hugo seized on the statement. 'It was that coat! Anyone might have mistaken him for a bear.'

'He is noisy,' the midwife complained as the man uttered a series of loud moans.

'Will he live?'

'Perhaps—if the wound doesn't go bad. Sometimes they live and sometimes—pouf!'

Hugo shuddered at the sound. 'When will we know?' he asked, unable to tear his eyes away from the feverish man.

'Tomorrow, or the next day.' She set the bowl aside. 'Or perhaps the day after.'

He fingered the rosary beads in his pocket. 'I will pray for him.'

'That is good. Talk to your god, and I will talk to mine. Perhaps together they can help.'

Hugo nodded, too miserable to be scandalized at the notion.

ON THE WAY HOME, he detoured to the church of Sainte-Chappelle. *There were three peals—or were they tolling?*

The housekeeper opened the priory door at his knock. She glanced down at his wet feet and soaked trouser legs and up again. 'Yes?'

'I must see Père Boudreau. Is he in?'

'It is late, Monsieur. and he is busy.'

'I must see him! My name is Hugo Gagnon, I am one of his parishioners.'

'Wait.' With a cross look, the housekeeper went to interrupt the priest's post-supper cognac. 'Father, it is one of your parishioners, a Monsieur Gagnon. His feet are soaking wet.'

'Gagnon?' The priest winced at the name. 'What now?' He gave a resigned sigh and swallowed the cognac. 'Send him in.'

'Monsieur Gagnon!' Father Boudreau rose to his feet as the housekeeper ushered the visitor into the room. 'Such a pleasant surprise to see you!' He gestured to an armchair, inwardly frowning at the wet shoe marks left on the carpet. 'How may I be of service to you?' He smoothed his long black soutane and composed his features, listening dutifully as Hugo spelled out his tale of woe.

'What shall I do, Father?' Hugo wrung his hands in torment after finishing.

'Do? You have already done everything required of you.'

'But if he should die? The poor devil is in the grip of a raging fever. The midwife says it's touch and go whether he will survive the night. If he dies his death will be on my conscience! The Holy Scriptures tell us that it is a sin to shed blood.'

'Did you not already say it was an accident?'

'It was, most assuredly.'

'And you helped him afterwards?'

'I did!'

'Then you stand in relation to him as the Samaritan to the wounded traveller.'

'I do?' Hugo's eyes widened at the suggestion.

'Certainly. You assisted a stranger in need, you have nothing to reproach yourself for.' The priest cast a longing glance at the cognac.

Hugo scarcely heard the words, his mind wrestling with the import of what the priest had said. *A Samaritan!*

'Monsieur Gagnon?' Père Boudreau was watching him. 'Are you feeling alright?'

'It's true!' Hugo sat up, a look of profound relief on his face. 'But for my intervention he would surely have perished by the wayside.' Saying the words he felt an intolerable burden slip from his shoulders.

'You see? There is no sin in what happened. It was an accident.'

'But I did shoot him, Father,' said Hugo, his conscience returning to prick.

'Then he is in your charge.' The cleric frowned. 'Did you say you left him with the midwife? The Indian woman?'

'I did, Father. He would surely have perished otherwise. He may still do so.'

The priest considered this. 'I have heard she has great skill with plants and potions?' He rubbed his sore knee. 'I wonder if—'

'But it was my bullet that struck him! Even though it was most assuredly an accident.'

'Yes, yes,' the Père answered testily. 'But have I not already explained that where there is no ill-intent, there is no sin?' Getting up, he motioned to the door. 'Say ten hail Marys for the man's safe recovery. And it wouldn't hurt to pay for a mass.'

'But Father, what should—'

'I am expecting the Bishop,' Père Boudreau apologised. *Someday!* he absolved himself. Murmuring words of comfort, he ushered the penitent Hugo—still pestering him with questions, from the room. 'Go with God, Monsieur!' he called out as the housekeeper closed the door behind the parishioner.

Returning to the study he uncorked the cognac, annoyed at the interruption to his post-digestive cogitations. *These wretched habitants and their superstitions!* He gulped back the glass and poured himself another.

WHEN HUGO RETURNED TO the cabin the next day the midwife was absent. The wounded man was still in the grip of fever, which seemed to have worsened overnight.

'Monsieur?' Hugo leaned over the man. 'Can you hear me?' To his fright the man went into a violent spasm, thrashing and jerking on the bed.

'Stay still—you will hurt yourself!' Hugo pressed the man's shoulders, attempting to confine him to the bed. He heard the door open behind him and turned to see the midwife enter. 'For God's sake, help me!'

Setting aside the basket she carried, the midwife dipped a cloth into a tub of water and pressed it to the man's brow while scolding and soothing in a mix of French and Mohawk. 'Hush now! *Wás sentáwha!*'

'What is happening?' he panted as the stranger continued to thrash about in spite of Hugo's attempts to restrain him. 'The fellow's strong as an ox!'

'It is his head—there may be swelling.' The midwife folded the cloth and laid it over the bloody bandage. Under her ministrations, the man gradually stopped thrashing and lay still. A gurgling sound issued from his throat. Suddenly his eyes opened, and he stared intently at some unknown presence, appearing to beseech the latter while speaking rapidly in tongues—or so it seemed to the alarmed Hugo. 'What in God's name is he doing?'

'Can you not see? He is talking to the spirits. *Nahóten sáton?*'

Hugo felt the hairs on his neck prickle. 'What spirits?'

'Sleep now,' the midwife said, and wiped sweat from the man's face.

'Will he live?' asked Hugo, noting with concern the stranger's ashen pallor.

'If the fever breaks; if not, he'll die.' The midwife's voice was matter of fact.

Hugo sat down in a chair, drained by the ordeal. 'If he dies, we shall have to bury him,' he said, his voice bleak.

'*You* will have to bury him.' The midwife sat down in a rocking chair and took out a clay pipe. She lit it, puffing it to flame. 'Someone may come looking for him.' She spat a shred of tobacco from her teeth.

'Who?' Hugo startled at the possibility.

'He must have friends, or a family. Why did you shoot him?'

'It was an accident! No one must know, do you understand? I will bring you more whisky and tobacco.'

The midwife surveyed him over the pipe, her face wrinkling in the tobacco smoke. 'Good whisky! The kind the Black Robes drink.'

'Yes, yes. Do everything in your power to cure him.' Hugo stood up, guilty and distressed at the man's suffering. 'I will return tomorrow.' With a worried glance at the patient, he hurried to the door.

LEFT ALONE, THE MIDWIFE smoked a fresh pipe, observing the feverish stranger in between puffs. 'What is your name?' she asked. 'Are you a ghost?' She leaned forward to peer at his haunted expression, 'or are you a bear? Perhaps you are a ghost in the shape of a bear. My father met one in the woods once when he was a boy. She cocked her head. 'Why were you in the woods, Ghost Bear?' She listened carefully as the man groaned and muttered, his face and hair drenched with sweat. '*Merde!* You did not say your father was a buffalo!' She smoked and rocked on this revelation, her face thoughtful.

The man became agitated again, calling out and attempting to sit up on the bed. With a mutter of impatience, the midwife hauled her bulk out of the chair. Bending over the log pile, she picked up a branch and placed it on the fire. Digging into a deerskin pouch around her ample waist she took out a pinch of coloured powder and tossed it into the flames. Returning to the table she retrieved a bunch of twigs tied together with sinew. She held the twigs over the fire until they began to smoke. She then brushed the smouldering twigs through the air above the wounded man while chanting in her native tongue.

She did this for some time, her voice rising and falling above his delirious moans. Setting the smoking twigs to one side she knelt down, groaning as her knees took the weight. Scooping a handful of compressed herbs and roots from a bowl she pressed the poultice onto his brow.

She began to hum and then croon. The man stopped twitching, his breathing becoming less ragged. She inclined an ear to his mouth as he muttered to himself.

'I do not know your name,' she said, lifting her eyes to observe his face, 'but you are Ghost Bear now.'

She listened for a moment further and then grunted. 'I am tired. I need to smoke.' She pushed herself up off her knees, grumbling with the effort. Lowering herself back into the rocker she looked around for the pipe, a vexed expression on her face. 'Where are you, little one?'

Surely, Thou Art Jacob

HE WAS LYING ON the floor beside a blazing fire. The acrid wood smoke stung his eyes, making them water. A splitting pain flashed in his skull, and he groaned. Putting a tentative hand to his scalp, he traced a bandage wrapped around his head. His fingers felt a pronounced welt or ridge beneath the binding. The stitched wound was tender, and he took a sharp breath at the feel.

A wave of nausea swept over him, and he waited for the dizzying sensation to pass before turning his head to survey his whereabouts. He saw a pine table and three chairs. A large trunk stood against the back wall. Shelves lined another wall, each shelf crowded with dusty glass jars. A large tub stood near a window. The air was musty with the smell of earth and plants.

His eye was caught by a soot-blackened deerskin nailed to the wall above the hearth. The hide was decorated with images of what appeared to be crudely etched pictographs of men and animals. In the heat and smoke from the blazing fire the images appeared to shimmer and dance. He blinked to clear his eyes before sinking back into sleep.

It was morning. A sick bowl had been placed beside his head and he vomited into it. When he opened his eyes again the bowl had been emptied. A woman was sitting at the table, busily mixing something in a glass jar. He tried to speak, and she looked up and said something in a foreign tongue. She came to his bedside, and spooned some liquid into his mouth, her black eyes curious as he choked it down. The liquid caused him to fall asleep again.

He dreamed a man leant over him, murmuring in a worried voice as he consulted with the woman. The stranger wore a crucifix around his neck, and he wondered if the man was a priest. He tried to say something—the effort exciting the man's attention.

'Who are you, Monsieur? the man asked. 'What is your name?' The questions echoed in his head as he fell back into an exhausted sleep.

After what seemed an eternity of waking and sleeping, he was able to remain awake for longer than a few minutes at a time. He was soaked in sweat and smelled of vomit and piss.

The door opened and the unknown woman entered, accompanied by a blast of cold air. She was carrying a dead rabbit which she set down on the table. She was enormously fat and wrapped in a blanket. A worn felt hat with a narrow brim sat on her head. A wool scarf was pulled around the hat crown and tied under her chin. Her face was smooth and brown, the plump cheeks pinked with cold. He was unable to guess her age. Approaching the fire to warm herself she grunted with surprise when she saw he was awake.

'So, you are not dead!' She chuckled. 'Your spirit is strong, Ghost Bear.'

She bent to peer at him. His nose filled with the smell of earth and musk as he shrank back under her gaze. She felt his brow and spoke to him in the same unfamiliar tongue.

He licked his dry, blistered lips and tried to speak. 'Water!' he croaked and pointed to his throat.

His eyes followed her as she dipped a cup into the tub and handed it to him. He glugged greedily, spilling water down his shirt. She refilled the cup, and he swallowed in similar fashion.

'I do not know your tongue, Englishman.' The midwife sat her bulk in the rocking chair, her face flushed in the heat thrown by the blazing fire. 'You must wait until the pale Frenchman returns. He has been here twice already, but you were off your head. You have been shot,' she explained, at his bewildered expression. 'They brought you here, to me. I dug out the bullet and put the bandage on your head.' She tapped her head to indicate.

'You were talking to the spirits,' she continued, rocking herself in the chair. 'It was the bear tongue, which I speak.' Her face was thoughtful. 'The spirits say you are from far away, but that you cannot remember your name or your people.' She pondered this while stretching her belly to rummage in the pouch tied around her ample waist. 'It is not a good thing to forget who you are. Although I knew a woman once who could not remember that she was a woman and not an owl.' She searched the table for something. 'But memory is a strange thing. Perhaps she was an owl who thought she was a woman.' Finding a pipe, she pushed a plug of tobacco into the bowl, tamping it down with her thumb. 'Just as you are Ghost Bear who thinks himself a man.'

When he awoke again the woman was stood over a bucket gossiping to herself as she stripped the rabbit of its fur. He picked up the bowl of water and sipped from it, the noise attracting her attention. She said something before continuing to skin the rabbit. When the rabbit was skinned, she washed the pink-grey carcass before cutting it up with a hatchet—the chopping sounds going straight to his head. She wrapped the portions in cloth before taking them outside. She left the door open while she hung up the portions, hooking the cloth bundles to nails hammered into the logs. Wintry air swept in, and he pulled up the bearskin to cover his throat.

The woman re-entered and washed her hands by pouring water from a jug. She came and knelt by his bed. She had that same potent smell of earth and musk about her that he remembered from before. Around her neck she wore a necklace of beads and leather and what looked like tiny bird claws. Each fat wrist was circled with similar beads. Her lank black hair fell about her cheeks as she began to unwind the bandage around his scalp. Clucking and muttering to herself she inspected the stiches.

'There was a man here,' he said, his voice hoarse. 'Who was he?'

The woman ignored the question as she finished retying the bandage. Filling a kettle with water, she placed it on the fire to boil. When steam hissed out of the spout, she carefully lifted it off the flames using a pair of tongs. Wrapping the handle with a cloth, she poured the boiling water into a mug. She scooped a handful of tree bark and pine needles into the mug and brought it to him. He sipped the liquid and grimaced at the taste.

She chuckled at his expression and sat down in the rocking chair. Picking up the pipe she began filling the bowl with tobacco. Getting up, she held a splint to the fire, using it to light the tobacco. She sat back down in the chair, inhaling and blowing out a stream of smoke. Rocking back and forth, she regarded him through the smoke.

'I saw you in a dream, Ghost Bear,' she said. 'We broke bread in my father's lodge. It was a good day. My father caught a fat partridge. You were clumsy, Ghost Bear!' Her face crinkled with merriment. 'You upset the cooking pot. My mother was mad, like a Huron!' She chuckled and sucked on the pipe, savouring the incident of the pot.

Outside, it was already dusk. An owl hooted. She cocked an ear to the sound. 'My uncle was a wise man,' she said after listening for a moment. 'They say he changed into a bird and flew away one day. I do not know if it is true, but he had a good memory.' A silence followed as a log crackled on the fire. She gazed at the flames while pondering on the pipe. 'Perhaps that partridge had a cousin,' she mused. 'If so, I pray that he may one day fly into my pot.'

She sighed and rocked, lost in the smoke of recall. 'I remember when I was a girl. I was slim as a fawn and could run like the wind. I had a race, once, with a girl from another tribe. I was faster, but a fucking Abenaki tripped me, and the girl claimed the race.' She grunted with displeasure. 'And now I am fat and find even walking difficult. But in my dreams I still run like the wind!'

He stared at her, haunted by a feeling of unreality. 'I don't understand a word you say,' he complained. A wave of dizziness overtook him and he groaned, feeling suddenly nauseous, and closed his eyes.

A MAN WAS SEATED in a chair pulled up beside the bed.

'How are you feeling, Monsieur?' The visitor leaned forward with the question. 'We spoke yesterday, do you remember?'

He barely had time to note that the man was the same visitor he had seen previously before he fell asleep again. Over the next few days the man was a frequent visitor, always bringing a gift for the Indian woman, whom he referred to as Sage-Femme, or simply Madame.

To his annoyance and frustration, he remembered little from these visits as he suffered a new and frightening complication—a series of convulsive fits that alarmed and exhausted him. The only warning he had of an impending seizure was a tingle in his scalp and a dull throbbing in his skull shortly before the onset. He quickly grew wary of such symptoms, tensing with anxiety while mentally bracing for the first tell-tale tremor in his limbs.

He awoke from the seizures fearful and confused, staring wildly about him and unable to recall the minutes before the convulsion. He woke up from one such fit to find that the midwife had placed a stick between his teeth to protect his tongue. He removed the stick, flexing his jaw to rid himself of the dryness and the wood taste.

'Where did you go, Ghost Bear?' The midwife was seated at the table sorting through a pile of twigs and plants.

He tried to say something, but the words wouldn't come out. He stared up at the timbers, a sense of dread paralysing his thoughts. *What happened to me?*

WHEN HUGO RETURNED TWO days later, he was gratified to find the stranger propped up against the wall next to the hearth. The bear skin lay across his legs. His face was wan and unshaven, his hair sticking out from under the freshly applied bandage The midwife was seated at the table slicing up a root between sipping a cup of whisky.

'*Ah! Monsieur. Dieu merci, tu es réveillé!* Pardon!' Hugo quickly added at the man's puzzled frown. 'I was speaking in French. I had quite forgot.'

'French? Where in hickory am I?' The man's voice rasped with dryness, and he took a sip of water from the bowl.

'You are in the town of New France.'

'I am?' The man looked astonished at the information. The astonishment gave way to wariness as he studied the visitor. 'And who are you?'

'I am Hugo Gagnon, sir. My companions and I found you in the woods. You had been shot—accidentally, by a hunter.'

'I was?' The man frowned to recall. 'Am I a hunter?'

'It is uncertain. Do you not remember being in the woods?'

'No.' He touched the bandage around his head.

'Do you remember what brought you here?'

'No, I don't.' The man looked concerned at the question. 'How long have I been here?'

'A week, no more.'

'A week!' The man stared in shock. 'What month is it?'

The question seemed to perturb his interrogator. 'January, of course.'

The stranger fell silent as he sought to absorb the information.

'And the year?' he asked hesitantly, as if fearful of the answer.

Hugo grimaced, perturbed further by the question. 'Why, 1900 of course. The new century.'

The man closed his eyes and, for a moment, Hugo thought he had fallen asleep. But he opened them again—a troubled expression on his face. 'Who am I?'

'What do you mean?' Hugo felt the hairs prickle on his neck.

'I mean I don't know who …'

'Monsieur?' Hugo touched the Englishman on the shoulder. 'He's passed out again,' he fretted to the midwife.

'He is still weak from the fever.'

'He claims he doesn't know who he is.'

'He is Ghost Bear.' The midwife took leaves from a jar and added them to a small pile on the table before her.

'Ghost Bear? Why do you call him that?'

'Because that is his name. He told me in his fever.'

Hugo's hand went to the crucifix beneath his shirt, as he recalled the rumours about the midwife's unnatural powers.

'Come back tomorrow, he will be stronger. Bring more whisky,' she said.

It was two days before Hugo returned to the cabin. The patient looked stronger and more alert as Hugo pulled up a chair to resume the interrogation. He unwrapped a small package he had brought with him. 'A cake, Monsieur.' He offered a portion. 'Carrot cake. My wife made it. We thought something not too rich.'

Raising it to his mouth, the man took a tentative bite.

Hugo stood up and placed a second package on the table, along with a bottle of whisky for the midwife. 'Where is she?' he asked.

'I don't know. She goes out.' The man licked crumbs from the palm of his hand.

'You are feeling better?'

The man rested his back against the wall. 'Yes. The woman, the ah …'

'Midwife.'

'Yes, the midwife. She resewed my scalp. She says a part of the bullet is still inside.'

Hugo cleared his throat. 'But you are feeling a little stronger? Good.' He hesitated, his expression becoming grave as he turned to the matter that had troubled him since his previous visit. 'Do you remember anything more about yourself, or where you are from?'

'I try, but my mind is a blank page.' The man grimaced with frustration.

'You do not remember anything?'

'I wish to God that I did. But so help me, I cannot recall a single thing about myself.' the man looked troubled at the admission.

The door opened and the midwife came in, her face flushed with the cold. 'You are here,' she said to Hugo and stamped her feet. 'My fucking toes are frozen.' Her eyes lit up as she saw the bottle on the table.

'I also brought you some of that tobacco you like, and some of my wife's cake.' Hugo pointed to the package.

'What does Ghost Bear have to say for himself?'

Hugo turned to find the patient had fallen asleep, his head slumped back against the wall. 'He is no nearer at remembering who he is.'

The midwife took off her coat and sat down at the table. 'I almost caught a rabbit, but he recognised me and ran away.'

'Will his memory come back?'

'The rabbit?'

'Him!' Hugo jabbed a thumb at the sleeping stranger.

'It depends.' She pushed some of the cake into her mouth.

'On what?'

'On *mmph!*' she said, her mouth choked with cake. She took a swallow of whisky. 'Ah!' Sighing in satisfaction, she laid a hand on her belly.

'When will he be well enough to leave?'

The midwife poured herself another shot. 'Two or three weeks, maybe. But we must be careful. He may suddenly get worse. I have seen it happen.'

Disturbed at the possibility, Hugo glanced at the sleeping man. 'Let us hope not,' he said.

On his return home, Hugo relayed the conversation to his wife. 'He swears he cannot recall a single thing about himself—not even his name. Can you imagine?' He shuddered at the prospect. 'Not to know one's own name!'

'Do you think he is telling the truth?'

'Why on earth would you say that?' Hugo stared in surprise.

Josette made a humming sound as she added wax to the cloth she was using to polish a brass jug. 'He might have cause to forget,' she suggested, her voice dark with the possibility.

'What in heaven's name does that mean?'

'Perhaps he has something on his conscience that he would prefer not to remember.'

'You cannot *wish* amnesia upon yourself!'

'Are you quite sure?' Josette raised her eyebrows.

He slept badly that night, haunted by images of the Englishman thrashing about on the floor and crying out in pain. He awoke in a cold sweat, his heart pounding madly, as if half expecting some banshee of vengeance to leap, screeching, from the shadows. 'I must make confession,' he muttered, and fell back to sleep.

When he returned three days later, the stranger looked in considerably better health. The colour had returned to his cheeks, and his eyes were alert as he greeted Hugo. 'Hello,' he said, his voice sounding stronger.

'Bonjour, Monsieur! I have something for you.' Hugo pulled the wad of soiled notes from his pocket. 'This was found between the pages of your Bible.'

'It was?' Surprised and gratified, the man took the notes.

'You don't remember putting them there?'

'No.' The man shook his head, busily counting. 'Two hundred dollars!' He looked gratefully at Hugo. 'Thank you, friend, for your honesty.'

'Of course. Now that you are feeling better is your memory starting to come back?'

'I wish to Jehovah that it would!'

Hugo noted the reference while pursuing the inquiry. 'Surely, you must now recall your name, at the very least?'

'No. Nor how I came to be in those infernal woods you speak of.' The man scowled. 'Nor the fool that shot me.'

'*Un accident, je n'en doute pas!*' said Hugo, lapsing into his native tongue in his haste. 'There are lots of hunters that stalk those woods. You were wearing a buffalo coat. It undoubtedly caused you to be mistaken for an animal of some kind. But I have news, Monsieur. I believe your family name is Wheeler.' He watched the Englishman's face for a reaction.

'Wheeler?' The man stared in puzzlement.

'It was written in the Bible you had in your possession when we found you.' Hugo looked around. 'I do not see it now, nor the haversack you were carrying.'

'It is here, beside me.' Tugging at the canvas bag, the man handed it to Hugo.

'*Merci.*' Taking out the water-stained Bible Hugo carefully turned the pages until he found the marriage plate. 'There.' He pointed to the inscribed names. 'The ink has run, but you can make out a name—Abe, for Abraham, Abraham Wheeler. Your grandfather, I presume?' He handed over the Bible and watched the other man's face for a sign of recognition as he studied the page. 'Does the name mean anything to you? Does it sound familiar?'

'I wish it did, but it means nothing to me.' The man muttered in frustration.

'But if the Bible is precious to you—as surely it must be since you carried it with you, then there must be a familial connection, do you not agree?'

The question was met with a hopeless stare.

'And since the only discernible name is Wheeler, Hugo continued, 'then surely, also, that name must hold significance for you? In which case, I shall address you, with your permission, as Monsieur Wheeler. Is that acceptable?'

The man contemplated this, twisting his mouth as he considered the proposition. 'It is,' he said grudgingly, 'since I have no other name by which to call myself.'

'Excellent!' Hugo smiled at the promising start. 'Tell me, Monsieur Wheeler. Do you intend to stay here—in New France?'

'Where else would I go? I have no home, no family, and no means of support.' The words were spoken in a tone of hopeless despair.

'You have some money, Monsieur. You are not penniless,' Hugo reminded him. 'And you have a friend, I assure you. Do you perhaps have a trade?'

'I don't recall.' Wheeler grimaced at the admission.

'Never mind. There is much need for capable workmen of all kinds in the town.'

'But I do not speak French.' Wheeler let out a long, hopeless sigh.

'Perhaps I may be able to help you there. I can teach you the language. It is a magnificent tongue and not difficult to learn. What do you think?'

Wheeler's eyes narrowed with sudden suspicion. 'Why put yourself to so much trouble on my behalf? After all, I am a complete stranger to you?'

'It is my Christian duty—the parable of the Samaritan.'

At the other's nonplussed stare Hugo pointed to the Bible. 'You may read it at your leisure.'

'Who will employ me—even if I could speak French? Heavens to a crow! I don't even know my own Christian name.'

Hugo was thoughtful for a moment. 'Perhaps there is a solution.' He picked up the Bible. 'Providence has provided us with your family name. Now let scripture do the rest.' As he turned the pages, his face brightened. 'Your grandfather was named Abraham, was he not?' He gazed at Wheeler for affirmation. Receiving none, he pressed on.

'Therefore, as night follows day, surely, thou art Jacob.'

'Jacob?' A baffled look crossed Wheeler's face.

'I congratulate you, Monsieur!' Hugo beamed in triumph. 'You shall no longer be *personne*, but Jacob!'

'Jacob?' Wheeler repeated the name wonderingly; already, it sounded hauntingly familiar.

Hugo was about to expound on the point when the door opened and the midwife returned, clutching a rabbit in her hand. She held up the rabbit, pleased with her success. 'He thought he could trick me for a second time!'

'Madame midwife, together we have discovered our friend's name. I present to you … Monsieur Jacob Wheeler!'

The midwife grunted. 'It is time he started to walk again. Tell him.'

ON SUNDAY AFTERNOON HUGO and Josette hosted his widowed aunt, Madame Ouellet, and her two daughters, Marguerite and Isabelle, on the occasion of the latter's seventeenth birthday. Isabelle could barely contain her fascination as Hugo recounted the tale of the mysterious Englishman discovered, half-murdered, in the woods. Eager to learn more, she peppered him with questions throughout the meal.

'Not murdered!' he hastily corrected over cassoulet. 'Wounded, entirely by accident.'

'Indeed.' His aunt sniffed, her distaste for the entire affair obvious. 'Perhaps he was a bandit, lurking to rob or slaughter.'

'He remembers nothing. Not even who he is. Imagine!' Josette passed around the bread, delighted to play hostess to the scandal.

'So, it is true—that he cannot even remember his own name?' Isabelle's eyes widened.

'He could not, but we were fortunate to find it referenced in the Bible.'

'What did you say?' His aunt's mouth dropped open in shock.

'In a page recording marriages. We found the family name written there, Wheeler. And from there we traced his Christian name, Jacob.'

'But he remembers nothing about himself?' Isabelle tried hard to imagine such a catastrophe.

'Nothing,' affirmed Josette. 'The bullet took away his memory.'

'Gracious!' Isabelle set down her spoon to ponder the notion. 'A man without a name!'

'He *has* a name, cousin. Have I not just told you? Jacob Wheeler, a perfectly good English name.'

'But, dear, did you not just say that he could not remember himself?' Josette glanced over her spoon.

'He did not, at first, it is true,' admitted Hugo. 'But since the improvement in his health, he remembers many things.'

'For example?' His aunt blew her nose.

'For example, that he was schooled as a child.'

'He said so?'

'There was no need. The fact is evident.'

'But he has no roots, no family?'

'Most assuredly, he did not give birth to himself!'

'But no history? No memory? Merciful God!'

'Isabelle!'

'Sorry, mama. It is just so … inconceivable. What will he do now, the Englishman?'

'When he is better, I will help him find lodgings so that he may move out of the midwife's cabin.'

'You? Why you?' His aunt fixed him a disapproving look.

'Exactly.' Josette raised her eyebrows.

'It is my Christian duty. I have spoken to Father Boudreau about the matter, and he tells me I stand in relation to the Englishman as the Good Samaritan to the wounded traveller.'

'That priest was always odd,' sniffed his aunt. 'I remember his eulogy for Pierre Langlois. No one in the congregation understood a word he said. I suspect the man was drunk.'

'But why you, husband?' Josette pressed. 'Surely it is the responsibility of the church, or a matter for the charities?'

'My dear—'

'Are there no other Samaritans?' interrupted his aunt.

'How will he support himself—given he cannot speak French?' asked Isabelle, unable to rein in her curiosity. 'Pardon, Mama.' She made a contrite face at her mother's frosty look.

Relieved to be able to fix on something tangible, Hugo gave his cousin a fond smile. 'I intend to tutor him in our language. And once he is able to express himself, I am sure he will find suitable employment. He strikes me as a capable sort of fellow.'

'He may yet prove to be a bandit! And what is more convenient for a bandit than to forget his memory? The authorities must be notified.'

'If you saw how pitiful he looks, aunt, then you would not think him so.'

'You say he is called Jacob?' queried Isabelle. 'Then he must be Christian. Is he Catholic?'

'I suspect he may be Protestant.'

'A Huguenot!' His aunt clucked in disapproval. 'They are everywhere these days.'

'Really, dearest. You are becoming obsessed with this Englishman.' Josette frowned to make clear her unhappiness.

'Strictly speaking, he is American.'

'*American* now!' His aunt shrieked the word.

'Compliments on the cassoulet,' said Marguerite, bored with the subject. 'Did you hear? Father Clement has taken ill.'

'Really? I didn't know. What happened to him?' asked Josette.

'Old age. The parish is too much for him. He stays shut indoors all day with only his housekeeper for company. They say that he has forgotten himself.'

'Another one!' Madame Ouellet's voice pitched with alarm. 'Let us hope the contagion is not spreading.'

After his relatives had departed, Hugo retired to the study where he sat down with a rare cigarette to ponder anew the entire, astonishing affair of the lost-but-found, nameless-but named, Jacob. Draping one leg over the other, he smoked on the oddity of fate that had crossed his path with that of the amnesiac American. And the longer he ruminated on the incident, the more the conviction grew that the hand of Providence was at work.

But for me, he would have surely perished in the woods, he reminded himself, the conceit of a New World Samaritan returning to enthral his conscience. Getting up, he fetched the Bible and turned the pages to Luke.

> *But a certain Samaritan, as he journeyed, came where he was: and when he saw him, he had compassion on him, And went to him, and bound up his wounds, pouring in oil and wine, and set him on his own beast, and brought him to an inn, and took care of him. And on the morrow when he departed, he took out two pence, and gave them to the host, and said unto him, Take care of him; and whatsoever thou spendest more, when I come again, I will repay thee.*

A certain Samaritan! The phrase entranced him, loudly declaiming to his fulsome piety. Was that not he? Had not Père Boudreau himself, said as much? And here was the stranger's story, adumbrated in the Bible! He turned the pages as he pondered, becoming sidetracked by a reference to pomegranates before landing at Genesis. *And Jacob dwelt in the land wherein his father was a stranger, in the land of Canaan.*

He sat back to take in the astonishing proof. For is not his father, whoever he may be, a stranger to New France? He passed over the notion that his beloved city might be considered Canaanite in the allusion as the conviction grew that the encounter in the woods was no accident but one divinely ordained. He found one more reference to add substance to the belief: *One law shall be to him that is homeborn, and unto the stranger that sojourneth among you.*

He set the bible on his lap to ponder the thorny phrase. *I am homeborn, and Jacob the stranger!*

And thus, by scriptural degrees, the nature of his stewardship advanced until he felt Jacob and himself bound by a mystical covenant. For did not the contrarieties prove the case? Frenchman and American; Catholic and Protestant; stranger and native-born!

He stood up and stared into the fire, astounded by the revelation. *A certain Samaritan.*

4

A Dream of the Pipe

HIS APPETITE HAD RETURNED and he was able to swallow solid food after what seemed an eternity of watery gruel. The hollowed flesh around his ribs began to fill out, adding weight to his emaciated frame and colour to his cheeks. He felt sufficiently recovered to take slow, tentative steps around the small cabin. Although subject to dizzy spells and severe headaches which left him drained and exhausted in their aftermath, he persisted in his attempts to regain his independence. To his dismay, he discovered his depth perception was unreliable, objects seeming simultaneously to be both near and far away. Venturing out onto the snowy porch one morning, he misjudged the step and almost stumbled down the stairs, only just saving himself by grabbing onto the post.

The midwife watched these faltering steps with an inscrutable gaze, puffing on the omnipresent pipe while offering occasional words of criticism or encouragement. '*Levez les yeux, pas le bas! Utilisez un bâton pour ne pas tomber!*' When he merely looked confused and irritable at the advice, she switched tongues, scolding and correcting in a language that seemed to Jacob utter gibberish.

'I don't understand you,' he complained, sinking into a chair across from where she sat at the pine table. 'You may as well be speaking double-Dutch.'

'It is strange you do not know my words, Ghost Bear, since they are of the woods.' She regarded him with a bemused gaze. 'Soon your strength will return. But you must not rush, like a foolish deer to the hunter.'

Fatigue and irritability got the better of him, and he made his way back to the bearskin bed. In spite of frustrating hours spent trying to recall some facts about himself, he was still no wiser as to his identity or how he came to be in New France. Who am I? he wondered for the thousandth time, staring up at the timbers. And how did I come to be here?

The single light in his gloom, was the hope that he had a home and family somewhere—the discovery of his name providing the only means to retrace his steps back to that source. If indeed Jacob Wheeler *is* my name, he wondered to himself. The name the Frenchman had bestowed upon him seemed equally real or unreal according to his mood or the time of day.

Nevertheless, he seized upon it in the faint hope it might jog his memory. 'I am Jacob,' he said aloud, in an attempt to retrace his steps backwards from that fact, however disputable. 'Jacob,' he repeated, unconsciously cocking an ear as if the word might evoke another sound or sensation and so that he might, by degrees, proceed from one scrap of self to another. But each attempt ended in failure and further frustration.

He examined the bible found on his person in the hope it might provide a surer clue to his origins. There is workmanship here, he noted, tracing his fingers over the worn leather cover and faded brass corners. It must be of some value—sentimental or otherwise, else why would I have carried it? Poring over the flyleaf, he tried to determine the water-blotted names inscribed there by some unknown hand or hands. Failing in this, he raised the volume to his nose and breathed in the musty odour, hoping by this means to stimulate some impulse of recognition or perhaps bring back the image of a forgotten face.

He turned the pages, reading the verses with curiosity rather than the warmth of remembered feeling. Whole sections were glued together, the pages stuck fast by dried moisture. He began to prise them apart when he yawned suddenly, his eyelids drooping. When the midwife returned, she found him fast asleep at the table, his head resting on the open book.

A sympathetic Hugo offered to help when next he came to visit, taking the bible and attempting once again to decipher the blotted names. 'It's useless. I'm afraid there is too much water damage,' he said, his voice regretful as he laid down the volume.

'The answer is not there anyway,' Jacob muttered, his countenance gloomy. 'It is inside me. I am my own vault and my own key.'

THE MIDWIFE HAD A great fondness for whisky, which she indulged in throughout the day, sometimes running two glasses at a time, forgetting the first and reaching for the second as she rummaged about the cluttered cabin. She took similar pleasure in her pipe, happily puffing as she reminisced aloud or gossiped about the creatures she had encountered during the day in the forest.

'That squirrel reminded me of André Papineau,' she mused as a cold gale blasted the frame of the cabin. 'He had the same nose. Papineau died two years ago in the woods. The fool accidentally shot himself with his own gun. I could do nothing for him. It is too bad, Ghost Bear, that you do not speak French or Mohawk.'

She slept in a corner of the cabin and cooked over the fire. During the day she set snares for rabbits or collected herbs and plants from the surrounding woods, filling the cabin with their earthy smell. When not foraging for food or plants, she sat at the table mixing potions and concoctions for the women who came to call on her services.

Word of the wounded Englishman had spread, and several people visited on the pretext of enquiring about potions, but really to see for themselves this mysterious figure sprung from the woods. The midwife was pleased to display Jacob as proof of the efficacy of her healing powers, happily showing off the bullet fragment she had dug from his skull. 'The white medicine could not have saved him,' she boasted. 'That is why they brought him to me.'

'Is it true—that he communes with the beasts of the forest?' asked one woman, eyeing the dozing Jacob with suspicion. She had travelled from the city on foot following the testimony of a neighbour that there was something fishy about the Englishman and his relationship with the midwife. It was a cold day, and her feet were wet from stepping in a puddle.

'He knows many things,' the midwife answered cryptically.

'Except his own name by all accounts.' The woman's voice held a spiteful edge to let the midwife know she was on to her cunning deceits.

'Names!' The midwife grunted as if such things were of no importance. 'What is it you wanted?'

'A love spell. Like the one you cooked up for Giselle Provencher.'

'I have some here.' The midwife got up and waddled over to the crowded shelves. She set down a small glass bottle.

The other woman sniffed. 'I want something freshly made up, not Giselle's leftovers.'

'Take it or leave it. That is all you get.' The midwife eased her bulk back into the chair.

'How much is it?'

'A dollar.'

'How do I know it will work?' The woman eyed the bottle, her voice suspicious. 'Giselle failed to land that carpenter she was so keen on.'

'A dollar if you want it.' The midwife struck a match and lit her pipe.

Grumbling, the woman paid and left with a last glance at Jacob. 'He looks odd!' she declared, casting the blame for her wet stockings and cold feet.

Hugo was a frequent sometimes daily, visitor the promptings of a guilty conscience combining with a genuine interest in Jacob's welfare. Of particular concern was Jacob's continuing inability to cast any light on his personal history, an omission that both intrigued and troubled the Frenchman.

'It is an unusual case,' he remarked to Denis Vachon, recounting a conversation he had held with a doctor in the town. 'It appears that the unfortunate bullet has disrupted that part of the brain where memories reside.'

'So, will it, his memory, come back?'

'The doctor was cautious on the question. It may, or it may not. He has seen examples of both possibilities.'

Denis raised an eyebrow. 'And if it doesn't?'

Hugo sighed. 'Then I fear he may never know who he really is.'

Denis stroked his chin while eyeing his companion. 'Have you mentioned to him about the … accident?'

Hugo cleared his throat. 'No.'

'And are you going to?'

'Do you think I should?'

'What does Serge say?'

'That what the Englishman doesn't know can't hurt him.' Hugo's gaze dwelt on Denis as if seeking approval for this opinion.

'True,' Denis grinned. 'I suppose you could say the same applies to all of us.'

Drawing a blank on medical advice, Hugo sought the counsel of Père Boudreau who adroitly evaded the question of prayerful dispensation, citing Jacob's Protestantism as an insuperable barrier.

'But what if he is Catholic? He might be, for all that we know.'

The priest considered this. 'Doubtful,' he reasoned. 'For one, he is English. For two, Catholics recognise each other,' he said wistfully, wondering if such a thing were possible.

'What do you mean?'

'There is a certain …*concordance* of feeling or sympathy, that one believer arouses in another. Do you not feel it?'

'I do!' exclaimed Hugo, the suggestion appealing to his mystical sense of faith.

'IS THERE NOT SOMETHING you can do to help him recover his memory?' Hugo asked the midwife on his next visit. He had arrived a few minutes earlier, his mood tetchy following an argument with his wife over repeated visits to the cabin.

'Are you his confessor or doctor that you should see him every single day and neglect your poor wife?' Josette scolded as she watched him put on his coat and hat. 'It's Sunday afternoon for Heaven's sake. You should be at home, not galivanting off into the woods to make merry with a complete stranger.'

He had taken the usual tram to the outskirts of town, torn between guilt and annoyance at her accusation. '*Galivanting!*' He muttered the word while gazing out the tram window at the grey, slushy streets and showers of rain. She wouldn't understand, he told himself. How could she? I barely understand it myself. I only know it is my Christian duty.

Arriving at the cabin he held his hat outside the door while shaking rain from the crown. The cabin was warm, the usual fire roaring in the grate. The midwife was sitting at the table shelling some hazelnuts. He placed a bottle of whisky in front of her. 'Where is Jacob?'

'He has gone to make a shit.'

'Oh.' He took a chair. 'Well?' he asked, repeating the question. 'Can you help?'

'I do not make miracles. Why do you not ask your Black Robes?'

'There must be something.' He eyed the cluster of bottles and jars sitting on the shelves. 'Some physic or potion?' he asked uncertainly, a Catholic qualm unsettling him.

'Memory is like a rabbit. If you chase it, it will run away.'

'So, you can do nothing?'

She snapped a shell with her teeth. Sweeping the shells aside, she motioned for him to open the whisky and pour her a glass.

'I will pay you, of course. For your trouble.'

'There may be a way,' she conceded, her eyes fixed on the whisky as he poured. She offered him some of the shelled nuts, which he refused. Taking up the glass she swallowed a mouthful of whisky.

'Yes?' he prompted, changing his mind and taking a nut.

Grunting with the effort, the midwife got up from the chair. 'Where are you?' she cooed in her native tongue. She listened for a moment, her gaze alighting on the large, brass-bound chest standing against the wall. 'I hear you!' Bending, she opened the chest, the woollen dress straining across her ample rear.

The door opened and Jacob entered, brushing rain from his shoulders. His face brightened as he saw Hugo. 'I did not expect you in this foul weather,' he said, shaking hands. He observed the midwife talking to herself as she bent over the contents of the chest. He turned a questioning glance on Hugo, who shrugged.

The midwife returned to the table, huffing from the exertion. She clutched a long wooden pipe in one hand, and a deerskin pouch and small muslin bag in the other. The pipe was coloured with red dye and hung with feathers.

'I have not smoked you for many days,' she said fondly, laying it on the table. She opened the muslin bag and held it to her nose, inhaling deeply. 'It is good. My grandmother gave it to me, long ago, when I was just a girl.' She scooped a pinch of ground root between her thumb and forefinger and pressed it into the bowl of the pipe. 'It will cost you a dollar,' she said to Hugo. 'Two dollars if it works.'

'What is she doing?' Jacob warmed himself by the fire as he watched.

'She may have found a way to jog your memory.'

Sitting down cross-legged on the floor, the midwife lit the pipe, sucking in deeply before emitting a stream of smoke which she fanned into the air around her. She took a handful of ochre coloured powder from the deerskin pouch and tossed it into the air. The powder combined with the smoke to give off a sweet, aromatic smell—like incense, it occurred to an apprehensive Hugo. He fingered the rosary in his pocket, anxious at being, *unknowingly*, a participant in a heathen ritual.

'Come.' The midwife summoned Jacob to join her where she sat on the floor. Picking up the pipe she offered it to him, holding it out with both hands. 'In the smoke you will see your people,' she said.

He hesitated before accepting, glancing at Hugo for direction. 'What nonsense is this?'

Hugo shrugged to show he was helpless in the matter.

The midwife closed her eyes and commenced a guttural, droning chant, rocking back and forth on her haunches.

Placing the pipe in his mouth, Jacob took a cautious inhalation. 'It's foul!' He grimaced and struggled not to spit out the taste.

While still chanting, the midwife tapped his knee and pointed to the deerskin above the fire. She then gestured to the pipe.

'What now?'

'I believe she wishes you to gaze at the hide while you smoke the pipe.'

Repressing his distaste, Jacob put the pipe to his mouth as the midwife rocked to and fro with closed eyes. He took a deep draught, spluttering as the potent mixture was sucked into his lungs. He choked for breath and felt as if he might be sick. He forced himself to take another draw, his eyes fixed on the deerskin as instructed. The unfamiliar smoke left him dizzy and light-headed, and the cabin walls seemed to sway. The midwife shook a small bone rattle in her hand and raised her voice in a throaty, hypnotic wail. The overpowering smell of sweet grass swayed his senses, and he closed his eyes to stop the room from spinning. He sucked on the pipe again, breathing in deeply as the heady smoke filled his lungs. To his amazement, the stick figures on the hide seemed to move and shimmer. He stared mesmerised as they flickered as if in a dance, forming a circle around the bulky creature in their midst.

All at once the hearth, the fire, and the deerskin vanished and vivid daylight greeted his eyes. He blinked. A woman was standing with her back to him in front of a window. She was gazing out at a tremendous yellow sky. He tried to speak but his voice remained lodged in his throat. A young girl went up to the woman and circled tiny arms around her waist, pressing her head against her side.

A door opened and a man entered from outside. He was lean and dark-haired, with a face burnt by the sun. He said something to the woman and sat down at the table to tug off his boots. A boy entered the room carrying what appeared to be a cockerel under his arm. He stood between the man and the woman, looking from one to the other. The living tableau was silent, bathed in the resplendent light of the sky outside the window.

He tried to speak, to alert them to his presence, but his tongue was thickly rooted in his mouth. The scene changed and he was in a different room. A man sat at a desk, writing. He looked up and called out something before returning to the task, the scene hauntingly familiar.

'Jacob! Jacob!' Hugo was shaking him, urging him to wake up. 'What was it? What did you see?'

'What happened?' Jacob blinked and recoiled at the taste of tobacco in his mouth.

'You seemed to fall into a trance. You were talking to yourself.'

'I was?'

'What did you see?' Hugo's eyes probed his face.

'I don't remember. Shapes. Figures. Nothing that made any sense.'

'Oh!' Hugo frowned in disappointment.

Jacob felt strangely drowsy. 'I must sleep,' he said. He got up and went to his bed, falling into a deep slumber as soon as he lay down.

'What is wrong with him?' A worried Hugo looked to the midwife who was seated back at the table, pouring herself a whisky.

'Nothing. It is the dream of the pipe.'

'Did it help him? Will he remember anything?'

'Perhaps. Perhaps not. Sometimes the smoke catches the rabbit. Sometimes the rabbit escapes.'

Shaken by the episode, Hugo returned home. He told all to Father Boudreau the following day in the confessional. 'It was a spell of some kind,' he admitted, tormented by the possibility that he had placed his immortal soul in peril.

'And what did the Englishman see?' The priest's voice was curious through the latticed grill.

'Nothing. Nothing he could remember.'

'So, it didn't work?'

'Work?' Puzzled, Hugo repeated the word.

'Never mind. What other sins have you committed? Any impure thoughts?'

'None, Father. None of which I am aware.'

There came a sigh from beyond the partition. 'Say a rosary for penance. And give something to the alms box.'

THREE WEEKS AFTER BEING carried, half-dead, into the small cabin, Jacob felt well enough to make a foray into the surrounding woods. The sky was a dismal grey with flakes of snow wafting through the air. Wrapped in the buffalo coat and with a woollen tuque provided by Hugo pulled down over his ears, he trekked through the snow to a clearing a half-mile distant. He stopped every now and then to catch breath, his exertions steaming into the air. The dull, throbbing headache that had bothered him since the accident had mostly disappeared, returning only when he was overly fatigued or when he tormented himself for too long trying to recall some shred of his past. Ever since the episode with the pipe he had struggled to determine the meaning of the scenes the ritual had evoked. The image of the man writing at the desk haunted him in particular, as though containing some significance that might, if deciphered, lead on to other clues.

As his strength and energy returned, the walks became longer as he strove to build up his physical endurance. His stride lengthened and his pace increased, in part in the unconscious hope that physical effort might somehow shake loose a nugget of gold from the pan of forgetfulness. Occasionally, a vague image leapt to mind, and he struggled to snare it before forgetfulness snowed in again. At times he felt like a man stumbling through a blizzard while catching glimpses of stray, ghostly figures through the blinding snow.

Once, chancing upon a familiar-looking cottonwood, he interrupted his exercise to press his hand against the rough bark, his face contorted with the attempt to recall the parental tree. Another time, the courteous hail of a passing woodsman invoked a half-remembered echo and he stared yearningly at the departing figure until the man vanished among the trees.

'I as good as have no past,' he muttered, bleakly resigned to the fact. The day was cold, a northerly wind gusting through the trees and blowing showers of snow across the frozen earth. He stopped to rest, panting, his hands on his knees. He looked around at the stark woods, wondering for the hundredth time how the devil he came to be in such a place. Was I with someone? Or was I fleeing someone? Why was I carrying a bible of all things?

A fox darted out of the trees, stopping to stare, its eyes bright. For a moment the two stared at each other before the fox sprang back into the undergrowth. Even he has a den somewhere, Jacob reflected ruefully, a place of his own to lay his head. He trudged on, intending to reach a maple that marked the extent of his previous walk. I may lack a past, he consoled himself, but I have a future the same as the next man. A future I may mould to my liking, despite my handicap. Reaching the boundary tree he turned to retrace his steps, his mind groping toward some notion of destiny. Behind him, the blowing snow was already erasing his footsteps.

HUGO RETURNED, ACCOMPANIED BY four other men who exclaimed with astonishment as they laid eyes on Jacob. They clustered around to shake his hand as Hugo introduced each one and explained their connection. 'They are fine fellows,' he said, 'and very pleased to see you up and about. Ignore their enthusiasm,' he added, irritated at the way his companions stared.

'He looks like a new man!' exclaimed Martin Cloutier, gawking at Jacob.

'You say his name is Jacob Wheeler?' Denis Vachon watched for a reaction as he said the name. 'See! He understands. Bonjour, Monsieur Wheeler!'

'Bonjour, Monsieur.'

Delighted by the response, Denis smiled broadly. 'Bonjour, indeed, Monsieur!'

'Bonjour.'

'By the Sacred Host, I cannot believe he survived!' Serge Villeneuve shook his head as he stared wonderingly at Jacob. 'I told you the midwife was capable, did I not?'

'When will she take the bandage off? Have you seen the wound?' asked Claude Charbonneau, peering at Jacob's scalp.

'Please, do not crowd around him. He is not an animal in the zoo!'

'Pardon, Monsieur Wheeler.'

'Bonjour.'

The friends withdrew to the porch to talk among themselves. The day was cold with fresh snow from an overnight flurry lying on the ground. 'He cannot stay here for ever, Hugo,' remarked Martin Cloutier. 'What will happen to him?'

'I have made enquiries. An acquaintance told me of a Madam Pepin who runs a respectable lodging house on rue des Martyrs. She may have a room available next month, at a reasonable rent. She will send word if such is the case.'

'Who will pay? Ah! the money found on his person,' said Claude, seeking in this way to remind everyone of the fact. 'Do you still have it?'

'I returned it to him. Did you imagine I would keep it?'

Serge grinned and poked Claude in the ribs. 'Did I not tell you!'

'So, Hugo. Do you really intend to teach the Englishman, French?' asked Serge.

'I do. Starting very soon.'

Denis grinned. 'Then can we expect him to speak like yourself, Hugo? He put on a fluting voice. 'On the one hand such a thing might be true. But on the other, equally, it might not!'

Hugo smiled good-naturedly. 'Would you rather he spoke like you, Denis?'

Claude guffawed. 'Let us hope not, for then he would never find work!'

As they were leaving, the midwife came up to Hugo. 'You'll have to pay me more money to feed the Englishman. I am not one of your Black Robe charities.'

Reaching for his wallet, Hugo took out three dollars which he passed to her. 'Take good care of him; and be assured, whatever you spend more, when I come again, I will repay you.'

'Hugo! Move your Jesuit arse, for God's sake. My balls are freezing!'

5

The Tongue of Angels

HUGO HURRIED HOME FROM work, his mind intent on how best to fulfil his pledge to educate Jacob in the French language. The streets were white and pure again, the grimy slush covered up by a fresh snowfall. A wagon lurched by, throwing a splash of icy water against his legs. By the time he arrived home his trousers were so soaked he had to change before sitting down to eat supper. He ate largely in silence, his mind preoccupied with verbs and conjugations as he conjectured a lesson on grammatical tenses. He was chewing on the construction of the relative clause when his cogitations were arrested by an exclamation from Josette.

'Hugo!'

He looked up, startled. 'What?'

'I was telling you about my meeting the curé in the middle of Avenue Courcelles. Did you not hear a single word I said?'

'Pardon, my love.' His voice was contrite. 'I have much to think on.'

She made a disapproving sound. 'What is it that preoccupies you so much that you ignore your poor, suffering wife?'

He set down his fork. 'I am about to start tutoring Jacob in our language, dearest. Imagine!'

She added a scoop of cream to the sugar tart. 'Why?'

He chuckled. 'Does it not make perfect sense? Since he intends to live and work in New France it goes without saying that he must command the language.'

'But why should *you* be the one to teach him? Are there not schools or tutors available for such a purpose?'

'My dear—'

'Have you not done enough already to make amends for what was an unfortunate accident? Really Hugo, you take too much upon yourself in regard to this creature.'

'Creature?' He frowned.

'This donkey of an Englishman! Do you not have time for me anymore? It's scandalous!' In a temper, she set down her napkin and pushed back from the table. 'All I hear about, night and day, is Jacob this and Jacob that.

Perhaps that is his real name. Jacob This!' She stood up, a cross look on her face as she brushed a crumb from her skirt.

'Charity, dearest. Father Boudreau—'

'Bother Father Boudreau! Let him tutor Jacob This and That.' And on that trumpet blast, she swept from the room.

With a resigned sigh he wiped his lips with the napkin. A few minutes later his wife re-entered the room, carrying a tray of coffee. Silently she set down the cups. 'Milk?' she asked, pursing her lips as she lifted the milk jug.

'Dearest, you know I always take milk.'

'Really? I hardly know any more,' she said, pouring the milk, 'between this and that.'

'You must remember, I am the cause of his suffering. I wish only to make amends for my offence.'

'Saint Hugo!' She gave a cat-like smile and sipped her coffee.

'Must we?'

'Must we what, dear?'

'Come, let us make up.' Getting up, he tugged her to her feet.

'Careful of the coffee!'

'Let us not quarrel.' He kissed her brow. 'I do it only because I must. If not me, who else speaks sufficient English for the purpose? And, sweetness, I *did* shoot him.'

She allowed herself to be kissed and caressed while noting where the wallpaper had peeled behind the ornamental side table. 'You will not devote too much time to it?' she asked, frowning at the peel.

'An evening or two a week, petal, no more. And perhaps the occasional Sunday. Not every Sunday!' he added, feeling her stiffen.

Disengaging herself from his arms, she sat down again. 'When do I get to meet this Englishman that so preoccupies you?'

'As soon as he has sufficiently recovered to mix with society.' He sipped coffee, pondering the question. 'At least not until he has a learned to introduce himself. After all, what would be the point of meeting if you could not converse?'

'Is he terribly disfigured?'

'Not at all. The scar is hidden by his hair.'

'All of it?'

'Yes. Why?'

'Sometimes a scar can be attractive—in a characterful sort of way.' She collected the dishes and put them on the tray.

Her husband chuckled fondly. 'You read too many romances.'

'Still.' She backed out the door, carrying the tray.

'Still what?' His voice followed her to the kitchen.

'Still nothing,' she said. She put the dishes on the table, her mind on the darkly handsome Andre Blanchet and the facial laceration he had brought to church one long-ago Sunday. Pouring heated water into the sink, she immersed the soup tureen, seeing again his startled look as she and her companions flocked around to coo and console.

'I shall be in the study, dearest.'

She gave a murmur in reply, brushing the tureen with warm, soapy memories.

'I AM MY OWN vault and my own key.' Haunted by the phrase, Hugo recalled it when he went to visit Father Pierre Marie Belanger, his former tutor in morals. They had maintained contact over the years, in spite of the latter's displeasure at Hugo's not entering into the order.

'I have heard of your Englishman,' said the priest, pouring two glasses of wine.

'You have?' Hugo glanced up in surprise.

'Father Boudreau mentioned him on his last visit. He also mentioned that the Englishman is under the care of that heathen woman?' Father Belanger stated the last with raised eyebrows.

'The midwife? She is very capable, Father, I assure you. She is undoubtedly responsible for saving his life.'

'Is she not rumoured to practice spells and enchantments?'

'Only the credulous believe so. She merely mixes up potions from the plants of the forest, the same as any apothecary might.'

'Even so, Hugo, take care. The devil has many cunning agents seeking to ensnare the unworldly.'

'I am protected at all times, Father.' Hugo pulled out the crucifix from beneath his shirt. 'And this—' He took out a small bottle of holy water from his pocket. 'Blessed by Father Boudreau for further assurance.'

'Good.' The priest nodded approvingly.

They were interrupted by a knock on the door.

'Monsieur Turgeon! Welcome!' said Father Belanger cheerfully as he escorted the visitor into the room.

The visitor's lined face was benign and dignified beneath the old-fashioned Paris beau hat he wore. His greatcoat collar was trimmed with beaver wool and beneath his arm he carried a polished walnut cane tipped with a silver knob. With the assistance of Father Belanger, he took off the greatcoat to reveal a grey frock coat and a blue, muslin cravat tied with a barrel knot.

'This is Hugo Gagnon,' said Father Belanger, introducing the two.

The visitor gave a courtly bow to Hugo, greeting him in the old style.

'Do you know each other?' asked the priest.

'Of course I am familiar with deputy Turgeon, even though I have not had the pleasure of meeting him until now. It is an honour to meet you, sir,' said Hugo, returning the bow. 'I am a great admirer of your work in the Assembly.'

'Gagnon?' The deputy regarded Hugo for a moment. 'You work in Government House, do you not?'

'I do, sir. In the archives.'

'Ah! I recall now. I am familiar with your family, Monsieur, through your father, a sterling fellow and proud patriot. I remember the day we stood side by side to defy the illegal tax edict issued by those upstarts in Quebec. The whole town manned the barricades, defying the troops to do their worst. A great day!'

The visitor took a seat, laying the cane against the armrest. 'But do not let me interrupt your conversation, gentlemen.'

'We were speaking of the Englishman,' said Father Belanger.

'Englishman? Which Englishman?'

'The one found in the woods—by our very own Hugo.'

The deputy, a lawyer and keen amateur philosopher, listened with attentive interest as Hugo recounted the story, giving a murmur of surprise as the account concluded. 'And you say he has no memory—not even of his own name?'

'None that we can identify.'

'And he speaks not a word of French? Astounding!' The deputy leaned forward. 'To discover a man with no memory and no language—at least no French—but he speaks his own tongue, English?'

'Most certainly. I converse with him in that tongue.'

'I, too, have some facility with the language,' said the deputy. He pondered for a moment, his face alive with speculation. 'So, to sum up. Your Englishman has no memory, no language, and no notion of how he came to be in the woods?'

Hugo nodded. 'In a nutshell.'

'This is unprecedented, my dear Monsieur Gagnon. Do you realise the import of such a case?'

'Import?'

'Indeed. In philosophical terms we might predicate it thus: a grown yet new-born soul, innocent of both himself and the world in which he finds himself. Remarkable! And his name is Jacob, you say? Might it not, just as rightly, be Adam?' The deputy smiled at the look on Hugo's face. 'In which case you might be said, in the language of the church, to have baptised him.'

The priest coughed and shifted in his chair. 'My dear René, I would hardly call the Englishman innocent. Who knows what crimes he may have committed, crimes unbeknown to us?'

The deputy nodded. 'I take your point, Pierre. But in the lexicon of philosophers, he holds great interest as a rare example of a man without knowledge of himself. Did Descartes not distinguish between self-knowledge and knowledge of the world? Perhaps our Englishman stands as an example of a person who is genuinely poised between the two—having no knowledge of language, as it pertains to his surroundings—or of himself, as he pertains to the world?' He considered for a moment. 'Monsieur Gagnon, if at all possible, I should very much like to meet your Englishman.'

'I shall arrange it sir, and gladly.'

The priest frowned. 'Do you think that is wise? Who knows what sort of fellow he is or what he has done in the past. Or, indeed, what he may do in the future?'

'Monsieur Gagnon will vouch for him, will you not?'

'I will. He strikes me as a thoroughly decent fellow who has had the misfortune to suffer a great calamity—like the parable of the Samaritan,' added Hugo. To his disappointment, neither the priest nor the deputy picked up on the allusion.

'I look forward to making his acquaintance. And now, Pierre, what news, old friend?'

Delighted at the encounter, Hugo returned home humming to himself. 'My dearest flower!' He lifted a surprised Josette into his arms and planted a kiss on her cheek.

'Goodness!' She helped him take off his coat. 'Did you fall into a pond and catch a fish?'

He laughed. 'Better! I have something to tell you.' Beaming at her sceptical expression, he steered her into a chair. 'Listen and be astounded!' He sat down and told of his discussion with the deputy. 'Well?' he said, chuckling at her expression as he concluded. 'What do you make of that?'

'The deputy said this?'

'He did! He as much as declared Jacob a person of immense interest!'

'And he expressed a wish to be introduced to him?'

'He did! Did I not tell you my saving his life was most providential?'

'You said it was an accident.'

'A providential one!' Hugo leaned forward. 'Do you not see? The deputy has taken a personal interest in the case.'

'Case?'

'A word he used, in the philosophical rather than the legal sense.'

Josette studied him, intrigued by the possibilities. 'This is an opportunity, Hugo. Who knows where it might lead? We could invite monsieur Turgeon for supper, to meet your Englishman. Imagine, the deputy in our house.'

'American.'

'Pardon?'

'He is American.'

'The deputy?' She held her composure for a moment before erupting into a peal of laughter. 'Your face!'

INSPIRED BY THE DEPUTY'S interest, he set about his task—nay, mission—to teach Jacob French. 'The tongue the angels speak among themselves in Heaven,' Father Ignatius had imparted to the row of solemn schoolboy faces gazing up at him. 'Yes, Gagnon?' he asked at the latter's tentative hand raise.

'Sir, is it not Latin—the language of the church—that they speak?'

The priest rubbed his cheek, his eyes ruminative. 'Latin in official matters, French for the sheer joy of it—for angelic discourse.'

Ever since, the distinction between the two had struck Hugo as obvious. Eager to impart the heavenly *patois* to Jacob, he rummaged among the bookshelves in his study, his mind brimming with the sacredness of the duty entrusted to him. "Perchance when he acquires the language might he not also acquire the faith?" The deputy's speculation added urgency to the task, he decided, reminding himself to take up the question with Father Boudreau.

Humming with intent, he took down volume after volume to leaf through the pages only to return each one with a murmured, 'That is not to the purpose.' To his delight, he spied a long-forgotten grammar squeezed between two large volumes of '*Letters of the Blessed Martyrs Concerning the Conversion of the Savages.*' With an exclamation of pleasure, he pulled the cloth-bound primer from its place. Brushing his fingers across the cover, he held the slim volume up to his nose. 'Ah!' he sighed, overcome with musty nostalgia for the Jesuit schoolroom of his youth.

He turned the pages, torn between smiles and tears at the childish notations written into the cramped margins of the text. Unable to resist, he took the book into the parlour where Josette was seated reading a romantic novel, an empty coffee cup on the small table beside her. 'Ahem!' He coughed to draw attention.

'Yes?' She looked up, arching her brow.

'I have found it!'

'Found what?'

'The very primer I used at the seminary.'

'Oh!' With a pout she returned to the novel.

Standing in place, Hugo proceeded to turn the pages with exaggerated sighs of pleasure and regret. 'I was whipped for that innocent mistake!' he protested, rigid with indignation twenty years after the fact.

His wife made a humming sound, engrossed in her book.

'Père Beaulieu awarded me a rosary for that answer!' He held up the volume, his eyes shining with remembrance. 'I believe I still have it somewhere. It has the wooden beads and the ivory crucifix.'

'Mm-hmm.' She lingered over a paragraph.

'To think! A precocious notation penned by myself on the insufficiency of nouns.' He thrust the page under her eyes.

'I feel a draught. Is there coal on the fire?'

For the remainder of the evening, Hugo immersed himself in the long-lost primer, making copious notes on sheets of paper and marvelling anew at the incomparable genius and elegance of his native tongue. Standing before the hearth, he delivered a brief and patriotic *extempore* to an imaginary audience on the sublime virtues of the partitive as a grammatical divisor, 'fully the equal of its mathematical counterpart!' Lecturing to the parlour curtains, he enumerated the wonders of the subjunctive, praising its elastic and unmistakeable Frenchness. 'For what other tongue so eloquently discriminates the essence not of the thing itself but of the beholder?' he enquired of the mantel clock.

Curious and exasperated at her husband's repeated turns and posturing in front of the fireplace, Josette complained to her sister, Claudette. 'Now he has it into his head to teach the Englishman how to speak French. One may as well teach a duck to bark!'

'But he is the cause of the Englishman's malady, is he not?' queried Claudette, being privy to the secret.

'Does that mean he is obligated to the fellow for the rest of his life?'

'I should like to see Hugo teach!' Claudette giggled at the thought.

'It will bring out the Jesuit in him.' complained Josette, piqued at the prospect.

'Well, then, dear sister, you know what you must do?'

'What?'

'Encourage him. Better teaching than preaching.' Claudette tittered at her own cleverness.

The next time he proceeded to practise his method of instruction, Hugo was surprised and gratified to see Josette arrange herself in the upholstered rose-print chair to observe. 'I may be able to offer some small but useful suggestions as to effect, if not means,' she suggested modestly.

Gratefully accepting her advice to loosen his shirt collar, 'so as not to unduly restrict the throat,' he prepared to orate only to be forestalled by an up-raised finger and apologetic smile. 'Your feet, dear husband.'

'My feet?' He looked down at his slippers.

'You stand like Father Boudreau about to give a sermon. Surely, a more relaxed posture is warranted?'

'Indeed. You are right.' He adjusted his stance. 'Like so?'

'Perfection!'

He had no sooner opened his mouth again than she tutted in mild disapproval. 'But not so, surely?'

'I beg pardon?'

'The hands, dear husband. To the sides, or loosely held in front, no? Is that not more natural? After all, you are not conducting an orchestra.'

'Ah! Like so? I am in your debt, dearest.'

He wet his lips. 'Regarding the nature of the predicate …' He stopped as Josette put a hand to her mouth.

'Yes, turtledove?' She coughed into her handkerchief. 'Pray continue. It is the air.'

'As you wish.' He cleared his throat and proceeded to wade into the murky waters of grammatical flux. 'One may take, as an example, the verb denotative of the present circumstance or *being*. Whilst manifestly perfect in its infinitude, it is, at the same time, the most irregular of its tribe.' Unconsciously, he steepled his fingers under his nose in imitation of his Jesuit tutors in the articles of faith. 'Indeed, of all its brethren, we may infer … Yes, petal?'

'Are you going to be instructing your *anglais* in the French?' she inquired with an innocent lift of her eyebrows.

'Merely to expedite matters, I assure you.'

'But the *anglais*—'

'Monsieur Wheeler,' he corrected.

'Monsieur Wheeler, *anglais*, surely does not comprehend the language sufficiently to allow for instruction in the same?'

Hugo muttered, annoyed with himself for the oversight. 'You're right. I had quite forgot in the moment. I must refresh myself on the English terms. Now, where was I?'

6

A Handcart of Nouns

O N A BRIGHT, CRISP morning in February, Hugo arrived at the cabin armed with the instruments of instruction. He was pleased to find Jacob there alone. 'Good morning, Jacob,' he said, rubbing his hands for warmth.

'Good morning, Hugo! A cold morning it is, too.'

'You have been outside?' Hugo set down the leather satchel he carried.

'A little walk. To the trees and back.'

Hugo stood back to admire, marvelling at Jacob's progress. 'It's hard to believe that, but a few short weeks ago, you were at death's door.'

With a proud grin, Jacob removed the toque he was wearing. 'See?'

Hugo started in surprise. 'You are without your bandage!'

'And heartily relieved to be rid of it.'

'May I see?' Approaching, Hugo studied the side of Jacob's head where the bullet had entered. The hair, shaved around the entry point, had begun to grow back, but not so much as to obscure the ugly ridge on the scalp where the skin had been stitched. Hugo placed a careful finger on the spot, wincing at this tactile reminder of his carelessness. 'I am heartily sorry, Jacob—for all you have suffered.'

'Aye, me too. I should love to bang the brains of the fool who shot me.'

Hugo coughed. 'Indeed.'

'I'm grateful to the midwife, but ready to leave here and resume my life.' Jacob looked at Hugo, a hopeful expression on his face.

'That is why I am here, friend. To begin your French instruction so that you may take your place in the world.'

'You mentioned a rooming house—in the city?'

'Madame Pepin assures me she will have a room available next month. Until then, we must take things a step at a time. Have the fainting fits disappeared?'

'Once or twice, only, and none for the past four days.'

'Excellent. Nevertheless, we must proceed cautiously. Today you take your first step in regaining your independence.' Opening the leather satchel Hugo took out a thick notebook. 'For you,' he said, 'to copy down the lessons and make notes.'

Jacob peered at the lined pages. 'I feel like a pupil again.'

'Again?' Hugo glanced up at the tidbit. 'Do you remember your schooling?'

'No. But I am certain I must have had some, at least. Else, where did I learn to read?'

'Quite so. I myself was educated by the Jesuit fathers in matters of faith and language.'

'And they also taught you English?'

'No.' Hugo paused from taking out a sheet of paper. 'When I was young, in my primary years, my father took it into his head to have me taught English. He intended me for a career in business, you see. He sent me to an English school in Ontario where I boarded for four years before he changed his mind again and summoned me back at the urging of Father Ignatius. I was then intended for the brotherhood. But then I met Josette, my wife.' He reflected a moment. 'I hope to introduce you soon,' he continued, 'but now to the business at hand.'

'You have nailed up the board as I asked? Good,' he said, rapping the flat board with his knuckles. He unfolded the paper to produce a large, foolscap sheet which he tacked to the wood, creating a makeshift blackboard. He stepped back, nodding in approval at the arrangement. 'Are we ready to receive instruction?' he asked, falling into the phraseology of his Jesuit masters.

'I am.' Jacob seated himself at the table, pen at the ready.

'Excellent!' Hugo took a deep breath, fully aware of the solemnity of the moment and his own position as celebrant of the sacred French tongue. '*Il est temps de commencer*,' he said, feeling the weight of Samaritan obligation.

Clearing his throat, he gazed solemnly at the blank sheet in imitation of Father Ignatius. 'In order to introduce verbs and their tenses, we shall begin with the rhetorical division of time.' Using a stick of charcoal, he drew a thick black line down the centre of the sheet, stepping back to observe the result. 'Good,' he said, and nodded to himself.

'Grammatical proximity,' he commenced, 'that is to say, the juxtaposition of a word, or words, in relation to an event, or events, is essential to grasping the genius of the French tongue.' His expression became grave as he folded his arms and fell into the fondly remembered voice of his schoolroom tutor. 'As I have had occasion to observe, such understanding is lamentably deficient in the Anglo-Saxon. In the Latin tongues we possess a more natural and altogether superior grasp of contiguity: that is to say, the relation of one thing to another in the time in which they occurred, have occurred, may occur or indeed, are occurring.' He paused to glance at his solitary pupil who was pouring himself a glass of whisky. He held up the bottle to Hugo.

'Time past, for example,' continued Hugo, shaking his head, 'may be apprehended as either singular or complex. If singular, to take but the first instance, one may say it is but the … *unambiguous* past.' He made a careful tick to one side of the charcoal line. 'If complex, or historical, it may be clearly apprehended as having relation to things that are of a hist– *epical* nature.' He drew a second tick and paused, pondering the diagram.

'Here, we have the illustration of time,' he summarised. 'Time as represented by this vertical line, so!' He stabbed the air with the charcoal stick. 'To the right—no, left, we have comp—historical time.' He placed a finger thoughtfully to his lip. 'To the other side, we have diurnal or … quotidian time. Chronological time, that is, figured in its quintessentially grammatical or rhetorical properties.' His voice trailed off doubtfully as he stared at the sheet.

He turned to Jacob, to observe him soundly asleep, his head on the table. 'Perhaps we shall defer the lesson to another time,' he conceded.

'IT WAS A DISASTER!' he lamented to Serge Villeneuve in the tavern. 'I put Jacob to sleep!'

'Why? What did you say?'

Drawing a deep breath, Hugo summarised the debacle to Serge who listened with an expression of astonishment on his face. 'You said that? Ye gods that is enough to put the angels to sleep. I understood hardly a word.'

Hugo sighed in agreement, his face a picture of misery. 'This business of imparting a language is more difficult than I had given to understand,' he admitted.

Serge drained his wine and beckoned for a refill. 'Perhaps the Englishman is best left to acquire his French naturally, from the air, as does a child.'

Hugo groaned. 'I simply must do better.'

Serge thought for a moment. 'How do you teach someone to fire a musket?'

'A musket?' Hugo frowned. 'I suppose you show him.'

'You mean you don't go off into some airy nonsense about the properties of gunpowder or the trajectories of flight?' Serge waited for Hugo's nod. 'Good. What you do is use simple words and allow him to feel the press of the gunstock against his cheek. Yes? You place his finger on the trigger and ask him to pull it when he is ready. Do you see what I am getting at,

Hugo? We instruct our novice by introducing him to the touch and feel of the rifle. You must do the same for your Englishman.'

Hugo blinked at the advice, astounded by its novelty. 'By heaven, you are right! In language, as in theology, simplicity is all. May I ask your advice on something else?' Before Serge could say yea or nay Hugo leaned across the table, his voice earnest. 'Should I confess to Jacob that it was I who shot him—all unbeknown of course! But I, nevertheless?'

Serge groaned. 'Haven't we gone over this already?'

'We have. But now that he is almost fully recovered, I feel a sense of obligation to speak truthfully and honestly about his injury.'

'Do you recall that time Madam Laurent accused you of possessing an over-zealous conscience?'

'I do.' Hugo firmed his lips at the memory. 'What does that have to do with the price of fish?'

Serge poured them both another glass of wine. 'What difference would it make to Jacob if he were to know who fired the bullet that hit him? Would it make him one whit happier about what happened? No. So hold your tongue. Say nothing. What he doesn't know can't hurt him. You show everyday how much the accident has affected you by your concern for the Englishman. So let us hear no more about confessions. Save that for Père Boudreau!'

THE FOLLOWING SUNDAY, FORTIFIED by Villeneuve's advice, Hugo returned to the cabin, determined to correct the mistakes of the previous week. Dispensing with the blackboard altogether, he sat across from Jacob. '*Table!*' he said firmly and rapped the pine with his knuckles in a business-like fashion.

Jacob hesitated and then rapped the wood. '*Table!*' he repeated, drawing a gratified smile from Hugo.

'*Chaise!*' Hugo pointed to the object.

'*Chaise!*'

The door opened and the midwife stepped inside, her head wrapped in a scarf against the cold. '*Femme!*' Hugo pointed.

'*Femme!*'

'What is this woman nonsense?' The midwife sat on a stool to tug off her boots.

'Jacob is learning French, Madame Midwife. Observe his progress.' Hugo pointed to himself. '*Homme!*'

'*Homme!*'

'*Femme. Homme. Table. Chaise.*' Hugo pointed to each in turn, brightening as Jacob repeated the words.

'He is making rapid progress,' he announced to Josette upon his return. 'He begins to understand the world around him in French.'

STILL PIQUED AT HER husband's inordinate interest in the Englishman, Josette went to visit her parents to celebrate her father's sixtieth birthday. Claudette and her husband, André, and a few of her father's friends had gathered for a light repast of cake, biscuits, cheese, and wine to observe the occasion. Following several toasts to the health of their father, Claudette took Josette aside to enquire about Hugo's progress in teaching the Englishman. André lingered on the edges of the conversation, curious to hear more about the mysterious stranger.

'The house is like a schoolroom,' Josette complained. 'I hear of nothing but indicatives and prepositions all day long!'

'And when will we get to meet this monsieur Wheeler?'

'God knows! When he can converse like a civilised person, I suppose.' Josette turned and raised her glass as her father was toasted by a former workmate. 'Good health, Papa!'

'They say he was found with a quantity of gold in his possession.' André discreetly covered his mouth with a napkin as both women turned to him in surprise.

'Gold?' Josette laughed. 'Nonsense! Where did you hear such prattle?'

André swallowed a mouthful of maple tart as his wife cocked an eyebrow in anticipation. 'Well?'

'It was Paul Moreau who told me.' Andre accidentally spat out a crumb, mumbling an apology as he continued. 'He had it from Gabriel Laurent who had it from Claude Charbonneau himself. Charbonneau being one of the finders,' he explained.

'Finders! Good Lord, is he a country or a scientific discovery? Next, they'll proclaim him the Second Coming.'

'Josette!' Her sister gasped at the blasphemy.

'Is this all anyone talks about—the wretched Englishman?' Josette clucked in disapproval.

'He himself is of no interest,' protested André. 'It is being said, that is all.'

'Being said? You sound like my husband!'

'It is strange, nevertheless,' her brother-in-law continued. 'Where did he spring from all of a sudden? And what was he doing in the woods? Is he a fugitive of some kind? Or a dissenter, sent to stir up trouble?'

'Are you suggesting he is some kind of criminal or spy? Ridiculous!'

'Bishop Drolet condemned him from the pulpit last Sunday,' divulged Claudette.

'What!' Josette stared in astonishment.

'Indirectly. He warned of unnatural signs and portents sent to test the faithful.'

'And to tempt,' put in her husband disappointed at the lack of gold in the tale.

'And you read the Englishman into that?' Josette gave a pitying smile while filing away the remark.

'Not … explicitly.'

'But implicitly,' confirmed her husband, 'as in a parable.'

'Good Heavens!' Josette stared. 'A parable? Have you both lost your minds?' She turned her gaze on her sister. 'Claudette?'

'What? Don't look at me! It's your husband you must ask.'

Returning home, Josette removed her coat and hat and sat down in the parlour, awaiting her husband's return from work. The clock ticked in the background as she waited, a determined crimp to her lips. At last, she heard the front door open.

'Josette?'

'What do you know of any gold?' she demanded as soon as Hugo entered the room.

'Gold?' He sat down to tug off his shoes, a perplexed look on his face. 'What in God's name are you talking about?'

'According to Claude Charbonneau, your Englishman was found with a quantity of gold in his possession—gold nuggets,' she added, scrutinising his face.

'And Charbonneau said this? Absurd!' Hugo laughed as he pulled off his shoe.

'He swears solemnly to it.'

Hugo frowned. 'Then he is a liar as well as a fool. But it is true that Jacob had some money in his possession, some American dollars.'

'You never mentioned that.'

'What was there to mention? Besides, it was a small amount.'

'How much?'

'Two hundred dollars, that is all.'

'And what happened to it?'

'I kept it for a while and when he was feeling better, I returned it to him. He now uses it to pay the midwife.'

'The midwife!' Josette sat back in the chair, a look of suspicion on her face. '*She* could have taken the nuggets.'

'There were no nuggets—gold or otherwise. And if Claude Charbonneau said so then let him repeat it to my face.'

'Poor Hugo.' Josette shook her head, her voice part bemused, part pitying. 'So innocent of the ways of the world!'

ANXIOUS TO FIND A place to live and to start earning money, Jacob badgered Hugo for a day when he might quit the midwife's cabin. 'I'm recovered now, and ready to start earning a wage,' he pestered. 'When will this Madame Pepin have the room available?'

'Any time now. Be patient. And use the time to practise French. For without it, you will not be able to find work.'

Jacob took the advice to heart, despite his frustrations with the language. It is the key to my livelihood, he reminded himself, and redoubled his efforts to achieve some sort of foothold on the slippery, baffling torrent of words that constituted the French tongue. He pored over the French-English dictionary Hugo had given him, painstakingly pronouncing words and attempting to retain their meanings. As cold, blustery winds announced the arrival of March, he uttered his novitiate words in the language, haltingly at first, and then with more confidence, as the sounds became less foreign in his mouth.

'*Merci*,' he said, when the midwife passed him a mug of tea heaped with sugar. '*Les cloches*,' he said on hearing the distant chime of bells.

'Where's the fucking pipe?' Scowling, the midwife upturned everything on the table.

'*La jolie pipe* … is on … *la chaise*,' he said, pointing.

'French, madame, I pray you,' he said on another occasion, begging her to address him 'in the original French' as she veered into Mohawk. 'For only thus will my ear improve.'

He made up word lists to memorise, further irritating the put-upon midwife by praising her cooking in the *pot de chamber*. '*Collier?*' he enquired on another occasion, pointing to his shirt.

She ignored him, sitting down in the chair as she thumbed tobacco into the pipe bowl. Jacob was bent over the dictionary, mouthing words to himself. 'Soon you will know the names of things,' she mused, emitting a stream of scented smoke. 'But the names are different in the Mohawk. The Mohawk names are the true ones.' Taking the pipe out of her mouth she rapped the table to gain his attention. '*Ka'nikáhta!*' She pointed to the tobacco pouch.

'What?' Distracted, he looked up from the dictionary.

'*Ka'nikáhta.*' She pronounced the word slowly, watching his face for signs of comprehension.

'*Tabac?*' he said.

She grunted. 'What is the English word. *Anglais?*' She pointed at the pouch again.

'Ah! Tobacco!'

'How can a thing have three names? It is absurd!'

'*Le tabac est sûrement sur le table n'est-ce pas?*'

On Hugo's next visit Jacob impressed his tutor by pointing to various objects in the cabin and haltingly enunciating the name of each in turn, stumbling over the pronunciation of 'egg.' 'I speak like a donkey!' he complained,

'Not so!' encouraged Hugo. 'The teeth need to sit like so,' he said, helpfully jutting out his lower jaw to demonstrate. 'This position imparts the required agility to the tongue. Like *thith*.'

'*Et comment va votre santé, Monsieur?*' said Hugo on another occasion, having decided it was time to introduce his charge to simple conversation. He stood up with the question, startling Jacob by sticking out his hand.

Jacob got up, a confused look on his face as he shook hands. '*Bien?*' he said.

'In a sentence, Jacob. Remember we talked about the verb of the present tense? *Ma santé est excellente, Monsieur. Merci d'avoir posé la question.* Yes?' he prompted at Jacob's baffled silence. He peered around the cabin in an exaggerated fashion.'*Veuillez vous asseoir, Monsieur Wheeler. Je ne vois pas la chatte ?*'

'La shat est dans le bucket, n'est-ce pas?

'*Et où est la sage-femme, cet après-midi?*'

'La sauge est une herbe de dame, n'est-ce pas?'

These early attempts at conversation floundered and jolted forward again on the handcart of nouns, the fragmented nature of the exchanges greatly frustrating Jacob. 'I feel like a child mewling his first words!'

'But you are!' exclaimed Hugo, struck by the truth of the statement.

THE COLD SPRING GALES gave way to milder winds as Jacob struggled to denote intention—wishes, desires and needs all devolving to the nearest concrete expedient: hunger being a rub of the belly, tiredness an exaggerated yawn, and puzzlement a finger-tap to the head.

Language, he brooded, sitting in front of the fire after another failed attempt at communicating with the midwife, must have been originally about *things*, its purpose being to signify objects, rather like an extension of the pointed finger. Thus, the idea of language as a *substitute* for substance, or at any rate an indicator of such, took root in his mind. The solidity of the object, contrasted with the vaporousness of the word, briefly fascinated him as he attached the sibilance of breath to the hardness of wood, the suppleness of leather, and the cold unyieldingness of stone.

The fact he could voice such notions at all came as a surprise and led him to believe that he was the product of extensive schooling.

One morning he caught himself humming a tune and stopped, intrigued at its provenance. 'Perhaps it is some chant or lullaby taught to me by my mother,' he speculated to Hugo. He hummed the ditty for the latter's enlightenment, being unable to recall the words.

Hugo did his best to hum along, impressed at this novel method of balancing the senses. 'Singing may indeed release the faculties,' he remarked approvingly to his wife on his return home. 'For do they not say that music is a tonic to the soul?' He hummed a few bars of an old French tune. 'Do you recall the air? It was my mother's favourite,' he recalled fondly, while beating time with his finger. 'Or perhaps she disliked it,' he said, his finger paused in mid-beat as an image of his piously observant mother came to mind.

The following day, while engaged in his employment duties, Hugo chanced to encounter the deputy. To his gratification, the latter greeted him by name in front of his fellow clerk. 'Monsieur Gagnon! How is your Englishman progressing?'

'He is almost fully recovered, sir. And has begun to learn French.'

'He has?' The deputy considered this. 'Then he is finding a pathway back into the world—the world he knows nothing of?'

'He is—slowly, and by degrees.'

'Slowly, and by degrees,' the deputy repeated, his face thoughtful. 'That is the Golden Way.' He turned to go before turning back again. 'I remain eager to meet your charge,' he reminded. 'As soon as my duties permit.'

'Simply say the word, sir.'

'I shall.' The deputy continued on his way, the tap of his cane echoing in the marble hallway.

'I did not know you were on terms with the deputy,' remarked his fellow clerk as Hugo retook his seat.

'We are socially acquainted,' Hugo advised modestly, happily filing away the exchange to share with Josette over supper.

Upon returning home he was presented with an envelope with his address carefully written upon the front. 'It is from Madame Pepin,' said Josette as he peered at the return address. She watched as he opened it. 'Well?'

'She has a room available.' He looked up, his expression pleased. 'I must tell Jacob.'

7

Old Town

TWO MONTHS AFTER HIS arrival, Jacob took his leave of the midwife, offering profuse thanks for her skill in saving his life.

'He is most grateful to you, midwife, as am I,' interpreted Hugo as they stood on the cabin porch. Jacob was wrapped in the buffalo coat, the thick wool toque pulled down over his ears. The small wagon Hugo had borrowed to drive them back into the city stood in the clearing. The March air was cold but clear, sunlight sparkling on the snow. The midwife was wrapped in a blanket, the battered felt hat pulled down over her head. Her hair hung in strands from under the hat, her cheeks rosy in the cold air.

'We should go,' said Hugo.

'Wait! Tell her I hope to repay her one day,' said Jacob, suddenly full of emotion.

'He hopes to be able to repay your kindness.'

The midwife grunted. 'For you, Ghost Bear.' She handed Jacob a pouch. '*Pour la tête*.' She tapped her head.

'*Pour la tête*,' he repeated, taking the ground-up herbs and nodding to show his understanding.

'Tell him to come back if he is troubled by strange dreams,' she said, already retreating behind the door.

'I am sure he will be alright. Goodbye, Madame. Farewell.' Hugo took Jacob's arm as they descended the porch steps. 'Watch your footing. There's ice beneath the snow.'

As the wagon trundled off, Jacob turned to look back at the cabin. 'She saved my life,' he said, 'and I don't even know her name.'

'Nobody does. Everyone calls her midwife. She's been living alone in the woods for as long as I can remember. My father pointed her out to me when I was a boy. She was enormously fat even then.'

'What tribe is she?'

Hugo shrugged. 'Who knows? Most probably Mohawk. But others say Huron, Cree or Algonquin. The credulous say she has magical powers and go to her for every ailment, including charms and love spells. We took you to her because we feared you would not survive the trip to the hospital.'

'I am grateful you did. I don't know what more the doctors could have done.' Jacob huddled in the warm robe as they proceeded, eager to experience the novelty and diversions of the town.

After travelling for some time, they emerged from the trees onto a dirt road. Other conveyances shared the road, the drivers muffled against the cold. Soon, the town fortifications came into view. Jacob's eyes widened at the sight of the high stone walls. Embrasures cut into the stone provided shelter for a row of cannon whose iron mouths protruded menacingly through the slits.

He turned to stare at the thickness of the massive walls as they lurched through the arched entrance way. 'The defences are formidable,' he remarked.

Hugo's face fell. 'It was all for nothing. The enemy was within.'

They approached a military barracks. A lone sentry idled against the ramparts, a pipe in his mouth. 'That's the garrison,' said Hugo. 'It's one of the largest in Quebec. The government claims it is there to protect us from the Americans.' He gave a dismissive laugh to indicate the falsity of the claim.

Leaving the barracks behind, they passed through an outlying *faubourg*, full of two- and three-storey row houses whose doors opened directly onto the street. 'The town is divided into upper, middle, and lower,' explained Hugo. 'This is the lower, or Old Town, also known as the Quarter. It contains the oldest buildings in New France.'

Freight wagons, omnibuses, carts, and cabriolets vied for space in the paved streets. In spite of Jacob's anticipation of the moment, the sights and sounds left him temporarily disoriented as the busy hubbub of the town displaced the snow-bound hush of the forest.

Hugo slowed the wagon to barely above walking pace as they passed under an arch linking two buildings. They entered a maze of cobblestone streets lined with shops and taverns. Pedestrians wrapped in scarves and hats hurried along the footpaths, their heads bowed against the blustery wind. Smells drifted in the air from bakeries, butcher shops and patisseries. A wagon creaked past hauling a cargo of firewood. '*Aller!*' cried the driver, cracking a whip. Jacob was diverted by the sight of a tradesman slowly ascending a ladder with a bucket balanced on his head. He glimpsed two women in a yard, singing in time as they folded a basket of laundered sheets between them.

'I had forgotten the world contained so many people!' he exclaimed, turning his head to take in every passing sight.

'New France is the third largest and oldest city in Quebec, after Montreal and Quebec City itself. Hup!' Hugo shook the reins. 'Rue Saint-Jean-Baptiste,' said Jacob, reading the sign attached to a stone wall.

'We are headed to rue des Martyrs, where Madam Pepin has her house.'

They passed under a gas lamp, set so close to the street that Jacob was forced to duck his head. 'Durn!'

Hugo grinned. 'The lower town is still lit by gas. But the streets and boulevards of the upper town all have electric lighting.'

'How much will it cost again?' asked Jacob, his voice concerned.

'Ten of your American dollars a month. Breakfast and dinner included. Don't worry. You have sufficient funds to tide you over until you find work of some sort.'

They continued for another half mile, embarking on a paved street lined with houses on either side. The houses had steep roofs inset with dormer windows.

'Here we are. Whoa!' Hugo drew the wagon to a halt in front of a house set on a corner. 'Come,' he said, climbing down, his body stiff from the seat. 'Meet your new landlady.' He chuckled. 'You'll find her a tad different from the midwife.'

Madame Pepin turned out to be a presentable middle-aged widow, her manner primly efficient. 'Good day, Monsieur Gagnon,' she said. 'Is this the gentleman you told me about?'

'It is, Madame. May I introduce Monsieur Jacob Wheeler.'

The landlady ran a proprietorial eye over Jacob. 'Good morning, Monsieur.'

'Good morning, Madame. The snow is cold, is it not?'

Madame Pepin raised an eyebrow. 'And he understands the conditions and the rules of the house?'

'He does, and is prepared to pay two weeks in advance, as per our agreement.'

Madam Pepin wiped her hands on her apron and stood aside. 'Then welcome, gentlemen.'

The house was old but clean, a steep flight of stairs leading up from the hallway. 'This is where you will take your meals,' the landlady said, showing the small salon. 'He understands that breakfast is not served on Sundays?'

'He does, assuredly so.'

'But how will I speak to him?' she whispered as Jacob idly inspected a bow-front commode.

'He is learning our language, Madame, and making much progress.'

'He conducts himself like an Englishman,' she said as Jacob peered out a window at the quiet street.

'He is actually American, Madame.'

'Indeed? This way, gentlemen.'

She led them up the flight of stairs to the garret, subdivided into two separate quarters. 'Monsieur …?' She turned enquiring eyes on Hugo.

'Wheeler. Jacob Wheeler.'

'Monsieur Wheeler's room is here,' she said, pausing before the first door. 'Monsieur Bedard, a carpenter, occupies the next room. He is a most obliging fellow and can be relied upon.' Opening the door, she stood aside to allow them to enter.

The room was surprisingly spacious and well lit, the dormer windows admitting plenty of light. The room contained a fireplace, a sturdy, upholstered chair, three wooden chairs, a table, a bed, an armoire, and a commode. A brass gas lamp was affixed to the wall. It struck Jacob as almost palatial compared to the cramped cabin he had, up until that day, occupied.

'It is very … pretty, Madame,' he said, the words stumbling from his tongue in French.

'Indeed, I had not thought so until just now,' she remarked in an amused voice. 'Well, I shall leave you two gentlemen to talk. I have things to do.' She paused at the head of the stairs, turning.

'Does he smoke?'

'He does not.'

'Good!' And with that she descended the stairs.

'I hope you like it here, Jacob.' Hugo spread his hands to take in the room. 'Don't worry. I have no doubt it will soon feel like home. And when spring finally arrives you can open the windows and gaze out over the street. The Old Town market is nearby where you may wish to buy some clothes and a pair of shoes. But wait for me before you do so. Those market sellers would filch a blind man of his eyes! And now I must go and return the wagon.' With a congratulatory smile, he shook Jacob's hand. 'Welcome, to your new home!'

Left entirely alone for the first time since his arrival in New France, Jacob wasn't quite sure what to do with himself. He sat in the upholstered chair and gazed about the room. He stood up and walked to the window, peering out. He pulled out the drawers on the armoire and inspected the bare wood panels. He sat on the bed, testing for sturdiness. He got up and walked to the window again, looking down onto the street. He sat on the chair once more, thrusting out his legs. He felt his coat pocket where the balance of his savings resided, minus the moneys paid out to the midwife and madame Pepin. Taking out the dollar bills he tucked them under the mattress, removing two, which he folded inside his pocket.

Feeling restless, and eager to explore his new surroundings, he stepped from the room, locking the door behind him. He glanced at the neighbouring room and listened for sounds.

Hearing none, he descended the stairs, the worn treads creaking beneath his feet. Madame Pepin stuck her head out of the parlour.

'You are going out, Monsieur?'

'Yes … Towards the market, is it not?'

'Be careful. There are thieves everywhere.'

'Bonjour, Madame,' he replied, mystified as to what she had said.

He walked towards the Old Town, looking about him to take in every landmark along the way. The street was lined with houses on both sides. At the bottom of the street stood a statue of a man carrying a paddle over his shoulder. He stopped to read the inscription, "Paul Noyé, voyageur". A gas lamp stood on the opposite corner. A brown guidepost gave the name of the intersecting street, rue Pascal Langlois. A finger post pointed in the direction he was going, Le Quartier. He turned to take in Madame Pepin's house on the street behind him. 'Number 87,' he said. 'Rue des Martyrs.'

Crossing the street, he continued towards the Old Town. The pavers seemed strange underfoot after the mud and grass he was used to. Grime-covered snow was piled in the gutters, and he was forced to step into the road to avoid several large puddles of melt water. For a moment, he half-wished he were back in the cabin with its familiar smells and the cheerfully vulgar midwife. The wind gusted and he tugged at the collar of the buffalo coat.

The street led to a large public market crowded with shops and pedestrians. The noise of commerce was loud in the air as stallholders shouted their wares or haggled with customers. He was shocked to note the number of poor and destitute occupying the dirty pavements. Entire families begged for food or coins, holding out small bowls for the purpose. Some individuals sat on the footpath, defeated and downcast, importuning passers-by with their eyes. Others, especially those afflicted by the loss of a limb, were more vocal, beseeching a spare coin or a piece of bread. One man, his crutches propped beside him, leaned against a wall, a bottle of wine in his hand, singing tunelessly in the hope of eliciting charity. A scruffy dog, as forlorn looking as its master, lay at the beggar's feet.

'Monsieur?' The man interrupted his song as Jacob passed. 'A penny!' he implored, holding out a trembling hand.

He hurried past, disturbed by the reminders of his own near fate. He wandered aimlessly through the narrow streets, the noise of so many French voices amidst the jostle of tradesmen, shoppers, hawkers and stallholders strange and discordant in his ears. His attention was diverted by the many statues that seemed to populate the Quarter. Indeed, it seemed to him that each corner possessed its own tutelary figure in bronze or stone gazing out blindly at the constant to-and-fro.

Turning a corner, he halted. A woman stood beneath a gas lamp, singing fervently, her apron spread to catch the occasional dropped coin. He lingered, struck by the plaintive tune and the mellifluous sound of her voice above the creak of a passing goods wagon. *'Chante, rossignol, chante. Toi qui as le cœur gai. Tu as le cœur à rire. Moi, je l'ai à pleurer!'* He was unable to grasp the words, but the mournful melody struck a chord in his own disoriented heart as the woman warbled above the indifferent bustle of the street. A hurrying tradesman bumped into him. *'Pardon, Monsieur!'*

'Pardon moi!' he replied.

Encouraged by this small interaction, he continued through the maze of streets, the busy sounds and strong smells of the marketplace flooding his senses. The houses and workshops were seemingly constructed with little thought for passage, each building crowding upon its neighbour. He passed several laneways, the openings occupied by old men seated on stools, seemingly to watch the world go by. Several returned his gaze and stared curiously as if he, not they, were the exotic object of interest.

He stepped back to give way to two workmen carrying a cabinet into a shop. A warning shout rang out behind him, and a man brushed past, a large wicker basket strapped to his back. The strange aromas and clamouring voices were overpowering as he continued, carried along by the motion of the passing throng as much as by his own volition.

The cobblestone streets became more congested as he penetrated into the historic heart of the Quarter. He found himself in a square hemmed in with weathered stone buildings that had the air of centuries about them. The ancient walls, the strange smells, and the incessant chorus of foreign voices on all sides induced a feeling of dizziness. He stopped to gather breath, aware of curious eyes turned his way.

Fixing his gaze on a statue across the cobblestone square, he crossed towards the figure, afflicted by a sudden and intense feeling of unease that seemed to have no discernible cause. He stopped before the statue—the life-size figure of a nun set on a concrete plinth. The stone figure held a rosary in one hand and a crucifix in the other. Her eyes were cast demurely downwards, as though to block out the vulgar noise of the street. An inscription, etched into a faded plaque, read, "Marguerite Bourgeoys 1650–1700."

As he gazed at the placid features, a suffocating anxiety constricted his throat making it hard to breathe. The loud clip-clop of a passing carriage resounded in his ears. Church bells tolled somewhere nearby, the brassy *dong!* echoing inside his head. A pale slick of sweat formed on his brow as his heart pounded in his chest. His limbs started to tremble as though the fever that had racked him at the midwife's had returned.

Consumed by anxiety, he sat on a bench to compose himself, his breath coming in shallow gasps. A carriage rattled past. Its sole occupant—a man in a flat wool cap—regarded him with a lingering and sinister stare. He sat there, dazed and disoriented, the object of curious glances by passers-by. A workman gave an aggressive look in his direction. A group of ragamuffin children pointed, their eyes drawn to the buffalo coat. Fearing he was on the brink of fainting, he didn't dare move from the seat.

After what seemed an age, he felt sufficiently himself to carefully retrace his steps to the lodging house. He climbed the stairs, glad Madame Pepin was not there to observe or ask questions. In his room, he threw himself down on the bed and closed his eyes, thankful for the quietness of the house. He was still struggling to comprehend the sensations in his head—fearful lest the excursion had somehow reignited his fever—when he fell into a troubled, dream-haunted sleep.

8

Monsieur Turgeon

THE DEPUTY LISTENED CAREFULLY as Hugo summarised Jacob's engagement with the French language, including his frustrations with having to 'hurdle from noun to noun' to explain himself.

'He said that—that language was a development from pointing?' The deputy pondered the observation. 'If so, then different qualities of each object, or noun, must be, self-evidently, a subsequent development, being secondary rather than primary in purpose.' He tugged at his ear while gazing at the window. 'Thus, it follows, does it not, that adjectives, being ascriptive in nature, must be a later invention of language, essence being corollary to fact?' he speculated. 'A most unexpected insight from a beginning student.'

Hugo made a humming sound in agreement, enjoying the rare privilege of taking tea with the deputy in his private chambers.

'And has he found employment?'

'Not yet, sir. But he is anxious to do so. He fears his lack of French will be an obstacle.'

The deputy considered this. 'I may be able to help. I am owed a favour by a certain Gustave Lascelles. Do you know the fellow?'

Hugo shook his head.

'He owns a leather-making business in Place Jeanne d'Arc—saddles, that sort of thing. Do you think your monsieur Wheeler might be interested in such an occupation?'

'He will be grateful for work of any description, sir, I assure you.'

'Good, then I will arrange it. But first, I would like to meet your mysterious Englishman.'

It was on the tip of Hugo's tongue to correct the deputy, but instead he asked, 'Shall I bring him here, to the Assembly?'

'No, no.' The deputy waved off the suggestion. 'Best to observe the fellow in his own habitat.'

Accordingly, the following Sunday Jacob responded to a knock on the door to find Hugo and a distinguished-looking gentleman standing outside in the narrow hallway.

'Jacob, I wish to introduce Monsieur Turgeon. Monsieur Turgeon is a deputy in the New France Assembly.'

'I am exceedingly pleased to meet you sir.' The deputy removed his hat and bowed.

Delighted that the esteemed deputy should be visiting her house, Madam Pepin insisted on bringing up coffee, offering a gratified smile at the deputy's compliments. 'It is a privilege, sir,' she said, and curtsied before exiting the room.

'And now, Monsieur Wheeler,' said the deputy, turning his attention to Jacob. 'I am given to understand that you are studying French. Forgive my own poor English,' he said modestly. 'I am not often called upon to use the tongue.'

'I try,' said Jacob, responding in French, with a glance at Hugo for affirmation.

The deputy nodded at this 'And how is your memory, sir? Has it improved since your unfortunate accident?'

Puzzled, Jacob looked to Hugo for interpretation.

'Never mind,' said the deputy, catching the look. 'Let us proceed in English.' he said and repeated the question.

'It has not,' answered Jacob, his voice rueful.

'You remember nothing of your former life?'

Jacob sighed 'Nothing, I am afraid.'

'Remarkable.' The deputy pondered for a moment. 'And what is your opinion, sir, of our fair city?'

'It is impressive, although I have seen only a little.'

'I intend to take him on a sightseeing walk as soon as I can find the time,' said Hugo.

'Good, good.' The deputy nodded, his eyes on Jacob in whom he seemed to take the keenest interest. 'Hugo tells me you are to look—pardon—you are *looking* for employment. Is that so?'

'It is. I am eager to earn an income.'

'And you do not remember your former trade?' The deputy sat forward in the chair, hands clasped on the knob of his walking cane, his coat gathered beneath him.

'I do not. I suspect I was an artisan of some kind.'

'What makes you say that?' The deputy cocked his head with the question.

'It is a feeling, that is all. I enjoy the open air. I am fit and strong and like to use my hands.'

'Do you see?' The deputy turned to Hugo with a delighted smile. 'The body remembers where the mind forgets! Forgive me, but your situation, unfortunate thought it may be, is of great interest to me,' he said to Jacob by way of explanation. 'You present an unusual example of a man sound of mind yet orphaned as to memory. Your mind represents what philosophers would consider a rare example of a blank slate—one that though organically mature is yet to be imprinted with language or knowledge of its surroundings. Pardon,' he added, seeing the look of confusion on Jacob's face. 'My scholarly interests outrun my manners.'

'But it is true what you say. I am new to your country, and new to your language.'

'A true New Frenchman!' The deputy smiled at the quip. 'Friend, you have the advantage of us.'

They talked for another hour, the deputy probing Jacob on questions of memory and perception before taking out and glancing at his fob watch.

'You must excuse me, Monsieur Wheeler,' he said, rising to his feet. 'I have taken enough of your time. But I am heartily glad to have gotten to know you. And in return for your forbearance, I offer the news that I am pursuing an employment opportunity on your behalf. Do you have any objection to working with leather goods, or indeed to an apprenticeship with regard to the same?'

'None, sir. No hesitation at all—to either prospect.'

'Excellent. Then I hope to return in time with an offer of employment. And in the meantime, I hope you shall count me as a friend—albeit an inquisitive one.'

'I should be most glad to do so.'

'Then farewell for now.' With a bow, the deputy departed.

TWO WEEKS LATER, JACOB received a note requesting that he meet deputy Turgeon outside the Spanish tavern in the Old Town marketplace at 9:30 a.m. the following day.

At the appointed hour, he waited for the deputy to appear. The April air was cool and moist under a cloudy sky. The market stalls were busy with early morning shoppers. The sensations that had assailed him on his previous excursion seemed nowhere in evidence and he pondered the troubling incident, mystified as to the cause. Strolling back and forth along the cobblestones he observed the passing traffic, looking forward to the time when he would share in such purposeful activity.

'Monsieur Wheeler!' The deputy approached down a steep side street, navigating the uneven cobbles with the assistance of his cane.

'Good morning, sir!' Jacob hurriedly advanced to offer his arm.

'How are you, friend?' The deputy's eyes were bright and engaging, his voice cheerful as he took the proffered arm. 'Shall we first take a cup?'

He steered Jacob into the premises of a nearby café. 'The coffee is excellent,' he promised, 'far finer than those in the Upper Town with all of their fancy linen.'

'You have enquired concerning my employment?' asked Jacob, loathe to enter without first receiving this assurance.

'Yes, yes, of course. Monsieur Lascelles looks forward to … seeing you?' The deputy raised an interrogative eyebrow.

'Yes. Seeing, as in meeting.'

'Ah!' Pleased at the choice of word, the deputy sat down at a small table, gesturing for Jacob to do the same. 'Are you hungry? Would you like something to eat?'

'No, thank you. I have eaten an excellent breakfast.'

'Madame Pepin?' The deputy smiled agreeably. 'I knew her husband. A rather scandalous fellow, if truth be told. But a true patriot.' He propped his walking cane beside him as he turned to survey the café. 'Do you know that the original establishment that stood on this spot was opened in 1675? It was the first coffee house in the then settlement of New France. And it was here, in this very room, a century later, that the English governor was forced by Jean-René Tremblay, great-grandson of the founder, to sign a document recognising the independence of the settlement and surrounding lands. There are still musket holes in the brickwork to show where fighting took place between the habitants and the redcoats.'

'Habitants?'

'Pardon. The word simply means 'inhabitant' but it takes on a special meaning in New France, and Quebec generally, by referring to the sons and daughters of the original settlers. It thus denotes a class of people close to the land and is a sort of shorthand—shorthand, yes?—for patriotic pride and attachment to traditional rural virtues. There is an established Patriotic Party in the New France Assembly—of which party I am a deputy—that strongly advocates for habitant values, which it considers the backbone of New France freedoms and independence.'

The coffee arrived and the deputy waited for Jacob to take a sip. 'Did I not tell you!' he exclaimed on seeing Jacob's reaction. 'The finest cup in the entire town.'

Although anxious to meet his prospective employer, Jacob listened politely as the deputy described some of the particular sights of the Quarter. 'The clock tower is where they hanged—hung?—the notorious bandit Black Jack Newsome, an English rogue who had taken up residency here. And the iron water trough outside is where Henri Cote fought the first duel in the history of New France, in 1685. He had accused another man, the merchant Samuel Benoit, of selling him sub-standard flour. He shot Benoit through the heart and was forced to flee the settlement shortly afterwards, hotly pursued by Benoit's relatives. But I talk as though I were debating in the Assembly! Hugo tells me that your French continues to improve day by day?'

'Hugo is too kind. I merely listen and repeat what he says as best I can.'

'I see.' The deputy dwelt on this for a moment. 'And you are otherwise fully recovered from your physical ordeal?'

'I am, I assure you. And entirely capable of work.'

'Excellent.' The deputy examined his fob watch. 'And now we must be off. Monsieur Lascelles will think we are avoiding him!' Draining his coffee, he stood up. 'Shall we?'

They strolled along rue Prospect, the Deputy raising his hat to several passers-by, who greeted him respectfully by title. 'I stood for her before the law when her husband was poisoned,' he remarked after one greeting by a spectre-thin lady who called out from across the street. 'That one!' He pretended to shudder following a cheery hail from a man labouring on a roof as they walked by. 'He came to see me with a petition to free his brother from prison—ten years early! I sent him on his way as soon as manners allowed.'

They approached a stone house with a blue plaque fixed to the wall. 'You must see this.' The deputy stopped to read the plaque. 'The house where Pascal Lavoie, poet laureate of New France was born. I studied him in school as do all children. His most famous poem is called "The Voyage" and is dear to the hearts of all citizens. It is our national epic and celebrates the legendary hero Gaston Tremblay, founder of our city.'

Some lines of verse were written beneath the inscription. The Deputy took out his glasses and perched them on his nose to recite—translating the lines for Jacob's benefit:

THE VOYAGE
I sing the matchless deeds of a hero bold
and chant of a city that shall never be old.
I sing of that dauntless hero fled
to dare the woods with faithful band
and find a home untainted by intendant hand.

'Splendid, is it not?' he said, turning to Jacob. 'Our very own Aeneas, as the poem elsewhere makes reference.'

'Perhaps we should continue, sir. I should hate to be late and create a wrong impression.'

'Quite right! Let us proceed.'

They turned left into rue Louis Riel and descended the winding street. 'There is where I went to school,' the Deputy said fondly, pausing to point with his stick at the Jesuit seminary situated behind a high stone wall. 'I believe our Monsieur Gagnon also attended in his time.'

They approached an intersection of several lanes, the junction forming a small square lined on each side by workshops, taverns, and other commercial establishments. In the centre of the square stood an elaborate monument to the Maid of Orleans. The Maid stood heroically erect, her body draped in a flowing banner with one arm extended dramatically to the horizon.

'Our destination,' said the Deputy, and pointed to a saddlery business standing on the far side of the square. Two large, blue-painted wooden doors faced outwards onto the street. Above the doors a faded sign bore the insignia, '*Sellerie et Maroquinerie.*' Below the sign was the name of the proprietor and the founding date of the business.

As Jacob started to cross the square, the deputy called a halt in order to assay the finer points of the marble monument. 'In the opinion of many judicious observers, this represents Paul Alois's finest work,' he declared, stepping back the better to observe the sinuous stone. 'It is rumoured that Madame Desirée Benoit was the model for the figure, although that may be malicious gossip as it was also alleged that she was his mistress. But certainly, one may suppose—Monsieur Wheeler?' He looked around for Jacob.

Jacob had crossed the square and was peering through a barred window into the dim recesses of the workshop.

'A moment!' called the deputy, hurrying after. 'Enter!' he said grandly as he caught up, jousting the air with his cane.

Jacob pushed open the door, breathing in the pungent odours of vegetable tannin, sawdust, and freshly oiled leathers. Racks of animal hides stood along one wall where two young boys were busily applying wax to a leather. Other boys were bent over a long workbench in the centre of the room, gossiping animatedly as they cut leather into shapes or glued them together. One or two looked up to acknowledge the presence of the visitors before returning to the task.

The deputy stood beside a saddle tree, admiring a half-finished saddle and complimenting the artisan on his craftsmanship as he ran his hand over the seat. The saddle maker, a grizzled individual with a permanent slant to his bearing from so many hours spent bent over the workbench, glowed under the praise. 'Merci, Monsieur Deputy!' he said, bobbing his head in gratitude.

'Monsieur Turgeon!' A burly man wearing a brown wool suit emerged from a small office to greet the distinguished visitor. He had slicked black hair, a moustache, flushed features, and a sharp nose over which were inlaid bright, suspicious eyes.

'Ah! Monsieur Lascelles!' The deputy took the proprietor's extended hand and shook it warmly, while enquiring after the man's wife and children. 'Your father was the finest boot maker I ever beheld,' he declared. 'Observe!' Putting a hand on Jacob's shoulder for support, he lifted one leather-clad foot off the floor for the proprietor to inspect. 'He constructed these very shoes after a fashion of my own design.'

'Such handiwork!' the proprietor exclaimed, bending to admire the shoe. 'I recognise my father's stitching.'

'And may I introduce Monsieur Jacob Wheeler?' The deputy planted his foot back on the stone floor and turned to indicate Jacob. 'He is the young man I told you about.'

'At your service, sir,' Jacob said, uncertain whether to bow his head or offer his hand. He did the latter, his voice betraying his nervousness at his scant French.

The proprietor took the proffered hand, his bonhomie cast aside as he attempted to size up the man standing before him. 'Are you acquainted with the leather trade, Monsieur Wheeler?' he asked, his eyes dubious as he inspected Jacob.

'He asks if you are familiar with leather,' said the deputy.

'Of the skin of the cow I am the most amiable,' Jacob assured the proprietor in reply.

'I can promise you, Monsieur Lascelles,' the deputy interjected as the proprietor looked to him in confusion, 'my young friend is eager to learn and is of a most able and energetic disposition.' Taking the proprietor by one arm, he led him aside. 'His command of the language improves with each passing day,' he whispered.

'But all the same, he is English, is he not?' the proprietor remarked as Jacob wandered over to inspect a rack of hides.

The deputy beamed. 'Indeed, he is. It is like the adage, is it not? "Such as the tree, such is the fruit,"' he quoted.

Lascelles knitted his brow. 'A most judicious observation, sir.' He scratched his chin as he watched Jacob bend to inspect a leather from the rack, breathing in the fragrant odours of pigment and dye.

'Well? What do you think?'

Lascelles hawed to himself, his face doubtful. 'I am prepared to take him on your word, Monsieur. I will give him a trial of six months, is that fair?'

'Indeed, it is, eminently so.'

'Good. Bid him be here tomorrow morning at seven o'clock sharp. We shall see if his hands are as competent as his nose. And now, Monsieur, a cup of coffee or a glass of wine perhaps?'

AFTER THREE MONTHS SPENT weighing and observing Jacob perform sundry tasks around the workshop, Monsieur Lascelles was sufficiently convinced of his industriousness to advance him to the workbench, assigning him a stool alongside the other apprentices in a display of conscious ceremony.

'Under the tutelage of my dear father, I myself mastered the craft of saddle-making on this very stool,' he said. 'And our own estimable Monsieur Guyot here shall be your teacher.' He gestured towards a frail white-haired man of some seventy years of age who had turned up in the workshop for the first time that morning.

'I am pleasing … to … encounter the father of the … master proprietor.' Jacob inclined his head to the old man. Two young boys, bent over the workbench, erupted with mirth.

'Quite so,' Monsieur Lascelles conceded, eyeing Jacob doubtfully. He frowned at the two boys. '"Such as the tree, such is the fruit!"' he scolded. Stroking his chin, he gazed pensively at the floor. 'Quite so,' he repeated.

Monsieur Guyot proved a painstaking mentor, systematically drilling Jacob in the names of the saddle-maker's tools. 'A wise father knows each of his children,' he counselled, indicating a row of wood-handled awls. 'Never mind,' he said at Jacob's puzzled look. 'Come with me.' He led the way to where a newly finished saddle rested on a bench. '*Selle!*' he pronounced, pointing at the object. 'Do you understand? *Selle!*' he repeated and laid his hand on the saddle.

'Selle,' Jacob repeated, as Monsieur Lascelles stepped out from his office to observe.

The elderly man shook his head. '*Selle!*'

'*Selle!*'

Under the eye of the watching Lascelles, the elderly man proceeded to name the various parts in a dry, trembling voice.

'*Pommeau!*' he said, taking Jacob's hand and placing it on the raised front of the seat.

'Pommeau.'

'*Troussequin.*' Guyot pointed to the cantle.

'Troussequin.'

Guyot frowned. 'Eh?' He repeated the word. '*Troussequin!*'

'*Troussequin!*'

'*Jupe.*' He placed Jacob's hand on the skirt.

'Jupe.'

'*Assiette.*' He tapped the seat.

'Assiette.'

The watching Lascelles intervened in the recitation. 'What is this part, in English? *Anglais?*' he said, placing his hand on a piece of leather extending from the skirt.

'Flap.'

'Flap?' The proprietor glanced at Monsieur Guyot, who made a dubious face. 'Carry on,' said Lascelles, and left with a scowling glance at the apprentices.

At the urging of his mentor, who privately praised his 'instinct for leather' to the proprietor, Jacob found himself employed on a greater variety of tasks as the weather warmed and the workshop doors were opened up to the street.

He soon learned how to fix leather to a stirrup and how to cut a noseband or bridle. The business of preparing the hides, as well as sweeping the workshop and keeping the braziers lit and full of coals, now fell entirely to the younger apprentices. If they resented his sudden pre-eminence, they showed no sign, greeting him with a respectful 'Monsieur', and willingly fetching tools or leathers at his request.

In spite of the repetitive measuring and gluing, Jacob found solace in the routine workshop labour. Over the following months, he became proficient in shaping and rasping the saddle bars and abrading the beechwood to a smooth finish. He acquired skill in shaving and fitting the leather saddle covers, tacking the latter into place before stepping back to allow Guyot to inspect the result.

'Shaping is important,' Guyot mused, running his hand over the ground seat. 'The leather must fit to the seat like a hand to a glove.'

The elderly man paused to ruminate, his mind drifting back, as it often did, to earlier days and earlier saddles. 'I made my first western saddle on this bench for a wealthy American who insisted on only the finest workmanship.' He pondered the American and his finicky demands for a moment before resuming his inspection of the leather. 'Continue,' he said, returning to his stool by the brazier. He sat there, warming his hands as he mused on Americans and the concordances of shaped wood.

AS SPRING TURNED TO summer Jacob became better acquainted with his fellow employees, learning the names of each of the young apprentices and drawing good-natured laughter at his attempts to converse in French. The young boys were high-spirited, mischievously telling him the wrong name for various objects and erupting into laughter when he innocently repeated it to Monsieur Guyot.

'Eh?' Guyot grimaced before casting a mildly disapproving glance at the giggling culprits. 'Boys, boys!' he reproached, shaking his head.

The apprentices were presided over by the shop foreman, a vindictive individual with a permanently sour face who frequently flew into rages at what he considered sub-standard work. 'Fool!' He slapped one of the apprentices—a boy scarcely ten years old—on the side of the head as he fumed over a badly stitched leather. 'Undo it and start again!' He flung the leather at the tearful boy with a warning glance at the boy's companion. 'You, too!' he shouted. To Jacob's surprise, the proprietor seemed to tolerate, if not countenance, such tyrannical displays, sometimes observing silently as the foreman, referred to only as 'Monsieur Barreau,' berated the cowed apprentices.

The man took a quick and open dislike to Jacob, seeming to consider his lapses into English a challenge to his authority. His lip curling in disdain, he muttered with derision at Jacob's attempts to master a new word or term.

'*Anglais!*' he spat, glowering at the malfeasance. In spite of this antipathy, he gave berth to Jacob—largely, the latter suspected, in deference to Monsieur Guyot—contenting himself with scowling and muttering under his breath whenever Jacob caught his eye.

The workday started at 7:00 am. and ended at 7:00 pm., except for Saturdays, when the business closed at 1pm. Jacob was started on an apprentice salary of six dollars a week, with the prospect of that sum increasing by an extra dollar at the end of the six months probationary period.

'In truth, the miser pays his apprentices less than three dollars per week, but he has doubled that in Jacob's case at my urging—and his indebtedness to me,' the deputy confided to Hugo. 'The debt?' he said, observing the unvoiced question on Hugo's face. 'It was a word from me that landed him the contract to supply the military with straps, reins, saddles, and stirrups. But perhaps do not speak of it,' he said and tapped the side of his nose.

His native proficiency with tools and clear willingness to learn slowly advanced Jacob in the estimation of the watchful Monsieur Lascelles.

'I can say that he has adept hands,' he conceded to the deputy when the latter enquired after Jacob's progress, 'and a vigorous disposition.'

In time, Lascelles became sufficiently impressed by Jacob's industry to revise his opinion of the trustworthiness of *les Anglais perfides*.

'Not all,' he cautioned, being naturally given to reservation, 'but some—one, in particular.'

TO ACCOMMODATE HIS NEW routine, Jacob rose at 6:00 a.m. every morning and breakfasted at 6:15 a.m. before heading off to the workshop carrying lunch—for which he paid Madame Pepin an extra seventy-five cents a week—in the worn canvas haversack. He returned to his lodgings by 8:00 p.m., retiring to his room after a simple meal of soup or bread and cheese.

One evening, bothered by elusive images whose nature or meaning he was unable to grasp, he sat on the bed staring at the leather cover of the weathered bible.

'What was I before?' he wondered. He studied his calloused hands a troubled look on his face. '*Who* was I before?'

9

An Invitation

AT THE END OF his six-month probationary period, Jacob received his one-dollar-a-week pay increase, his employer announcing the fact with grudging approval. 'Be sure to tell monsieur Turgeon,' he told Jacob. 'And I expect no decline in the standard of work,' he warned, waving Jacob from the office.

'I got half of that,' Jacob muttered to himself.

'I must sound like an idiot,' he complained to Hugo the next time the latter arrived to give a lesson. 'I barely comprehend one-tenth of what is said to me. And why in blazes do people always raise their voices when addressing me—as though I'm deaf!'

In spite of Hugo's protestation that he was 'but a hair's breadth' from sufficiency, his attempts at deciphering the rapid, idiosyncratic speech that flew between his fellow apprentices at the workbench frequently left him with a throbbing headache.

'Yesterday I mistook old Guyot's instructions and almost ruined a leather,' he told Hugo. 'I fear monsieur Lascelles will lose patience one of these days and turn me out the door.'

Driven by this anxiety he practised harder than ever to increase his understanding of the language. On Hugo's advice, he stopped people on the street, pretending to enquire after directions—screwing up his face as he attempted to understand the replies. He entered shops, pointing at the bread or cakes as if deciding on a purchase. Indeed, on more than one occasion, he found himself exiting a bakery with an unwanted loaf tucked under his arm. He listened in on the gossip and banter of his fellow employees, grimacing as he attempted to untangle the patois. He engaged his neighbour, the carpenter Bedard, in rudimentary conversation, nodding as though fully comprehending the replies. He did the same with Madame Pepin, praising the soup or the Sunday goose, and watching closely to see if she understood.

And slowly, gropingly, as the weather turned colder, he began to discriminate between sounds and inflections, his ear attuning to the subtle stop, which turned *verre* into *verte*, or the shape of the mouth, which turned *cou* into *cul*. He drew praise from Hugo for correctly judging that *châssis* was a permissible substitution for *fenêtre*, and a look of surprised delight when discriminating between *sortir* and *partir* as the latter took his leave.

Monsieur Guyot nodded approvingly when Jacob asked for *un tournevis*, or stretched out his hand and enquired, unselfconsciously, for *le poinçon rond*. Once, tacking a strip of leather, he overhead one of the apprentices mutinously refer to the shop foreman as '*un ver sal!*' and chuckled, drawing a startled glance from the speaker.

His halting fluency improved further as, to the stockpile of nouns, he added the elusive filament of *being*, which yarned the words into companionable speech. By late fall, he was responding in simple sentences to the instructions of Guyot, the Frenchman squinting at his progress.

One morning, Guyot pointed at a leather belt. 'What do the English call this part?'

'Buckle. It is a word … like as … the similar to … the French.'

Monsieur Guyot considered this for a moment. 'The Indians believed, so it is said, that to name something is to gain power over it. What say you, Jacob?'

He pursed his lips. 'The puissance … of the named thing?' he ventured, grimacing his way through the sentence.

Monsieur Guyot murmured at this piece of wisdom.

'Names … words, are strong, like this leather,' he said, and tugged the belt between his hands. 'This, the heathens believed, or so I am told.' He stared into space for a moment, pondering savage ways. 'It is important to keep the fingers warm,' he said distantly after a pause. Scratching the grey stubble on his chin, he resumed the lesson.

As the months passed, Jacob's conversations flowed more vigorously into tuneful French while yet resisting the final abandonment of his littoral tongue. 'Your French is leavened with an Anglo-Saxon sensibility, my dear Monsieur Wheeler,' the deputy proposed following one chance meeting on the street. 'Like yeast,' he explained in response to Jacob's puzzled expression.

'One wonders if this is not some precursor of our future as Frenchmen,' the deputy mused to a like-minded colleague over a glass of brandy. 'Yeast to our dough,' he speculated, staring into the fire. 'Of course—' he brightened at the thought—'it might turn out the contrary, that the unsurpassable eloquence of our native tongue might yet colonise the language of Shakespeare—or, at the least, give it a French accent!' His eyes twinkled at the prospect.

IN SPITE OF HIS determined progress, Jacob's impatience frequently out-ran his ability, leading to misunderstandings and, on certain days, linguistic backsliding. 'I speak as a child might speak,' he complained to Hugo one particularly frustrating day over coffee in their favourite tavern. 'And see like a child might see. Things are the same yet grasped differently.' He stirred in sugar, uncertain of his own meaning. 'It is as if I were learning the world anew.'

'Many a whole mind hath half the wit,' Hugo remarked to his wife over breakfast the next morning, repeating a quip the deputy had made upon learning of Jacob's observation.

'There is a poetry in half-learned speech, is there not?' the deputy had remarked, going on to praise the innocent profundity of children and mental defectives. 'For they, too, have their way of grasping the world,' he pointed out in response to Hugo's startled look.

Having given much thought to the matter, Hugo decided his wife's approaching birthday was the ideal time to introduce Jacob into society. 'It's next week, the 19th of October,' he announced to Jacob. 'I've arranged a small *soiree* in her honour. She is eager to meet you. Will you come?'

Jacob frowned. 'Do you think my French good enough?'

'Of course it is! You've come on by leaps and bounds since your arrival here.'

Jacob wavered, hesitant at the prospect of meeting people in a social setting, however informal.

'Do come! Josette has heard all about you. You needn't worry about making conversation as you will hardly get a word in edgewise. My cousin Isabelle will be there, too. She is dying to meet you.'

'I have no clothes to wear,' protested Jacob, 'only my work clothes.'

'There is an excellent clothier in the Quarter, on rue du Fournier. He will sell you a complete outfit for less than twelve dollars. Shall we say six o'clock?'

Rueful at the expense, Jacob nevertheless visited the said provisioner and purchased a wool jacket, some rather baggy trousers that almost matched the jacket, a white shirt, suspenders, a necktie, waistcoat, socks, and leather shoes.

Finishing work at noon on Saturday, he attended a barbershop for a haircut and shave. Later that afternoon, he examined himself in the full-length gilded mirror provided for his room. He turned from side to side, observing himself in the glass while frowning, as if uncertain of his own reflection.

His appearance drew a double-take from Madam Pepin. 'Well, cats could fly! You are out to conquer the world, Monsieur Wheeler,' she said, as she held open the front door for him.

He had dipped further into his savings to purchase a wool overcoat, relieved to dispense with the heavy buffalo robe. Wearing the coat, and his new Dominion fur hat, he made his way through the winding streets of the old town. The day was cold and brittle with a freezing wind that warned of the coming winter.

Leaving the Old Town behind, he made his way through more affluent neighbourhoods to the Middle Town, where Hugo lived. The streets were wider and cleaner than those of the Quarter, cast-iron gas lamps lining both sides of the street. The two-storey town houses were made of stone with gabled roofs. The uniform facades were distinguished by three upper windows and two lower ones set either side of the front door. In the majority of houses, the window frames and front doors were painted a matching red. He found the harmony pleasing, although he couldn't have said why.

Arriving at rue Henri Brisson he made his way to number 34. Taking a deep breath, he smoothed his hair and knocked. *I am enchanted to make your acquaintance, Madame Gagnon.*

'Jacob!' A cheerful Hugo answered the door. 'How are you?' His eyes widened as he took in Jacob's appearance. 'You look a new man!'

Taking off Jacob's coat—and complimenting the feel—Hugo led his guest into the drawing room where his wife and the other guests sat sipping coffee. As Jacob was ushered into the room they glanced up, the conversation coming to a halt. The faces shone with anticipation, and it struck him that the conversation had been about him.

'Friends, may I introduce Monsieur Jacob Wheeler. Jacob, my darling wife, Josette.'

A pleasantly featured woman with rich chestnut hair rose to greet him, a smile on her face. 'My dear Monsieur Wheeler! I am charmed to at last meet you. Hugo has told me so much about you!' She extended her hand. Nervously forgetful of Hugo's instructions, he shook it, drawing a stifled guffaw from one of the male guests.

He coughed, conscious of the faux pas. 'I am enchanted to make your acquaintance Madame Gagnon,' he said, repeating the rehearsed words as a beaming Hugo looked on. 'I wish you a happy birthday,' he said, extending the spray of blue asters and white Japanese anemones he had purchased for the occasion on the recommendation of his landlady.

Josette oohed in delight. 'Asters! My favourites! So thoughtful.'

'It is too … nothing,' he stuttered, feeling as if he were some exotic savage introduced for amusement.

Hugo laid a hand on his shoulder. 'Allow me to introduce my wife's sister, Claudette, and her husband, André Petain.'

'Enchanted,' he said as the couple observed him with intrigued stares. The husband got to his feet and stuck out a hand. 'Very pleased to make your introduction, sir!' He had weepy eyes and a drooping moustache. His wife remained seated, eyes glued on Jacob, her mouth slightly open.

'And my cousin, Isabelle.'

The young woman—not much more than a girl—rose from her chair to greet him. She was of medium height, with a smooth skin the colour of nutmeg, and inquisitive brown eyes. Her black upswept hair was fastened in place by an artfully pinned silver brooch. She was dressed in a cream, embroidered blouse and a long brown skirt, the high waist emphasised by a beige-coloured belt. 'I am delighted to meet you, Monsieur Wheeler.' Her eyes were bright with curiosity, her lips parted in a warm smile. 'Hugo has talked of nothing else but you for months!'

'I am very enchanted …,' Running out of words, he swallowed, his eyes dwelling on hers.

'And this is Jules Desjardins.' Hugo introduced the other male guest, who had regarded the exchange with amusement. 'Jules is second cousin to Isabelle and visiting from New York.'

Desjardin stood nimbly to his feet. 'Pleased to meet you, old bean!' he said in English, showing off his careless mastery of idiom. He was slim and dressed in the latest New York style, his three-piece suit notable for its contrasting waistcoat and cuffed trousers. He sported a fashionable, curly moustache and very short hair, parted in the middle. He stuck out a hand. 'I had heard you were English, but you sound very much American.'

'As I am.' He shook the other man's hand, relieved to find another English speaker among the guests.

Desjardins grinned. 'We French tend to treat all English speakers as Englishmen, whether they are or not.'

'Let us eat,' said Josette, taking Jacob's arm and escorting him to the dining room. 'I am sure Monsieur Wheeler must be hungry.'

'I know I am!' said Jules.

A table stood in the centre of the room, set with a tablecloth and glass-ware and china dishes. Three covered dishes and a platter of sandwiches served English style, with egg and cucumber sat on the table along with cheese and biscuits. A vase of fresh, brightly coloured chrysanthemums formed an ornament in the middle of the table.

'For our special guest,' said Josette, indicating where Jacob should sit. She motioned Isabelle to take the chair opposite.

'André, you sit beside Monsieur Wheeler.'

Petain did so, as his wife took the chair next to Isabelle. Jules sat across from André while Josette seated herself at one end of the table, and Hugo the other.

'Wine?' asked Hugo, holding up the bottle. He filled Claudette's glass and turned to Jacob.

'I'm sure Monsieur Wheeler would prefer the taste of good old Yankee Jack.' Unscrewing a flask of bourbon, Jules splashed the liquor into a whisky glass and handed it to Jacob. 'All the way from Kentucky.'

'Surely not until after we have eaten?' protested Hugo.

'Nonsense! Bourbon is America's wine.'

'Just so long as you don't offer any to my cousin!'

'What do you say, Isabelle. A shot of hellfire?' Desjardins held up the silver flask.

She laughingly refused. 'Mama would have a fit!'

'Shall we eat?' Josette removed the covers from the hot dishes. 'Isabelle darling, please pass around the tourtiere.'

The guests made small talk, directing a few politely worded questions in Jacob's direction, having been warned by Hugo to avoid the topic of his unexplained arrival in New France.

'So, Monsieur Wheeler, how do you like our dreadful weather?' Jules addressed the question in English. The conversation halted as the other guests listened to hear his reply.

'The weather is … raining ducks,' Jacob replied in French.

'Bravo!' Hugo clapped hands, a delighted smile on his face. 'Did I not tell you! His ear is quite remarkable.'

'And do you enjoy living in the Quarter, Monsieur? I hear it can be quite lively.' Claudette speared a piece of baked fish.

'My sister-in-law asks how do you like living in the Old Town?' said Hugo.

'Yes, thank you,' he answered in French. He took a sip of bourbon, his eyes on the pretty girl opposite. She sat slightly forward, a smile on her face as if eager to catch his every word.

'Monsieur Wheeler. I understand that you cannot recall—'

'Isabelle darling do try the devilled egg,' interrupted Josette. 'I've added the pepper you like. Hugo, pass the plate, there's a dear.'

'More bourbon?' Without waiting for an answer, Jules refilled Jacob's glass.

'Your French is excellent, Monsieur Wheeler,' complimented Josette.

'I think not, Madame. But … to your husband, I am in the obligation.'

'See! But scarcely eight months ago, not a word!'

'Josette has told us of your tireless dedication, Hugo.' Claudette smiled teasingly at her sister. 'Indeed, she speaks lavishly and admiringly of your splendid—'

'Pardon. Hugo dearest, the wine?'

Jacob sipped a glass of water, mistaking it for the bourbon in his nerves. He tried his best to answer a convoluted question from Petain, turning to Hugo for assistance. His ears seemed made of cloth, his tongue also, as he tried to follow the conversations taking place around him. The young woman observed him from across the table, a question on her lips that she seemed to be trying to suppress. He gave her an encouraging smile.

Flustered, she averted her eyes, but soon returned them, hard put to contain her fascination with the handsome stranger. His slightly bewildered air as he tried to follow the conversations, his mysterious past, his shy glances in her direction, all conspired to inflame her already brimming interest. At a pause in the conversation, the question she had been dying to ask ever since he was introduced, leapt unbidden to her lips, her pent-up curiosity over-bursting the banks of propriety. 'Why were you in the woods, Monsieur Wheeler, if I may ask?'

'Cousin!' Hugo gave a shocked glance.

'My delightful cousin asks what you were doing in the woods?' interpreted Jules, a sardonic note to his voice as his eyes selected among the sandwiches.

A silence fell, all eyes turned upon Jacob, as they awaited a response. The exasperated Hugo himself awaited the reply, his own admonition seemingly forgotten.

'I don't know, I was shot,' he added, the reply drawing gasps.

'An accident!' Hugo hastily interjected. 'A stray bullet from an over-eager hunter no doubt.'

'No doubt,' echoed his wife, a wondering look on her face as she regarded Jacob.

'And you lost your memory as a result? I cannot comprehend,' said Isabelle, her voice sympathetic, 'what it must be like to live without a memory?'

'Less of a burden, if you ask me,' said Jules, deciding on the ham and cheese.

'But to not—'

'Cousin! Can we not speak of more salubrious things?' Hugo frowned.

'But I would like to know too!' chimed Claudette, her eyes on Jacob. 'Wouldn't you, Andre?'

Her husband cleared his throat. 'I agree with Hugo. Hardly a time to discuss such matters.' His voice, however, was reluctant.

'I only wanted to know what it feels like to—'

'Good heavens, cousin! You will distress our guest, I am quite certain, by continually referring to his unfortunate accident.' Hugo suspended his raised wine glass, his voice sharp with disapproval.

'Pardon! It was thoughtless of me. I apologise, Monsieur Wheeler, for my rudeness.' Isabelle gave a smile that contrived to be both arch and contrite at the same time.

'My cousin apologises for the interrogation,' said Jules. 'She hopes you will forgive her.'

'Tell her I take no offence,' answered Jacob, before remembering his own French. 'I take no offence, Isa—Mademoiselle,' he corrected hastily, the slip drawing an exchange of looks between Claudette and Josette.

'Someone shoot the elephant!' joked Jules, drawing puzzled looks.

'Isabelle do tell us what inspired you to make that blouse, it is so elegant,' praised Josette.

'Jacob, more fish?' Hugo passed the platter. 'Eat up!'

'How is the bourbon? André—another glass?'

As the evening continued, the conversation—so different from that of the workshop!—flew by Jacob in spite of the occasional question directed his way. He caught stray words and once thought he recognised the phrase, 'drowning in a glass of water'—one used habitually by Hugo. Throughout the meal, he darted glances at his beguiling interrogator, smitten by her lively manner and graceful gestures as she passed the milk and sugar.

Isabelle for her part was acutely aware of his interest, rewarding him with shy yet eager smiles as their eyes met across the table. *What would mama say?* She giggled at the thought and pressed a hand to her mouth.

'Isabelle?' Josette turned inquisitive eyes on her.

'Oh, nothing! I was just thinking.'

'About?'

Jacob was watching, his eyes intent. 'Oh, just something Marguerite said. Hardly worth a mention.'

'And where is Marguerite?' asked André. 'I haven't seen her in an age.'

'She volunteered to stay home with mama, who is unwell,' said Isabelle.

'That frightful flu?'

'Perhaps. A touch only.'

'A toast!' Hugo raised his glass. 'To Monsieur Wheeler. Welcome to our beautiful city!'

'Monsieur Wheeler!' The guests raised their glasses.

Cheese and biscuits were passed around as Hugo, the expansive host, uncorked a bottle of cognac. 'Just a little,' he urged his sister-in-law.

Claudette put her hand over the glass. 'It gives me the most frightful headache.'

'Very well. Josette?'

'No, thank you. Jules, let me try a drop of that bourbon. Just a drop!'

'Isabelle … Isabelle?'

'Oh, pardon! No thank you, Hugo.' She had been distracted, aware of Jacob's gaze, and emboldened by the wine. Although, in truth, she had drunk barely a glass.

'I hope it wasn't too much of an ordeal,' whispered Hugo as the guests stood in the hallway to take their leave.

'No!' he said, his eyes drinking in Isabelle as she teased her cousin on some point or other.

'And has our Monsieur Wheeler had a chance to see the sights of our fair city?' Jules broke off his conversation with Isabelle to address Jacob.

'I intended to show him around myself,' answered Hugo on Jacob's behalf, 'but, alas, where does one find the time nowadays?'

'Then Isabelle and I would be pleased to act as guides. Isabelle, what do you think?'

'Oh yes! Please!'

Her enthusiasm drew a laughing protest from Josette. 'Do you not think your mother may have something to say about that?'

'Mama won't mind—as long as Jules chaperones me. He can talk her into anything.' Isabelle turned sparkling eyes on Jacob. 'Wouldn't you like me to show you our splendid city, sir?'

'She wishes to know if you will accompany her on a walking tour of the town,' said Jules.

'Yes! I am … enjoying to walk?' Momentarily forgetting himself, he turned to Hugo for assistance,

'Good enough!' Jules smiled merrily. 'Shall we say next Sunday? Two o'clock at the cathedral square? Excellent! We shall meet you there!'

10

A History Lesson

THE FOLLOWING SUNDAY, HE ate an early lunch of steamed fish and *Pommes lyonnaise* before making his way towards the square. 'Follow the bells!' Madame Pepin called out. She watched him depart along the street. *Isabelle Ouellet? And her mother—such a sour milk!*

The weather was cold and overcast, with a gusty wind blowing scraps of litter along the pavement. He made his way through the winding streets of the Old Town as the peal of noon bells beckoned him toward the cathedral. He walked purposefully, looking forward to seeing the Upper Town for the first time, but most of all, eager to remake the acquaintance of the graceful and attractive young woman who would be his guide. Why did Hugo not speak of her before? She cannot be more than sixteen—seventeen at the most. Her warm laugh sounded again in his ears. What sort of impression did I make upon her?

Beggars and the destitute were out in force, counting on Sunday observances to loosen the purse strings of those scarcely more fortunate than themselves. He stepped into the road to avoid a man and a woman huddled beneath a blanket and sleeping sideways on the pavement. The man snored with rasping breath. The woman's eyes were open, staring blankly, one arm thrown across her partner's chest. He walked up a street that ended in a flight of stone steps cut into the side of a hill. He climbed the steps, moving aside to give way to a descending pedestrian. A blast of wind caused him to clutch the lapels of his coat. 'Snow before the morrow,' his neighbour, the carpenter, had forecast.

Reaching the top of the steps, he headed up a steep street lined with shops and taverns. The shops struck him as more prosperous looking than those of the Quarter. He glanced at the street sign set into the wall, *Rue Marian*. He heard the sound of horses and wheels as he approached an intersection at the top of the street. The noise of traffic became louder as he emerged onto a wide boulevard. Despite it being the sabbath, a constant flow of landaus, phaetons, caleches, and omnibuses traversed the busy thoroughfare, their wheels rattling against the paved stone. Across the boulevard he saw a large square dominated by an imposing cathedral at the far end.

A party of schoolchildren, shepherded by nuns, approached, the children laughing and gossiping and seemingly unbothered by the cold. He followed them to a crossing where a policeman wearing a fur cap with earmuffs held up a flag and blew piercing blasts on a whistle. As they prepared to cross, a horseless carriage clanked past, exhaust smoke billowing up in a cloud. The green leather top had been rolled back, in spite of the weather, and the driver and passenger sat high above the rear-mounted engine. The children clapped and cheered at the sight. He stared after it, intrigued that the unusual conveyance didn't astonish. *My mind is not blank! I have not lost all prior knowledge*, he told himself, excited at the implication. *The horseless carriage is familiar to me*, he pondered, as he gazed after the conveyance, *but not my own yesterdays*.

He continued across the boulevard and into the expansive square. The mostly empty space contained benches and shade trees and, in the middle of the concourse, a monumental stone fountain. Only a few muffled figures occupied the benches beneath the bare trees. From one of these benches, a figure leapt to his feet and waved an arm in greeting. 'Monsieur Wheeler!'

He recognised Jules and waved back, disappointed not to also catch sight of Isabelle alongside her cousin.

'My dear Jacob!' Jules advanced to meet him, holding out a leather gloved hand. He wore a Derby hat and a silk scarf tied around his throat. 'What weather! We must wait before my cousin joins us. She is inside the cathedral with her mother, who insisted Isabelle attend a baptism with her. She will be occupied for another half hour or so.' He glanced at Jacob, who was out of breath. 'Shall we walk while we wait? Or do you prefer to sit?'

'Sit, if you have no objection. It is a steep climb from the Quarter.'

'One I avoid whenever possible!'

Their path led them past the stone fountain, and Jacob stopped to admire its architecture. Modelled on the grand Italian style, it consisted of winged cherubs blowing trumpets while perched tiptoe on the topmost of a series of descending basins, water splashing from bowl to bowl. The bronze sculpture of a naked woman rose above the cherubs, her arms spread as if to acknowledge her surrounds

'The 'Spirit of New France," said Jules, gazing at the figure alongside Jacob. 'It was cast by Emile Poirier, one of our most notable sculptors. It is said to be modelled on the daughter of Gaston Tremblay's great-grandson, Henri, the self-proclaimed president of New France. We are known as the city of monuments,' he explained as they continued across the square. 'You will have noticed them all over the place. They are an obsession with the town. Outsiders joke that if a cow takes a shit in New France the inhabitants raise a statue.'

They reached the bench and Jacob shaded his eyes as he took in the magnificent façade of the cathedral. 'The Cathedral of the Blessed Virgin,' explained Jules. 'It is the most important building in New France. It was built over the course of a hundred years by stonemasons under the direction of Claude Giroux and his descendants. It was finished in 1791 and is considered to be the finest stonework in all of North America.' Reaching inside his bespoke wool overcoat he retrieved a cigar. 'Would you care for one?'

Jacob shook his head as his companion took out a box of matches. 'I acquired the habit in New York, and now I can't give it up—not that I wish to!' Striking a match, Jules drew the cigar to flame while glancing at Jacob. 'What shall we talk about—to pass the time until Isabelle joins us? I dare not show you around the square without her say-so.'

'Anything but me,' said Jacob, fatigued at the mere thought of answering more questions.

'Quite right!' Jules chuckled. He gazed around the deserted square, ruminating for a moment. 'What do you know of your new home?'

'Nothing. Except that it is very cold—and windy.'

'Good! Then let us begin with that.' Jules flicked ash from the cigar as he gazed at the fountain while collecting his thoughts. 'New France is the third oldest and third largest city in Quebec. Only Montreal and Quebec City itself are older. We were founded in 1667 by Gaston Pierre Tremblay. You will doubtless hear much of him, particularly from Isabelle who is madly in love with the fellow. Tremblay was an early explorer and fur trader. He came to New France in 1665 with Jean Talon, the first intendent or administrator of the colony. The two had been childhood friends. But for obscure reasons they fell out soon after arriving. Some say it was to do with unscrupulous dealings with the Indians. Others say it was simply jealousy on the part of Tremblay. At any event, their friendship ended in a bitter quarrel. A short time later, Tremblay departed the colony with some three dozen followers, vowing never to return.

It is said that the exiles wandered the woods for six months before stumbling across the Mercier River which in turn led them to this spot. At all events, Tremblay founded a settlement here in 1667. Legend has it that he announced the spot as the true and pure New France. Why that name? Some think it was to stick a finger up the arse of his former friend. But more reliable historians claim it was a clever ploy to attract badly needed women to the new settlement. By calling it New France he managed to lure a shipload of women who arrived from Paris hoping to find husbands in the colony.'

Jules paused and smoked the cigar for a moment before resuming. 'Tremblay was a capable fellow and a superb administrator in his own right. He did much business with the Indians around the settlement, winning favour by his open and honest dealings. The success of the new settlement, along with its prosperity on the back of beaver pelts traded from the Indians, attracted settlers from Montreal and Quebec who were disenchanted with the new regime for their own reasons. They brought their wives and families and set up farms and businesses.

In fact, the new settlement was so successful, it soon began to rival Montreal itself, angering Jean Talon. After various threats, he despatched an expeditionary force to compel the settlers to either return to the colony or submit to his authority. With the help of his Indian allies, Tremblay defeated the force at the battle of the Three Rivers, so called because of the intersecting streams. It was a glorious victory for the new settlement and thereafter they were allowed to live in peace. But the battle provoked an enmity between the settlement and the Colonial authorities in Quebec which exists, in part, to this day.' He paused to look at Jacob. 'Is that too much history?'

'No, not at all. I am eager to discover as much as I can.'

Jules reflected on this for a moment. 'Quite,' he said, before continuing. 'Anyway, the settlement grew and grew, attracting its own settlers from France as the habitants, as they called themselves, sent letters home urging relatives to join them. By the time Tremblay died, the settlement had grown into a prosperous town with a church, several taverns, and a school. The settlers made a solemn vow to honour Tremblay's memory by always maintaining their independence. Over the next two hundred years this determination continued, in spite of the pressures from, first France, and later, England, and still later, Canada, to come back into the fold. Indeed, the habitants fought the British, the Indians, the Americans, *and* their fellow Canadians to preserve their independence.

When Quebec joined three other provinces in 1867 to form the Confederation that made up Canada, New France stubbornly refused to join, asserting it was a separate country. We remained a thorn in the side of the union for almost twenty years, resisting both blandishments and threats to give up our independence. Finally, the City Fathers gave in to the pressure and agreed to join Confederation as an autonomous region of Quebec province. The proviso demanded by the citizens was that they retain special powers relating to language, culture, and administration.'

Jules halted to tip ash from the cigar and reflect on what he had just said. 'We are, in some respects, a state within a state, with our own Charter of Autonomous Rights and an Assembly of elected deputies. The Assembly has the right to pass local laws subject to approval by a provincial governor appointed by Quebec. The governor has the power to cast a veto over any proposed laws that conflict with the Canadian constitution or, indeed, provincial legislation. It's an uneasy balance, and one constantly changing. Our city acknowledges the authority of the federal and provincial governments while steadfastly insisting on its unique historical privileges.

Less than ten years ago there was an uprising—or civil disturbance as the federal government chose to name it—which was put down with the loss of over two dozen lives. And the resentment and distrust lingers. Did you notice the military barracks on the way into the city? The people claim they are there not to protect New France from attack by expansionist Americans, as the authorities insist, but to impose the will of the federal government in the event of another disturbance.'

Jules paused to puff on the cigar. 'So you see, Jacob, beneath this veil of harmony—' Jules made a sweeping gesture with the cigar, 'lies a festering hotbed of discontent, ready to erupt again at any time. The city is riven by factions. You have the habitants—largely descendants of the original settlers—who make up the Patriot Party. They are fiercely protective of the city's history and traditions and are generally obsessed with the past— and statues. Our dear friend, Head-in-the-clouds-Hugo, counts himself a habitant. Isabelle's family, also. Her mother's maiden name is Tremblay, and they claim Gaston Pierre as a direct ancestor. The party is led by Rene Turgeon, with whom you are already familiar.

Then you have the Reformist Party, largely made up of businessmen and professionals, led by Bernard Benoit. The Reformists favour modern ways and methods and urge for a full merger with Quebec and stronger trade ties to the United States. The two parties make up the bulk of the deputies elected to the Assembly where they fight for pre-eminence and generally squabble over everything from French language instruction to the price of eggs.'

The cathedral bells struck two o'clock. They sat in silence as the sonorous peals boomed out across the square, leaving a resonant vibrato in the air when they fell silent.

'And then there is the church,' Jules continued, with silent reference to the bells. 'The clergy are protective of their influence over the habitants and are constantly at odds with both the Reformists and the provincial legislative assembly in Quebec City—whom the church fears for its alliance with the Reformists.

I find it all intensely irritating and left as soon as I could. I went to school and university in America and have lived, ever since, in New York where I work in a bank. There you have it, my friend. The history of New France in a nutshell, nuts and all!

Finally!' Jules stood up as the doors of the cathedral opened and figures began to emerge. 'I think I see Isabelle,' he said, shading his eyes.

They walked across the square to where a group of congregants were gathered on the steps of the cathedral. In their midst stood a bare-headed cleric, a black cassock hanging down beneath his coat.

'See that fellow—in the long coat? That is Bishop Drolet, a wily old fox. He plays habitant against Reformist and both against the Quebec Government. He has as much to do with prayer as a cat with a dog. His only concern is with protecting the authority of the church.'

They arrived at a sweeping flight of steps that led up to the cathedral entrance. Jacob sought out Isabelle among the faces. 'There she is,' said Jules. 'Isabelle!'

At the hail, the young woman turned, her face lighting up as she saw them. 'Jules!' She beckoned with her gloved hand. She wore a sensible wool coat and leather boots laced up the front. Her dark hair was tucked under a fur hat. In the cold air, her cheeks were tinged with pink.

As they stopped on the step below, she turned to an elderly lady wrapped in a fur coat and hat, her hands thrust into a fur warmer. 'Mama, may I present Monsieur Wheeler?'

'So, this is your Englishman?' The old lady cast a frosty glance in Jacob's direction, her eyes piercing with disapproval.

'How do you do, Madame?' he said, anxious to create a favourable impression.

'Hmph!' She raised an eyebrow.

'And this is Monseigneur Drolet, Bishop of New France.'

The bishop glanced at him without interest, his attention clearly on Jacob's companion. 'Jules!' he exclaimed. 'You have returned to us.'

'Alas, no.' Jules spread his hands in apology. 'A short visit only, to see my family.'

The bishop, a saturnine individual with cropped grey hair and distant blue eyes, nodded. 'Perhaps one day,' he remarked, his gaze turning to Jacob. 'This is the Englishman you told me about?' he asked, glancing at Madame Ouellet.

'Yes, Monseigneur. The one without a mind.'

'Memory, mama! His mind is sound!' Isabelle cast a horrified glance at her mother.

'As you say.' Madame Ouellet made a grudging sound in her throat.

The severely embarrassed Isabelle turned to the young woman standing beside her. 'Monsieur Wheeler. This is my sister, Marguerite.'

"'Ow do you do?' said Marguerite, in her best imitation English, drawing a giggle from the mortified Isabelle. She was dark-haired like her sister, and, like Isabelle, dressed in a wool coat and fur hat.

'Mademoiselle,' said Jacob, bowing his head.

'You are of the Protestant faith, Monsieur Wheeler?' The bishop clasped his hands in front of him. A large crucifix suspended from a heavy black rosary was visible beneath his coat.

'He asks if you are Protestant,' said Jules. 'Tell him you are Hindu if you like. He dislikes all faiths equally.'

'I think I must be,' answered Jacob, shocked at Jules' rudeness. 'Tell him I have a bible.'

The answer seemed to amuse the monseigneur. 'Then all is not lost!'

'The old goose speaks not a word of English,' assured Jules with a breezy grin.

'Mama, it is cold. Let me hail you a cab to take yourself and Marguerite home.'

'And you still intend on showing the Englishman around the city—in this wretched weather?'

'I will take great care of her, aunt, I assure you.' Jules extended an arm to assist the elderly lady down the steps.

Marguerite took the other arm while making big eyes at Isabelle. *Go ahead!* she urged silently. *I will take care of mama.* She guided her mother down the broad steps. 'Careful!'

The two proceeded slowly across the square to the boulevard.

'Farewell, Madame Ouellet!' The cleric raised a hand, as if in blessing. 'The cold!' he shivered, regretting his impulsive decision to venture outside without his clerical hat. 'Farewell, Monsieur Wheeler,' he said, turning to leave. 'I hope one day to see you at Mass—with our own Jules!'

'He will convert you yet, Jules!' Isabelle chuckled. She turned to Jacob. 'Ask Monsieur Wheeler if he wishes to see the inside of the cathedral.'

Jules sighed and turned to face Jacob. 'Do you wish to see inside? It's as boring as old wood.'

'Yes! I mean *oui*, Mademoiselle.'

Jules made a face. 'Then let us at least wait until old pate head goes in ahead of us!'

THE INTERIOR WAS HUSHED and dim, the air musty with the smell of incense and candle wax. An ornate high altar rose at one end of a broad, rectangular nave which was lined on both sides with pews. A series of thick pillars separated the nave from the various aisles. The ceiling soared high above, its weight supported by a series of rib vaults that ran down to the great pillars. A number of high-arched, stained-glass windows were built into the wall along one side, the coloured glass lending an atmospheric light to the interior. Jacob turned in a half-circle to take in the great, echoing space. Isabelle observed his reaction, with a pleased expression. Jules fiddled with his coat buttons, looking bored and impatient.

'It took over one hundred years to build,' said Isabelle, repeating what Jules had said to him in the square. 'It was designed by Phillipe Giscard and built by Claude Giroux. Both lie buried over there.' She pointed to a chapel in the aisle. 'And Gaston Trembly, the founder of New France, lies buried over there.' She pointed to another chapel.

'In spite of the fact he was a notorious unbeliever,' added Jules. 'It was the poem that made him a saint.'

'Come!' Isabelle led the way across the nave to the aisle and the series of stained-glass windows. 'They depict scenes and figures from our history,' she explained, Jacob struggling to understand. 'Tell him!' she urged her cousin.

'They are scenes of banditry, mostly,' Jules interpreted. He plonked himself down in a pew as Jacob moved forward to observe the sumptuous, glowing panes.

Isabelle pointed to the nearest window. 'That is Gaston Pierre Tremblay negotiating with the Iroquois.'

'Gaston Pierre, robbing the Indians,' said Jules from his pew.

Jacob stared at the depiction of a bearded woodsman surrounded by respectful Indians.

'And that one—' Isabelle moved along to the next window, 'shows Jacques Gauthier breaking the soil for the first habitant farm in New France.' She stared up at the window, her face alive with admiration. After a moment she led the way further down the aisle, a disgruntled Jules getting up from the pew to follow.

'*Saint Joseph des Iroquois*, the patron saint of New France.' Isabelle halted in front of a rose window depicting a man seated at a desk, a feathered quill in his hand and a gold halo around his head. 'He was martyred by the Indians,' she said, half to herself as Jacob strove to understand the words, Jules having wandered off.

'And this is my favourite!' Isabelle stopped in front of a window magnificently composed of red, blue, green, and yellow panes. It depicted a canoe manned by what looked like hunters or woodsmen, along with several Indians huddled together and dressed in furs, one of whom was pointing to the wooded shore. A bearded man stood in the stern, one hand gripping the steering oar, his head turned in the direction indicated by the Indian guide. Isabelle turned to Jacob, her face shining with history. 'The work of Paul Durand, our finest glassmaker.' She spoke in a half-whisper, her voice filled with ancestral pride as she gazed up at the illumined scene. 'It shows Gaston Tremblay discovering the future site of New France. You understand?'

She gazed at Jacob as if he might have understood.

And it seemed to him, that he did. '*Oui*,' he said, entranced by her animated expression.

She gave a gratified smile, convinced that something about the holy air inside the church facilitated understanding. It is the miracle of tongues, she imagined.

A shaft of sunlight illuminated the glass and bathed her in a roseate glow. Jacob stared, his breath taken by the sight. In that moment she seemed a figure in the tableau, the colours projecting into the dim, dusty light of the church and falling around her. He forgot to breathe, captivated by her pale, ethereal features as she gazed up at the window.

'Jacob?' A bored Jules had re-joined them.

'Pardon! I was lost in the window.'

Jules glanced up at the stained glass. 'Isabelle's favourite! It shows the founding of New France. According to the church, it's an allegory. Some nonsense about the founding of Jerusalem—although the import changes with the season.'

'I know nothing of such things,' confessed Jacob, staring up at the window. 'But aren't they supposed to be religious—like in the bible?'

Jules burst into laughter, the sound echoing in the stone silence and drawing a scandalised look from Isabelle.

'Jules! Compose yourself!' She glanced around to see if the laughter had attracted attention. In the almost empty church, a few parishioners knelt in front of the high altar.

'Pardon!' said Jules, seeking to stifle his mirth. 'It is the incense in the air. It tickles my nose.'

'Come—before we are asked to leave!' A cross Isabelle led off through the pews to the opposite side of the nave.

Taking Jacob by the arm, Jules whispered in his ear. 'It depends on your definition of religious, my friend. To the habitants, Gaston Pierre is, you might say, a secular saint. They worship his memory as such.'

Several side chapels lined the aisle, and Isabelle led past the first two, stopping at a third. 'The tomb of our founder, Gaston Tremblay.' She dipped a knee and crossed herself before a stone sarcophagus engraved with the figure of a reclining man reminiscent of a medieval knight.

'He died of old age,' said Jules, his voice unusually solemn. 'Which was something of a miracle in itself, given he had so many enemies. They dug up his remains after the cathedral was finished and moved them here, in spite of objections that he was, in fact, a heretic.'

Isabelle had moved along to the adjoining chapel. 'The Blessed Mother Marie Dumoulin, sister of one of Gaston Tremblay's original followers,' she explained. She waited as Jules interpreted for Jacob's benefit. She genuflected before the plaster statue that presided over the chapel from a niche in the wall. A triple row of candles in an iron votive stand cast a flickering light. Isabelle knelt on a faded red leather cushion and bowed her head. Her lips moved in earnest prayer as she looked up at the face of the pale virgin in the shadowy recesses of the chapel.

'Is all this not strange to you?' Jules whispered to Jacob. 'I understand that Protestants worship without incense?'

Unwilling to disturb the kneeling Isabelle, Jacob whispered a reply. 'Perhaps. I have no memory of attending church or chapel.'

'You don't?' Jules' voice expressed surprise. 'Then perhaps you are not of the Protestant faith after all—in spite of the bible you are said to have carried?' He pondered this conjecture for a moment as he fingered his moustache. 'Could it be that you are a freethinker? Or perhaps the unfortunate injury released something in you?' He studied Jacob, his face full of speculation.

'What do you mean by released?'

'Perhaps the injury altered your thinking?'

'In what way?'

Jules shrugged. 'Who can say?'

Isabelle crossed herself and got to her feet. She went over to the rows of candles and dropped a coin into a small metal box. Taking a taper from its holder, she lit a candle before turning to look at Jacob. 'For you, Monsieur Wheeler,' she said, her expression grave, before dropping to her knees again in prayer.

'She is lighting a candle—for your memory.'

'My memory? I don't understand.'

'She says the Blessed Mother may grant to bring your memory back.'

Touched by the gesture, Jacob expressed gratitude as Isabelle crossed herself and stood up again. 'Thank you, Mademoiselle.'

She smiled at his response. 'Do you think it would be improper if I invited him to call me Isabelle?' she asked her cousin.

'I don't see why not. The fellow and I are already on first-name terms.'

'Isabelle, if you please, Monsieur,' she said, looking at Jacob.

'She wishes you to address her by her name,' said Jules.

'Oh! Isabelle,' said Jacob, the name sounding like music on his tongue. 'And me—' He pointed to himself, 'Jacob.'

'Jacob, I know,' she said laughingly.

'Done!' said Jules. 'And now that you're both baptised, may we please go back outside?'

'First, ask Jacob what he thinks of our historic church.'

'She wants to know what you think—of all this?' Jules gestured at the interior.

'Tell her I am profoundly impressed.'

Jacob watched as Jules conveyed the sentiment, wondering at his use of the word. 'profoundly' Is that a word I customarily use? If not, have I indeed been changed by the accident? The troubling thought was forgotten as Isabelle turned pleased brown eyes upon him.

'*Alors tout va bien!*' she said.

No sooner had she spoken than the church bells struck 4 o'clock, the peals reverberating through the cavernous space.

THEY EMERGED TO FIND the sun disappearing behind a layer of dense grey cloud. 'Snow within the hour!' predicted Jules. 'We shall have to call off the tour, for now. Besides, it's getting late. What?' he said as Isabelle leaned in to speak with him, her eyes on Jacob.

After a brief discussion, Jules turned to him. 'We will walk with you to rue Marian. It will take you back to the Lower Town. Agreed?'

'Perhaps we can finish the tour some other time?' said Jacob, disappointed at the conclusion. At that moment a sunbeam shot through the clouds to illuminate the square. Isabelle's smooth features shone in the ray of light, reminding Jacob of the stained windows and the caught brilliance of the illumined faces.

'Yes, certainly,' said Jules. 'Shall we proceed?'

They set off along the grand boulevard, still busy with horse-drawn traffic as flakes of snow drifted through the air. They passed another square, one fronting a magnificent structure crowned with towers and turrets and topped by a green copper roof that gleamed in the overcast light. Two massive flagpoles projected from the roof, the flags fluttering in the stiff breeze.

'Remember the local Assembly I told you about?' said Jules. 'Well, this is it—Government House, where the deputies sit and pass local laws subject, of course, to the governor's approval. Our friend Hugo works here, in the archives. What?' He moaned in mock protest as Isabelle tugged him towards a large statue that fronted the building. He looked cheerfully back at Jacob. 'Did I not warn you?'

Isabelle waited beside the monument to introduce the figure that stood atop the plinth. 'Gaston Pierre Tremblay, the founder of New France,' she announced, her face flushed with pride.

The bronze figure was rendered in dynamic pose, as if caught from life. It leaned forward, one arm extended, a finger pointing to the distance. The other hand grasped a flintlock musket. The man's face was turned back over his shoulder as if urging some unseen companions to follow. A patina of verdigris, streaked by weather and pitted with grime, had attached itself to the bronze skin, imparting a dauntless solemnity to the voyageur's appearance. The limbs were artfully distributed so as to achieve the sensation of suspended motion—the backwards glance pulled into balance by the muscular torso as the epic figure leaned forward into destiny. In the fading light and drifting flakes, it was almost possible to imagine the ghostly founder turning to encourage or shout a warning.

'The bronze was cast more than a century ago by Robert Courtois, the foremost sculptor of his time,' said Jules, his voice touched with emotion. 'Forgive me,' he said. 'All from New France are afflicted by this cursed sensitivity to reminders of our past.'

Jacob wandered around to the front of the pedestal. A faded brass scroll inscribed with a lengthy citation was affixed to the plinth. "Gaston Pierre Tremblay," he said, bending to read the name inscribed on the plaque.

"I sing the matchless deeds of a hero bold, who founded a city that shall never grow old," quoted Jules. 'That's the opening of *Le Voyage*, the epic poem by Pascal Lavoie. The poem celebrates the founding of the city by Tremblay after his flight from Montreal, allegedly pursued by troops sent by an angry Jean Talon. It tells of Tremblay and his loyal supporters braving the woods and rivers in search of a refuge. It's our great patriotic verse. Every schoolboy and schoolgirl must learn it by heart.

Doubtless it's full of legends invented by Lavoie. But don't tell Isabelle I told you that, she believes it in every word. Did I tell you we are known as the city of statues and monuments? I did? Behold the proof. There are a dozen or more similar representations around the city. On Founder's Day, half the town makes a pilgrimage from one to the next, like worshippers observing the Stations of the Cross.'

Jules paused, then began to recite from the poem as if to prove to himself he still remembered the words, 'And where the lovely trees did shade, They saw a mountain topped with firs … They raised a cross upon that holy hill and knelt to pray …' He faltered, trying to recall the words.

—'Beseeching He who dwells above for grace,' a smiling Isabelle joined in, her voice rising to join with her cousin's, 'That He might blessings pour upon that place!'

Jules laughed. 'When you can recite that, word for word, then you know, Jacob, that you are a true habitant.'

Returning to the boulevard they resumed their progress, passing a hotel, expensive-looking shops, and a grand-looking restaurant lit with electric light. 'The Golden Plate,' said Jules as they passed the latter. Its broad windows showed diners drinking wine and smoking cigars at linen-covered tables. White-jacketed waiters carried covered dishes back and forth on the lushly carpeted floor. 'Our finest restaurant. It will cost you a day's salary for just a glass of wine.'

Arriving at a sign set into a wall, they stopped, Jules pointing across the street. 'Rue Marian. That will take you home, Jacob,' he said. 'Downhill all the way. Mind you don't slip on the steps and break your neck.'

In spite of the cold, the drifting flakes, and the approaching dusk, Jacob was reluctant to take his leave. 'My thanks to yourself and your cous— Isabelle, for the tour,' he said.

'Yes?' Jules gave ear as Isabelle spoke, her eyes on Jacob. 'My cousin bids you well in your new life here in the city. And wishes you continued progress in your commendable studies of the French language.'

'Is it permitted to ask if I may see her again?' His eyes were on Isabelle, drinking in her warm prettiness amidst the failing light.

Jules reflected as he smoothed his curled moustache. 'I advise you to wait, friend. Society here in New France is not as … progressive, as it is in America. You will need her mother's permission.'

'What are you talking about?' asked Isabelle, piqued to be shut out of the conversation.

'He wishes to see you again.'

'And what did you say?'

'I advised him to wait.'

'Good!' She gave a winning smile at Jacob. 'But not too long. Don't you dare repeat that!'

11

Isabelle Ouellet

S HE AWOKE FROM A vivid dream—of what, she couldn't recall, and lay under the warm covers, trying to remember. The sound of bells pealed in the distance. Sunlight flooded in through the window as though it were spring outside, not winter. She stretched languorously, thinking back to the previous Sunday and her tour of the cathedral with Jules and Jacob. 'Jacob!' She repeated the name, basking in the sound, her mind returning to his wide-eyed expression as he stood amidst the magnificence of the cathedral, clearly overwhelmed by the splendour surrounding him.

What must it be like—not to know who you are? She shivered in spite of the warmth of the bed. And all because of an accident, a stray bullet that forever robbed him of himself! The thought that fate could be so capricious evoked a murmur of protest at such random, wanton tragedy. Could the world be so cruel? Could God? The horrifying prospect caused her heart to beat with fright. She breathed against the pillow, stifling her fear, before her thoughts returned to Jacob. Where did he come from? Who were his parents? Did he perhaps have a wife or sweetheart somewhere, waiting in vain for his return? Surely, family and friends would look for him … issue missing posters or employ private investigators?

The bells fell silent as her mind returned to that moment in the cathedral where they both stood—suspended in the instant as it seemed—before the window of Gaston Tremblay. Something had passed between them—a look, an understanding even. Jacob had felt it too, she was certain, a deep, instinctive sympathy that was hallowed by the sacred air of the church. He had understood her, had intuited her meaning in spite of lacking the words.

She heard Marguerite singing to herself in the next room and turned down the covers, loathe to get up from the warm bed.

Marguerite smiled as she entered. 'Good morning, sleepy head.'

'What are you doing standing there by the window?'

'I am waiting to see the new curé. He is said to walk down the street at eight o'clock every morning, without fail. And there he is!' Marguerite pressed her face up against the glass.

'Let me see!' Pushing in beside her sister, Isabelle peered at the figure proceeding along the street below. He wore a black coat over a cassock and a prelate's hat on his head. He walked with head bent forward, hands clasped behind his back. 'He walks like a duck! What is his name?'

'Martin Simard.'

'Is he related to Marie Simard?'

'He is a third cousin, so Marie claims. Admit it. You dreamt of him!' Marguerite blew warm, teasing air against Isabelle's neck.

'Who?'

'You know who! They say he has long, thick fingers.'

'The curé?' Distracted, Isabelle twisted her neck.

Marguerite chuckled. 'Your Englishman!'

'Merciful heavens! Is that all that preoccupies you—his fingers?'

'Poor, innocent Isabelle!' Marguerite kissed her hair.

'Girls!' Their mother's voice came from downstairs. 'Hurry up! Breakfast is ready.'

They were still chatting about Jacob as they sat down to breakfast, much to their mother's displeasure. 'You are made giddy by that Englishman,' she complained, spooning pork spread onto a slice of toast.

'He is American, Mama, not English.'

'The same thing.' Her mother bit into the toast. 'Are you attracted to him?'

'Mama!'

'No use denying it. I see by your face that you are.'

'And why not? He is obliging and well-mannered and has an honest face.'

'He is an oddity. A man without a memory. Whoever heard of such a thing?'

'It wasn't his fault. He was wounded in the head.'

'Nevertheless, I forbid you to see him again.'

'That's not fair!'

'So, you did intend on seeing him?' her mother said, her teeth embedded in a piece of toast.

'No, not exactly. I just would not wish to ignore him if he wished it so.'

'Well, you have my decision. It's time you started getting serious about your future. There's Madeline Chauvin's nephew, that nice young Henri. They say he is going places and is looking for a wife.'

'But I am not looking for a husband!'

'Then its high time that you did. Look at your sister, she has Dominic Beaulieu wrapped around her little finger.'

Marguerite spluttered into her coffee but did not dispute the assertion. 'Do you expect me to snub Jacob if I meet him in the street?'

'Jacob is it now?' Madame Ouellet raised her eyebrows.

'We broke no formalities. The situation called for it.'

'No matter. He is a pauper, with no money, no prospects, no family, and no memory.' Her mother shuddered. 'You have the whole of New France to choose from and you make a fool of yourself over a … *vagrant*.'

Isabelle put down the spoon, tears in her eyes.

'Mama, do you not think you are being harsh?' interceded Marguerite.

'I am being a mother!' said Madame Ouellet grandly and added a dash of milk to her coffee.

'We saw the new curé,' said Marguerite, with a sympathetic glance at her sister.

'I don't care for him.'

'But you've never even seen him—let alone heard him say Mass.'

'I don't care. I prefer Father Laurent. He has a fine singing voice. Your poor father often remarked on it. He would have been sixty this month.' Madame Ouellet's hand trembled and she set down the cup. 'I can see him there, reading the newspaper and complaining about the cost of bus tickets. His last words were to look after you, his beloved daughters.' Her eyes grew moist, and she plucked a handkerchief from her sleeve.

'Do not upset yourself, mama.' Getting up, Isabelle put her arms around her mother.

'Never mind,' said her mother and blew her nose as Isabelle sat down again. 'Why is Father Laurent being replaced?'

'He is not being replaced. He is retiring.'

'Retiring? Is there such a thing—for a priest?'

'He has asked to be transferred back to Clairvaux. The new curé will take over the parish.'

'Isabelle, has the cat got your tongue?'

'Do you really forbid me to see him?' Isabelle's voice was tearful.

'Who? The curé?'

'Jac—Monsieur Wheeler.'

'I do. And for you own sake, even if you refuse to see it. You are a naïve young girl with no experience of the world. God knows what your poor father would say. Heavens!' Their mother glanced up at the clock. 'We shall be late for Mass. Hurry!'

Ten minutes later, dressed in ankle-length skirts, Moroccan leather shoes, cream-coloured shirtwaist blouses and contrasting ribbon ties, they presented themselves to their mother for inspection. She looked them up and down, a disapproving expression on her face. 'A bit fashionable for church, don't you think? The bishop would have something to say.'

Marguerite hooted. 'He would prefer to strap us all in corsets!'

'Mama, it's the twentieth century. Besides, we'll be wearing our coats.'

Their mother sighed. 'Well, go and put on your hat and gloves. And wear a scarf!' she called after them. 'That old cathedral has more draughts than a barn!'

THE CATHEDRAL WAS FULL, many, like themselves, hoping to satisfy their curiosity as to the new curé. Isabelle squeezed into their regular pew alongside her mother and sister. She looked around the crowded nave, absurdly imagining that perhaps she might glimpse Jacob. Was it too fanciful to imagine that he might have returned to catch a glimpse of her? Already, the visit—visitation!—she sucked in her breath at the faintly blasphemous thought that fused Jacob in her yearning devotions with stained glass, candlelight, and incense. The unfairness of her mother's edict rankled in her breast as she took out her rosary, stringing the coloured tear-drop-shaped beads between her fingers. Kneeling, she offered up a prayer for the memory of her father, followed by another for her mother and sister, and yet another for the memory of Gaston Tremblay.

Sitting back down, she turned her head slightly and caught the eye of Marie Pelletier across the aisle. Marie smiled and she smiled back. Madame Desrochers returned her nod and Celeste Allemande gave a discreet wave. Lucien Amaury, the butcher's son, gazed boldly at her and she looked away. Marguerite gave a discreet cough and, leaning forward, motioned with her eyes to where Sulpice Benoit sat wearing a stylish wool hat and a red silk scarf around her throat. As she stared, Sulpice smiled, causing Isabelle to compress her lips and quickly turn back to face the altar.

There was a shuffle of feet from the pew behind and a hissed, 'Odile!' directed at her mother.

Turning, Isabelle saw her aunt, Delphine, together with her husband, Henri, and daughter Hélène squeeze into the pew, murmuring apologies as they proceeded. 'Pardon! Pardon!' Aunt Delphine warbled as she stepped on the toes of Roger Charpentier, drawing a frown from his fiancé. With a bustle of coats and a creaking of wood, the family settled into the pew. Isabelle's uncle Henri beamed at her, and she smiled in return. Delphine leaned forward to whisper into the ear of her sister while Roger Charpentier's fiancé stared rudely, causing Isabelle to face back to the front.

Music sounded from the organ loft, and Isabelle closed her eyes, imagining for a moment that she was back in her warm bed. The congregation rose in a noisy and prolonged shuffle of feet as Bishop Drolet entered. He was followed by the curé, the attending acolytes, and two altar boys, one carrying a cross, the other a thurible. The bishop was dressed in a silk chasuble embroidered with an orphrey of gold braid and a blue background emblazoned with a representation of the Blessed Virgin. The curé, by contrast, was dressed in a plain white surplice over his black soutane. The focus of all eyes, he walked with his gaze raised towards the high altar, his lips moving with the words of the entrance hymn.

Marguerite leaned back behind their mother to catch Isabelle's eye. '*He looked at you!*' she mouthed.

'*He did not!*' Isabelle mouthed back and poked out her tongue.

Sunlight streamed in through the stained-glass windows, and the smell of incense filled Isabelle's nose as the bishop gave the first reading, from Ecclesiastes. The reading was followed by the responsorial psalm sung by the choir. The congregation knelt for prayer and then sat again for the second reading. Glancing across the aisle, Isabelle saw Sulplice Benoit in her stylish hat pluck a handkerchief from her sleeve and dab her lips, looking the picture of boredom.

An acolyte gave the reading, his voice sounding like an echo in the spacious church:

"Wherefore I perceive that there is nothing better, than that a man should rejoice in his own works; for that is his portion: for who shall bring him to see what shall be after him?"

Isabelle bent forward to catch Marguerite's attention, but her sister was sitting with her eyes shut while idly twisting the rosary around her fingers. *Dreaming of Dominic no doubt.* She was still mulling the import of the reading when the congregation stood for the blessing. The bishop took his seat on a red leather bench to one side of the altar. The congregation coughed and sat down in a collective bustle.

An expectant hum rippled through the pews as the curé mounted the circular steps to the ornately panelled pulpit to deliver the sermon. Isabelle noted his polished black shoes as he climbed the steps. He was tall, and she wondered if he had a permanent stoop, recalling the way he walked along rue Mercier. Clearing his throat, he began speaking in a rather high-pitched voice that echoed through the nave.

'Brethren in Christ! On this rock, Christ hath built his church!'

The clever reference to the ledge of rock which formed the highest part of the city and upon which the cathedral was constructed, drew approving murmurs. Isabelle listened carefully for the first few minutes as the curé established his nativity by briefly recalling his early days as a novitiate in the self-same cathedral. His eyes swept the pews as though he might single out individual persons for acknowledgement, the prospect titillating Isabelle. Her interest waned, however, as he went on to his principal message which was to affirm the moral authority of the church over the state, a familiar and favourite theme of the bishop's orations. The latter nodded approvingly as the curé embarked on the homily.

Her attention drifted as she dwelt on Jacob's sparse yet charming French. *I love the way he pronounces my name. He makes it sound different. It makes me sound different. Mama is so unfair! She barely knows him.* She heard a chorused 'Amen!' from those around her and listened in again as the curé praised the piety of rural life as a defence against the evils of secularism.

'For did not God Himself ordain as much?' he challenged, sweeping the pews with his gaze.

The question awoke the dozing Marguerite, who bent forward to catch Isabelle's eye while mouthing her verdict: '*Boring!*'

'*Hideous!*' she mouthed back.

With a glance at the bishop, the curé turned his homily to the early days of New France, causing Isabelle to sit up and take notice.

'Virtue was everywhere in those days,' he praised, his voice pitched with nostalgia. 'It was in the soil, in the rivers, and in the hearts of men, especially those brave souls who perished for their faith.'

For the next several minutes, he recited verbatim from the book of Jesuit martyrs, declaiming the sufferings of the blessed in a resonant vibrato that carried to every corner of the church. As he described the terrible torments endured by Père Abelard, the first Jesuit missionary to the nascent settlement of New France, his voice darkened, and he began to tremble with barely suppressed emotion.

'His skin was flayed with brands dipped in burning oil!' The curé stared at the congregants, his voice full of wonder at the ingenuity of the Iroquois torturers. 'How he must have yearned for Paradise!' His hands gripped the pulpit, his body trembling as though he might swoon. The bishop coughed into his fist and the curé brought the homily to an end with a hurried blessing. Isabelle glanced at Marguerite who made wide eyes in return.

She lined up for communion, standing behind Richard Fortin and his sister, Coralie. Head bowed, she knelt at the rail to receive the Eucharist. The bishop placed the wafer on her tongue, and she sipped from the chalice held by the curé. Crossing herself, she got up and made her way back to the pew.

Her gaze lowered, she bumped into Claude Martin who made a silly face, which provoked her to giggles in spite of the solemnity of the moment. She suddenly missed Jules, who had taken the early train back to New York, declining her mother's suggestion he stay to attend Mass. 'Business will not wait,' he had responded, making his farewells.

'How very American he has become!' was her mother's only comment as she closed the door behind him.

FOLLOWING THE MASS, THE congregants gathered in groups to visit with friends and relatives as they exited the service. Clouds chased across the sky in between patches of bright sunshine. A blustery north wind swept the square and cathedral steps.

'At least Father Laurent had the decency not to speak of blood and savages on a Sunday morning!' Madame Ouellet took a small mirror from her handbag to examine her face.

'Yoo-hoo!' Aunt Delphine waved excitedly, bustling toward them through the press of worshippers milling outside the cathedral. 'Odile, darling!' Delphine embraced her sister and turned to Isabelle, showering her niece with kisses and hugs. 'You look so pretty!'

'Where is Désirée?' asked Madame Ouellet, searching the crowd for their other sister.

'There she is! Désirée! Over here!' Delphine waved to catch her sister's attention.

'Good morning, ladies!' Charles Dumoulin gave a cheery hail as he passed, his voice jovial in the morning sunshine. He twirled his top hat to one and all. The collar of his expensive black coat was edged with felt in the latest Parisian style. 'I'm off for a good old champagne breakfast!' he announced, descending the broad steps to the square where a number of carriages awaited.

'My, but he's grown fat!' whispered Delphine as Madame Ouellet raised a gloved hand in acknowledgement.

'My dear Odile!' Aunt Désirée kissed her older sister on both cheeks. She then kissed Delphine and Isabelle, exclaiming over Isabelle's coat. 'And you made it yourself? You could sell it in the stores of Paris! Where is your sister?'

Isabelle looked around for Marguerite and saw her gossiping with their cousins. She was about to call to her when she was diverted by yet another hail.

'Madame Ouellet!' Emile Lessard leaned from the window of a departing carriage, doffing his hat with the greeting. 'My best wishes to you!' he called out, a smile on his face, as the carriage drew away

'And my greetings to your dear mother!' Odile called back.

'Yoo-hoo!' Delphine waved as she spotted a friend. The woman, carrying a parasol, waved back.

'Look!' Désirée poked Odile in the ribs, addressing her sister in an urgent whisper.

A short, extremely stout woman dressed in black descended the steps toward them. She leaned heavily on a stick, escorted by the bishop on one arm while the curé danced attendance on the other.

'Hauteur Benoit!' Isabelle stared at the woman.

The trinity paused on the bottom step, madame Benoit peering about for her carriage. She caught sight of the Ouellet women and sniffed, turning up her nose as her gaze swept past them.

'Did you see that? Isabelle's mother turned to her sisters with a look of outrage. 'The impertinence!'

'Indeed! The creature is an infamous whore!' exclaimed Delphine.

'There's Gideon Martel!' Delphine clutched her sister's sleeve as they watched madame Benoit's reputed lover descend the steps, holding tightly to the arm of his daughter.

'Will they acknowledge each other?' Isabelle spoke in a hushed voice, fully mindful of the gossip about the scandalous pair. To her disappointment, the frail, elderly ex-deputy passed by his former mistress without so much as a glance.

'It was rumoured he had his way with her in her husband's chamber while the Assembly was in session,' Delphine whispered, her eyes fastened on madame Benoit.

'Even as the vote was being called!' exclaimed Désirée, huddling close to her sisters.

'She screwed half the Reformist Party in her time,' Delphine hissed, the lapse into habitant vernacular so near the church doors drawing a surprised glance from Isabelle.

'And gave a promissory note to the other half!' giggled Désirée.

'Did you know she once bared her breasts in the Public Legis—Madame Verreau! Yoo-hoo!' Désirée waved animatedly to an acquaintance.

They returned their gaze to madame Benoit as the bishop struggled to assist the stout matron up onto the step of her carriage.

'He has his hands full!' joked Delphine, causing her sister to snort with laughter.

'She was once light as a feather,' remarked Madame Ouellet, regret and satisfaction mingled in her voice.

'And so pretty!' Désirée conceded. 'But look at her now! Her nose has fallen into her chin.'

'Did you hear about Father Clement?' Delphine's eyes gleamed with gossip. 'They say he passed away two nights ago in his sleep.' She fell silent as the bishop walked back up the steps, flanked by the curé, both men dispensing blessings as they made their way through the respectful parishioners.

'His mental faculties, poor man, were gone,' Delphine resumed. She looked about her before lowering her voice to a whisper. 'At the end, he thought his housekeeper was his mother. Imagine!'

'I heard he mistook her for his wife—even though he was a priest.' Désirée pursed her lips to confirm the rumour.

The three sisters looked at each other, each waiting for the other to speak first. 'You shall hear no malice from this mouth.' Delphine firmed her lips.

'God forbid one should speak ill of the dead,' agreed Désirée, her eyes on Odile.

'So, there was something—the housekeeper?' Odile raised an eyebrow.

'All I will say is that the poor man was without his wits at the end.'

Odile gave a shuddering sigh. 'Another one!'

'My dear sister-in-law!' Désirée's husband approached through the crowd of parishioners. He kissed Odile on the cheek. 'Isabelle!' He stooped to allow his niece to kiss his cheek in return.

'Frédérick, have you seen Henri?' Delphine searched the crowd for her husband.

'He stopped to speak to René Couture.'

'Good Lord, that grump! It's a wonder he's sober enough to attend. Was his wife with him?'

'She was gossiping with Marguerite. How pretty you look, Isabelle. The boys must be chasing after you!'

'Pfff! She is infatuated with a beggar. Some Englishman found lost in the woods!'

'Mama!'

'The Englishman? Désirée has mentioned him. I hear the poor fellow has lost his mind.'

'Not so, uncle! He has a name and an occupation.'

'So does the Devil!' Her uncle laughed, exceedingly pleased with the *bon mot*. He turned to see if others had bought into the quip.

'Henri! Where have you been? We were about to send for the constable!' Delphine clucked in exasperation as her husband approached.

'Mixing, my darling. Didn't you complain just last week that I was like a tortoise in its shell?' He removed his hat to kiss Odile on the cheek. 'Hello Odile. Good morning, Isabelle.' He looked around. 'Where's your sister?'

'It's true!' Delphine chuckled. 'I did call him a tortoise!'

'Over there, with Camille Couture … Marguerite!' Isabelle gestured for her sister to join them.

'I saw you in conversation with René Couture,' said Delphine to her husband. 'What did the scoundrel have to say?'

'Full of complaints, as usual! Marguerite! Come, give your uncle a kiss!'

'Isabelle, come here. Your collar is crooked.' Madame Ouellet smoothed the offending item.

'Monsieur Lapointe! Hello!'

'Did you see Sulplice Benoit?' Delphine made eyes at her sister. 'That colour—on a Sunday!'

'Henri! Don't wander off, it's time to go. Where on earth is Hélène?'

'And I said, so does the Devil!'

'GIRLS!' MADAM OUELLET PEERED at her reflection in the mirror and adjusted her hat. 'Hurry up!' As she was putting on her gloves, her daughters descended the stairs. 'Isabelle, have you even brushed your hair? Marguerite, are you wearing that blouse?'

'What is wrong with it?'

'The colour, for one. It's far too cheerful. Never mind, we shall be late. Madame Herbert is due at eleven o'clock for a fitting. Are we ready?' With that their mother opened the door.

The three women made their way down rue Mercier arm in arm. A recent snowfall had partly melted, leaving large puddles of water on the street. Unlinking arms, they carefully navigated each one, cautious not to wet their shoes. Towards the bottom of the street a heavy goods wagon passed by, its wheels throwing up slush.

'Watch out!' Their mother clutched her coat as water sprayed over her shoes. The driver ignored her angry look, peering straight ahead as the two large horses pulled the wagon, their hooves clattering on the cobblestones. 'Such a dolt!'

Passing through a small alley on rue Legrand, they encountered a dishevelled woman, her feet wrapped in strips of cloth. A ragged shawl was pinned around her pitifully thin shoulders. She was accompanied by two small children, as malnourished and dirty as herself. Next to them was a soiled blanket and flattened packing box that served as their sleeping quarters. 'Please Madame, spare a coin. The children have not eaten.' The woman held out her hand as they passed.

'Make way!' Their mother continued past the woman.

'Please, Mama. Can we not spare a penny?' Isabelle had tears in her eyes as she beheld the wretched children. They regarded her with wide eyes, their cheeks hollowed for want of food.

'And who will feed us?' Her mother's voice was sharp. 'Come! Don't encourage her.'

Isabelle glanced back. 'She looks familiar, somehow.'

'And why not? she is there every day.'

'It's a shame,' said Marguerite. 'Can the church not do something? There are so many like her.'

'The church cannot be expected to feed every beggar in the city. There would be no end.'

The small dressmaking shop was located on rue Bishop Lavoie next to a tobacco shop, the proprietor of which was outside on the pavement, sweeping the shop front clear of melted snow.

'Good morning, ladies!' He raised his cap, his cheeks flushed with exertion.

'And a good morning to you, Monsieur Tobin.' Their mother fished in her purse for the shop key. 'Pray God we have a short winter!'

'Young ladies!'

'Good morning, sir.'

His eyes took in Marguerite's slim figure as she followed her mother into the shop. To his delight, she glanced back, a pert expression on her face. With a grin, he resumed sweeping.

The shop was cluttered with rolls of yarn and muslin. A sewing bench and a tailor's dummy stood next to a chest of drawers containing buttons, pins, eyelets, and various other knick-knacks of the dressmaking trade.

Madame Ouellet took off her coat and replaced it with a pinafore, her daughters doing the same. She shivered. 'Marguerite, light the fire at once. And Isabelle, start on those buttonholes. Madame Herbert will be here at any moment.'

Shortly after noon there was a commotion on the street outside, an angry shout drawing all three women to the window.

'What is it?' Their mother drew a tiny gap in the lace net curtains. On the pavement outside, monsieur Tobin was using his broom to sweep the unfortunate family they had passed earlier from the front of his premises.

'Go beg elsewhere!' he cried, whisking the broom in the direction of the mother, who shrank back.

'I beg pardon, sir.' The proprietor stepped aside to allow a man in a fur hat and wool coat to pass. 'Off with you!' he said, resuming his indignation as the man passed. The mother hurried away, her two girls clinging close to her side.

'Damn'd riffraff!' The proprietor glared after the interlopers, shaking the broom once more before retreating inside the shop.

'Can't we do something?' Isabelle looked beseechingly at her mother.

'The children looked starved,' added Marguerite.

'Am I a private charity?' Grumbling to herself, their mother nevertheless fished in her purse for a coin. 'Here. Run after them and give her this,' she said, handing the coin to Isabelle. 'And tell her not to expect any more.'

'I will, Mama. And thank you!' Opening the door and scooping up her skirt, Isabelle hurried after the family. 'Pardon!' she called out as she caught up.

The woman looked back in alarm. 'We want no trouble!'

'For you, Madame.' Isabelle held out the coin.

The woman took it, depositing it into the pocket of her tattered coat. 'Thank Madame Ouellet,' she said, drawing the shivering children to her side.

'You know my mother?'

'Know her?' The woman gave a harsh laugh. 'I was her favourite seamstress!'

12

An Opportunity

FOLLOWING THE CATHEDRAL TOUR, Jacob could think of little else save the winningly pretty young Frenchwoman. Over and over, he recalled her luminous expression as she gazed up at the stained-glass window, colours falling about her. Something rare and mysterious had occurred that day, he convinced himself; something momentous that, ever since, had inserted itself like a warm glass pane between himself and the daily world of stitched leather, burning coals, and wood shavings.

'Did your cousin speak of our little outing?' he asked Hugo over Saturday lunch in the tavern.

'Oh, she may have mentioned it,' replied Hugo, absorbed in the newspaper.

'What did she say?'

'Say?' Hugo glanced up, a bemused look in his eyes. 'She said you inspected the cathedral, what else?'

'Oh.'

'Ah!' Hugo set down the newspaper. 'You mean did she say anything about *you!*' He smiled in self-congratulation. *Josette will see that I am not such a dunce in the ways of the heart after all!* 'As a matter of fact, she did— not about the church, but about the dinner party.'

'Yes?' Jacob was all ears.

'She said she thought you a perfectly decent chap, with good manners.'

'Oh.'

Hugo chuckled at the disappointment in Jacob's voice. 'That's praise, my dear fellow. You made a favourable impression.'

'Your cousin is utterly fetching. And very pretty.'

'Do you wish me to tell her that?' Hugo eyed him with amusement.

Jacob thought for a moment. 'Yes. Would you?'

'Let me see … fetching and pretty. Yes, I think I can manage that.' Hugo returned to his newspaper.

'What are the … conventions, should I wish to see her again?'

At the question, Hugo closed the newspaper, a considered look on his face. 'We are careful about such matters in New France. Relations between men and women are very much governed by the church and tradition and, above all, parental approval. In my cousin's case, that means Madame Ouellet. Not a person to be trifled with, I assure you. Now, another glass?'

The conversation with Hugo added more coals to Jacob's smouldering hopes. Isabelle was, he decided, beyond charming, her sense of humour a delight, her smile enough to melt a blind man's heart! And her eyes!—full of a warmth that seemed to reach out and embrace the listener. And the way she spoke his name! He was bursting to see her again. But what if he had a rival? The sudden thought poured cold water on his fanciful projections and plunged him into dejection—a mood that worsened when he pictured Madame Ouellet standing like a mother dragon between himself and her offspring. With a frustrated mutter he tried to focus on the saddle before him.

His fixation on the young woman was briefly diverted by a small triumph that happened one morning at breakfast, a year after his arrival in New France.

Madame Pepin stuck her head around the parlour door. In her hand she carried a freshly boiled egg balanced on a large spoon. 'Would you like another egg, Monsieur Wheeler?'

'No thank you, Madame. I am quite full from the toast and spread.'

She looked at him in some surprise before withdrawing. It was only after wondering at the expression on her face that the cause struck him. I answered without hesitation! He sat back in the chair, delighted with the fact. I didn't have to search for the words—they were just there! That the response was simple, and a repetition of previous answers, seemed to him of small account beside the fact of it being spontaneous and unmindful. Basking in the incident, he took every opportunity to engage madame Pepin in conversation as she cleared away the dishes until she pointedly remarked that she had work to do.

'Yes, Madame. I understand the utmost nature of work.' She gave him an odd look and returned to the kitchen.

This new and seemingly overnight comfort in the language gave him the confidence to join in the banter of his fellow apprentices at the work bench. He laughed off their increasingly ineffective attempts to trick him into asking the foreman for *le marteau élastique* or to provoke old Guyot by urgently enquiring after *un baiser* to finish the saddle. Giving as good as he got, he amused his workmates by asking if they had eaten *un avocat* for lunch, and, if so, had the robe got caught up in their teeth?

Lascelles observed this flurry of linguistic prowess with a sceptical visage, being overheard to remark that 'a parrot may talk but is still a parrot.'

One Sunday afternoon Jacob took an exercise stroll around the neighbourhood, nodding to fellow strollers. The market had closed but he sat on a bench in the square to enjoy the mild sunshine. A beggar wandered up and he rewarded the fellow's enterprise with a coin, watching as the latter touched his forelock in gratitude before shuffling off. 'Don't tell your friends!' He called out after the man.

Jules Desjardin's suggestion that the near-fatal bullet wound had 'released' something in him came to mind as he idly watched a woman walk a small poodle across the square. Is it possible? he asked himself as she stooped to pick up the small dog. He saw a pair of vagrants approach and stood up. I was once even lower than you, it occurred to him as he headed off back to rue des Martyrs.

'Good afternoon, Monsieur,' a passer-by greeted him.

'And good afternoon to you, sir,' he replied with the same instinctive reflex as his answer to Madame Pepin.

And as his ears became more fully adjusted to the quicksilver intonations of his new language, so too—to his surprise—did his eyes, the urban surrounds of streets, houses, and roofs transmuting into an altogether altered landscape, one less precise and immutably solid in the hazy winter light. He discovered a pleasure in renaming things, the languid *herbe* seeming to signify an essential quality absent from the harshness of his native 'grass', and *un célibataire* reflecting an altogether more elevated acknowledgement of his bachelor status.

The binary division into male and female that his new tongue insisted upon, began to seem less strange and less arbitrary, the designations leading him to notice things formerly hidden in the diurnal laxity of his native speech and awakening a suspicion that society and the world itself was altogether more layered, ambiguous and complex than he had hitherto given awareness to. '*There is a puzzlement to the world,*' he noted in a margin of the dictionary, staring at the words with some perplexity as though they had been written by someone other than himself.

'Sometimes I seem to be someone else,' he remarked to Hugo upon recounting the triumph of the egg.

'How can one be someone else?'

'It is how I sometimes seem to myself.'

Hugo repeated the remark to the deputy, drawing a bemused look from the other man. 'He said that?' The deputy tapped his fingers on the walnut desk. 'I read, not long ago, an article in which the author speculated that we are all composed of several different selves, and that we can gain access to each one through dreams or hypnosis.' He mused on the thought, unsure where to take it. 'Does Jacob ever refer to his past?' he asked.

'No, sir.'

The deputy stood up and walked to the window where he looked down at the Gaston Tremblay monument in the square below. 'Your American continues to surprise,' he ruminated. 'One might conceive of him as a voyageur of sorts.'

'Sir?'

'He is constantly opening up new regions of inquiry, is he not?'

'I have never thought of it that way.'

'Jacob the Voyageur.' The deputy smiled to himself as he gazed out the window. 'Who knows? Someday they may raise a statue in his honour.'

ISABELLE! DO LOOK AT what you're doing!' Madame Ouellet tutted in annoyance as she picked up the fabric her daughter was cutting. 'Follow the lines! The pattern is ruined.'

'Sorry, Mama. My mind was elsewhere.' Isabelle took back the fabric, an apologetic expression on her face.

'Do you think we are made of money? Who will pay for it if we cannot use it?'

Marguerite looked over her mother's shoulder. 'Don't work yourself into a fuss, Mama. See, a snip there and everything is mended!' She pointed to the spot.

'Thank God at least one of my daughters hasn't lost her mind. And over whom, I wonder?' their mother added, her voice sharp.

'You still think of him?' Marguerite asked Isabelle that evening after supper, her voice full of sympathy.

'You know I do.' Isabelle sat in a chair next to the window, stretching out her legs and tapping her toes together. 'I can't help it.'

Marguerite's eyes widened. 'You are in love with him!'

'Not love,' Isabelle demurred, her voice unconvincing. 'I am not like you, dear sister, to fall in love at the drop of a hat.' She hesitated. 'I suppose you could say I am … *taken* with him.'

'Isn't that the same thing?'

'No. There are differences … of degrees,' ventured Isabelle.

'Seriously, darling.' Marguerite sat down and stroked her sister's hair. 'Is Jacob all you can think of?'

'Yes,' Isabelle confessed, her voice miserable. She looked at Marguerite with moist eyes. 'Do you think he has forgotten about me?'

Marguerite chuckled and kissed Isabelle's brow. 'Impossible! Once this horrid weather clears up, I'm sure he'll be pounding on the door.'

'Do you really think so?' Isabelle clutched Marguerite's hand, her eyes entreating.

'Well, not pounding perhaps, but he's sure to come calling.'

'And mama?'

Marguerite sighed. 'Mama is mama. She'll come around in time—once she sees you are heartfelt. But there are other boys, sweetness. You are too young to be so besotted by one man. What about poor Henri? He dotes on you.'

Isabelle made a face that caused Marguerite to smile. 'Try kissing a boy,' she suggested. 'Any boy. That might divert your mind from Jacob.'

'Marguerite!'

'Why not? I kissed a few before I settled on Dominic. And then went back and kissed a few more to make sure.' Marguerite's smile broadened at Isabelle's shocked expression.

'I'm certain the curé would have something to say about that.'

'Bother the curé. Let him kiss his housekeeper.'

'Marguerite! That's ... that's ...'

'What?'

'Funny!' Isabelle burst out laughing, her sister joining in. 'Can you imagine mama's face!'

Marguerite kissed Isabelle's cheek. 'Now, go to bed,' she said in a mock-stern voice. 'And no dreams of you know who!'

Humming to herself, Marguerite turned down the covers, fondly recalling the first time she had kissed Dominic with her tongue. Or was it Claude Lavoie that time behind the church? She climbed in between the sheets, hard put to remember.

JACOB WAS PAINSTAKINGLY SEWING a saddlebag at his workbench when he was distracted by a loud voice calling from the doorway. 'Bonjour! Bonjour!'

Monsieur Barreau, the foreman hurried over to greet the visitor, monsieur Lascelles being temporarily away from the workshop on business. Jacob had returned to his sewing when he was summoned by Barreau, an annoyed look on his face.

'Yes?' he said, going over to where the foreman stood with the visitor.

'Speak to him—he is English.' Barreau was dismissive as he motioned to the visitor—an imposing, fortyish individual wearing a Stetson hat, leather boots, and a thick fur coat.

'Yes, sir,' said Jacob. 'How may I help you?'

The caller gave a surprised look. 'God Almighty, if you don't sound American!' He scrutinised Jacob, his gaze sharp and appraising. 'Are you?'

'I am.' Jacob grinned, pleased to hear the sound of his native tongue.

'Well, I'll be! I was hoping to find a Frenchie who spoke 'merican and find the genuine article instead. Don't that beat all!' The man stuck out his hand. 'Gus Ferguson, New York State.' He spoke in a booming, confident voice.

'Jacob Wheeler. Pleased to make your acquaintance, sir.'

The foreman observed the exchange with a sullen face. 'What does he want?' he said rudely.

Jacob was about to reply when they were interrupted by the return of monsieur Lascelles, carrying a parcel under one arm. 'What's going on, and who is this?' he asked, his eyes suspicious.

'Some American. He just walked in without a by-your-leave.'

'What does he want?' Lascelles addressed the question to Jacob.

'Is this the boss man?' asked Ferguson before Jacob could reply.

'It is. His name is monsieur Lascelles.'

'Well, tell the monsewer I come to do business.'

'Sir,' he said, turning to his impatient employer. 'His name is monsieur Ferguson, an American from New York. He says he is here to do business.'

Lascelles looked the visitor up and down. 'What sort of business?'

'The kind that's going to make monsewer Sourface a lot of money,' said Ferguson after Jacob had relayed the question to him. 'Tell your boss I come to buy his goods.'

'Ah!' Lascelles' expression changed at Jacob's explanation. 'Please monsieur, my office.' He extended a hand to indicate the way. 'You come too,' he instructed Jacob. 'Return to work,' he said to the foreman, who shot a vindictive glance at Jacob before turning away.

Lascelles ushered the visitor to a chair. 'Sit down, sit down,' he said, taking the other chair. Jacob remained standing.

Lascelles pushed aside some invoices on the desktop. 'Ask him what sort of business he has in mind. A moment!' Getting to his feet, he stuck his head out the door, a cross look on his face. 'Keep it quiet out there!' He returned to the chair. 'Now,' he said. 'What sort of business?'

'IT TURNS OUT THE American was a godsend!' Jacob laughed over a mug of beer as he sat in the tavern on Saturday night, regaling his companions with the tale. 'He owns a large, carriage-making business in Albany, New York State, and he's looking for a cheap and reliable source of leather for upholstery and harnesses. He's opening up an office in New France for the purpose and wants Lascelles to supply the materials. *Lots* of materials!' he added triumphantly. 'And what's more, he wishes for me to act as liaison. All communication must go through me as the only English speaker in Lascelles' employ.'

His companions listened admiringly as Jacob recounted how his employer's initial hesitation turned to ingratiating satisfaction as the American explained the range and scope of his requirements. After Jacob finished the tale, they broke into smiles, reaching out to clap him on the shoulder.

'So, the Americans come to New France to do their business?' Denis Vachon whistled in surprise.

'What chance led him to your door?' asked Martin Cloutier.

'We weren't the first choice. He went to two other workshops, but nobody there spoke English.'

'Play your cards right and there may be something in this for you.' Serge Villeneuve tapped the side of his nose.

'You have doubled your value to old Lascelles,' agreed Claude Charbonneau.

Jacob grinned, unable to contain himself at the stroke of good fortune. 'Already Lascelles treats me differently. Just yesterday he invited me into his office for a coffee. Imagine!'

'Be careful not to overplay your hand,' cautioned Serge. Lascelles is well known for his cunning. Aye, and his temper.'

'I've seen glimpses,' agreed Jacob, sobered by the advice.

'But never mind.' Serge raised his beer. 'A toast—to Jacob! Your French is coming on marvellously,' he said, putting down the mug. 'So, Hugo, you have taught him how to fire a gun,' he teased Gagnon.

'How is your head?' asked Martin, peering at Jacob's scalp.

'See for yourself,' he said, pulling aside his hair while inclining his scalp to their inquisitive looks.

'Astonishing!' exclaimed Martin, half-standing to better examine the scar. 'If you didn't know, you'd never suspect!'

'It is proof of miracles, is it not?' asked Claude, turning to Hugo.

Hugo nodded. 'I do so believe.'

'Balls! It's proof that the midwife knows her trade,' scoffed Serge. 'What say you, Jacob?' The others waited expectantly for an answer.

'It is true, Serge. The midwife has balls,' he said, his voice solemn '—leather ones'.

The table regarded him in silence for a moment before Serge exploded into laughter, the others joining in.

Denis clapped Jacob on the shoulder. 'Your first joke in French!' he declared.

Hugo was staring at Jacob, surprise on his face. 'Did you mean it—the way it came out?' he asked.

'I did,' he said, laughing at Hugo's expression and setting off the table again.

The drinks continued to flow as Jacob conversed with his companions, laughter filling in where understanding faltered. Liberated by the alcohol, he shamelessly paraded his newfound patois as Hugo watched on, a proud look on his face.

'A miracle!' Claude repeated endlessly, whether in reference to Jacob's French or his recovery, or both.

'To health!' cried Denis Vachon, holding up his beer. 'And to Hugo who, for once in his life, hit the target!'

The toast drew a gasp from Cloutier and earned Vachon a sharp kick under the table from Serge.

'To Jacob!' Claude leapt into the breach, raising his mug while flashing a recriminating look at the chastened Vachon.

'To Jacob!'

To Hugo's relief the remark passed unnoticed by Jacob, basking as he was in the warmth and goodwill of his companions.

Arm in arm, the two made their way home through the darkened streets, laughing and joking in a melange of English and French.

'*Bonjour!*' Jacob called out to passers-by. '*Bonsoir!*' he corrected, turning and hailing.

'They are fine fellows, Hugo. And you are a fine fellow!' He embraced his companion.

'We are all fine fellows,' agreed the considerably more sober Hugo. *Even that dolt Vachon!* he fumed under his breath.

TRUE TO HIS WORD, a few days later, Ferguson brought over the designs for the carriage interiors. Unrolling the sketches in Lascelles' office, he explained the quantity and quality of leather required as Jacob interpreted.

'Tell him the measurements are all there,' Ferguson said, pointing to the sketch. 'Suppose we start with an order for one carriage,' he suggested, 'to try things out? I take it that's agreeable?' He glanced at Lascelles.

The business concluded, Ferguson shook Jacob's hand. 'I depend on you to keep everything hunky dory,' he said.

After Ferguson had departed, Lascelles turned to Jacob. 'I want you to help supervise the staff. Make sure they understand what is required and see to it that the cuts exactly match the measurements supplied by the American. Start today. There is plenty of leather to choose from. What did the American say to you?'

'He merely wished that all would go well.'

He spent the next several days overseeing the softening, cutting, and stitching of the leather upholstery in line with the instructions specified by Ferguson. The foreman looked on with barely suppressed wrath as Jacob oversaw the process, laughing with good humour as one apprentice held up 'the American cow', for inspection.

A week later, Ferguson returned to inspect the finished leathers. An intent look on his face, he held each one up to examine the quality and stitching, stopping to refer to the sketched diagram. Lascelles hovered close by, as did the anxious stitchers and cutters, all awaiting the American's verdict.

'OK.' Ferguson laid the last leather back on the bench. He thought to himself for a moment. 'Tell Sourface I'll take these and raise him another six orders. The same cut and stitching.' He winked at Jacob. 'That's poker for I want to do business! And throw in the tack as discussed.'

'Complete?'

'Reins, collars, straps, buckles, the whole kit and caboodle.' Ferguson stuck out his hand. 'Put it there, partner!'

Observing Lascelles' frown at the handshake, Jacob quickly relayed details of the order. 'He wishes you to provide the entire upholstery for six carriages as well as the harnesses,' he explained.

Lascelles' frown disappeared, replaced by a triumphant look as he comprehended the full extent of the order. Clapping his hands, he ordered the apprentices back to work before inviting Ferguson into his office for a celebratory glass of wine. 'You, too,' he said as an afterthought, turning to beckon Jacob.

Upon departing, Ferguson paused in the doorway. 'We should have dinner sometime and speak American,' he said to Jacob.

'Gladly.'

'What did he say?' asked Lascelles when the American had departed.

'He said we should have dinner sometime, as fellow Americans.'

Lascelles stood in the office doorway as Jacob returned to work, a thoughtful look on his face. A half-hour later he called Jacob back into his office. 'This is a good opportunity for you,' he began, motioning Jacob to a chair. 'As you are my … emissary to the American, I will raise your salary by an additional two dollars a month. How does that sound?' He regarded Jacob closely as he made the offer.

'It is very generous, sir.'

'Then let us shake hands, to seal it.'

In spite of the meagre increase, Jacob was glad of it. A quarter of his monthly salary went to Madame Pepin for room and board. Of the remainder he set aside half to deposit in a savings account at the *Banque de crédit de la Nouvelle France,* and half for incidentals and the occasional tavern meal. The deposit, along with his increasing comfort in the language, provided for, he felt, a surer purchase on life. In a moment of optimism, he reckoned his position, much like a merchant might tally his stock: a job, a few trusted friends, some small savings, and a pleasant room at Madame Pepin's with whom he was on familiar, although respectful, terms.

Following the departure of Monsieur Bedard he now enjoyed the minor distinction of senior lodger. His new neighbour was a quiet, morose fellow who worked in a tobacco warehouse and who once offered to pay madame Pepin a pound of tobacco in lieu of rent, a proposal she indignantly refused. Further ingratiating himself, Jacob made small repairs around the house and shovelled snow from out front in winter.

One afternoon, his services were called upon to coax the landlady's pet cat down from a tree where it had taken spitting refuge from an aggressive dog.

'Thank you, Monsieur Wheeler.' Madame Pepin cuddled the frightened cat, clucking and scolding all at once. 'An extra serve of pie for you!'

13

Saint-Jean-Baptiste

IT WAS LATE SPRING before he saw Isabelle again—the occasion a chance meeting in the streets of the Old Town where Isabelle, accompanied by her mother and sister, had come to shop at the market.

'Isabelle!' He crossed the street unable to contain his delight at the unexpected encounter. 'And Madame Ouellet!' He bowed his head before smiling at Marguerite, who smiled back.

'Come Isabelle!' Her mother flashed a look of displeasure at having her daughter's name called out in the street. 'At once!' She turned to go into the market entrance.

'Mama, a moment, please?'

Her mother's brow puckered with disapproval. 'A moment only, we have shopping to do. Marguerite, stay with your sister. I shall be at the butcher's.' With a pinched look, she swept by Jacob and into the market.

Marguerite made eyes at her sister before discreetly wandering off into the surrounding stalls.

'I am delighted to see you again!' Jacob resisted the impulse to reach out and touch her arm.

'And I, you!' Her smile dazzled amidst the throng of shoppers. She wore a floral bonnet and a summery jacket and skirt.

'I, I, think, that is …' His French faltered and vanished in the moment. Reduced to the importuning stares of his first days in the town, he gazed fervently, his heart swelling up in his chest. 'Your hat is very pretty!'

'Thank you, sir!' She gave a mock curtsey, delighted at her effect on him. But in truth, as she acknowledged to herself later—on pretending to browse the market stalls with her mother—she was as ardently breathless and as fervently tongue-tied as her would-be suitor. 'And how are you, Jacob?' She could not resist saying his name.

'I am in good health, Isabelle.' And no more could he.

'Your French improves each time I see you.'

'Thank you. I hope that—'

'Isabelle!' Her mother's voice rang through the crowd.

'I must go. I hope to see you again, soon.'

'It is my dearest wish.'

The words drew a beaming smile. 'Goodbye Jacob.'

'Goodbye Isabelle.'

'Coming mama!' She flashed a backwards glance as she stepped into the shadow of the market. He was standing in place, his mouth half-open as he gazed after her.

'Oh my!' A smiling Marguerite caught her arm. 'Two Jacobs and two Isabelles!'

'Three, if you count mama's!' Laughing and clinging to each other, they continued into the market.

I truly am in love! Isabelle decided that night. The notion astonished and yet did not. Her childish dreams of being swept off her feet by a Gaston Tremblay look-alike to raise a family of irrepressible habitants, as devoted as herself to New France, paled and vanished, replaced by a bewildering yet intoxicating passion for a stranger, an outsider, a man with no memory, 'and no prospects!' said her mother's voice inside her head.

'It is incredible!' she told herself. 'Unbelievable.' Her heart, as transparent as the stained-glass windows of the church, had arranged itself into a tableau in which Jacob knelt at her feet, proclaiming his undying love, while Gaston Pierre himself peered down approvingly from the topmost corner pane. A golden light washed over the scene, the grass impossibly green, the Mercier River sparkling in the sunlight as it flowed past. A homely cottage with a whitewashed door stood in the shade of the lushly flowering trees. 'Mary, Mother of Jesus, let it be true!' she beseeched, her lips quivering in prayer. 'And let Jacob feel it too!' And thus love, that gleeful cherub, slipped into her maidenly dreams and she was Isabelle no more, but Isabelle-Jacob.

MAY MELTED INTO JUNE, the long, warm days scarcely easing his frustrations as he struggled to comprehend his feelings for Isabelle. That she should have entered his life—his lost, wayward existence—seemed to him little short of a miracle. That she should return his feelings, to whatever degree, left him in a state of astonishment. I have no future but with her, he told himself. He was shocked, therefore, to learn of a cruel embargo placed upon his hopes, one pronounced by Isabelle's mother and conveyed by an apologetic Hugo.

'Forbidden to see her?' His mouth opened in protest as Hugo announced the edict. 'Why? Have I done something to upset her? I barely know the woman! I've only ever met her on two occasions.' The words tumbled from his mouth as Hugo tried to assuage his dismay.

'Unjust, I know. I agree with you Jacob. But Madame Ouellet is her mother and feels that Isabelle needs protecting.'

'From me?' Jacob gaped in astonishment. 'I wouldn't harm her for the world! You must know that.'

'From herself, I mean. From her own vulnerable heart. Please, Jacob, sit down.'

Jacob sank into a chair, a look of intense frustration on his face. They were in his room, Hugo heading there after being summoned to Madame Ouellet's house on Rue Mercier. There, he was subjected to the gimlet-eyed stare of the matriarch as she laid down the law regarding Isabelle and 'the feckless Englishman'.

'I am disappointed in you, nephew, that you have invited this … this … *gypsy* into our midst.'

'But aunt, Jacob is a fine fellow—decent, hardworking and honourable. I don't see—'

'He is without family or memory, English, and a Protestant—worse, a so-called freethinker—into the bargain.' She said the last with a raised voice as though incredulous that such creatures existed.

Outside the room, sitting on the stairs to listen, her daughters exchanged breathless glances.

'But aunt, we do not know his full circumstances. It is not his fault he was injured so severely as to lose his memory. And he has full command of his other faculties. He is intelligent, as shown by his quick command of French, and diligent—witness his occupation—and respectful of your daughter.'

'Nevertheless, I have made my feelings clear. Let that be the end of the matter.'

From the stairway came the sound of a gasped breath.

'Really, aunt, are you not being harsh? If you could hear how fondly he speaks of Isabelle, you would change your mind.'

'He *speaks* of her?' Madame Ouellet stared down her nose.

'Only in the most respectful terms.'

'Then let him respect her altogether by staying away!'

'If you would only give him a chance. He has the most honourable intentions.'

'And do those intentions include becoming a Catholic?'

Hugo sighed. 'I cannot say.'

'And does he intend to regain his memory?'

'I am sure he *wishes* to remember, but cannot, owing to the severity of the injury.'

'What prospects does he have?' she demanded, her voice frosty.

'Prospects? Why, I imagine he will work for monsieur Lascelles for a few years, or so ...'

'Yes?'

'Really, I am not a fortune teller!' Exasperated at her intransigence Hugo sat back in the chair.

'And is that what you wish for your cousin—to be married to a ... *saddle-maker* with no memory, no fortune, no prospects, no family, and no faith?'

He muttered at the catalogue, his face glum, unable to think of a reply.

'I expect you to convey my wishes to him.' The mandate was accompanied by a severe glance. 'As Isabelle no longer has a father, you must stand in his place. Besides, are you not the Englishman's friend?'

'American,' he corrected wearily. 'Very well, I'll pass along your message, although I can hardly say I approve of the contents.'

Putting on his hat in the hallway, he cast an apologetic look at Isabelle where she sat on the staircase, her face strained as she gripped the hand of her sister. '*Sorry!*' he mouthed, and opened the door, glad to be back outside in the warm air.

'So, there you have it,' he explained to the stricken Jacob. 'Her mother is quite immovable on the subject, I'm afraid. But she may come around in time. Leave it with me, my dear fellow. I shall do my best to change her mind, I promise.'

'And what did Jacob say?' asked Josette when Hugo recounted the details over supper.

'What could he say? The poor fellow was shocked and upset. Isabelle's mother is being most unjust. What?' He shot a look at his wife. 'You don't agree?'

'Did I say anything?' she asked, her face a picture of pained innocence.

'But?'

'You must admit, Hugo, he lacks any prospect for advancement in the world. I'm sure Isabelle's mother wants more for her daughter.'

'Her husband was an insurance clerk!'

'Which perhaps explains why she wishes more for Isabelle. Look at Marguerite's intended, Dominic Beaulieu. He is a lawyer, with a promising career ahead of him in his father's practice.'

Hugo groaned and put a hand to his head, feeling a headache coming on. 'Jacob may surprise you yet.'

'It is not me he must surprise.'

NO SOONER HAD HER cousin departed than Isabelle hurried into the parlour to confront her mother. 'Mama, it is unfair!'

'You were listening? I told you to go to your room.'

'She is right, you're being monstrously unfair, to both Isabelle *and* Jacob,' insisted Marguerite, following her sister into the parlour.

'Had I not forbidden you to see him? And yet you flirted shamelessly with him on the street!' Her mother turned a stern gaze on Isabelle.

'We bumped into each other! By accident! Would you have me run away every time I see him?'

'Mama, be reasonable, she can hardly hide away indoors for fear of encountering Jacob on the street.'

'Nevertheless, she must avoid him at all costs. Your sister is still a child. She needs protecting.'

'I am not a child! Besides, he has done nothing wrong.' Isabelle eyed her mother tearfully. 'Is it because he is not French?'

'Or not Catholic?' put in Marguerite.

'It is because you are too young and innocent to know your own mind. Now run along, I wish for some tea.' Their mother waved a handkerchief. 'Put the kettle on.'

'It's cruel!' protested Isabelle, tears falling down her cheeks.

'It's life!' Her mother's voice was sharp. 'And what do you know of that—with your rosary and your daydreams? Life is hard, and one must be sensible and clear-eyed to avoid disappointment. I do it for your own good. In six months you will have forgotten the Englishman ever existed. Find a nice, sensible Frenchman, like Marguerite has. And then you can rely on a safe, happy life together, as I had with your father.'

Madam Ouellet's voice softened as she regarded Isabelle, who had sunk into a chair, her face distraught. 'You will want to have children and to raise them as good Catholics. You will want to secure their future. —Yes,' she insisted as Isabelle opened her mouth to protest, 'these things are important. You will want a house and furniture and enough money to tide you over the hard times. And believe me, they will come. And when they do, you will need someone who understands you, and whom you understand in return.' She clicked her tongue as Isabelle tried to interject. 'I am tired of discussing it. You have my decision. There must be no further contact with this Englishman. I wish to hear no more about it. Not a word! Marguerite, where is the tea?'

JACOB PLEADED WITH HUGO to intercede with Madame Ouellet on his behalf, only to be met by *umming* prevarication each time, his friend clearly unwilling to 'bait the bear' as he put it. 'She has put on armour against you Jacob. You understand?' Hugo made a motion as if to pull on a chainmail coat. 'Give it time, my friend. She may come around.'

'Can you not say something to change her opinion of me?'

'I shall try.' Hugo laid a sympathetic hand on Jacob's shoulder. 'But she is formidable once her mind is made up.'

'Could you not speak to my aunt on Jacob's behalf?' Hugo complained to Josette over dinner. 'He is driving me mad with his constant imprecations.'

'Why me?' Josette raised an eyebrow. 'She is your aunt, after all.'

Hugo swallowed a mouthful of pie, mumbling as he did so.

'Yes?'

'Pardon, dearest.' He cleared his throat. 'She may listen to another woman.'

'Indeed? And what would you have me say?'

'For one, point out she is being entirely unreasonable.'

'And is she?'

He gave a surprised look. 'You don't think so?'

Josette poked at a morsel of pie, a thoughtful look on her face. 'I like Jacob, but is her mother being so unreasonable in wishing to safeguard her daughter's happiness? After all, your own mother was not so taken with me, do you remember?'

'That was different. She had hopes I would take holy orders.'

Her eyes narrowed at the reminder. 'Jacob ought count himself fortunate there are no Jesuits involved.' *Except you!* she almost added, her lips firming just in time.

Nevertheless, as she admitted to her sister, the impasse between the would-be lovers and madame Ouellet intrigued her. 'I should like to help bring them together. But the dragon is fierce in defence of its young.'

'Hugo?' Claudette tittered.

Josette ignored the jibe, knitting her brow to find a way past the formidable obstacle that was Isabelle's mother. 'There must be something that could change her mind.'

'Perhaps if he converted to the true faith?'

'He could become a monk and still she would object!'

'Then perhaps the only solution is for them to run away together.' Claudette's eyes widened. 'Think of the scandal!' She deliberated a moment, her expression thoughtful. 'Is she so besotted with him?'

'Entirely. According to her mother, it is nothing but "Jacob" from morn 'til night.'

'Really?' Claudette pondered this. 'And his feelings—they are as strong?'

'Stronger!'

'It must be nice,' Claudette remarked, a note of envy in her voice. 'I never felt that way.'

'For André?' Josette raised an eyebrow.

Claudette looked suddenly despondent. 'For anyone.'

'I BUMPED INTO YOUR aunt at the patisserie,' Josette announced to Hugo a few days later.

'You did?' He paused from tugging off his tie. 'And what did she say?'

'What do you suppose?' She set down the blue-patterned porcelain tea pot. 'I didn't even have to bring up Jacob. She launched into a tirade before I could even ask. Imagine!'

'And?' he asked, the tie suspended around his neck.

'She complained! What else? Jacob is apparently at fault for her daughter's disobedience, her wilfulness, her own insomnia. She even holds him at fault for the wet weather! And, do you know, she will not even mention him by name. It is nothing but the "wretched Englishman" this and the "witless interloper" that. I could hardly keep up.'

'And what did you say?' He tugged off the tie.

'What could I say! I hardly opened my mouth the entire time. And when she did catch breath, it was only to denounce him in stronger terms than before. The woman is deranged in her opposition.'

'And what of Isabelle?'

'Ah!' Josette blew out an exaggerated sigh. 'According to your aunt, the poor darling has had her head turned by a cunning Casanova who arrived in New France for the sole purpose of seducing foolish, unworldly young virgins.'

Hugo stretched out his legs, taking off the heel of one leather shoe with the toe of the other. 'That is it, then. We may as well tell Jacob the truth—that there is no hope. There are other fish in the pond, as they say. Let him cast his line elsewhere.'

Josette gave a pitying look. 'Do you really think it that simple?'

Hugo frowned. 'I am not the simpleton in affairs of the heart you think me to be. I have no doubt it will be a wrench, but Jacob must accept the reality of her mother's opposition, as must Isabelle herself.'

'And love?'

'Really, Josette.'

His tone piqued her. 'You accept every airy notion in theology, yet scoff at the idea of love?'

'Airy notion? Please, do not price walnuts against eggs. And since when did you become a champion of love?'

As soon as the words were uttered, he realised his mistake. 'Not, my dear, that you were ever anything but!' he said, hastening to make amends. 'I meant simply that …' He shifted uncomfortably at her narrowed gaze. 'Who knows what I mean!' And with that he kicked off his remaining shoe in surrender.

Hugo was still tiptoeing around his offended wife when Jacob stopped by on Saturday after finishing work.

'What a morning!' exclaimed Jacob, sinking into the upholstered mahogany chair. 'Lascelles berated the apprentices for a solid hour over some childish mischief that resulted in the glue pot being overturned and spilling glue all over the floor. He had them in tears before he finished. We were still clearing up the sticky mess when Ferguson stopped by with the requirements for a new order. I thought Lascelles' eyes would pop as he apologised for the mess. Since the military contract ended, all his hopes lie with Ferguson, and he is mortally afraid of losing the business.'

The small talk continued for a few more minutes before Jacob steered the subject around to the real purpose of his visit. 'And have you had a chance to speak to your aunt since we last spoke?'

Hugo glanced at his wife who was carrying a tray of coffee and glazed petit fours into the room. 'Josette?'

'Try these,' she said. 'I got them this morning from the new bakery on rue Baptiste. Madame Ouellet? I spoke to her the day before yesterday.'

'I asked that Josette speak to her on your behalf,' volunteered Hugo, drawing an exasperated glance from his wife.

'Hugo is under the impression that women have some mysterious affinity when it comes to communicating with each other. Pastry?' Josette picked up a petit four with a pair of silver tongs.

'Not affinity but divinity!' Hugo beamed with the quip.

'And what did she say?' Jacob accepted the pastry, eager for news.

Josette gave a sympathetic smile. 'Alas, nothing to encourage one.'

'Oh!' With a heavy sigh Jacob sat back. 'The woman detests me!'

'I am sure she is merely being protective of her daughter.'

'And surely there are other fish—'

'As I was *saying*,' Josette darted her husband a withering look, 'there is no need for despair. Love will find a way. That is, if you *believe* in love,' she added, and tossed her chestnut hair as her husband took refuge in his cup of coffee.

'Then it is hopeless.' Jacob muttered, his face a picture of gloom.

'However,' Josette nibbled on the confection, 'she did complain that Isabelle swoons around like a moon-struck calf.'

'She did?' His face brightened.

'You see?' said Hugo, his voice jovial. 'Did I not tell you not to despair?'

'It is my lack of prospects,' Jacob conceded. 'And truth to tell, I can hardly blame her.'

'Come, let us talk of merrier things! Tell me more about this American— what is his name?—Ferguson.'

An hour later, Jacob rose to take his leave, offering thanks for their efforts on his behalf.

'It isn't over,' promised Hugo as they stood in the doorway. 'We shall redouble our efforts to bring her mother around, won't we dearest? Goodbye, Jacob.'

Jacob had just turned away when he was stopped by a hissed summons. 'Jacob!' Pulling the door behind her, Josette stepped into the street. 'Do you have a message for Isabelle? Be quick!' She darted a glance back at the door.

'Indeed I do! Ask her to meet me—on Saturday. At the … ah … *market* where we met before. She will remember. A thousand thanks!'

'Sunday is better!' Josette whispered the words although the street was empty. 'That is Saint-Jean-Baptiste Day. There will be festivities.'

'Sunday then.'

'When?'

'Pardon?'

'What time?'

'Oh! Two o'clock.'

'I'll pass on the message. And Jacob!' Josette pressed a conspiratorial finger to her lips. 'Just between us, you understand?'

AT THE APPOINTED HOUR, a newly shaved and fresh shirt-wearing Jacob hovered nervously in the shadows of the market building, his heart pounding each time he checked the empty street. From the nearby park he heard the sound of a brass band. Sickened by the fear Isabelle might not turn up, he patrolled restlessly back and forth, tapping and scratching his chin as he watched and waited. A family hurried by on their way to join the festivities in the park, the children breathless with excitement.

'Happy Saint's Day, sir!' The boy raised his cap as he dashed past.

He paced some more, certain it must now be 2:30 p.m. *What if her mother—*

'Jacob?'

He whirled at the sound of her voice. Isabelle stood behind him, a joyous smile on her face. To his dazzled eyes she seemed a vision of loveliness in her white-linen and lace dress and matching summer hat embroidered with a silk ribbon bow. Marguerite stood alongside her sister, stylishly dressed and holding a yellow parasol.

'Isabelle! I thought—' he stuttered, forgetting what he had thought.

'We came the other way,' laughed Marguerite, 'to avoid certain persons.'

'Marguerite?' Isabelle looked pleadingly at her sister.

'Of course. I will wait for you on rue Lalonde, outside the library. Remember, we promised mama to be home for tea.' She pecked Isabelle on the cheek. Directing a brilliant smile at Jacob, she headed off, the parasol artfully balanced on her shoulder.

'Shall we walk?' Swallowing with nerves, Jacob extended his arm. His heart leapt as she placed her hand on his sleeve. They walked slowly up rue Père Abelard to the gardens adjoining the Quarter. The park was full of strolling families enjoying the holiday. An ice-cream seller served treats from a stall. A military band played across the ornamental pond on which ducks swam. They walked in silence, following the circular path around the pond. Elated that she had hold of his arm, Jacob held his head up proudly as other couples strolled past.

They stopped to watch a small boy feed the ducks, tossing bread crusts from a bag. The child stamped at an over-eager duck, and they turned to each other, smiling, eyes sparkling. The child's mother hurried forward as the toddler advanced to the edge of the pond. 'Jacques!' She swept the protesting child up in her arms and they laughed together, finding the sight irresistibly amusing. Isabelle held tighter to his arm, and he clasped her fingers—or did she clasp his? No matter, clasped and joined, they continued down the path, finding the trees never before so green, the summer sky bluer than recall, the shouts and laughter from playing children a balm upon their bursting hearts.

'Did I mention that you look beautiful,' he said, unabashedly falling into the language of love. And she wooed in return, brushing an imaginary speck from his sleeve, licking her lips and tucking a stray hair into place under her oh-so-becoming straw boater with its pink ribbon tied around the crown.

They found a bench under some trees. He guided her to take a seat before sitting down beside her, holding his breath, inching closer so that he could feel her warmth—or was it the sun? He scarcely knew, or cared, his whole attention fixed on the young woman at his side as she blushed and trembled and lowered her gaze and glanced up again.

'Will your mother not permit me to call upon you?' The words leapt out of their own accord, nervousness betraying the hours he had spent mentally rehearsing the scene while bent over the saddle tree.

'She will not.' A shadow passed over her face, her words uncharacteristically sober, as if similarly much dwelt upon. 'I tried and tried but could not change her mind.' Anxiety tugged at the corners of her eyes. 'She is stubborn. She means well, but ...' Her voice trailed off in a despondent sigh.

'But you came, nevertheless!' He leaned in with the question.

'I did!' The assertion was as bold as it was plain and simple. She fiddled with the lace on her collar, her face looking up, flushed, uncertain. He swallowed and kissed her—oh so lightly!—on the lips, drawing back, an anxious look in his eyes. She had hers closed, holding her mouth up, bashful yet ardently so. He kissed her again, longer this time. She did not kiss back, but pressed, oh so slightly!

'Isabelle, dearest!' He gazed into her now open eyes, her lips slightly parted, a breathless look on her face. He kissed her again, tentatively at first, and then more firmly, laying his hand on her own where it rested on her knee. They drew back, panting, gazing at each other like the first lovers that ever sat on that bench or walked in that park or ran, laughing through the trees, when the world was overrun with forest and Indian maidens made sport among the shadows pursued by their eager suitors, faces daubed with colourful dyes and hair shining with grease. '*Coo!*' they called, imitating the woodland birds while fluting love calls through the untrodden green as they shadow-danced from tree to tree—long before New France, before conquest, before time was marked on sundials, and long, long before the last eastern elk vanished from beneath the canopy of red and gold maple.

By the time he guided her back to reunion with her sister, his heart was irretrievably meshed with hers. His hand linked with her tiny yet strong fingers, and hers clasped back. They kissed again, uttering fevered yet soothing promises, youthful charms immune to frowning mothers or watchful, miserly employers.

The conspirators rendezvoused with smiling faces and blushing yet prideful intimacy, which Marguerite took in at a glance before embracing her radiant sister. Whispering in Isabelle's ear, Marguerite turned to Jacob, a dazzling smile on her face. 'Isabelle will meet you again, if you like. Next Sunday, around the same time?' And with that, she escorted her sister away, tugging Isabelle as she looked back, her cheeks flushed, her eyes sparkling, her face shining with the afternoon of love.

He scarcely remembered walking home, or what he had for supper—mumbling in response to questions from his landlady, or mounting the stairs to bed, or undressing and turning back the covers, eager only to fall asleep and dream!

14

Argumentum ad Misericordiam

'Isabelle! Marguerite! Come down here at once!' Madame Ouellet stood in the hallway looking up at the stairs, a wrathful expression on her face.

Isabelle's heart sank as she descended the stairs and took in her mother's angry features. 'Mama, whatever is the matter?'

'In here!' Her mother disappeared into the parlour.

'She knows!' Marguerite hissed to Isabelle as they followed their mother into the parlour.

Madame Ouellet stood before the fireplace with hands clasped, her face stiff with censure. 'What, pray tell, were you doing sitting in the park on Sunday making shameless love to a man I had forbidden you to see?'

'Making love! Mama, we were just talking—perhaps holding hands, that is all.'

'To a man I had expressly forbidden you to consort with!'

'They were just talking, mama. There is nothing to upset yourself about.'

'And you! The one I trusted to chaperone her!' Madame Ouellet glared at Marguerite.

'I did chaperone her. It was harmless conversation, nothing else.'

'Harmless?' Their mother gasped. 'You lied to me—your own mother! Do you have no care for your sister's reputation?'

'Please mama, don't upset yourself. As Marguerite said, it was nothing. There is no need to fuss.'

'Fuss?' It was all too much. With a sobbing wail, Madame Ouellet collapsed into a chair, fumbling for her handkerchief as Isabelle rushed to comfort her.

'Mama!'

'That I should be so deceived!' Their mother gasped for breath.

'I'm truly sorry. Forgive me. It was just that I so badly wished to see him, and …' Isabelle choked, unable to finish.

'Air! I need air!' Madame Ouellet picked up the ivory Chinese fan. 'How could you,' she fanned accusingly, 'go so wantonly behind my back?'

Isabelle sniffled. 'I'm sorry,' she said, thoroughly miserable.

Marguerite gave an exasperated sigh. 'Mama, they are in love. You cannot simply—'

'In love!' Their mother shrieked the words. Feeling faint she sank back into the chair, fanning herself strenuously. 'What will people say? What will the church say?' Her bosom heaved at the thought. She turned a furious stare on Isabelle. 'I absolutely forbid you from ever seeing that … that *foundling!* ever again, do you understand? Answer me!'

'How can you forbid her from seeing somebody? Is she to walk about the streets wearing a blindfold?'

Eyes blazing, Madame Ouellet rounded on her eldest daughter. 'Better be blind than a shameless strumpet! Honour thy father and mother! Does the Bible not command this? Or have you contempt for scripture also?'

'But I love him!'

The desperate cry drew a screech of horror. 'Foolish child! What do you know about love? You are barely old enough to catch a bus by yourself! If your father were here to witness … Thank God, he was spared this at least.' Furiously, she fanned the sentiment.

'There is no need to carry on so, Mama,' protested Marguerite. 'You will make yourself ill.'

'Ill? It will be the death of me! Such scandal! To flirt so shamelessly with a complete stranger. In the park! On the Saint's Day!' Overcome by the ghastliness of it all, their mother gave a distraught moan.

'It was innocent, I promise you!' Isabelle sank to her knees by her mother's chair. 'I don't know what you may have heard, but—'

'What I have heard chills my blood! To think you were such a dutiful daughter—until corrupted by that fiend.'

'Corrupted?' Isabelle burst into astonished tears.

'You have no right to forbid her from seeing him.'

'I have every right! I am her mother. And as such, I strictly forbid any more contact with the English heretic!' She stood up, her face strained. 'Out of my sight! Both of you. You are forbidden to come downstairs again until supper. Go!'

'JACOB, WHAT HAVE YOU done?' Hugo rose from his chair as Jacob entered the tavern.

'Me?' Taken aback by the abrupt greeting, Jacob stopped short. 'Nothing I can think of to cause concern. Why?'

'Then you didn't publicly consort with my cousin on Saint-Jean-Baptiste Day in spite of her mother's wishes?'

'Consort? We sat and talked. Her sister was nearby. Nothing untoward took place, I assure you.'

'No?' Hugo raised an accusing eyebrow. 'Then you didn't meet her in the park? Nor sit with her on a bench while making amorous … overtures?'

'Good God man! We barely touched lips. Is that so wrong?' Heads turned in the busy tavern.

'May I remind you that this is not New York!'

'But all we did was sit and talk. The kiss was innocent. A spur of the moment thing. Surely, that cannot be held against me?'

'Oh, but it can—*can* and will be. Her mother is quite beside herself. I spent the whole evening yesterday trying to calm her down. I'm exhausted!' Hugo let out an exasperated sigh. 'There is no easy way to say this, Jacob, but the fact is her mother has forbidden Isabelle from ever seeing you again.'

'But that is absurd! I meant no offence—either to Isabelle or to her mother. Madame Ouellet has no cause for alarm, I assure you.'

'I grant that you meant no offence,' conceded Hugo, 'but you must remember my cousin has only just turned eighteen.' He paused, to let the fact sink in. 'Isabelle is naïve, an idealist, and that is how she sees the world.' He turned a searching look on Jacob. 'No matter the reality of a person or circumstance, Isabelle perceives it—transforms it you might say—like light through coloured glass. She is innocent of worldly matters. She sees only the ideal. That is why her mother and sister are so protective of her. They understand how vulnerable she is to heartache and all the slings of the world. She is instinctively given to following her heart rather than her head, no matter the risk to herself. Do you understand me, Jacob?'

'I do, I swear to you! I would not see her harmed for all the world.'

Hugo considered for a moment. 'Then you will understand that, as her closest male relation, it is my duty to protect her. And as her cousin I must ensure that she is properly chaperoned at all times.'

'But she was! Her sister was there with us the whole time. Really, Hugo, you have no need to work yourself up over this.'

Hugo gave a vexed groan. 'My God, you still don't understand. This is a conservative society. The church, quite rightly, commands great influence. People know each other. They gossip. Persons, young girls in particular, must be protected from scandal. Her mother is mortally afraid for Isabelle's reputation.'

'I really am sorry.' Jacob's face was crestfallen.

Hugo vented a loud sigh, visibly deflating. 'Hopefully, it will blow over.' His voice, however, gave faint hope that he believed that such would be the case.

THE JOY JACOB HAD felt but a few scant days before—the first moments of real happiness he had experienced since his arrival in New France—vanished like dew on a summer's morning as he struggled to come to terms with Madame Ouellet's ban on any communication with her daughter. How can she be so heartless! Does she have no care for her daughter's happiness? He roamed aimlessly through the streets of the Old Town as he grappled with the despairing thoughts that careered through his mind.

On several of these distraught perambulations his footsteps led him to the dress shop on rue Bishop Lavoie in desperate hope of seeing the beloved—for so he now thought of her. And once he did, catching a glimpse as she exited the shop with her mother and sister. He hung back behind a fruit seller's stall as she passed by on the opposite side of the street, linked arm-in-arm with her sister. Her face was pale beneath a dark-blue headscarf. It was all he could do to prevent himself calling out her name and rushing to her side. He watched until they disappeared, and then set off for his lodgings, his heart sorely laden, his tongue bemoaning his fate. How sad she had looked! How forlorn!

August arrived, the hot humid days an oppressive counterpart to the winter chill. The air inside the workshop was stifling in spite of the open doors. Trade was now entirely reliant on the business brought in by Ferguson, the American's carriage business flourishing in New York State.

'I've introduced a new line of eight-seater carriages,' he revealed to Jacob. 'My partner is sending up the paperwork. We'll need a whole new set of leathers. I'll bring over the designs in a few days.'

It was the first intimation Jacob had been given of a business partner. He kept the morsel to himself, although unsure why, when explaining the new line to Monsieur Lascelles.

The proprietor nodded, an avaricious gleam in his eyes as he took in the details. 'Assure the American we can meet all of his requirements,' he said. 'And make sure you keep everyone on their toes. Best workmanship only, understand?' Getting to his feet he trailed Jacob to the door, his eyes following as the latter walked over to the water barrel. With a motion of his head, he summoned the watchful foreman to his side. 'Any problems?' he asked, eyes still on Jacob.

'None, sir.'

'He seems preoccupied—look at the long face on him! Does he properly instruct the cutters?'

'He does. Although …'

Lascelles glanced sideways, his suspicions instantly aroused.

'Although what?'

'Sometimes he is too easy on them.'

'But they follow his instructions?'

The foreman shrugged. 'Well enough. He has airs about him, if you ask me.'

Lascelles thought for a moment, itching the stubble on his chin. 'Does he ever speak about the American or their connection?'

'No, not that I have heard.'

'Keep an eye on him. Let me know if anything changes.'

'Most assuredly, sir.'

HE WAS WALKING HOME when he heard his name called. 'Jacob?' Isabelle stepped out from an alley beside a warehouse.

'Isabelle!'

With a sob, she rushed into his arms. 'I've missed you so much!' Her body trembled as she clung fiercely to him. A woman passing on the other side of the street turned to look.

'My darling!' He kissed her brow, her hair, her cheeks, her eyes, tasting her tears on his tongue.

'I am so happy to see you!' Sniffling, she smiled, her trusting innocence in that moment a wrench to his heart.

'Does your mother know you are here?'

'No! I told her I was going to confession. But we must hurry. She will expect me back soon.'

'Then let me walk you home. We can talk on the way.'

And talk they did, exchanging love vows and heartfelt declarations, the embargo placed by her mother only serving to release pent-up passions as they smiled and swapped tender looks and stole quick kisses. All too soon, they turned into rue Mercier.

'I must go!' She kissed him on the lips, her eyes shining.

'When can I see you again?' He held onto her hand, reluctant to release it.

'Soon! I will come to you. Goodbye, dear heart!' And with that she was gone, hurrying up the street with one final, backwards glance.

They met several more times as summer gave way to fall, strolling hand-in-hand in the park, sipping coffee in an out-of-the way restaurant, or simply sitting on a bench to watch the world go by. Happily united amidst the falling leaves, they spoke longingly of a future together that already seemed passed, the nostalgic yearning in their voices hearkening to a time when they could be together freely, their love unencumbered by parental fiat. He spoke optimistically of advancement at work or perhaps some new occupation altogether, which would provide the wherewithal for them to marry.

She spoke glowingly of a home, children, married bliss, and future happiness as proud habitants. The eldest boy will be called Gaston Pierre, she dreamed, leaning her head on Jacob's shoulder in the cloud-speckled day. Neither one mentioned faith, nor language, nor her mother's opposition, the breeze being placid and the bursts of autumn sunlight warm on their blissful cheeks.

One Saturday afternoon as he returned from work, Madame Pepin accosted him in the hallway. 'You have a visitor,' she said as he was about to close the door behind him. 'A young lady—madame Ouellet's daughter.' Her eyebrows peaked in disapproval. 'You may use the parlour,' she said, her voice leaving no doubt as to the impropriety of a young woman visiting a gentleman, unchaperoned, in his quarters.

Murmuring thanks, he hurried into the parlour. Isabelle sat there, a handkerchief twisted in her hands.

'I am sorry. I had to see you!' She jumped to her feet, her face pale.

'What is it?' His concern at her expression dashed his delight at seeing her again.

'It is mama. She has discovered our meetings. Someone saw us in the gardens together.' Her lip trembled. 'She was so angry! I am forbidden to ...' Her voice trailed off, her eyes—so sparkling at their last rendezvous, now full of despair. She pulled away from him in spite of his attempts to embrace her. 'I must go. She will be waiting.' Distraught, she allowed him to kiss and embrace her before disentangling herself. 'Goodbye, dearest!'

Overcome with emotion, he followed her to the street. 'When will I see you again?'

'I don't know—she watches me like a hawk! It was all I could do to steal away.' She kissed him on the lips. 'I'll send a message—with Marguerite. Goodbye!'

He watched her hurry up the street towards Pascal Langlois, raising her long skirt and running to catch the omnibus as it clanked along the rails.

'Goodbye,' he said, half to himself, watching until she boarded the electric tram. And then he turned, to be confronted by the steely glare of his landlady.

15

Père Boudreau

'I AM AT MY WIT'S end! She is wilful and disobedient ever since she met the wretched Englishman.' Madame Ouellet's voice shook with dismay, her sisters listening sympathetically as she poured out her woes. They were gathered in Delphine's parlour sipping coffee as they conferred on the matter.

'She is obsessed with the creature! She stole away to meet him in secret—despite my explicit instructions to avoid him.'

'That is not like Isabelle,' conceded Désirée.

'It is him! He has—' the distraught Madame Ouellet was about to say 'ruined' but checked herself. 'He has caused her to rebel against me, her mother! Her mind is on him every minute of the day. What am I to do with her?' She drained the coffee and held out the cup for more.

'Are they still seeing each other?'

'Good heavens, no.'

Désirée exchanged glances with Delphine.

'What?' Their sister bristled at the silent entente. 'She is hardly ever out of my sight.'

'Do they perhaps write—exchange notes?'

'Of course not! Do you think me blind?'

'Have you tried introducing her to other young men—to take her mind from him?'

'Yes!' Désirée chorused. 'What about Henri Chauvin? You said he was keen.'

'I've tried, God knows.' Overcome with emotion, Madame Ouellet wept into a handkerchief as her sisters made soothing noises. 'What on earth does she see in the oaf? He can't even remember his own name!' She shuddered and wept again.

'Hugo speaks well of him,' offered Delphine, glancing to Désirée for assistance.

'And he's working—at that—what is it? Oh yes, a leather monger's shop in the square.'

'Which one?' asked Delphine.

'That Gustave Lascelles. You know, the one with the suspicious eyes.'

'I hear his wife is a fright, always surly when you meet her in the street.'

'That is because of her dreadful upbringing.'

'What do you mean? I had not heard—'

'Sisters!'

'Pardon.' Désirée placed a comforting hand on Odile's knee. 'Do not distress yourself, darling. Isabelle is still hardly more than a girl. By spring she will have forgotten all about him.' She turned to Delphine. 'Is that not so?'

'Of course. Is that not the nature of young girls? Do you remember when we were her age?'

Désirée chuckled. 'I remember pining over Jacques Langlois. I carried his likeness to bed with me each night.'

'And I was madly in love with Justin Fortier. I remember kissing him behind the church after service.'

'And you, Odile!' They turned eyes on their sister. 'I distinctly remember seeing you snuggle up to Joseph Laurent at the Saint's Day picnic,' recalled Delphine, 'in spite of papa's disapproval.'

'You kissed him!' reminded Désirée.

Odile sniffed. 'It was on the cheek only. A peck.'

'Liar! It was on the mouth!'

'Blessed Mother!' Madame Ouellet looked crossly at her sisters. 'Never mind about Joseph Laurent! What am I to do about Isabelle?'

'Have you considered talking to Father Simard?'

'The curé? He couldn't find his arse without the bishop holding it.'

The vulgar remark brought a shriek of laughter from Delphine, Désirée joining in while Odile sat stone-faced.

'Father Boudreau, then,' said Delphine, recovering herself. 'I went to see him that time when my Hélène was being so rebellious. Do you remember?'

'We're not even in his parish.' Odile twisted the handkerchief between her hands.

'Pudding!' Delphine waved away the objection and looked to Désirée for support. 'What do you think?'

'Why not? said Désirée turning to face Odile. 'Your Isabelle is nothing if not Catholic. Who knows, she may listen to the Church if all else fails?'

'I have no faith in Father Boudreau. His ears are too pointed for one thing. The man is little short of a charlatan in my opinion.'

'Odile!'

'It's true. I once heard he questioned the Holy Trinity. He flat out declared such a thing an impossibility.'

'Who told you that?'

'Camille Desrochers. She had it from her cousin, Agatha.'

'That gasbag!'

The exclamation brought a snigger from Delphine. 'Still,' she said, pouring more coffee, 'what have you got to lose?'

'It's true,' Désirée chimed in. 'Isabelle has always been respectful of the Church.'

Madame Ouellet pondered the suggestion as she took the tram home. They may be onto something, she conceded, her daughter's Catholic piety a frequent occasion for pride. Accordingly, and in spite of her reservations over the character of the cleric, she made a visit to the rectory at Sainte-Chappelle the following Saturday.

'Madame Ouellet, what a surprise!' Father Boudreau rose to greet her as she was ushered into the rectory. 'What brings you here?'

She frowned, the question being somewhat odd in her opinion. 'I came to seek your advice, Father,' she said, her voice stiffly formal.

'Please, sit.' He did so himself, grimacing as he sat. His sore back had been playing up all morning and all he longed for was to lie down in a darkened room, preferably after a snifter of brandy. And now this disagreeable woman was detaining him from said pleasure. Nevertheless, he put on an attentive face as she enumerated her complaints over her daughter's infatuation with the 'wretched stranger.'

'Which stranger?' he interrupted. 'The town is full of them these days.'

'That Wheeler fellow!' She could not bring herself to mention his first name.

'Wheeler?'

'That miserable creature found skulking in the woods!'

'Ah! The Englishman.' His brow furrowed as Madam Ouellet launched back into her complaint. *The fellow had been nothing but trouble ever since he turned up in the town. Sent by the Devil, one could suppose! First there was that pious bore Hugo Gagnon, and now this termagant.*

'Well, Father?' she concluded, her face clouded with worry. 'What should I do? She is intoxicated with the fellow!'

Father Boudreau sighed and stroked his chin. *She was related, was she not, to the arch-unbeliever Tremblay, himself?* 'Have you thought of sending her away—to a relative, perhaps? A period away from home may help her to see things differently?'

His visitor looked faintly scandalised. 'Send her away? I imagined you were going to suggest something more … Catholic.'

'Such as?' He raised an eyebrow.

'Confession—perhaps penance, or at the very least, prayer.'

'Prayer?' Intrigued, he stared at the floor.

'YOU HAVE DECEIVED ME!' Hugo's face was pale with anger.

'In what way?

'Don't play me for a fool! You know in what way.' Hugo stood, arms crossed, before the window of Jacob's room, having refused the latter's invitation to sit.

'Oh! That. We met a few times. What of it?' Jacob's voice was breezily defiant.

'What of it?' Hugo stared as though he could hardly believe his ears. 'Did I not explain the situation to you in a way that was perfectly clear?'

'You did. But I saw no reason to agree to such … tyranny! Her mother is impossible. We had no recourse except to meet—'

'Behind her back, and mine!' Hugo glared with the words.

'—anyway, we could. I am tired of this quarrelling. Can we not simply agree to disagree on this?'

'You think it that simple?' Hugo stared in amazement, as though reasoning with a child.

'What do you mean?'

'I mean …' Hugo searched for words, 'I mean it's not that simple! This can't be fixed by an apology or admission of wrongdoing.'

'Wrongdoing?' Jacob stared rebelliously. 'Look here, Hugo, I'm willing to accept fault in this, but her mother—'

'Her mother has sent her away.' The words echoed like a pistol shot in the confines of the room.

Shocked, Jacob searched his companion's face. 'Sent her where?'

'She is with a relative. Where, I cannot say.' Hugo threw himself into a chair, his limbs sprawled in exasperation.

'She cannot do that!'

'Cannot?' Hugo's voice was strained. 'She can and has. Isabelle has left the city.'

'Left?' Jacob stared, horrified. 'To go where?'

'Does it matter?' Hugo's voice was bleak.

'Yes!'

'Ah! So that you may follow?' Hugo shot a critical glance at Jacob. 'So, my aunt was right—in this, at least. Just how deeply involved are you two?'

'Does it matter?' Still reeling with the news, he threw his companion's words back at him.

'I cannot say where.' Hugo blew out his lips. 'Her mother has forbidden me to tell you—made me me swear on the Bible.'

'The woman is a monster!' Jacob jumped to his feet to pace up and down the room, his face agitated.

'You must try and see it from her point of view—understand why she is so upset. She is a respectable woman, and in the matter of courtship there are norms and decencies she expects to be observed.'

'Are you suggesting we acted indecently?' Jacob glared with the question.

'Her mother most certainly thinks so. She is acting as she feels is proper, in defence of her daughter's honour.'

Jacob bristled. 'And you think I would endanger that?'

'No, I don't.' Hugo's voice softened. 'But then I am not the widowed mother of a young woman with a reputation to protect.'

'What if I go to her mother and apologise—explain that we behaved properly at all times, no matter what she may have heard?'

'She would not see you.' Hugo's voice was blunt. 'I said it before, give it time, observe our customs. Go about it slowly and with proper ... etiquette, and my aunt may soften. She loves her daughter and wants only for her to be happy. In the meantime, she has made Isabelle promise not to get in touch with you. And, as your friend, I would expect no less from yourself.'

'When will she be allowed to return?' asked Jacob, a sick feeling in his throat.

'In due course. Her mother may relax her opposition, who knows?— especially if you respect her wishes and refrain from contacting Isabelle. But until then I advise patience and, above all, restraint.'

'Do I have a choice?'

'No, you don't. And there it is, I'm afraid.'

Jacob walked to the window. Outside, the autumn sky was blue. He heard birds singing, and the voices of children playing in the street.

'Jacob, do we have an understanding? Will you give me your word not to contact Isabelle?'

Jacob nodded, too distraught to speak.

'ARE YOU HAPPY NOW Mama?' Marguerite's voice was upset, her look accusing. They were sitting in the parlour of Madame Ouellet's house, having just returned from the train station where a tearful and protesting Isabelle had been despatched to the care of her Aunt Jeanne in Montreal.

'Marguerite, dear, your mother had no choice.' Delphine placed a consoling hand on her niece's arm.

'It's all for the best,' agreed Désirée. 'In a few weeks she will forget all about this mad obsession.'

'Obsession?' Marguerite looked as if she was about to burst. 'Isabelle is not the one who has the obsession!' With a fierce glare at her mother, she stalked from the room.

'Let her go,' said Madame Ouellet as Désirée made to follow her niece. 'She will be angry with me for a time, and then let go of it. I know her. Trust me.'

'Jeanne will meet Isabelle at the station, don't worry about a thing.' Delphine picked up the Chinese fan to admire the workmanship. 'Désirée, be a dear and pop the kettle on.'

'I had no choice.' Madame Ouellet's voice was trembling but defiant. 'She needs to be protected from her own foolish heart.'

'Of course you didn't.' Delphine stroked her sister's hand.

'As you say, in a few weeks she will have forgotten all about him. Jeanne will take care of that.'

They went into the kitchen and sat at the table as Désirée poured boiling water into the teapot. 'Isabelle will have that many suitors in Montreal her head will spin,' continued Delphine.

'See?' agreed Désirée arranging the cups and saucers. 'Next thing you hear she will be engaged to some banker's son and happy as a lark.'

They sipped the tea, halting only when Marguerite passed by and went out the front door without a word, shutting it loudly behind her. Delphine looked at Désirée and both shook their heads. Their sister sat frozen faced at the rudeness, her hand gripping and twisting her handkerchief.

When her sisters had left—after lavishing her with kisses and trilling over the potted rose mallow on the hall stand—Madame Ouellet sat at the kitchen table where she wept intermittently for the remainder of the morning. The strain of the past few months was etched upon her face as she lamented her own foolishness. 'I was impulsive,' she sniffled. She glanced across the table at where her husband sat in his accustomed chair, a censorious expression upon his face. 'There is no need to say so!' she accused, suddenly spiteful. 'I have done my best in your absence.'

Going upstairs to change, she sat at the dressing table in the bedroom, studying her face in the mirror. She put a hand to her hair, grimacing at the greyness and the lines on her face. An inexpressible sadness enveloped her as she stared at her image. To have lost a husband *and* a daughter! Tears trickled down the face in the mirror. It was for your own good, she told the face, although betrayed by the anguish in the reflected eyes. Perhaps the

Englishman isn't such a bad catch, she conceded. He has employment, at least. But immediately the negatives swarmed in to counterbalance the single positive. He has no family, no history—he could be a murderer for all anyone knows. He is not French, not Catholic, not anything! The last qualifier caused her lips to stiffen, her formidable self staring back once more. Wilful child!

SENSING A COOLNESS BETWEEN himself and Jacob ever since Isabelle's departure, Hugo bemoaned the fact to his wife. 'I know he pins the fault on me—even though I am entirely blameless in the matter.' He kicked off his shoes in frustration. 'Why could he not have fallen in love with someone else—anybody but my cousin?'

'Perhaps it was meant to be.' Josette brought the soup tureen to the table.

'Meant to be? What in Heaven is that supposed to mean?'

'As in ordained.' She sat down and took up the ladle, her whole attention focussed on the soup.

He gave an irritable glance as she began spooning the lentil and tomato soup into a bowl. 'There's nothing ordained about it. It's chance, pure and simple.'

She made a humming sound as she passed him the bowl. 'Come now, dear. Was it by chance you found him in the woods? Was it by chance that you … you know …'

'Know what?'

'Need I say?'

He sat largely silent through the soup, the preposterous notion that there was something pre-ordained about Jacob's infatuation with his cousin nevertheless appealing to that same Catholic notion of a guiding Providence that had mesmerised him from his first encounter with Jacob.

'Do you think so?' he asked as his wife collected the empty bowl.

'It is possible,' she answered, the expression on her face showing she was fully cognisant of what he had been thinking. 'Why not ask Father Boudreau?' She sprinkled some chopped basil over the steamed fish that was the next course. 'After all, who better to ask about love than a priest?'

HUGO INVITED JACOB TO meet him in the tavern the père following Saturday afternoon. 'Serge and Denis will be there, along with Martin and Claude,' he said, encouraging Jacob to attend. 'It will cheer you up, and they are eager to see you again.'

To his relief, Jacob turned up, doing his best to put a brave face on his misery. He received the warm commiserations of his companions—all of whom had heard the tale through Hugo—while tossing back glass after glass of wine and brandy until a concerned Hugo steered him from the premises.

'For God's sake,' he said, observing Jacob's wretched state. 'Don't let Madame Pepin see you like this. She will throw you out onto the street.'

He brought Jacob to his own home instead. 'Sleep there,' he said, depositing him on the parlour couch. 'And don't move until morning!'

'He is heartsick,' he apologised to Josette on going upstairs. 'What could I do? I couldn't let Madame Pepin see him like that.' He sat on a chair to pull off his socks.

'Would it not be easier to tell him where Isabelle is and have done with it?' she asked, smoothing the bedcover over her legs.

He stared in shock, a sock suspended in his hand. 'I swore an oath—on the Bible!'

'But I didn't.' She arched an eyebrow with the suggestion.

Horrified, he paused from pulling off the other sock. 'No! I forbid it.'

Josette pouted, a frown creasing her brow. 'Really, Hugo. You are being overly severe. She is your cousin, not your daughter. Surely, she is old enough to be able to decide for herself whom she loves?'

Hugo stared in amazement. 'Have you forgotten your own father—how protective he and your mother were of both you and your sister?'

'And have you forgotten how determined I was?'

He sighed. 'No. I have not. But at least you had—have—a father to guard you. Isabelle has only her mother.'

'And you!' Josette clicked her tongue in frustration. 'It is hard for a woman. Harder than men realise. We have the Church on one side, and our families on the other. I feel sorry for Isabelle. A woman ought to be allowed to decide for herself, as much as a man.'

'But you do. You make the final choice, do you not?' he asked, crawling into bed.

'I wonder,' she said, wincing at the touch of his cold feet. 'I wonder if we truly do, or if we choose only to please others?'

'What are you saying?' He propped himself up on an elbow. 'Did you not choose me of your own volition?'

His face was so stricken at the possibility that she could not help but smile. 'Darling Hugo!' She stroked his cheek. 'Of course I did. And I had to fight the Jesuits into the bargain! Do you not remember? But for me, it would be Father Hugo sharing my bed!' She laughed at his shocked expression.

'I am very glad you chose me!' He kissed her cheek.

'But not all women have the power to choose,' she said, unwilling to let go of the thought. 'That is all I am saying. Look at Isabelle. Between you and her mother, the poor girl has nowhere to turn.'

'You make me sound like a tyrant! I have only her best interests at heart.'

'But how do you know what is best for her? Do you know better than herself?'

He groaned. 'I'm tired, cannot this wait until morning?'

'It is horribly unfair, that's all I am saying.' She half-raised her head, too piqued to let go of the point. 'Don't you agree? Hugo!' She poked him.

'I must sleep!' he protested, his voice muffled by the pillow.

She sighed and sank her head back on the pillow. 'A woman deserves ...' She closed her eyes with the thought unfinished.

JACOB RETURNED TO MADAME Pepin's early the next morning in time for breakfast, proffering the explanation that Hugo had invited him to supper and insisted he spend the night.

'I see.' Madam Pepin's searching gaze spared nothing of his wretched state. 'Your shirt is stained,' she said, turning away, 'place it in the laundry basket.'

He uttered a mumbled 'thank you', eating only an egg for breakfast before stumbling up to his room where he flung himself on the bed. In the distance, church bells tolled to summon the faithful and those of clear conscience to worship. 'What to do?' he groaned and buried his head in despair.

16

A Scandal of the Petite Bourgeoisie

JACOB WAS WALKING ALONG rue St. Madeleine in the Upper Town, taking advantage of the lingering days of an Indian summer, when he was startled to hear his name called. 'Monsieur Wheeler?'

He turned to find Marguerite walking behind him, the first time he had laid eyes on her since her sister's exile the previous month. She wore a fashionable hat decorated with ribbons and feathers and carried the same yellow parasol he had seen before. She was accompanied by a young man dressed in a morning jacket, striped trousers, and a boater hat.

'Marguerite!'

'Monsieur Wheeler, this is my fiancé, Dominic Beaulieu.'

The man glanced at Marguerite as if surprised by the introduction. After a moment's hesitation, he extended his hand towards Jacob. 'Good morning,' he said, his voice cool.

Marguerite cast an appealing glance at her fiancé. 'Dominic, a moment, please, if you would be so good?'

The young man looked discomforted at the request, but agreed, wandering off a short distance, his hands thrust in his jacket pockets, a slight frown on his face.

'How are you Monsieur Wheeler?' The formal address added to Jacob's apprehension that Marguerite held him to blame for the breach between her mother and sister. Her expression, normally so cheerfully flirtatious, was grave beneath the parasol. She looked into his eyes with a frank, unabashed gaze, so different from—and yet so reminiscent of!—her younger sister.

'I am well, thank you,' he answered. He was conscious of the strolling pedestrians, the shrill blast of a police whistle in the distance, and the stares of the fiancé as he fidgeted a few yards away.

He was wondering whether to enquire after her sister, when Marguerite forestalled him. 'I had a letter from Isabelle,' she said, surprising him with her directness. She studied him as if to gauge the effect of her words.

'Did she ask about me?' Realising the faux-pas, he quickly apologised. 'Pardon. I meant to ask if she is well?' And yet his eyes held hers, unwilling to drop the question.

'She is well, although most unhappy at being sent away.' Marguerite turned the handle of the parasol, her eyes weighing as she regarded him. 'She misses you greatly and wonders if you miss her in the same way?'

'Miss her?' He echoed the question, a horrified look on his face. 'I am desperate without her!'

She glanced at her fiancé before returning her gaze to him. 'Isabelle is, as you must realise, naïve in the ways of the heart.'

Uncertain whether the remark was a rhetorical *non sequitur* or a question that awaited a reply, he was about to offer a response when she continued, her voice ruminative so that he strained to hear above the noise of the busy street. 'Do you know what I consider to be the greatest of crimes, Monsieur Wheeler?'

'Pardon?' He squinted in the sunshine, confounded by the question.

'The ruination of innocence.' Marguerite's expression was grave as she once again subjected him to a searching look. He was struggling to come up with a reply when she continued. 'My sister is vulnerable to her intense feelings. So far, her life has consisted of home and church, with not much in-between. In many ways she is an innocent, especially when it comes to affairs of the heart.' She broke off as two families strolled by the members engaged in loud, cheerful conversation. The waiting fiancé glowered and folded his arms across his chest, clearly put out at the *tête-à-tête*. Her eyes lingered on him for a moment before she spoke again.

'Once my sister gives her heart, it is given, in spite of all obstacles, as you are so plainly aware. With Isabelle, there is no withholding, no taking back, no matter the provocation. That is why mama is so fiercely protective. Do you understand me, Jacob?' Her eyes peered into his.

'I do! And I swear to you that my feelings are as strong and sincere as her own!' He licked his dry lips, his throat constricted with anxiety as her eyes dwelt on his answer.

'I suspected as much.' For the first time since their encounter, she relaxed her formal posture. She glanced at her impatient fiancé, a sigh escaping her lips. 'Then do not despair. All may be well, in spite of everything.'

Reaching into the small, beaded purse that dangled from her wrist she withdrew a square of folded paper. 'From Isabelle.' She thrust the paper into his hand. 'If you wish to write back, give the letter to Josette. She will pass it on to me.' She waited a moment before speaking again, her voice bright. 'A pleasant afternoon to you, Monsieur Wheeler!' And with that, and with a look of silent encouragement, she re-joined her scowling fiancé.

Taken aback by the encounter, Jacob gazed at where Marguerite and her fiancé had already disappeared into the crowd of strollers. He stared at the letter in his hand, his breath catching in his throat. Sitting down on a nearby bench, he eagerly opened the twice-folded page. While couples and families promenaded by in the autumn sunshine, he smoothed the paper—briefly holding it to his nose to savour the scent of perfume—before devouring the words, written in Isabelle's trusting, breathless voice.

My dearest Jacob!

I am terribly sorry that mama caused such a frightful fuss! I am exiled here, to Montreal, to mama's cousin, where I languish in unspeakable misery! I think only of you—of us—and weep throughout the day and dream of you at night. My aunt is not unsympathetic. She consoles me and reassures me as best she can but is hesitant as to the question of my return. (She knows mama well!!) I cherish the memory of those brief hours we spent in the park—the happiest of my life! Write to me, Jacob. Marguerite will arrange it. Jules—you remember my cousin from New York?—has gotten wind of this 'scandal of the dressmaking class' as he jokingly calls it and writes to cheer me up with funny little stories and tales of New York. He is on our side and bids me pass on his 'Yankee good wishes.' I beg you, please write and tell me your heart. Your loving Isabelle!

He stared at the letter, tears in his eyes. A man sat down beside him, taking off his hat to fan himself. 'The heat will slaughter us! What say you, friend?' He was a portly middle-aged gentleman, his brow glistening with sweat. 'I was walking up Joseph Dumont—you know the street? —when I was accosted by some fellow demanding a hand-out. He refused to let me pass. Can you believe? Scandalous!' He stared at Jacob, his face alive with the incident. 'The fellow was dangerous, I have no doubt! I threatened him with the police and the scoundrel laughed in my face. What do you say to that?'

'Pardon.' Jacob got up from the bench, his heart bursting in his chest. He walked away, his seatmate staring after him with astonished indignation.

All the way home he repeated the sentiments of the letter, while scarcely aware of the passing crowd. Back in his room he read the letter again, this time with the aid of the dictionary to ascertain subtleties of meaning that might have escaped him. He looked up 'languish' and 'unspeakable', repeating the definitions until they were part of him. And then, unable to contain his joy, he sat down at the table and penned a reply.

My dearest, darling Isabelle! I rejoice at receiving your precious words! I have the letter before me as I write. He stopped to check both the dictionary and his grammar, muttering with impatience as he looked up the tenses. *Forgive my poor words as I am more used*—another frustrating pause followed as he searched the dictionary—*to speak rather than to write. Nobody will tell me where you are! I worry lest you feel abandoned.*

Then, foregoing correct usage altogether, he declared his bursting affections in a frantic jumble of misspelled words and grammatical tense infractions that cannoned off the page margins as he employed both English and French to pledge eternal devotion, signing off with '*Your loving and heartfelt admirer, Jacob.*'

Folding the letter, he stared at it for a few moments, his heart beating madly, his imagination picturing them joined hand-in-hand, love-flushed and gazing into each other's eyes, their lips touching in a kiss. What torture to be without her! He groaned and put his head in his hands. He stayed that way until suddenly recalling Marguerite's instruction to pass the letter to Josette. *Then, surely, Hugo cannot be party to it.* A picture of his friend's certain displeasure should he discover the deceit provoked a pang of conscience. The hall clock struck downstairs as his eyes lingered on Isabelle's missive. But it cannot be helped—his lips tightened with the acknowledgement. After all, what he doesn't know cannot hurt him.

'ISABELLE? THE COFFEE IS made.'

'Coming, Aunt.'

Inspecting herself in the mirror, she tucked a strand of hair behind her ear. Unable to resist, she picked up Jacob's *billet-doux*, for what seemed the hundredth time that morning, her eyes again devouring the words. She tucked it into her chemise, the paper crinkling against her heart as she descended the stairs to the parlour where her aunt waited with the coffee and cake.

'You have a blush on your cheek,' her aunt said, pouring coffee into a dainty cup.

'Do I?' She shot a hand to her cheek.

'No!' Her aunt laughed. 'It is just that you seem more cheerful since receiving the letter from your sister.'

'She always cheers me up somehow,' she said, sipping the coffee to avoid her aunt's gaze.

'And your mother? She is well?'

'She is.' She set down the cup. 'She sends her affectionate greetings.'

Her aunt cut a slice of almond cake for each of them, handing Isabelle her portion on a china plate decorated with wavy blue lines. 'And has her mood improved somewhat?' She peered over the coffee cup with the question.

'It has. But not, I am afraid, where Jacob is concerned. Her mind is still set firmly against him.'

Her aunt made a humming sound as she sipped the coffee. 'Give her time, sweetness.'

'Time! It has been eight weeks!' She almost put a hand to the letter within her dress.

'Is your time here so very unpleasant?' Her aunt cocked her head.

'No, I am so sorry. I did not mean to disparage … that is, I am grateful …'

Her aunt gave a merry peal of laughter. 'Goodness, I am teasing you!' She put a hand to her lips as a crumb of cake lodged there.

'Oh!' Isabelle attempted a smile, her thoughts returning to the letter. How despairing he sounded!

'And you still harbour … fond thoughts for this Jacob?'

'I do,' said Isabelle, her voice at once miserable and defiant.

'Ah!' The aunt nodded to herself with the information. 'But you must acknowledge that your mother knows best in this unfortunate situation,' she said, her voice sympathetic but firm. 'She sent you to me because she is concerned for your welfare, not to mention your reputation.' The sentence ended as a question, accompanied by a raised eyebrow.

'She is suspicious, and without reason!' The petulant words burst out before Isabelle could think. 'My mother imagines we are still in the last century where the permission of the Church is needed for each and every occasion—how to dress, how to think, who to love! It is just that, for once, I would like to make up my own mind, without being told what to do,' she finished, embarrassed at the outburst.

'Indeed?' Her aunt considered this, lifting her silver fork to spear another crumb of cake. 'Modern love,' she said, and smiled, liking the phrase so much she repeated it, 'modern love.'

In spite of her aunt's efforts to introduce her to eligible young men—acting at the behest of her mama, Isabelle had no doubt—she resisted all such entertainments or, if she did attend out of a sense of obligation to her well-meaning aunt, smiled politely and rebuffed any and all attempts at intimacy.

'You must be more accommodating, dearest,' her aunt whispered at one soiree where the eligible son of a respected surgeon attempted to engage her interest. 'Monsieur Riboulet is quite taken with you,' she added, smiling at the smitten young man where he stood next to the buffet, a hopeful look on his face.

'Thank you, aunt but I am feeling a little under the weather. Have we not stayed long enough?'

In further attempts to divert her niece, her aunt took her on tours of the city, hoping the bustling energy of the metropolis would spark feelings of excitement or, at least, enthusiasm. But to her disappointment, no such conversion to the humming rhythms of the city streets took place.

Her only interest was in the basilica, which she compared, unfavourably, to your own cathedral. She also seemed taken by several monuments around the city, in particular, the recent monument to de Maisonneuve, which, she said, reminded her of the statue of Gaston Tremblay, 'only not so fine'. Honestly, Odile, do you not think the poor child has suffered enough? She misses you terribly, in spite of the disagreement between the two of you. I really do not think much more can be gained by keeping her here—in spite of her delightful personality. She attends Mass three times a week at Our Lady's—you will recall it from your last visit here. She invariably stays after the service to pray and light a candle. She is a fine young woman who impresses all that meet her with her modest and becoming conduct. Robert is much taken with her and regrets, I suspect, that we do not have a child of our own. She spends much time in her room and resists all my efforts to introduce her into society. It is clear that she pines for this Jacob who so concerns you. Her heart seems set upon him. I know you, Odile, and your character. Your mind is quite inflexible, once made up. But are you so certain of your dislike? Might this Jacob not be Joseph to her Mary? (Is that blasphemy? If so, may God forgive!) You ask if she might not be in secret communication with him? If so, I have seen no evidence of it.

FALL USHERED ITSELF IN with a flurry of snow, the streets a brief white oasis before the grime and smoke of the city turned them slushy and grey. Isabelle helped in her uncle's tobacco shop during the day and, insofar as politeness allowed, mostly kept to her room at night. Her aunt was a fine cook and she enjoyed helping her bake cakes and prepare fish while hearing about her mama's younger days. 'And that's how she met papa?' She laughed on hearing the tale. The laughter turned to pensiveness later, as she undressed for bed. Why must my own courtship be so fraught by comparison?

She knelt to say her prayers, including, as always, a special plea to St Valentine for herself and Jacob. 'And pray, let him find also the true faith,' she added in a whisper.

Before climbing into bed, she tucked the latest missive from Jacob underneath her pillow, reminding herself to remove it in the morning. As much as her aunt was kind and accommodating, she had no doubt that she was under strict orders from her mother to report on any communications from Jacob. Indeed, she had suspected the motherly woman of sifting through her books and papers on more than once occasion in search of such a breach. She shivered at thought of the *billets-doux* she had carefully hidden behind the chest of drawers. Her letters in return, secretly scribbled after she had retired to bed, had been as a temperature chart, the drafts notating her intense emotions as they progressed from conventional words of love to swelling declarations that would have scandalised her mother. By the third missive, her suppressed emotions had erupted in naïve, yet heartfelt, sentiments that stripped bare her unregulated passion. To her joy, Jacob had responded in kind—anxious expressions after her welfare quickly blossoming into bold and ardent declarations of love that made her long to cast aside all conventional restraint and fly to his arms.

She lay with her head on the pillow, listening to faint noises from the street. The yellow light of a streetlamp shone through the window, illuminating the engraved glass and casting pale halos on the bed cover. 'Please let mama come around', she whispered to the pillow, the dutiful Catholic daughter asserting herself before sleep. 'But if not, Jacob has my entire heart', murmured her lips, the rebellious, heretical sprite wreaking anarchic sport in her dreams.

JACOB MADE HIS WAY home through the wintry streets, his mind churning over Monsieur Lascelles' latest interrogation as to Ferguson's plans for the future. The American's repeated informal invites to spend some time together was of particular interest, his employer quizzing Jacob on whether he had in fact taken Ferguson up on the latest invitation.

'No, sir. The invitation was informal and not to be taken seriously—something common among Americans.'

The explanation seemed to satisfy his employer, who dismissed him with a wave of the hand, his eyes following Jacob out the door.

That he had not heard from Isabelle in over two weeks was another source of anxiety. 'Perhaps she has met someone in Montreal—who knows, she must be bored?' he muttered jealously to himself, deeply suspicious of Madame Ouellet and her intentions.

'It is true that she is ambitious for Isabelle,' acknowledged Hugo when Jacob expressed his fears, 'but you have no cause to worry. Isabelle is loyal to a fault and excessively devout in her affections.' He wrapped an arm around Jacob's shoulder. 'I admire your patience and am grateful that you respect her mother's wishes. Who knows but the old girl may take it as a favourable sign and drop her opposition?'

His conscience niggled at him as he made his way through the dark, snow-covered streets. A freezing wind swept the Quarter, and he huddled deeper inside the buffalo coat he had taken to wearing again. The robe was a source of amusement to the apprentices, who tried it on, laughing as it draped along the floor. Once, to general merriment, the youngest, half buried in the coat, galloped back and forth across the workshop floor, hooting and snorting in imitation of a buffalo. The laughter abruptly stilled when the workshop door opened and Lascelles and the foreman stepped inside, the latter immediately scolding such frivolity.

He was thankful for the coat's warmth as he crossed an intersection and was swept by another freezing blast. 'I shall never get used to this damnable wind,' he moaned, his teeth chattering. He had purchased a new set of leather boots for the winter, along with a pair of wool-lined mittens and a beaver-fur hat with earmuffs to combat the bitingly cold gales that pushed the January temperatures to well below freezing. Has Josette received a letter? he wondered, resolving to call upon Hugo at the earliest opportunity. His friend's reaction, should he ever discover the betrayal, sent a shudder through him, and he pushed the disturbing thought from his mind, bending his head into the wind.

His troubled conscience lasted only until the moment he opened the front door and spotted a package lying on a silver dish with his name written on it. At the sight, all scruples vanished, and he eagerly took up the package, recognising Marguerite's hand.

'A boy delivered it this afternoon,' said his landlady, emerging from the kitchen. 'It has no stamp,' she said, her eyes upon him.

'It is a friend,' he said. 'Serge Villeneuve. Probably an invitation to go for a meal or something.'

'And does your friend indulge himself in perfume?' Madame Pepin raised her eyebrows and stepped back into the kitchen, not requiring an answer.

Sitting down at his desk, he carefully opened the package, glancing at the slim volume enclosed before turning to the letter, his heart racing at the familiar hand.

Dear, Dearer, Dearest! Jacob!
I miss you more with each passing hour, if that is possible. It has now been five months since I was despatched here like a parcel in the mail! I have written to mama, telling her how cruel this exile is, and how hard it has been on me. But I fear my pleas fall on deaf ears. She is quite impossible when in this mood! Marguerite has suggested I write to Father Simard, or even the bishop, and beg their intervention in the matter, but I worry that such a stratagem would only infuriate her more. She communicates with me only through Marguerite, thus intensifying her displeasure. I attend Mass three or four times a week at a quaint little church on rue Marchand, close to the house. Aunt Jeanne accompanies me. She is a very pleasant woman and does her best to lift my mood by introducing me to her social circle. But to no avail! I long only to be reunited with you. I cannot bear this exile much longer. I send you lots of kisses and my pledge that your love is the only thing that sustains me! Kiss! Kiss! You see? Your most loving and affectionate Isabelle.

He wrote back at once, a dictionary and grammar at his elbow.

My Darling Isabelle! Your letter is like a ray of sunshine on this bleak, wintry day. You say five months have passed? It seems more like five years! But you must trust we shall be together again, sooner rather than later. Do not despair. I have hopes that my position will improve and that your mother will alter or abandon her opposition altogether. Just last week I received a small increase in salary. I would have wished to celebrate by buying you a mug of that sweet hot chocolate you like at the café on rue René Descartes. See? I remember every minute of our delightful day in the park! I had supper with Hugo recently. He expressed fond thoughts of you and the wish that we would be together some day. He promises to work on your mother to this effect. Meanwhile, Josette sat there, a sphinx-like smile upon her lips! I feel wretched at deceiving Hugo, he is so trusting of me. But he would surely put a stop to our communications if he knew. Marguerite laughingly refers to him as 'Father Hugo!' You praised my French in your previous letter, but if you knew how many hours it takes to compose each one—a dictionary in one hand, a grammar in the other—you would pity me and admire my persistence! And still, I make mistake after mistake—which only your kindness prevents you from pointing out. Write again soon, and I shall endeavour to reply at once. You lamented my tardiness in your last letter, but I must depend on seeing Josette who must then slip the letter to your sister—without your fearsome mother seeing it! Both Hugo and Marguerite still refuse to give me your address, the former for his promise to your mother; your sister for fear a direct letter, mailed by me, would most certainly alert your aunt. Thus, I must depend on this hand-to-hand conveyance. But all is worth it for a reply from you! Farewell, my love, for now. I await with trembling heart your next letter! Your loving Jacob.

ON HIS NEXT VISIT to the Gagnons, he surreptitiously slipped the letter to Josette in a moment when Hugo left the parlour in search of a modern grammar he had picked up. She took the letter and folded it into her bosom. 'Trust me!' her lips whispered.

'Here is the book I was telling you about.' The returning Hugo pressed the grammar into his hand. 'Take it. Tell me what you think next time we meet.'

'Thank you. And now I must go,' said Jacob, slipping the volume into his pocket.

'Cheer up!' Hugo slapped him on the back. 'Who knows what fortune tomorrow may bring!' Opening the door, Hugo shivered. 'Rather you walk home than me!' The night was cold, the snowy street outside deserted and hushed under the starlit sky. 'Oh! I have invited Madame Ouellet for tea next week. I shall put in another good word for you!'

'Marguerite will accompany her!' Josette trilled over her husband's shoulder. To Jacob's alarm, she held up her hand and shook an imaginary sheet of paper.

'Goodnight and thank you!' He bid a hurried farewell, furious at Josette's levity.

'Why did you say that?' Gagnon asked, a puzzled look on his face as he closed the door behind Jacob.

'Say what?'

'About Marguerite accompanying her mother? What is that to Jacob?'

'For something to say, only, dearest. There is some cake left over. Would you like a slice before bed?'

17

A Surprising Offer

FERGUSON PULLED THE WORKSHOP door closed behind him. '*Brrr!*' He shivered, stamping snow from his boots. Howdy, Jacob. It's like a Chicago. winter!' he declared, pulling off his mittens. 'See these?' He held them up for Jacob to inspect. 'Warmer than gloves. Calf leather lined with lambswool.'

'Monsieur Ferguson!' Lascelles emerged from his office, an ingratiating smile upon his face. 'To what do we owe this pleasure? Ask him what he wants,' he said to Jacob.

'Why in heck ain't he put a telephone in?' Ferguson said, frowning at the proprietor. 'That's how business is done these days.'

'Sir, he wishes to know why you haven't put in a telephone?'

'Tell him I am waiting for the lines to be put in. This isn't America.'

'He assures you he will install a telephone as soon as the lines are put in.'

'No matter.' Ferguson blew his nose. 'Darn cold! Anyway, it's you I came to see. How about you take supper with me on Saturday night?'

'Certainly. It would be a pleasure.'

'Good. The Golden Plate Restaurant on Boolevard Champlain. You know the joint?'

'I do.'

'Say, six o'clock?'

'I'll be there.'

'Jim-Dandy. Goodbye, Monsewer!'

'What was that about?' Lascelles demanded as Ferguson went back out into the cold.

'He invited me to dinner, on Saturday.'

Lascelles stared. 'Just you?'

'Yes.'

'I heard my name mentioned?'

'Just to say goodbye.'

'If there is any business to be discussed I should be there.' Lascelles' face was suspicious.

'I am certain he just wishes to dine with a fellow American.'

'You are not authorised to discuss business matters—of any sort.'

'Of course not, sir.'

With a last, distrustful glance, Lascelles stepped back into his office.

ON SATURDAY EVENING, JACOB arrived at the restaurant, a glittering affair of starched table cloths and glass chandeliers. The evening was very cold and he wore the buffalo coat over his suit. The *maître d'hôtel* showed him to the window table where Ferguson sat alongside another man dressed in an expensive wool suit. The man looked younger than Ferguson. He was plump and partly bald, his face mottled with pink veins.

'Jacob!' Ferguson got to his feet. 'This is Morgan Selt, my business partner from Albany.'

'How do you do, Jacob. I've heard a great deal about you. All of it good!' The other man stood up to shake hands. His voice was bluff, like Ferguson's and just as confident sounding.

'Shucks, we don't stand on ceremony here, boys. We're 'merican! Jacob, sit down. Morg, pour him a glass of wine.' Ferguson raised his glass. 'To the good old USA!'

They made small talk while ordering from the leather-bound menu, Jacob interpreting and questioning the waiter on behalf of his two companions. After the meal had been ordered, Ferguson arranged himself comfortably on the plush seat. 'Why don't you tell us about yourself, Jacob? How did an American end up in this god-forsaken neck of the woods?'

'The whole shebang don't leave anything out,' added Selt.

Both men expressed surprise as Jacob unfolded his history—his account of getting shot and the aftermath drawing a gasp from Selt.

'Jesus H. Christ if that ain't something!' Ferguson shook his head as Jacob concluded the tale.

'And you're still carrying a piece of the slug in your head?' marvelled Selt, sitting back as the waiter refilled their glasses.

'So, I'm told.'

'And you don't remember a thing about where you came from?' an equally amazed Ferguson asked, 'or where your folks are at?'

He shrugged. 'I'm afraid not. And believe me, I've tried.'

'And you've been stuck here the whole time?'

'I have. Through necessity as much as anything.'

'And that Injun woman you said healed you, she still around?'

'She is, although I haven't visited her in some time.'

'If that don't beat all. Tuck in gentlemen!' said Ferguson as the waiter arrived with the steaks.

The meal passed quickly, both Ferguson and Selt making small talk and questioning Jacob on local habits and customs. 'There are goddam statues everywhere,' Selt complained at one point. 'And bells!' He shook his head.

'Don't mind Morgan,' chuckled Ferguson. 'He can't stand to see a statue that ain't of himself.'

Following dessert, Ferguson ordered whiskies while Selt took out a cigar. 'Jacob?' He offered one across the table.

'Me too!' Ferguson grinned as Jacob declined the offer. 'Like sucking on grass!'

'So, you've decided to become a Frenchie now?' probed Selt, reclining with the cigar.

'No, still American. But after two years, I'm starting to feel at home here.'

After quizzing Jacob on further aspects of his story, the two men exchanged looks.

'So, Jacob, what are your intentions for the future?' asked Ferguson. 'Are you intending to stay on with this Lascelles fellow?'

'I haven't given too much thought to it, to be honest. I'm just grateful to be employed. There are many that are not so fortunate.'

'I never saw so many goddamn beggars,' agreed Selt, flicking ash from the end of his cigar.

'Morg, why don't you tell Jacob about our plans?'

'Sure 'nuff.' Selt leaned his elbows on the table, emitting a stream of smoke as he regarded Jacob. 'You may be wondering why we came to this burg to do business and not Montreal?'

'It's bigger,' put in Ferguson, 'Montreal, that is, and lots more English speakers.'

'Lots more English speakers,' agreed Selt, 'and it's on the railroad line— not that this burg ain't. But things are more expensive.'

'A lot more.' Ferguson nodded.

'Also, more competition. The limeys have got a grip on business, and they don't welcome newcomers. This joint is different.'

'This town is more Frenchified,' agreed Ferguson.

'There's an opportunity here—for the first man in, so to speak.' Selt puffed on the cigar, regarding Jacob through a cloud of smoke. 'And we've got plans.'

'Tell me something,' interrupted Ferguson. 'What's the beef between this town and Quebec City? We met a government fella there and he about spat teeth when he heard we were going to set up business here, in New France.'

Jacob smiled, happy to be able to contribute to the conversation. 'It almost certainly goes back to the historic rivalry between the regional Assembly in New France and the Provincial Assembly in Quebec. The habitants—the locals, that is—are generally suspicious of anything the Quebec government proposes and would just as soon keep them at arm's length.'

'I did not know that.' Ferguson glanced at his companion. 'See, Morg. What did I tell you? local knowledge.'

'You got that right, Gus. Anyway, on with the story,' said Selt, looking at Jacob. 'We figure that we could save a pile of dough by transferring all of our upholstery business from New York State to right here. And not only that—' he glanced at Ferguson—'we plan to build carriages here—both for the American market over the border, and the French one both here and in Montreal. Expanding the business, see?'

'Selling premium rigs to the Frenchies, as well as to Americans.' 'We reckon it's cheaper to do all that right here in New France. Labour's cheaper—even when you figure in the costs of transportation.'

'And there's plenty of skilled, unemployed craftsmen, as you pointed out.' Selt sucked on the cigar. 'What do you think of that?'

'We'd like to hear your opinion,' said Ferguson.

'Monsieur Lascelles will be delighted. I'm sure he would be more than happy to supply all your upholstery needs.'

His dining companions glanced at each other. 'You said you see your future here, in New France?' asked Selt.

'I do.'

'And you don't have any other prospects in mind—apart from Lascelles?'

'Pardon?' Jacob furrowed his brow at the question.

'What he means ...' Ferguson leaned forward, 'is how'd you like to work for us—as our man in New France?'

'You want me to work for you?' Jacob's mouth opened in surprise.

'Why not? You're a competent fellow. I saw how you instructed those Frenchies.'

'We need someone who understands the lingo.' 'Someone we can trust,' added Ferguson.

'An American,' said Selt, his face solemn. 'Somebody we can count on to handle our business here.'

Jacob grimaced, unsure whether he understood the offer. 'But I have no experience in running a business. I wouldn't know where to start.'

'No problem. Morg here would work with you for the first few months, and we'd send up our best numbers man to take care of the books.'

'We plan to open a factory here,' added Selt. 'We'll send our carriage master up from Albany to take charge of building the rigs. We'd depend on you to hire competent workmen, arrange supplies, order materials, take charge of sales, and oversee shipping—back to the States or anywhere in Canada. Think you could handle that?'

'Yes, I do!' He gulped the answer, breathless as he suddenly understood the opportunity being dangled before him.

'Good man. And I guarantee you'll be well rewarded.' Ferguson glanced at his companion, who nodded.

'At least three times what that skint Lascelles is paying you.'

'Plus, a bonus if you meet sales targets.'

'You know what I earn?'

'To the penny.' Selt grinned. 'We're businessmen, Jacob. We do our homework.'

'Due diligence.' Ferguson nodded. 'What do you say? We've put an offer in on a building over on roo Burgeron. This could be your big chance, Jacob, to set yourself up in the world.' Ferguson waited for an answer.

'Yes!' In his excitement Jacob barely restrained from a gladsome *whoop!* 'That is, if you're sure I could handle it.'

'We do. Business know-how a man can learn from experience. But he's got to have the right foundations. Right, Morg?'

Selt puffed agreement. 'It starts from the ground up.'

'I'll do my level best not to let you down.' Jacob felt giddy and gulped some of the wine.

Ferguson laughed. 'That's the spirit! Can you imagine the look on Lascelles' face?'

At mention of his employer, Jacob's exuberant mood abruptly deflated. 'What about Monsieur Lascelles?'

'We'll keep him on as a supplier—until we establish our own supply chain.'

'When would you want me to start? I owe Monsieur Lascelles at least a week's notice.'

'Give him three or four weeks. It will take that long to settle all the legal work and complete the building permits. After that you can start with us. Morg here will explain what we want you to do, show you the ropes. And after that you deal with Lascelles on your own—from our side of the table.'

'The American side.'

'What do you say, Jacob? Shall we shake on it?' Ferguson stuck out his hand.

Jacob took a deep, steadying breath and shook the other man's hand. 'Thank you, sir!'

'And there!' Selt leaned forward, extending his hand.

'*Garcon!*' Ferguson snapped his fingers. 'Bring over some good old Yankee whisky!'

HE WALKED HOME UNMINDFUL of the cold, his head still spinning from the conversation. Did I dream it?' he asked himself over and over. Is it really true? '*We'll pay you three times what you're getting from Lascelles.*' He did a rapid calculation. Seventeen hundred dollars a year! The dizzying figure took his breath away. Is that what Ferguson had intended? Or was it a mistake, an overestimation of his present salary? It can't have been a mistake, he told himself, trying to temper his jubilation. They are too smart for that. Seventeen hundred dollars!—plus a bonus!

He laughed with delight, drawing glances from a couple passing by. Isabelle flashed to mind—the image quickly followed by the frowning face of her mother. The heartless shrew will have to reconsider! His heart leapt as he sucked in the cold night air and laughed his great good fortune up to the brilliant stars. In his jubilation, they seemed to tremble and dance, revelling in this entirely unexpected bonanza.

Thus, this man of excellent prospects made his way home through the winding streets of his adopted city, his heart rejoicing as he contemplated the future.

In spite of the late hour, he wrote immediately to Isabelle to share the splendid news. After regaling her with accounts of the dinner, spilling into English in his excitement, he concluded the letter with a fervent wish: *I intend to share the news with Hugo as soon as possible so that he may [might?] pass it on to your mother. I am hoping that she will change her opinion of me as a suitor when she learns of my advancement. But first, I must hand in my resignation to Monsieur Lascelles.*

Putting down the pen he pondered the sentence.

'AND HOW IS OUR friend Jacob doing?' The deputy stepped into the doorway of Hugo's cramped office where he was bent over a dusty volume of '*The Annals of Old Quebec,*' reading it by the light of a small window as the bright winter sun streamed in.

'Oh! I didn't see you, sir!' Hugo jumped to his feet. 'Jacob? He does well, thank you.'

The deputy nodded, his lined face seeming at home amidst the piled shelves of antique books, manuscripts, and letters. 'Monsieur Lascelles speaks favourably, but grudgingly, of his progress —no slight on Jacob, I assure you—but simply the man's nature. He even complimented his workaday French.' 'Workaday?' Hugo puzzled at the adjective.

'He refers to Jacob's quick mastery of the terms of his trade—the naming of tools, leathers, saddle parts, and so forth.'

'Ah?'

'A novel term, don't you agree? But that is not why I came to talk to you.' Suppressing a sneeze in the mote-speckled air, the deputy looked around to survey the crowded shelves. 'How long have you worked in this position?'

'Ten years, sir, ever since leaving the seminary.'

The deputy chuckled. 'I remember with great fondness my days there. We had a Greek tutor, a monsieur …? What the devil was his name? I can see his face, but the name quite escapes me.'

'Sir! Forgive me. Would you like to sit?' Gagnon hurried to offer his chair.

'No, no, my boy. Sit down. I shall be but a minute.' Resting his hands on the cane, the deputy cleared his throat. 'I have an opening for a private secretary. Dependable old Laurent has handed in his notice of resignation, due to age, you see, the bugbear of us all.' The deputy sighed. 'At any rate, I thought you might be interested. The duties are light—to maintain records of meetings, help to draft bills or motions, attend the Assembly when in session, write correspondence, greet visitors, that sort of thing. The post is only guaranteed until the next election of course, but do you think it might interest you? The pay is probably better than you are earning now and—who knows?—you may decide to stand for the Assembly yourself one day in which case the experience would prove invaluable. What do you say? Would you like time to think it over?'

Hugo sat there, his ears uncertain whether they had heard correctly. 'You wish me to work for you?'

'As my private secretary. If you would like time to think upon it, I would understand.'

'No need!' Hugo leapt to his feet. 'I accept at once, sir, and with the utmost thanks!'

'Excellent! Come up to my office this afternoon and I'll introduce you to old Laurent. He will make all the necessary arrangements.'

'PRIVATE SECRETARY? TO THE deputy?' Josette echoed the words as they poured out of her jubilant husband's mouth. He had swept her up in his arms immediately after stepping in the door and before removing his hat.

'Will it mean more money?' she asked.

'Yes! Probably. But don't you see, sweetheart, the advantages?' He clasped her hands, his eyes sparkling with ambition. 'I shall get to see the innermost workings of the Assembly. I shall get to attend meetings as his assistant. He even mentioned the possibility of one day standing for nomination myself!'

'Oh goodness!' Josette regarded him, eyes wide, as the realisation sunk in. She looked around for her fan and saw it lying on the side-table. Picking it up, she fanned the emotion, smiling, already telling her sister, and seeing the look on the face of Sulplice Benoit when she heard the news. 'The deputy's wife!'

'MONSIEUR LASCELLES?' JACOB TAPPED on the square of glass set into the office door. Lascelles was sitting at his cluttered desk sorting through papers.

'Come in Jacob. I want to discuss the terms of the American's contract with you. See here?' Before Jacob could put in a word, Lascelles held up a sheaf of papers. 'Damn Americans and their lawyers! Sit down!' He offered Jacob a chair. 'Shall I put on the coffee?'

Surprised at the unusually obliging nature of his employer, Jacob sat down, a sense of foreboding in his heart as he cleared his throat.

'What can I do for you?' Lascelles sat back in the upright chair. 'The dinner!' he suddenly remembered. 'How did that go? What did the American want?' His expression was affable, the lingering effects of the pleasant breakfast he had enjoyed that morning.

'That is what I wished to speak to you about.'

'What? Did he raise the question of business?' Lascelles frowned with the question.

'Yes, but in an entirely unexpected way,' Jacob temporised, his courage suddenly deserting him.

'Well? What did he say?' Lascelles leaned forward on the desk.

'He, uh, offered me a position.'

'What's that?' Lascelles blinked, as though he might have misheard.

'He, monsieur Ferguson, asked me to come and work for him—as his agent in New France.'

The affable look on Lascelles's face changed to one of suspicion.

'His *agent*? And what did you say?'

Jacob took a deep breath. 'I said yes. I could hardly say no. The offer was too generous.'

There was silence in the room. Lascelles grimaced and rubbed his jaw as though he had difficulty comprehending the information. 'He offered you employment—as his agent?' He stared out the door of the office. 'What were the terms?' he added, almost as an afterthought.

'I do not wish to go into the details. There are things still to be sorted out. Suffice to say that soon I shall be representing monsieur Ferguson in all future dealings with you.' He swallowed. 'Regretfully, sir. I must inform you of my intention to quit my employment with you—in two weeks' time, if that is agreeable?'

'And if it is not?' The question was rudely blunt.

'Then whatever date you think agreeable.'

Lascelles said nothing for a moment. He picked up the pile of papers on his desk and shuffled them into a square. 'So, you are going to work for the American?' he said, as if still having trouble with the concept. He slapped the papers back down on the desk, a frowning expression on his face.

'Yes, sir. I am most grate—'

'Get out!' The shouted words were startling in their ferocity. His face livid, Lascelles stood up, knocking back his chair. 'Get back to work while I think about what is *agreeable*.' He glowered at Jacob, his teeth bared in an ugly snarl.

Taken aback, Jacob hastily left the office and returned to the workbench, shaking his head at a silent question from Guyot.

Lascelles sat at the desk, his body rigid with fury as he contemplated the shocking betrayal. *And I offered him work! Who else would make such a generous offer to a … pauper! An idiot who had not a word of French! I put bread in his mouth when he had nothing! And this is how he repays me!*

His immediate instinct was to seize the ungrateful wretch by the collar and throw him out into the street—the mere contemplation of which afforded him an instant of dizzy, vengeful pleasure. But the hard-headed businessman in him gave rein to such violent impulses. *He is to be the American's representative. That means business is to continue.* The prospect of continued business was counterbalanced by a cold, seething rage at the thought of having to treat the filthy English backstabber as an equal. *An equal!*

The notion almost caused him to choke as he tasted that morning's breakfast in his mouth. *God's curse on the traitor! But be careful, he* admonished himself in the same breath. Profits are at stake. He took a deep controlled breath as he looked out at the workshop floor. There would be a reckoning, he promised himself through gritted teeth. Oh, yes! There would be a return for this insult, or my name isn't Gustave Lascelles!

SHE READ THE LETTER again and again, her hands trembling with joy and excitement at the astonishing news. Heady with delight, she repeated the astronomical salary beneath her breath. They would be able to afford a house! They would be able to help her mother—perhaps even allow her to close down the shop! Her thoughts in a daze, she mumbled her way through afternoon tea with her aunt, it being on the tip of her tongue to burst out in triumph with the news. Instead, she reined in her excitement, deciding to await her mother's reaction—surely, Hugo would have conveyed the news by now?

'Isabelle. Are you dreaming?'

'Pardon aunt. What did you say?'

'More tea?' The teapot was poised.

'Thank you.' She held out the cup.

'You look like the cat that got the cream!' Her aunt added milk to the cup.

'Sorry, I was thinking.'

'Of the price of eggs, no doubt?'

Isabelle smiled and sipped the tea—the rich milky mixture tasting like nectar on her tongue. Her aunt was studying her, a shrewd expression on her face. 'The letter this morning, it contained pleasing news?'

'Oh, yes!'

Her aunt raised her eyebrows. 'Well? Are you going to share?'

Isabelle hesitated, and then blurted out what she had intended to keep secret. 'Marguerite has informed me of a most wonderful advancement for Jacob!'

'Indeed? And may one know of what sort?'

'He is to be promoted—with another company, an American one, with a great increase in salary.'

Her aunt knitted her brow. 'And you imagine that this changes things with your mother?'

The unexpected response was like a splash of cold water. She bit into a sugar and cream biscuit, the buttery flakes bland against her tongue.

'It may change the young man's prospects,' her aunt continued, her voice not unkind, 'but there are other considerations for your mama.'

'Such as?' Thoroughly miserable, she waited for the response.

'Well, the fact he is a complete stranger, an American, for one.'

'That's unjust. He cannot help who he is.'

'Perhaps. But your mother doesn't see it that way. She has long dreamed of you marrying a nice young Frenchman and settling down like a good Catholic wife. And that brings up the second of your mama's objections. This Jacob is of the Protestant faith, I understand?' Aunt Jeanne raised her eyebrows with the question.

'It is uncertain,' answered Isabelle.

'Uncertain?' Her aunt set down her cup. 'How on earth could anyone be uncertain as to their faith?'

'He cannot remember his own religious instruction—but he was impressed when I showed him the cathedral. Perhaps it brought back memories.'

Her aunt chuckled. 'Hardly an endorsement as to his beliefs!' Her face grew solemn again. 'Your mother suspects he may be a so-called free-thinker,' she said, her nose wrinkling with distaste at the notion.

'Really, aunt. It's the twentieth century. Do we still need to make these distinctions?'

'Blessed Mary!' Her aunt almost spilled tea into the saucer. 'Our faith is who we are, as good Frenchwomen!' She gazed at Isabelle, her mouth open in dismay. 'Your mother feared this would happen.'

Apologetic at being the cause of her aunt's distress, Isabelle offered reassurance. 'Do not worry, aunt. I could never abandon my faith, not even for love.' She set down her cup as a further sign of sincerity.

'I am very glad to hear it!' Her aunt dabbed at one eye with a linen handkerchief drawn from her sleeve. 'Very glad!'

Upset by the conversation, Isabelle stood by her bedroom window later that afternoon, looking out over the grey street. Rain had started to fall, the weather as dismal as her changed mood. Jacob where are you? she wondered. What are you doing now? And how long must I endure this exile before mama relents and allows me to return home?

She pressed her palm against the window, peering at a man holding an umbrella over the head of his female companion. She watched the pair walk down the street huddled together under the umbrella. Dear Blessed Virgin. Will you not take pity upon me? What have I done to deserve this?

She felt against her breast for Jacob's letter and withdrew it to read yet again. '*I am hoping that your mother will change her opinion of me as a suitor when she learns of my advancement.*' Tears filled her eyes, and she whispered a prayer beneath her breath. Outside, the grey wintry light grew darker and electric lights came on along the street. '*I love you wholeheartedly and live only to see you again!*' She smiled through her tears at the sentiment, written in haste and in English. It had taken frowning concentration over the pages of her own English-French dictionary, purchased soon after her liaison with Jacob, to determine the exact meaning of 'wholehearted', since when it had become her favourite English word. 'Wholehearted!' she had exclaimed. 'With the whole of one's heart!'

Downstairs, she heard her uncle return home and listened for a moment, the conversation with her aunt returning to trouble her. In spite of her instinctive defence of Jacob, his indifference towards religion was a source of disquiet that grieved her and was the cause of much prayer on his behalf. Her one consolation was the fervent hope that he might one day embrace the true faith and draw the same comfort from it that she herself did. The words of her cousin Jules came back as she stood gazing out the window. 'He embraced the French language, did he not? Then why not Catholicism too? One is as good as the other!' he joked, before apologising at the look on his cousin's face.

'Isabelle?' Her aunt called from the foot of the staircase. 'Your uncle is home. Time for supper!'

18

An Unexpected Visitor

Six MONTHS AFTER STARTING his employment with Ferguson-Selt Quality Carriages, Jacob strode along rue Jean-Jacques Boisard, his heart overflowing with optimism. Spring had flowered into a glorious summer, and he now boasted the grand title of general manager, earning a princely salary of $1,700 per annum plus bonuses. He hummed with self-satisfaction, drawing a glance from a passing woman and rewarding her with a cheery grin before she quickly looked away.

In spite of his newfound prosperity, he had retained his room at Madam Pepin's and took her modest, prepared lunches to work exactly as before. But instead of overalls, he wore a custom-made brown wool suit, polished leather shoes, and a Derby hat with a low crown and 'dash' brim. Leaving his lodgings at 6:30 am on the dot, he walked through the Old Town market square and up Saint-Gabriel to avenue Marian, where he turned right onto rue Bergeron, arriving at his office at 7:00 am. Armed with a pot of coffee, he sat at his desk until lunchtime, answering correspondence, filling out forms, checking bills and inventories, and planning work schedules.

The adjacent office was occupied by the unassuming Dwight Raskin, the 'numbers man' sent up from New York to take care of the accounts. Jacob had hired a secretary, an obliging middle-aged spinster called Madame Bisset who collated employee hours, kept track of appointments, and answered the newly installed telephone. She took dictation as required, employing Pitman's shorthand in cryptic French phonetics, which she later transcribed onto a typewritten sheet for his signature. He installed a time clock on the shop floor below his office to ensure the punctuality of his employees. Inside his own office he had placed a small pendulum clock. When the clock struck noon, he took out his lunch, eating at his desk, sometimes with Dwight for company.

Once a week he made a telephone call to Albany to update his employers or to receive instructions. He enjoyed his new position and the authority that went with it, although irked at times by the excessive paperwork—much of which he delegated to Madame Bisset. The busy schedule kept his mind occupied and distracted him from the frustrations of his distant and secretive relationship with Isabelle.

In the middle of each month, he made a round of his suppliers, who greeted him with elaborate courtesy as he inspected materials or made suggestions for changes. All of the upholstery work was now carried out in-house, requiring only the supply of leathers and buckles. The break with Lascelles necessitated by this decision had been messy and acrimonious, his former employer heaping the blame on him for the decision not to renew the contract and thereby gravely imperilling the Frenchman's business, nay, his very livelihood itself. 'There will come a day when he regrets his arrogant high-handedness!' Lascelles vowed to his foreman after Jacob made a final visit to close out the contract. 'Mark my words,' he swore, a venomous expression on his face.

On one of his supplier rounds, he passed Serge Villeneuve on rue Madeleine, his friend walking by without so much as a glance. 'Serge!'

Villeneuve turned, staring in puzzlement before his eyes widened. 'Jacob! Is that you?'

'It is indeed.' He smiled as the other man gaped in amazement while studying him from head to toe.

'By the Pope's tail! I never would have known you.' Serge tipped the carpenter's cap back on his head. 'You look like a bank manager!'

'Hardly. Merely a spoke in the wheel,' laughed Jacob.

'No, more than that.' Serge scratched his chin, marvelling at the man in front of him. 'You've risen in the world, Jacob. And to think …' He shook his head in wonder.

'It's still the same old me, Serge. Would you like to meet at the tavern on Saturday night for a drink?'

Villeneuve grinned. 'Why not? I'm there most nights.'

Pleased, Jacob continued on his way, filing away the gratifying encounter to include in his next missive to Isabelle.

Whenever bored with the papers piled on his office desk, he wandered down onto the workshop floor to watch as his employees applied the finishing touches to the half-a-dozen carriages in various stages of completion. Two of these—large, six-person vehicles custom-ordered by a transport firm in Montreal, stood resplendent in newly applied paint and varnish. He watched for a moment as a workman fussed over the interior trim.

'Sir?' The workman stopped what he was doing when he became aware of Jacob watching.

'Nothing, keep going. Will it be ready in time?'

'Yes sir. I just have to fix the lamp.' The man pointed to the brass light fixture sitting on the floor.

'And the other one?'

'Same thing. I should be finished in couple of hours.'

'Good. We'll ship them on Tuesday's train.' He made a mental note to tell Madame Bisset to make the necessary arrangements.

Occasionally, he took off his jacket and rolled up his sleeves to lend a hand, finding the physical labour a relaxing break from the endless rounds of paperwork. Frank Horton, the American craftsman imported from New York to oversee carriage construction, disapproved of this participation, irritable at the dilution of his authority as the French apprentices looked between himself and Jacob for direction. But as he observed Jacob's obvious enjoyment in the work and willingness to take instruction, he relaxed his opposition. 'You'd make a handy coach-maker yourself,' he remarked one day as he watched Jacob help manoeuvre a wheel onto a greased axle.

'I like mechanical things,' said Jacob, wiping his hands, 'and moving parts. I like the way they all fit together.'

'Then you've the true heart of a craftsman.' Horton stopped as he observed one of the young apprentices sand down an oak log intended as an axle tree. 'Smooth strokes!' he barked. 'And shave off that knob! Don't try and sand it.'

Horton demonstrated, using a hand plane to level the protuberance before vigorously sanding and smoothing the spot as the chastened youth looked on.

'Where did you find that simpleton?' he muttered as the apprentice took over the task.

Jacob laughed. 'He's a fine boy, I know his uncle. Give him time.'

As he approached the third anniversary of his mysterious arrival in New France he was, to all outward appearances, an industrious, ambitious young man confidently making his way in the world. But of late he was increasingly perturbed by fleeting images that suggested someone other than the self he presented to the world—an 'original' self as he came to think of it, struggling to show through the veneer of Frenchness and newfound bourgeois prosperity.

The memories—if that is what they are, he speculated—disturbed him inasmuch as he was increasingly content with the life he had fashioned out of such unpromising raw materials. The flashes of perception that percolated through his dreams tantalised him with glimpses of another life, albeit one increasingly remote and distant. On occasion, the nocturnal images intruded into daylight—born and vanishing before he was consciously aware of their presence. As he paid more attention, he came to realise that they were often evoked by the physical activity of the moment—whether tinkering on the workshop floor or helping to manoeuvre a new drill press into position. Despite the fact that he had all but abandoned hope, or interest even, in recovering his memory, the ghostly images convinced him that physical labour was the cipher that might, one day, unlock the hieroglyphs—those sensations and intuitions of a former life—and thus reveal his true identity.

Somewhat reluctantly, he discussed the phenomena with Hugo. 'But of course, as soon as I consciously think upon these things, they vanish like fireflies in the moonlight,' he complained. 'It is as if they were purposefully designed to tease and provoke me.'

Hugo, who had watched his friend's rapid rise in the world with a mixture of pride and astonishment—and not a little envy, reported the conversation to the deputy, correctly guessing the conundrum would fascinate the scholarly politician, who had continued to follow Jacob's progress with paternal interest.

The deputy pondered the description, much taken by the account as Hugo had surmised. 'He said that—like fireflies in the moonlight?'

'He did. Although professing to hold no interest in his past, it clearly still haunts him.'

The deputy pinched his jaw, a ruminative look on his face. 'Often-times, when I try to recall something, it altogether escapes me,' he observed. 'But then, when I am resting or thinking of something else entirely, the answer pops into my head. You could advise Jacob to try this method. He may find the answer he seeks, or at least the simulacrum of such. It is useful to focus on a piece of music or a favourite poem to open the gates of perception,' he added, having read of the practice in a psychology journal.

Although sceptical when the method was suggested to him, Hugo nevertheless urged Jacob to try it, implicitly claiming the novel theory as his own. 'What have you got to lose?' he cajoled the reluctant Jacob. 'Don't you wish to find out all that you can, whichever way you can?'

Jacob's unwillingness, as he admitted to himself, arose from his increasingly ambivalent feelings about the past now that he was making such impressive headway in his new life. Who knows, but I may not like what I find? he pondered, raising a new and disturbing element of doubt about his antecedents. Why risk stirring up a hornet's nest?

Nevertheless, unsettled by the phantom images, he agreed to test the theory. One night he closed his eyes and lay perfectly still, willing himself into that brooding half-state which, Hugo had suggested, would render him receptive to the quicksilver flashes of memory that teased his mind like fish darting beneath the surface of a murky pond. But after a few minutes of passive observance, he promptly fell asleep. He tried the experiment several more times with the same result before abandoning it.

'It's a relief,' he confessed to Hugo. 'The truth is I no longer care about my past. It is the future which interests me the most. However,' he conceded, 'the practice is an excellent means of inducing sleep.'

The deputy blinked upon hearing the admission, reading it as a statement on the political controversy currently bedevilling New France.

'Again, he confounds us all! His eyes look forward only—as eyes are designed to do—while we Frenchmen look backwards, as though the future lay in the past rather than before us.' The more he considered the analogy, the more taken by it the deputy became. 'The figure relates to biology, in particular the organ of the eye,' he ruminated, gazing out the window. 'But then might not such biology—of the particular organ—dictate our beliefs about the nature of the world?'

He turned to Hugo, his face alive with speculation. 'Deafness, for example, might persuade a man to observe and understand the world as an infinite series of convergent signs that are read quite differently from, say, the vibrations in the ear experienced by someone not deaf. One might perhaps perform a useful experiment by asking a blind man, and a deaf one, to sit in a room and describe their separate impressions of the world.' He sat back in the chair, ignoring the Assembly bill he had been contemplating minutes earlier.

'Sir, the House meets in less than an hour.' Hugo glanced at the clock.

'Of course!' The deputy turned his eyes to the bill. 'But an idea worthy of inquiry perhaps?' he remarked.

ONE SUNDAY JACOB HAD just finished writing a letter to Isabelle when he heard a knock at the door. He found Hugo standing in the hallway clutching two bottles of wine. Alongside him stood a slim, tousled-haired man dressed in a homespun linen jacket offset by an old-fashioned, and slightly rustic, neckcloth. The stranger was bareheaded, in contrast to Hugo who wore a straw hat, set back upon his head at such a rakish angle that the sight caused Jacob to laugh.

'Pardon!' he apologised. 'I am not used to seeing you dressed in so … bohemian a fashion!'

Hugo grinned. 'It is the effect of my companion,' he said. 'Jacob, meet my good friend Alois Giroux. Alois is one of New France's finest sculptors, if not *the* finest.'

'Hello.' With careless informality, Giroux stuck out his hand. 'How much does she charge for the room?' he asked, peering over Jacob's shoulder.

'You must excuse us,' said Hugo as Jacob stood aside to welcome them in. 'I was strolling with Alois, whom I have not seen in an age, when it occurred to me that you two should meet.'

'I am glad you stopped by. I was becoming quite bored with myself.'

'Hugo, you did not tell me his French was this good,' remarked Giroux, looking around to inspect the room.

'I taught him!' Hugo beamed with pride.

'Indeed, you did. I could not speak a word when I first arrived.'

'And yet now you speak like a genuine habitant,' suggested Giroux, inspecting a small, framed picture on the wall.

Over a bottle of wine, Hugo lavished praise upon his companion's renown as a sculptor whether working with, marble or bronze. 'Jacob, you are familiar with the bronze sculpture on rue St-Germain? You know, the one of Henri Brisson that you pointed out was also the name of my street?'

'The one of the voyageur seated in a canoe?' Impressed, Jacob turned to the visitor. 'You did that?'

'I did.'

'It is magnificent! One of my favourite pieces.'

Giroux accepted the praise with modest good humour. 'I am quite fond of it myself.'

'And he did the marble of Catherine Sienna on Promenade Samuel-de Champlain. You know, the one where she is holding up her hands in prayer?'

'I think so.' Jacob frowned to recall. 'There are so many statues in the town.'

Hugo chuckled. 'And most of them created by Alois and his family!'

'Far from most,' demurred Giroux. 'Thirty-seven to be exact.' He eyed Jacob curiously. 'Hugo has told me of your history,' he said, with disarming candour. 'I find it intriguing.'

It was Jacob's turn to be modest. 'Hardly. I am a creature of fortune swept along by luck—including meeting good old Hugo here.'

'But that in itself is remarkable, is it not?' Giroux's restless blue eyes were suddenly intent. 'One could fashion it into a play or a novel.'

'Or a statue!' joked Hugo.

Jacob opened the second bottle of wine as the conversation drifted off into talk of New France politics, Hugo gossiping freely about the current concerns of the Assembly. 'It's always the same,' he announced in reply to a question from Jacob, 'nothing but language, taxes, education, and language again.'

Jacob frowned. 'I don't understand. What do you mean by education?'

'The Reform Party is pushing to allow the formation of Protestant schools and to allow English as the language of instruction in such schools. The Patriots are understandably furious and won't have a bar of it.'

'There can't be that many Protestants in New France, surely? And as for English speakers—they are as rare as hens' teeth.'

'All that may have been true at one time,' agreed Hugo. 'But times are changing. Witness yourself and your employers. There has been an influx of English speakers, and they are pushing, no, demanding, the right to set up schools in their own faith and language.'

'And what does Monsieur Turgeon think of this?'

'Old Turgeon? He is given to the middle way,' interrupted Giroux. 'Moderation in all things, right Hugo?'

'Indeed, and what is wrong with that? I myself subscribe to the self-same philosophy.'

'Really?' Giroux raised a teasing eyebrow. 'You, such a staunch Catholic and zealous habitant?'

'There are exceptions to moderation,' protested Hugo. 'We Frenchmen are nothing without our faith. And certainly nothing without our language. Such birthrights must be protected.'

'So, no Protestant schools and no English language?' persisted Giroux, with a sly wink at Jacob.

'In places like Montreal, where a third of the population is English, yes. But here in New France …?' Hugo shook his head. 'No.'

'Hugo!' Giroux raised his eyes in mock horror. 'You are becoming a radical!'

'In matters of faith and language only.'

'Can radicalism be limited to certain areas only or does it not spoil the entire barrel?'

'French and faith!' said a stubborn Hugo, repeating the popular maxim.

'Tell me Hugo,' said Jacob, changing the subject, 'has the deputy heard any further from Gustave Lascelles? I saw him on the street the other day and the rogue walked by me without so much as a by-your-leave.'

Hugo chuckled. 'He has done the same to both the deputy and myself. It is as if we no longer exist. What an extraordinary creature he is! Oh, but you do know he has lost his business?'

'No, I didn't. What happened?' Jacob frowned at the news.

'His charming personality, I should think. It drove off buyers, who were more than happy to take their custom elsewhere. In the end, he had no choice but to close the business.'

'And his employees?'

'Gone, I suppose. Who knows where?'

'That must have come as a blow,' said Jacob, his voice regretful.

'The fellow survives like a cockroach. I hear he now works as a labourer on a building site.'

The conversation drifted on, fuelled by wine and a packet of biscuits. Giroux seemed increasingly bored by the topics of discussion, getting up to gaze out the window at the street below and then turning his attention to the small bureau upon which stood Jacob's collection of grammars and dictionaries. 'Hello, what's this?' he said, withdrawing a volume. 'Do you mind?' he asked, holding up the volume.

'Not at all. It's the bible found upon my person when I was discovered in the woods.'

'It is elaborately bound.' His eyes full of curiosity, Giroux took the bible to the table and set it down. With a glance at Jacob for permission, he opened the battered cover, pausing to examine the water-stained flyleaf. 'It has been through the wars,' he said, peering at the blotted names.

'Yes. I imagine I dropped it in the snow. Perhaps more than once.' Giroux pored over the volume, his stone-roughened fingers turning the pages with respectful care. 'I myself do not have a word of English,' he said.

As Jacob and Hugo resumed their conversation, the topic turned to Marguerite Ouellet and her forthcoming marriage to Dominic Beaulieu. 'Will Isabelle be there?' asked Jacob, his ears, and his hopes, pricking up at the possibility.

'I think she will be,' said Hugo. 'Surely,' he added.

'And after the wedding, her mother will allow her to stay?'

Hugo shrugged. 'Perhaps. But who knows?'

Giroux sifted through the pages, only half listening to the conversation, his eyes full of professional interest as he admired the illustrations. 'Such workmanship!' he exclaimed of a coloured plate. 'Hello. What's this?' He took out a creased charcoal sketch tucked between the pages and spread it open upon the table. 'Figs and fishes!' He studied the drawing, whistling with appreciation.

'That was among the pages. I keep meaning to get it mounted and framed.'

'A winged buffalo!' Giroux marvelled at the sketch. 'But are those wings?' He peered more closely at the page. 'Lances! Spears of some sort?' He turned his focus to Jacob, his eyes burning with curiosity. 'It is quite marvellous. Did you draw it?'

'Heavens, no. It was in between the pages. I have no idea as to its origin.'

'Would you object if I made a copy?' Giroux drew out a small sketchpad from his jacket pocket.

'Go ahead.'

For the next few minutes, the sculptor made several copies of the sketch, absorbed in the task. 'Quite a find!' he said, putting away his pen. 'I would be most interested to learn about the artist.'

'As would I. But you have the entirety of its history there before you.'

'Would you like me to frame it for you? The glass would protect it against fading and discolouration.'

'Would you? I would be obliged.'

'Say no more.' Giroux carefully folded the sketch. 'Hugo. Your satchel.'

'It means a lot to me—as a clue to my origins,' said Jacob, having second thoughts as he watched Hugo tuck the sketch among the papers in his satchel.

'Don't worry. I shall take excellent care of it.'

'And now, we must away!' Hugo stood up. 'By St. Peter's beard!' he chuckled, suddenly unsteady on his feet. 'Just how much wine did we drink?'

Tipsy but feeling cheerful in the wake of the visit, Jacob wrote a short note to Isabelle as soon as his guests departed.

> *Soon, I shall be able to afford to buy a small house. I have already inspected one on avenue Le Coq d'Or, not far from Hugo's street. It is a clean and pleasant dwelling, with views of the town from the upper windows. It has a plumbed sink on the public water system. I am hoping that you will like it as much as I do.*

The letter, with its implied promise, sat on the table while he nodded off from the effects of the wine. When he awoke, his eyes fell on the letter, and he blew out his lips in frustration. It would be so much easier if I could simply pop it in the post!

A YEAR AFTER SENDING Isabelle to live with her aunt, Madame Ouellet's displeasure continued unabated, the old woman's frosty demeanour unmoved by pleas from Marguerite, from Hugo, from Jules, and from her sisters to end her youngest daughter's exile. 'She may return when she promises to abandon this foolish infatuation of hers, and not before,' she declared, her mouth set in haughty disdain.

Although publicly adamant in her refusal, privately she longed for the estrangement to be mended, and to welcome her daughter back home with forgiving arms. But a fear of scandal, concern for Isabelle's vulnerability, and above all, the Church's disapproval of any liaison between a Catholic and a Protestant, demanded the exile continue. Thus, when her nephew Hugo came to visit, bursting with news of Jacob's sudden elevation to the ranks of the *bourgeoisie*, she still refused to budge, dismissing the news as irrelevant to his continuing status as non-Frenchman, non-Catholic and, horror!—orphan.

'How can he be an orphan, aunt? Just because he cannot remember his family does not mean they do not exist.'

'Not to be remembered is not to exist,' she pronounced.

'He now speaks very commendable French. And would, I'm sure, be willing to entertain adopting the faith.'

'How very strange your words are! "Entertain … adopt." Is Catholicism a foundling to be taken pity on?'

'Now, aunt. You know I did not mean—'

'Really Hugo. From you, of all people. I remember how proud your mother was when it was thought you would take Holy Orders. More tea?' She held the teapot aloft.

'Please. Thank you, aunt.' He held out his cup, wondering what words might convince her of Jacob's sincerity. 'He has observed your wish not to communicate with Isabelle. Is that not worth something?'

'I would expect no less. Even a freethinker may lay claim to morals.' She hesitated over the teacup. 'You are quite certain—that they are not in contact?'

'I am. He has given me his assurances on several occasions. Why? Does Aunt Jeanne say differently?'

'She does not,' Madame Ouellet conceded, setting down the cup. 'At least one may hope he is not a liar.'

'Far from it!' protested Hugo. 'Jacob is an honest man. If only you would be willing to meet and talk with him, I'm sure you would find him a decent person who sincerely loves and respects your daughter.'

'Enough to make shameless love to her in a public park?'

'He was new to the city, he didn't understand our ways. And can he be blamed for that?'

'Another biscuit?' She held up the plate.

'Aunt, please.'

'If he converts to the true faith. If he agrees to abide by the strictest rules of conduct, then I may be willing to consider.' She nibbled on the biscuit, her teeth delicately severing the shortbread.

'And Marguerite—the wedding plans go well?' he asked, changing the subject before she could change her mind.

Her features softened. 'She is like a busy bee, buzzing from one thing to another!'

'And the bishop will perform the ceremony?'

'Of course. Although he had the temerity to propose the curé. Can you imagine?' Her eyebrows rose at the thought.

'Surely, Isabelle will be allowed to attend?'

Madame Ouellet dunked her biscuit in the tea, staring at the sodden wafer before answering with a vague murmur that might have meant anything.

'She is unmovable on the subject,' Hugo complained to Josette on his return home. 'She lists condition after condition. Jacob must be French. He must be Catholic. He must, somehow, produce a family.'

'And his new prospects mean nothing?' Josette set down her embroidery.

'He could be the richest man in New France and still his lack of faith would be held against him!' Exasperated, Hugo ran a hand through his thick hair.

'It wasn't so long ago, dearest, that you yourself would have shunned the companionship of a Protestant.'

'That was then. I have learned since. Besides, Jacob is different.'

'How so?'

'He is not so much a Protestant as a …' He frowned, searching for the apt word.

'A man who has forgotten God?' she suggested.

'Good heavens!' He stared at her. 'What makes you say such a ghastly thing?'

'He forgets everything else.' She tugged at a stitch. 'Why not his faith?'

'He is Protestant. We have established that fact,' he said, his voice irritable.

'We have? How?' She pulled the needle and thread.

'If he were a fellow Catholic, I would sense it,' he said, and stood up to take off his jacket as she opened her mouth to object. 'Is dinner ready?'

MADAME OUELLET'S RESOLVE FALTERED only when Marguerite brought her own formidable artillery to the field as the two sat having breakfast a month before the planned nuptials. After some desultory conversation about invitations and dresses, Marguerite deployed her forces. 'Mama,' she said, her voice careful yet determined, 'you realise that it is unthinkable that I should get married and not have Isabelle there to act as my bridesmaid?'

Madame Ouellet buttered a second slice of toast, her lips pursed.

'Mama?'

'She has disobeyed my wishes, and *still* will not renounce this foolish infatuation.'

'Has this nonsense not gone on for long enough?'

'Nonsense you call it?' Her mother sniffed. 'Since when is wilful and continuing disobedience a matter of nonsense?'

Marguerite brought the artillery to bear, her voice as determined as her mother's. 'If Isabelle is not there, I will not get married.'

Her mother spread sliced egg on the toast, her face creased with annoyance. 'I am exhausted by the entire affair!'

'Then end it! Please mama, I beg you.'

Madame Ouellet set down the toast to blow her nose. 'What do the wishes of a widowed mother count for these days?'

Sensing a weakness, Marguerite wheeled out the reserves in a flanking movement. 'Father would be horrified at what has happened. Can you imagine! He would urge you to forgive and to mend this estrangement. You know I am right.'

Her mother made a grudging sound as she bit off a piece of toast.

'Admit it mother. You are as anxious to see her as I am.'

Suddenly overcome with emotion, the elderly lady trembled with tears, her own longing for her daughter as moist as the toast in her mouth. 'I do miss her!'

'Then end this quarrel.' Tears brimmed in Marguerite's eyes as she observed the toll the estrangement had taken on her mother. 'I know it affects Isabelle as much as it does you. Will you permit her to return?'

Her mother nodded in surrender, too overcome too speak.

'You will? Oh Mama!' Jumping up from her chair, Marguerite flung her arms around the elderly lady, raining kisses on her head. 'I shall write to her at once! She will be so happy.' Then, taking advantage of the moment, she fired the grapeshot. 'I intend also to invite monsieur Wheeler to the wedding.'

'Invite the devil if you wish!' Her mother blew her nose again, the last of her resistance crumbling to ashes.

ON SATURDAY, JACOB LEFT work early and took a tram to the outskirts of the city. Dismounting at the last stop, he walked a mile and a half through the verdant woods, a bulging sackcloth bag slung around his shoulder. A lumber wagon approached from the opposite direction, and he stood aside to let it pass, lifting his cap in response to the driver's hail. Whistling, he continued, cutting through the trees from the wagon path while enjoying the fresh scents of pine and maple.

He found the midwife bent over a shrub, tugging at it and muttering to herself. She glanced up at his greeting.

'Ghost Bear! So, you have returned.' She wiped sweat from her brow as she blinked in the sunlight. In spite of the warm day, she wore the familiar patterned blanket around her shoulders. Her eyes took in the bag over his shoulder. 'You have brought me gifts?'

'Of course!' He chuckled, glad to see her again.

Inside the cabin he took in the familiar smells, glancing at the floor near the hearth where his bed used to be. Reaching into the bag, he took out a bottle of whisky, followed by another, and then a bottle of wine. 'And this …' He took out a loaf of fresh bread, followed by a box of chocolates, and another of savoury and sweet pastries. The latter caused her to coo with pleasure. Picking up a pastry, she ate it with gusto, humming with delight and sinking into the rocker as she eyed a second confection.

He poured two generous shots of whisky as her fingers hovered between a *canelé* and a chocolate éclair.

'To your health.' He raised the glass, unsurprised to see that she had not waited for the toast, having drained the whisky in a gulp. She chose the éclair, smacking her lips as she savoured the rich taste.

He spent most of the next half-hour telling her about his business success, the account interesting her not one whit as she passed over the subject.

'Tell me of your love life,' she said. 'Do you need a potion?' She indicated the overflowing shelves. 'I have fresh prickly pear root.'

He cleared his throat before answering, discomforted as always by her frank way of speaking. 'I have no love life,' he admitted. 'Isabelle—the young woman I told you about—is still in exile.' The midwife made a scoffing sound in reply.

He rationed himself on the whisky as the afternoon wore on, the midwife happy to sit and smoke her pipe as a warm breeze blew the scent of pine through the open door.

'You never did tell me what those figures mean,' he said, his gaze turning to the soot-blackened deerskin tacked above the fireplace.

'They do not mean anything,' she said. 'They tell a story.'

'What story?'

'I forget.' She puffed contentedly on the pipe.

Well used to her peculiarities, he got up to inspect the hide, the images smudged by smoke.

'What do you see, Ghost Bear?'

'Bunch of Indians, I guess.' He leaned in closer to pick out the blackened figures. '…Waving spears at a buffalo or something. Or maybe they are worshipping it?' He turned to her for elucidation.

'Do you know the buffalo?' she asked.

'Know it? How in tar would I know it?'

'It has a brother.'

He sighed. 'Don't go getting all Indian on me. As far as I know I've never even seen a buffalo.'

'There was one in your holy book.'

'My holy …' He blinked. 'You mean the sketch? *That* buffalo?' She said nothing, her eyes on him as she smoked.

He sat down again, feeling the sensation of going around in circles.

'Why do you hide from your friend, the pale Frenchman?'

'Hide?' He furrowed his brow at the question. 'How am I hiding?'

'Does he know about your letters to his cousin?'

'Heavens to a crow!' He stared in shock. 'How do you know about that?'

She chuckled, showing her blackened teeth, but made no reply.

He frowned, mystified as to where she might have obtained the information. 'You have been talking to Marguerite? Or perhaps Josette? Do they even know you?'

She blew out smoke, ignoring the question.

Suddenly curious he leaned forward. 'Do you know what will happen? Will her mother come around to me?'

'Do I have eyes like an owl that can see into the future?' Her voice was offended.

'Pardon, I thought …' He shrugged. 'I don't know what I was thinking.'

She chuckled with glee at his woebegone expression, her fat rolls shaking. 'Do not be like a miserable Blackfoot with the whisky!'

She pushed the empty glass back across the table, her smooth brown face crinkling with mischief. Humming to herself, she pulled a mixing bowl towards her and sampled the contents. Wincing at the taste, she got up and took down a jar from the shelf. Opening it, she added a pinch of ground herbs to the compound. She began to chant softly, her eyes closed as she stirred the mix with a spoon. 'Soon you will have a visitor,' she said, opening her eyes.

'Who? Hugo?'

'Not the Frenchman.' She added more herbs to the bowl.

'Then who?'

'Someone else.'

'The deputy?'

She pointed a finger to her ear, indicating her deafness had returned.

It was still light and feeling energetic he decided against taking the bus from the city limits, walking all the way back to rue des Martyrs. On opening the door to his room, he was surprised to find a note slipped underneath. He opened it, recognising the handwriting as Hugo's. *'Dear Jacob. Sorry to have missed you. I came by with news. It's Isabelle. She's coming home!'*

19

A Return Home

BESIDE HERSELF WITH EXCITEMENT, Isabelle pressed her face to the window as the train chugged into Gaston Tremblay station. She glimpsed Marguerite eagerly scanning each car as the train steamed slowly alongside the platform. 'Marguerite! Yoo-hoo!' She signalled frantically to catch her sister's attention.

'She sees me!' Tears of happiness sprang to her eyes as Marguerite shrieked her name while waving madly at the carriage.

'Is your mother with her?' asked aunt Jeanne, shading her eyes as she peered through the window.

'I don't see her.' Disappointment tempered Isabelle's excitement as she searched the faces of those gathered on the platform.

'Never mind. I am sure she is anxiously awaiting you at home.'

The train had no sooner shuddered to a halt than Isabelle jumped down into her sister's embrace. 'Marguerite!'

'Isabelle, dearest! You have returned to us!' Weeping and laughing, Marguerite showered her with kisses. 'And how you've grown! You have become a woman!'

'Welcome home, Isabelle.' Dominic stepped forward, a grin on his face. He kissed Isabelle on both cheeks as Marguerite and Jeanne embraced.

'Where is Jacob?' Isabelle searched among the waiting faces, an eager smile on her face.

The first word out of her mouth! Marguerite's eyes widened in affected shock. 'He isn't here, sweet pea. And you mustn't see him before the wedding. I promised mama.'

'Oh!' Isabelle's face fell at the news.

'Don't look so woeful.' Marguerite clutched her arm. 'Mama is dying to see you!'

'She is?'

'Of course, sillykins!'

'And how is mama?' she asked, still getting over her disappointment at not seeing Jacob.

'She is herself.' Margaret laughed merrily, her eyes sparkling. 'Come!'

THE TWO PLIED EACH other with questions on the cab ride home, Isabelle quizzing Marguerite on every detail of her wedding plans while Marguerite insisted on learning of the latest Montreal fashions. Dominic and Jeanne sat on the opposite seat, smiling as they tried to follow along. The day was cloudy, patches of bright sunshine interspersed with drifting cloud shadow.

'Everything looks different.' Isabelle peered out the window as the horse clip-clopped through the familiar streets, 'yet just the same.'

'That is because you are different and yet the same!' Marguerite kissed Isabelle's cheek. She had not let go of her arm the entire journey.

'Have you seen our house?'

'Which house? What are you talking about?'

'The house Jacob has bought for us? You know, the one on avenue Le Coq d'Or?'

Marguerite glanced at Jeanne, who stared back, a look of alarm on her face. 'I've absolutely no idea what you are talking about.' She squeezed Isabelle's arm in warning. 'Now, tell me about the hats the ladies are wearing in Montreal.'

Suddenly aware of the danger, Isabelle nervously laughed off the remark. 'I am joking, dear sister! Now, about the hats …'

The cab pulled up outside the house and Isabelle's excitement turned to nerves. She glanced at Marguerite for reassurance.

'Go on! She's breathless to see you.' Her sister pushed her out of the carriage door.

She stood outside the familiar front door, her heart in her mouth with anxiety. Suddenly the door opened, and her mother was standing there, the paleness of her cheeks emphasised by pink rouge.

'Isabelle!' The elderly woman's voice trembled as she beheld her daughter.

'Mama!' Flinging herself into her mother's embrace, she burst into tears.

DESPITE HER JOY AND relief at being home again and the excitement of her sister's approaching nuptials, the atmosphere inside the house over the next few days was strained in spite of the calming presence of her Aunt Jeanne. Isabelle and her mother treated each other with elaborate yet respectful courtesy while holding their tongues, as if by mutual unspoken agreement, on the explosive subject that threatened the fragile accord.

'Am I forbidden to say his name!' Isabelle hissed to her sister at one point, her mother having made abundantly clear that any mention of

Jacob was unwelcome, no matter how tentatively Isabelle tried to broach the subject.

'Give her time, sweetness. She is still getting used to having you home again.'

'How much time does she need—a century?'

They were sitting in Marguerite's bedroom with the door closed as they discussed the wedding, and Jacob; the wedding dress, and Jacob; the reception, and Jacob, until Marguerite finally exclaimed in exasperation. 'Is Jacob all you can think of?'

'I'm sorry,' said Isabelle, her face contrite. 'I know it is your wedding we should be discussing, but I simply must see him. It's unfair, being so close and after all this time—almost a year!' Tears sprang to her eyes.

'Isabelle, you promised. And you nearly gave the game away. Did you not see Aunt Jeanne's face when you mentioned the house? I'm sure she caught on. It is a blessing she adores you. Now, please, no more mention of Jacob, for an hour at least!'

'I didn't promise. You did.'

'On *your* behalf. Now you must swear not to upset mama by seeking out Jacob. Promise?'

'And what if I bump into him on the street—by accident?'

'No accidents!' Marguerite gave Isabelle a peck on the cheek. 'Promise?' Her eyes searched for a reply.

'Well then, when can I see him?'

Marguerite blew out an exasperated sigh. 'I told you—at the wedding. Not before. Not this minute, not this hour, nor, indeed, tomorrow or the day after.' She put on a stern expression. 'Agreed? Good. Now turn your mind from Jacob and look at this seating plan. I have seated Madame Rosineau next to Sophia Gallois. Will that work? Or will they scratch each other's eyes out?'

On Friday, Isabelle accompanied her mother, sister and aunt to confession, the four women walking in linked pairs through the streets to the cathedral. While waiting her turn to enter the confessional, Isabelle lit a candle and said a prayer for Jacob. 'Blessed Mother, let me see him soon!' When Marguerite emerged from the confessional, shortly after going in, it was Isabelle's turn to enter the darkened booth. Kneeling, she crossed herself and recited the familiar invocation. 'Bless me Father, for I have sinned, and it is four days since my last confession.'

'And what sins have you committed, my daughter?'

She barely registered the voice of the curé as she bowed her head. 'Disobedience, Father.'

'Yes?'

'I think of my fiancé, even though it troubles my mother.'

'It is natural to think of a fiancé. Why does this trouble your mother?'

'He is not my fiancé—not in name.'

'Then what is he? Is your relationship sinful?'

'No! It is just that my mother forbids me to see him.'

'And you disobey her in this?'

'No—but I wish too.'

'The Bible commands us to honour our mother and father.'

'I do!'

'And what does your father say in this?'

'He has passed away.' She crossed herself with the words.

'Then you must be especially careful to honour your mother's wishes.'

'And not see Jac—my fiancé?'

'If that is what she commands.'

'But I love him!'

There came a silence before the shadowy voice beyond the grille resumed. 'Have you indulged in any unlawful relations?'

'No!' She was certain they heard the cry beyond the confessional.

'Is this man of upright character?'

'Yes! He is very upright!' She hesitated. 'But he is not Catholic.' She listened for the effect of the admission.

'Then what is he?' The voice sounded puzzled.

'He is Protestant, I think.'

'You think?'

She sighed. 'It is complicated.'

'Your mother is concerned for your spiritual welfare and—'

'But love cannot be wrong!'

'You are certain you love him?'

'With my whole heart!' Her voice broke.

'Nevertheless, it is your solemn Catholic duty to obey your mother's wishes. You say that he is not a Catholic? That is troubling to the Church and a matter of grave concern. Many an innocent girl has been led astray by her heart. Say a rosary and beg God's forgiveness for your disobedience. May the Blessed Virgin Mary and all the saints help you to grow in holiness; and may Jesus Christ grant you eternal life. Go, my daughter, and sin no more.'

With a heavy heart, she left the confessional and knelt at the altar to recite the rosary. She looked up tearfully at the figure hanging on the crucifix. In the candle-lit shadows she was uncertain if the expression on the plaster face was grieving for, or forgiving of, her disobedience. 'Please, dear Jesus, my heart lies with Jacob. You would approve of him if you—I will try to bring him into the holy church after we are married.'

'Amen,' she finished, and rose to her feet. Genuflecting, she crossed herself. She lingered as she thought of Jacob, whereupon she bobbed again and kissed the rosary beads clutched between her fingers.

RELIEVED TO HAVE HER daughter back, but unwilling to relax her ban on contact with, or mention, even, of Jacob, Madam Ouellet said a silent prayer that her daughter's mad infatuation with the Englishman would soon end. Seated downstairs in the parlour conversing with her cousin over a glass of wine, she gave passionate vent to her emotions, bemoaning the fact that the wretched fellow had ever ventured into New France.

'Why could he not have lost his way to Montreal! It's all a frightful mess. And he is entirely to blame. What is your opinion, cousin?'

Jeanne measured her silence over the wine glass before replying, her voice carefully neutral. 'Over the past year I have gotten to know my niece very well. She is utterly delightful, and as strongminded as yourself, Odile.' She tipped the glass, studying the wine. 'Has it ever occurred to you that what you term infatuation may, in fact, be something else? I ask you to consider the possibility as your daughter's happiness seems deeply linked to this man. I am convinced that her affections for him are genuine.'

'Really! I had expected better from you.' Madame Ouellet sucked her breath in dismay. 'Do you not realise that the man is not French, not Catholic, and not of sound mind?'

'Nevertheless, her heart seems set on him. And the more you try to interfere …'

'This affair will be the death of me.' The older woman blew her nose, her eyes moist.

'Do not torment yourself, cousin. Honestly, when you first sent Isabelle to me, I was willing to be your accomplice in the matter. But now, after observing her, and after becoming better acquainted with her hopes, I find myself in sympathy with her feelings.'

The declaration provoked a flutter of horror. 'You, too!'

'What does one do when confronted by a charging bull?' asked Jeanne, quoting one of her father's favourite sayings.

'A charging bull? Good heavens what does that have to do with any-thing?' Madame Ouellet sniffed, a waspish look on her face.

'The answer is that when confronted with a charging bull one steps aside. To do otherwise is to court disaster. Do you understand me?'

'Is that what you call it—this mad infatuation—a charging bull?'

'You will get trampled, I fear, unless you accept it for what it really is.'

'And what is that?' The question was accompanied by a severe glance.

'Love, my dear cousin.'

'Love!' Madam Ouellet stared as if her cousin had lost her wits. 'How can it be love? She is scarcely more than a child!'

'She is a young woman. One who knows her own heart and mind. She will not be deterred. That is plain to see. Better to let the affair run its course. If it is an infatuation, as you insist on calling it, then it will burn out of its own accord.'

They heard a door open upstairs and the sound of laughter as Isabelle and Marguerite descended the stairs. Jeanne made eyes at her cousin that said, *'Remember, Odile. A charging bull!'*

20

A Reunion and an Estrangement

NOW THAT ISABELLE HAD returned—and so close!—Jacob was beside himself with the desire to see her again and sweep her into his arms. The love-by-correspondence had ignited an even greater passion within his breast—the cruel separation stoking the flames of his longing to such an inferno that he felt it might consume him if he did not see her upon the very instant. With fuming impatience, he acceded to Hugo's appeal to observe her mother's wishes and restrain himself until the day of her sister's nuptials.

'Wait but just two weeks for the wedding day,' Hugo had urged. 'Then you may legitimately see and speak to her, and your patience will receive its just reward.'

To preserve his sanity, he exhausted himself through long days at the factory followed by lengthy rambles through the city streets, his footsteps taking him ever closer to rue Mercier in spite of his pledge. There is no breaking my promise should I accidently encounter her, he reasoned, becoming bolder and more desperate as the days passed.

One afternoon, as dusk fell and gas lamps were lit along the street, his footsteps led him yet again to rue Mercier. In an agony of suspense, he walked the footpath on the opposite side to her house, casting yearning glances up at the darkened bedroom window.

As he passed back—this time on her side of the street—a light came on and he could not prevent himself from stopping, catching his breath as a shadow—her shadow!—passed behind the lace curtains. He stood with bated breath, his heart pounding as he looked up. *Isabelle!* The hushed, desperate plea flew upwards in the warm starry night. The shadow appeared once again behind the curtain. *Isabelle!* Surely, she heard him, heart calling to heart!

A cough disturbed his vigil. 'Pardon!' He stepped aside to allow a man to pass. The man gave a look that betokened distrust. He walked three or four houses past where Jacob stood before turning into his own house. His hand on the doorknob, he turned, fixing Jacob a stare that left no doubt as to his suspicions.

'Good night!' called out Jacob and turned on his heel to walk away, berating himself for his folly. He could call the police—have me arrested on suspicion. Her mother would go mad! What am I doing?

It might have comforted—or further dejected him—to know that, soon after his departure, the beloved herself pulled back the curtains to gaze yearningly into the silent street, hoping against hope that her Jacob might step forth from the shadows to declare his earnest, undying love—Romeo to her Juliet!

After watching for a while she dropped the curtain and sat on the bed, thoroughly miserable yet immeasurably thrilled at the prospect of seeing the beloved in less than two weeks. Following prayers, she crawled beneath the sheets, her heart reaching out across the city rooftops to rue des Martyrs. 'Jacob!' she breathed. She turned on her side to watch the full moon trace patterns though the lace curtains. And, like countless maidens before her, she prayed to the orb, albeit in disguise. 'Please, dear Lady, let us be reunited—to never again be parted!'

ONE WEEK BEFORE THE wedding, Hugo and Josette hosted a bridal supper for Marguerite and her intended. Jules Desjardins attended along with Clara, his fiancée, having taken the train from New York. Denis Vachon and his wife Yvette were among the guests, as was Camille Couture, Marguerite's friend from her days at the convent, and her husband René the cheesemaker, notorious for being overly fond of his wine. Claude and Anna Charbonneau sat across from Serge Villeneuve and his wife, Marie. Martin Cloutier and his wife Danielle were quietly bickering with one another, the latter annoyed with his insistence on rushing her toilet.

Isabelle sat with Josette on one side and Josette's sister, Claudette, on the other. Across from them sat Hugo and Andre. The guests of honour, Marguerite and Dominic, sat in the middle of the extended table. All were dressed in the latest fashionable clothes of the French bourgeoisie—the women in silk gowns, the men in lounge suits and shirts with starched collars.

An air of merriment enlivened the table as wine bottles were passed around and glasses refilled.

'A toast!' Hugo stood up, his glass raised. 'To the happy couple. May their days be many and blessed!'

'And may their children always know their father!' mumbled a flushed René Couture, already in his cups after lunching on a bottle of homemade grape wine. A shocked silence from both his wife and the other guests was promptly vanquished by a peal of laughter from Marguerite. 'I would hope!' she chortled, clasping her discomforted fiancé's hand.

As the supper progressed and the hum of conversation and the clink of wine glasses filled the air, Claudette whispered in Isabelle's ear. 'A penny for your thoughts, dear cousin?'

'They are not worth a penny.' Isabelle pulled a face.

'Let me guess.' Claudette, five years older than Isabelle, fixed her with a playful glance. 'One word?' she hazarded. 'Two syllables?' She smiled at Isabelle's blushing protest. 'Biblical?' she continued teasingly. 'The husband of …'

'Rachel!' prompted Hugo, leaning across the table. 'And,' he added mysteriously, 'another.'

'What do you mean, another?' André Petain frowned, trying to recall his scripture.

'Yes! A help for us poor sinners who are not as piously learned as yourself, Hugo,' added Claudette.

'A help?' Hugo thought for a moment and then motioned with his head towards his wife.

'Josette? Jacob was married to a Josette?' Claudette scrunched her nose. 'Are you certain? I don't recall that name from the bible?'

She was interrupted as Josette stood up, tapping her wine glass with a spoon. 'A game!' she announced. 'To help digest the maple pudding!'

'What game?' René Couture, who had dozed off, opened his eyes.

'Hush, dear husband,' his wife said, even as he appeared to nod off again. 'A disquisition! A game of love!'

The announcement drew claps and laughter.

'How is it played, you ask?' Josette touched a delicate hand to her ear, the gesture drawing chuckles. 'It is simple. Camille dearest, pass around the paper and pencils.'

When this had been completed, Josette smiled at the eager faces. 'Good! Now all you need to do is complete the sentence starting with, 'Love is …' followed by a single word, or … if you use two words, then one of them must be an article. Do you understand?'

'No.' Denis Vachon put up his hand. 'What do you mean, an article?'

'For example, Love is … a flower!'

'Denis wishes to know which one is the article!' piped up Jules Desjardin, prompting laughter.

'Dearest, disquisition' is the wrong word,' Hugo pointed out. 'I believe the word you mean is 'apothegm'?'

Loftily ignoring the remark, Josette beamed at the guests. 'Shall we begin? You have one minute! Do not overthink your answer. Spontaneity is truest and best. Hugo, darling, you are appointed timekeeper.'

'But I wish to take part!' he protested, drawing a giggle from Claudette.

'Do so. But keep the time!'

The guests took up their slips of paper, casting humorous glances at each other as they wrote. Camille Couture nudged her husband awake and placed a pencil in his hand, which he stared at in befuddlement.

'Start!' Hugo announced, his eye on the mantel clock. And then, a minute later, 'Pencils down!'

'I shall begin,' said Josette, 'followed by Hugo as timekeeper and so forth around the table.' She drew herself up in the chair as her eyes surveyed the guests in a dramatic pause. 'Love is … a tyrant!' The comment drew hoots and applause.

'Too true!'

'Hugo, old pear, she means you!'

'Your turn, dear tyrant,' said Josette, sitting down, her eyes sparkling with mischief.

'Tyrant?'

'Go on! We haven't got all night.' She poked him under the table.

'Very well.' Clearing his throat, Hugo gazed around the table. 'Love is holy,' he pronounced, his voice solemn. The guests looked at each other as Hugo continued, '… and being so, is thus proof of God's grace.'

The contribution drew silence before a loud exaggerated groan issued from Jules, followed by a roll of the eyes from Josette that inspired guffaws.

'I call foul!' Denis Vachon slapped the table, making the cutlery jump.

'Too many words!' ruled Josette. 'We are after apothegms, not disquisitions.'

'But the definition itself met the rule—' Hugo's protest was cut off by his wife.

'Next!'

'Love is undying!' declared Danielle Cloutier, drawing applause.

'Love is a nightingale!' followed her husband, determined not to be outdone.

The game went on, around the table until reaching Marguerite. 'Love,' she said, drawing her lips into a flirtatious pout as she regarded her besotted fiancé, 'is willing!'

The remark drew delighted gasps—and a toast from Jules.

'Bravo, cousin!'

'What does it mean?' Yvette Vachon looked confused.

'Next!' Josette clapped her hands as eyes turned to Camille Couture.

'Love,' she said softly, 'is understanding.'

The pronouncement drew respectful murmurs as eyes turned to her dozing husband.

'Love,' declared Yvette Vachon, a triumphant smile on her face, 'is divine!'

'We bob before such wisdom!' Jules drew laughter as he jumped to his feet and bent in an elaborate bow.

'What I said!' protested Hugo, 'since divinity is holiness and thus a gift of Grace.'

'Oh, hush, Hugo! You've had your turn.'

'Love is a rose, a beautiful rose—always in bloom,' contributed Anna Charbonneau to applause.

'Love is a song,' declared Marie Villeneuve with a smile at her husband, 'that is always in the heart!'

'Love is a strong wine that never runs dry,' said her husband, Serge, Hugo's attempted protest drowned by laughter.

And so the game worked its way around to Isabelle who sat with parted lips, a flush on her cheeks.

'What have you written?' Thinking her cousin shy, Claudette leaned over and picked up Isabelle's slip of paper as an expectant hush fell over the table. 'Oh! It's blank.'

'The winner!' declared Jules merrily. 'The true face of love!'

'Shhh! Let her speak.'

'Do you wish to pass, cousin?' asked Josette.

'No.' Isabelle cleared her throat. 'Love,' she whispered, 'is Jacob.'

'Who?' asked someone.

In the confused silence, the remark was trumped by a slurred declaration from René Couture, who had awoken again. 'Love?' he called out, lurching to his feet and spilling his glass of wine, 'is a strumpet!' He glared at the startled faces, a trickle of wine dribbling from his mouth as his mortified wife tugged at him to sit down.

'Did he say trumpet?' asked Jules, a mock hand to his ear. At which point the table roared with laughter.

THE MID-SUMMER SKY WAS warm and blue as the bells tolled. Trembling with anticipation, Isabelle waited in the vestibule with her sister and mother and uncles and aunts. The cathedral was full of friends and relatives, as gaily bedecked as the happy day itself. Marguerite wore a white silk gown she had sewn herself, the artfully plain style ornamented with a lace bodice and sleeves. Her hat had a folded brim with a short gauze veil pinned to it. She carried a wedding bouquet of lavender, jasmine and roses, which she fiddled with constantly.

'You look positively angelic.' Isabelle, dressed in a white, cotton gauze gown embroidered with floral bouquets, brushed a hair into place. 'Dominic's eyes will pop out of his head.'

'They had better! Did you see Jacob?'

Isabelle put on an aloof face, her lips crimped together as she refused to answer.

'Don't deny! I saw you earlier peeping out from the carriage.'

Isabelle collapsed into a nervous giggle. 'Big eyes!'

'Was he there? Did you see him?'

'I couldn't tell. So many people were coming in.' She made a fretful sound. 'It's been so long. I can't wait to see him again. What if he doesn't come?' A look of horror crossed her face at the thought. 'What if he stays away—on account of mama?'

'I'm certain he's inside.' Marguerite's voice was reassuring. 'Probably with Hugo and Josette for protection.' She smiled in sympathy. 'Poor Isabelle. Your time will come.' She used a finger to wipe away a tear on her sister's cheek. 'No tears! it's bad luck. How does my hat look?'

'Perfect! as are you. And they are tears of happiness!' Isabelle kissed her sister.

Their mother glanced back, her normally severe features softening as she beheld Marguerite. Madame Ouellet wore a floral hat and a dark coat over her best dress. Her gloved hands held a rosary. Delphine and Désirée, together with their husbands, stood beside her. Jeanne stood close behind, arm-in-arm with her husband, who had arrived from Montreal the evening before.

The organ swelled and the two sisters exchanged a breathless glance. Their Uncle Frédérick turned and mouthed the word, 'Soon!' Next moment, the bishop and the curé, both clad in white chasubles—the bishop's embroidered with a gold brocade—appeared in the doorway. 'Are we ready?' asked the curé, his eyes taking in the bridal party.

Beaming, Uncle Henri held out his arm to Marguerite. 'A vision!' he pronounced. Uncle Frédérick took the bride's other arm The entrance hymn began and smiling faces turned to greet the bride as the bishop led the procession down the nave towards the high altar.

Although trying her best to be demure, Isabelle's eyes darted from side to side as the processional continued. *Where is he?* She arched her eyebrows to Danielle Cloutier and gave a tiny wave of her hand to Marie Villeneuve, her eyes searching the happy faces. *Surely, he came. Was he not as desperate to see her as she was him?*

And then! Her heart leapt as her eyes picked him out standing next to Hugo and Josette. He had a look of great eagerness on his face as he gazed ardently back at her. '*Jacob!*' she mouthed, thrilled to at last see him again. *He looks so handsome!* His eyes were locked on hers as she passed, his lips slightly open as though breathless. Hugo and Josette smiled at her, but she hardly noticed, her eyes filled with the beloved.

'Oh!' She murmured an apology as she bumped into Uncle Henri where the bridal party had stopped in the chancel. Dominic and his best man stood waiting on the altar steps, the groom beaming with pride. Sunlight streamed through the stained-glass windows. The organ fell silent, and the bishop gave the greeting.

Isabelle felt dizzy and took a deep breath, inhaling the smell of incense. She risked turning her head to glance at the pews and saw Jacob, his gaze still fixed on her. She trembled and felt she might faint with intense desire. She squeezed her wrist to control the rapid beating of her heart. As the bishop continued, her thoughts leapt forward, imagining Jacob and herself in the stained-glass light, waiting to be joined in solemn and ecstatic union—like that of Gaston Pierre and his beloved Lisette! She gave an involuntary moan at the thought, drawing a sharp glance from her mother.

Embarrassed, she bowed her head and stared at her shoe as the guests stood for the Gathering Rite. The Bishop raised a hand in blessing. 'Heavenly Father. You have ordained that the sacrament of marriage be a holy mystery, a metaphor of Christ's love for his church ...'

The guests sat down again as the bishop gave the first reading. Marguerite glanced at Isabelle—eyes sparkling behind the veil, a look of ... amusement! on her lips that somehow recalled her definition of love at the supper party. Isabelle barely restrained herself from laughing out loud at the recollection. Placing a hand over her mouth, she pretended to cough.

And after, when they were gathered on the steps to congratulate the radiant Marguerite and her proud husband, she searched for Jacob, impatient to see him. And there he was!—pushing eagerly through the throng of well-wishers toward her.

'Jacob!' She was tongue-tied, incapable of anything but gazing into his eyes.

'Isabelle!' He clasped her hand, his eyes so full of desire that she felt she might swoon. And then, impulsively, and to the shock and horror of her watching mother, she rose up on her toes and kissed him full on the mouth.

'I THOUGHT HER MOTHER would have a heart attack!' giggled Josette as they walked home through the streets, the scandal of the very public kiss having dominated the aftermath of the wedding.

'It was a sight to behold.' Hugo shook his head, uncertain whether to be chagrined or shocked by his cousin's impulsive reaction to seeing Jacob. 'Jacob, what do you think?' he asked for the tenth time that night.

'I'm just over the moon she was happy to see me.' Heady with joy, Jacob danced a wine-affected waltz step, an imaginary Isabelle in his arms.

'And did you expect anything else?' teased Josette.

The electric lights guided their steps to rue Henri Lamont where they would part ways. The night was warm and balmy, a perfect end to a perfect day. Jacob felt like shouting out his love, his heart as rapturous as a warbling bird.

'You could hardly take your eyes off her the entire service.' Hugo laid a fond hand on his shoulder. 'All that waiting was worth it,' he added.

'And all those letters—' Josette halted, a stricken look on her face.

'What letters?' Hugo's voice was humorous, as he turned to his wife. 'What letters are you—' He stopped as he took in his wife's expression. Perplexed, he turned to Jacob. 'What letters is she talking about?' His eyes widened. 'Did you communicate with my cousin—in spite of your solemn promise?'

'I didn't exactly promise,' demurred Jacob, the words unconvincing, even to himself.

'But you did! You gave me your word!'

'Calm yourself, dear Hugo. It was innocent. Two people in love.'

Hugo spun to face his wife. 'You knew!'

'A few notes, only. Hardly letters at all.' She tried to make light of the matter, her face pale.

As the full enormity of the deception dawned on him, a horrified Hugo stared accusingly at Jacob. 'I gave my solemn assurances to Isabelle's mother—on your behalf!'

'It was, as your wife said, entirely innocent. Nothing for anyone to be concerned about.'

'Innocent?' Hugo's voice rose with astonishment. 'Do you not understand? You have lied to me—as well as to Isabelle's mother!'

'Darling.' His wife caught at his arm. 'Calm yourself. This is the wine talking.'

'We meant no harm—simply to console each other. You must understand, we were both desperate at being apart.'

'But that is not the point!' Hugo's voice cracked as a growing sense of outrage began to displace his shock at the revelation. 'You swore to me that you would not contact my cousin—and I trusted you! I vouched for you with her mother. And you lied!' He gasped as the full import struck him. 'My God, you were in communication all along!' A passer-by lingered, pretending to examine a shop window.

'And how did you pass the messages along, given that—' Hugo cast a furious look at his wife. 'You! You aided and abetted the deception!'

'Hugo do control yourself. There are people—'

'Not a word, I pray you!' Hugo turned back to confront Jacob his face livid. 'How could you lie to me like that!'

'I am truly sorry Hugo.' Jacob's voice was contrite, his happiness of but a moment ago thoroughly deflated.

'No doubt you are!' Hugo's face was grim. 'But not as sorry as I am. You have deceived me—and enlisted my wife into the deception. Did you enjoy making a fool of me?'

'Hugo. Please let us not quarrel and spoil a joyous day,' begged Josette.

'Hugo, can we not discuss this tomorrow? We are both tired and—'

'What is there to discuss?' Hugo grabbed his wife's hand. 'Come Josette!' He stormed off, dragging a protesting Josette along with him, the ruins of his friendship with Jacob lying strewn like so much confetti in his wake.

21

A Matter of Faith

THE DAY AFTER THE quarrel, Jacob wrote a letter of abject apology, accepting full blame for the deception and pledging to do his utmost to regain Hugo's trust and so repair the breach in their friendship. To his great disappointment, Hugo replied via a short note acknowledging Jacob's regret but affirming the impossibility of maintaining a friendship 'given such a blatant and calculated betrayal of trust.'

Remorse weighed heavily on Jacob even as the responsibilities of his new position made ever greater demands on his time and energy. A month previously, his employers had made a successful bid for a tender issued by the Plattsburg public transportation department across the US border.

'Ten omnibuses!' Dwight jubilantly announced as he flourished the acceptance letter. 'I told you it was worth the expense!'

That expense had included a brief trip south—Jacob's first foray into the land of his birth in three years—to meet with his employers as they wined and dined the officials involved in assessing the bids. The private dinner included a bevy of attractive women brought in from Albany by his employers for 'sociability'. As the transport commissioner buried his face in a young woman's bosom, Selt winked at Jacob. 'It ain't the hook that lands the fish, but the fly.'

Before leaving, Jacob walked briefly around the populous streets, imbibing the sights and sounds of the newly incorporated city. 'I felt quite French,' he admitted to Dwight on his return. 'And then, when I came back, I felt quite American as it all caught up with me again.'

Quite what the 'all' constituted, he was unsure, other than experiencing a pang of regret at being unable to discuss the experience with his erstwhile friend. Frustrated by Hugo's continuing refusal to accept his apology, he was pondering other avenues of reaching out when he bumped into Denis Vachon while walking through the Lower Town.

'Denis!' He stretched out a hand in anticipation. And then it occurred to him that Vachon might be aware of the quarrel and the deception that caused it. He hesitated, searching the other's face.

'Jacob!' Vachon grinned broadly, his cheerful manner a relief as he warmly shook the extended hand. 'What's this I hear about you and Saint Hugo!'

'So you heard?' he asked, wondering how intimately Vachon was acquainted with the details.

'Only what Yvette tells me—from Josette.' Vachon smirked, seemingly amused by the incident.

'It is most unfortunate.'

'He'll get over it. What is a little deception between friends?' Vachon winked. 'Now I must be off. I have an appointment.'

The remark puzzled Jacob for a few days until he put it out of his mind in an effort to make contact with Isabelle. The brief encounter at her sister's wedding had left him desperate for more, like a parched man offered a sip of water. Now that his emissary was unavailable, he was entirely in the dark about Isabelle's circumstances—half dreading that her mother had decided to send her back to exile in Montreal. Thus, it was with mixed eagerness and anxiety that, strolling along Boulevard Champlain, he spotted Marguerite heading towards him on the arm of her husband. He hastened to greet the happy couple, offering profuse congratulations on their recent nuptials.

'Thank you, Jacob. I am so glad you were able to attend.' Marguerite flashed a radiant smile, looking the very picture of marital happiness.

'And Isabelle—she is still here—at your mother's?' he blurted out, noticing a frown cross Dominic's face as he did so.

'Still here, and still desperately missing you.' Marguerite glanced at her husband, the look instantly melting his frown. 'I assure you, she will not be returning to Montreal. Aunt Jeanne has already left with her husband.'

The reassurance brought forth an audible sigh of relief that in turn drew a sympathetic smile from Marguerite. 'I am sure everything will work out as you and Isabelle wish. And what's this I hear about yourself and Father Hugo?' she asked, an amused glint in her eyes. 'Don't worry,' she laughed at his look of dismay. 'This is New France, remember? Everyone knows everyone's business!'

'I wish he would accept my apology and regret,' he said.

'No matter.' She laid a hand on his arm. 'I am half the cause,' she said, looking not the least bothered by the admission. 'He'll get over it. Just give him time.'

Dominic cleared his throat. 'Come dear, we must go. We will be late to meet the Cloutiers.'

'Goodbye Jacob. We will talk again. Do not be discouraged. Remember, all things in time!' With a consoling smile she departed on the arm of her husband.

'In time?' The expression irked him as he continued along the street. Everything is time! Hugo is time. Isabelle is time. The world is time! Disappointed not to hear more encouraging news of Isabelle, he bumped into another pedestrian. With a muttered half-apology, he brushed past the affronted man, leaving him to glare in his wake.

ISABELLE SAT BEFORE THE dressing table brushing her hair while regarding herself in the mirror. *Girding myself before battle.* She grasped a handful of hair and ran the brush through the strands, wondering briefly at the expression as she clutched another handful of hair. She put down the brush, a determined set to her lips as she took a last look in the glass.

'The house seems empty without your sister.' Madame Ouellet looked up from the newspaper as her daughter entered the room. 'I sometimes think—' Her expression abruptly altered as she noted Isabelle was wearing a coat and hat. 'Where are you going?'

'To see Jacob.'

'That man again!' Madame Ouellet flared with anger. 'Has he not caused enough trouble!'

'I miss him, Mama, and I wish to see him.'

Her mother snorted. 'After that scandalous display at the church? Impossible!' She rustled the newspaper and returned to her reading. After a few moments she glanced up. Isabelle had not budged, a pale yet defiant look on her face.

'Did you not hear me?' Her voice was sharp.

'It was a kiss. And nothing I regret.'

'Nothing you regret. Good heavens!' Her mother put a hand to her chest as if to feel her heart. 'I certainly regret it, as did the entire church congregation that witnessed it. Madame Leblanc has talked of nothing else since. I am embarrassed to show my face in the church. I shall have to attend Sainte-Chappelle with that strange Father Boudreau. Now please go and change and make me a pot of tea.' Shuddering at the ghastliness of it all, she returned to the newspaper.

A moment later, she set the newspaper down, her eyebrows raised as she saw Isabelle had not moved. 'Are you paralysed? Go and put on the kettle.'

'I'm sorry you disapprove, Mama. But what happened was no fault of Jacob's.' Isabelle's voice was determined. 'Yvette Vachon will accompany me, as chaperone.'

'As chaperone? Then you have arranged this!'

'I am old enough to make up my own mind as to whom I wish to see.'

Her mother gasped at the impertinence. 'Do you disobey me so wantonly?'

'Jacob is not—'

'Not of our faith! Do you imagine you could ever marry him? Think, girl! He is a freethinker, at best! Will he insist on raising the children as such? You condemn their immortal souls before they are even born. And even if I were to give my permission, you could never marry in the church. The bishop would not permit it.'

'Then I shall marry in a barn.'

Her mother's mouth fell open in shock. 'Good heavens! I might have expected such nonsense from your sister, but from you?'

'Our Saviour was born in a barn, why can't I be married in one?'

'Such blasphemy! Do you hear yourself?' Madame Ouellet regarded her daughter as she might a deranged person. 'There are lots of other young men—Catholic and French available, why him?' The last word was spat from her mouth.

'Because he is the one I choose.'

Too shocked to reply, Madame Ouellet could only open her mouth to form a wordless 'Oh!' At any other time she might have admired her daughter's calm resolution, but in the moment she was rendered speechless by the unprecedented display of defiance. '*What do you do when confronted with a charging bull, Odile?*'

She made a noise in her throat, her nerves intensely brittle as she stared at her rebellious daughter. In the fraught silence the clock struck twice in the hallway. Suddenly feeling every one of her years, she released a pained, drawn-out sigh. 'When will you be back?' Her voice quavered with the question.

'Before supper.' With the same composed manner, Isabelle kissed her mother on the cheek. 'Do not worry, Mama. You have nothing to be concerned about.'

After the front door had closed behind her daughter, Madame Ouellet sat unmoving at the table, her face drawn. I tried. I did everything a mother could do. Her lip trembled as she took in the empty room. She sat there for a quarter hour, her body stiff, her mind blank. She felt cold and drew the shawl around her shoulders. The clock struck the half hour and she started at the sound. The conversation came rushing back and she closed her eyes, her face etched with tiredness. What else could I do? She uttered a loud despairing cry that shattered the silence. The clock ticked in her ears, the noise echoing in the bare hallway. Unable to contain her feelings, she buried her face in her hands and wept.

'YOU HAVE A VISITOR, sir.'

Absorbed in paperwork, Jacob looked up at his secretary. 'Who?' He stood up straightening his tie. 'Who?' he repeated, momentarily confused by the expression on Madame Bisset's face.

And then he was astonished to glimpse Isabelle over his secretary's shoulder, a look of joyous eagerness on her face. 'Isabelle!'

Yvette Vachon appeared behind Isabelle. 'Hello, Jacob,' she said, with an impish smile.

'I don't understand?' He gazed from Isabelle to Madame Bisset, both women regarding him with humorous expectation. Confused, he inclined his head as Isabelle kissed him on the cheek.

'Buy us coffee and cake and I will explain all.' Her eyes sparkled with merriment as she tugged at his arm.

'Madame Bisset, I will be back before—' He glanced at the clock, 'three thirty.' And with that he allowed himself to be tugged out of the office.

Over coffee he listened with incredulous ears as Isabelle told him of the quarrel with her mother, her voice breathless as she poured out the details. Yvette lingered outside the restaurant, inspecting the window of a nearby shop.

'Mama does not approve,' admitted Isabelle, finishing her account, 'But I am confident she will no longer oppose.'

The simple words seemed to Jacob a momentous declaration, like a battlefield general stating his intention to lay down arms.

'Heavens to a crow!' he stuttered, too astonished to think. Before he had time to say more, Isabelle surprised him further by inviting him to tea a week on Sunday, a mischievous smile upon her lips.

'At your mother's?' He stared in disbelief.

'Where else!' She laughed gaily, seemingly divested of a burdensome weight. 'You'll come?' Her eyes lit up with amusement at his bewildered expression. 'She won't bite—I promise!'

'Of course I'll come!' He shook his head, marvelling at the turn of events. 'Of course!'

Feeling giddy with laughter at the incredulous look on his face, Isabelle stroked his hand, her cheeks flushed with reflected light from the window. 'A sign of the Second Coming!' she joked, then reconsidered and whispered a hurried repentance under her breath.

Her delight faltered only when the conversation turned to the falling out with her cousin. 'He is awfully upset with me, too,' she admitted, her face downcast. 'But I know Hugo,' she said. 'He cannot hold a grudge for long. It is not in his nature.'

'I hope so,' he said, before quickly returning to the subject of her mother's miraculous conversion. 'I can hardly believe it!'

Still in a daze a week after the revelation, he completed negotiations for the house on avenue Le Coq d'Or, hurriedly signing the paperwork.

Standing in the unfurnished parlour, he made plans to paint and repair the cracks before taking Isabelle to view it. I shall propose to her in this very room, he decided, making a note also to strip and replace the wallpaper. Gazing at the bare room, he pictured a festive table adorned with glassware and candlelight, the chairs filled with friends and well-wishers. He saw Hugo, their friendship repaired, sitting alongside Josette, the latter sharing a joke with her sister, Claudette. Marguerite sat with Dominic, the latter standing up to propose a toast. And then he pictured Madame Ouellet at one end of the table, a look of glowering disapproval on her face as she stared in his direction. Is she really reconciled? he questioned, or is this some cunning stratagem? With a last look around he left the house.

THE FOLLOWING SUNDAY, HE arrived at the modest residence on rue Mercier with a floral bouquet in one hand and a basket containing wine, chocolates, cheese and grapes in the other. Each item was of the finest quality as testament to his status as general manager. Nervous at the reception he might get, he knocked lightly on the door. To his great relief, Isabelle answered, a delighted smile on her face as she beheld him. 'Jacob!'

Pulling him inside, she kissed him on the lips before taking his hand and leading him into the parlour. Her mother sat there, an unreadable expression on her face, her eyes looking past him at the window.

'Good afternoon, Madame Ouellet.' He bowed in the old style and would gladly have kissed the elderly lady's hand had she raised it.

Instead, she turned distant eyes on him. 'Good afternoon, Monsieur Wheeler,' she said, her voice and manner aloof.

'Mama! See what Jacob has brought us!' Isabelle laid out the offerings on the table in front of the matriarch. 'Oh! What is this?' She glanced at Jacob before picking up a small box wrapped in gift paper. 'For me?' With another glance for confirmation, she peeled off the paper and opened the box. 'Goodness!' She drew out a rosary of dark-coloured beads upon which was suspended a silver crucifix. 'Jacob?' She gave a look of wonderment.

'It's beautiful! Look Mama!' She held it between her hands for inspection. The old lady gazed at the object and mumbled, whether to express approval or disapproval, Jacob was uncertain.

'I had bishop Drolet bless it,' he said, pride in his voice.

'You did?' Isabelle stared in surprise, as did her mother, the old lady's mouth opening in shock.

'The bishop!' Isabelle turned to her mother, her voice filled with delight at what seemed very much like a *fait accompli*. 'Do you like the gifts, Mama?'

The old lady grunted. 'I am a little tired. See to our guest, Isabelle.' She got to her feet, her eyes fastening on the rosary for a moment. 'Bishop Drolet?' Her voice was faint.

'Himself.'

'And you explained it was a gift—for my daughter?'

'I did, Madame. Madame, before you go—' He glanced nervously at Isabelle, 'I have something I wish to discuss with you.'

'Later, perhaps.' She made a whistling noise through her nose and, to his disappointment, slowly left the parlour. 'I shall be in my bedroom,' she said over her shoulder to Isabelle.

Surprised to be left alone, Isabelle turned and took his hands in her own. 'Tea?' she asked, smiling. 'What's the matter?'

'Now I have to summon up the courage all over again!'

'But don't you know the answer?' She made a pouting face. 'Unless it is mama you intend to marry?'

'MARRIED! WHEN? WHAT DID mama say?' Marguerite's eyes widened.

Isabelle laughed merrily. 'One thing at a time!' They were seated in the parlour of Marguerite's new house on avenue Montaigne where Isabelle had just broken news of her engagement. 'It won't be for a year at least. Mama insists on a twelve-month engagement. I think she is desperately hoping I will change my mind.'

'But you have spoken to him—the curé?' Marguerite was breathless over the news.

'I have.'

'And?'

'He has agreed to marry us. But he won't dare defy the bishop. He will marry us in the old church hall on rue Jacques Martin.'

'He will? Even though Jacob is … whatever he is? But darling, you've always dreamed of a church wedding ever since you were a child.'

'It can't be done. The bishop won't allow it.' Isabelle made a rueful face.

'But he will permit Father Simard?'

'Yes. He is willing to turn a blind eye as long as it is not in the cathedral.'

Marguerite took a moment to absorb this. 'But what else? Tell me everything. Leave nothing out! Why, for example, did you not ask Father Boudreau?'

'I did, but the bishop has forbidden him to perform any priestly function.' She waited, with an anticipatory smile, for Marguerite's shocked response.

'Why?'

'It seems he questioned the Immaculate Conception—during the sermon! It's said he also described the idea of papal infallibility as stuff and nonsense.'

'He never did!'

'It's true. In fact, it's rumoured the bishop is in the process of getting him dismissed from the priesthood.'

Marguerite stared, too amazed to say anything.

'It seems mama was right about him being an odd fish.'

The sisters gazed at one another. They heard Dominic in the next room as he opened and closed a drawer in search of something.

'Goodness, so much to take in! Will mama attend?'

'She has not yet said yes or no. You know mama.'

'And what does Jacob say?'

'He is beside himself with happiness. As am I!'

'So, my little sister is ready to be a wife?'

'Jacob's wife!'

Marguerite kissed Isabelle on the forehead. 'Congratulations, Madame Wheeler! What is it?' she asked as a shadow crossed Isabelle's face.

'Everything would be so much simpler if Jacob would accept the faith. Nothing would make me happier. But he point-blank refuses even to discuss it.'

'I couldn't have imagined you marrying anyone other than a patriotic, and very devout, habitant. But who knows,' consoled Marguerite, 'perhaps Jacob will indeed accept the Church one day.' She reached out to clasp Isabelle's hand in her own. 'It may happen, in time. You must have faith.'

'Faith I have,' said Isabelle, a rueful twist to her mouth. 'It's Jacob's I worry about.'

BISHOP DROLET EMERGED FROM the vestry following evening prayer to find Madame Ouellet sitting in a pew waiting for him. 'Ah! Madame

Ouellet!' He gave what he hoped was a graceful smile while noting the look of displeasure on her face.

He sat next to her, sighing as he did so. 'It's the rosary, isn't it?' The smell of incense lingered in the air. A few parishioners still knelt before the altar. 'What could I do? The fellow asked. I could hardly refuse.'

'How much?' Her voice was blunt.

'I beg pardon?'

'How much did the English heretic pay for you to bless the rosary?'

The bishop looked shocked. 'Heavens! One could hardly refuse such a request.'

'How much?'

'A donation, that is all. Toward the upkeep of the church. It would have been unchristian to refuse.'

'And marriage?'

'Marriage? That is out of the question.' His voice was adamant. 'In the church, that is,' he added.

In her ire, she missed the qualification. 'Come. Do you think me a child? He must have raised the question.' Her sharp gaze probed his reluctance. 'Did he request a dispensation—as part of the donation? Surely you cannot countenance joining a Catholic and a Protestant in church? It would be a sin.'

'As I told you, Madame Ouellet. He cannot, and will not, be married in the church. That I can assure you.'

'Then why did my daughter let slip that Father Simard would perform the service?'

The bishop cast a longing glance at the wooden figure of Christ hanging from the cross above the altar. 'Father Simard may do as he wishes, as long as he does not perform a church ceremony.'

'As he wishes? You are the bishop, are you not? Then forbid it!'

The prelate uttered a heartfelt sigh. 'You must realise, Madame, that times are changing.' He glanced around as if to make certain they were not being overhead. 'There are forces at work,' he muttered.

'Forces? What on earth are you talking about?'

The bishop wound the rosary around his fingers. 'The Church has many enemies, Madame. We must pick and choose our battles and be careful not to give ammunition to those who oppose us.'

'And who are these people?' she demanded, wondering if the bishop was losing his mind. 'And what does that have to do with the Englishman requesting a dispensation?'

'Everything and nothing,' he said, sighing. 'Now, you must excuse me, I have much to do.'

'But he is not of the faith!' she insisted as he rose to leave.

'Our Lord's blessings be upon you,' he said, signing the air over his shoulder. Before Madame Ouellet could respond, the bishop fell to his knees in front of the altar, leaving her to fume in her seat.

IT WAS JOSETTE WHO finally brokered the peace, sending an olive branch in the form of a supper invitation to celebrate the engagement. "*M. and Mme Hugo Gagnon are pleased to arrange a small formal supper to mark the occasion of the engagement of M. Jacob Wheeler and Mlle Isabelle Ouellet. Saturday afternoon, June 12, at 5pm.*"

Her husband picked up the hand-written card and studied it, an unhappy expression on his face.

'What?'

'I don't know if I can go through with it.' He placed the card back on the table.

'Hugo, we've discussed this. It can't go on. She is your cousin, after all. Do you intend to miss the wedding as well?'

'The wedding is one thing, but a supper party …?' His voice trailed off. 'Anyway, I must go. I'll be late for the Assembly.' He stooped as she offered her cheek, brushing it with his lips.

After he had gone, she sat and quietly wept, folding and refolding the handkerchief as she dabbed at her eyes. Three months had passed since the bitter quarrel and it was no nearer resolution, in spite of her attempts to conciliate her husband.

'This is a new side of him,' she complained to her sister. 'Who would ever have imagined he would prove so stiff-necked over such a trifle!'

'A trifle?' Claudette raised an eyebrow as she offered her sister more coffee. 'My dear, to be honest, it was something more than that, do you not think?'

Josette pouted as she took in the remark. 'It was supposed to be romantic,' she said. 'Little more than an adventure, like those silly opera plots.'

'But you know Hugo, what he is like about these things.' Claudette's voice, while sympathetic, was also admonitory as she added sugar to her coffee.

'But to carry on like he has!' Josette lifted the coffee cup to her lips.

'And how is that?'

'You know, sulking in that tiresome way that men do. Looking hurt and accusing at the same time. Really, you'd think I'd had an affair!' She set the cup down without sipping.

'And has he said anything to Isabelle?'

'He avoids her! As if she didn't have enough to cope with, given her dreadful mother and all!'

'Well then, you shall have to make amends.'

'Me? Why me?' Josette looked offended at the suggestion.

Claudette waited, eyeing her sister over the cup. 'Do you expect Hugo to apologise?'

Josette gave an exasperated sigh under her sister's gaze. 'It's the Jesuit in him. It always comes out at such moments. He has no humour about such things.'

'Humour?' Claudette considered this. 'My dear, you did, after all … go behind his back.' She met her sister's arch look.

Josette sniffed. 'I am not the only one to keep a secret.'

'What do you mean?'

'I mean Jacob! Who else shot the poor man in the brain?'

'Josette!'

'Well, is it not hypocrisy to condemn me for that which he does himself?'

'I hardly think the two are the same, do you? More sugar?' she asked, offering the bowl.

'And how are they different?' Josette waved away the sugar.

Claudette suspended her cup. 'Well, one involves a … deception, the other …'

'Exactly!' Josette pounced on the hesitation. 'They both involve a deception. The one harmless, really, the other amounting almost to murder, albeit by accident.'

'Sister!'

'Truth be truth.' Josette set her lips in a *coup de grâce*.

'Have you suggested that to him?'

'Once. But he got so angry I dropped it.'

'And the engagement supper?'

'It's still a week away. But I dread the prospect. They might fling knives at each other for all I know.'

'Then you must first resolve it between yourself and Hugo. You have the week.'

JOSETTE STEWED ON THE advice for another day before deciding to act.

'Hugo, dearest.' She sat and took his hand in hers after supper, having made his favourite fish pie.

'Yes?' He looked at her.

She noted that his expression was warmer and more Hugo-like than it had been in the months since their quarrel.

'I am deeply sorry about the … thing with Isabelle and Jacob. You know I—'

'Thing?' Some of his restored warmth vanished.

She took a deep breath. 'Deception. It was thoughtless of me. I really did think of it as something harmless, simply bringing two lovers together in spite of her mother's opposition. You know, like Abelard and Heloise?' Tears filled her eyes. 'But I can't live with this coldness between us. Can you forgive me?'

His eyes grew moist. 'My dear, I already have.'

'You have!' She pulled her hand away before quickly putting it back again.

'Yes. What you perceive as coldness is merely hurt on my part.' He sighed heavily. 'I am aware of my own … sensitivity to such things. But I confessed my anger and forgave you at the same time.'

'Confessed?' Her eyes narrowed. 'Who to?'

'To Father Simard in the confessional. He advised me to forgive and forget. The first I have done, the second … will come in time.'

'And Jacob and Isabelle?'

He made a disapproving sound. 'That may take a little longer. And do not forget, there is another injured party to consider.'

She frowned to think.

'Isabelle's mother! Madame Ouellet.'

'Of course.' She raised his hand to her lips and kissed his fingers. 'But what about the engagement party? I have invited Isabelle and Jacob for coffee to discuss the arrangements.'

Hugo considered for a moment, his face solemn. 'Let them come. Let us settle this one way or another.'

'One way or another?' She furrowed her brow.

'My dear, you cannot control everything.' Leaning forward, he kissed her tenderly on the lips.

'Darling Hugo!' she said and stroked his cheek. *I must get in some of that chocolate cake Isabelle likes.*

'COME IN!' JOSETTE STOOD at the door, cheerfully beckoning them inside. Jacob hesitated, uncomfortably aware he hadn't seen Hugo since their quarrel.

'Hugo will be down in a minute,' said Josette, and ushered them into the freshly wallpapered parlour. To one side was a small, polished table on which stood a decanter of wine, several glasses, a tray of cakes, and a colourful arrangement of pink and blue irises and peonies. Jacob sat down, feeling ill at ease as he waited for Hugo to appear.

'Wine?' Josette poured from the decanter. She smiled at Jacob as if to say, 'Don't worry!'

Momentarily reassured, he was promptly discomforted again when Hugo made his appearance, a composed expression on his face. He greeted Isabelle, kissing her on the cheek, but made no attempt to shake hands with Jacob, simply giving the briefest of nods in his direction before sitting down to accept a glass of wine from his wife.

'Come, dearest. Why look so glum? The happy couple are here to greet you.' Josette held up her glass. 'To Isabelle and Jacob!'

Hugo half-raised his glass. 'To the happy couple,' he said, his voice cool in spite of the sentiment.

Jacob was about to break the awkward silence when Isabelle forestalled him. 'Hugo, I am terribly sorry—about the letters. It was utterly wrong of me. Please don't blame Jacob. I arranged everything.' Her voice was tearful as she made the apology.

'With the aid of my wife,' Hugo pointed out.

'Hugo, darling. I thought—'

'I should like to hear from Jacob,' he said, cutting her off. For the first time, he looked directly at Jacob.

'It was wrong of us—of me, Hugo. And I am truly sorry.' He was about to add to the apology but decided brevity was the safest course. He looked apprehensively at the other man, desperate to put the quarrel behind them. 'Hugo, you have been my dearest friend since my first days in New France. I hate to think that my actions may have ruined that friendship. I humbly ask for your forgiveness.'

'I see.' Hugo weighed this as he stared into his wine. 'And your mother?' he asked, directing the question to Isabelle. 'You have apologised to her?'

'Many times!'

'And Jacob?'

'Good God, no! It would make things worse!'

'And your promise to me?' He looked directly at Jacob.

'Broken.' Jacob took a deep breath. 'Most regrettably and ashamedly so.'

'Hugo?' prompted Josette in the silence that followed.

Hugo, however, yet refused to bend leaving his wife and the visitors in suspense.

'I was brought up to believe in the sanctity of an oath,' he said finally, his voice solemn. 'To break one's word is no small thing. One simply does not lie to a friend. But—' he held up a hand as Josette made to interrupt—'apologies, too, are of great moment and if sincerely given must be accepted with a forgiving heart.' Leaning forward, he extended his hand to Jacob. 'I accept your apology,' he said, his voice thick with emotion. 'Now let us shake hands and put the matter behind us once and for all.'

Jacob felt tears come to his eyes as he clasped the offered hand. 'I have greatly missed our friendship.'

Josette smiled at Isabelle as the latter sniffled into a handkerchief. 'Well, thank goodness that's over with and we are all friends again. Isabelle darling, some chocolate cake?'

22

A Brand-New Age

SIX YEARS INTO HIS marriage, Jacob carried himself with that air of contentment indigenous to personal happiness and material success. His mother-in-law, the formidable Madame Ouellet, was a doting grandmother to his three children despite clinging to her frosty opinion of their father. Over the years, he had formed a small but trusty circle of friends, and a larger circle of acquaintances, many of them professional people met during the course of his business.

His marriage to Isabelle, the bedrock of his happiness, was as serene and gratifying as he might have wished, her careful stewardship of house and family a daily pleasure to observe. The one sticking point to their otherwise blissful union was his resistance to converting to the Catholic faith, his freethinking beliefs a source of unhappiness to his wife that he deeply regretted, but nevertheless robustly maintained. He frowned but held his tongue when she placed a large crucifix over their bed and adorned several walls with pictures of the Madonna. And he kept his reservations to himself as each of their three children was, in turn, splashed with water from the baptismal fount, Isabelle standing next to the curé with a proud smile on her face.

Fully embedded in his new life, he rarely bothered with thoughts of the past, increasingly indifferent as time passed, as to whether the amnesiac fog would ever lift to allow in some penetrating light. He was, as he might have described himself, Jacob Wheeler: businessman, husband to Isabelle and father to Gaston, Louis, and Marie-Odile. 'Monsieur' Jacob Wheeler, he might have amended for the enlightenment of an interested observer.

Thus, it was with an air of prosperous contentment that he sat down to breakfast one morning in the sunny dining room as Isabelle fussed over their sons and nursed the infant Marie-Odile.

'Mr. Ferguson and Mr. Selt arrive this morning,' he reminded her as she wiped Louis' mouth. 'I shall be dining with them this evening. Gaston, sit still. See how Louis copies you?'

The serving girl they employed five mornings a week cleared the breakfast dishes as he returned to the *Daily Register*. 'Did you see this?' He held up the front page for Isabelle.

She glanced at the newsprint. 'What does it say?'

'They are planning a new square, to be named after Gaston Tremblay.'

'Really? Where?'

'You know the old square on rue Saint-Joseph? Well, they're enlarging it and knocking down some of the surrounding houses. They say it will be the largest square in the city.'

Her eyes widened. 'Larger than Cathedral Square?'

'It says so.'

'The bishop won't like that. Open wide!' She held the spoon up to Louis' mouth.

'They've commissioned Alois Giroux to build a monument to grace the new square,' he said, returning to the page.

Isabelle knitted her brow. 'But there's a statue there already—of St. Marie Dufour. Gaston, wipe your nose.' Leaning over she dabbed at her son's nose with a napkin.

Jacob smiled. 'Are you personally acquainted with every statue in the city? Anyway, they are pulling it down.'

'What?' She looked up in shock.

'Sorry, relocating it—to the street alongside the square.'

'The idea!' Scandalised at the notion of pulling down a statue, she spooned some pulped fruit into her mouth, tasting it for flavour. 'What monument?' she asked, wiping Marie-Odile's chin.

'Pardon?'

'You said they had commissioned a monument. What sort?'

'It doesn't say. Just that it will be grand as befitting the new square.'

'As long as it's not some modern monstrosity. Let's hope it's of Gaston Tremblay. After all, the square is named after him.'

'Don't we have enough statues of the fellow? They are everywhere.'

'As they should be. Are you full, little angel?' Cooing, she kissed the infant.

'I must go. I'm late.' He got up, stooping to kiss the baby. 'Goodbye sweet pea!' He kissed his wife next before mussing the hair of both boys. 'Be good and listen to your mother.'

AN HOUR LATER HE waited to greet his employers as they arrived at the carriage factory direct from the railway station. Dwight waited alongside him, running a comb through his hair.

'Hello, sir!' Jacob shook hands with Ferguson and then with Selt as they got down from the Hansom cab. 'I trust you had a pleasant journey?'

'Hello, Jacob. Good to see you again. Morning, Dwight.' Ferguson inhaled a satisfied breath as he gazed around the busy street. 'Things are thriving, I see.'

After escorting his employers around the workshop floor and showing off the latest carriages under construction, Jacob brought them back to his office. There they sat over coffee and ledgers while the Americans questioned himself and Dwight on all aspects of the business.

'All's ship-shape and hunky-dory!' pronounced Selt, closing a ledger. 'My compliments, gentlemen. The business is in fine shape.' He lit a cigar. 'That will be all, Dwight,' he said, thanking the accountant.

Ferguson waited until the door had closed before turning to Jacob. 'Well, Jacob, you've done exceptionally well,' he said, a genial note to his voice. 'Indeed, you've exceeded our expectations this last quarter. Wouldn't you say so, Mort?'

'Hit a home run, I'd say.' Selt blew out a stream of smoke with the remark.

'Thank you, sir. I have hopes of landing a new contract next week, to supply—'

'But there's no future in the business.'

'Pardon?' Jacob started, taken aback by the words.

'What Gus means,' said Selt, flicking ash from the cigar, 'is that the carriage trade is finished.'

'Busted,' said Ferguson. 'Times are changing. We are getting out of it, here and in the US.'

Stunned by the pronouncement, Jacob looked from one man to the other. 'I didn't expect that,' he said, confused and not a little upset.

'Now don't look so crestfallen,' chuckled Ferguson. 'It ain't that we plan on sinking the ship, just changing course.'

'A new tack,' echoed Selt.

Jacob stared, puzzled. 'A new tack?'

'The future of transportation is in the motor car industry,' explained Ferguson. 'No one wants to ride a horse when they can drive an automobile or take a bumpy old carriage when they can sit comfortably in an electrified tram.'

'Why would they?' asked Selt.

'Automobiles are the wave of the future, and we aim to get on board,' said Ferguson, careless of the mixed metaphor. 'The fact is, Morg and I have long discussed jumping ship and getting into the automobile business entirely.'

'Entirely?'

'We've already started,' elaborated Selt.

'You have?'

'Almost two years ago, down in Albany,' said Ferguson. 'We partnered with an auto maker and opened a factory to make and sell motor cars.'

'It didn't work well,' interjected Selt. 'Too many mad ideas. The fellow was a genius inventor but hopeless at business. So, we decided to go our own way. We bought him out and started our own company. We own the plans and hand-build the automobiles.'

'Sold over two dozen last year,' added Ferguson, nodding in self-congratulation. 'We aim to double that this year.'

Jacob sat open-mouthed with surprise.

'We planned to set up shop in Rochester—turn the carriage workshop there into an automobile factory, and close down this place. But then Morg here had the bright idea—'

'It was both of us together,' interrupted Selt, blowing a modest ring of smoke.

'Anyway, we figured we already got New York State covered from Albany, so there wasn't much point in keeping Rochester open. So why not close it down and set up here, north of the border?'

'This way we cover our bets, north and south,' added Selt.

'What do you think, Jacob. Would an automobile factory fly in New France?' Both men looked at him with the question.

The audacious idea took him back for a moment. But the more he considered it, the more it appealed to him. 'I don't see why not. It is, as you say, the way of the future.'

Selt glanced at Ferguson, who nodded. 'It would be small scale at first. No actual manufacturing, just assembly. We'd ship the parts up from Albany, and you'd put them together here and sell the finished product.'

'We intend, eventually, an assembly line, like that Olds fellow in Detroit.' At Jacob's puzzled look Ferguson elaborated. 'He had the bright idea of getting others to make the parts, then his factory puts them all together. Kind of like what'll you'll be doing, only on a grander scale.'

'A conveyor belt,' confirmed Selt, 'with each man given a particular task.'

'So, what do you think of that, Jacob?' Ferguson sipped his coffee as he waited for an answer.

'I don't know what to say.' Jacob considered for a moment. 'There are some automobiles in the Upper Town. They run on steam. Is that what you plan?'

'Heck no. Our model—we call it the Runabout—operates on gasoline.'

'It's the durndest thing you ever saw,' said a proud Selt. 'A single-cylinder engine that will get you twenty miles per hour and run all day long.' Rummaging in his briefcase, he took out a sheaf of papers. 'Here. Cast your eye over these.'

Curious, Jacob leafed through the papers. Several showed photographs of an upright vehicle with two upholstered seats and, in some instances, a canopy. He was surprised to come across a colour photograph, one which showed in vivid detail, an automobile with a blue chassis, handsome white tyres and red upholstery. He whistled in appreciation.

'An autochrome,' explained Selt, referring to the picture. 'Took all morning to get it right.'

'That's it, the Runabout.' The pride in Ferguson's voice was unmistakable as he leaned forward to peer at the photograph.

'How much does one cost?' asked Jacob.

Ferguson winked at Selt. 'To the point, as always! Guess?' he challenged.

Jacob shrugged, mentally comparing the automobile with its equestrian counterpart. 'I'd hazard six or seven hundred dollars,' he guessed, hoping he wasn't too far off the mark.

'Close! We aim to sell these buggies for under six hundred dollars.'

'Given the lower production costs in New France,' added Selt.

'We figure at first the main market will be back over the border, in Upper New York State.' Ferguson took another sip of coffee. 'We'll ship the parts up here, you put them together, and then send the finished article back over the line.'

'But eventually, we see a market right here in New France and the entire province of Quebec.'

'Not to mention Ontario,' added Ferguson. What?' he asked at the doubtful look on Jacob's face.

'I'm not sure how many would be willing to lay out dollars on such a machine. They tend to be conservative around here, and tight with their money.'

'You can't fight progress,' said Ferguson, his voice firm. 'Once they see the benefits, they'll want to invest in the future.'

'But it might take some arm-twisting at first. You up for it?' Selt fixed Jacob a probing look.

'I believe I am. Yes sir, I most certainly believe I am,' he repeated, with more conviction.

'Good man!' exclaimed Ferguson. 'I knew we could count on you. And to show our confidence, we're going to throw in a sweetener, right Morg?' He addressed his partner without turning his head, his eyes on Jacob.

'Sugar sweet.'

'Rather than a salary, we're prepared to offer you a twelve percent share of the new company, to grow to fifteen percent in the event of reaching sales targets. We'd like an investment of, say, ten thousand dollars on your part as a buy-in.'

Jacob's eyes widened at the proposal. 'You want me to buy in—for ten thousand dollars?'

'In return, you'd get part-ownership and a percentage of profits, rather than a salary. How does that sit?' Selt viewed him through a haze of cigar smoke.

Jacob hesitated, taken aback at the proposal. 'Instead of a salary?'

'That's right,' affirmed Ferguson. 'You'll take twelve percent of the sales profit, minimum. Put it this way. If we sell twenty-four automobiles the first year—either here or back in the States, it doesn't matter where—you'll pocket around seventeen hundred dollars as your share.'

'And from there, it only goes up,' contributed Selt.

'You'd be an owner, rather than a worker. Isn't that what you'd want?'

Still hesitant, Jacob temporised, tapping his fingers as he mentally ran the numbers. His employers waited patiently. 'Think of it, Jacob, you'll be a partner,' encouraged Ferguson. 'And who knows, your share could grow beyond fifteen percent in time.'

'Imagine an automated assembly line,' added Selt, 'with autos coming off the line every quarter hour.' He motioned with his cigar as if to the future.

'You could be rich in a very short time!' Ferguson beamed with the enticing prospect.

'Manufacturing automobiles will be the new wealth of America,' prompted Selt.

Still Jacob hesitated. 'It sounds very generous. But I'm the first to admit, I don't know a thing about the automobile business.'

'Just as you didn't know a thing about making carriages!' said Ferguson, his voice jovial. 'But you're a quick study, Jacob. And that's worth a deal to us. We'll take care of the engineering side, while you and Dwight run the books and grease the palms like before.'

'We figure if we can sell two dozen automobiles the first year, and four dozen the year after, we can make this horse run,' said Selt.

'So, do we have an agreement?' asked Ferguson.

'Strike while the horse is still running,' urged Selt.

Jacob scratched behind his ear. 'Ten thousand is a lot of money. I don't know that—'

'What'd I tell you, Morg! Always drives for a bargain!' chuckled Ferguson. 'There's no need to put the entire dough up front. It will take at least a year to get everything up and running.'

'Would I be on salary for that year?'

'Gee whiz!' laughed Selt. 'I'd say we made the right choice, Gus.'

'How about this?' Ferguson leaned forward with an offer. 'We'll guarantee your salary right up until this place closes and the new business opens. After that, you're on profits, same as us. How does that sound?'

Jacob drew a breath and took the plunge. 'Then count me in!'

'Good man!' Ferguson gave a beaming smile and reached out his hand.

'Welcome aboard, partner!' Selt followed, offering a hearty handshake. 'Congratulations!'

'When do we start?' asked Jacob, buoyed now that he had made the decision.

'Depends,' said Selt. 'How long will it take you to finish up here?'

'We've got existing work for the next five or six months.'

'Fine. It will take at least that long to get everything properly set up. We intend putting in an offer on the business next door to increase space. And maybe the business next to that one too, if the price is right.'

'A reasonable price,' affirmed Selt.

'Then there's the logistics. We need to set up a supply line, arrange for freight …' Ferguson looked at Selt.

'Get this place up and running,' continued his partner, 'equip the workshop with tools, bring in gasoline, put in a gas pump, and train mechanics. We'll send up our own people from New York, like before. They'll train the locals on how to put the autos together and how to keep them running smoothly.'

'And in the meantime, you can come down to Albany to check things out,' said Ferguson.

'Sure. Stay for a few weeks. Learn the business. See how the automobiles are put together.'

'If all goes to plan, about a year from now we re-open as Ferguson-Selt Automobile Company.'

'Reliable autos at a reliable price,' quoted Selt.

'Up here it ain't like it is in the States,' said Ferguson. 'We'll have the jump on our competitors.'

'There's a shake-out in the market down South,' confirmed Selt. 'Everybody and his dog is keen to make the next Model T.'

'But we ain't greenhorns.' Ferguson grinned. 'We got the capital, and we got the know-how.'

'It's the future,' affirmed Selt. 'Soon, automobiles will be everywhere. And that's a fact you can take to the bank.'

'Talking of which. My throat's as dry as a buffalo's fart!' Ferguson got to his feet. 'Let's go drink on the deal. Come on partner!'

'AND HOW ARE THINGS at home?' Marguerite lifted her youngest, Etienne, onto her lap as she sat across from her sister.

'I couldn't be happier. Gaston do stop rolling about on the carpet. Are you a cat?'

'You sound like mama.' Marguerite chuckled.

'Where is she?'

'She should be here any moment.'

'She came to tea last week, to see our little angel!' Isabelle kissed the infant on the forehead as she snuggled her in her lap. 'She dotes on her.'

'And who wouldn't?' Marguerite leaned across to tickle the infant under the chin. 'Coo-coo!'

'She's sleepy. May I set her down?'

'Of course.' Marguerite pointed to the cot. 'Etienne is outgrowing it.' She watched Isabelle place the already sleeping Marie-Odile in the cot. 'And how's Jacob, now that he's a wealthy partner?'

Isabelle laughed as she returned to her chair. 'Hardly! But he's happy with the new direction the company is taking.'

'Automobiles?' Marguerite shook her head, marvelling. 'We live in a brand-new age.'

'That is why we must stick to our roots, or else get swept away by all this change.'

'I hear that Lucien Gaudreau is arguing to open another English school—in the Old Town, of all places.'

'The Assembly will never allow it. That would make three.'

'Don't be so sure, if it goes to a vote. At least that's what Dominic thinks.'

'And he is in favour, I suppose?'

Marguerite raised an eyebrow. 'Haven't you said that Jacob intends bringing up Americans and their families to work in the new factory? They'll want their children to be schooled in English, surely? Besides, I hear Bernard Benoit is now arguing that all French schools in New France should include an hour of English instruction each day.'

Isabelle looked shocked. 'What next? Lessons in Anglicanism?'

'And how is your own instruction going?' Marguerite pursed her mouth, speaking in her best imitation English. ''ello! What a fine day we are 'aving.'

'Spoken like a native! A very confused one.'

'Can you converse with Jacob—in English, I mean?'

'A little. But it's frustrating when I can't remember the right word. And the grammar is frightful.'

'And the children?'

'He's happy for them to speak French. Although later I suspect he'll want them to learn English.'

'Case in point. And their faith? He's still content for them to attend Mass and so forth?'

'Of course.' Isabelle frowned. 'That is not even a question.'

'He dotes on you, my dear. If you wished to raise them as monkeys, he'd agree.'

'What a thing to say!'

Marguerite cuddled Etienne. 'I have my own little monkey! Mwah!' She kissed his forehead.

'I've asked Jacob to take me with him the next time he visits the midwife.'

Marguerite looked up in surprise. 'The midwife? Why?'

'I've heard so much about her, I simply wish to meet her in person.'

They heard a knock on the front door and exchanged glances. 'Mama.' Marguerite got up and set Etienne on the floor. 'Play with your new toy,' she said, placing a lead soldier in his hand.

'Not a word about the midwife!' cautioned Isabelle.

Madame Ouellet looked cross as her daughter relieved her of her coat. 'The cab driver almost collided with a milk cart. I told him in no uncertain terms what I thought of him! Don't get up.' Bending, she kissed Isabelle on the forehead before picking up Etienne. She lavished kisses on him as he struggled in her grasp. Setting him down, she walked to the cot to gaze fondly at the sleeping Marie-Odile. 'How peaceful she looks! God grant us all such innocence.'

'Sit here, Mama.' Marguerite pulled up the comfortable chair.

Arranging herself in the chair, Madame Ouellet looked around the room. 'New drapes? They're rather bright, don't you think?'

'Tea, Mama?' Marguerite poured into a small china cup. 'And try these pastries, Isabelle brought them.' She placed a pastry on a small plate and set it beside the cup.

'And how are you, Mama?' asked Isabelle. 'Is your leg any better?'

'It isn't, but God sends these things to try us.' Madame Ouellet made a sour face as she sipped the tea. 'Marguerite! You know I take sugar.'

'Just coming, Mama.' Marguerite placed a china bowl heaped with sugar next to the saucer.

Isabelle watched as her mother stirred sugar into the tea. Her face looks pinched, she thought, full of sympathy.

'I've missed seeing you, Mama. It's been almost a week. The children miss you, too.'

Madame Ouellet's face melted as she gazed at the cot. 'Sweet little darling! Of course she misses her grandmother.'

Marguerite put down her teacup as she remembered something. 'Did you read in today's *Tribune* about Father Boudreau? Only its monsieur Boudreau from now on.'

Isabelle gasped. 'You mean he's been dismissed from the church?'

'Laicized,' according to the *Tribune*. 'It means he can no longer perform his functions as a priest.'

'About high time,' sniffed their mother. 'Didn't I tell you the fellow was a secret non-conformist?'

'As I recall, you blamed him for being odd, like a fish,' said Marguerite.

'And so he is. The creature now denies the most fundamental tenets of our faith. And to think he had the nerve to hear confession all that time. Good riddance to the fellow.'

'What will he do now? Where will he go?'

'Vanish, hopefully.'

'A former priest can't have too many options,' said Isabelle. 'The poor man, I feel sorry for him. What must it be like—to lose your faith?'

'Like losing your memory, I should imagine,' her mother said, studying her tea.

'Isabelle tells me she is planning to visit the Indian midwife.' Marguerite glanced mischievously at her sister, who made a cross face in return.

'The midwife?' Madame Ouellet set down her cup, 'Why? What business do you have with the woman?'

'She is a respected healer. And she saved my Jacob's life.'

'But why on earth must you visit her? Are you ill? Do they not have perfectly good, civilised doctors in the town?'

'I'm curious. I've heard so much about her from Jacob over the years.'

Madame Ouellet bit into a pastry, an odd expression on her face.

'What?' Isabelle and her sister glanced at each other. Their mother shook her head and chewed.

'What?' they uttered in unison.

'You have already met her.' Madame Ouellet dipped a corner of the pastry into the tea.

'When?' Isabelle stared in amazement.

'You were just a baby, no older than little Marie-Odile.'

'Mama, the details!'

'It was your father,' Madame Ouellet said, her voice crisp with disapproval. 'He had a pain in his arm the doctors were unable to get rid of. Someone, that awful Brodeur woman I recall, suggested the midwife and your father was impossible to dissuade.' She took a bite of the moist pastry.

'Go on.' Isabelle leaned forward, prompting her mother to continue.

'That's all. We ventured out into the woods and visited her at that stinking shack she inhabited.' Their mother's face wrinkled with distaste at the memory.

'And where was I?' asked Marguerite.

'You were there too. Your father carried you, I carried Isabelle. The heat was frightful.'

'And did she cure him?'

'Who?'

'Papa, of course.'

'Oh, I don't know. She rubbed some stinking poultice or other into his arm.'

'And did it work?'

'He claimed so, but then he was always credulous in such matters. It probably healed by itself.'

'So, I met her?' Isabelle shook her head, surprised at how life threw up such odd coincidences. *Jacob will be dumbfounded when I tell him.*

LATER, PUSHING THE PRAM home from the boulangerie with her two youngest inside and Gaston trudging alongside, she stopped to tie his shoelace. 'You'll trip and fall and bang your head, and that will be the end of you,' she admonished, kneeling at his feet.

'Who is that, Mama?' He was looking up at a bronze statue mounted on a stone plinth. The figure leant against a full-size paddle.

'That is Martin Moreau. He was a famous voyageur.'

'What's a voyageur?'

'A person who paddles a canoe.'

'Why?'

'Why what?'

The boy looked up at the imposing figure. 'Why is he up there?'

'So that we may remember him. He was a famous man back when New France was just a small village.'

'Did he fight Indians?'

'Probably. Now, look where you're going. Come on.'

Crossing rue Amboise, she stopped to point to another statue on the opposing corner. 'There's your namesake, the person you were named after,' she explained, stopping the pram so that her son could get a better look. She clicked her tongue at his puzzled expression. 'Gaston Pierre Tremblay, the greatest man in the history of New France, and your direct ancestor. You will learn all about him at school.'

'I don't want to go to school!'

'Then perhaps you would rather catch fish or grow apples?'

Gaston held onto the pram as they continued, intrigued with a picture of himself standing beneath a giant apple tree laden with fish.

23

All Chants Sound Alike

‘There used to be more trees,’ Jacob remarked as he and Isabelle strolled through the leafy green woods. ‘I wonder what happened to them all. Ah! There's your answer!’ he said as they heard shouts and the sounds of chopping and sawing ahead of them. They came across a clearing where a lumber crew was gathered around a fallen tree. The men were busily chopping and stripping the branches. Several more trunks, similarly stripped, lay stacked to one side.

‘Good morning!’ Jacob called out.

‘Good morning, sir!’ One of the men doffed his cap.

‘I see you've made an impression,’ he said, with a glance at the stripped tree trunks.

‘This area has been marked for logging,’ said the man as his companions took advantage of the interruption to roll cigarettes and drink water from bottles placed in the shade.

‘How much of it?’

The other man wiped sweat from his brow. ‘Until we have enough logs.’

Jacob considered this, not caring for the way one of the crew was staring at his wife. ‘Good day to you,’ he said.

They continued for another half-mile through the woods. Sunlight filtered through the leafy canopy, the air drowsy with summer motes.

‘They brought you all the way here—in the back of a wagon?’ Isabelle's voice was loud in the forest hush.

‘I'd be dead if they had continued on to the town.’

She mentally crossed herself at the thought, making a note to thank her cousin the next time they met.

‘Look! There she is.’ Jacob's face broke into a smile as he glimpsed the midwife sitting on the porch. She appeared to be dozing, the ever-present pipe in her mouth. The much worn felt hat shaded her eyes.

‘Good morning, midwife!’ he hailed, cheerful at seeing her again.

‘Eh!’ She blinked and looked around before seeing him. ‘Ghost Bear!’ Her plump face creased into a toothy grin.

‘I've brought my wife to meet you,’ he said, mounting the steps.

‘Hello, Madame. Jacob has told me so much about you. I wish to thank you for saving his life.' Isabelle smiled her warmest smile, her eyes taking in the patched dress, lank hair, and plump brown face of the other woman. She tried to place her age, but could not, defeated by the midwife's unwrinkled skin and considerable girth.

The midwife squinted up at her. 'You were just a babe in arms the last time you came to see me. I undercharged your father for that potion,' she said, vexed at the oversight.

Isabelle glanced at Jacob in amazement. He grinned with a 'told you so!' expression on his face.

The midwife's eyes strayed to the bag Jacob carried across his shoulders. 'Did you bring me whisky?'

'And pastries. The ones with crème that you like.'

'My belly hungers already!' Grunting, the midwife lifted herself out of the rocker. 'Come!'

Isabelle held her breath as she crossed the threshold into the dim, musty-smelling hovel. She looked around at the cluttered shelves and cramped space.

'That's where my bed was—where she tended me.' Jacob pointed to a spot near the fireplace. 'I was off my head for the first week with a raging fever.'

For the first time, the reality of the oft-told story hit Isabelle as she gazed at the plank floor and pictured the scene.

Jacob pulled out a chair for her as the midwife rummaged through the shoulder bag, a gleeful look on her face. 'Whisky!' She chortled with pleasure as she withdrew two bottles. Groping into the bag again, she withdrew a bottle of wine and a box of pastries tied with a red bow. She ripped open the bow to chuckle at the contents. 'I see you!' Without ado she scooped up a pastry and crammed it into her mouth. Jacob gave a wry look at Isabelle, as if to intimate 'I told you so!' a second time.

'Shall I open the wine?' he asked.

'And the whisky!' The midwife smiled happily, flecks of crème, sugar and pastry clinging to her mouth.

They passed a pleasant hour chatting and reminiscing, the midwife drinking the whisky while Jacob and Isabelle sipped the wine. Isabelle could not keep her eyes off the other woman's enormous bulk and the rolls of fat that jiggled on her arms. The midwife's face was very Indian-looking she thought, eyeing the necklace of coloured beads suspended around the plump neck by a leather string. She stole covert glances at the necklace before realising that the small decorative objects between the beads were made up of bird claws and tiny bones—perhaps from a bird also.

She glanced at Jacob, but he seemed perfectly at home, chatting with the midwife in-between sips of wine.

'My belly thanks you!' The midwife sighed with contentment as she finished off a third pastry. Relighting the pipe, she leaned back in the chair, her eyes resting on Jacob. 'They say you will make the carriages that run without horses,' she said.

A delighted Jacob shot a glance at Isabelle. 'You probably knew before I did!'

The midwife beamed. 'A little bird sang to me,' she said, and puffed on the triumph.

'That is a most unusual necklace. Did you make it yourself?' asked Isabelle.

The midwife nodded, lost in some thought or other.

Isabelle raised her eyebrows to Jacob, who grinned as she recalled his advice. '*She may not say anything for minutes at a time. It just means she is thinking.*'

A few minutes later he stood up. 'Excuse me, ladies. I will be back soon.'

Left alone with the midwife, Isabelle coughed discreetly, bothered by the unaccustomed tobacco smoke.

'Why do you call my husband Ghost Bear?' she asked. 'Jacob explained once, but I never really understood.'

'Because that is his name.' The midwife was staring out the open door, a peevish look on her face. Isabelle followed her gaze to where a raven sat cawing in the branches of a sugar maple. The midwife sank back in the chair with a grunt of annoyance. 'That bird is very rude!' Opening a tobacco pouch, she took out a pinch, tamping the tobacco into the pipe bowl with chubby fingers. 'It is so that I do not forget,' she said.

'Pardon?'

'The necklace.' The midwife struck a match and drew the pipe to flame.

'Forget?' Isabelle's brow wrinkled in confusion. 'Forget what?'

'Does your husband remember anything about who he was before?'

'No,' said Isabelle, unsure if she was following the conversation, 'and he has stopped trying. It is no longer important to him.'

The midwife lapsed into silence as she considered this. 'The bullet has not come out from his head?'

'Bullet? Oh! No, it hasn't. The fragment is still there.'

'And it does not trouble him?'

'I don't think so. He never mentions it. Why?'

The midwife fell silent again. Shifting her bulk in the chair, she reached out a foot to drag a wicker basket toward her. Reaching down, she fetched out a necklace similar to her own made with dried animal parts interspersed with shells and coloured beads and threaded with a thin leather strip. 'Take it.' She held out the necklace to Isabelle.

Isabelle took the necklace, trying not to shudder as she felt the dried claws and beaks beneath her hand. 'Thank you, but …' Not knowing what to say, she held on to the necklace, wishing Jacob would hurry up and return.

'He has gone to make water.'

'Pardon?'

'And then he will walk through the woods. Ghost Bear has a gift.'

'A gift?'

'Not to remember. Just as your gift is not to forget.'

Isabelle frowned, now thoroughly confused. 'How can it be a gift both to remember and to forget?'

'There are some things that it is good to forget.' The midwife mused on this as she picked out another pastry. 'Do you know this flower?' She indicated a dried plant, its flowers still apparent.

'Fireweed, I think,' said Isabelle. 'But is it a flower? I thought it was a weed?'

'That is the flower of forgetfulness.'

'It is?' She glanced out the door for Jacob.

The conversation lapsed again. Isabelle sat back in the chair, looking around the weathered cabin. The notion that her father had been here almost thirty years earlier struck her as incredible. She wondered if he had sat in the very same chair she now occupied. She was pondering the coincidence when she was startled by an entirely unexpected sound.

The midwife had begun to chant, rocking herself in the chair as she crooned in a low, wavering voice. Taken aback, Isabelle wondered if she were intruding. Everything—the coincidence of her father's visit, the stuffy, strange-smelling cabin, and the woman rocking and chanting in front of her—seemed suddenly unreal as if she were in a dream. *The wine must have gone to my head.*

The pungent odour of tobacco smoke made her dizzy and she blinked to clear her eyes. The midwife seemed to have forgotten—or perhaps was indifferent to—her presence as she crooned, absorbed in the monotonous, repetitive chant. Isabelle began to feel nervous and wondered if she should go and look for her husband.

'Pardon, ladies!'

'Oh!' She jumped as Jacob re-entered the cabin, an apologetic smile on his face.

'I couldn't resist taking a short walk over familiar ground. It's time we started back,' he said, picking up the empty shoulder bag. The midwife had stopped crooning to reach for her pipe.

'Walk well, Ghost Bear,' she said as they bade farewell. Her eyes followed as they descended the porch steps and started off back through the woods.

'Is anything the matter, dear?' asked Jacob as they walked. The noon heat had cooled, and it was pleasant walking in the shade. 'Was it the midwife? I know she can take getting used to …. Darling?'

'Oh! Pardon. I was thinking.'

'About what?'

'I do think she is the most peculiar person I've ever met.'

Jacob chuckled. 'I did warn you. She has her own ways. What is it?' he asked, noticing the perturbed look on Isabelle's face. 'Did she say something to upset you?'

'No, not really.'

'Then what?'

'It was something she said—or at least something I *think* she said.' She knitted her brow as she thought back.

'You mustn't let all those rumours about her supposed powers affect you. They are just old wives' tales.'

'It was a mishmash, really,' said Isabelle, as if he hadn't spoken. 'She sang to me.' She said the words in a wondering voice. 'I *think* it was to me. Perhaps it was to herself.'

'Ah! She chanted, you mean. She does that every now and then.'

'It sounded like … the singing in church.'

'No doubt all chants sound alike.' He breathed in the forest air, relishing the rare opportunity to be away from the noise and smells of the town.

'But the odd thing is I seemed to understand it. At least I think I did. It was the wine,' she said, a peeved note to her voice, 'and that dreadful smell of tobacco. How did you ever stand it?'

'The Indian incense.'

'Pardon?'

'That first time you showed me around the cathedral, the smell of incense reminded me of the midwife's pipe.'

'Oh!' She didn't know what to say.

'And what else did she say?' He was really more interested in the leafy woods.

'Something about … a great forgetfulness she said was coming.'

'She said that? Don't worry. She likes to appear mysterious when it suits her.' He squeezed Isabelle's hand, enjoying the feel of the grass beneath his feet.

'Did it really upset you?' he asked at the troubled expression on her face. He scratched the side of his cheek, suddenly irritable. 'Her usual tricks! It was the whisky talking, no doubt. And what was that she gave you?' he asked, spying the necklace clasped in her other hand.

'She said it would help me to remember—or not to forget—I forget which.'

He laughed, thinking it was a joke. 'Sorry,' he apologised at her pained expression. 'But take what she said with a fistful of salt. She's always pronouncing on this or that as if she had a crystal ball to peer into. As for the necklace, it's simply a knick-knack. She makes such things all the time. She usually sells them to the credulous. Did you hear her talk with the birds? It's remarkable. At times she is so intent you actually believe that she is communicating with them. Jinks!' he exclaimed as he stumbled against a tree root.

'She said that forgetfulness was like a fireweed, poking up everywhere.' Isabelle's voice was fretful, unable to let go of the thought.

'Look,' he said, attempting to change the subject. 'The woodcutters are still at it.'

'What do you think she meant?'

'About fireweed?'

'About a great forgetting?' Suddenly frightened, she stopped and looked into his eyes, her face a greenish pale in the shade.

'Nothing.' He kissed her brow. 'As I said, it was the whisky talking. She must have drunk half the bottle. Come on, let's get home and have supper. I'm starved. I wish I had eaten one of those pastries!'

SHE AWOKE TO THE tolling of the matins bell. She listened, half-awake, as the great bronze bell, cast by Claude Yachine a century and a half past, rang out its slow, clangourous peals across the silent rooftops of the city. Drowsily, she turned towards the shutters, glimpsing bright blue sky between the cracks. Beside her, her husband slept noisily, breathing heavily and muttering in a dream. She closed her eyes again, content in the warmth of the wool blankets and the soft mattress. In slumbering fancy, she floated through the closed shutters of the bedchamber and into the morning air outside. Light as a feather, she drifted high above the cobbled streets. An old woman was singing in a tremulous voice as she swept the laneway below. She strained to hear, recognising the tune. *'I've loved you for so long, I will never forget you.'*

Buoyant in the bright air, she floated high above the rooftops of the houses and the turreted, green-domed public buildings. Below, she could see her mother's house on rue Mercier with its familiar red door and matching dormer windows. She was now drifting towards the cathedral itself where it sat high above the city at the top end of rue Marian, it's great spire piercing the blue sky. In her dream-state she saw through the stone walls of the bell tower as the great, pealing bell swung massively back and forth on its wheel. Birds scattered in fright as the deep, brassy *dongs* reverberated in the clear air.

In the pregnant silence following the last plangent peal, the city seemed caught in sunlit splendour. The Mercier River glittered in the distance and the surrounding farmlands lay golden and open to the sun. Beyond the farms and the river, the green mass of forest stretched as far as the eye could see. She murmured against the pillow, shifting uneasily as the dream changed and the houses, squares and statues abruptly melted away like snowdrops in the sun. Wild grass sprouted through the cracked foundations of the city. She uttered a protest as the reinforced walls of the cathedral slowly crumbled and the formidable stone facade crashed to the earth. Deer prowled through the silent woods, stopping to peer through the trees at the broken ruins of the bell tower lying shattered in the grass. Foxes tumbled and played around a giant stone head half-buried in the undergrowth.

'Mother of God!' She muttered in terror as the graves in the churchyard split open and coffins spilled their grisly remains onto the grass. Her limbs were paralysed, and she was uncertain whether she was awake or dreaming. Beside her, her husband snored with a rasping sound in his throat. She fought to wake herself and sat up, her heart pounding, and clutched the nightgown to her throat. The street outside was silent once more. She turned her head to look at the shutters and the reassuring cracks of blue sky.

She sank back against the pillow, her mind grappling with the midwife's prophecy—for such it seemed to her. 'Everything will be forgotten, even love,' the strange woman chanted. And then she stopped, looking blindly at Isabelle as if seeing her in a dream. *'Which is worse: to forget or to be forgotten?'*

A sudden sensation of hysteria made her want to scream. 'But I won't forget!' she vowed. 'Not ever!' The thought was monstrous, striking at her very essence. To forget Jacob, the children, New France, myself? The dreadful litany made her want to burst into tears. Her gaze fell on the midwife's necklace where it lay on the chair next to the bed. She clutched at it, her fingers gripping the beads. 'God would not allow such a dreadful fate!' Frightened, she slid back under the covers and embraced the warmth of her sleeping husband. Closing her eyes, she recited to herself. 'Our Father, who art in Heaven, hallowed be Thy Name …'

SHE WAS STILL IN a daze as she fed and clothed the children and kissed her oblivious husband good-bye. 'Be careful!' she called out after him, causing him to turn his head and glance back. Still unable to shake off the dream vision, she left the two youngest with the serving girl. 'I'm off to Mass,' she said. 'I should be back before lunch.'

Taking a protesting Gaston by the hand, she set off to take communion, deciding, on a vagary, to attend at the church of Sainte-Chappelle. Kneeling to receive the host, she pinched Gaston as he squirmed at the rail beside her. The new priest, a young seminarian on his first parish, held up the host to bless. She closed her eyes, feeling the cool wafer as the priest laid it on her tongue. 'This is my communion,' she murmured as the host, the church, the city and her family all melted into one. She bowed her head in prayer.

'Praise the Lord!' Gaston piped in a loud voice, drawing a suppressed giggle from the young girl kneeling beside him.

'Hush!'

Following the service, she was about to leave when a voice called out to her. 'Isabelle!'

'Hugo?' She smiled, surprised to see him.

'Hello, nephew!' He squeezed Gaston's nose as he sank into the pew beside Isabelle. 'How have you been, cousin?'

'I had an extraordinary visit.'

'Yes?'

She briefly described the visit to the midwife, her eyes wide with the telling.

'She said that?' Hugo's voice was as concerned as her own.

'What does it mean?'

'Who knows! She's probably a bit touched in the head,' he said, laying a reassuring hand on her arm. 'All that mumbo-jumbo about plants and spells. I can still remember the stench!'

'Spells?' Isabelle started with the word.

'Not spells, exactly—I don't know.' Hugo shook his head and frowned. 'I wouldn't pay her any mind,' he said, his voice unconvincing. 'People will believe any nonsense.' He stood up from the pew. 'I must go. The Assembly is in session this morning.'

'You behaved like a savage at mass,' she reprimanded Gaston as they made their way home. 'Your poor grandfather wouldn't know where to put his face for shame.'

'But uncle Henri told us Grandpa didn't go to church.'

'He did when he was your age, clever socks.'

An elderly man tipped his hat as he walked towards them. 'A very good morning, Madame Wheeler!'

'Good morning, Monsieur Boucher.'

'That was Marcel Boucher,' she said to Gaston as they walked on. 'He was a great friend of your grandfather's.

'I wish I was a bull,' Gaston complained.

'Whatever for?' She blinked in surprise.

'Then I could gallop at things!' Sticking his fingers beside his head he made a dash at a cat nesting on a nearby gatepost. The cat hissed and leapt into the air, vanishing behind an iron fence.

'Stop that,' she said, and pulled the resistant boy by the hand.

THE REST OF HER day was busy with the children and a visit from her mother. While the latter fussed over her grandchildren, she took the moment to scribble 'Remember not to forget!' on a piece of paper, the words having assumed tantric significance in her mind.

'Isabelle. Where are you?'

'Coming, mama.' Folding the paper, she slipped it in between the pages of a book. 'I need to pop out to the shops for a moment,' she said. 'Can you watch the children?'

Her mother looked up in surprise. 'The shops? You've only just got in.'

'I won't be long.' She was already pulling on her coat.

'If you must,' her mother sighed. 'Gaston, get down off that chair!'

Still unable to shake off the oppressive mood that had clung to her all day, she walked aimlessly through the streets, vaguely intending to visit her sister. But her feet took her instead toward the Old Town. She took the back streets, wrinkling her nose with distaste at a row of dilapidated houses on rue Vernier. A group of men sitting on the steps of a charity house looked up as she hurried by. Turning a corner, she came across a beggar woman sitting against the wall, a cap for pennies at her side. Stopping, she searched through her purse before depositing some small change in the cap. The woman looked up at her through bleared eyes but said nothing.

She found herself on an unfamiliar street, full of noisy children dressed in ragged clothes. Their mothers sat on the steps of a run-down house, chatting and smoking.

'Good morning, Madame! Are you lost?' one called out in a bold voice that caused her companions to laugh.

She headed towards the main town again, relieved to find herself back on a street she recognised. Passing by St Joseph's Orphanage, she peered through the iron railings at the arched doorway leading into the building. She continued, feeling the weight of a formless apprehension that was resistant to the clearing skies and the reassuring solidity of the pavement beneath her feet.

Turning down the steeply cobbled rue Thierry Vaillant, she put one hand out against the wall for balance. She stopped briefly by the statue of Marietta Dubois to examine the inscription, repeating the words beneath her breath. Passing the Épicerie Moulin, she was hailed by a young girl leaning from an upper floor window. As the sky began to cloud over again, she crossed over to avenue Giroux and walked alongside the high grey stone walls of the convent.

'Madame Wheeler!'

She looked up to see Sophia Vasseur, daughter of Henri Vasseur, the architect. 'Did you know Mathieu Caron has died?' The young woman was breathless with the news. 'He was out of his wits at the end—he thought he was a cat!' The young woman put a hand to her mouth. 'Imagine his poor wife?'

'Mathieu Caron is dead,' she said to her mother as she walked into the house and removed her hat.

'Who?' Madame Ouellet looked at her in surprise, her mouth open, a half-eaten apple in her hand.

'He thought he was a cat,' said Isabelle, staring at her reflection in the glass and vaguely wishing the day would start over again.

24

A Boundless Future

O N THE 15TH OF July 1910, the *Daily Register* published a rare front-page photograph. The grainy black-and-white image showed Ferguson, Selt and Jacob standing in front of a large sign announcing the opening of the automobile factory. The newspaper, renowned for its liberal, anticlerical views, trumpeted the announcement with a dash of progressive bombast:

Today marks a bright new era for New France, one with the opportunity to transform it from an agrarian backwater to an epicentre of modern industry. The announcement, by Messrs Ferguson and Selt, both from Schenectady, New York, is a triumph for our city. The new automobile factory catapults us ahead of both Montreal and Quebec City as the base for the first assembly-line production in French Canada. The enterprise, to be managed by M. Jake Wheeler, an experienced businessman and long-term resident of New France, heralds a boundless future for our proud city. The local manufacture of automobiles offers rich opportunities for commercial growth and development. One important benefit will be in training local craftsmen in the skills required by modern industry. The first vehicles will be assembled in New France from parts sent up from the USA. But according to M. Ferguson, the long-term goal is to manufacture and assemble automobiles right here. This includes the possibility of producing the first vehicle manufactured entirely in Canada. The first product will be the Roadster, a 30-horsepower vehicle assembled under licence from a brand-new design by the famous American engineer Alcott Williams. The vehicle is expected to sell for just over $600. Monsieur Ferguson predicted over 50 automobiles will be assembled in the first full year of production.

The headline and accompanying story caught the attention of Bernard Benoit, prominent businessman and leader of the Reform Party. He praised the new enterprise in the Assembly, holding up the newspaper headline to declare that it signified a new dawn for the region. 'No longer are we beholden solely to agriculture,' he declared, drawing applause from his colleagues on the Reform benches. 'The forces that would hold back our beloved city are now left grasping for reasons why we should continue to lag behind the rest of the industrialised world.'

He was interrupted by more applause as well as boos and catcalls from the Patriot benches. 'I intend to be the first to purchase one of these splendid conveyances,' he continued, defying the catcalls. 'The honourable opposition may prefer to ride horses!' he taunted. 'But as for me, I prefer the comfort and convenience of an automobile!'

He sat down to applause and jeers as the Speaker called for order. The noise of dissent died away as deputy Turgeon took to his feet in reply.

'It is indeed, a new age,' he conceded, his voice strong and vigorous in spite of his years. 'And all in New France welcome progress—contrary to the beliefs of our distinguished colleagues across the floor.'

'Here comes the but!' joked Bernard Benoit to his colleagues in a loud stage whisper.

'However!' The deputy smiled amidst laughter, 'we do not, nor will not, forget the foundations that made and make our province great … Church and hearth, gentlemen … Church and hearth!'

Amid noisy applause from the Patriot Benches, Benoit leapt back to his feet. 'Correction, Monsieur Speaker! Correction! The honourable deputy said 'province'. We are most certainly no such thing! I ask that he withdraw the remark!'

Eyes turned to the deputy, who stood once more. 'Withdrawn … special autonomous region,' he conceded, pronouncing the term with distaste. 'Once an independent country!' he added to cheers as he retook his seat.

BACK IN HIS CHAMBERS, Benoit sat with a few colleagues discussing the news story on the opening of the automobile factory. Copies of the *Daily Register* were laid out on the desk.

'What do we know of this Wheeler fellow? Joseph?'

The question was addressed to a compact man wearing a striped business suit. A prominent Windsor-knotted tie bulged above the shirt collar.

'Wheeler? I've run across him several times in the course of business. A capable fellow. His company built the charabancs for the New Cross line. An American originally.'

'He sounds like he might make a useful ally.'

Henri Grenier, owner of a cardboard box factory, yawned and scratched himself. 'He's married into the Ouellet family.'

'Is he now?' Benoit frowned. 'Does he agree with their politics?'

Grenier shrugged. 'Uncertain. I believe he's a freethinker, for what it's worth.'

'My wife says he never attends church with his family,' confirmed Joseph Bélanger, a fellow deputy.

'He's most certainly a capitalist,' remarked Georges Lamond, the fourth member of the group. A youthful looking, fashionably dressed man, he lounged in the chair his legs crossed at the ankle. 'He's a partner in the business, which says something.'

Benoit nodded as he took in the information. 'What does the *Catholic Tribune* say?' he asked, referring to the Catholic daily that represented the conservative voice of New France.

Lamond gave a jeering laugh. 'The usual rubbish! A warning not to let progress muck with traditional pieties!'

'Henri. Can you arrange a meeting with the fellow? I'd like to learn more about him.'

'Certainly.'

'Did you hear that old fool, Turgeon, in the House?' Lamond snorted in derision. 'I wish he'd trip and impale himself on that stick!'

RELIEVED TO AT LAST be making something, Jacob stood at the door as his employees trooped through the factory door, respectfully doffing their caps as they passed and each in turn calling out, 'Good morning, sir!'

Four demonstration tables had been set up in the cavernous space. An expert from Albany stood behind each table accompanied by an interpreter. Several automobile chassis stood on the workshop floor, their bare frames awaiting the addition of the machine parts stacked in neat piles along the wall.

He watched as the men put their lunches in the employee kitchen. They then gathered in a large group around the shop foreman, who held a clipboard in his hand. Reading from a list, he assigned each employee to one of the four training stations.

Jacob joined the nearest group, listening in as the speaker explained the function of a radiator and gave instructions for bolting one to the chassis. 'This will be your job. Learn this and do nothing else.'

He moved to the second group as the instructor demonstrated the procedure for mounting the headlamps. 'One on each side,' he said, holding up one of the large brass objects for view. The headlamp drew admiring comments as the employees gathered around to examine it. 'The lamps are driven by electricity,' the instructor announced, and led the group to a series of batteries set up on a nearby bench.

Jacob moved on to a third group, who respectfully stood aside at his approach. 'Keep going,' he said, motioning them back to the table. The instructor balanced a tire on the table as he explained its properties. 'This is a Goodyear wrapped-thread detachable tire,' he said. 'It is filled with compressed air to take the weight of the automobile and passengers. Tires are the most important part of an automobile. Think of it like the shoes on a horse. If the horse throws a shoe he can't travel. Well, nor can a motorist if he blows a tire. The good thing about this fellow is that it doesn't require any special tools to remove it from the rim. I'm going to show you how to fit and remove it.'

The fourth group of trainees were standing in front of a large blackboard on which was posted a cut-away illustration of an automobile engine. 'The engine is four-cylinder, thirty horsepower,' the instructor explained. 'Inside are the pistons,' he said, pointing to the illustration. '*Pis-ton*,' he said, repeating the word in French. 'The pistons drive the power to turn the wheels.' He made a churning motion with his hands to illustrate.

Leaving the groups, Jacob climbed the stairs to the first-floor offices and walked past the newly hired secretaries, nodding to Madame Bisset. The office adjoining his own had a brass name plate with *Bookkeeper* inscribed on it. He stopped and stuck his head in the doorway. 'Hey, Dwight?'

Dwight looked up. 'Hi Jacob. Everything's new and raring to go!' He gestured to the wooden shelves lined with books and ledgers.

'It doesn't look like the old buggy,' said Jacob, looking at a large, coloured poster on the wall. The poster displayed a gleaming automobile with the word 'Roadster' written underneath.

'Nope. We are far past that, thank God,' agreed Dwight. 'This new baby is all-fired modern. Thirty-horsepower. Imagine! She'll sell like hotcakes,' he predicted.

'Let's hope so,' said Jacob. He opened the door to his own office, fitted with glass along one side so that he could look out onto the factory floor below.

'Tea, if you please, Madame Bisset,' he said, pausing at the door. He sat down at the walnut desk he had retained from the former business. The noise of hammering came to his ears, and he wondered again at the wisdom of situating the offices so close to the factory floor. He was still debating this when Madame Bisset arrived with the tea.

'You needn't have fetched it yourself,' he protested. 'One of the girls could have done it.'

'I don't mind. Shall I pour?' she asked, setting down the tray.

He sipped the hot milky liquid, his thoughts preoccupied by his dwindling bank balance. Through careful management of his finances, he had paid off more than half of the required 'buy-in' amount, thus easing his anxiety somewhat about the wisdom of such an outlay. The absence of a guaranteed salary had distracted his mind for months in the build-up to the opening. His last pay cheque had been cashed the month before, and since then the family had lived on his savings. Only partly reassured by the clanging and ringing from the factory floor, he added more sugar to the tea.

'At least two-dozen fully assembled cars in the first six months,' Ferguson had remarked, considerably upping the earlier figure. 'We need to recoup our outlay,' he said, in response to the surprised look on Jacob's face. 'It's the way business works—earn back the investment as quickly as possible and then watch the profits roll in.'

'I hope so,' Jacob had muttered to himself, mindful of Isabelle's worried reaction when he broke the news that there would be no more salary.

Anxious to convince her of the wisdom of the arrangement, he had tried to reassure her, 'Fixed salary, no? But a salary arising from sales and profits? yes. I'll be a partner, dear, an owner. In a few short years, once the business finds its feet, our income could double or even triple.'

'And if it doesn't … find its feet?'

'I'll make sure it does,' he vowed.

JUST TWO WEEKS AFTER opening, the first Roadster stood fully assembled on the factory floor. Inviting the office staff to accompany him, Jacob walked around the finished automobile as the factory hands stopped work to watch. The open-topped vehicle looked resplendent in polished brass, red leather upholstery and black rubber tires. The engine compartment had been left open to reveal the copper and brass tubing and red water pump. The shiny black metal encasing the vehicle had been polished to such a degree that he could see his own reflection. Climbing up onto the seat he sat behind the maple-wood steering wheel to a round of cheers and applause.

'By golly!' he exclaimed as he climbed back down. 'I can't wait to drive it.'

In the large, fenced lot at the rear of the factory, he took his first driving lesson under the instruction of the senior American mechanic. As Dwight and Madame Bisset watched, the mechanic patiently explained how to prepare the vehicle by setting the spark lever and turning on the gas. 'Okay, now you use this.' The mechanic held up a hand crank, which he inserted into the motor, demonstrating the correct hold. 'Don't grip it too tight or you risk breaking your arm,' he cautioned. 'Are you ready? It should start on a half-turn.'

Jacob gave a quick, half-turn as instructed. The engine spluttered and caught, the sound like music to his ears.

Exhilarated by the experience, he slowly manoeuvred the Roadster up and down the wide yard, learning about the clutch, brake and gears with the mechanic sitting alongside issuing instructions. After a quarter-hour he felt confident enough to operate the automobile by himself as the instructor watched. He drove three times around the spacious yard before bringing the vehicle to a stop in front of an admiring Dwight.

'Holy cow!' exclaimed Dwight as Jacob climbed down. 'There goes the horse and buggy!'

A WEEK LATER, AFTER much repolishing, the Roadster was officially unveiled to the public. Journalists from the *Daily Register* and *Catholic Tribune* were invited to attend, along with a host of dignitaries including the mayor and deputies from both political parties. A group of fiddlers had been hired to entertain the guests. Instructed by Jacob to play 'cheerful, robust tunes, not dirges!', the musicians nodded to one another before launching into *C'est L'aviron* to the accompaniment of stamping feet and rattling spoons.

Ferguson and Selt were present for the occasion, mingling and shaking hands with the guests gathered on the workshop floor and clearly pleased with the turnout. The musicians finished to applause and Ferguson mounted the platform, an interpreter beside him, as the photographer they had hired for the occasion took pictures.

Ferguson extended an arm, a genial look on his face. 'Welcome all! Honourable deputies … Monsewer le Mayor … Gentlemen … *bienvenue!*' Tucking his thumbs in his waistcoat pocket, he proudly introduced the Roadster. 'A work of art!' he proclaimed as heads turned to admire. Referring to a sheet, he read off a list of facts about the gleaming centrepiece. 'How much would you pay for one?' he challenged the audience. 'How much would you pay for a superior piece of horseflesh that worked non-stop from dawn 'til nightfall … and never bothered you for so much as a bag of hay!'

The interpreted remarks were met by laughter. After a few more anecdotes in praise of the automobile, Ferguson concluded his remarks. 'And now my partner, Mr. Morgan Selt would like to say a few words. Morg?'

Morgan Selt, dressed in a checked suit and fancy necktie, spoke for a further fifteen minutes, praising the virtues of New France as a place to do business while also taking the opportunity to plead for increased tax incentives for new enterprises.

'Let's marry Yankee know-how to French can-do!' he finished, stumping the interpreter and puzzling the crowd.

'And now, Jacob Wheeler, the man in charge!'

Selt stood aside as Jacob took the centre of the platform to a round of applause. The interpreter stepped down as Jacob looked out over the assembled guests. Following brief remarks praising the American owners for their faith in New France, he turned his attention to the assembled automobile.

'Gentlemen, you are looking at the very first automobile assembled in New France! Soon, every family will be able to afford one. The advent of the automobile age will promote new opportunities for work and travel. It will prompt investment in new roads, new factories, and new filling stations,' he declared, borrowing the latter phrase from the Americans. 'I see a future of boundless prosperity lying before us. And that future starts here—not in Montreal or Quebec City, not even in Toronto, but in New France!' The crowd burst into patriotic applause as he clenched both fists and raised them in the air in a triumphal gesture.

Standing amid the invited officials, Bernard Benoit turned to a companion, eyebrows raised in approval.

Jacob continued, his voice rising in conviction. 'Since time immemorial, man has depended on the strength and power of the horse to plough fields, draw loads, and transport him wherever he wished to go. No more! A new age has begun, gentlemen. For the first time in history, the horse has been replaced—not by another animal—but by a mechanical engine so ingenious it will change how we live and work.

Gentlemen …' His eyes swept the expectant crowd, 'I give you the future!' He extended his arm to indicate the automobile, drawing enthusiastic applause.

Dismounting the platform, Jacob walked up to the Roadster, pausing before hauling himself up to allow the cameras to record the moment. An employee cranked the engine as the assembled guests and officials stood to one side. Jacob engaged the clutch as his beaming partners looked on. To shouts of acclaim, he steered the shuddering automobile past the admiring onlookers and out onto the cobbled street. Blasting the klaxon horn, he set off down the street as the guests swarmed onto the pavement to cheer his progress.

OVER THE NEXT FEW weeks, Jacob became a celebrity in the town, his name frequently mentioned on the front page of the *Daily Register* and its rival the *Catholic Tribune*. The former ran a front-page photograph of Jacob standing with his foot on the running board with the caption 'The new face of New France.'

With a proud Isabelle sitting next to him on the passenger seat cradling Gaston or Louis in her lap, he drove around the entire town, each drive drawing admiring glances as he honked the horn for effect. One sunny Saturday, he risked driving through the narrow streets of the Old Town, carefully manoeuvring past the church of Sainte Chappelle while slowing to overtake carts and carriages. As pedestrians turned to gawk, he overtook a horse and carriage, startling the horses as he motored past. Reaching the Upper Town once more, he sped up to twenty miles per hour, enjoying the feel of the wind against his face. 'Why leave it here?' said Isabelle as he parked outside the house. 'It blocks half the street.'

'Advertising,' he answered, smiling as neighbours flocked around to admire the gleaming carriage.

He was greeted by an effusive Dwight as he entered the factory next morning. 'Twenty orders!' Dwight flourished an order book. 'And a further ten promised.'

Jacob telephoned Ferguson with the good news, hearing a sigh of relief down the telephone line.

'That's real good, Jacob. Now go out and reel in some more fish!'

Shortly after the launch, he received an embossed invitation in the mail inviting him to address a meeting of the Chamber of Commerce.

Hugo raised his eyebrows as Jacob read out the details. 'You are going to accept?' They had met by chance in the street and taken the opportunity to retire to a café.

'Is there a reason I shouldn't?'

Hugo handed back the card. 'You do realise that they're all members of the Reform Party?'

'And what's wrong with the Reform Party? I share many of their views.'

Hugo frowned. 'Do you know what those views are?'

'Hugo, don't patronise me.' Jacob lifted a hand to signal the waiter. 'I'm perfectly well aware of their aims and policies.'

'To bring in English schools, a liberal curriculum and to rein in the authority of the Church?'

'Sounds good so far,' chuckled Jacob.

Hugo stiffened. 'We are not Montreal, or Toronto, for that matter,' he said, his voice prim. 'Our culture is distinctly French, Catholic and agrarian.'

'Hugo, my fine fellow. I've heard the same a thousand times. You are always turned towards the past. How can you go forward if you don't face where you are going?'

'And how can we maintain our culture and identity if we don't look back at where we came from?'

Jacob laughed, still jubilant at the invitation. 'It's just a meal. I talk, and then we eat.'

His companion studied him, his gaze sceptical. 'Perhaps,' he said.

A week later Jacob, wearing a new tie for the occasion, entered the gilded premises of the Chamber. A lectern had been set up in front of a number of dining tables. A crowd of perhaps sixty men sat at the various tables talking and drinking wine and spirits. Waiters carrying trays trooped back and forth from the kitchen replenishing drinks.

'Monsieur Wheeler?' A neatly groomed man dressed in an expensive suit approached, extending his hand. 'Bernard Benoit,' he said, introducing himself. 'We met briefly at the launch of your splendid automobile. I have already put in my order for one.'

They shook hands before Benoit turned to introduce three men standing alongside him. 'May I introduce my companions: Joseph Grenier, Henri Bélanger and Georges Lamond.' The men each shook his hand in turn, their manner hearty and welcoming.

'See, we don't have horns!' joked Lamond, who was dressed in a brown suit with a contrasting beige waistcoat and bright red tie.

'Georges is president of the Crédit Mutuel,' explained Benoit. 'Founded by his family over one hundred years ago. It is the third largest bank in Quebec.'

'Second largest,' corrected Lamond, with eyes on Jacob.

'Of course! second largest,' smiled Benoit. He laid a hand on Jacob's shoulder. 'Now, everyone is waiting to hear about your marvellous new enterprise.'

Jacob spoke for approximately twenty-five minutes, referring to the notes he had made, and reiterating his theme that the automobile factory opened the way for a change in New France's perception of itself. The speech was received with prolonged applause and shouts of *bravo!*

'Excellent speech,' praised Benoit, guiding Jacob to a chair at one of the tables. 'Come and enjoy a splendid supper. See that fellow over there, in the grey suit? That's Arnauld Archambault, Speaker of the Quebec Legislative Assembly. He was in town and requested to hear your speech. And that chap with him in the grey suit? That's Chesaire Bonifay, owner of the largest private insurance company in Canada. I'll introduce you later.'

Following the meal, and numerous introductions, during which he received gushing congratulations for his speech, Benoit led Jacob off into a private room. The three men he had been introduced to earlier sat in upholstered leather chairs smoking cigars.

'Please, sit.' Benoit gestured to an armchair. 'Brandy?' He poured from a crystal decanter, handing the glass to Jacob. Arranging himself in another chair, he offered Jacob a cigar. 'No?' He lit his own, moistening the tip with his tongue. 'Jacob—do you mind if I call you Jacob? We are all friends here, no stuffy formalities.' At Jacob's nod he continued. 'We were most impressed by your splendid talk.'

'Hear, hear!' put in Joseph Grenier as the others nodded in approval.

'It was just the sort of thing we like to hear,' continued Benoit. New France needs men like yourself, Jacob. Smart, modern captains of industry not afraid to venture an opinion.'

Jacob smiled agreeably as the conversation veered off into small talk, mainly concerning news items from Montreal and Toronto. Mention of a proposed language bill provoked animated discussion.

'What's is your opinion, Jacob?' asked Benoit, turning to him.

'About the language bill?' Benoit nodded.

'People should be allowed to speak the language of their choice,' he said to appreciative looks.

'So, you don't see English schools as a threat?' queried Henri Bélanger.

'My own factory depends on workmen imported from the States. Some will stay on here after training the locals. They will wish to educate their children in English, and who can blame them?'

'Who indeed?' echoed Bélanger to murmurs of approval from the others.

'Tell us,' coaxed Joseph Grenier, a short, sober-looking individual dressed in a plain black suit. 'What are your plans for the future?'

The others listened keenly as Jacob made a series of mostly non-committal remarks centred around expanding the automobile production line to ensure the continuing prosperity of the business.

'And your wife, Madame Wheeler, she is happy to support you in this endeavour?'

Put on notice by the question, Jacob took a sip of brandy before replying. 'Naturally,' he answered, the response occasioning an exchange of glances.

'As I said, Jacob,' said Benoit, taking the lead once again, 'the interests of New France depend on men like yourself. Needless to say, the Reform Party agrees with your views and is best placed to advance those interests.'

'He means us,' said Lamond, the sly quip bringing chuckles from his companions.

'The fact is, Jacob, the seat of Old Town is coming up for nomination early next year and we'd like to propose you as a candidate on behalf of the party. It's a tough seat, one we've never been able to win. But with you as a candidate, we feel we have at least a chance. What do you say?'

Jacob hesitated, taken aback by the offer. 'I don't know. I'd have to think on it.'

'Of course.' Benoit blew out a puff of smoke.

'There are plenty of advantages to being a deputy, both business and personal,' said Grenier.

'Better you than a son of the soil,' urged Bélanger.

'A son of the nightsoil!'

The quip from Lamond drew a guffaw from Bélanger.

'You would be welcomed among like-minded friends,' added Benoit, directing a frown at Lamond. 'Many are businessmen like yourself. But the professions are well represented too, such as journalists and academics. All share the view that New France must modernise if it is to progress.' He looked at Jacob, inviting a response.

'Give me a week or so to consider.'

'It would be one in the eye for that old frog-face Turgeon!' chortled Lamond.

Jacob frowned, irked by the jibe. 'I'll have you know that deputy Turgeon is a personal friend of mine.'

'Pardon. We meant no offence,' said Benoit, smoothing over the difference as Lamond apologised, his face twitching as he did so.

'The deputy is an honourable man, held in high esteem,' Benoit continued. 'But' he added, measuring his words, 'he remains attached to an old and nostalgic viewpoint, one which is diametrically opposed to progress and innovation. His party does nothing but frustrate our attempts at meaningful reform.'

'It would be good for business—being a deputy,' put in Joseph Bélanger. 'You'll make many new contacts, all anxious to buy those automobiles of yours.'

'The deputy prefers his horse and carriage!' sniffed Lamond. 'Horse shit and faith!'

'A crude way of putting it,' said Benoit, directing a severe glance at his companion. 'But not unjustified,' he said, turning back to Jacob. He poured more brandy from the decanter. 'But let us hear more from you, Jacob. What are your thoughts on New France and its future?'

HE THOUGHT BACK OVER the evening as he sat in his office the next morning, idly gazing out at the shop floor. Deputy Wheeler! The words sounded pleasingly congruent in his mind, the notion of rising from an anonymous, impoverished *personne* to such an august rank flattering to his self-esteem. He pictured himself strolling the Old Town—perhaps with a cane! he edited humorously—as people bowed respectfully and gave way before him. And further glory beckoned—had he not been introduced to the Speaker of the Quebec Legislative Assembly? The man had requested to hear my speech!

For a moment he thought of phoning Ferguson with the news that he had been asked to stand as the member for Old Town. 'Take it, take it!' he heard the other man urge, 'politics is pure business.' An image of Isabelle—a dismayed look on her face as he announced his acceptance of the offer—sobered his fanciful thoughts.

He muttered uneasily as the pendulum swung back the other way. 'Damn'd habitants!' Bélanger's scornful dismissal of Isabelle and her entire social class, came back to his ears. 'Not class, but caste!' Lamond had quipped, to laughter. With a frown, Jacob pushed the conversation from his head.

Isabelle was happily talkative over supper, regaling him with news of her day and the children's latest escapades as she cajoled Louis to eat more of the steamed fish. 'How was the dinner last night? You never properly said.' She held a spoon to Marie-Odile's mouth, coaxing the infant to part her lips.

'Oh, boring! I'm becoming sick of the sound of my own voice.'

'It's a very charming voice, darling. Louis, doesn't your dear papa have a charming voice?'

After the children had gone to bed, her good mood continued as she enjoyed her 'Jacob hour' of sitting in companionable silence, embroidering while he finished the newspaper. 'Read something to me,' she said, 'in your charming voice.'

'What?' He regarded her over the newspaper.

'Anything but politics.'

He debated her emphasis on the word. 'You dislike them that much?'

'Who?'

'Politics. Politicians.'

'Oh!' She tutted and shook her head.

'You wouldn't like to be a deputy's wife?'

'Good Heavens no!' She held up the embroidery. 'See?'

'Very pretty. What do you have against politicians? Somebody has to run affairs, collect taxes, build schools.'

She gave a disparaging hum. 'Is that what they do? I thought they sat around all day and listened to the sound of their own voices.'

'Is that what you think of monsieur Turgeon?'

'He's different.' She held up the embroidery to inspect the pattern.

'Different how?'

'He defends our interests against those scoundrels in the Reform Party.'

'Why scoundrels?'

His interest made her look up. 'Because they would destroy everything I value about New France. Our language, our culture, our faith.'

'Come now. Isn't that being a little unfair? They just want what's best for the city.' He returned to the paper, turning a page to read about the latest dispute in the Assembly over a Patriot proposal to increase the tax on business. *I could be there, speaking my piece.*

'Jacob?' Her voice was hesitant.

'What is it?'

'Will you come to church with me and the children on Sunday?' She set down the embroidery to gaze at him.

He groaned at the question. 'Dearest, I thought we had settled that?'

'The children are beginning to question your absence. Even Louis notices. They see Marguerite and Dominic and all the other families and wonder why their father doesn't attend with them, as other fathers do.'

'I've told you, dearest. I am not a believer. Must we go through this again?' He gave an exasperated sigh.

'It would mean a great deal to me, and to the children.' She picked up the embroidery.

'You know my feelings about religion. You promised to stop asking. Can you do that?'

'I don't think I can.' She teased out a false stich, a note of sadness in her voice. 'One day you may realise that something is missing from your life. And on that day, God's grace will embrace you. That is my prayer for you,

Jacob.' Her voice, calm and regretful, pierced his heart. Remorseful, he got up and kissed her tenderly on the forehead.

Lying in bed beside her, he felt a pang of guilt as he listened to her soft breathing. *Perhaps I should go, to please her.* He dwelt on the thought, his mind drifting back to Benoit's proposal. *She could never accept it. It goes against all she believes in.* It briefly occurred to him that he might stand for the Patriot Party instead, but the thought of advancing notions of Church and soil caused him to mutter. 'I'm a businessman. A rationalist. I don't share this obsession with the past, with superstition—with statues!'

He thought he heard a sound and listened, wondering if either Gaston or Louis had got up again. *I could go just the once, I suppose. But that would create an expectation. Maybe at Christmas, or Easter.* Feeling sleepy, he turned on his side, reaching out for Isabelle in the darkness.

'WHAT A DARLING LITTLE girl!' Josette bounced Marie-Odile on her lap. 'She looks more like her mother every day.' She rubbed her face against the infant while gazing sideways at Isabelle. 'I'm so glad you could stop by,' she said. 'Marguerite and Camille will be here at any moment. But why look so glum?' she asked, taking in Isabelle's expression.

'It's Jacob. I can't convince him to come to church with me.'

Josette thought of a witty reply but held her tongue in deference to the upset look on her cousin-in-law's face. 'Is it necessary that he does?'

Isabelle looked faintly shocked at the reply. 'Yes! If he is to be a proper father to his children.'

'Is he not … proper? *Coo-coo!*' Josette nuzzled her face into the giggling child.

'Yes, of course he is. I meant …' Isabelle tugged at her dress sleeve. 'I meant that he could be … you know, like Dominic, Marguerite's husband. He is at church with the family every Sunday.'

'But I have observed that Dominic is not as affectionate with his children as Jacob is.'

'Really?' Isabelle looked up, gratified at the remark.

A knock sounded at the front door. 'Here they are.' Handing the infant back, Josette went to greet the arrivals. 'Hello, my darling! Come in! And you have brought little Etienne with you! But where is Camille?'

Isabelle cocked her head as her sister's voice lowered to a whisper in reply. She heard a muffled gasp from the hallway.

'Isabelle!' Marguerite entered, her face flushed from the walk. She kissed Isabelle on the cheek, her lips cool from the fresh air. 'And darling little

Marie-Odile!' She picked up the infant and gave her a resounding kiss. 'Such an angel! How old is she? A year and a half already! Where does the time go? Etienne, come here and say hello to your cousin.' She sat down and lifted Etienne up onto her lap.

'What were you saying about Camille?'

Marguerite made a woeful face. 'That worthless husband of hers.'

'What has he done this time?'

Marguerite cupped her mouth and whispered so that Etienne couldn't hear.

'What? I can't understand you.'

Marguerite pointed to her right eye and made a tiny circle with her finger, her expression solemn,

'No!'

'Yes.' Marguerite nodded. 'I just came from there.'

Isabelle paled with anger. 'The bishop ought be informed—or the magistrate!'

'Exactly what I said!' Josette sat down on the plush sofa alongside Marguerite.

'And what would poor Camille do then?' Marguerite looked to both women for an answer.

'At least she wouldn't have to put powder around her eyes!'

'Never mind the wretched fellow. How is your Jacob, dear?'

'In the same breath!' Isabelle furrowed her brow in mock outrage.

'Did you hear about that ridiculous new law in Ontario? Hugo's frightfully upset.' Josette leaned over to rub Etienne's arm. 'Steam was coming out of his ears.'

'What law?' Isabelle glanced at Marguerite, who looked as perplexed as herself.

'It was in the *Register* this morning. You didn't see it?' Josette looked around for the newspaper. 'It's called Regulation 17, if you can believe. Such a silly name.'

'What about it?'

'They intend making English the only language permitted in Ontario schools. No more French language schools throughout the entire province.'

'Isabelle's eyes widened. 'Why?'

'The same old rubbish. They fear it will introduce Catholicism by the back door.'

'Exactly!' Isabelle's resounding endorsement brought surprised looks from her companions.

'Whatever do you mean?' asked Josette. 'I thought you, of all people, would be as upset as Hugo?'

'I am of course, but this is the reason why we should forbid English language schools in New France. If Ontario can ban French, then why shouldn't we ban English?'

'What are you afraid of?' teased Marguerite. 'English or Protestants?'

'This isn't funny.' Isabelle's brow creased in annoyance. 'Our very culture is at stake. Don't you see that?'

'All I know is that it put Hugo quite off his poached egg. He rushed out of the house a quarter hour early—no doubt to discuss it with monsieur Turgeon. Ah!' Josette said to herself. 'That is where the paper went.'

'Catholic or Protestant, what does it matter? They are both of the Christian faith, are they not?' said Marguerite. 'This eternal wrangling is such a bore.'

'Does it not concern you in the least? asked Isabelle.'

'Why should it? They can do as they please in Ontario, although I expect Dominic will have lots to say about it. He's become quite obsessed with politics lately.'

'We need our own ... What did you say it was called?' Isabelle asked Josette.

'Regulation 17,' said Josette. 'It sounds like the St Mary's dress code. I remember my very first run-in with Sister Ignatius—'

'That horror!' Marguerite shook her head. 'I swear I still have the scars from when she caught me talking to the boys over the fence.'

'But it didn't stop you,' chuckled Isabelle.

'I almost forgot the cake!' Josette jumped to her feet. She re-entered the room moments later carrying a large tray bearing two cakes. 'Chocolate or fruit?' she asked, setting down the tray.

'Which one is the more Catholic?' asked Marguerite, her eyes sparkling with mischief.

'The fruit, I imagine,' said Josette, setting out three china plates.

'Why the fruit?' questioned Isabelle.

Josette picked up the cake knife. 'Isn't there some talk about fruitfulness in the Bible?'

Isabelle laughed. 'Your knowledge of scripture is commendable, Josette, as always. What?' She looked perplexed as Josette giggled.

'Sorry! I was thinking of a conversation between Hugo and monsieur Turgeon.'

'Do tell,' prompted Marguerite.

'When the two of them get together over wine, it's all airy-fairy notions of this, that and the other. And the more wine that gets drunk, the more ridiculous they sound. And afterwards Hugo preens like a duck, as if they had discovered the secret to happiness or some such nonsense.'

'Go on!' The sisters smiled at each other as the same words tumbled out of their mouths.

Josette pursed her lips and put on an affected voice. 'The origin of the peanut?' She swept out a dramatic hand. 'Why, it started out life as a humble seed in the earth. No,' she corrected herself, 'before emerging from the twig it was but the *essence* of seed, the *potentiality* of peanut.'

'Really?' Marguerite shook her head in bemusement. 'Why do men never talk of the really important things? They are such airy creatures, always mistaking politics and business for the world.'

Detecting a note of frustration in her sister's voice, Isabelle exchanged looks with Josette. 'Dominic?' she asked.

Marguerite forced a smile. 'Sometimes,' she confessed, 'I would rather he talk about peanuts.'

'They just need prodding,' said Josette, her voice sympathetic.

'They are mostly dense about matters of real importance.' The three women looked at each other, their faces solemn.

'I'll boil some more tea, should I?' asked Josette brightly.

Marguerite blew out her lips. 'May as well,' she said.

25

An Anniversary

To accommodate their growing family and reflect Jacob's increasing prosperity, they had moved from the modest house on avenue Le Coq d'Or to a much larger, free-standing house on rue Sainte-Monique in a desirable area of the Upper Town. The stone-built, double-storey house boasted plumbing, gas for lighting and cooking, a dining room, parlour, kitchen, library, and four above-stairs bedrooms.

The house also boasted a spacious front garden, much to Isabelle's delight. She promptly planted a series of rose bushes along the front of the house, taking pleasure in watering, nurturing and pruning the red, pink, and yellow roses. So successful was she in this endeavour that the roses drew admiring attention from neighbours and passers-by who praised her green thumb and asked for cuttings to decorate their homes.

Jacob was now a prominent figure in New France society, although his decision to turn down Benoit's offer to stand for the seat of Old Town as a Reformist candidate continued to bar him from access to the highest levels of influence. Benoit had approached him twice more with the offer, and each time the temptation to accept had increased before his reluctant refusal. However, he continued to cultivate close business relationships with the Reformist Party members, making it known that he shared their views—even accepting further invitations to address the Chamber of Commerce. He largely kept these ties from Isabelle, rationalizing that such relationships were inevitable for a man ambitious to succeed in business. How else am I to sell automobiles? he asked himself.

But these considerations were put to one side as Isabelle bustled about the house preparing for the dinner to celebrate their tenth wedding anniversary.

'The soup is divine!' she praised a beaming Madame Rodier, the cook they had employed for the occasion. 'Fleurette, come and taste.' She watched, lips parted with anticipation, as their maid sipped from the ladle.

'Excellent, Madame!'

'And you, Dominique?' she asked the servant girl hired to assist for the evening. She looked around for Jacob. 'Darling, where are you? Come and taste the soup.'

Jacob was in the dining room sipping from a glass of brandy as he admired the table setting. A glittering array of china, glassware and cutlery was laid out upon the heavy, starched tablecloth. Flower bouquets, each one including a freshly picked rose, were set at intervals. He picked up one of the formal seating cards, written in Isabelle's careful hand, and laid before each place setting.

'Jacob, where were you,' said Isabelle as she entered the room. 'I wanted you to try the soup.'

'Everything looks splendid, dear.' He kissed her brow.

'Do you think so?' She glowed at the compliment.

'I absolutely do. I'm a very lucky man.' He smiled with satisfaction. 'Ten years. And look how far we've come.'

'All down to your silly automobiles.' She pecked him fondly on the cheek.

'Careful,' he teased, 'you'll be signing me up for the Reform Party next.'

She made a face. 'I've asked Fleurette to put the children in their rooms early. Although I feel guilty. Perhaps we should permit them to stay downstairs for a while longer?'

'And do what—drink wine with the guests?' He squeezed her hand. 'They can bear it for one night.'

'WELCOME, DEAR FRIENDS!' JACOB waited until the chatter died down before continuing. 'A special greeting to you, Monsieur Turgeon, you honour us with your presence.' He smiled at the venerable deputy, now an intimate friend and frequent guest at the house. 'And to all of our dear friends who join us to celebrate ten years of happy marriage.'

'To Jacob and Isabelle!' Jules Desjardin raised his glass, the other guests following suit.

'Hear, hear!'

'And many more!'

Amidst the congratulations he bent and kissed Isabelle on the cheek. 'Ten glorious years!'

The two servers brought in platters of poached fish, maple ham, and roast chicken dressed in pepper sauce to join the bowls of broiled corn, honey-glazed carrots and mint peas already on the table.

'My compliments to the cook,' said Serge Villeneuve slicing into the ham.

'How many cars did you sell today, Jacob?' joked Denis Vachon. 'Oh yes, some more of those delicious peas,' he said as his wife placed the bowl before him.

'Not enough!'

'It is said you are a modern King Midas,' proposed an admiring Claude Charbonneau. 'Everything you touch turns to gold.'

'Then for God's sake, don't touch the fish!' Martin Cloutier's quip was greeted with laughter.

The clink of crystal and china, and the noise of animated conversation brought a burst of satisfaction to Jacob as he gazed around the table, taking in the familiar faces. Jules Desjardin had taken advantage of the dinner to introduce his second wife, Elodie, proudly declaring her the 'jolliest' of company. Jacob eyed her chatting gaily to Claudette Petain. *She looks just like the first.*

At the other end of the table, Claude and Anna Charbonneau shared a joke with Marguerite while Dominic was deep in conversation with the deputy. Isabelle was coaxing Hugo to try the roasted potatoes. 'They are cooked in duck fat and taste superb!' Jacob's gaze lingered admiringly as she scooped a potato and placed it on the plate of her protesting cousin. In the soft candle glow, she struck him as prettier than ever, the passing years serving only to enhance the smiling warmth of her face. *I must remember to tell her how beautiful she is.*

'What do you make of the situation in Europe, Monsieur Turgeon?' The question, from Denis Vachon, momentarily stilled the noise of conversation.

'Must we?' protested Josette. 'Hugo talks of nothing else all day long.'

'I should like to hear Monsieur Turgeon's opinion,' said Claude Charbonneau.

'Me too!' declared Martin Cloutier as eyes turned to the deputy.

The deputy wet his lips with wine, taking time to gather his thoughts before answering. 'I fear that Germany is spoiling for a fight. And both France and England are running out of patience. Unless a miracle happens, war seems inevitable.'

The sombre words cast a shadow over the celebratory mood.

'But surely it won't affect us, being so far removed?' asked Marie Villeneuve, dismay in her voice.

The deputy sighed. 'Once the tiger is out of the cage, no one is safe.'

'Legally, if England goes to war, then so do we,' said Jules.

'Which is a monstrous state of affairs,' objected Hugo, 'especially for Quebec.'

'Agreed,' said Serge Villeneuve. 'It is not our fight. Besides, we have only a handful of soldiers and barely a navy to speak of. Let Europe settle its own differences.'

'Hear, hear!' declared Claude Charbonneau to a chorus of agreement.

'If we do go in, will it mean conscription?' asked Denis.

'Not here, I should think,' said the deputy, 'although English Canada is likely to think differently.'

'It would be an all-around disaster,' argued Hugo, growing upset at the prospect. 'Let English Canada fight if it is determined to be so foolish. And let us hope that the Quebec government keeps our noses clean and well out of any European war!'

'Dessert!' Marguerite clapped her hands as the door to the kitchen opened, and the serving girl entered bearing a large platter of cheese and biscuits.

'Champagne!' someone called out as Fleurette followed, holding two bottles in her hands and cradling a third under her arm.

After the corks were popped and glasses filled, Jules Desjardins rose to propose another toast. 'To my darling cousin—who tolerates my humour,' he said to laughter. 'And to her husband and my good friend, Midas—sorry, Jacob,' he corrected to more laughter. 'I envy you, Jacob,' he said, suddenly solemn. 'To have made such a happy marriage.'

'And for all those automobiles!' interjected Claude Charbonneau to another burst of laughter.

Jules raised his glass: 'Health and happiness!'

'Health and happiness!'

JACOB SANK INTO AN armchair with a glass of cognac as Isabelle supervised the clearing of the table and the washing of the dishes and cutlery. He heard her call out as she bade goodbye to the hired help. 'Goodnight and thank you!'

She joined him with a tired expression on her face. 'What an evening!' She sat down, fanning herself with the ivory Chinese fan that had belonged to her mother. 'Did you enjoy it, darling?'

'It was wonderful, sweetheart. An evening for us to remember.'

She smiled. 'It was, wasn't it?'

'And we get to do it again in another ten years,' he joked.

'Papa?'

'Goodness!' Isabelle put down her fan as a tousled-haired Louis peeped around the door. 'Why aren't you in bed?'

'I can't sleep. Papa, will you tell me a story?'

'Papa's tired. Come here, sweet pea,' said Isabelle, and held out her arms.

'It's alright, I'll see to him.' Jacob got up from the chair. 'Come on, little fellow!' He hoisted the child into his arms. 'One story,' he said, 'and then you must sleep. Agreed?'

The child nodded sleepily. 'About the brave donkey,' he said.

'Goodnight my little angel.' Isabelle blew a kiss. 'Sweet dreams!'

Jacob joined her in the bedroom not five minutes later, an amused look on his face. 'He nodded off before I had barely started.' He sat down to take off his slippers. Isabelle was sitting at the boudoir removing her face powder.

'Those stories you tell the children each night—' she studied her cheek in the mirror and wiped a spot of powder, 'where do you get them from? Marie-Odile was prattling on half the morning about a duck named Hector?'

'Cockerel,' he smiled.

'Pardon?' She peered at him in the mirror.

'Hector is a cockerel, not a duck.'

She pursed her lips in the mirror. 'And just who is this Hector?'

'Just something I made up.'

'Really?' She half turned.

He shrugged. 'The children got tired of the old lumberjack tales. They asked me to make up a story about a fox. So, I did. Both boys liked it, so I made up a few more.'

'I didn't know you had a talent for storytelling.' She dabbed her face with a moist cloth.

'It pleases the children.' He tugged off a sock.

'Can I hear one?'

'Lord no!' He laughed and tugged off the other sock.

'Why not?'

'They are just nursery tales. Something to amuse the children.'

She suspended the cloth as she regarded him in the mirror. 'Write one down.'

'What?' He furrowed his brow.

'I'd like to read one. Perhaps I'll read it to the children during the day when I'm trying to get them to nap or quieten down. Besides, it will be good for your style.'

'Style? What are you talking about?' He stood up to remove his shirt.

She tucked a stray hair into place as she gazed in the mirror. 'Aren't you always complaining that your written French lags behind your speech? Well, this is a way to improve. It's how I improved my own vocabulary as a child.'

He said nothing, turning down the sheets.

'Jacob?'

'I don't have the time.'

'To write a little story? You could dictate it to Madame Bisset—in your charming voice.'

'She would think me an idiot.'

'Seriously, Jacob. It would please me.'

He grunted, secretly pleased at her interest. 'I'll think about it.'

'Good!' She stood up and took off her dressing gown before climbing into bed next to him. 'What did you make of Jules' new wife?'

'She looks remarkably like the first one. What was her name?'

'The first wife? Clara.'

'No, this one.'

'Elodie. Do you think so?'

'Your feet are cold!'

'Warm them, please!'

Grumbling, he allowed her to press her feet against his. 'We are invited out tomorrow night, don't forget, the Government House dinner.'

'Oh, that! Do we have to go? You know how I feel about those stuffy old bores.'

'The Premier will be there.' He waited for a response. 'Isabelle, did you hear?'

She mumbled into the pillow.

'What?'

'I sometimes think …'

'Think what?'

'That the world is changing so fast,' she said. 'We are in danger of losing ourselves … who we are.'

'We change as the world changes.'

'My poor dear mama used to say that what's remembered on Monday is forgotten by Thursday.'

'What on earth does that mean?'

'I'm not sure. But she was fond of saying it, the poor dear.' She was sad for a moment, thinking back.

'Drat! The lights.' He got up to turn out the lights.

She felt him press against her as he climbed back into bed. 'Goodnight, darling,' he said, his voice drowsy. 'Happy anniversary.'

'And you, Monsieur Wheeler.' She snuggled against him. 'Whatever happened to that old Indian woman?'

'The midwife? What on earth made you think of her? I haven't a clue. I haven't seen her for ages.'

'She told me something important, about forgetting.'

It bothered her that she couldn't recall the exact words, and she tried to think as Jacob began to breath heavily against the pillow. She was half asleep before the words flashed into her mind. '*Remember not to forget.*'

26

The Buffalo Redux

IN AUGUST 1914 THE long-delayed Gaston Tremblay square opened in the centre of town. The opening attracted great popular interest, briefly pushing news of the outbreak of war in Europe from the front pages of both dailies. Speculation mounted as to the nature of the giant bronze cast by Alois Giroux to form the centrepiece of the immense space. Giroux had created the sculpture in great secrecy, permitting only a few trusted apprentices—each sworn to silence—to assist him with the work. He himself was untypically silent on the subject and its meaning, answering all questions with a cryptic, 'wait and see'. His desire for secrecy was so intense that the massive bronze was put into place behind a temporary wooden fence and concealed beneath a scaffolding of canvas sheets.

The secrecy, hailed as a 'brilliant ploy to create public interest' by the *Catholic Tribune*, inspired a burst of speculation as to the subject of the hidden artwork. Illicit bookmakers took large sums of money from gamblers waging on a monument to Gaston Tremblay himself, while others wagered on rumours that it was a tribute to New France or to French civilisation. Speculation grew so frenzied that the mayor announced a 24-hour police guard to watch over the monument until the public unveiling. Subsequently, one of the officers was sent home in disgrace, having attempted to peek under the canvas in order to place a winning wager. From then on, more ropes were added to make the bronze impossible to access.

On the appointed day, Jacob and Isabelle took their places among the invited dignitaries as a large crowd gathered to witness the historic event. A military band played martial and patriotic airs as the leaders of both political parties gathered on the speaker's platform erected to one side of the mysterious sculpture. The Quebec flag flew on one side of the artwork, the traditional white and green colours of New France on the other—the defiantly equal prominence of the latter secured only after a flurry of last-minute negotiations with the Provincial Government.

The band finished playing and the Lieutenant-Governor stood up from the row of chairs hosting the official guests. He was greeted with applause by the good-humoured spectators, although a few scattered boos could also be heard. After opening remarks that delicately praised New France for retaining its 'special characteristics within the province', he stepped aside in favour of the Speaker of the New France Assembly, who spoke for a quarter hour in front of the increasingly restive crowd. Next to speak was deputy Turgeon, the popular and highly respected figure greeted with warm applause. He spoke glowingly and eloquently, praising the square and the yet-to-be-seen sculpture as emblematic of the town's glorious history. 'Long live New France!' he concluded to enthusiastic cheers as the Lieutenant-Governor tried valiantly to conceal his discomfort.

The deputy was followed by Bernard Benoit, who heralded the square as part of the region's dramatic transformation, both industrially and culturally. 'New France!' he proclaimed and stopped to observe the crowd. 'New!' he repeated meaningfully. 'That means that our town, our region, must always renew itself in step with the changing times. This is what our glorious founders intended—that we stride into the future full of confidence, knowing who we are and where we came from.' The sentiments were greeted with applause.

At a signal from the organiser, the band struck up as attention turned to the canvas-shrouded monument. The Lieutenant-Governor posed for the cameras as he waited to cut the ribbon that held the canvas covers in place.

'What do you think it is?' Isabelle asked Jacob as excitement mounted.

'I haven't a clue. Alois held it so tight to his chest that even Hugo couldn't get a word out of him.'

With great fanfare, the dignitary cut the rope and the canvas shrouds fell away to cries of anticipation. The cries gave way to gasps as the monumental artwork stood revealed as a colossal bronze in the form of a winged bull. One foreleg was half-raised as if the creature was poised to charge forward. The fierce face and flaring nostrils emphasised the impression of strength and barely controlled ferocity. The massive sculpture towered above the speaker's platform, the outspread wings extending on either side as though prepared to loft the triumphant creature up into the heavens.

'What is it?' Isabelle turned to Jacob, a look of confusion on her face.

He stared, unable to suppress a grin of recognition. 'The buffalo!'

'Buffalo?' She repeated, more confused than ever. 'What does that have to do with New France?'

The initial puzzled reaction of the crowd quickly turned to cries of admiration as the full effect of the majestic bronze made itself felt. The sculptor was introduced to 'hurrahs!' and a rapturous ovation as he stepped forward to bask in the adulation. Standing with a delighted smile on his face, he raised a hand in acknowledgement as the dignitaries on the platform rose to join in the applause.

THE MONUMENTAL ARTWORK QUICKLY became the talk of the town, hundreds gathering each day to view the imposing beast. They gazed up in wonder at the flared nostrils and outspread wings and paid the opportunistic free-lance photographers to take their picture standing in front of the towering sculpture. The *Daily Register* was effusive in its praise, quickly declaring the monument a masterpiece.

> *The splendid bronze is fully in keeping with the new square, anchoring the vast space with a magnificent sculpture that is sure to come to symbolise New France now and into the future. The imposing monument was poetically described by the Honourable Sir François Langelier, Lieutenant-Governor, as an 'audacious masterpiece' entirely befitting the new concourse. Various allegories have been suggested for the mysterious creature: that it represents the spirit of nature—the greenery of the ancient forests that once covered the land, challenging the modern predominance of stone and iron; that it represents the enormous potential of a New France poised to charge into the future—a reading naturally favoured by the secular, liberal elements of the populace. The more philosophical claim that it represents a metaphysical, quasi-mystical creature meant to remind us of eternal, transcendent values. Perhaps one day a meaning will be settled upon. Meanwhile, the sculptor himself remains enigmatically silent, refusing to comment on the symbolism of the giant bull or the inspiration for the bronze while, no doubt, rejoicing in the controversies it has stirred. The plaque beneath the massive sculpture simply reads 'Winged Bull,' and perhaps, in the end, that is all that needs to be said.*

'Did you not recognise it?' asked Jacob on their return home. Taking Isabelle's hand, he led her into the library to stand before the framed charcoal sketch.

'I never gave it much notice,' she confessed, making up for her neglect by studying the sketch with new interest.

'Alois wants to keep the bull's origins a secret, a guessing game to tantalise the curious.'

'And will you keep his secret?' she asked, peering at the sketch. 'Those … spears, do look like wings, I must admit.'

'Of course. If Alois declines to reveal the inspiration then it is not for me to reveal it. Besides, it's not as if I owned the likeness. He has transformed it from a buffalo into a bull, but you can clearly see the original creation, can you not?'

She pursed her lips. 'When did you say this was sketched?'

'God knows. I wish I knew the story of how it came about.'

'It looks old,' she said. 'But I can see why Alois was so taken with it. There's something about it, don't you think? It's quite striking, as if the artist was determined to capture something.' She reached out a hand to straighten the wood frame. 'Perhaps the reason you kept it was because the artist was famous, in which case it may be of great value?'

He chuckled. 'I doubt it. Probably some western ranch-hand with time on his hands.'

They stood and stared at the sketch for a moment before the clock struck the hour and they turned to more immediate matters.

PROMPTED BY THE NEW monument, although he might have puzzled to make the connection, Jacob decided to visit his old friend the midwife. The mid-summer day was hot and humid, and he mopped his brow as he walked. He exclaimed with surprise as he beheld dozens of new houses standing on the large area of ground cleared from the woods just beyond the city walls. A tarred road connected the houses to each other and to the main road leading into the city. He was further surprised to note a bus stop at the end of the tarred road. A large wooden billboard announced a new housing project, "The Woodland Estate," to be commenced in the near future.

Stepping off the tar and onto the grass, he walked a half mile before entering the woods proper. He gave a sigh of satisfaction as he finally left the expanding town and its environs behind. Birds chirped in the trees as he enjoyed the familiar woodland hush. A deer emerged from the under-growth, and he stopped in his tracks to observe. The animal held one foreleg in the air as if suspicious of the surrounding brush. It stood there on trem-bling legs for a moment before lowering its head to the grass. He stepped out from behind a tree and the startled deer bounded off into the woods.

The midwife was seated on the porch, smoking and rocking herself. 'Ghost Bear,' she said, taking the pipe from her mouth and eyeing him as he approached. She sat with the familiar blanket around her shoulders in spite of the warm weather. She was bareheaded, her silvery black hair tied in long plaits.

'Hello old friend! You are looking well,' he greeted as he mounted the steps to the porch.

Unusually, she didn't follow Jacob inside to rummage through the gifts he carried. Instead, she watched from the rocker as he took a bottle of whisky and another of wine from the bag and set them down on a stump that served as a side table. The midwife struck him as preoccupied and fretful, her face drawn into a frown as she sat in the rocker.

'Soon I shall be able to take a bus the whole way here,' he said, his voice cheerful.

She grunted in reply, clearly irritable at the suggestion. 'They frighten the birds and drive away the deer.'

'I saw a deer,' he said, pouring her a glass of whisky and himself a glass of wine, 'so they can't all be gone. I brought you some of the pastries you like.'

He set the box down in her lap. To his surprise she ignored it, leaning forward in the chair, her eyes fixed on the woods.

'Is something wrong?' he asked. 'Are you expecting someone?'

She said nothing, intent on the trees. Vexed, he sat back in the other chair, telling himself she was in her 'Indian' mood and would speak when it suited her. The summer afternoon was warm and hazy, the breeze barely a whisper in the air. The midwife rumbled phlegm in her throat and leaned forward to eject a gob of spit into the dirt.

'Do you miss your buffalo, Ghost Bear?' she asked, settling back in the rocker.

'Buffalo?' He stared in surprise. 'What buffalo?'

'You sang of him in your fever.'

'I did?' Taken aback, he studied her face to see if this was one of her enigmatic jests.

Tapping burnt tobacco from the pipe bowl, she sat back to consider the pastries. Picking one up, she took a small bite before returning it to the box. She then took a sip of the whisky.

'Is everything all right?' he asked, bemused at her behaviour. When she again made no answer, he sighed and stretched out his legs, more than content to humour her mood and sit in silence to enjoy the summer day.

She rocked herself for a few minutes before turning to him, a glint in her dark eyes. 'Of what do you dream these days?'

'I do not remember my dreams.' He refilled his glass and swallowed at a gulp, reprimanding himself for using the wine to quench his thirst.

The midwife's attention was once again fixed on the nearest trees. She muttered to herself, a cross look on her face. The drowsy air and forest stillness combined to make him feel sleepy and he leaned his head back against the wall of the cabin.

He woke with a start. The midwife was still seated in her chair, smoking the pipe. The sun was already well past the zenith. Crickets chorused loudly in the grass. 'Good Lord, how long did I sleep for?'

The midwife grunted and held out her empty glass. 'What does it matter?' she said.

She seemed more her old self, and he noticed pastry crumbs on the front of her dress. Around her neck she wore the familiar bead necklace.

He repeated his earlier question. 'Is everything alright?' He spoke softly so as not to provoke her ire.

She regarded him with a long, probing stare that struck him as distinctly odd.

'Did the birds tell you something?' he asked.

Instead of replying, she began to sing in a quavering voice that gathered strength as she continued. He thought he recognised something in the chant. 'Is that the story you told me when I first arrived? The one about the moon and the maiden? I remember that the moon hid its face so that her enemies would not find her.'

She ignored him, continuing the soft wail. Perhaps it is something else, he told himself, perplexed at the lack of her usual chuckling welcome. Maybe she's angry. After all, she hasn't seen me for ages.

'What do you know of stories?' she asked suddenly, her voice grumpy.

'All I know is that they have a beginning, a middle, and an end,' he joked, hoping to lighten her mood. 'Don't you agree? It's the way of things,' he added, adopting her own cryptic mode of speech in the hope of provoking a conversation.

'Who are you to say what is the way of things?' She scowled, as if insulted by the notion. 'A story must have its tail in its mouth, like a snake.'

'You talk in riddles, as always,' he objected, annoyed at her continuing ill-humour. They sat in silence for a further half-hour, the midwife rebuffing all of his attempts at conversation. Finally, he stood up. 'Isabelle must be wondering where I am.'

The midwife gave no response, seemingly absorbed in the pipe. 'Farewell,' he said, disappointed with the visit. To his surprise, she leaned forward to clutch his hand.

'Go well, Ghost Bear.' She squeezed his fingers, squinting up at him. 'Remember your name.'

He studied her face, unable to read a meaning there. 'Of course I will. How could I forget?'

27

A Nursery Tale

GENTLEMEN!' GENTLEMEN! THE SPEAKER shouted to make himself heard above the noise. 'Do we have a motion?'

'We do, Monsieur Speaker.' The noise fell away as Bernard Benoit rose to his feet. 'It is a joint motion. And I defer to my august colleague, deputy Turgeon, leader of the Patriot Party, to put the motion before the Assembly.' The announcement was greeted with applause.

'The chair recognises deputy Turgeon.'

The veteran deputy rose to his feet. 'I thank you Monsieur Speaker, and also express gratitude to my esteemed colleague, deputy Benoit.' He bowed in the direction of the Reformist benches. Someone coughed, the noise loud in the hushed Chamber as deputy Turgeon adjusted his spectacles to read. 'The motion, presented with the utmost seriousness and after much discussion between both parties, is as follows:

Notwithstanding that our great nation, Canada, finds itself at war with Germany,' he began, his voice strong and sincere, despite the occasional quaver due to age, 'and notwithstanding the deep love, affection—and loyalty,' he continued, with a glance at the attentive benches, 'that each of us feels toward our homeland … this Assembly, in solidarity with our parent Assembly in Quebec City, categorically rejects the notion of conscription for French Canada, as has been proposed by the Federal Government.'

His voice rose as the motion was greeted with cheers and applause. 'Notwithstanding our strong objection to conscription, we express confidence and faith that in this great struggle between the European powers, right and justice will prevail.'

'I NEVER THOUGHT I'D live to see the day.' Turgeon fanned himself with the motion paper as he relaxed in his private chambers with Hugo Gagnon following the vote.

'It was unanimous?'

'Ha!' The deputy gave a dry laugh. 'God is not that merciful! There were two abstentions and one vote against—by that strange fellow Dupont, who has all sorts of axes to grind. But it was as unanimous as these things can be.'

'And your amendment?'

'Defeated, I'm afraid. Not that it had much of a chance to begin with. "French schools for French children," was never going to be popular, even in my own party—some of whom regard Ontario as a foreign country.'

'But you knew that,' sympathised Hugo. 'It was more of a reminder.'

'So it was intended. Why should we fight for a government that denies French Canadians the right to an education in their own language simply because they happen to reside in Ontario or Manitoba? What is in the papers?' The deputy indicated the newspapers lying on a side-table.

'More riots in Montreal.'

'Against conscription?'

'No. Against rising prices and the loss of jobs.'

'I fear the same will happen here.'

Hugo made a grumbling sound. 'This is not our war. Let English Canada fight it as it wants. It has nothing to do with us, and yet we suffer from it.'

The deputy pinched his jaw while gazing at the floor. 'Enough of politics,' he declared. 'Right now, I'm off to see your delightful cousin for some tea and sanity.' He looked around. 'Where in the moons of Jupiter did I put my hat?'

'MONSIEUR TURGEON!' ISABELLE SMILED warmly as the maid showed the deputy into the parlour. 'How nice to see you again.'

'My dear Isabelle!' He kissed both her hands. 'How are you my dear?'

'Right as rain!' she said in English. She laughed at the look on his face. 'Jacob has been teaching me English expressions. Do you know that one?'

'I do. It is raining cats and dogs,' he said, and chuckled at the confusion on her face. 'You will come to it in time. An odd, if picturesque, language!'

'Jacob is in the library. I'll put the kettle on and make tea—and bring in some of those biscuits you like, the chocolate ones,' she said, leading him to the study.

'You are too kind!'

'Monsieur Turgeon!' Jacob greeted his friend with a glad handshake before showing him to a chair.

'Thank you, Jacob. I have just come from the House.'

'Ah! The conscription vote. And?'

'Roundly condemned—by both parties. However,' sighed the deputy, 'I do not imagine that will be the end of it. Ottawa won't be impressed.'

'Did you hear about the riots in Montreal?'

'I did. I expect the same to happen here. People are fed up with the rising prices. Ah! My dear!' He smiled as Isabelle entered the room balancing a tray.

'Here you are.' She set down the tray and placed the silver teapot and two cups on a side table along with a milk jug, sugar bowl, and a heaped plate of biscuits.

'An angel come to minister!' he praised as she poured the tea.

'I shall be disappointed if you leave a single biscuit on the plate. Jacob?' She handed her husband a cup of tea. 'Now, I shall leave you two to talk.'

The deputy watched admiringly as Isabelle closed the door behind her. 'You are indeed fortunate, Jacob, to possess such a wife. She is a fine upstanding woman, as was her mother before her. "A good woman is a treasure beyond jewels," he quoted.

'I tell myself every day, I assure you.'

'And how are things with you, friend?' enquired the deputy, taking a biscuit.

'Much the same. I can't complain.'

'And the factory?'

'We are now turning out a dozen ambulances a week, thanks to the new assembly line.'

'And they are being shipped to France?'

'They are. Mind, I shall be glad when we are able to get back to producing automobiles again.'

The deputy bit into a biscuit, his face lighting up with pleasure at the taste. 'Hello, what's this?' he asked, his eyes lingering on a handwritten page next to the plate.

'Oh, that's nothing. A short tale I wrote to read to the children at bedtime.'

'Indeed? May I?' Intrigued, Turgeon picked up the page, looking at Jacob for permission.

'Of course.' Jacob shrugged with embarrassment as the deputy took out his reading glasses. 'It's nothing really, a means to improve my written French and what Isabelle refers to as my atrocious spelling. It's very simple, as a child might write.'

The deputy said nothing, already absorbed in the page.

And it so happened that a certain dormouse, fed up with being cold and hungry for the winter, ventured into the house of a rich man who owned a cat. The cat was known for its bad temper and ferocity in catching and devouring mice. Thus, the dormouse proceeded cautiously, anxious to avoid the cat, but eager to look for crumbs from the rich man's table. As the dormouse feasted happily on a few such morsels he received the fright of his life as he was pounced upon by the cat—a grey monster who had appeared from seemingly nowhere to grasp him in its sharp claws. 'Please do not eat me, sir!' he pleaded, desperate for some way to save himself from the jaws of the terrible creature.

'And why should I not?' demanded the cat in a gruff voice. 'You are stealing food from my master's table!'

'A few crumbs only,' pleaded the shivering dormouse. 'I steal only that I may not starve!'

'What is it to me if you starve or not, so long as you do not steal from my master? Convince me of the rightfulness of your action and I shall let you live,' answered the cat, his eyes menacing as he licked his lips.

The poor dormouse seized upon the chance to escape the fearsome jaws. 'Then, sir, I challenge you to solve a riddle. Which is best. To live or to die?'

The cat frowned. 'To live is the better choice. Who could dispute that? That is no argument at all!'

'Then what if it is in a person's power to grant life or death, which is the better choice, for that person?'

'You shall not trick me!' the cat hissed in a fury. 'You were caught stealing, that is quite another case!'

The dormouse quivered with fear but continued his plea. 'But where the weight of evidence is clearly against the accused, as in this matter, would you not agree that to grant life in such a case reflects even more favourably upon the judge?'

The cat hesitated. 'Perhaps,' he conceded.

'Then, being an honourable cat, do you not think that showing mercy to me will bring more satisfaction to yourself in the long run, since reputation outruns all else?'

The cat considered this for a moment. 'You mean that by sparing your life I gain the benefit of a good reputation?'

'Exactly!' The dormouse trembled with sudden hope. 'You will win renown among your fellow creatures for your wisdom and good sense.'

'But my dear dormouse, what does reputation mean to a cat?' And with that the cat swallowed the dormouse in a single gulp.

The moral of the story, dear reader, is that appealing to self-interest only works if the other person agrees on what is at stake. A cat's reputation depends on devouring mice. That is how he gains the regard of his fellow cats!

The deputy looked up from the page, a delighted look on his face. 'You wrote this Jacob?'

'I did, to read to the children.'

The deputy took off his glasses. 'Then, in my opinion, you have succeeded marvellously. The style is entirely suited to the subject matter.' He pondered for a moment. 'Did you show any literary talent before?'

'I would hardly call it talent. It's all new to me.'

'Remarkable.' The deputy dipped a biscuit into the tea. 'And how did you come upon this particular style or method of presentation?'

'I don't really know. It just seemed suited to the tales.' Jacob thought for a moment. 'Although I suppose I remembered the stories the midwife used to tell me. They were colourful and each one had a lesson to be learned. And they mostly featured animals that spoke like men.'

The deputy's face lit up with the reply. 'Fascinating—an aboriginal de la Fontaine!'

'Pardon?'

'A small observation, no matter. And only your children have heard them?'

'The children and my wife.'

'Do you have any more?'

'I do, six or seven others.' Abashed at the deputy's praise, Jacob opened the desk drawer and passed over two more handwritten sheets. 'This one I only just finished writing down yesterday.'

Taking another sip of tea, the deputy adjusted his glasses and began to read.

One morning, a curious and lively cockerel, let us call him Hector, ventured out from the farmyard and down the road in search of adventure. He was a brave and fearless cockerel, eager to find out more about the world beyond the farmyard. He had not travelled very far when he came upon a horse and wagon stopped by the side of a flooded stream. The driver, a dishevelled man with long black hair and a doleful face, looked up as the cockerel strutted up. 'Good morning, Master Cockerel,' he said. 'As you can see, I am stuck on this side of the stream, waiting for the water to go down before I can cross. Will you tell me a story to cheer me up while I wait?'

'I suppose I could,' said Hector, 'if you tell me what is on the other side of that stream. For I have never dared to cross it and am eager to find out.'

The man considered this. 'What is on the other side is exactly the same as on this side.'

The cockerel looked disappointed at the reply. 'Oh,' he said, 'I was hoping it was something marvellous and different.'

'Such as?' The man asked, curious at such a remark.

'I was hoping it was a land where cockerels could talk and never be afraid of getting their heads chopped off,' answered Hector.

The man, a freight-carrier by trade, looked bewildered at the answer. 'But you are a cockerel, and you can talk already. So why do you wish to exchange the other side for that which you already have here?'

'You are right,' answered Hector, 'but my fate depends entirely upon the farmer. And one day, when I least expect it, he will decide to chop off my head and eat me. Across the stream I am hoping to find a world where farmers do not chop off heads and cockerels may live happily ever after.'

The man thought about this. 'Would you like me to carry you across to the other side? Perhaps you will find what you wish for.'

Hector brightened. 'Oh, would you? I should be most grateful. And I shall pay for my passage with a story.'

Happily, he told several tales before the driver stood up and announced the water was low enough to cross. Picking up the cockerel he placed him in the back of the wagon. Then, climbing up onto the seat he urged the patient horse into the water. Half-way across the river, the water rose suddenly and swamped the wagon, overturning it. 'Help!' cried Hector, fluttering above the water. 'I am afraid I shall drown!'

'Sit on my head,' called out the man, and I will swim us to shore. And he did so, although the unfortunate horse drowned.

'But we are on the same shore we set out from,' objected Hector as his feathers dried and his courage returned.

'Then wait another day, Master Cockerel, and perhaps another wagon may ferry you across.'

Hector thought about this. 'No,' he said, 'I have decided I am quite happy where I am.'

'But aren't you afraid of getting your head chopped off and being eaten?'

'I was,' answered Hector, 'but I no longer am.' And with that he set off back to the farmyard where he was happily greeted by the adoring hens. And for the rest of his days, he never again ventured away from the farmyard.

The lesson of the story, dear reader, is that we should accept what life has given us, with all its joys and misfortunes. For across the river things may not be so good as they might seem. And it is better to accept life as it is than to pine for some imagined paradise.

With a delighted chuckle, the deputy finished reading and laid the sheet back on the desk. 'And do your children enjoy the tales?'

'They do. They particularly like knowing that they are invented just for them.'

'Have you thought of publishing them?'

Jacob's eyes widened. 'Good Lord, no! They are not worthy of that. They are simply nursery tales to entertain my children at bedtime.'

'But they are charming. You have a natural gift for expression. What does Isabelle think?'

'She enjoys them. She says that they are improving my French.'

'Michel Verreau, publisher and editor of the *Catholic Tribune* is a good friend of mine. Do you mind if I show him your little tales?'

Taken aback, Jacob stared at the deputy. 'You mean he might print them?'

'If he agrees with me on their worth, yes.'

Jacob rubbed his jaw, pondering the prospect. 'I don't know. I am a businessman. The tales may not sit well with the public. Mr Ferguson might think them frivolous and at odds with my position.'

'Then print them anonymously. Michel will agree to that. No one need know you are the author. In fact, I will keep your name from Michel himself if you agree to me showing them to him.'

Jacob considered this further, picking up the teacup to nurse it as he sat in the chair. 'In that case, why not?'

A FEW DAYS LATER, as he made his way home from the factory along rue Bergeron, Jacob heard chanting accompanied by shouts and whistles emanating from rue Marie Françoise-Thérèse. Hurrying through an alleyway that connected the parallel streets, he halted in surprise at the sight of thousands of protestors filing down the thoroughfare holding up banners condemning the rise in food prices. Several also denounced the same Military Service Act that had been condemned in the Assembly. Scores of policemen shepherded the marchers as they paraded past, their faces angry and determined in the November sunshine.

'There were thousands of them,' he said, recounting the protest to Isabelle upon his return home. 'The deputy was right. What's happening in Montreal is now being repeated here.'

'I'm not surprised.' Isabelle passed him the bowl of buttered broccoli. 'Prices are going up everywhere. Soon people won't be able to afford to eat. Louis, don't play with your food.'

'I spoke to Mr Ferguson just yesterday and brought up increasing the men's wages a fraction to compensate.'

'And?'

'He wouldn't hear of it.'

'Perhaps this demonstration will change his mind?'

'I doubt it. He blames French Canada for not enlisting in the war, says it serves them right.'

'He said that? That's not very Christian of him.'

'His faith is capitalism, not Christianity, I'm afraid.'

'And the two are incompatible?' she asked, leaning to dab Marie-Odile's lips with a napkin.

'As far as he's concerned, yes.'

Isabelle shook her head in frustration. 'This is what my father always feared. That our beliefs and way of life would suffer the further away we moved from our values and traditions. Cannot you insist upon an increase? After all, you are a partner.'

'A junior partner,' he reminded her. 'A very junior partner. I have little say in the overall running of things. Besides, the war which is causing all of this hardship is being fought in the name of God, is it not?—on both sides.'

'Not in God's name. In the name of religion.'

'The two are different?'

'When they no longer represent each other.'

'I haven't heard back from old Turgeon,' he said, fearing the conversation was upsetting her. 'He was supposed to show my little stories to that newspaper friend of his. I'm sorry,' he apologised, seeing the expression on her face. 'I shouldn't have brought politics to the dinner table.'

'It can't be helped.' She attempted a smile. 'After all, they are like vegetables nowadays served up at every meal.'

'THEY ARE, AS YOU say, charming.' The newspaper editor placed the pages down on the desk.

'So, you will publish them?'

Verreau thought for a moment. 'Yes. I think our readers will enjoy them—take their minds off all this conscription folderol. Let's start off with one each week, to see how they are received.' He tapped a pen against his teeth as he studied the deputy. 'But I would much prefer to print the name of the author rather than Anonymous. The readers would like to know.'

'I am certain that they would. But I have given my word.'

Verreau hummed. 'You can tell me, in confidence. I will respect his wishes.'

The deputy placed a finger against the side of his nose. 'Sorry.'

'Is it Hugo Gagnon? I can hear his voice in the tales.'

'Hugo? Goodness, no!' The deputy chuckled.

'Then that other fellow—the one that caused such a fuss in the Assembly?'

'Dupont?'

'Yes, him.'

The deputy shook his head. 'It is no one you are personally acquainted with, I assure you.'

'Not acquainted with. Now there's a clue!' Verreau was about to make a further guess when they were interrupted by a commotion in the street outside. Opening the second-floor window, Verreau looked down at a procession of chanting protesters marching along rue Camille toward Government House.

'Who are they?' The deputy moved in beside him to observe.

'More protestors against conscription.'

The deputy squinted, making out the wording on a large banner held up by two of the marchers. 'Say No to the English war!' was written in large black letters. He clucked disapprovingly. 'The federal government is making a huge mistake. Their actions only reinforce anti-English sentiment.'

Verreau frowned. 'I agree. They can hardly take away our rights on the one hand and expect us to fight their war on the other.' He leaned further out the window to follow the line of marchers. 'Perhaps your anonymous friend and his enchanting little tales couldn't have come along at a better time.'

'When will you publish them?'

Verreau considered, still looking at the marchers below. 'Soon,' he promised. 'Soon.'

THE RIOTS MANY HAD feared happened early the following year when the federal government began to enforce the conscription bill. Those found without registration papers were arrested, further fuelling anger at the widely despised bill. The anger exploded in a series of riots over the Easter weekend. Alarmed at the violence, the federal government sent in troops from Ontario to control the disturbances. The nervous and badly trained conscripts opened fire, killing a handful of protestors and wounding many more. Jacob had no choice but to close the factory for a week as the shocked city tried to recover from the event.

The irony, as René Turgeon pointed out in his memoirs years afterwards, was that the war ended just seven months after the riots.

"And then the authorities in their arrogance thought it wise to declare a state of emergency in Quebec Province, despite warnings that this would only fan the flames of resistance. The result was a country split along linguistic lines; and within that divide lay a smaller fracture: a sharpened sense that New Frenchmen could not trust anyone other than themselves to protect their interests. Thus, the chaff of one conflict germinated the sparks of another. That same momentous year also brought the terrible flu epidemic as well as the first newspaper publication of the well-known Fables of Jacob Wheeler."

'Charles?' He half-turned in the chair. 'Charles.'

'Yes, sir?' His manservant stuck his head in the door.

'Be a good fellow and read me the date of that framed copy of *The Catholic Tribune* hanging on the wall by the stairs.' He waited a few moments.

'Which one, sir?' came the man's voice. 'There are several.'

'The one with mention of the Nursery Tales on the front.' He waited again.

'Ah! May, sir. May 21st, 1918.'

'How very long ago it all seems,' the deputy mused before writing the date. 'A fabled year indeed. If only poor Jacob knew what lay in store.' He sighed and put down the pen. 'Not that any of us suspected.'

THE FABLES, PUBLISHED UNDER the pseudonym, "Tales of a Habitant," were greeted with immense popular acclaim. The Saturday edition of *The Catholic Tribune* sold out as people purchased copies to read to their children or themselves while waiting eagerly for the next week's issue. The characteristic tendency of the citizens to allegorise ran riot as each new fable was interpreted according to the hopes and beliefs of the interpreter. "The dormouse is New France. The cat is English Canada!" proclaimed one letter to the editor. "The fable is meant to instruct us on the dangers of dealing with a distant government that knows or cares nothing of our values."

"Hector is a pious Catholic, passively accepting his preordained fate without protest or hope for a better future—just as the Church would have it!" argued another letter-writer. "On the contrary," argued still another. "Hector is a symbol of suffering humanity, finding consolation in that which he yet cannot accept. He thus symbolises Everyman and the dilemma of being born into a universe without meaning or purpose."

"The cockerel represents the ignorant past," opined yet another writer. "Hector abandons his hope for a better future out of fear of the unknown, preferring to cling to what he has been taught to think rather than trust his reason. 'The other side of the river' is not heaven but knowledge, knowledge that would free him from his fear of death."

Most of the wildly differing interpretations read politics or religion, or both, into the fables, as speculation ran rife as to the identity of the unknown author. "He writes the purest prose since Voltaire," declared one voice. "The author is evidently a person of the deepest sensibility and steeped in the glories of the French language. To write prose of such plain and simple virtue is a skill to be admired. He is most certainly a scholar, probably a professor at the university."

"He is without question a native-born habitant or someone profoundly intimate and respectful of all aspects of habitant life and culture," opined another. "The writer is a person of faith, a true son of the Church who values tradition, language and religion above all else. The tales reflect the author's unhappiness at what is happening to his beloved New France. They are a rallying call to all who would oppose the tyranny of the provincial and federal governments."

Verreau, delighted at the reception, promised more pieces by the same author while pestering the deputy to coax more tales from the pen of the unknown writer. 'Give me his name, and I shall make him famous!' he declared, hoping to tempt Turgeon into revealing the secret. But the deputy refused to budge, simply assuring his friend that more tales remained to be published.

The *Daily Register*, meanwhile, watched the success of its rival publication with jealousy and amazement, pouring scorn upon the simplistic style of the tales and professing amazement that gullible townsfolk could be so easily taken in by the 'childish' subject matter.

The so-called fables are nothing but a hash of recycled fairy tales—anachronistic and backwards-looking. They reject the future and yearn for an imagined past when New France was supposedly a paradise of simple, faithful habitants toiling at the plough or kneeing before black-robed clerics. Surely it is time, as Deputy Benoit argues, to accept that the world is changing, and that we must change with it.

But as the fables continued to be avidly discussed in homes, schools, taverns and coffee houses, the *Register* belatedly ran a series of its own, employing a team of staff members to pen stories that extolled the virtues of science, modernity and secularism. The results were so vapid, and the scorn with which they were greeted so widespread, that the newspaper quickly and quietly dropped the series.

JACOB WATCHED ON WITH astonishment as the controversy over the meaning and authorship of his little 'scribbles' as he called them, briefly pushed alarm over the growing schism with the provincial government from the front pages. To his bemusement, and secret satisfaction, he over-heard the tales being discussed on every street corner. His own employees were not immune, Madame Bisset praising the stories to the secretaries while he covertly listened in, flushed with guilty pride at her lavish endorsements.

This vicarious pleasure lasted until the publication of the fifth tale when, sitting in a tavern, he overheard a man at a nearby table viciously condemn the tales as the handiwork of an ultramontane cleric. 'It's the revenge of the old guard, their last stand against modernity,' the man pro-nounced to a companion.

Turning his head, and pretending to look for someone, Jacob caught sight of an intense looking, heavily bearded fellow, who might have been a professor or an artist, hectoring his companion with his opinion of the unknown author. 'Once discovered the writer ought be shot or hanged!' Angrily slapping the table to make his point, the man cursed all clerics and their 'mystical mumbo jumbo.' 'Shoot them all and have done with it!' he declared in a loud voice, careless of the dark looks he drew in the famously habitant tavern.

'You must promise not to tell anyone of my authorship,' Jacob instructed Isabelle upon returning home. 'Else all of this may well land on our heads like a ton of bricks.'

Isabelle, who was delighting over the latest contrary claims in the letters page of *The Catholic Tribune*, looked up in surprise, 'But darling, I am so proud of you! You have the entire city ablaze with speculation. And not just New France either.' She flourished the newspaper headlines. 'See, they are all the rage in both Montreal and Quebec City! You are famous in both places.' She stopped as she saw the look on his face. 'Do you not wish to claim them as your own?'

'No. I think it wise not too, at least for the moment.'

His refusal dismayed and confused her. 'And why ever not? Is it because of what your Mr Ferguson might think?'

He bent to untie a shoelace. 'That's a small part of it. But you have seen the demonstrations in the streets? Passions are running high. People are angry—over the war, conscription, prices, the imposition of emergency powers, and God knows what else. They are looking for someone to blame. You have read for yourself the absurd interpretations people place on the stories. Someone may take particular offence one way or another, and ...'

'And what?' Alarmed at the implication, she put down the newspaper.

'Who knows what people are capable of these days? All I know is that I won't risk placing our family in danger.'

She placed a shocked hand to her mouth. 'Do you really think people are capable of such madness—over a children's tale?'

'I think people will do almost anything to advance their cause, particularly if violence breaks out, as the deputy fears it will. Already I regret giving my permission to allow them to be published. The times are too volatile.' He grasped her hands in his own. 'Can you promise to keep my authorship secret?'

'I have already told Hugo and Josette—and Marguerite.' She thought for a moment, 'and Yvette Vachon, who will certainly tell her husband.'

'That cannot be helped. But you must swear them to secrecy—for all of our sakes. Can you do that?'

Concerned by the urgency in his voice she searched his eyes.

'I promise.'

28

A Celebrated Man

THE END OF THE European war found Jacob in an enviable position. Four years of guaranteed income—brought about by the various wartime contracts to supply the military with vehicles—had allowed him to retain his workforce—who were designated essential workers—and at the same time fine-tune the increasingly sophisticated assembly line production methods. He had established a healthy bank balance and almost paid off the mortgage on the house. With the factory now retooled to produce automobiles once more, he had ambitious plans to produce a car designed, engineered and produced in New France. But for the moment, the majority of vehicles that rolled off the production line went south, across the border to New York State.

In addition to business success, his masked fame as author of the popular fables gave him a warm glow of achievement, albeit one shared by only a small circle of friends. His self-esteem was further bolstered by the continuing friendship of deputy Turgeon, who maintained his role as intermediary between Jacob and the editor of *The Catholic Tribune*. Inspired by his good fortune, new tales poured from his pen as the little creatures he created each week were rapidly absorbed into habitant folklore. Lisette the wise owl was a particular favourite, as was Sylvan the inquisitive squirrel. Indeed, the names acquired a vigour of their own, one deputy accusing another in the Assembly of acting like Eduard the donkey, who ate his neighbour's apples. And in a notorious court case that gripped the city, one woman accused her rival in an adulterous affair of being descended from Celeste the duck, who unwisely fell in love with a cat. The remark occasioned an outbreak of hilarity among both witnesses and court officials and was gleefully picked up by the *Daily Register*.

His marriage to Isabelle continued to be the bedrock of his happiness. He made substantial contributions to charitable causes at her behest and paid for the replacement of the chapel altar rails at the cathedral. His continuing refusal, however, to adopt the Catholic faith remained a source of discontent between them, Isabelle professing sadness at his estrangement from religious belief. He obliged her at Christmas and Easter by attending services at the cathedral, his presence drawing looks and comments as Isabelle sat proudly at his side.

'There, that wasn't so bad, was it?' she remarked following a Good Friday church service. They had just returned home, and the maid was boiling water for tea.

'It was so long!' He took off his tie, eager to sit in his favourite armchair and finish reading yesterday's *Daily Register*, the newspaper having joined *The Catholic Tribune* as a subscription.

'Did you notice how happy Camille Couture looked with her swollen belly?'

'I did, as it happens,' he said, unbuttoning his shirt. 'Has that husband of hers stopped beating her?'

'Jacob!' She glanced around to make sure none of the children were within hearing.

'Come on, it's an open secret. The fellow is only tolerated in social circles because of his wife.'

'Perhaps a baby—especially a late-born one—will prompt him to mend his ways,' said Isabelle, her voice wistful. 'I believe that with God's grace anything is possible.'

'Perhaps,' he said, without conviction. 'And then there's this,' he said, holding up the previous day's headline. "Flu plague strikes Montreal. Hundreds dead." The paper showed a picture of police constables in Montreal, all wearing masks. He put down the paper. 'It's starting to happen here, too.'

Isabelle crossed herself, her face pale with fright. 'God preserve us!'

The contagion, blamed on returning soldiers, quickly spread from a few initial cases in rural Quebec to infect half of Canada, it's frightening virulence putting everyone on edge. Reports filled the newspapers of overwhelmed hospitals and morgues as the number of dead rose to unimaginable figures. Rumours spread of a thousand people dying in a single 24-hour period as fear and panic overwhelmed the populace. Horror stories abounded—of a tram driver dying at the controls; of passengers dying between stops; and of people keeling over in the street. Bodies were disposed of in mass graves and unattended burials.

On his way to work, Jacob increasingly came across dead bodies in the street. Some lay outside houses where their relatives had dragged them, waiting for the City Morgue Wagon to stop by and pick them up. Frightened pedestrians gave the corpses wide berth, muffling their faces or holding their breath as they passed by. The provincial government enacted a law requiring people to wear face masks and imposing quarantine restrictions as social life all but ground to a halt. 'People are dropping like flies' became the repeated catchphrase as the plague tightened its grip on the country. The virus spread to the most remote regions, decimating entire populations on Indian Reservations as the public health system threatened to collapse under the weight of sick and dying patients.

The flu seemed to die down during the summer months and the city breathed a collective sigh of relief, thinking the crisis had passed. But it flared up again in the winter, becoming, if anything, more deadly. The usual death tolls from influenza and pneumonia quickly tripled and then quadrupled, provoking mass hysteria as people searched desperately for ways to protect themselves against infection. All kinds of panaceas were touted, some so ridiculous as to prompt the police to threaten to arrest purveyors of the so-called cure.

Jacob lost almost a quarter of his workforce to the disease and seriously contemplated shutting down for the winter, arguing with a reluctant Ferguson that he lacked sufficiently skilled employees to continue turning out automobiles. The decision was taken out of his hands, however, by a decree from the provincial government ordering all enterprises employing more than ten people to close.

He phoned Ferguson to give him the news.

'Shut down?' He heard cursing at the other end of the line. 'For how long?'

'Hard to say. At least for a month I should think. People are afraid to leave their homes.'

'Drat! Did Morg tell you? We've only just started to build a new factory down here?'

'You have?' He frowned. 'At this time?'

'Sure, why not? There's all these soldier boys coming home with money in their pockets. And they all picture themselves driving a gal around in an open-top roadster. We'd be fools not to take advantage of the opportunity. The thing is, we were counting on the money from your end to help finance the operation.' There was silence on the other end of the line for a few moments before Ferguson spoke again. 'Oh, what the hell. We'll just have to make out somehow. Bye Jacob. Gotta go.'

He sat in his office in the deserted factory, thinking over the call.

'Stick 'em up!' Dwight stuck his nose in the door, his face masked by a large colourful bandana.

The sight caused Jacob to laugh. 'You only need a red nose!'

Dwight untied the mask. 'You may laugh,' he said, grinning. 'But I wear this all the time out on the streets. You can't be too careful.'

Jacob nodded, pointing to his own mask lying on the desk. 'Did you know Ferguson is building a new factory down in Albany?'

Dwight's eyes widened with surprise. 'Since when?'

'Since now, I guess. What?' He said, seeing the doubt on Dwight's face.

'Is this the right time to be splashing out cash? People are dropping like flies all over the country.'

Jacob gave a humourless grunt. 'What I said. But you know Ferg, he'll charge ahead anyway.'

'What does Selt say?'

He shrugged. 'He agrees, as far as I know.'

On his walk home, he caught up with a morgue wagon as it creaked down the street to pick up another corpse. His fellow pedestrians crossed themselves and hurried past the conveyance. He held his mask against his mouth as he went by, glimpsing bare feet stuck out from under a canvas sheet.

Isabelle met him at the door, her eyes reddened from crying. 'I had a telephone call from Anna Charbonneau.'

'Yes?' Concerned, he took her fingers between his own.

'Her brother, Francois, and his family'. She began to cry.

'Good God, what happened?'

She sniffled, her eyes full of tears. 'Anna said they took ill at breakfast yesterday and were all dead by 11 o'clock that night.'

'The whole family?' He stared, his face incredulous.

She could only nod, too upset to speak.

'The funeral?'

She shook her head, her eyes filled with tears. 'They're gone already, a mass grave, in the park.' She looked at him through despairing eyes. 'There was no one there to say goodbye.'

They remained largely housebound through December and January as the newspapers ran ever more alarming headlines and the death toll in the country grew to equal that of all the losses suffered in the war.

A second, even deadlier, wave of the epidemic prompted authorities across the country to close down schools, ban all church services, and urge people to remain at home as much as possible. But in spite of these measures, the number of deaths spiralled each day as wild theories abounded as to the cause of the scourge. The faithful blamed it on an epidemic of sin and godlessness; fearmongers blamed it on the recent influx of refugees from the war, returned soldiers, or the native Indians. One unfortunate man had to be rescued by the police as he was violently attacked for coughing and sneezing in the street.

Isabelle kept the children locked indoors and prayed daily for divine relief from the ravages caused by the plague. Rumours spread that Bishop Simard, successor to Monseigneur Drolet, had taken ill with the disease. Two days later it was announced that he had succumbed to the illness. *The Catholic Tribune* reported the news on a black-bordered front page. A week later came the church announcement that a Bishop Chretien from Quebec City had been appointed as a successor. Even in the midst of the epidemic, the appointment drew fierce criticism that a successor had not been appointed from within the New France Catholic hierarchy.

'Why bring in a complete outsider—someone who knows nothing of our history or traditions?' complained deputy Turgeon to Jacob. 'I would demand an answer in the House but for this pestilential flu.' He paused. 'It's obvious why—it's another attempt by the government to bring us back onto the leash.'

Jacob was prompted to ask which leash—clerical or political?—but withheld the question, deeming it wiser to simply nod and imply agreement.

IT WAS THE FOLLOWING year before the authorities finally declared the epidemic over and life slowly began to return to normal. The shops were full of goods once more, and automobiles began to roll off the factory floor. Trucks and cars became an increasingly common sight as the horse-drawn wagons began to disappear. Business was flourishing, and the city seemed more crowded than ever. In June, a prosperous and contented Jacob surprised Isabelle by throwing a banquet to celebrate their sixteenth wedding anniversary.

'A toast!' A clearly inebriated Denis Vachon got to his feet, almost sweeping his plate to the carpet in the process. 'To my old friend Jacob! You've come a long way since that day we found you in the woods,' he declared, to a hum of praise from the invited guests. 'You are now a captain of industry. A celebrated man!' he insisted, his voice slurred. 'Author of his own tale!'

The last proclamation drew a furrowed brow from Jacob and a gasp from Isabelle. 'Don't worry! Your secret is safe with me!' Vachon gave a conspiratorial wink, further alarming his host.

'What secret?' asked Claude Charbonneau.

'Why, that he intends to be even more successful in the future!' The remark drew laughter, and a relieved breath from Jacob.

'Seriously, though,' hiccupped Vachon. 'You have outgunned us all, Jacob.' He looked around in puzzlement as he forgot what he was saying.

'Including your French!' admonished his wife, Yvette, to more laughter.

'To Jacob and Isabelle—your health and happiness!' Dominic Beaulieu raised his glass.

'Jacob and Isabelle!'

'Reply! Reply!' Josette clinked her glass. Glasses began clinking all around the table as Jacob stood up.

'Dear friends, Isabelle and I thank you for joining us in this celebration. You too, Denis,' he quipped to laughter. 'I remember those early days in New France. They seem but a dream now.' He paused, feeling emotion well up inside him.

'A pleasant dream, I hope?' piped up Martin Cloutier.

'Very pleasant! And none of it possible without my guiding light, my star in the heavens, my true and trusted partner amidst war, struggle, and disease.' His voice choked as he turned to Isabelle, who had tears in her eyes. 'My dearly beloved wife!' He bent to kiss her upraised lips.

'To Isabelle!' Jules Desjardins raised his glass.

'To Isabelle!'

The supper continued as the merriment increased, the travails of the recent war and the ravages of plague forgotten as the wine flowed and ever more elaborate dishes were carried out from the kitchen.

'Oh, say! Have you read the latest tale in *The Catholic Tribune*?' Claude Charbonneau chuckled. 'It's the one about the billy-goat and the fox? Have you seen it?'

Jacob cleared his throat as the eyes of those few in the know cast covert glances in his direction. Charbonneau launched into an animated account of the fable—printed by *The Catholic Tribune* to mark the definitive end of the influenza epidemic. He finished the summation by declaring the tale 'jolly good!' and the anonymous author 'jolly clever!'

'Who the devil is the author, anyway?' asked Serge Villeneuve. 'I should like to shake his hand.'

'Jacob who do you think?' asked Josette, a mischievous smile on her lips.

Put on the spot, he took a sip of wine. 'I don't—'

'I know!' All eyes turned to Isabelle.

'Who, for God's sake? I'm dying to know!' Camille Couture sat forward, urging Isabelle on.

'The bishop!'

'The bishop?' Mouths opened in astonishment.

'Or the curé ... or Father Provencher ... or ...'

Anna Charbonneau, not being privy to the secret, looked accusingly at Isabelle. 'You don't have a clue, do you?'

'Not really.' Isabelle gave an apologetic smile. 'Sorry!'

'Time to move on!' Josette clinked her glass. 'A game!'

The guests groaned in pretended protest. 'What is it this time, the sack of Rome?' demanded Jules to laughter.

'No. It goes like this …'

As Josette explained the rules, Jacob leaned over and kissed Isabelle on the cheek. 'Thank you!' he whispered.

'A close thing!' said Hugo, leaning in *sotto voce*. 'But you are right, Jacob, to keep it to yourself. These are uncertain times.'

Isabelle gazed fondly at her husband, a proud smile on her lips as glasses clinked and voices rose in merriment. '*My darling husband!*' she mouthed, her face flushed with happiness.

Hugo Gagnon watched the loving exchange, his eyes thoughtful, as they had been throughout the toasts and, indeed, the entire evening, the good-humoured tributes casting Hugo's mind back to earlier days and the squalid little cabin in the woods, so different from the glittering mansion that now surrounded them.

'He has far outsoared me,' he mused to himself. 'Outsoared us all.'

'I give you Monsieur Automobile!' someone joked.

Jacob bowed his head with affected modesty, drawing laughter.

'Monsieur Automobile!' went up the cry as glasses were raised in a joyful toast. Hugo raised his own glass, watching as Isabelle gazed at her beaming husband, her eyes shining with devotion. *For surely, thou art Jacob.*

'GREAT HEAVENS!' RENE TURGEON collapsed in a chair in his private chamber, his face flushed. 'What a to-do! Did you hear the outcry in the Chamber? They were like savages in there!'

'I've never heard it so loud before. What happened?' Hugo poured a glass of water.

The deputy pulled a handkerchief from his pocket and mopped his brow. 'In a word—anarchy!' he complained, accepting the water. 'That shout you heard—' he gulped a mouthful of water—'that was the new Reformist fellow—what the devil is his name? Gendreau, I think. Anyway, he had just finished asserting the claim that English, being a minority language of longstanding in New France, deserved equal prominence with French in matters of education. When, pardon'—he took another swallow—' … when Andre Charpentier jumped to his feet and declared that since the Mohawk language met the same conditions, did it not also deserve equal protection and prominence? The Reformists lost their heads and began to bray and shout like madmen!'

'It was a clever thing to say.'

'I wonder.' The deputy sighed.

'Sir?'

'I fear our friend may have inadvertently introduced a new and troubling dimension to the debate.'

'How so?'

'Rights are a tricky question—how far to extend them, and where to draw the line? If rights are extended to one group, can they be withheld from another?'

'But New France has always been French. Its laws and customs are based upon that fact and should remain so.'

'New France was originally Iroquois,' pointed out the deputy. 'Thus, to extend your argument backwards, one might argue that Iroquois language and customs should prevail.'

Hugo muttered in exasperation. 'I'm sick to death of all this division. It's always the same: faith and language, language and education—faith, language and education. When will it all end?'

'When we no longer have language and faith to divide us, I imagine. Not until then.' The deputy took a sip of water as he studied his secretary for a moment, his face thoughtful. 'Hugo?'

'Yes, sir?'

'I feel my age. And now that the war is over it seems a good time to pass on the baton, as it were.' He stopped to take a considered breath, his eyes still on Hugo. 'How would you like to take my place?'

'Sir?' Hugo felt his heart leap.

'Not now, but in a few weeks, after I've had time to canvas my party colleagues on the matter. They know you and respect you as a loyal habitant, so I don't anticipate any problems there. Of course, they will have to decide who will replace me as leader, but that is another question. I would stand down—resign—and nominate you as my successor until the election. You could be sworn in before the Speaker. There'd be no need for a vote until the next election—but what do you say to the idea?'

'Forgive me. But this is so sudden …' Hugo swallowed, lost for words.

'Sudden in its announcement, perhaps, but something I have given much thought to. I think you would make an excellent deputy. So, your thoughts?'

'If you think I am able …' Hugo swallowed again. 'Sir, it would be an honour!' In a daze, he stood up and took the deputy's extended hand.

'Deputy!' Josette felt her head spin on hearing the news from an ebullient Hugo. 'Deputy!' She sank into a chair, hardly able to grasp the prospect. Hugo stood before her, a delighted smile on his face.

'Are you sure that's what he meant?'

'Of course, I'm sure! We shook hands on it.' Hugo laughed, an exhilarated yet nervous sound. 'Deputy Gagnon!' he said, not certain himself whether he believed it.

'We shall have to throw a party … inform people.' Josette was up and out of the chair, her mind working rapidly as she planned the announcement. 'Blessed Mary!' She gazed at him, her eyes sparkling. 'Deputy Gagnon! Wait until I tell Claudette!'

'Not yet,' he cautioned. 'Wait until I am sworn in first, then you may tell whom you like.'

'Oh!' Her face fell only to brighten again. Just think—you'll be the equal of Jacob!'

'His equal? What do you mean? I thought I already was?' Hugo frowned, his tone vexed.

Josette kissed him, placing her arms around his neck. 'I mean in terms of influence, in terms of the weight your voice will carry.' She felt his body stiffen and drew back her head. 'Are you a tiny bit jealous of all his success?' Her eyes probed with the question.

'No. Certainly not! … It's just that he has risen so high in the world, from such unfortunate beginnings …'

She peered into his face. 'And you don't feel just the tiniest bit of envy?'

'To the contrary, I rejoice in his success.' He embraced her, holding her close so that she was quite unable to look into his eyes.

29

An Unwise Decision

JACOB HAD BARELY ENTERED the office before the operator put though a call from Ferguson. 'Is everything alright?' he asked, detecting a strain in the voice over the line.

'Everything's jim-dandy.'

'And Morgan is in good health?'

'Sure! Old Morg's a goer. Listen Jacob, the reason I'm calling. We've run into some problems financing the new plant down here. Morg and I have already put in a hundred grand each. We'd like you to put in less than a third of that amount, $30,000.'

'$30,000 dollars!' His mouth dropped open in shock.

'It's to cover the costs of the new production line as well as to pay for licencing fees and to cover the shut-down while we make the change-over.'

'I don't have that kind of money,' he objected. 'Everything's tied up in the house.'

'But you can raise it?' Ferguson's voice was impatient.

'I don't know—even with a bank loan. But I don't understand why—'

'This is part of being an owner, Jacob. You've profited, haven't you? We all have. To keep those profits rolling in we have to reinvest, modernise, take advantage of the changing times. It's smart money, Jacob, just like your original investment. And as a sweetener, Morg and I have agreed to immediately up your share to 15%. How does that sound? Once the new plant is up and running, we expect to make our money back ten times over. Are you in or are you out?'

Jacob stared at the desk, his mind in a whirl. 'I don't know. I'll have to think about it. It's a lot of money.'

'Not when you consider what Morg and I are putting in, and have already put in. We need you, Jacob, as a willing partner. Are you on board?'

'I'll have to speak to the bank.' His voice tightened. 'I have hardly a tenth of that much cash on hand.'

'I knew we could count on you!' Ferguson's voice resumed its familiar joviality. 'I'll expect to hear from you as soon as possible. We've bills to pay. Keep selling those autos!' And with that, the line went dead.

Jacob stared at the receiver, his mind blank.

Halfway through the morning he received a telephone call from Morgan Selt. 'Good morning, Jacob!' Selt's voice was breezy down the line. After a few pleasantries he quickly got to the point of the call.

'We have run into a bit of a cash-flow problem down here. Has Gus talked to you about it?'

'Yes. He called two hours ago. He wants me to contribute $30,000 to the plant expansion.' He listened, hoping Selt would declare it all a mistake.

'Splendid! Can we count on you?'

With a sinking heart, he prevaricated. 'It's an awful lot of money.' Hearing no response he continued, making no attempt to hide the reluctance in his voice. 'I would have to take out a substantial loan to raise the full amount.'

'You don't have it on hand?'

'Good God, no.'

'Well, wire us the money as soon as you secure the loan. Can you do that?'

Jacob hesitated, his hackles rising at the pressure. 'Is it that much of a rush?'

'We have suppliers down here wanting payment before they'll continue with the work. This is what ownership is all about, Jacob, taking risks and reaping the rewards.'

'As I said, I'll have to see what I can manage.' His tone now verged on open defiance.

'Good man! I'll expect that wire transfer as soon as.' Selt ended the call.

He deliberated before summoning Dwight to his office. 'Have you heard anything—from down south?'

His arms folded, Dwight leaned against the door frame.

'Like what?'

'Like how it's going with the new factory?'

'Okay, far as I know.'

'As far as you know?'

'They run their own shop.' Dwight's brow furrowed in puzzlement. 'They don't tell me everything. Heck, you'd know more than me.'

'So, you haven't heard anything?'

'What sort of thing?'

'Any rumours or speculation, anything like that?'

'No. Why, what's this about?'

'Nothing.' He waved a hand. 'Just checking out a hunch.'

'You *have* heard something!' Dwight straightened up.

'They need more money—to finish off the plant expansion and pay the licencing fees.'

Dwight shrugged. 'No surprise there. I hear they intend doubling the size of the production line.'

Unable to shake off a sense of unease, Jacob did some sums on a sheet of paper. Looking at the figures, he scratched his jaw, tempted to call Ferguson back and decline the request. *This is part of being an owner, Jacob. We need you. Are you on board?*

He leaned back in the chair and called out to the youngest secretary. 'Marie? Coffee, please.'

Drinking the coffee, he stared at the figures. He made a few adjustments and set down the pen, rubbing his hands against his face in deliberation. I should talk it over with Isabelle. Get her view on things. The clock struck eleven, and he made up his mind.

'Marie? Put me through to the operator.'

While waiting for the call to go through he was tempted to hang up. His mind was so conflicted he reacted with a start when the bank manager's voice came on the line.

'Certainly, I can see you today, Monsieur Wheeler,' said the obliging manager. 'Say, two o'clock?'

Later that afternoon he negotiated a loan for the entire $30,000, using the house, two investment properties, his savings, and his shares in the business as security. 'Thank you, Monsieur Alfont,' he said, standing up to shake hands.

'Nonsense! You are one of our most important customers.' The manager showed him to the door. 'I'll complete the paperwork today, and the money will be wired to the nominated bank first thing tomorrow morning.'

Disturbed at the large amount of debt he was taking on, he walked through the streets of the Upper Town before making his way back to the factory, his mind heavy with unease.

Following a sleepless night, he went to the factory early and sat at his desk, impatient for Dwight to arrive. When the latter did so, he summoned him into his office before he even had time to remove his coat.

'Dwight, you have plenty of contacts down south. Do me a favour, call them. Ask if everything's hunky-dory.'

'Is there something I need to know about?'

'Nothing I can put my finger on. A feeling, that's all.'

'I'll get right on it.'

Unable to concentrate, he fiddled with the papers on his desk while waiting for Dwight to make the call. A short time later, Dwight re-entered his office.

'Well?' he demanded.

Instead of sitting down, Dwight remained standing, tapping a knuckle against his teeth.

'What?'

'There is something.'

'Like pulling teeth! What?'

'I spoke to Lester Hornchurch. You know him—the accountant from Albany?'

'And?' he barked.

'There's some scuttlebutt.'

'Goddammit!' He clenched his fist, his suspicion bearing fruit. 'What?'

'I don't know. Lester was vague. But things are … up in the air.'

'Now you tell me!' Furious, he glared at Dwight, who held up a hand in protest.

'I didn't know!'

'What else?'

Dwight looked unhappy. 'As I said, he was vague. I suspect he's been told to keep his mouth shut.'

Jacob cursed at the implication, feeling a cold sweat on his brow. 'Call him again! Right now.'

'Now?' Dwight stared. 'I just spoke to him!'

'Just make the call!' He felt light-headed.

'Okay! Hold your horses.'

'And ask him directly! Don't let him fob you off.'

It took the operator ten minutes to place the call, ten minutes during which he simmered with an anxiety verging on panic. Finally, just as he was about to be consumed by his fears, he heard the operator put the call through. Jumping up, he went to Dwight's office and listened in as Dwight spoke to the unknown voice.

'Really? Holy cow!' Dwight's eyes widened, intensifying Jacob's fears. Clenching and unclenching his hands he watched Dwight's face as he spoke into the receiver.

'Okay, I promise. Not a word—to anyone.' Reassuring his informant, Dwight ended the call.

'Well?' Jacob felt his heart pounding.

Dwight blew out his lips, trying to sort his impressions. 'That was Herb Thompson. He helps Lester with the books. According to Herb, something's definitely up. The production lines have stopped rolling and an investigator from the US tax department spent the morning nosing around asking questions.'

'Jesus! What for?'

'All kinds of stuff. He had a warrant of some kind and took away the accounts ledger along with all the other finance records.'

'What did Ferguson say?' He felt on the edge of full- blown panic.

Dwight shrugged. 'Nobody can seem to get hold of him—or Selt, for that matter. What the hell's going on?'

'I'll tell you later.' Returning to his office he picked up the phone.

'Operator, get me the Commerce Bank on rue Langlois, please.' Cursing with impatience, he waited for the connection. 'Hello? The manager, please. It's monsieur Wheeler calling. Tell him its important.'

A short while later the manager's voice sounded through the receiver. 'Ah! Monsieur Wheeler. Not to worry, the money was wired first thing this morning. I supervised it myself.'

'You've sent it already?' Fear gripped him.

'Yes, I can assure you. Not two hours ago.'

'Can you stop it—reverse it?'

'Pardon?' There was a puzzled silence on the other end of the phone.

'There's been a mistake. They don't need the money. Can you get it back?' His voice had risen with panic.

'I shall have to see. It may have been picked up already.'

'Please try. And call me back straightaway.'

He spent an agonising quarter-hour pacing the office before the telephone rang again. He snatched at the receiver. 'Yes?'

'Monsieur Wheeler?' The manager's voice was apologetic. 'I am sorry to inform you that the money has been collected already—by a Mr Morgan Selt.'

'Selt? Not Ferguson?'

'Um, Mr Selt, according to the bank. Is something wrong, sir?'

He gave a heavy sigh. 'No. Thank you. That is all.'

He placed the receiver back on the stand, his mind numb. After a while he stood up and put on his coat. 'Madame Bisset. I am going out for the morning.'

Several employees greeted him as he walked through the factory floor, but he ignored them, his eyes blind to all but his own fears. Stepping out onto the street he took a deep breath, his mind reeling. The sky was a dismal grey and it felt like snow. He headed up rue Asselin, walking mechanically, his senses too dazed to take in the activity around him. *Perhaps I am overreacting. Perhaps all is in order.* Yet he felt sick to his stomach, his gut insisting on the truth of his instincts. He walked for a mile, right up to the cathedral, before turning and retracing his steps. *The house is at risk. My shares in the business, too. I shall be ruined.* He stopped, suddenly dizzy and fearing he might faint in the street.

He returned to the office to be greeted by a worried-looking Madame Bisset. 'Sir, Monsieur Ferguson has called you half a dozen times.'

She helped him off with his coat, her normally unflappable demeanour clearly flustered. 'He sounded angry,' she said, 'upset.'

At that moment the telephone rang. 'That will be him,' she said, her voice nervous.

He picked up the receiver. 'Hello?'

'Jacob! Jesus Christ where have you been?'

'What's the matter?'

'The money! Did you send the money like I asked?'

'Yes. It went through early this morning. Why?'

'It did?' There was a pause at the other end of the line. 'Where did you send it?'

'To the bank account, of course.' His brow furrowed. 'Did you not—'

'Christ on a stick! The business account?' Ferguson's voice was frantic.

'Yes. Where I always—'

'I told you to send it to the other account. The one I use to avoid tax questions.'

'I'm sorry. In my haste I forgot. But Gus, what in blazes is happening? The bank manager here said the money had already been collected.'

'Selt!' The word exploded from Ferguson's mouth, followed by a string of curses.

'Gus. Speak to me. Tell me—' He stared at the receiver as the line went dead. Now more than ever convinced at his madness in agreeing to the loan, he put his head in his hands.

'Jacob, is everything alright?' Dwight stood in the doorway.

'No,' he muttered, feeling sick. 'I think we're in trouble, Dwight.'

'How so?' A clearly worried Dwight sat down on the other side of the desk. 'We've met our sales targets. Our order book is healthy—'

'Not us. The US plant. That was Ferguson on the phone, he was in a panic.'

'So, Herb was right—something is afoot?'

Jacob stood up, feeling light-headed again. 'Hold down the fort, will you?'

'Sure. Where will you be?'

'At home.' And with the startled eyes of the other man on him, he collected his coat and left the office.

HE PICKED HIS WAY through supper, drawing concerned looks from Isabelle. 'Are you coming down with something?'

'No. It's not the flu—Spanish, French, American or any other kind, I assure you. I am quite well.'

'It wouldn't matter even if it was the Spanish flu. I would look after you. It wouldn't part us.' Isabelle spoke in a quiet, matter-of-fact voice as she placed a spoonful of peas on Gaston's plate. And thus, she missed the expression of gratitude and wonderment on Jacob's face as he looked at her.

He retired to the library where he sat brooding before the fire. The door opened and Marie-Odile peeped in. 'Papa, will you read me a bedtime story?'

'Not now, darling. Perhaps mama can read it to you.'

He was still agonising over his foolish decision when the telephone rang. He heard Isabelle call out in surprise from the dining room. 'Who would call at such an unearthly hour?'

'Jacob?' It was Dwight's voice, sounding anxious. 'Sorry to disturb at such an hour, but I figured you'd want to know right away.'

He felt his heart constrict. 'Know what?'

'I called Herb again and pumped him for the straight goods. It seems Ferguson and Selt are being investigated for war profiteering, fraudulent trading, and unpaid creditors. Herb is convinced that the government will bring charges. The factory is shut down and all assets frozen.'

He hung up the phone, feeling nauseous.

'Is everything all right, dearest?' Isabelle asked as he joined her in the bedroom.

'Sure. Just work stuff.'

'Jacob. I know when something's worrying you.' She studied his face. 'What is it?'

'Really, it's nothing. It will all be sorted tomorrow.'

'You'd tell me if something was wrong?'

He kissed her cheek. 'Of course, dear. Goodnight.'

The next morning Dwight was waiting in his office.

'Have you seen this? It just came in from Albany.' Dwight passed him the *Albany Advertiser*. 'The box at the bottom,' he said, pointing to the front page.

Auto Factory Closes. Owners Charged. A complicated web of insolvency, bankruptcy and fraudulent trading obscures the closing down of the well-known Ferguson-Selt Automobile factory located in the town of Colonie, Albany County. Rumours of money siphoned off from creditors to pay for personal debts surround the owners. At the time of printing, it is alleged that the relevant authorities have ordered the arrest of the two principals and the seizure of the factory and all of its assets. The closure puts approximately 125 employees out of work.

'I can hardly believe it.' Dwight shook his head. 'Gus and Morgan under arrest?'

'What's our position?' Jacob fought to keep his voice under control.

Dwight shrugged. 'We come under US tax law insofar as we are a branch operation. I expect we'll be shut down any day.'

He stared past Dwight at the factory floor. 'And my own position?'

Dwight shrugged. 'Hard to say. You are a partner, so …'

IN THE DAYS OF uncertainty that followed, he continued all factory operations in compliance with the instructions of the US law firm hired by the company to protect its assets. A week later one of the firm's lawyers arrived at the premises.

'It's hazy, gentlemen, hazy.' The lawyer, an affable fellow who drank his coffee with a considerable dash of whisky, blew his nose as he outlined the situation to Jacob and Dwight.

'I guess you fellows are alright,' he said, tucking the handkerchief back in his pocket. 'You in particular, Mr Wheeler, as part-owner. There are no allegations of wilful negligence against you, at least not at this stage. And your operation here is running at a profit. But everything else—the factory, the tools, and the remaining automobiles are all sequestered awaiting court rulings in the US. In other words, gentlemen, you are to cease trading, with immediate effect.' He paused to let the words register as he sipped the whisky-drenched coffee.

'And the employees?' Jacob glanced out the office window at the busy factory floor.

The lawyer followed his glance. 'Pretty well screwed, I'd say.'

Jacob and Dwight exchanged looks. 'That's not right. There must be something we can do out of our assets here in New France?' argued Dwight.

'Not your assets, gentlemen. They belong to the parent company and will be added to the assets quarantined to pay off the list of creditors. Things are different up here, so different laws may apply. But I fully expect that to be the case. It depends on the reach of the US tax office. It's all very messy. More I cannot say at this stage.'

Jacob turned pale. 'And me, personally? My house … that's safe?'

'Did the company buy it or loan the money for it? No? Then it should be safe, far as I can tell.'

'As far as you can tell?'

'The law is a tricky business, friend. And tax law? Ye gods!' The lawyer rolled his eyes.

'And the money I loaned to Ferguson and Selt?'

The lawyer took out a flask from his pocket and poured a splash of whisky into the empty cup. 'That? Gone, I'm afraid.'

'Gone? Gone where, exactly?'

'Into their pockets, I'd say. I certainly don't see them handing it over to the creditors. But I'll add it to the list.'

'Will I get it back?'

'In all likelihood it's been spent already. You could sue one, or both of them, for its return, but what's the point? They've already declared commercial and personal bankruptcy.'

'When?'

'At least a month ago. I don't recollect the exact date.'

Jacob glanced at Dwight. 'Before they asked for the loan,' he said, his voice bleak.

''Fraid so,' said the lawyer.

'Christ Almighty!' Dwight's face showed his disgust. 'I'm powerfully sorry, Jacob.'

He felt sick, barely able to focus as Dwight asked, 'What will happen to them—Gus and Morgan?'

'Hard to say. The authorities will have to prove their case of fraudulent trading but …' the lawyer paused as he sipped from the cup, 'my guess would be that both gentlemen are facing a long term behind bars.'

'Richly deserved!' declared Dwight.

'Well may you say!' agreed the lawyer and took another sip.

HE SOLD OFF THE two investment properties and the Roadster to raise more cash. But he was still left with a debt of almost $20,000. A 'rainy-day stash' he had secreted away years earlier on the advice of Jules Desjardin was now the single, slender margin standing between himself and utter ruin. He considered selling the house and moving into smaller and cheaper housing but couldn't stomach admitting his foolishness to Isabelle and the children. *The bank will seize it anyway.* The reminder brought on a throbbing headache.

Faced with a dire future, he winced as news of the factory closure became public and rumours began to circulate. To his alarm, a reporter phoned the residence, seeking information. He had no sooner hung up, with a terse "No comment', when there was a knock on the front door.

'Monsieur Wheeler?' called out the maid. 'There is a gentleman here to see you.'

'Monsieur Wheeler? Good morning, sir. I'm a reporter for the *Daily Register*. I'd like you to comment on the closing down of the automobile factory.' The man waited expectantly, pen poised for an answer. 'Awful business isn't it?' he prompted as Jacob made no reply. 'For the employees, certainly, as well as yourself.'

'Good day to you!' snapped Jacob and shut the door.

'And Madame Wheeler? What does she think?' demanded the voice through the closed door.

'Who was that?' Isabelle came down the stairs wearing her coat and hat, Marie-Odile beside her.

'No one, a journalist. Where are you going?'

'To visit Marguerite. Why? Is something wrong?'

'Wait until later,' he said, unbuttoning her coat.

She was confused as he tried to tug her arm out of the sleeve. 'Why? Tell me what is going on?'

'It's a reporter—asking questions. Wait until he's left. Please, dear.' He tugged off the coat.

'A reporter?' Her face showed alarm. 'Is it that bad, Jacob? You must tell me.'

'Mama! I thought we were going to visit Aunty?'

'Not now, sweet pea. Something's come up. We'll go later. Why don't you read your book and I'll call you when it's time. Jacob?'

She turned to him, a worried look on her face. 'Tell me.'

'It's Ferguson and Selt. They've got themselves into trouble.'

'Oh!' Her mouth parted. 'Does it involve you?'

He shook his head. 'No, but I'm afraid the factory will be shut down and all the assets seized. But don't alarm yourself,' he said as she gasped. 'We are quite safe. Quite safe,' he repeated, feeling a rush of guilt at the frightened look on her face.

'I can't believe it! You are certain they won't be coming after you?'

'Hush,' he soothed, and laid a hand against her cheek. 'This has nothing to do with me. It's Ferguson and Selt who created this mess, and they're the ones who are going to have to pay. Only, there'll be all kinds of talk in the newspapers,' he warned. 'Be prepared.'

Next morning, the closure was front page news in both the dailies. The *Catholic Tribune* was measured in its approach, treating the episode as a morality tale while hinting at the 'Yankee malfeasance' behind it. The lengthy account wove the factory closure into the "influenza crisis" that had taken such a toll upon New France, the paper decrying the "disastrous consequences of modern industrial capitalism on an agrarian populace largely innocent of such perils."

The *Daily Register*, by contrast, reported the closure as a direct consequence of criminal activity on the part of the American owners, pointedly excluding "the Canadian operation" from blame.

> *Investment in New France will continue, despite this setback. Indeed, it may be argued that opening the factory in the first place encouraged other investors and entrepreneurs to consider our region as a possible locus for more, not less, investment. The example of the Ferguson-Selt automobile factory is a cautionary tale, but not a fatal one. After all, are we to abandon the automobile following an accident and return to the days of the horse and buggy?*

Following publication of the forced closure, Jacob fielded numerous telephone calls from friends concerned at the effects on himself and Isabelle. Several came to the house to offer their condolences—as well as to discover more details about the looming scandal. He was reserved in his reception of such visitors, retreating into vague allusions to the American owners while claiming little knowledge of events beyond what was reported in the newspapers. The Chamber of Commerce sent a letter of sympathy, assuring Jacob, "you will be back on your feet in no time." The letter was signed by Bernard Benoit.

Three days later, while the closure was still being reported and gossiped about, Dwight came around to formally tender his resignation. 'I guess I'll head back to the States,' he said as they discussed the situation over a glass of wine. 'Not much point in staying, is there? Unless you think I could be of some use?' he added, his voice hopeful.

'I'm afraid I don't see how.' Jacob shook his head, utterly despondent.

'Does your wife …?' Dwight didn't finish the sentence, his voice dropping to a whisper.

'No, not all of it. I'm hoping I can find some way out before telling her.'

Dwight nodded, his face solemn. 'Have you tried contacting Ferguson or Selt?'

'Ha!' His voice tightened with contempt. 'That pair of hucksters? They are either on the lam or in jail. I don't care which.'

'Still, it's a powerful shame it had to end like this.' Dwight stood up and extended his hand. 'All the luck in the world, Jacob. If I hear anything, I'll let you know.'

He stood up. 'Goodbye Dwight.' He remembered something. 'How is Madame Bisset doing? Have you heard?'

'Not since last week. We had coffee. She's still in a bit of shock.'

Jacob made a rueful face. 'So say we all.'

30

A Confession

THE GENERAL MOOD OF post-war recovery was rudely jarred when, on the 13th of April 1921, The *Catholic Tribune* printed a headline that electrified its readers: "*Legislative Assembly votes to abolish special Charter of Rights.*" The headline was followed by a series of sub-heads: "Bill, if passed, will end unique status of New France; Local Assembly to be abolished; Region to lose autonomous rights relating to language and education."

'I don't believe it!' Hugo Gagnon, newly installed deputy, exploded with anger as he read the newspaper. 'This is a coup!' he cried, and jumped up from the chair with such violence that he rattled the cups and spilled the coffee.

'Goodness, you gave me a fright!' Josette scolded as she used the napkin to wipe the front of her dress.

'Do you realise what this means?' Hugo thrust the newspaper in front of her face. 'No more Assembly! No more autonomy! We will fall under the direct rule of those idiots in Quebec!' He was so agitated that she begged him to sit down.

'I'm sure the Assembly won't pass it,' she said, pouring herself more coffee.

'The Assembly?' He stared at her as if she were mentally deficient. 'It's not up to us! We have no say in the matter. It's the Legislative Council in Quebec City that will decide our fate. If anything, the Reformists will pass a motion in favour of the bill. It gives them everything they ever wanted. Imagine—two public school systems, one for French Catholics, the other for English Protestants! And we have no say in the matter!' He sat down, his face pale, the prospect too ghastly to contemplate.

The Dissolution Bill, as it was dubbed, caused an uproar in the Assembly, the Patriot Party deputies so incensed at Reformist support for the proposed bill that fistfights broke out. The Speaker himself was subjected to assault as he tried in vain to restore order. The anger quickly spread to the streets, spontaneous protests breaking out across the city as people vented their outrage. Shopkeepers put up shutters as the demonstrations turned violent. Alarmed at the scale of the protests, the authorities called in police reinforcements amid rumours that the Quebec government was on the brink of intervening and declaring a state of emergency.

Despite fierce Reformist opposition, and against the objections of the governor, who denounced the measure as illegal, the Patriot Party forced a motion through the Assembly calling for a referendum on the proposed constitutional changes. The result, when it became known, caused wild public celebrations as it was revealed that a commanding majority of over 80% voted against any changes to the Charter, which had guaranteed regional language and educational rights ever since New France had become a reluctant partner in Confederation.

The resounding 'no' vote provoked alarm in the provincial capital where Charles Pelletier, Minister of Internal Affairs, summoned his security advisor, Colonel Marcel Soubry, to express his displeasure. 'Did you see the papers?' Pelletier jabbed a finger at the pile of newspapers on his desk. '*The Sun* is calling for the bill to be postponed, *The Herald* is demanding it be withdrawn altogether, while *The Star* is demanding that we bring it forward and pass it immediately.' He thrust his hands into his jacket pockets as he stared moodily out the window. 'What do those crazy bastards want?'

'The newspapers?' ventured a cautious Soubry.

'Those damned so-called habitants! They're now agitating for separation altogether. Imagine!' Scowling, the Minister turned away from the window. 'I want you to sort it out. Understand?'

Colonel Soubry made a coughing sound. 'Sort it out?'

'Yes, handle the situation. Stop the god-damned riots for one thing.'

'There are riots?' The colonel tried, surreptitiously, to read the headlines of the nearest newspaper.

'There will be, once the bill goes through, or haven't you been following?' Pelletier fixed his subordinate an irate look. 'Can you handle it, or should I send for Dupay to do it?' he said, naming a rival officer.

'No, no. I shall take care of it, sir. Leave it in my hands.'

Back in his office, the agitated Soubry immediately sent for his adjutant, Captain Adrien Perrault.

'Where in blazes were you?' he demanded as Perrault was shown into his office. 'I sent for you a half-hour ago.'

'Pardon, Colonel, I was on the parade ground whipping the new recruits into shape.'

'Have you heard about that nonsense in New France?' Soubry pointed at the newspaper. 'What do those crazy bastards want, eh? That was a question, Perrault!' The gruff, bewhiskered officer glowered at his subordinate.

'Pardon, sir, may I?' Perrault gestured to a chair.

'You certainly may not!' The colonel barked at the insolence. 'Answer the damn question! You're supposed to be my intelligence officer—or have you forgotten?'

Perrault, a tailored, saturnine fellow with a neatly manicured moustache, drew himself up in a formal, yet somehow loose posture that infuriated his superior. 'I hear that the townspeople, the so-called habitants, are against the changes to a man—or woman, for that matter' he added.

The insouciant manner of the reply, one that blithely ignored the colonel's irritation, further incensed the latter. 'No matter! The government is afraid of an insurrection. I'm sending you to the cursed town. You're to leave on tomorrow's train. Take a detachment with you. And for God's sake, don't draw more attention to yourselves than is absolutely necessary.'

Eyes narrowed, he studied his subordinate for a sign of disquiet at the posting. To his dismay, he found none. Rather, he suspected the officer welcomed the idea. Disappointed, he briefly considered withdrawing the order.

'Well? What the devil are you waiting for?'

'My instructions, Colonel. What am I to do there?'

The innocuous question was somehow laden with insolence.

'Do there?' Soubry sighed heavily, making it abundantly clear he did not suffer fools gladly and that it was one of the latter tribe that stood before him. 'You're to *handle* the situation. Let that idiot of a governor think he is calling the shots, but I want you to maintain law and order, at whatever cost.' His eyes narrowed again. 'Do you understand me, Captain?'

'Yes, Colonel. At whatever cost.'

The sardonic way his words were repeated, unsettled the colonel. He waved a hand in dismissal. 'Go! Carry out your orders.' He watched Perrault come to attention—was that languid salute a deliberate provocation?— before turning on his heels and leaving the office.

Muttering, Colonel Soubry rummaged through the papers on his desk looking for the transportation orders and wondering what Charles Pelletier meant by 'handle'. I should have asked for written orders—to cover my arse. I'll do so at once. I can just see the shit falling on me if anything goes wrong. Perhaps I should have passed it on to Dupay. The disquieting thought entered his mind that the Minister had already sounded out his rival, who had declined the task and thus passed it on to him. Perturbed at the possibility, he unearthed the order forms, scowling as he pictured Perrault lording it over the stupid peasants, a gloating look on his face. Hopefully, those dammed rebels will fry your arrogant nuts in boiling oil!

ISABELLE HAD FOLLOWED THE newspaper reports on the factory closing with mounting concern as stories emerged of unpaid employees and a growing list of creditors. Some of the latter placed blame on Jacob, accusing him of knowing the dire financial straits of the parent US company but trading freely nevertheless. A monsieur Molineux stepped forward to claim he was owed one thousand dollars for the purchase and installation of a lathe and several other items of machinery. "Who will pay me now? How will I feed my children?" he demanded, pointing the finger directly at Jacob while voicing dark suspicions of complicity.

Threats of lawsuits were bandied about, including one by the laid-off employees. To Isabelle's vast relief, these were redirected to the US courts where a trial was pending as the tax authorities there pursued their investigations. She was conscious of looks directed her way in the street. Merchants who were once eager to offer a line of credit now waited, it seemed to Isabelle with unseemly eagerness, for her to open her purse and pay for purchased goods. 'I am so sorry that monsieur Wheeler has lost his position,' one merchant had the temerity to offer while carefully perusing the shopping list she handed over.

To reduce the household budget, she let go of the maid and practiced domestic economies, dispensing with fine cuts of meat in preference for cheaper, less quality cuts that could be stretched into soups and casseroles. She mended clothes rather than replacing them—her dressmaking skills rendering the task an easy one—and forewent the purchase of those small luxuries that her husband's prior fortune had made easily attainable.

'I'm sorry, dearest,' Jacob apologised, on seeing all the changes, 'but I'm confident of soon finding another position. Monsieur Turgeon and several others have promised to help.'

'It's not your fault, Jacob. You have nothing to reproach yourself for. We are still very fortunate compared to many. The house is almost paid for. We have the savings—and the investment properties. We can sell them if we have to. And I certainly won't miss that noisy Roadster. I'd rather take the tram in any case.'

It was on the tip of his tongue to confess, to reveal all, but Louis wandered into the parlour and the chance was lost.

'Don't take it too hard,' consoled Bernard Benoit when the two met by chance in the street. 'As businessmen, it's a risk we run every day. I'm confident a man of your experience and know-how will be eagerly sought-after. If you like, I'll make enquiries on your behalf.'

Jacob accepted the offer, pleased and a little surprised at the other man's genuine sympathy.

But his mood remained downcast, his confidence in his own judgement severely shaken as more stories emerged of employees losing homes to the banks or relying on charity to make ends meet. The prospect that he might soon have no alternative but to declare personal bankruptcy simply to keep his head above water, kept him from sleep as he brooded over ways to restore his fortune—or at least protect what little remained. He lost his appetite, chewing half-heartedly on a slice of toast for breakfast while pretending to be cheerful for the sake of Isabelle and the children.

'An alarming business in the boulevard the other day,' he said, reading from the newspaper. 'A bunch of hotheads attacked the provincial government office.'

Isabelle tutted in disapproval and motioned to the children. Looking up a few minutes later, he saw them staring, their faces apprehensive. 'Heavens to a crow!' he exclaimed, returning to the newspaper. 'It says here that they've discovered a boy with two noses!'

'I worry about Jacob,' Isabelle confided to her sister when the two met for coffee at Josette's. The morning paper had reported the suicide of a former employee, neglecting to mention the man was heavily indebted to a gambling syndicate. 'All of this has taken a terrible toll upon him, although he pretends otherwise. He blames himself for what happened. It's not fair. It was all the fault of those dreadful Americans.'

'At least you're not on the front page anymore,' consoled Marguerite, 'this political nonsense is all anyone talks about.'

'Did you read the *Catholic Tribune* this morning?' Josette walked into the room reading from the newspaper. 'Some of the protestors are now calling themselves separatists. They are demanding that New France declare independence and the severing of ties with Quebec and Canada altogether.' She set down the newspaper as if tired of reading such nonsense.

'Can you blame them?' asked Isabelle, relieved to turn the conversation away from Jacob and the factory closure.

'And what does deputy Hugo make of it all?' teased Marguerite.

'Oh, the usual nonsense.' Josette affected a languid yawn to cover her pride in the title. 'He said the Assembly more resembles a lunatic asylum with every passing day.'

'What happened yesterday? I hear it really was bedlam.'

'That self-important bore Benoit got up to drone on about the future. You know, the usual fishcakes about the freedom to be educated in one's own language, freedom to worship—or not—in a church of one's choosing, and some other pudding about a person's right to this or that. I can't recall it all. But I do remember Hugo saying Benoit called them the three "oughts" of modernity, if you can believe.'

'And what did dear old Hugo say?' asked Isabelle.

'He didn't say anything. But Devoir, the new leader, jumped up and dismissed the "oughts" as the blessed trinity of secular liberalism.'

'Quite right,' declared Isabelle.

Marguerite rolled her eyes. 'Such a habitant!'

'And you are not—a habitant?'

'Always, I am Marguerite!' answered her sister, affecting their mama's voice and grand manner so precisely that Isabelle could not help but laugh. 'But I do miss her,' said Marguerite as tears sprang to her eyes. 'What wouldn't I give to hear her voice again?'

THROUGHOUT THE WINTER JACOB tried, with increasing desperation, to find some way out of the financial morass he had created for himself, the stash funds depleting with alarming speed. After an hour's negotiation with the bank manager, he handed over the house title deed, with the proviso that his family continue to live in it for the next six months. He added a last-minute stipulation that the bank give him first refusal in the event of his fortunes being somehow miraculously restored.

He was relieved when the telephone rang to distract his increasingly frantic thoughts.

'Jacob? It's Bernard Benoit. My secretary told me you rang.'

'Yes, I was wondering if you had managed to turn up anything suitable?'

There was a brief pause on the line. 'Why don't we meet tomorrow for lunch? You know the bistro on rue Madeleine—the one with tables out front? Good. Shall we say noon? See you then, goodbye.'

'Where are you going?' Isabelle asked the following day as Jacob put on his hat and coat.

'I've arranged to meet Bernard Benoit for lunch. He's promised to try and help. Hopefully, he has something for me.' He smiled to reassure her, disturbed at the anxiety he saw in her eyes.

She stood at the door to watch him leave. Benoit? Isn't he the advocate for all I despise about the way New France is changing? She watched her husband cross the street. How careworn he looks! Overnight it seemed, her husband's purposeful, confident carriage had disappeared, replaced by a slower, hesitant slouch that seemed to suggest the huge weight on his shoulders.

She watched a moment longer before closing the door. She leaned against it, her eyes taking in the mirrored hall stand—chosen with such care for fitness and style. Next, she contemplated the polished oak staircase to admire the pleasing lines and uniform sturdiness of the railings. Her eyes lingered on the tasteful floral wallpaper—chosen over Jacob's preference for a less ostentatious design. I hope we won't have to sell the house, she worried. The solidity of the door against her back, the sturdy railings, the bold wallpaper—all spoke out in protest at the prospect that they might one day belong to another family and another woman's gaze. Jacob wouldn't allow it, she told herself. I know he'll find a solution.

'What are you doing, mama?' Louis stood in the hallway, a perplexed look on his face.

'Holding up the door in case it falls in!' Putting on a smile, she advanced to stroke his cheek. 'Have you finished your chores?'

THE LUNCH WITH BENOIT was a failure—the Reformist leader too exercised with the volatile mood in the town to pay much more than polite attention to Jacob's situation.

'Those absurd so-called separatists!' Benoit angrily rustled the newspaper as Jacob sat down. 'Anarchists, if the truth be known. The people are being led astray by fanatics like that scoundrel Chaban. Next, they'll be demanding their own flag and anthem.' He folded the newspaper and set it aside.

'Don't they already have a flag?' asked Jacob. 'I see it waving everywhere,' he said, referring to the gold and green flag of pre-confederation New France.

Benoit snorted. 'That is a cultural flag, not a political one. It's supposed to signify heritage, not an independent state—no matter what that lunatic Chaban has to say.' He poured wine into Jacob's glass.

'Until then?' said Jacob, hoping to steer the conversation back to the purpose of the meeting.

'Ah, yes!' Benoit's expression was sympathetic. 'I've spoken to half-a-dozen colleagues, and while there's immense appreciation for your experience and business abilities, I'm sorry to say there is nothing suitable available—not yet. But who knows what may happen in a week or a month? Now that people are aware of your availability, an offer may be forthcoming any day.'

'So, there's nothing?'

His bleak summation drew an apologetic shrug from Benoit. 'Not for the moment, I'm afraid.'

The news plunged Jacob into gloom, which he did his best to hide by sipping on the wine.

'Tell me,' said Benoit, breaking off a crust of bread, 'what is happening to your former partners?'

'From what I hear they've been found guilty on each charge and will be sentenced shortly.'

'To imprisonment?'

'Hopefully, for years to come,' said Jacob, unable to keep the bitterness from his voice.

'And the factory? There's no prospect of reopening—even backed by local investment?' Benoit tutted at Jacob's grim head shake. 'The perils of capitalism,' he commiserated, 'although don't don't tell your friend Gagnon I said so!'

They ate a lunch of seasoned pork chops and sage and garlic potatoes, Jacob barely tasting the flavours. Benoit was unable to resist turning the conversation back to his *idée fixe*. 'God knows what will happen next. One hears all sorts of rumours. They say that Chaban is up to his old tricks. The villain! How he must relish this. They will not rest until we are separated down to our breeches. Damn communards! But what about you, Jacob?' He eyed Jacob across the table. 'You must be caught between the proverbial rock and a hard place, given your own progressive views?'

Jacob set down his fork, unable to finish the meal. 'I stand with my wife in this as in all things.'

'In spite of your own opinions?'

'Opinion is one thing, love and loyalty another.'

Benoit made a humming sound as if the sentiment might be possible, or even true. 'What is it the Americans say? A house divided against itself cannot stand?'

'There is no division. There never will be.'

Benoit nodded, a thoughtful look on his face. 'I have always said that madame Wheeler is a remarkable woman, as was her mother before her, in spite of our differences. Her family and mine have been at loggerheads ever since the founding.' He sighed. 'I sometimes think our obsession with the past is the curse of New France. Everyone here has the memory of an elephant.'

'I am not so burdened.'

'No, of course not, being originally from America.' Benoit refilled their glasses. 'It's rumoured that Chaban is planning a major protest in Tremblay Square for Saint-Jean-Baptiste Day. Do you plan to attend?'

'I don't know. Isabelle may insist on going.'

'Then take care, for your family's sake. I happen to know the authorities are determined not to tolerate any riotous behaviour. And did you know they have planned a counter-demonstration—to show the country that the protestors do not represent all of New France? And with extremists on both sides …?' Benoit shuddered. 'Just be careful. Don't get caught in the middle—of the square!'

Feeling dejected and out of sorts following the lunch, Jacob decided against going directly home. Instead, he headed towards Old Town, suddenly nostalgic for reminders of his earliest days in New France. Arriving at rue Marian, he descended the steep street, taking the familiar steps cut into the hillside as he made his way towards the market square.

Arriving at ground level again, he walked alongside the market building passing a row of beggars where they had made temporary shacks out of crates and boxes. The tenants sat outside their refuges begging for coins. The sight struck him as more melancholy than usual, an air of hopelessness clinging to the occupants. A woman clutched at his trouser leg as he passed, holding up her hand, her eyes beseeching. 'I'm sorry, Madame,' he said. '*Truth be known, I am scarcely better off than yourself,*' he muttered under his breath. The realisation struck hard as he continued along the row, shocked at the number of men and women fallen on hard times as a result of the war or the lingering effects of the deadly flu pandemic. He came upon a woman crouched on the pavement, her skirts lifted as she urinated on the street.

Disturbed at so much poverty and distress, he was about to cross the street when he heard his name called. 'Monsieur Wheeler!' A man sat outside one of the makeshift shelters looking up at him. The fellow was dressed in little more than rags, his face marred by the ravages of disease. He had a bruise beneath one eye. 'Monsieur Wheeler, do you not recognise me?' The man's voice was raspy, his lips and gums covered in sores and blisters. 'Jacques Côté. I was your employee.'

Shocked, he stared at the man, dimly recognising the face of one of the first workers hired when the factory opened. 'Jacques? What happened to you?'

The man gave a hoarse laugh. 'When you closed the factory, I was left penniless. I could not afford to pay for my room, and the landlord tossed me out onto the street. This is my new home.' He motioned with his head to a large crate covered by a scrap of tarpaulin behind where he sat.

'You could not find other work?'

'Where?' The man croaked and had a coughing fit. 'I like a drink,' he said, gasping and wiping his mouth with a dirty hand. 'So here I am.'

'I'm sorry.' Embarrassed, Jacob put his hand in his pocket and withdrew a few coins, thankful that Benoit had insisted on paying for the lunch. 'It's not much,' he apologised, 'but I'm a bit short myself at the moment.'

The man took the coins and began to laugh, his emaciated frame shaking as he chuckled. 'A bit short,' he repeated, as if finding the remark irresistibly funny. He laughed again, tears appearing in his eyes.

'Well, I wish you the best for the future,' said Jacob, chagrined at the reaction.

He walked away as the man shook with laughter, his bony hand pointed at Jacob. 'A bit short!' he cackled as Jacob hurried to cross the street.

He returned home defeated and dispirited. After a tired account of the lunch to Isabelle, he retired to the study where he sat brooding before the empty fireplace. I must tell her. There's no way around it. He grappled with the best way to broach the subject, his mind frantically searching for a time and a setting. Perhaps after supper—or maybe I could accompany her to church, just the two of us … I could ask Marguerite to be present. A feeling of deep shame vetoed that stratagem. In the event, all of his agonised deliberations came to nought as the confession simply tumbled out of him.

Isabelle had come into the library carrying a cup of coffee, which she set down beside him. 'Don't look so worried, darling. Something will turn up, I'm sure. God will not let anything happen to us.' She kissed his brow.

'Dear, wait,' he said as she made to leave the room. He went to the door and closed it before turning to speak, his voice strained. 'There's something I must tell you.'

31

An Evening Stroll

S HE DID HER BEST to hide her profound shock as Jacob revealed the full extent of their financial distress. 'The house?' She thought she might faint. 'And the investment houses—both of them?' She couldn't help but repeat what he had told her, as if she might have misheard the first time. 'And all of our savings?' She felt nauseous and gripped the apron between her hands.

'We are not destitute.' His voice became desperate as her eyes widened with shock and her face paled to the point he feared she might become physically sick. 'We still have the money Jules advised me to hide away—for which, thank God.'

The information shook her. She hadn't known of that either. 'And how much is that?' Her voice was faint, reflecting the panic she felt rising up to engulf her.

'Precious little,' he confessed, his voice little above a murmur, 'considering our needs.'

'Oh!' It was all she could say. She sat there, hands folded in her lap, a dazed look on her face.

'I am desperately sorry.' His voice was abject. 'I should never have agreed to the loan.'

'I wish you would have discussed it with me first.' Her tone was quiet, reasonable almost, not the shrill, accusatory voice she heard in her head.

'I wish to God I had.' His voice was bitter, despairing.

'What will we do now?' She looked at him as if expecting an answer, a way out.

'I may have no choice but to declare bankruptcy.' He dropped his eyes, too wretched to meet her gaze.

'Oh!'

They sat in complete silence for a few minutes before she stood up. 'I must get dinner ready.' She left the room, closing the door quietly behind her.

In the kitchen, she leaned against the table, feeling light-headed as she struggled to absorb the news. Bankruptcy, he said. Where would we go? A cheap rental—in the Old Town perhaps? She thought of her parsimonious mother and her strict insistence on accounting for every penny spent. Images of poverty, of charity, rose before her eyes. She shivered as she recalled the homeless woman outside her mother's shop all those years ago. Was that a sign—a portent? Had her head been turned by her husband's material success—and was this retribution for that sin? She held onto the table, still unable to grasp what her shame-faced husband had revealed. She pictured the look on Marguerite's face upon hearing the news—of Hugo and their friends. Pitying, no doubt. Shocked, certainly, as she had been. '*And you didn't know?*'

She pulled a bowl of unpeeled potatoes towards her. It hurts most that he did not tell me. Did he not trust how I would take the news? Picking a potato from the bowl, she distractedly brushed a blemish with her finger. Does he not know me better? She picked at the blemish—a bruise, really— her mind occupied by a new and terrible doubt. The wall of trust that was the impregnable fortress surrounding their marriage vows was breached. She saw it clearly, a tiny crack near the foundations which let in … what? Light. Betrayal. *Unfaithfulness?*

She picked up the paring knife and began to peel, revealing the white glistening flesh beneath the brown skin. Exchanging the paring knife for a carver, she placed the peeled potato on the chopping board and began to slice—then, changing her mind, cleaved it in half.

He had remained in the chair after she left the parlour, a feeling of profound self-disgust holding him in place. The look of betrayal in her eyes, a look she had tried to hide by turning her head away, tormented his conscience. I was a fool. An absolute fool! Through me, we've lost everything. Feeling he might choke from remorse and shame if he stayed in the house a moment longer, he got up and put on his hat. 'I shan't be long,' he said, stopping by the kitchen. He hesitated as she continued peeling. 'I need to clear my head …' She didn't look up.

PUBLIC HOSTILITY TOWARDS THE Dissolution Bill had muted throughout the long winter, but continued to bubble beneath the surface, like liquid water trapped under ice. The outrage simmered in newspaper columns and in letters to the editor. With the return of warmer weather, popular resentment boiled to the surface once again. Strikes, demonstrations and marches demanded the withdrawal of the bill. The government, increasingly nervous at the growing unrest, tried several measures to appease the public, even promising to establish a commission to inquire more fully into the issue. The offer was roundly and scornfully condemned as a blatant ploy to buy time. With emotions running feverishly high, the city was, the *Catholic Tribune* reported, "sitting on a powder keg and waiting for the spark that would ignite it."

Jacob followed the newspaper reports without interest, his thoughts fixated by his own crisis. Unable to see an escape from the noose he felt tightening around his throat, he petitioned for bankruptcy.

'I'll find a way to put us back on our feet,' he vowed to Isabelle as her eyes fell upon the legal papers,

She sat in silence, her face ashen.

'Isabelle?'

'I heard you,' she said, the quietness in her voice adding to the shame and despair he felt.

In the days after he lodged the petition, he either avoided her gaze or cast anxious looks in her direction, his manner so subdued that Marie-Odile asked her mother if he were ill.

'Your father has a lot on his mind,' she was told. 'Now set the table. You too, Louis.'

He was sitting in the library when the phone rang, startling him.

'Jacob? It's Hugo. I wonder if you would like to meet for a glass of wine?'

FOLLOWING A SHARED BOTTLE of wine, during which he did his best to deflect the conversation from the 'American affair' as his friends and acquaintances referred to it, talk turned to the civil unrest provoked by the constitutional crisis.

'Did you hear the joke?' asked Hugo in an attempt to lighten his companion's downcast mood. 'Three languages, two faiths, one people. The third language being Mohawk,' he explained at Jacob's puzzled expression.

'Anyway,' Hugo continued, 'someone, I forget who, countered with 'one language, one faith, one people'. To which our dear friend monsieur Turgeon quipped, 'a blessed trinity!' Someone else objected that we are not one people anymore, given the number of outsiders who've flocked into the town, to which dear old Turgeon responded that in which case, our campaign slogan should be … two-thirds of a trinity!' Sorry,' he chuckled at the perplexed look on Jacob's face, 'you'd have to be raised Catholic to appreciate it.'

They were returning through Gaston Tremblay Square when they came across a demonstration. A small crowd had gathered under the figure of the winged bull to listen as a speaker standing on an upturned crate vigorously denounced the proposed constitutional changes. A dozen policemen stood by, looking on. 'Bravo!' cried Hugo, raising his fist in the air. 'Bravo!'

Two or three of the demonstrators turned in their direction. 'Thank you, Monsieur Deputy!' called out one.

'Alas, a deputy without an assembly.' Hugo muttered the words, his voice regretful as they continued.

'Will you miss it?'

Hugo shrugged. 'I hardly had time to get used to it.'

'Nevertheless, they recognised you,' said Jacob.

'I've become quite involved in the movement,' said Hugo, pride in his voice.

'Movement?'

'The resistance.'

Jacob stopped in alarm. 'Resistance? You're swimming in dangerous waters, old friend.'

'I have no choice. Our very birthright is at stake.' Hugo's voice was emotional as they resumed walking 'If this bill passes, we lose everything that makes us distinct. It would be a betrayal of our forefathers and all that they fought for. There's a huge march planned for next month—for Saint-Jean-Baptiste Day.' he said as they exited the square onto rue Saint-Joseph. 'We plan to mobilize the entire city. We'll follow up with strikes that will shut down all commerce and force the provincial government to repeal the bill.'

'We?' He stared. 'Who do you mean by we?'

Hugo gave a weak smile. 'Jean Chaban has formed a steering committee to organise the resistance. He's asked me to sit on it.'

'Chaban?' Jacob frowned at the name. 'Isn't he that mad fellow that's always in the newspapers?'

'Don't believe the lies. He's actually a very reasonable man who just wants New France to go back to the way it was under the Charter.'

'They say he's a leader of the separatists. In which case, he wants it to go back even further … to independence. Surely, you can't wish for that?'

'And why not?' Hugo's voice was defiant. 'If they insist on taking away our rights, we may have no choice but to separate and forge our own destiny once again.'

'This isn't you.' Jacob's face betrayed his surprise at the fervent declaration of his usually temperate companion. 'Chaban is dangerous, a zealot. You should steer clear of such people.'

'He's not a zealot. He's a loyal habitant who objects to the humiliations forced upon us by the federal and provincial governments.'

Jacob shook his head. 'And what does Josette say?'

'Josette will follow where I lead.' Hardly had the bravado tumbled from his mouth than Hugo hesitated. 'At least she says she will.' He glanced at Jacob. 'There's a meeting of the steering committee next week to arrange things. Serge, Claude, Denis, everyone will be there. Will you at least attend so you can see for yourself who's involved and what we are doing?'

'I don't want anything to do with it. I've enough troubles of my own.'

'Troubles? What troubles?' It was Hugo's turn to look concerned. 'You mean the factory closing?'

Jacob nodded. 'There are still matters to be decided.'

'But you are alright? You and Isabelle and the children?'

'Of course. But there are legalities that must be settled.'

'You'd let me know if they weren't? I could help. All of your friends would do whatever they can.'

'Thank you, Hugo, but that won't be necessary.'

'Can I not persuade you to attend next week's meeting?'

Jacob wavered, feeling obliged by the offer of assistance. 'Alright,' he agreed, 'but only as an observer.'

'Good!' Hugo clapped him on the shoulder. 'You'll be surprised, I promise.'

SHE HAD TRIED TO busy herself after Jacob left—dusting the furniture, mopping the kitchen floor, even pruning the roses. All the while her mind screamed so loudly she imagined the neighbours could hear. Feeling nauseous, she hurried to the toilet where she threw up, her body reacting to the fear and panic that smothered her. She splashed water on her face and stared at herself in the mirror. How could he let it happen? Why was he so foolish as to lend the money? I would have certainly advised against it. She did not need her mother's voice in her head to assure her of that.

She deliberated about confiding in her sister, but something—shame, loyalty to Jacob, or simply depression at thought of the conversation and Marguerite's reaction—held her back. The continuing stories in the *Daily Register*—which had sent a reporter to Albany to dig deeper into the affair and report on the legal proceedings—added to her anguish as more details came to light of deception, bribery, tax evasion and outright fraud. The newspaper's failure to make clear that none of these malfeasances were connected to Jacob or the New France division distressed her so much that she made an angry phone call to the editor. To her mortification, details of the conversation were included in the next issue, her denials made to seem like attempts at self-justification amidst the financial imbroglio. To add to her frustration, the leaked phone call reignited the scandal in the pages of not only the *Daily Register* but the *Catholic Tribune* as well.

'You were unwise to provide them with ammunition,' Hugo tutted when Isabelle called in at her cousin's house to discuss the sensationalist newspaper account and clarify the context. 'Say nothing further,' he advised. 'The newspapers lack morals and will scandalously misquote every word you say.'

Marguerite gave similar advice but could not resist making a furious phone call of her own to the same editor, accusing him of 'monstrous behaviour' and calling him a 'sleazy guttersnipe'. The allegations were promptly and prominently included in the next edition, provoking, variously, outrage or amusement among readers eager for fresh gossip and titillation.

Jacob dismissed the reports as concoctions, being far more concerned with the effects of his admission on Isabelle. Several times he tried to broach the subject, only to desist at the hurt expression on her face. Retiring to bed each night, he sought her hand under the covers and squeezed it, only to meet with a limp, indifferent response. His hesitant 'good night, dear,' was met with a cheerless, muffled reply as she kept to her side of the bed, her back to him. Throughout breakfast she was formally polite in passing the toast or the salt, while engaging in endless, forced conversation with the children. Miserable to his bones, he slunk off to the library with a cup of coffee as soon as it was decent to do so. He sat there for most of the morning, wrestling with stratagems for restoring their fortunes. To his dismay, his many calls to the business acquaintances he had met through attendance at the Chamber of Commerce or through his cultivated patronage of the Reform Party went unanswered.

'It's as if I no longer exist,' he complained in a telephone call to Dwight. 'I may as well be a ghost.'

'You terrify them because you stand as a reminder of what might befall them. Try not to take it to heart. Once your fortunes are reversed, they will come swarming back as you will then stand as a reminder of how a person might recover from such a blow.'

He found solace in the company of Villeneuve, Cloutier, Vachon, Charbonneau, and other close friends from his first days in New France. He began to spend more and more time at the tavern, reluctant to return home and be reminded of his failures as a husband and provider.

'The old pieties keep him warm, I suspect,' remarked Hugo to his wife after one such session. 'How now his commerce, his well-shod friends, and his claims on the future?'

'You sound … satisfied.' Josette gave a cryptic glance across the supper table.

'No! Not at all. It's simply that it is well to remember that Fortune is a wheel that never stops turning.'

'And you have told him this?' She raised an eyebrow.

'Of course not!' He flashed her an indignant look. 'One does not kick a dog when it is down.'

'Dog, now?' Her eyebrow went up even further.

'Stop imputing things!' He frowned with guilty annoyance and dug into the baked ham.

The simmering tension between Jacob and Isabelle came to a head when he returned home one evening late for supper and the worse for wear after a drinking session with Serge Villeneuve and Denis Vachon.

'I believe I shall forgo supper,' he said with inebriated courtesy, stumbling as he made his way to the library.

'Pappa! Will you read to me?' Marie-Odile plucked at his sleeve. 'Pappa?'

'Leave your father, darling. He is tired and needs to sleep.' Isabelle took the girl's hand. 'I will read to you.'

'But pappa!' The girl squirmed out of her mother's grasp and ran to the library.

'Pappa! Will you read me a story?'

'Pappa is indisposed,' said Isabelle as Jacob looked up with bleary eyes. 'Come, let's put you into bed.' she said, steering the upset girl from the room. She turned out the light as she left. And when Jacob came to bed, well after midnight, she lay still as if fast asleep while he stumbled and muttered as he undressed in the dark.

The next morning, she went to confession and poured out her anguish and disappointment, indifferent as to whether or not the shadowy presence behind the grille recognised her from the details.

'Life is so unfair,' she mourned. 'I expect me and my children to be turned out of our own home and put out into the street any day now.'

'God sends these trials that we may overcome them, and in so doing, prove our trust and devotion to His divine plan.'

She was silent, her hands tented in prayer—or despair.

'Sister?'

'I am just so upset.' Her voice trembled.

'With your husband?'

The reply hovered on her tongue.

'Madame?'

'With myself.' The awareness was like a flash of lightning in the darkened cloister.

'You have nothing to reproach yourself for. It was not you who betrayed the marital trust.'

'Please, give me my penance, Father, for my sins.'

'For *your* sins?'

'Yes, the sins of pride and hard-heartedness.' She was in tears.

Afterwards she knelt at the altar, her fingers gripping the rosary Jacob had given her as she bowed her head. '*Open my heart, Lord, that I may forgive and beg forgiveness in return.*' She raised her eyes to the crucified figure, tears rolling down her cheek. Getting to her feet, she wandered over to the stained-glass windows and stood for a moment, bathed in the prismatic light that soothed her soul. Her gaze sought out Gaston Tremblay, the great hero of her youth, as he stared resolutely at the wild shore. For a moment, she imagined herself riding with him in the birch-bark canoe as it tossed and bounced on the turbulent stream. She pictured herself taking his hand as she stepped onto the sacred soil, her feet wet from the bilge water, her garments blown by the brisk wind. The coloured panes were a glowing tapestry of light and suspended time. It was possible, she felt, to imagine the figures were moving, breathing, alive somehow in the captive glow. She felt light-headed and took slow, deep breaths in the hushed, radiant air. '*Lord, let Thy light shine upon me.*'

HE HAD PUT OFF going directly home, his feet taking him to the cathedral and then all the way back to Tremblay Square, his mind raw with self-recrimination. The protestors had gone, replaced by the usual sightseers admiring the bull. He joined them to look up at the outspread wings, the flared nostrils, and the air of barely restrained ferocity. The visitors swapped astonishments as they beheld the towering figure. 'It reminds me of something, but I don't remember what,' a woman remarked to her male companion.

'It must have cost a pretty penny or two,' replied the man. 'Look at the wings alone. All that bronze. How much do think its worth—the whole thing, I mean?'

'What do you mean—if you carried it off?'

'No, silly. If it were melted down, say.'

Other sightseers wandered up. 'Bet I could climb up there and ride it!' bragged a young boy.

'You'll do no such thing!' his mother scolded. 'Show some respect.'

'Should we get a photograph?' a man with her asked.

The sightseers moved off and left him alone in its soaring shadow, the monumental beast offering the consolation of scale and perspective to his wretchedness. He stood on tiptoe and reached out a hand, pressing it against the cold, hard bronze. You did yourself proud, Alois. I'll keep your secret. Not that it matters where you took the inspiration from. The achievement is all your own. The thought stayed on his mind as he rested against the great plinth that supported the winged beast. His mind strayed to the charcoal sketch, and he wondered, for the hundredth time, which hand or hands were responsible for carving the original. 'From stone to bronze,' he mused, 'from prairie grass to city square.' *From pauper back to pauper.* The bitter jibe further soured his mood.

I should be getting home, he told himself. But still he lingered, taking solace from the breeze, the vast open space of the square, and the mighty beast half-footed above him. A church bell sounded in the distance, and he straightened up as another party of sightseers approached. A young girl smiled at him in her excitement at seeing the bronze. He gave a preoccupied look in return before setting off across the square in a sudden anxiety to return home.

'JACOB?'

'Yes?' He closed the door behind him, flushed from the walk.

'Where have you been? I was waiting for you.'

'Where are the children?' He stared. 'And why are you wearing your coat and hat?'

'Because, my heart, we are going for a walk—another one!' She pecked his lips, surprising him. 'Don't worry about the children, they are with Marguerite.'

He groaned. 'My dear. I really don't feel like going out. I've only just got in. Can we not postpone it for another time?'

'Most certainly not!' She took his arm. 'Come with me, if you please.'

'Where are we going?' He protested, still reluctant.

'A surprise!'

The late afternoon was warm and lovely as she guided him towards the Old Town. He glanced sideways several times, wondering at her intentions. She seemed her old self again for the first time since he had confessed his foolishness. Unwilling to risk upsetting her good mood, he put aside his reluctance and the disappointments that had, thus far, shaped his day. To his gratified amazement Isabelle smiled and joked and hugged his arm, her determinedly high spirits lifting his own.

The market square was plastered with posters and graffiti denouncing the Quebec government and urging citizens to rise up in defence of New France. Splashed in white paint on a wall was a protest condemning the provincial assembly as a monster sucking the lifeblood of the people. A message scrawled in ink announced a protest rally to be held in the Old Town the following Saturday: "*Come join your fellow citizens in defending our historic rights!*"

He paused to examine one poster that showed a likeness of the Quebec premier with an 'x' painted across his face. He tried to read the words beneath the image but Isabelle dragged him on, determined to ignore the graffiti.

The park was full of strollers and people enjoying the spring sunshine. Several recognised Jacob, tipping their hats in acknowledgement as they passed. Some even offered a respectful, 'Good afternoon, Monsieur and Madame Wheeler.'

'See, everybody knows you!' Isabelle teased.

'At least they don't blame me.' He gave a heavy sigh.

'And why would they? What happened wasn't your fault.' She led him towards a bench. 'Do you remember this seat?'

'Naturally. It almost got me banished from New France.'

She laughed. 'I *was* banished.'

They sat down to look at the passers-by. After a while, he turned to her, his heart burdened with remorse. 'Isabelle, dearest. I want to say again how terribly—'

'*Shhh!*' She pressed a finger to his lips. 'Look!' she whispered, directing his attention to where a young couple lingered under a tree to gaze into one another's eyes. 'That was us, once.' She contemplated the oblivious lovers, a wistful look on her face. And as they sat, bathing in the memory of that glorious day, his despairing mood melted into something approaching resignation or perhaps even acceptance.

'What is it?' he asked, as he felt her tremble. 'Do you wish we could live that day again?'

'No, not that.' She turned to look at him, her face grave. 'Love is all that counts, Jacob, love. Not factories, or automobiles, or even our present troubles. It will all end sooner or later. And when it does, the only thing that will matter is the love we had for each other.' Her voice trailed off, her eyes bright with tears.

Moved beyond words, he kissed her lips.

The light was beginning to fade, filtering through the trees as they sat with clasped hands to observe the passing parade. Couples strolled the manicured grass, arm in arm. The leaves of a nearby silver maple rustled in the breeze, casting a pattern of light and shade. As he gazed on her face, warm and trusting in the chequered light, his heart was pierced with an unbearable love. 'You remind me of that day in the cathedral when we first met,' he said. 'The light from the stained glass was falling all around you, and I thought you a vision of love—then and now.' With infinite tenderness he kissed her brow.

Smiling with gratitude, she hugged his arm, moving closer so that there was no space between them. They sat there in perfect silence as the light began to fail. The green, rustling leaves whispered an ancient, murmurous song that held them in a kind of spell as they leaned against each other, faces rapt, even as dusk crept in to claim the bench, Isabelle, Jacob, and, last of all, the restless, wind-stirred grass.

32

Fire in the Night

AGAINST HIS BETTER INSTINCTS he attended the meeting at Hugo's house. When he arrived at the appointed hour, he was surprised to find the parlour crowded with twenty or more attendees, seated in chairs or standing around the walls. Several women were in attendance. He recognised Serge Villeneuve, deep in conversation with Claude Charbonneau, and Denis Vachon as he took a seat beside the latter. Turning his head, he caught sight of several others whom he knew by acquaintance. Three of the organisers, including Hugo, sat behind the dining room table which had been moved to face the room. A fourth chair was empty. Hugo raised a hand in greeting as their eyes met, a smile on his face.

'So, he roped you in too,' remarked Denis as Jacob sat down.

'You're here unwillingly?'

'I'm like you, a cynic,' said Denis. 'But Serge here is a true believer.' Just then Serge saw Jacob and called out a surprised greeting, leaning across Denis to shake hands.

Josette entered, carrying a tray of coffee which she placed on the table. She returned minutes later with a platter heaped with sandwiches. 'For you, gentlemen—to fuel the fire!'

'Thank you, Madame, a true daughter of the revolution!' The words were spoken by a man seated at the table next to Hugo.

'Who's that?' asked Jacob, guessing the man's identity.

'That's Jean 'Loup' Chaban,' confirmed Denis. 'He's the one organising everything.'

He observed Chaban as the latter engaged in animated conversation. The fellow struck him as an unnaturally intense individual, his scruffy beard and unkempt hair—pulled back into a tail—proclaiming his status as someone indifferent to social conventions. He wore a working man's jacket over a corduroy vest and grey denim shirt unbuttoned at the collar.

The door opened and another man entered, wearing overalls. Muttering apologies for being late, he took his place at the table in the empty chair reserved for him.

'And who's that?'

'Armand Joubert, an ally of Chaban's, and a notorious firebrand.'

The conversation fell away as Chaban finished his discussion and looked up.

'Comrades, are we ready to begin?' He played with the cuff of his jacket as he began speaking in a rough voice that rang with the patois of the Old Town.

'He's actually from a rich family in the Maples,' whispered Denis, naming an upper-class district of the town. 'He puts on that accent for effect.'

Chaban paused to take a sip of water. 'The purpose of today's meeting, brothers and sisters, is to confirm our plans for Saint-Jean-Baptiste Day, the day we force the government to hear our voice.'

'And show the bastards who's boss!' Joubert's interjection brought good-humoured laughter.

Chaban gave his comrade an indulgent smile before introducing, with breezy informality, the men seated at the table. 'Brother Hugo here has agreed to sit on the steering committee to help organise the resistance. Andre Lagarde you already know. And this is Armand-come-lately-Joubert!'

Joubert scowled as the room chuckled at the joke.

Chaban then proceeded to outline plans for the demonstration, his intensity alarming Jacob as he discussed methods for forcing entry into the square should the authorities, as now expected, forbid the gathering. 'There'll be cops stationed at all the openings, but we have the numbers to force our way through at the rue Saint Joseph entrance. The men first, to make passage for the women and children. If the cops don't give way, then we keep pushing until they do.'

The declaration brought approving voices and a resounding, 'Yes!' from Joubert.

Jacob's alarm grew as he saw Hugo nodding along with the words. Leaning past Denis, he saw Serge equally receptive, his face fierce with resolve.

'How many do we expect?' said Chaban in answer to a question. 'Fifty thousand at the very least.' The figure drew gasps.

'Hopefully, more,' continued Chaban. 'Comrade Armand has been organising for people to come in from the rural areas to support us. How is that going, brother? he asked, turning to Joubert.

'Expect at least eight, and maybe up to ten, thousand. The rural workers hate the proposed bill as much as we do.'

Charbonneau spoke up. 'And what about the Church? It would help if the bishop, at least, was present. It might prevent the cops from breaking heads.'

Chaban gave a scornful laugh. 'The bishop is just as likely to attend on the side of the cops!'

'Not true!' Recognising the voice, Jacob turned around to see Charles Mercier, a long-time neighbour of Hugo's, seated behind him.

'Isn't it?' Chaban's face soured at the objection. 'Chretien speaks out of both sides of his mouth. I wish Simard had not died, at least you knew his conscience was in the right place. This Chretien is a wily, slippery fellow—a toady appointed at the behest of the provincial government. Remember, he's not even from New France.'

'The Church must balance opposing forces,' demurred Hugo, looking unhappy at the remarks.

'Why balance?' demanded Joubert, leaning forward to engage with Hugo. 'There is only one side for it to take.'

'Its own,' quipped Chaban, 'as it has always done throughout our history.'

'Then you must not be very well acquainted with our history, Monsieur Chaban.' Mercier's voice was sharp. 'The church has always stood with us.'

'No matter!' Chaban waved a hand in arrogant dismissal. 'We have a list of speakers who will address the crowd, including Brother Hugo here. A group is working on banners and flags. We need to form another committee to organise the strikes that will follow the demonstration.' He paused and inclined his head as Hugo whispered in his ear. When he looked up, his eyes fixed on Jacob. 'We need another man to sit on the strike committee. Somebody who understands business and where to hit early and hard. Comrade Jacob, we are all aware of your recent troubles and sympathise. Brother Hugo assures us you are a man with exceptional organisational talents and nominates you to the committee. Do you accept?'

Furious at the nomination, Jacob glared at Hugo. Chaban sat forward as he waited for a response.

'No, I do not.' The blunt refusal provoked an intake of breath from the crowded room. Unfazed by the reply, Chaban regarded Jacob with an appraising gaze. 'That's too bad, comrade. We could use a man of your talents.'

'You are a wealthy businessman, perhaps you are on the side of the Reformists?' The challenge, from a sneering Joubert, drew mutters.

'I have my reasons.' Jacob returned Chaban's stare as a hush fell over the room.

'I trust we can at least count on your support?' The question, from Chaban, eased the tension.

'Of course you can! Jacob is one of us.'

Serge Villeneuve's vehement endorsement drew a nod from Chaban. 'No one is forced to do anything,' he said. 'We are not the government.'

A man rose from his seat. 'There are rumours of soldiers being brought in to help out the police.' The possibility provoked alarm among those present.

'They are not rumours, but fact.' Chaban's voice was uncompromising. 'A train brought them in at night not two days ago. They were observed entering the barracks.'

The confirmation caused consternation among the listeners. 'Will they be in the square?' a voice demanded. 'There'll be women and kids there!'

'We don't know. But be assured, we'll be prepared if they attempt to harm the people.'

To Jacob's shock, Hugo nodded in approval.

'I hear they're organising a counter-demonstration. Is that true?' The question came from Serge.

'It is. We can expect the bastards to try and rush us out of the square.'

'Half their luck!' A voice called out, to a chorus of support.

Another man spoke up. 'Pardon, but how many did you say would gather?' Jacob dimly recognised the speaker as a baker from the patisserie on rue Pierre de Frasnay.

'Gather? That word shows you do not yet understand,' sneered Joubert. 'We are not talking about a prayer meeting!'

The rebuke brought an indignant response from the baker. 'Then what word would you suggest?' he asked, his face flushed.

Chaban directed a warning glance at the bellicose Joubert. 'At least fifty thousand,' he repeated, 'along with several thousand from the rural districts.'

'Thank you, comrade,' said the baker, directing an offended look at Joubert. 'That is all I wanted to know.'

'I now hand over to Brother Joubert to tell us more about the strike action. Brother?'

'We'll shut down the fucking city!' Joubert made a clenched fist, his eyes blazing. 'No trams, no shops open, no trading, no factories working, nothing!—just like Winnipeg! We'll force the arrogant shits to listen!'

The remarks brought claps and hoots of approval.

The door opened and Josette poked her head in. 'More coffee?'

'WHAT DO YOU MAKE of Chaban?' Jacob asked Denis Vachon as they made their way home following the meeting.

'A charismatic fellow, dedicated to the cause. But I do wish that Joubert would shut up! The loudmouth gets on my nerves.'

'Something puzzles me. They seem to be opposed to the Church. As habitants, shouldn't they be on its side?'

'Not all habitants are religious. Some of them, like Chaban, are more interested in an independent New France. They see the habitant movement as a useful means to an end, and don't much care for the Church's restraining influence over the people. Remember, Gaston Tremblay himself was said to be a non-believer.'

'Claude told me Chaban and Joubert are the leaders of the separatist faction.'

'It wouldn't surprise me. Chaban has his fingers in every pie. And they are not the only ones.' He glanced sideways at Jacob. 'Did you know Serge is now a full-blown separatist?'

'Serge?' Jacob thought about it for a moment. 'Mind you, it shouldn't surprise me. He's never hidden his allegiance. Anyone else that we know—? Wait!' He took Denis by the arm. 'Not Hugo, surely?'

Denis made a wry face. 'Perhaps. But if not, it won't take much to push him over the edge. He's infatuated with Chaban. He calls him the spirit of Gaston Tremblay.'

'The fellow is dangerous. I fear his influence.'

'And you're right to. I heard a whisper that he and Joubert are not waiting for Saint-Jean-Baptiste Day, but intend springing a surprise ahead of it, as a warm-up.'

'What kind of surprise?'

Vachon shrugged. 'Who can tell? But knowing Chaban, something big no doubt.'

Returning home, Jacob sat down and recounted the meeting to Isabelle, profoundly grateful that their former intimacy seemed fully restored. She listened carefully, asking questions and professing surprise at her cousin's open involvement. 'It's not like Hugo to be so ... zealous,' she said, 'excepting in matters of religion, and language,' she added.

'It's the influence of that Chaban fellow.'

'Maybe. But losing his deputyship so soon after getting it must be galling. I know Josette was crushed.'

Jacob took her hand in his. 'Dearest, I know your heart is set on attending the demonstration, but I urge you to reconsider. After listening to the firebrands at the meeting, I'm afraid they are intent on troublemaking. Also,' he said, squeezing her hand as she opened her mouth to protest, 'the government is organising a counter-demonstration, and don't forget there are plenty of Reformists as dangerous as Chaban and his ilk. The mood in the city is far too volatile.'

'Nevertheless, I intend to go,' she said, her face determined.

'And what if there's fighting?'

'I have no choice. This is everything we stand for—who we are. We simply cannot sit by and let those thieves in Quebec City steal away our birthright.'

'That word again—it's the one Hugo used.'

'Hugo is right. We must fight to protect our heritage.'

Jacob sighed, his face troubled. 'I wish you would reconsider. There's a real possibility of violence. Remember what happened with the Easter riots? People lost their lives, and I fear this will be much worse. You should have heard them at the meeting. They are already talking of forcing their way into the square if need be. And they are promising a crowd of at least fifty thousand.'

'Nevertheless, all the women will be there, even Josette. I cannot let them down, I must stand beside them. It will be expected I attend as a direct descendent of Gaston Tremblay.'

Seeing the look on her face, he relented. 'Then, if you must, you must. Of course, I will go with you.'

She gave a grateful smile. 'I know that you don't agree with all of our ideas, Jacob. You must think us silly for fighting over the past. But this affects the future as well, and the sort of city we wish our children to live in.'

'I am not so opposed as you might think,' he admitted. 'I've seen, for example, how the lust for profits can corrupt. And I've seen, also, how individual greed can harm the public interest.'

Isabelle smiled. 'Jacob Wheeler! We'll make a habitant out of you yet.'

He had just retired to the library when Isabelle stuck her head in the door. 'Jacob? Marie-Odile has asked you to read to her.'

'What would you like to hear, pumpkin?' he asked, sitting down on the side of the child's bed.

'Lisette the Owl,' she replied firmly.

'But didn't I read that to you just two nights ago?'

'She's my favourite!'

'What do you like about her?' he asked, amused and curious at her preference.

'She is clever and good!'

'Just like you! Let me see.' He shuffled through the sheaf of hand-written pages. 'Here we are, the clever and good Lisette herself!' He cleared his throat and began reading.

Lisette the owl was respected among all the creatures of the woodland for her wisdom and good sense. Whenever the deer, the wolves and bears, the racoons and porcupines, or even the little field mice had a dispute to settle, they called upon Lisette to judge the merits of their particular case. One day, Pierre the beaver came to the branch where she sat, demanding she settle a dispute between himself and Gerbaud, the bad-tempered bear.

When the case became known, the creatures of the forest gathered to hear, listening eagerly as an indignant Pierre gave the details.

'Every time I build a home out of sticks for myself, Monsieur Gerbaud comes along and knocks it down!' complained Pierre. 'I am at my wit's end how to provide a house for myself and my family!'

The accusation drew cries of 'Shame!' directed at the bear, amid much sympathy for Pierre who, after all, was only a tiny beaver by comparison.

And now all eyes turned to Gerbaud to see how he might defend his actions. 'Well, Monsieur Gerbaud, what do you have to say for yourself?' asked Lisette, turning her head and large yellow-brown eyes upon the bear, notorious for his surly moods and bullying ways.

'He builds his house in the pond where I fish!' growled Gerbaud. 'Is it my fault if he chooses to live where I must eat? For two pins I would knock both him and his house down!' The ferocious reply drew murmurs from the assembled spectators. 'He makes an excellent argument,' conceded Phillipe the field mouse. 'After all, a bear has to eat!'

'I disagree,' objected Fabien, the white-tailed deer. 'Let the bear eat elsewhere and leave poor Pierre and his family in peace!'

Having heard the arguments on both sides, all eyes turned to Lisette where she sat on the branch listening. Her wise head turned from side to side as she deliberated. 'How will she decide?' The onlookers wondered. 'And will Gerbaud accept the judgement if it goes against him?' For the bear was feared for his hot temper.

'I have heard the evidence,' said Lisette and fluffed up her feathers. 'The case comes down to two simple questions: the right to eat versus the right to live and sleep in safety. My decision rests on which of these two rights is of more importance.' Murmurs of approval greeted the words.

'As always, she hits the nail on the head!' declared Emile the porcupine. 'I was against the bear at first, because of his size. But now I see that he has a right to eat.'

'But what of poor Pierre?' objected Henri the racoon. 'Does he not have an equal right to live in the pond where he might gather sticks to build his house?'

'Shhh!' came from those around them. 'Lisette is about to speak!'

Lisette fixed the spectators with her unblinking stare. 'Since the right to eat is no more or less important than the right to live in safety, there can be no clear advantage found to either party. Therefore, both parties to the dispute are equally in the right,' she declared.

The unexpected verdict left the animals confused. 'What then is to be done?' asked someone, 'if no one wins?'

'Life,' answered Lisette, 'is not always about winning or losing. If I decide for Pierre, then Gerbaud must go hungry. And if I decide for Gerbaud, then Pierre has nowhere safe to live and sleep. And yet, a decision must be made in order to keep the peace.

She turned her head to survey the breathless onlookers as they awaited a judgement, confident that Lisette's wisdom would find a way in spite of the difficulty of the case.

'The solution is that Gerbaud must fish in a manner that does not tear down the house Pierre has built, and Pierre, in turn, must understand and respect Gerbaud's right to fish in that spot. That way, both of their rights are protected. Can the parties agree on this?'

Pierre looked at Gerbaud as the others waited with bated breath for his reaction. Slowly the bear extended a paw and the two shook hands, to applause from the other creatures. That applause turned to cheers as they turned to hail Lisette for her wisdom.

The moral of the tale, dear reader? Oft-times in a quarrel, there is right on both sides. Wisdom comes from recognising this and seeking a solution which does not favour one side over the other as arguments that are settled by force rarely end well. Which goes to prove the adage that a handshake is more powerful than a fist!'

Marie-Odile had her eyes closed, a smile upon her face.

'Good night, sweet angel,' he said softly, and kissed her cheek. 'Sleep soundly—like little Pierre!'

He was awoken from sleep barely an hour after going to bed. It was dark outside, but the sounds of a commotion could be heard in the distance.

Isabelle, too, was awakened by the noise. 'What is it?' She sat up, her heart pounding. They heard the sound of bells as a fire wagon rushed along the street.

Jacob went to the window to peer out. He saw a red glow on the horizon, across the rooftops. 'I'm not sure. Something's on fire.'

'Where are you going?' she asked, as he put on his dressing gown.

'I'm just going downstairs to check. Don't worry.'

The noise of bells and the sound of rushing firewagons grew louder as he opened the front door and stepped out into the street. A cab was pulling up a few houses down and he hailed the passenger as he stepped out, stumbling and almost falling as he did so. 'Monsieur Vanier! What is all the commotion?'

The man approached at Jacob's hail. He was dressed in a formal suit and top hat. 'I've just come from a do in the city,' he said, his face showing a yellow cast in the illumination from Jacob's opened door. 'It's bedlam! Some rascals have set fire to the governor's mansion.' His voice was slurred, and he swayed on his feet. 'The cab driver claims he heard shots.'

'Who? Which rascals?'

The man stared at him, his eyes tired and bloodshot from the liquor he had consumed at the event. 'Who? Those damn'd rebels, that's who. They ought to be strung up! Every last one of them. Goodnight, Monsieur Wheeler!' And with that the man staggered off back to his residence.

When Jacob peered out of the window again next morning, he could see a column of smoke rising up into the air. The papers were full of lurid accounts of the incident, the *Daily Register* denouncing it as a "flagrant attack on the state itself." The *Catholic Tribune* was more temperate, decrying the "imposed constitutional changes which inspired such a desperate act."

'According to the police it was the work of the separatists,' said Jacob, reading from the paper to a worried Isabelle. 'And there were three wounded, including one policeman. The mansion was burnt to the ground.' His mind went back briefly to Vachon's warning of 'something big' in the works. He put down the paper. 'You realise what this means? You can't possibly go to the square on Monday. It will be far too dangerous. Emotions will be at boiling point.'

Isabelle set her lips, her face defiant. 'It is even more important that we go, to show solidarity with the people. More than ever, they will expect to see a Tremblay there. We cannot let our friends down.'

He sighed in surrender. 'Very well—but we leave at the first sign of trouble, agreed?'

He turned back to the newspaper accounts of the attack, which the *Daily Register*, quoting from Benoit's final speech in the Assembly, characterised as "a deliberate assault on progressive, liberal values." The rebellion of the "Three Oughts," as it came to be known, had begun.

33

The Square

RUE SAINT-JOSEPH WAS A riot of colour and noise. Green and gold flags waved proudly in the air, drums pounded, and a solitary trumpeter gave forth strident, out-of-tune blasts as the festive column, marshalled by organisers from the union movement, headed towards the square. Other marchers streamed in from nearby streets to swell the ranks as the assembled column sent up a collective chant defying the provincial government. Women and children carried banners demanding the restitution of the Assembly and the Charter of Rights. Other banners demanded '*Sovereignty!*' '*Justice*,' and '*Historic Rights!*' while one forlorn placard pleaded for an end to cruelty to horses.

'There must be tens of thousands!' Isabelle turned to Jacob, shouting to make herself heard about the noise noise, her cheeks flushed with excitement.

'At the very least!' Jacob shouted back, caught up in the festive mood despite his apprehension. Rumours of trouble ahead flew down the column as the police attempted to block entrance to the square. In the end, they had simply given up the attempt and stepped aside, unable to resist the tide of marchers forcing their way past the barricades. The vast concourse was already filled with demonstrators cheering and chanting in triumph as they congregated beneath the winged bull. Willing hands erected a platform beneath the monument, guarded by protestors in the event the police might try to tear it down. On the far side of the square, held back by a thin line of helmeted police, a far smaller crowd of counter-demonstrators waved the white and blue fleur-de-lis of Quebec and the Canadian Red Ensign while shouting insults and hurling abuse at the jubilant protestors.

They had begun the march in the company of the Villeneuves and Vachons but had since become separated in the tumultuous sea of protestors. Jacob tried to find them but abandoned the attempt as the crowd swelled in number.

'There's Hugo!' Isabelle pulled Jacob's arm, directing his gaze to where Hugo stood on the platform, his face exultant with pride. Someone had passed him the New France flag and he waved it from side to side to massed cries of patriotic fervour. Gaston Joubert prowled the stage like a caged tiger, urging on the crowd by punching his fist into the air. Jean Chaban stood with a megaphone in hand waiting to address the cheering mass of supporters.

'Self-Rule!' chanted the crowd. 'No more union!'

Chaban shouted into the megaphone. 'Brothers and sisters, reclaim your historic birthright! Demand the right to live in a free and independent New France!'

Excitement rose to a fever pitch as the mob roared back its approval. Chaban's voice boomed out across the square as he exhorted the volatile crowd to ever greater displays of defiance. Planting himself at the front of the platform, he led the cheering mass in the separatist chant: "One faith! One tongue! One folk!"

Jacob paid scant attention to the outpouring of fevered patriotism, more concerned to keep an eye on what was happening elsewhere in the square. He stood on tiptoe but was unable to see past the forest of flags and banners. He thought he detected the shrill blast of a police whistle and listened anxiously, frustrated by the noise of the crowd. There! He heard it again, followed by several more blasts. Something was happening across the square, he was convinced. He became acutely aware of the suffocating crush of bodies.

'We must leave!' He tugged Isabelle's arm to get her attention above the full-throated roars for independence.

'I want to hear!' She joined in the chants while pulling him towards the platform. Hugo Gagnon had taken a turn at the megaphone, shouting out something Jacob couldn't hear, but which was greeted with cheers by the crowd. Stretching on tiptoe to see above the surrounding heads, he caught a glimpse of helmets. It seemed to him that the line of riot police separating the rival demonstrations had pushed closer.

'We must go!'

Isabelle uttered a protest as he dragged her behind him, fighting to push through the mass of tightly packed bodies.

The shriek of police whistles split the air. He thought he heard cries of fear or anger—he was uncertain which—and pushed on with more urgency toward the street exit. Risking a glance back at the platform, he glimpsed Chaban pointing to some disturbance in the crowded square. The raucous cheers gave way to uncertainty and confusion as those around them began to sense something was amiss. Isabelle had caught his alarm and clung to his hand as he barged through the resistant sea of bodies. Screams sounded above the noise of the chanting crowd, followed by shouts of fear. A crackle of gunshots provoked a wave of panic as the crowd—now a frightened mob—recoiled from whatever was happening in the centre of the square.

In the turmoil, Isabelle's hand was torn from his grasp. He turned in time to see her swallowed up in the struggling mass of bodies as she cried out his name. He fought through the crowd, frantic to reach her as the sounds of gunfire grew louder and the panicked mob tried to flee the violence. People were running on all sides. He was sent flying as someone slammed into him. He tried to scramble to his feet but was knocked down again. Men and women rushed over him in a terrified stampede as he tried to protect himself, curling up to make himself as small as possible.

The rush of people seemed to last an eternity before the crowd at last thinned and he was able to sit up, his body bruised, his head dazed and aching from several kicks. Badly shaken, he took a few moments to recover his breath before climbing unsteadily to his feet. 'My God!' He exclaimed in disbelief as his stunned senses took in a scene of devastation. Dozens of bodies—men, women, and children—were strewn across the ground, some with their limbs twisted in grotesque fashion.

He stumbled past the fallen, crying out Isabelle's name while seized with dread lest he find her lying among the still and broken bodies. A small child sat next to a woman who appeared to be dead or unconscious. The child sobbed tearfully while shaking the woman's arm to rouse her. On all sides injured protestors were moaning in distress and pleading for help.

Desperate to find Isabelle, he made his way past the confused, milling figures still wandering the square—many in shock like himself. The fighting appeared to have died down and he found himself in the shade of the giant bull. He called out Isabelle's name, his voice now a hoarse croak. The clang of fire bells sounded in the distance and the smell of smoke drifted on the air. A man rushed past, his face frantic with fear. 'They are shooting! Save yourself!' The temporary lull ended as members of the rival factions surged into the space around the monument, attacking each other with guns, knives and cudgels. As if in a dream, he saw people clamber onto the plinth, attempting to hoist themselves up onto the bronze wings in a panicked attempt to escape the violence.

A cop appeared before him with raised baton, a frenzied look on his face. He barely had time to raise his arms before blows rained down as he tried to shield himself. The blows continued and he fell to his knees beneath the vicious assault. The blows stopped suddenly, and the baton clattered to the ground. He struggled to his feet, thinking only to flee. The cop turned astonished eyes on him. It was then that he saw the knife protruding from between the man's ribs. The cop moaned, his face a deathly pale colour, and slumped into Jacob's arms.

Shouting for help, he struggled to support the wounded man. He saw a face he thought he recognised, but it disappeared in the melee. The cop was abruptly wrenched from his arms as his comrades arrived on the scene. Jacob's frantic protestations of innocence were buried beneath a vengeful hail of baton strikes. He cowered, desperately trying to protect himself before shock and darkness engulfed him.

'JACOB!' A VOICE WAS calling his name. He tried to open his eyes, but the pull of sleep was irresistible. 'Jacob!' The voice was insistent. A hand gripped his shoulder. 'Jacob!'

He groaned as a fierce pain shot through his head.

'Jacob? It's me, Denis. Thank God you're alive!'

He opened his eyes, struggling to focus on the face that loomed over him. 'Denis?'

He tried to sit up but gasped at an agonising pain in his ribs. 'Best not to move for a while. You were knocked out.' Vachon's face was smudged with dirt, his eyes bloodshot. 'The bastards gave you a good going-over. Your ribs may be broken. Your face is black and blue. What in God's name happened to you?'

'Isabelle?' He gripped Denis' arm.

Denis shook his head, his face grim. 'I don't know—about her or my Yvette.'

Disoriented, he turned his head. He was lying on what felt like a pile of straw. At least a dozen men sat slumped against the side of a stall, despairing looks on their faces.

'You remember Antoine?' Denis motioned to one of the seated men. The man gave a tired glance and raised a hand in response.

He sucked in his breath at the piercing pain in his side. 'Help me sit up!'

Denis did so, easing Jacob back against a wood partition. He grimaced as pain shot through his ribs. A strong smell of shit and piss came to his nose. 'What in the name of God is that stench?'

'We're in a stable, inside the barracks. The cops dragged us here from the square.'

'What happened?' He tried to remember.

'There was a riot. Not us, the other bastards.' Denis' voice was bitter. 'Someone fired a shot. Next moment there were shots everywhere. It was bedlam. Women and children were screaming, everyone trying to get away from the fighting. They say dozens were killed.' He regarded Jacob, his face sombre. 'Your clothes are bloodied.'

Jacob stared at the blood stains on his jacket as flashes of memory pierced his confusion. 'There was a cop! He was beating me.' He tried to recall the details, his mind dazed. 'And then I remember he just groaned, and I was holding him up. I saw a knife—in his side.' He stared wildly with the recollection, clutching Denis in spite of the intense pain in his ribs. 'But I never hurt him, I swear! I don't know who did.'

Denis frowned. 'Maybe that explains why you're not with the others.'

'Others?'

'Hugo and Chaban. They are in the next stall, accused of murder, along with at least a dozen others. Serge is in there, too.'

'My God!'

They heard footsteps as someone approached. Denis put a finger to his lips, a warning look in his eyes.

'Quiet in there!' A man's head appeared over the top of the stall. He was wearing a military cap. 'No talking!' He glared for a moment and then left.

'*Soldiers?*' He mouthed the word. Vachon nodded, his face solemn.

'What will happen to us?' he said as the footsteps retreated.

Denis' expression was grim. 'A trial, I suppose. Hopefully a proper, legal one in public. If not, then a military court will decide our fates. In which case, God help us!'

'I CAN'T FIND JACOB!' Her voice frantic, Isabelle collapsed into her sister's arms as soon as Marguerite opened the door.

'My poor darling! I was so worried about you!' Marguerite pulled Isabelle inside as she saw black smoke curling up over the rooftops. She had scarcely steered the distraught Isabelle into a chair before the front door was thrown open again. 'Dominic!' She sobbed with relief on seeing her husband. His clothes were dishevelled, and he had a shocked look on his face. 'Thank God you're safe!' she cried and threw her arms around him.

'They are burning down the city!' he shouted, as if unaware he was back indoors.

'Who is?'

'I don't know! Someone!' He pulled himself free of Marguerite's embrace, a dazed look in his eyes. 'They were shooting! It's absolute chaos. The cops are arresting everyone.' He sank into a chair, his voice trembling. 'I've never seen anything like it.'

'Did you see Jacob?' Isabelle's eyes were wide with fear.

'I didn't see anyone!' His face white, Dominic stared up at his wife. 'It was madness! Absolute madness!'

'You are certain you didn't see Jacob?' Isabelle pleaded.

'I was glad to get out of there alive!' Dominic stared in shock, as if Isabelle hadn't spoken.

Declining Marguerite's pleas to stay with her for the night, Isabelle insisted on returning home to the anxious children. 'I must be there when Jacob returns,' she said. 'I'll send word of any news, and you do the same.'

'Be careful, the streets are dangerous,' warned Marguerite, trying to change her mind.

'The children are alone. I must go.'

She hurried through the streets, past police patrols and other pedestrians as confused and frightened as herself. 'Please, Blessed Mother, let Jacob be safe,' she prayed, fear hastening her steps.

Once home she stayed up until well past midnight, staring at the clock and starting at every sound from outside. Finally, at two o'clock she fell into a fitful sleep, only to awaken again before dawn, her face wet with tears. 'Jacob!' she wept. 'Where are you?'

By mid-morning, she was beside herself with panic. She rushed to the door at a knock to find Marguerite on the doorstep, her face as exhausted as Isabelle's own. 'Marguerite, thank God! Come in!' The sisters embraced before Marguerite sank into an armchair next to the distraught Marie-Odile. Isabelle went to the window and pushed aside the curtain, staring out into the street. Gaston stood by the fireplace, an angry look on his face as he observed his distressed mother. Louis wandered in and out of the room, seemingly uncertain where to sit or what to do.

'I should have listened to Jacob!' Isabelle abandoned the window to pace back and forth, her voice filled with remorse. 'He warned me against going, but I wouldn't listen. God forgive me!'

'Tell me again what happened in the square,' prompted Marguerite in an attempt to take Isabelle's mind off her increasingly frantic fears for Jacob.

'I don't know! One moment I was clinging to Jacob, the next we were separated. There was a mad panic. People were screaming and shoving and pushing. I was almost knocked down and trampled. The mob carried me to the street outside the square. I tried to get back to look for Jacob, but it was impossible. People were pouring out of the square and sweeping everyone before them in a panic. I heard shots—lots of them! And then

Marie Villeneuve appeared out of nowhere and grabbed my arm. 'We must leave!' she shouted. 'They're shooting everyone!' She sobbed at the recollection and sank into a chair.

'Mama!' Marie-Odile jumped up from Marguerite to fling her arms around her mother while bursting into tears. Isabelle kissed and hugged the frightened girl as an anxious-looking Louis joined them, kneeling by the chair to embrace them both.

'If anything should happen to Jacob …' Isabelle pressed her forehead against her daughter, unable to bear the thought. 'What's that!' She started up in hope at a frantic knocking on the door. 'Jacob?'

Marguerite hurried to open the door to find a hysterical Josette standing outside. 'Josette! Come in. What's happened?'

'They've arrested Hugo!'

'Hugo? Why?'

'They've accused him of being one of the ringleaders of the riot!' Josette burst into tears.

'Accused him? Who?'

'I don't know—one of those arrested. Everybody's turning on each other, naming names in hopes of getting themselves released.' Josette's voice choked. 'Why my Hugo? He wouldn't hurt a fly!'

'Do you know where he is?' Isabelle put a hand to her chest, anxiety flooding through her.

'No.' Through sobs, Josette tried to continue. 'Monsieur Turgeon told me of the arrest. But that was all he knew.' She wept with despair as Marguerite held her.

Suddenly, a fist pounded on the door. 'Blessed Mary!' Isabelle put a hand to her mouth.

Gaston turned from the window, a frightened look on his face.

'It's the cops!'

34

Aftermath

A SHOCKED LULL HELD THE city in suspense as its citizens absorbed the bloody events of the square. The *Catholic Tribune* reported, "a sort of daze descended on the streets" as citizens went about their business in a withdrawn, subdued fashion as though still at home and asleep in their beds. Even the normally boisterous Old Town with its famous market was deserted, the paper noted: "Stall holders report a sharp diminishment in trade."

The *Daily Register* devoted an entire issue to what it termed, in a lurid headline: "Massacre in the Square!"

The violence is alleged to have started when one group of marchers—witnesses differ on who was to blame—charged the other, sparking a general melee and mass panic. Eyewitnesses disagree on when the shooting started and who was responsible. Some blame the police; others blame anarchic individuals on both sides who came for the express purpose of igniting violence. It is alleged that at least one hundred people, including five policemen, were killed in the intense fighting that broke out as hostilities boiled over. A full count is expected to be released later today. According to survivors, many of the victims were trampled to death in the ensuing panic. Other bodies bore the marks of gunshot wounds. Police sources confirm that many of the dead are children whose parents unwisely permitted them to attend what was supposed to be a peaceful demonstration. Houses and shops around the square were set on fire—by whom is not yet known. The bloody event has been roundly condemned by the governments of Quebec and Ontario as well as by the federal government in Ottawa. The Prime Minister issued a public statement deploring the violence, which, he said, "will forever stain the beautiful new square, recently opened with such pride and optimism for the future." The premier of Ontario called upon all citizens of New France to accept their privileged status as "beloved and indispensable members of the Canadian family." Our own premier has lashed out at the "extremist elements that refuse to accept the broader will of the people." He has called for an end to self-exclusion sought by those who look backwards to an imagined golden past while violently rejecting the present. He described the popular demand for independence as the "pipe dream of a few dozen malcontents and provocateurs who have succeeded in deluding otherwise decent and law-abiding citizens." He concluded his remarks to the legislature by demanding the harshest possible measures against those found responsible for the shocking and bloody violence. Police, meanwhile, have rounded up dozens of suspected rioters who will be charged with various offences against the public order. More serious charges await those responsible for organising and inciting the deadly violence. Those arrested are in the hands of the authorities amid rumours of the imposition of martial law. Their whereabouts are unknown at the time of publication. Captain Perrault, the senior military officer in the city, refused to comment except to threaten that those found guilty will "pay the heaviest price, and suffer the most severe penalties."

The whereabouts of the missing men was on everybody's lips. Feverish rumours circulated: they had been transported to an internment camp in the far north of the province; they had been sent to a secret army post to await execution; they had been despatched to Ontario, or even to the United States, under cover of darkness. But the most persistent rumours pointed to the military barracks just inside the city walls as the place where the detainees were being held pending trial by a military court. The usually nondescript barracks was observed to be under heavy guard amid claims of a great swell in the number of its occupants due to more arrested suspects being spirited there in the dead of night.

Unable to discover if Jacob were alive or dead, Isabelle made increasingly desperate attempts to find out where the arrested men had been detained, only to be frustrated at every turn, the authorities deeming the information too sensitive and the situation in the city too volatile to reveal the location of the arrested or even to release their names.

"It is no surprise," The *Daily Register* informed its readers, "to find that visitors and locals alike avoid the historic Old Town area with its central market for fear of being caught up in another outbreak of violence. Meanwhile, the hunt for the organisers and perpetrators of the dreadful carnage in Gaston Tremblay Square continues."

CONFRONTING HER WORST FEARS, Isabelle visited the makeshift morgue where the bodies of those killed had been taken. A sympathetic nurse ushered her past the police barrier and showed her a list of names of the dead. 'We are still waiting to identify all of the bodies, Madame. But I know monsieur Wheeler, my husband worked in his factory. His body is not here.' The middle-aged woman took her hand in sympathy.

'Thank you, Sister!' Relieved to tears, Isabelle pressed the woman's hand. A door opened and a man dressed in uniform exited the room. Over his shoulder, she glimpsed rows of bodies covered in sheets.

Shaken at the sight, she went straight to the cathedral where she beseeched the Blessed Mother to safeguard and protect Jacob. She stayed for two hours, alternately praying and weeping in the dim shadows. Finally, she dried her tears and lit several candles, uttering a prayer over each one.

She walked home through the subdued streets—many of the shops boarded up in anticipation of further disturbances. Police patrolled in groups of four or more for safety as the authorities braced themselves for more violence. Alarming rumours of mass shootings and reprisal attacks circulated throughout the city as the authorities clamped down on any signs of defiance.

Crossing the street to avoid a police patrol, she fished out her key. 'Any news?' she asked as soon as she stepped inside the front door.

Gaston looked glum. 'Aunt Josette sent word that monsieur Turgeon is making inquiries on our behalf, but so far he has come up with nothing. He thinks the men are being held in the military barracks. But uncle Henri telephoned to say he heard a rumour they have been sent to Montreal on special trains.'

'Mama,' said a worried-sounding Louis, holding up a china pot. You must eat something. Aunt Marguerite sent over a casserole dish for us.' He took the lid off the pot so that she could smell the contents.

She touched his cheek and forced a smile at the anxious look on his face. 'You eat. I'm not hungry.' I must stay calm, she reminded herself, the children are as fearful as I am.

She attempted to comfort Marie-Odile, her youngest still traumatised by the police interrogation the previous day as the cops ransacked the house searching for alleged conspirators.

On the same afternoon, Dominic Beaulieu hid in the coal bin to escape the brutal search of his home, emerging afterwards blackened with coal dust, his face pale under the smudged dirt.

'Have they gone?' His voice trembled as Marguerite clung to him, blackening herself with coal dust in the process.

The following day Josette described the harrowing scenes as her own house was searched and her neighbour arrested. 'They dragged poor Charles out onto the street with his wife clinging to her husband and screaming at the top of her lungs. It was dreadful!'

Isabelle lay sleepless in bed that night, her mind conjuring frightening scenarios as she prayed for Jacob's safety. The street outside was silent save for the occasional sound of police whistles or fire bells in the distance. Moonlight filtered through the lace-patterned curtains. Her hand reached out to Jacob's side of the bed as she was overcome by an aching sense of desolation and despair. Her fingers clutched the rosary Jacob had gifted her and she pressed the silver cross to her breast. '*Dear Father in Heaven. You who see all. Do you not see and pity your servant Jacob who has committed no wrong? I know he is not Catholic—and not religious,*' she thought it best to admit, '*but he is a good and kind man who loves his family.*' She turned on her side, her face resting in a halo of moonlight. '*They say that those arrested have been taken to the military barracks for interrogation. If you see Jacob there, Lord, please let him know that we love and miss him and long only for his safe return.*' She stretched out her arm, resting it upon his pillow. '*I am weary without him.*'

MORE ARRESTS WERE CARRIED out across the city as the authorities sought to prevent further protests. The heavy-handed tactics provoked a violent backlash amidst simmering popular resentment. A mob descended on the St. Charles Police Station and burnt it to the ground, the officers barely escaping with their lives. The violence increased as rival mobs fought each other in the streets amid rumours of another huge demonstration. Alarmed at the spiralling violence, the authorities declared martial law and rushed in additional troops to help control the situation.

"What have we come to," lamented the *Catholic Tribune*, "when citizen fires upon citizen and armed troops patrol the streets? Is this the New France we grew up in? Is this the legacy of our forefathers?"

The next day, military censorship was imposed, the newspapers permitted to carry only the blandest of assurances from the authorities that the violence had been quelled and the 'anarchists' detained for questioning.

AS TWO WEEKS PASSED with still no word of the missing, Isabelle joined with Marguerite, Josette, Marie Villeneuve and Yvette Vachon to form the "Women's Committee for the Release of Those Unlawfully Detained." They marched on the cordoned-off square carrying placards and demanding the authorities reveal the names and whereabouts of the missing men. They discussed a proposal to sneak into the square at night and chain themselves to the monument in protest. Plans were underway for this when word came from monsieur Turgeon, who had made tireless efforts on their behalf, that the men were, of a certainty, being held at the military barracks. 'And what's more,' he added, his voice filled with relief, 'Jacob and Hugo are among them!'

'It's a sad day when we rejoice to find our husbands are in prison—for that means they are alive, not dead,' remarked Isabelle when she hung up from the former's-deputy's phone call. Tears came to her eyes as a relieved Josette embraced her. 'Call Marie and Yvette,' she said, wiping her eyes. 'Tell them to contact everyone they can. Tell them we meet here at noon tomorrow to march on the barracks.'

The following day Isabelle headed a group of more than three hundred women as they marched on the garrison. Singing and chanting, the procession made their way through the streets of the Old Town as bystanders cheered and called out encouragement. Dozens of women spontaneously joined in as alarmed police sent for reinforcements, fearful of another riot breaking out.

The women arrived at the barracks to find their way barred by a line of soldiers, rifles crossed against their chests. The column of aggrieved women halted and spread out to stand face-to-face with the soldiers. The air was tense, the soldiers nervous and sweating inside their uniforms as wives, mothers, sisters, daughters and grandmothers looked them in the eye, daring them to deny passage. Behind the soldiers rose the high stone wall of the barracks where Captain Perrault and a half-dozen aides stood on the ramparts to observe the fraught stand-off.

The sergeant in command, a hardened, no-nonsense veteran of Artois and the Somme, stepped forward to confront Isabelle and her fellow organisers as they stood with linked arms in defiance of the soldiers.

'Go home!' he barked. 'This is no place for women!' Sweat gleamed on his forehead. He was close enough to Isabelle that she could smell the garlic on his breath.

'It is no place for innocent men wrongly arrested, either' she retorted, to cries of support from her companions.

'Innocent?' The sergeant laughed harshly. 'Your innocent men slaughtered women and children!'

'If you seek justice, then arrest those truly responsible—the authorities!' Isabelle's defiant reply brought cheers from those around her. The sergeant scowled, his eyes narrowing at this insubordination.

'Is this why you fought in the war—to imprison your brothers?' demanded Marie Villeneuve.

The sergeant took a deep breath. Ignoring the others, he leaned his face towards Isabelle. 'I'm not here to argue with you. I'm here to tell you to piss-off back to your kitchens—and bedrooms,' he added with a belligerent snarl.

She refused to flinch, looking him boldly in the eye. 'Many of those imprisoned men fought beside you in the war. They are your brothers-in-arms.'

'They are not my brothers! I don't come from this shit hole of a town! Now be off with you—before my men clutch at those pretty skirts!'

The menacing vulgarity brought shocked protests from the women.

'Pig! You have no right to speak in such a manner!' A furious Marie Villeneuve spat in his face.

The incensed sergeant used his tunic sleeve to wipe the spit as Marie, yelling insults, was restrained by her friends.

A strange look came over the sergeant's face—an expression Isabelle found more unsettling than his open hostility. 'Go home,' he said, his voice dangerously soft and distant sounding, as though he were back in the trenches peering over the sandbags at the advancing enemy. 'Go now, before it is too late.'

'We demand to speak to your commanding officer!' Isabelle stared up at the figures looking down from the ramparts. She raised her voice to a shout. 'We won't leave until we do!'

Captain Perrault looked down and nodded at the sergeant, whose manner changed yet again.

Leaning forward, he hissed directly into Isabelle's ear, his voice doling out each word with measured violence. 'Take your whores and yourself back to the gutter … before I give you the treatment you deserve!'

Shocked, she slapped his face. With an oath, he raised his hand as though to strike, his eyes ablaze with fury.

'Sergeant!' was barked down from the ramparts.

The sergeant sucked in a breath, visibly controlling himself as he lowered his hand, his face crimson with anger.

'Go home, ladies!' The same voice shouted down. 'You have no business here!'

'We are going nowhere!' Isabelle yelled up at the aloof figure. 'And it is you who have no business in New France!'

'I said go! Before I lose patience!'

In response Isabelle began to sing, softly at first, her voice growing in strength as first one, and then several, and then all of the women joined in, raising their voices in a ringing chorus of defiance.

Sing, nightingale, sing! you of the joyous heart!
Your heart smiles while mine weeps.
I have loved you for so long, I will never forget you!

'Do you hear that? Listen!' One of the prisoners called out for silence as the voices of the women reached into the barracks. A hush descended as the men gathered to listen, straining to hear as the familiar song floated above the solid stone walls and penetrated the grim surroundings of their captivity. They wept freely at this reminder of a world that still existed—their suffering and despair temporarily forgotten. 'They know we are here!' one man cried, his bearded cheeks wet with tears. 'They have not forgotten us!'

35

Martyrs of the Resistance

THE BRIEF FLOWERING OF hope among the captives was forgotten the very next day as rumours spread of a gallows being erected in the exercise yard. The subsequent noise of hammering and sawing confirmed their worst fears. Over the preceding week, many of those judged the most serious offenders had been hauled before rotating panels of junior officers to be interrogated on their involvement in the riot. Following a summary inquiry, the men had been allocated to different stables based on their perceived level of culpability.

In spite of vigorously protesting his innocence, Jacob was transferred, along with several others, to a stable kept under close twenty-four-hour guard. Shackles were placed on his wrists and feet, and he was escorted, shuffling, to the makeshift cell.

'Jacob!' Hugo Gagnon got to his feet, moving awkwardly in the shackles as Jacob was led in. 'Thank God you are alright! I feared you had been harmed in the violence!' Hugo's face was pale, his once scrupulously shaven cheeks now stubbled and gaunt looking.

'Hugo? Am I relieved to see you!' They embraced as best they could.

'Hello Jacob, welcome to hell!'

He turned at the sound of the familiar voice. 'Serge! You, too?' He held out his hands as Villeneuve climbed to his feet and extended his shackled wrists.

'It's good to see you, Jacob,' said Serge, grasping his hands, 'even in this shithole! But you are hurt?' he said, on seeing Jacob wince.

'A few cracked ribs, that's all. At least they let me see the surgeon. He put a bandage around them.'

'They want you healthy for the rope!' Jean Chaban was seated with his back against a wooden partition. Joubert sat alongside his comrade, each man shackled like Jacob.

'So, Wheeler. They arrest businessmen too?' Joubert spoke the words in a sour voice.

'As you see. And why are you here?'

'I sent two of the bastards straight to hell.' Joubert grinned with the reply.

'Hush!' Chaban nudged his companion as one of the sentries stationed outside the stall turned, a hostile expression on his face.

Joubert scowled at the sentry, his renowned defiance asserting itself. 'Toad! Fuck off back to your hometown and leave mine in peace!'

The sentry gave a grim smile and raised a hand to jerk an imaginary noose around his neck.

'But Jacob, why are you here?' Hugo' voice was hoarse. A glimpse of his usual groomed demeanour peeked through the facial stubble and lank, uncombed hair. Wisps of straw stuck to his clothes.

'They think I killed a cop.'

'You?' Joubert snorted in disbelief.

Hugo's eyes widened. 'What happened?'

'He was beating me when someone—I don't know who—stabbed him as they ran by. They blame me for his death, but I swear it wasn't me!'

'Ha!' Chaban exclaimed. 'Do you think they give a *sou* whether you did it or not? Someone has to pay! Why not you?'

'But what about you, Hugo?' asked Jacob, ignoring the jibe.

Hugo bit his lip, as he struggled to control his emotions. 'It's as Jean said. They are seeking to make an example. And who better than an ex-deputy?' He shuddered with the words.

'And you, Serge?'

'I admit I cracked a few heads. But they were trying to crack mine.'

'Do they have any evidence against you?' asked Hugo.

Jacob shook his head, his face wrenched with frustration. 'I don't see how. I demanded they produce evidence or a witness. They couldn't seem to make up their minds. They told me I was being held for further investigation. But then they put me in here.' His voice dropped with the implication.

'Have you seen anyone else?'

'Denis is—or was—in the next stable. I don't know where he is now.'

'Have you heard from Isabelle?'

'No!' Jacob's heart leapt with hope. 'Have you heard anything?'

Hugo shook his head, a despairing look on his face. 'Jean said he overheard one of the guards say the women were forced away after demanding to speak to us. At least they know we are here, thank God.'

As the interest stirred by Jacob's arrival died down, Hugo motioned him to a corner of the stable. 'What do they intend to do with us?' he whispered as he glanced at the others.

'I don't know, hang us, perhaps,' Jacob answered, his voice bleak.

'But why?' Hugo lowered his voice further as he glanced at Chaban and Joubert. 'They've admitted to killing people, we haven't.'

'Have all of these men confessed to murder?' Jacob looked around at the dejected captives. With a start he recognised a former mechanic at his factory. The man felt his gaze and looked up and then away again, a hopeless expression on his face.

'Hardly any of them, I think. But then why put these shackles on us unless they have in mind the same fate?' Hugo stared in desperation. 'I do not want to die here, like a common criminal. Surely, even a military court is obliged to allow us our rights?'

Jacob shook his head, unable to offer any comfort.

THE CONDEMNED MEN PASSED the day in an agony of suspense as the noise of hammering continued. For dinner, they were fed a single cup of water and a bowl of thin gruel.

'You are required to feed us, not poison us!' Joubert shouted and threw the bowl against the wall.

The action drew a blow to the side of his face from the affronted soldier dispensing the meal. 'You'll be feeding the worms soon enough! See if they complain.'

The threat intensified the strained atmosphere inside the stable. Shortly after the meal the sound of hammering abruptly stopped and the men glanced at each other. 'It won't be long now, boys—unless they've run out of nails,' Joubert's attempt at jocularity fell flat in the strained silence.

'They can't do this! They have no legal basis. It's murder!' a man protested.

'But who can stop them, brother?' responded Chaban. 'We must accept our fate like men.'

'We die as martyrs,' declared Joubert, his face defiant. 'Remember that when you stand up on the scaffold.'

Hugo swallowed at the words, his pale face turning, if possible, even paler.

Bound together by a dreadful fatalism, the captives spent the night in silence as each man kept vigil over his emotions. Jacob thought obsessively of Isabelle, his mind tracing her face, her smile, the soft accommodating warmth of her body, and the steady gaze of her eyes, shining with love. The thought that he might never see her again was a torture worse than the fear of being hanged. He slipped into a despairing slumber, his hand reaching out to rest on a mound of straw as he whispered her name.

When he opened his eyes again, it was still dark. He looked around in the lantern glow. In spite of the gallows awaiting them in the morning, several of the men were asleep. Hugo sat with his knees drawn up, his face haggard in the dim light. He held a rosary in one hand as his lips moved in prayer.

Jacob's eyes met with Serge Villeneuve's, but the latter's gaze was lifeless, as if he had already departed the world. His former mechanic sobbed quietly, his face buried in his hands. Chaban and Joubert were talking softly together.

'*We will hold you while we investigate further.*' Jacob closed his eyes, clinging to the words like a drowning man clutches at a rope.

They were given no breakfast, listening without protest as the prisoners in the adjoining stables were fed a ration of weak coffee and buttered bread. The military chaplain entered, holding a bible in his hand. He offered last rites to the shackled men, kneeling to lead them in prayer. As the prisoners knelt around the priest with bowed heads, Jacob noticed Chaban and Joubert listening to the side, paying silent heed to the familiar incantations of their childhood. Hugo was telling the rosary beads, a fervent expression on his face. At least he has that solace, thought Jacob, a comfort denied me.

Late in the morning, the surrounding stalls and stables were emptied as the prisoners were led out a dozen at a time. Their turn came last, the condemned men knowing instinctively what that meant.

'Be brave, comrades!' urged Chaban as they were roughly ordered to their feet. Surrounded by sentries, they stumbled out into the bright sunlight of the exercise yard, Jacob and Hugo bringing up the rear. The gallows occupied one side of the yard, the lumber smelling fresh and new in the sunlight. Steps led up to a platform where the hangman stood, a black hood hiding his face. The chaplain and an officer Jacob knew as Captain Perrault stood to one side of the steps. The other prisoners were assembled behind a line of soldiers and forced to watch. The day was warm and benign, the air pungent with the smell of horse dung, piss, and straw and leather.

A soldier approached and hustled Jacob and Hugo away from their comrades.

Stand there!' he ordered, pushing them to one side.

Hugo shot Jacob a look of the profoundest relief, tears springing to his eyes.

Their shackled comrades were led towards the scaffold steps. A lone drummer beat a tattoo as they were positioned in a line at the foot of the steps, Chaban first, followed by Joubert. The shackles were removed, and their hands bound behind their backs.

Serge turned his head, an expression of angry defiance on his face as his eyes found Jacob's. 'Tell Marie I love her!' he shouted, his voice hoarse as it broke the silence. 'Tell her I die without fear or regret as a martyr for New France!'

The guards seemed surprised by the outburst and said nothing. Chaban was led up the steps to the steady tap of the drum. He was positioned above the trapdoor where a heavy rope noose with a large knot was placed around his neck. The hangman then proceeded to place a sackcloth hood over his head, only for Chaban to resist.

'I wish to say some last words!' Chaban turned to the captain. 'I have that right!'

The hangman glanced at Perrault for instructions. The captain shook his head.

'Let him speak you bastards!' Joubert's voice rang out as the hooded and struggling Chaban was re-positioned over the trapdoor. The drumbeats stopped and an awful silence prevailed among the watching men. Jacob's heart was in his mouth as he watched. With a sudden motion, the hangman pulled the lever. Chaban dropped like a stone. He struggled and kicked for what seemed minutes before hanging limply in the noose. His body, still wearing the hood, was taken down and laid on the ground in front of the scaffold where the hood was removed for reuse.

The captain signalled the sentries and Joubert was led up next, his face defiant. 'No hood!' he demanded, turning aside his head. The hangman paused to glance at the captain, who nodded. Joubert gazed at his fellow prisoners, his voice ringing out in the tense silence. '*Long live free New France!*' He barely got the words out before the trapdoor opened beneath him.

The other executions followed with swift and lethal precision. Serge Villeneuve also refused the hood, turning a fatalistic gaze on Jacob and Hugo as he braced himself for the drop. The remaining men, their faces ashen, awaited their turn. One turned and pleaded his innocence before the captain.

'I am innocent of any crime, sir!' he begged, his voice shrill with fear. 'I did not hurt anyone!'

The captain remained expressionless, merely nodding for the hangman to continue his grisly work. Jacob's former mechanic was led up next, trembling so violently he had to be assisted up the steps. He wept and prayed as the noose was placed around his neck. At the last moment, he raised his eyes as if to reassure himself with one final glimpse of the shining blue sky.

All sixteen bodies were laid out in front of the scaffold, their faces fixed in a grimace of bloodless horror at the swift and certain departure of warmth and life. Captain Perrault stepped forward, his stony gaze taking in the subdued observers.

'What you see before you, is justice done. These men were each found guilty of the most heinous crimes and have paid the penalty.' His eyes lingered on the chastened prisoners. 'Have no doubt but that more will follow.'

NEWS OF THE SUMMARY executions provoked an explosion of public anger. Defying martial law, huge crowds marched in the street demanding the release of the remaining detainees. A crowd estimated at 100,000 ignored orders to disperse and gathered in Tremblay Square to call for justice for the 'St Jean-Baptiste-Martyrs.' The women's committee organised nightly vigils outside the barracks, the candlelight protests attracting thousands of supporters who sang in hopes that the imprisoned men might hear their voices.

Both newspapers bravely ignored the censorship laws to demand a halt to the executions. The *Daily Register* drew raised eyebrows by using the term "innocents" to describe the hanged men. "*Being on the side of progress, liberalism and modernism doubles our moral duty to speak up in defence of the defenceless,*" it editorialised. "*Although this newspaper has long disagreed with the position of the so-called habitants, it defends their right to justice and a fair and public trial under the guaranteed right of due process. We call for an end to martial law and the immediate release, of those not charged with any crime.*"

Not to be outdone, the *Catholic Tribune* described the "dreadful scene" of the executions based on purported eye-witness testimony. "*His beliefs failed him at the end,*" it reported of Abel Lothaire, a noted opponent of the Church. "*He was an atheist, who called out despairingly to God as the noose was placed around his neck.*" The unsubstantiated claim drew severe criticism as a spiteful libel on the defenceless Lothaire. Shortly after publication, the editors of both newspapers were arrested and locked up in a cell in the public safety building to await trial.

Amid appeals for calm, more violence broke out. The new bishop, under intense pressure from his congregation, announced a special mass for the martyrs, whereupon he was promptly summoned to the barracks to face an irate Captain Perrault.

'You can have your mass—for the good it will do—on condition you stop referring to the accused men as martyrs or innocents. If you break this rule or attempt to praise them as heroes in any way, it will go the worse for you,' Perrault threatened, barely able to contain his temper.

Bishop Chretien raised his voice in protest. 'You place me in an impossible situation! I know these people—they will be expecting the Church's sympathy and support. I cannot deny them that. It is my solemn duty as bishop.'

Perrault regarded the fretful cleric across the desk. 'I notice you were very quiet during the riots. Were you in the square, alongside your flock?' He raised his eyebrows with the question.

The bishop played with the heavy crucifix around his neck, a defensive look on his face. 'These are fraught times, as you yourself must realise, Captain. The Church must tread a delicate path between those who sympathize with the mar—condemned men and those who support the abolition of the Charter and Assembly.'

'But are not those people—the so-called reformists—the same ones opposed to the authority of the Church?' The captain posed the question with a sneer. 'Surely, your first responsibility is to your flock, not to the wolves?'

The bishop gave a tortured sigh in response. 'The question is complicated. The Church finds itself in a complex position, buffeted by conservatives on the one side, and reformers on the other. In response, the Church must fulfil its historic mission to heal and console, and not to further inflame passions.'

Perrault waved a hand, suddenly bored. 'Go! Hold your mass. But remember my words.' He watched as the bishop left, his face pinched with contempt. *That fool of a colonel was right. These people are backward, credulous, mired in superstition. Do we even want such primitives in Quebec?*

RUMOURS CIRCULATED THAT THE next round of executions was scheduled in two days. In preparation, the cases of several 'undecideds' were being adjudicated by Captain Perrault himself. Armed with a sheaf of papers and the single-sentence recommendations of the military tribunals established to try the arrested rebels, as they were now officially referred to, he interrogated a succession of detainees, deciding on hanging or imprisonment with a meticulous stroke of his pen.

'Next!' The captain fanned himself with a folder, his mind savouring the succulent creature he had spied from the ramparts the day before.

'Name?' he snapped as his adjutant led in the next prisoner.

'Wheeler. Jacob Wheeler.' Jacob pulled himself up straight, eyeing the officer and the stack of papers on the desk before him.

Captain Perrault took his time, reading from a file before looking up at Jacob. 'Well, what do you have to say for yourself?'

'I demand to know on what authority I am being detained. You have no right to keep me here. I have done nothing wrong, committed no crime, nor broken any laws.'

'Emergency powers, my dear fellow.' Perrault's voice was languid as he appraised the prisoner. 'I can keep you standing there until the crack of doom, if I so choose.'

'I have done nothing wrong.'

'So you say.' Perrault sat back in the chair and draped one leg over the other. 'Wheeler?' He placed the tip of a pen between his teeth. 'You are English?'

'American.'

The captain raised his eyebrows. 'Profession?'

'Businessman.'

'What kind of businessman?'

'I make—did make—automobiles.'

'Really?' Perrault looked at the adjutant. 'Did you know that Charest?'

'No Captain, I did not.'

Perrault picked up a paper from the desk. 'It seems you murdered a police officer.' He cocked an eyebrow with the accusation.

'That's absurd! I didn't murder anyone.'

'Absurd? You don't think killing someone a serious business?' The captain frowned as if trying to comprehend such wilfulness.

'Yes, of course it is! I'm just saying I didn't murder anyone. I'm innocent.'

'Innocent.' Perrault pondered the word. 'You were seen,' he continued, as if speaking to a child, 'kneeling over the dead officer after having plunged a knife into his heart.'

'It wasn't his heart, it was his ribs!' Jacob cursed himself as the words leapt, unbidden, from his mouth.

'Really?' The captain's eyes gleamed. 'Hear that Charest? He admits to the crime.'

'No! I meant only that I saw the knife handle. It was sticking out from his side. Someone must have stabbed him as they ran past.'

'As they ran past?' Captain Perrault wrinkled his brow in bemusement. 'And who was this someone?'

'I don't know. I didn't see him.'

'Stabbed by someone running past, whom you didn't see?' The captain made a pretence of deliberating on the words as if they might carry weight.

Unable to maintain the pretence he threw back his head and laughed merrily. 'Come now,' he said. 'Do you think me a fool?'

'I swear to you that is what happened.'

'Indeed.' Perrault composed himself. 'We have a witness.'

Jacob's mouth fell open in disbelief. 'A witness? That can't be. He's lying!'

'Lying? You haven't even heard what he has to say.'

'I don't need to. He's a liar, whoever he is.'

'Charest. Fetch the witness.'

'At once, Captain.' The adjutant went to the door and stuck his head out, speaking to another man in the corridor.

As he waited, Jacob's mind was in turmoil, wondering who this alleged witness might be. The captain was doodling on the file, bending forward to inspect his creation.

'Captain?' The adjutant waited for Perrault's permission as Jacob strained to see past him at the half-open door. At a flick of the hand from his superior, the adjutant opened the door and a dishevelled figure, his hair unkempt and face heavily bearded, entered.

'Lascelles!' Jacob exclaimed in shock, barely recognising his former employer. Lascelles stared back, his face full of malice.

'So, you two know each other?' asked Perrault, perking up with interest.

'Indeed, Captain,' answered Lascelles. 'I employed this man when he was no more than a penniless vagrant. He repaid my charity by forming a league with some American thieves, who were later sent to prison. Together they conspired to ruin me.' Lascelles' voice was hoarse, his lips cracked and covered with sores.

'Liar!'

'Yes, yes.' Perrault clucked with impatience. 'And you swear that you saw the prisoner in the square?'

'I do, sir.'

'Tut!' Perrault held up a warning hand as Jacob made to interrupt. 'And what did you see, exactly? Be sure and tell the truth now.'

'Sir, I saw him murder the policeman.'

'Another lie!'

'How?'

'Pardon Captain?'

Perrault sighed. 'How did he murder the cop?'

'Sir, he pulled out a knife and stuck it in the man.'

'Where?'

'Where?' Lascelles frowned in confusion. 'In the square, Captain.'

Perrault shook his head at the adjutant, an expression of great weariness on his face.

'Where … did … he … *stab* the victim?'

'Oh. In the chest, sir.'

'See?' Jacob whirled to face the captain. 'Did I not tell you? Tripped up on his own falsehoods!' He glared at Lascelles, who appeared bewildered.

'It says here,' Perrault flicked at the file on the desk, 'that the victim was stabbed in the side, between the ribs.'

'Oh! I meant the ribs, Captain. I was confused. So much was happening.'

'And you are certain of what you saw?'

'On my life, sir!' Lascelles' voice trembled with eagerness to please.

'Damn you for a liar!' Enraged, Jacob stepped forward as Lascelles flashed him a look of pure hatred.

'Stand still!' The adjutant pulled him back.

'That wraps it up then.' Perrault looked at Jacob. 'Unless you have anything to add?'

'Add? Good God, can't you see he's lying through his teeth? The scoundrel has a grudge against me. He is a false witness!'

'Nevertheless, what he says accords with the facts.' The captain smiled, pleased at his own cleverness. He motioned to the adjutant as Jacob continued to vehemently insist on his innocence. 'Take him away!'

In turn, the adjutant summoned the guard. 'Take him back to the cells.'

'Come on you!' The sentry dragged Jacob, still protesting, from the room.

'Sir? Your promise?' Lascelles looked beseechingly at Perrault.

'Yes.' The captain gave a great sigh. 'But keep your mouth shut else you will find yourself back in here again, and it will not go easy for you. Do you understand?'

'I do, Captain. I assure you.'

'Then go!' The captain waved a hand in dismissal. He picked up the pen and made a notation on Jacob's file. 'To be hanged.'

THE BISHOP PEERED NERVOUSLY though the vestry door. The cathedral was full, every seat taken, even the aisles occupied. Closing the door, he leaned back against it, sweat forming on his brow. 'They seem angry!'

The acolyte, a thin, stooped specimen with a thatch of red hair grimaced. 'It is the executions they are angry about, Monseigneur.'

The bishop gnashed his teeth at the miserable creature. 'I know why they are angry, fool! But why do they blame me?'

The acolyte shrugged and spread his hands. 'They accuse the Church of betraying them in their hour of need.'

'Get out there and check that everything is prepared!'

As soon as the door closed behind the creature, the bishop poured himself a large glass of communion wine, his heart palpitating. *I should never have agreed to this. Damn that curé! And where is he, anyway?* He froze in fright as he heard voices outside. Listening with his ear to the door, he closed his eyes, his face pale. *They blame me. Why, in God's name? I wasn't there. I didn't order the shooting—or the hangings!* Perrault's face leapt to mind, and he shuddered. Someone pushed against the door and he jumped with fright. The acolyte stuck his head inside. 'Everything is ready, Monseigneur.'

'How do they seem?'

'Who?'

'Mother of God! The congregation, who else?'

'Oh.' The acolyte's voice dropped to a whisper. 'Not good.'

'Not good? What the devil does that mean?'

'I mean they look displeased, Monseigneur.'

The bishop blanched, lamenting his fate at being posted to this den of savages.

'Monseigneur, they are waiting.'

Taking a deep breath, the bishop opened the door. The curé, his face pale, stood there along with several servers,

'Let's get on with it,' the bishop muttered, feeling the soul leave his body.

He mounted the altar, acutely aware of the fraught atmosphere inside the church and the angry stares directed his way. Throughout the first part of the Mass, he studiously avoided looking at the congregants, closing his eyes and staring upwards as he gave the blessing.

As the time approached for the homily, one he had drafted and redrafted a dozen times, his nervousness increased at the palpable tension among the congregation.

'*Your Holiness, they will be expecting a personal address commiserating with their suffering. It is what Bishop Simard—*'

'*Do you see him here?*' *Seething with nerves and frustration, he snapped the words at the wretched curé standing before his desk,*

The curé raised his voice in mild protest. 'I meant only—'

'*I meant only!*' *he mimicked the curé in a mincing voice. 'Go away and allow me to finish!*'

He passed in front of the altar, forgetting to observe the blessing in his anxiety. Mounting the pulpit, he coughed and gripped the rails. A deathly hush had fallen over the congregation. Raising his eyes, he at last risked glancing at the crowded pews. His gaze alighted on several grim-faced women dressed in black near the front, and he shuddered. *And that fellow over there with the sharp eyes, is that one of the captain's spies?*

Peering at the scripture, he read in a tremulous voice the passage he had marked for the occasion. "O deliver not the soul of thy turtledove unto the multitude of the wicked," he began. Overcome by a rush of lightheadedness, he risked a second glance at the congregation. Greatly alarmed by the hostile stares that greeted him, he returned to his text in a faltering voice. "Have respect unto the covenant: for the dark places of the earth are full of the habitants of cruelty."

'Where was the Church in our hour of need?'

The question rang out like a pistol shot, causing him to blanch with fright. Marie Villeneuve, dressed in mourning, had risen to her feet. Angry voices rose in agreement as a ripple of discontent ran through the congregation. The bishop felt a sensation of otherworldliness as other women, also dressed in black, rose to their feet in a silent yet terrifying tableau of grief and betrayal. He put his hands over his face, revisiting the agony of Christ and certain he was about to keel over in a dead faint.

'Where was the Church when they hanged my Serge from the gallows like a dog!' Her voice acidic with scorn, Marie Villeneuve pointed an accusing finger.

As if of one mind, the entire congregation rose to its feet in condemnation. The bishop glanced up at the organ loft where the petrified curé had taken refuge, his face a ghostly white. The bishop gripped the rail as the church began to spin about him. And then he fainted.

36

A Proposition

UNNERVED BY THE OUTPOURING of rage incited by the hangings, and further alarmed by critical reports in both Canadian and American newspapers condemning the summary executions, government authorities in Ottawa and Quebec held several emergency sessions to discuss the crisis. The consultations culminated in a military despatch to Captain Perrault ordering him to halt the executions 'forthwith' and to cease from scheduling any further hangings while the situation was being evaluated. He was further ordered to permit relatives to visit the detained men and to release those with no proven charges against them.

Perrault read the despatch with contempt before tossing it onto the desk. 'Idiots!' He was in such a foul mood for the rest of the morning that no one dared say a word in his presence.

The news that they were permitted to visit drew cries of delight from the women who had maintained their vigil outside the barracks. As word of the concession flew around the town more women flocked to the gates, clamouring for entrance. A vexed Perrault was informed of a mob gathered outside. In response, he climbed the ramparts to look down on the boisterous women, who broke into jeers as they caught sight of him.

'Let them in, no more than two dozen at a time,' he ordered the man standing by his side, a corporal with a badly broken nose.

His eye roved over the angry, upturned faces. 'That one,' he said indicating the choice morsel he had sighted previously. 'After she's seen her husband, escort her to my office.'

'Yes sir.' The broken-nosed corporal eyed the woman with professional interest.

'JACOB!' ISABELLE'S HEART SKIPPED a beat as her husband was led into the visiting room. Her joy turned to horror at the pitiful sight he presented. His clothes were soiled, bits of straw and chaff stuck to his jacket and trousers. His gaunt, unshaven face was scratched from itching, his hair greasy and unkempt. 'My poor darling!' she rushed to embrace him. 'You look so thin!' Moaning in distress she clung to his breast as he cradled her in his arms.

'It's alright, dearest. This will soon be over. Please, don't distress yourself.' Tears of gratitude fell from his face as he held her in his arms.

'I've brought you clean clothes.' Her face wet with tears, she tried to put a smile on her face. 'The children send their love.'

They sat down, Jacob clasping her hands between his own. How warm they felt! How soft!

'There is a rumour that they will be freeing some of the men—those with no charges proven against them. Surely, that will include you?' Her voice full of anxiety, she gripped his fingers.

'It is uncertain.' He licked his dry lips, loathe to cause her further distress.

'Has something happened? Tell me!' She searched his face, alarmed at his expression.

'My dear.' He reached out to stroke her tear-stained cheeks. 'Do you remember when I worked at the saddlery in place Jeanne d'Arc all those years ago?'

She nodded, too apprehensive to speak. 'Then you may recall the name of my wretched employer, Gustave Lascelles …'

SHE HAD BEEN WAITING an hour to see the officer in charge, her fears mounting as she recalled the tortured look on her husband's face. Her repeated queries were met with the explanation that the captain was busy and would see her the moment he had a chance. In exasperation she finally stood up and demanded to see him.

The guard leered at her. 'I imagine he'd be very glad to see you.' He laughed at her outraged look. She drew the collars of her blouse together and sat back down again.

After waiting a further half-hour, the door at last opened and she was summoned inside. An officer sat behind a small desk busily scribbling on a pad. 'And who is this?' he asked, without looking up.

An aide whispered in his ear and the officer glanced up, his eyes taking her in from head to toe. 'Alright, Charest. Leave us.' He got to his feet as the door closed behind the adjutant.

'Please, sit down.' Moving behind her, he pulled out the chair.

'My name is Captain Perrault. How may I help you, Madame?'

She looked up in confusion. 'You asked to see me.'

'I did? Hmmm.' He pondered for a moment. 'Ah, yes, I recall now. Your husband, the conspirator—'

'He is no conspirator! I assure you, Captain, my husband is a peaceful, civilised man. He had nothing to do with any conspiracy.'

'He didn't?' Perrault picked up the folder on the desk, frowning as he looked over the contents. 'It says here he was clearly observed up on the platform with the arch-conspirators Chaban and Joubert?' He set down the folder. 'Both of whom were hanged, as you no doubt are aware?'

She shivered at the reminder. 'But my husband is not like them! He was there to protest, not to fight!' Her eyes filled with tears. 'I promise you Captain, he is entirely innocent.'

'I am truly sorry for your misfortune, Madame.' The captain got up and leaned against the desk in front of her, his voice sympathetic. Taking a handkerchief from his pocket, he bent forward and attempted to dab her eyes.

'Stop! What are you doing?' She recoiled from the gesture.

'Pardon. I simply wished to offer some comfort in this trying time.' He held out the handkerchief, which she refused, tugging out her own damp handkerchief.

'I am sorry to cause you distress.' Perrault sighed regretfully. 'But I must inform you that your husband's name is among those scheduled for execution.'

She gasped in horror. 'You cannot! He has done nothing wrong. Sir, I beg you. He is a good man, innocent of any crime.'

With a gentle clucking sound, he placed his hand over her own. 'Alas, I can do nothing. The tribunal has decided.' He stood up from the desk, a sorrowful look on his face.

'Sir! I beseech you! My husband is a godly man, a devout believer in Jesus Christ, as you yourself surely are?' she pleaded, her eyes full of tears.

He picked up the folder again and leafed through the papers, giving the impression of studying the contents.

'Please Captain! I am begging you as a man of honour!' Her husband's frightened face loomed before her, a noose around his neck.

Perrault hummed thoughtfully as he considered the folder. 'It says that he helped organise the violent demonstration that led to the deaths of many men, women and children—not to mention five valiant police officers simply doing their duty.' He shook his head and closed the folder. 'I believe you to be sincere, Madame. I wish there was something I could do ...'

'Please sir!' She threw herself onto her knees in anguish. 'You would be executing an innocent man! My husband abhors violence of any sort. He is a believer, a devout Christian who attends church without fail every Sunday.' She looked up with desperate, tear-filled eyes. 'Please, I beg of you! Show mercy!'

'Come now, no need for that.' Taking her arm, the captain assisted her back into the chair. 'Perhaps if I were to give a favourable opinion to the tribunal, your husband may yet be saved.' He mused on the thought as she stared, desperate for him to continue.

'Who knows—they might even consider him worthy of early release?'

Sitting on the desk again, Perrault leaned forward and brushed a tear from her cheek. 'You are such a handsome woman, Madame. I doubt anyone would be able to resist your charms … least of all a soldier such as myself.' His eyes roamed over her blouse.

She stared at him, feeling the blood drain from her face. 'What are you implying?' she asked, her voice faint.

'Implying? Nothing at all.' His voice was soothing as he took her hand, clasping it between his own. 'I am simply saying that it is within your power to see that the court receives a favourable opinion of your husband. That is all.' He caressed her hand, his eyes regarding her much as a snake would regard a delectable mouse.

'This is outrageous!' She snatched back her hand, a shocked look on her face. 'I shall report you to the authorities!'

He laughed. 'My dear Madame. I *am* the authorities! Nevertheless, I see that your mind is made up.' He stood up from the desk, his voice and manner suddenly brisk. 'The guard will show you out. The execution will take place tomorrow morning. Go on now. Be off with you! Do not waste my time!'

He sat down and picked up the folder, his eyes busily inspecting the contents. 'What? Are you still here? Shall I call the guard?' He stood up again and made as if to do so.

'Wait!' She held up a hand, her face deathly pale. 'Please, give me a moment.'

NEWS SPREAD QUICKLY THAT no more executions would take place and, furthermore, that fully a third of the detained men were to be released as a gesture of conciliation. The announcement sparked jubilation and relief among the townspeople and apprehension among the prisoners as they waited to find out who among them would be set free.

On a blustery autumn day, the captives were led out to the yard to exercise. Jacob was talking with Roland Abreu, a leading figure in the resistance movement, when they were distracted by shouts from one end of the yard. Puzzled, they went to investigate. Their fellow prisoners were flocked around a post, calling out names as they jostled to read a notice nailed to the wood.

'What is it? Let me through!' Abreu shoved through the excited prisoners to read the notice, which consisted of a list of names, in alphabetical order, of those to be released. Turning to Jacob he shook his head. Jacob pushed to the front, determined to see for himself. To his dismay, the list of names concluded with 'Vichy'. He read the list again, more carefully, surprised to see Hugo's name included among those granted amnesty.

Swallowing his severe disappointment, he sought out Hugo where he stood accepting congratulations from a group of fellow detainees also scheduled for release.

'Well done, Hugo!' Jacob embraced his companion.

'Maybe you will be on the next list,' consoled Hugo, trying to conceal his joy at this unexpected development. 'I have no doubt but that there will be more set free in the coming days. It is a crime that you are in here at all.'

Later, as the fuss died down, Jacob found himself in a corner of the yard along with Denis and Roland as the amnestied gathered in a separate group, talking among themselves as they awaited instructions from the guards.

'What do you think?' asked Denis, his eyes on the jubilant prisoners.

'About?' asked Jacob, although knowing full well what Denis implied.

Denis frowned. 'I can't understand why Hugo's name is on the list. He was in the same cell as you, Jacob. Why release him and not you? Or Séjour, or Tissier?' he added, naming some of the more innocuous prisoners. 'It doesn't make sense.'

'I think they all have pretty wives,' joked Roland.

'I can't figure it,' continued Denis, his gaze resting on Hugo. 'Why not you, Jacob? Or me?'

'Hey, don't forget me!' protested Roland.

'Lascelles!' Jacob spat the word.

Denis' face darkened. 'That scoundrel! The word is he was set free for his own safety straight after speaking against you. It's just as well—for the sake of his miserable neck!'

'DEAREST!' A WEEK LATER, Isabelle embraced him in the visiting room 'Have you heard anything?' Her eyes searched his face as they sat down.

He shook his head. 'Nothing yet.'

She moaned in frustration. 'The whole town talks about nothing else but the amnesty. Josette, of course, is over the moon to have Hugo safely back home. I'm glad for them, of course. But why him and not you? It's so unjust keeping you here when you have done nothing. And all because of that wretch Lascelles!'

Moved by her distress, he kissed her hand. 'My poor darling, this has been so hard on you.' He did his best to console her, his eyes moist. 'Don't be discouraged. The amnesty means that the government is having second thoughts. Who knows, I may be among the next to be released?'

'Do you think so?' Hope lit her face as she gripped his hands. 'But what about Lascelles?' she remembered.

'Everyone can see the man's a notorious liar. Everyone, that is, other than Captain Perrault,' he said, his voice bitter.

A guard called out that the visit was over, and Isabelle took her leave, promising to light a candle at the cathedral daily until his release. 'God will ensure that the truth will come out,' she said.

He kissed her tenderly, moved by her staunch faith. 'I am certain it will. It is only a matter of time.'

As she was leaving, she was surprised to be stopped by one of the guards, an older man with a broken nose. 'Madame Wheeler? The captain wishes to speak with you to discuss your husband's case.'

SHE STARED AT HER image in the tram window, a numbness encasing her mind and body. Her reflection struck her as pale and ghostly. She wondered if the other passengers noticed as her mind struggled to blot out the captain's lustful eyes as they observed her with leering intent.

'I fear for your husband's fate, Madame.' He had moved closer with the words, placing a hand on her knee. Shocked, she pushed it away. Undeterred, he attempted to caress her cheek with his fingers, his voice cajoling. 'These are desperate times, Madame Wheeler, and your husband is among desperate men. Who knows what could happen to him?'

'How dare you!' She shook off his hand, her face filled with revulsion.

He leaned his face close to hers, so close she could smell his breath. 'Come now, you're a grown woman, don't play the coquette with me. I know what you habitant women are like. Give me what I want, and you shall have what you want, I promise.' And with that he forced his mouth onto hers, pressing even as she fought to resist.

'Be still!' he threatened, and pinned her back against the chair, his hand groping her blouse.

Struggling, she freed her mouth and screamed.

'That won't help you,' he menaced, angered at her resistance as she struggled to free herself from his grip. 'It will only take a moment,' he soothed, his manner changing again.

'Monster!' Freeing her hand she slapped him across the face.

'Damn you!' Placing a hand to his cheek, he glowered at her, his face flushed.

She hurried to the door, which she found locked. She shook the handle and shouted for help as Perrault advanced toward her again, a look of thwarted aggression on his face.

'Captain? Is everything all right?' A hand tried the door from outside.

'No! Help me!' she shouted.

'Captain?'

Perrault halted, breathing heavily. 'Everything is fine! Get back to your duty!' With a glare of pure malice, he reached into his pocket and took out a key. She backed away as he inserted it into the lock.

'Bitch!' he hissed, his eyes bright with fury. 'You'll be an old maid before your husband ever comes home to you. Do you understand?' With a snarl, he pulled open the door and stepped aside.

'Get out!' he shouted as the sentry stood at attention. 'Do not attempt to sway me with your false charms! Go back to the gutter!'

Feeling unable to breathe on the crowded tram, she got off and walked for two blocks, making her way through the busy streets in a daze. She paid no attention to the passers-by, her mind recoiling from the shock of the officer's lust-filled eyes and hot breath as he pressed his mouth on hers.

Despite the setting sun, children still played on the footpath. She passed a group of young girls playing hopscotch, hopping up and down the chalked squares with squeals of laughter. One girl turned to look at her and she recognised herself in the curly hair and wide, innocent eyes.

In the sanctuary of the cathedral, she lit a candle and knelt to pray. Tears spilled from her eyes as she clasped her hands and bowed her head. '*Please, Lord, have pity on your servant, Jacob. Show mercy that he may be released and returned home to his family. You, who see all things, know that my Jacob is innocent. Please, I beg you, in your divine grace protect him against harm and false witness.*'

Crossing herself, she rose and sat back in the pew. In her hand she threaded the rosary Jacob had gifted her—how long ago! The cathedral was almost empty. On the high altar, an acolyte was extinguishing candles. She sat for a further half-hour in the shadows, the hush, and the cloying scent of incense and wax, bringing familiar solace as these things soothed her troubled soul.

She looked up at the stained-glass windows, now darkened, their glowing colours lost to night. Picking out her favourite window, she imagined she could see the figure of Gaston Tremblay as he gazed upon the sacred woodland that would become New France. A tear rolled down her cheek. Pressing the rosary to her lips, she kissed the crucifix. '*I pray that my Jacob may one day find your divine grace and the peace of your blessed love. Grant him this, O Lord, in return for his unjust suffering. Let him find his way to you as the lost lamb seeks the shepherd.*' She suddenly longed to go back to when she knelt as a child at her mother's side during Sunday Mass. *One day my children will kneel here and light a candle in my memory.* She crossed herself at the thought and bowed her head in prayer.

'*I know what you habitant women are like!*' An image of the Captain's leering face intruded upon her prayer, and she gasped in revulsion. Her gaze rose to take in the crucified Christ where he hung suspended from the cross, his face drawn with anguish. Her lips moved again, not in prayer, but in protest. 'Why should my Jacob suffer while evil men prosper?' She waited, as if for an answer, and then let out a deep, inconsolable sigh.

PERRAULT STARED AT THE closed door, the empty room seeming to mock his humiliating rejection. *Damn woman! Who does she think she is!* He opened the file lying on the desk. *To call him*—Captain Adrien Perrault, a decorated soldier—*a brute and a monster!* Grinding his teeth he wrote in a bold, revengeful hand, 'To be imprisoned for life'. He closed the file. *Let her come crawling back on her hands and knees!*

Upon reading of the sentence in the *Catholic Tribune*, a shocked Isabelle marched straight to the barracks and furiously demanded to see the captain. When this demand was refused, she demanded, in equally forthright terms, to see her husband. This request was also refused. Glancing up, she saw Perrault smirking down at her from the ramparts.

Infuriated, she shouted up at him. 'You shameless scoundrel! I demand that you let me see my husband this moment or I shall go straight to the newspapers with a report of your infamous conduct!'

'Go ahead!' he shouted merrily. 'See if they print your lies!'

Beside herself, she did as promised, pushing her way past the receptionist and into the editor's office of the *Catholic Tribune* where she stopped short, confronted by a man in military uniform seated behind the desk.

'Where is Monsieur Verreau?' she demanded.

'He is on leave,' the man said, climbing to his feet. 'How may I help you Madame?'

On the verge of hysteria, she collapsed in tears. The hapless censor signalled for the receptionist, who assisted her into a chair and fussed over her.

'Monsieur Verreau is in prison,' the woman whispered, offering Isabelle a cup of tea to calm her nerves. 'The government now oversees the newspaper. Drink some tea, Madame, it will help,' she said, raising her voice as the officer approached to check on Isabelle.

NEWSPAPERS IN THE REST of the country were not so constrained. *The Globe* published a front-page editorial denouncing the 'secretive tribunals' set up to mete out the sentences. It demanded the solicitor-general investigate the "entire unsavoury process", with a call to launch a public inquiry into the events surrounding the executions. It's rival, the *Toronto Star*, went further, demanding the release of the imprisoned men "until such time as their guilt or innocence can be established by normal judicial procedures, freed from the taint of military influence." The editorial appeared just above a brief account of the discovery of the body of a certain monsieur Gustave Lascelles, found hanging from the neck of the giant bronze in Gaston Tremblay Square, a noose around his throat, hands firmly tied behind his back.

37

A Suspicion

S HE HAD BEEN FORCED to move out of the beloved home on rue Sainte-Monique, the bank foreclosing shortly after the imposition of martial law. She moved into a dilapidated row house on rue Marguerite Bourgeoys in the heart of Old Town, close to the public market. There she lived 'in respectable squalor' as she termed it with Louis and Marie-Odile, refusing pleas from her sister and cousin to live with them. 'I need a place for Jacob to return to,' she explained. 'And it's not so bad. One gets used to the smells after a while.'

Her new neighbours viewed her arrival with suspicion, some openly scornful of the high and mighty wife of the prosperous businessman reduced to such penurious circumstances. Others were kinder, mindful of her husband's arrest and pitying her straitened situation as a sacrifice for justice and habitant rights.

When a year had passed and still with no word of when Jacob might be released, she wrote pleading letters to the Legislative Assembly in Quebec City and to the Federal Parliament in Ottawa. She received official letters in return explaining that her husband's case was "under continuing investigation and/or review" with the assurance that it would be "resolved as expeditiously as possible." Increasingly desperate, she wrote letters to newspapers across the country, urging the federal government to intervene and correct what she termed "an outrageous injustice, which is a stain upon the conscience of the nation."

Relatives of the imprisoned men organised a silent protest outside the provincial government office where they held up banners demanding the release of the remaining "martyrs." One night Isabelle and six other women chained themselves to the winged bull, reviving an action Isabelle had first proposed following the initial arrests. Workers crossing the square in the morning rain blinked with surprise when they observed the women standing beneath the monument, secured to it by chains. The police were summoned and cut the chains, arresting all seven women on charges of disturbing the public order. After a morning spent in the city watchhouse, they were released with stern warnings as to their future conduct.

The stressful campaign to free her husband, along with the demands of running the impoverished household, took a toll on her physical and emotional health. During a bout of influenza, she was forced to rest in bed for a week as Marguerite moved in to look after her and the children.

'Why won't you come and live with Dominic and me?' fretted Marguerite, disturbed by her sister's exhausted appearance. 'Honestly, he is all for it. And the children, too. It would be so much better than this.'

'Please, don't upset yourself,' replied Isabelle. 'This is our home, and we must make the best of it until Jacob returns.' In spite of her mild voice, her eyes showed her determination to stay.

'You are running yourself ragged, poor thing!' Tutting in dismay, Marguerite brushed Isabelle's hair back from her cheek. 'And you are frightening Marie-Odile and Louis. You must slow down. You cannot expect Jacob to be freed overnight. These things take time, sweetness. You ought to understand that better than anyone.'

'It's just so unfair.' Isabelle's voice choked. 'I pray for him every day.'

'I know.' Marguerite clucked in sympathy. 'But things are changing. Did you hear of the report in *The Star*?'

'I did. But those villains in the legislative assembly won't be moved by an English newspaper.'

'It's not just *The Star*. Voices are being raised in Ottawa and elsewhere demanding an end to martial law.'

'That's good.' Isabelle's voice dropped off to a murmur. Seeing that her sister had fallen asleep, Marguerite left the bedroom, quietly closing the door behind her.

Two days later, Isabelle felt well enough to receive René Turgeon downstairs, in spite of Marguerite's remonstrances. 'I feel quite well,' she insisted, smiling to illustrate. 'Now run along, dear sister, and see to your husband, or he'll think you have divorced him.'

A half-hour later, the ex-deputy knocked on the door bearing a bouquet of tulips. She smiled warmly at him. 'Why, Monsieur Turgeon, what a pleasure to see you!'

'Good morning, Isabelle!' Raising his hat with one hand, he held out the flowers with the other.

She took the bouquet. 'Tulips! My favourite.' She hesitated and drew back as he tried to kiss her cheek. 'Better be safe than sorry,' she apologized. 'I couldn't forgive myself if I passed on the flu to you, even though I am feeling much better. Please, do come in.'

'So, how are you my dear?' Turgeon studied her over a cup of coffee, his observant gaze noting the tiredness about her eyes.

'Well, thank you,' she said, deflecting his concern. 'I seem to be over this bothersome flu at last.'

'And the children?'

'Gaston is staying with my aunt Jeanne in Montreal and working as an apprentice mechanic. Louis is a trainee with the Post Office. Marie-Odile is still in school, of course. She is almost as tall as me.'

Turgeon shook his head in bemusement. 'How time flies! I remember her sitting on your lap, all curls and dimples! And Hugo? I haven't seen him in an age.'

'Still employed at the library. He jokes it is similar to the Assembly archives, only not as dusty.'

Turgeon made a rueful face. 'I had great hopes when he succeeded me as deputy ...' He sighed. 'Still, we ought to be thankful for small mercies. It's a miracle they released him without charge.'

'And yet they charged my Jacob.' Her voice was resigned rather than bitter.

'True. When did you last see him?'

'Almost a week ago. I brought him a clean shirt, and they allowed me a half-hour—but only after I kicked up the most dreadful fuss. There are rumours of another amnesty. Do you think it will include Jacob?'

Turgeon's voice was careful as he replied. 'I sincerely hope so. That odious creature Captain Perrault seems to have taken against your husband, for whatever reason. But my dear,' he exclaimed on seeing her distress at the remark, 'this is upsetting for you. Tell me, how are you managing? It must be difficult.'

'We manage—but without the restaurant meals.' She attempted a smile but failed. 'Our friends are very generous and help wherever they can. And Jules, my cousin in New York, sends a cheque every month to pay for the rent.'

'And the bank?' He broached the question with the same careful regard for her feelings.

'They still bother me every now and then, but since we surrendered the house, less so. I think even the bank understands that we have nothing left to give.'

'Won't you let me help?' Turgeon sat forward, his lined face full of concern.

'No need, but thank you.' She put on a brave smile. 'Your friendship is the best gift you could give.'

She stood at the door to wave goodbye, watching as he proceeded slowly along the narrow street to the bus stop, leaning on his cane. She wrinkled her nose at the smell coming from the rubbish collected in the gutters, missing the scent of roses from her former garden. The vinegar wagon trundled by, and the driver looked at her. 'Vinegar?' he called out in a mournful cry. She shook her head.

A woman stared at her from the house opposite, a sour look on her face. She closed the door, shutting out the smells of garbage and the odours of cooking. Thinking back on the ex-deputy's visit, she sighed and leaned her head against the door. She heard the bells of Sainte-Chappelle peal through the air and reminded herself to attend the church and light her daily candle.

THE QUEBEC LEGISLATIVE ASSEMBLY dug in its heels at criticism of the heavy-handed actions in New France, pointing to the sporadic acts of resistance that still occurred on a regular basis as justification for the continuing imposition of martial law. The latest outrage, as the pro-government newspaper *Le Devoir* described it, was an attack by rebels on the military barracks. "Disaster was only averted by the prompt and vigilant action of the sentries who caught and detained the would-be arsonists. They are now locked up in the same prison they had sought to burn to the ground."

Inspired by the audacious attempt, a man described as an anarchist by the authorities, set fire to one of the new English schools that had opened in the city. A fierce inferno reduced the school building to a smoking ruin before the flames could be extinguished. The school reopened in a new location under around the-clock armed guard. In spite of this deterrence, a second man was caught trying to set the new premises alight. Both the arsonist and his imitator were punished with ten-year prison sentences, the men dragged from the court while shouting the defiant phrase of the resistance, 'Long live free New France!'

In an effort to quell simmering public resentment, the authorities announced a second amnesty, news of which soon reached the barracks. As the appointed day approached, the hopeful inmates gossiped and wagered on which of them would be included. The prisoners flocked around as a soldier nailed the list to a post.

'Stay back!' he ordered.

In spite of the warning, they pressed forward, attempting to read the sheet as the soldier hammered it against the post. Amid the pushing and shoving prisoners, Jacob strained to see his name. His heart sank with disappointment at the realisation he was not included.

'No surprise.' Denis Vachon stood beside him to scan the names.

'They must have missed me!' Roland Abreu joked as he pushed through the prisoners to stand beside them. 'Gentlemen, we are still guests of the government.'

Later, after the fuss had died down, Jacob approached a guard to seek permission to see the captain. 'It's important,' he said.

The guard laughed mockingly. 'Of course it is. There are a dozen more 'importants' ahead of you!'

A harried Captain Perrault was in no mood to listen to pleas for clemency.

'Tell them it's their bad luck!' he snapped, waving away a soldier who enquired if the prisoners might see him. Sitting at his desk, he stared at the latest military despatch, his foul mood deepening as he re-read the order. In blunt language, the despatch once again denied his oft-repeated request for a transfer to a more honourable duty than that of commander of a military prison. *"You're doing a fine job, Perrault. Keep at it!"*

He ground his teeth as he recognised the gloating, scrawled jibe as that of his superior. He sat with his elbows on the desk, pressing his cheeks between his hands as he dreamed of taking revenge on the smug, sanctimonious colonel. *The fat disgusting pig! I ought run him through with a sabre!*

'What?' He looked up, still seething, as Charest respectfully tapped on the door.

'Sir, a prisoner is demanding to see you.'

'About the damn list?'

'Aye, Captain. Shall I send him away?'

Perrault listened as the prisoner outside the door protested the decision.

'Tell him I demand to see him! Captain?' The voice shouted through the closed door.

Perrault's ears perked in recognition, something about the voice sounding familiar. 'Charest! Bring him in.'

He scowled as Jacob was escorted into the room. 'Well? What is it? Can't you see I'm too busy to be wasting time with the likes of you!'

'Captain, why wasn't I included in the latest amnesty? I have been unjustly detained now for over a year—'

'Unjustly detained for over a year!' Perrault savagely mimicked the words. 'Why? Because you're a murderer and a scoundrel, that's why! Now get out of here and back to your cell.' He signalled Charest.

'But I'm neither!' Jacob struggled to remain in the room as the soldier seized hold of his arm. 'You must know this! I told you Lascelles was a notorious liar. And now that he is unable to bear false witness, you have no lawful cause to keep me here!'

'Ask your wife why!' Perrault took brief, malicious enjoyment at the look of confusion the remark elicited before returning to dark fantasies of the colonel, his fingers twitching with the compulsion to strangle the oaf.

Isabelle hardly had time to hand over his fresh clothes on her next visit before Jacob fired the question that had consumed him all week, the captain's taunt having ripened into a festering wound amid the boredom of prison life.

'You met with Perrault—after I was first sentenced. Do you remember?' Jacob studied her closely.

She nodded, paling at the question.

'What happened—you never said.' The question came out like an accusation, in spite of his resolve to remain calm.

'It was nothing. He called me into his office—'

'And?' His gaze was fierce.

'Jacob, what's the matter? What's gotten into you?'

'And?' he repeated, his voice demanding.

'And ...' she took a deep breath, 'he made an improper suggestion.'

His stomach tightened as a cold rage seized him. 'I knew it! What happened—exactly?'

'He proposed,' her voice faltered, 'an exchange ... of favours. Must we talk about this?' She laid her hand on his, her voice pleading. 'The man is a scoundrel, can't we leave it at that?'

'Damn him to hell!'

The unaccustomed violence in his voice frightened her. 'Jacob, promise me you won't say or do anything rash! He is the commandant here. He has the power to make your life miserable, even extend your sentence. Promise me!' The guard, lounging in a corner, was staring. 'Jacob, are you listening? It was nothing! I put him in his place and left the office at once.'

He buried his face between his hands, breathing deeply as he sought to bring himself under control.

'Jacob?' She stroked his wrist.

'I'm alright,' he muttered. He took her hands in his. 'I knew the man was a brute, but this ...?'

Anxious to take his mind off the captain, she told him about Turgeon's visit and Marie-Odile's success in her exams. 'I baked her favourite cake as a reward!'

He nodded absently as she talked, a distracted look on his face that concerned her.

A short time later, the guard announced the visit was over. 'Move your feet!' he shouted, ordering Jacob back to the cell.

'I'll be back next week!' Isabelle called out as he was led away.

He turned his head to see her standing by the chair, a hopeless look on her face.

'REALLY, WHAT IS TO be gained by such senseless acts?' Josette poured Isabelle a glass of wine as she posed the question. It was the last day of summer and she had insisted that Isabelle join herself and Hugo, Isabelle's sister Marguerite and husband Dominic along with Claudette and her husband, Andre, for supper. 'One would think the very last thing the city needs is more fighting and more arrests,' she continued.

'The fools are playing into the hands of the authorities,' Claudette agreed. 'They provide the politicians with every justification for continuing the occupation,' she said, using the word on everyone's lips to describe the imposition of additional emergency powers declared by the authorities. 'Now we have to put up with a curfew on top of everything else!'

'Which will only provoke more trouble,' added Marguerite.

'Did you hear they've installed Bernard Benoit as a temporary governor? Benoit!' Hugo grunted in annoyance. 'Why him? Don't they understand it will only make things worse?'

'It shows the habitant spirit is alive and well,' volunteered Andre Petain, taking the conversation back to the arson attacks. 'Beneath the boot heels of the occupiers the thirst for our traditional freedoms is still there.'

Can you have a thirst beneath boot heels? wondered Marguerite to herself.

'Enough of all this talk about violence!' Claudette looked to Josette for support. 'Let us enjoy one day at least without talking about politics. Honestly, it's become an obsession. It's all anybody talks about.'

'But we are under occupation,' her husband objected. 'What else do you expect?'

'How can French soldiers occupy a French city? Besides, we are already a part of Quebec. It's foolish to maintain this fiction that we are somehow a separate country.'

'Claudette!' Her husband's mouth fell open in shock.

'Well, it's true,' she persisted. 'Don't you think so, Marguerite?'

'If only things could go back to the way they were,' lamented Marguerite.

'But that's exactly what we demand,' interjected Hugo. 'We are fighting to regain our traditional rights to control our destiny.'

'Hear, hear!' agreed Dominic. 'Rights that have been brutally taken away without our consent.'

'How are you coping, dearest?' Josette leaned in to whisper the question to Isabelle as the discussion continued. 'Your dress is so pretty. And what have you done to your hair? It looks marvellous!'

Isabelle smiled weakly. 'There's no need to flatter, Josette. Honestly, I'm quite recovered. But I'm afraid I'm not very good company.'

'Nonsense! You just sit there and speak or not. You are among family and friends. What now?' Josette furrowed her brow as the conversation turned argumentative.

'I'm just saying,' Andre insisted, talking above his wife who tried to interrupt. 'What kind of a world do we live in where innocent men are falsely condemned and imprisoned based on nothing but blatant lies and untested allegations made in secret?'

'Hush Andre! You will upset Isabelle.' Claudette turned an apologetic glance in her direction.

'Pardon,' Andre apologised. 'At least you were lucky, Hugo.'

'We both were!' Josette laid an affectionate hand on her husband's arm.

'A toast to that!' Claudette raised her glass. 'To luck!'

As the dinner ended, Hugo insisted on walking Isabelle home despite her protests. 'It's not necessary,' she insisted. 'And you'll have to walk all the way back again, by yourself—and reach home before the curfew.'

'Nonsense. A walk will do me the world of good. I've eaten so much tourtiere I'm bursting! And I'll take a cab back. Plenty of time.'

The summer twilight was warm, the air loud with twittering birdsong as they cut through a laneway to rue Saint-Honoré. They passed a squad of soldiers patrolling the area, Isabelle pointedly looking away as they walked by.

'What a fine evening,' said Hugo, anxious to restore Isabelle's mood as the soldiers turned a corner. As discreetly as he could, he raised the question of finances, gently probing to discover if she had sufficient funds to pay the bills and keep food on the table. 'Josette and I are quite flush at the moment,' he said. 'You'd oblige us by relieving us of some of the burden.'

'Thank you, Hugo. But between Gaston and Louis' contributions and my sewing work we have enough to get by. Josette is so happy you are home.'

He sighed, his mood changing. 'I am too, of course. But why do I feel so guilty? I had nothing to do with it. It was sheer luck, I suppose.'

'Perhaps Josette worked her magic on that dreadful Captain Perrault,' she suggested, stealing a sidelong glance at her cousin.

'Who knows?' he shrugged. 'She said the fellow merely listened to her protests and said nothing of any consequence.'

They walked in thoughtful silence until they reached her door. 'Goodnight, dear cousin!' She kissed him on the cheek. 'And thank Josette for the splendid meal.'

Bidding Hugo 'be careful!', she watched as he walked off along the darkening street in search of a cab before closing the door.

'Mama!' Marie-Odile rushed down the stairs to embrace her.

She smiled, kissing the girl's wavy brown hair. 'Where is your brother?'

'In bed asleep already!' said Marie-Odile, helping Isabelle off with her coat.

'Where you should be, darling. Go along now, I'll be up to kiss you in a few minutes—and remember to wash your face.'

JACOB WAS EXERCISING IN the yard when Captain Perrault happened to pass through, accompanied by a party of government officials sent by the Quebec legislature to inspect the prison and to see what, if anything, could be done to relieve the situation. The party, deep in conversation, stopped near enough for him to listen in on the discussion.

'You must understand, Captain, this situation cannot go on indefinitely. The governments, both in Quebec and in Ottawa, are anxious to put the troubles behind us and return the situation to normality as soon as possible.' The speaker, a man in a black suit and bowler with a neatly trimmed goatee, looked at Perrault, waiting for an acknowledgement of his concerns.

'No more than I!' Perrault grimaced. 'Do you think I enjoy nursemaiding a bunch of criminals and anarchists? I fought in the war, sir, at Neuve Chapelle and the Somme! I was gassed and wounded for my efforts.'

'I'm sure you were a valiant soldier, Captain, and I understand this posting is a difficult one. But that is precisely why we need a man of your calibre to make it work.'

Mollified, the captain was about to continue the tour when his eye fell on Jacob. 'One of the chief anarchists!' he said loudly, a look of contempt on his face. 'A murderer and a rebel!'

Stung, Jacob answered back before he could prevent the words leaving his mouth. 'Did you tell the gentlemen about your lechery towards our wives?'

The accusation startled the visiting dignitaries, who half-turned to Perrault for an explanation.

'As well as a notorious liar and provocateur!' added Perrault. Flashing a venomous glance at Jacob, he steered the party across the yard.

'Do you think that was wise?' Charest came up beside Jacob.

'It's the truth!'

'Perhaps.' Charest's voice was sober. 'But you have caused him great offence, in public. He is not a man to forget such an insult.' With a cautionary glance at Jacob, he followed the officials.

Jacob recounted the episode to Denis and Roland, surprised at the looks of alarm that crossed their faces. 'You should have held your tongue,' counselled Denis, 'there are other ways to take your revenge. Roland?'

'I agree.' Roland nodded, his expression grave. 'One does not poke the bear unless it is in a cage.'

'What can he do, lock me up?'

All the same, in the privacy of his thoughts he regretted the outburst. It was stupid and childish, he reproached himself. *I promised Isabelle.*

Annoyed with himself, he lay back on the bed. Damn the villain, anyway! But slowly his anger gave way to guilt, and then remorse as he recalled how forlorn Isabelle had looked as she watched him led away. A hopeless sigh escaped his lips as he pictured the straitened circumstances she was forced to endure. Fool! he berated himself over the run-in with Perrault. He thought of Hugo, envying his freedom. The knowledge that over eighteen months had now been stolen from his life with his family drew a groan of torment. Hugo was released, why not he? And then a sudden notion dashed all other thoughts from his head as his eyes widened with shock. *Josette!*

'NO TALKING!' THE SOLDIER scowled at him. 'Move!'

Avoiding the man's gaze, Jacob lowered his head and continued his walk around the yard. To his surprise, the usual group of detainees was joined by a fresh influx of prisoners who took part in the shuffling column that rounded the dirt square. The day was cold and overcast and he crossed his arms in front of his chest to keep warm. He heard a hiss from behind and acknowledged the sound by lifting, but not turning, his head. 'What?' he said, recognising the voice of Roland Abreu.

'I have news, friend. They say the federal government itself is now demanding the release of all political prisoners.'

'Is that likely?' asked Jacob, the boredom of prison life constantly enlivened by rumours that proved as transient as they were false.

'Hopefully not, as I'd miss the old place dreadfully.'

'Who are these other men? Where did they come from?

'The word is they are common criminals, sent here due to overcrowding at the penitentiary.'

The whistle sounded and the men turned towards the stable door that led back inside.

He was on his bunk, pulling off a shoe to inspect a blister on his foot when the cell door unlocked, and a man entered dragging an iron bed frame behind him. Jacob looked up in surprise. The prisoner was followed by a guard who carried a thin mattress and blanket.

'Over there.' The guard pointed to the wall opposite Jacob's bunk.

'What's this?'

'You've a new cell mate,' the guard said, throwing the mattress down on the bunk. 'Make sure you get along.'

Dismayed at the intrusion, Jacob studied the new inmate, a frowning, wispy-haired fellow with an incessant grimace, his face twitching with every second breath.

'What's your name?' he asked as the guard left, locking the door behind him.

The man gave a vacant stare before sitting down on the bunk, his eyes flicking past Jacob as if he were no more than an item of furniture. 'Jacob,' he said, thinking that perhaps the man was in shock at his new surroundings. He stuck out his hand.

The man looked at it and then at Jacob before lying back on the bunk, his gaze fixed in the same vacuous stare.

Perturbed at the man's behaviour, Jacob kept a close watch on him for the remainder of the day. The fellow grimaced and muttered, chattering to himself for minutes at a time. More disturbingly, he seemed not to notice Jacob, as if he were invisible. Once, the man alarmed him by suddenly talking loudly as if to a third person in the cell.

'What is the matter with you?' demanded Jacob in fright. 'Are you a lunatic?' The man continued gibbering as if Jacob wasn't there.

Greatly concerned at his cell mate's mental condition, he approached one of the friendlier guards to request the man be moved elsewhere. 'He obviously belongs in an asylum, not a prison,' he said.

The guard observed him, his face sympathetic. 'Diaz? The captain specifically ordered he be put in with you.'

'Me? Why?'

The guard shrugged. 'He doesn't explain himself to the likes of me.'

'But the fellow is obviously a lunatic. What's he in for?'

'He started a blaze that killed three people as they slept.'

'Good God! On purpose?'

'That's what the court found. He would have hung but for his lunacy. They gave him thirty years instead.' The guard turned to go, glancing back at Jacob. 'Be careful when you fall asleep.' The warning was given soberly, with no hint of a jest.

From then on, he maintained a state of vigilance around his cell mate. One night, shortly after talking to the guard, he awoke to find Diaz standing over him in the darkness.

'What do you want?' he shouted, half in warning, half in alarm.

The fellow regarded him in silence before turning back to his own cot.

His heart beating fast, Jacob remained watchful until hearing the other man begin to snore. Taxed by the vigilance, he fell into a disturbed sleep.

'Ah!' He struggled for breath as a pillow was pressed against his mouth, suffocating him. He felt a body kneeling astride him, determinedly pushing the pillow into his face. He lashed out in fear, twisting and kicking in a desperate bid for air. His flailing hands gripped some fingers, and he twisted them with all his might. His assailant gave a cry of pain and released the pillow. Gulping for air, Jacob jumped up and pummelled his attacker, striking him with repeated blows while shouting for help. It was pitch black, the only light coming from a bulb somewhere in the hallway.

'Jacob? What is it? Are you alright?' The commotion had awakened Roland in the adjoining cell, and he called out to alert the guard.

Jacob heard the sound of a lock and the door being pulled open. Next moment, strong arms were shoving him back onto his bunk. 'Sit down and don't move!' Another guard knelt over Diaz, holding up a lantern to examine the insensible man. 'We must take him to the infirmary,' he told his companion with a glance at Jacob. 'What happened?'

'He tried to kill me! He's a lunatic!' Jacob trembled with shock.

'You don't have to answer to me,' said the guard. 'It's the captain you must convince.'

His companion gave a humourless laugh as they dragged the senseless Diaz from the cell.

The incident was the talk of the exercise yard the following morning, the men clustering around to listen as Jacob explained to Roland what had happened. 'The lunatic tried to smother me in my sleep! The man is deranged. He belongs in an asylum not a prison.'

'Quiet there!' The guard motioned for the men to separate. 'Back into file!'

'Why did he attack you?' Roland's voice followed closely behind him as he walked.

'Because he's a lunatic!'

'Do you think that's the only reason?'

Jacob stopped, the question arousing his own suspicions. 'What do you mean?'

'I mean, why put the lunatic in with you? There's an empty cell next to Denis. They could have put him in there, but they didn't. Why not?'

Jacob thought about the remark when back in his cell, the bare cot across from him only deepening his suspicions.

Before noon, he was summoned to Captain Perrault's office. He went, expecting the worst, only partly reassured by the guard's sympathetic remark. 'Diaz is utterly mad. Even the captain can't deny that. He should never have been sent here in the first place.'

The captain looked up as he entered, a malicious look on his face. 'So, not content with murdering an innocent cop, you try and slaughter your cellmate?'

'The man is a lunatic. He should never have been sent here,' he said, fortified by the guard's admission. 'He tried to murder me in my sleep. I acted in self-defence.'

Perrault grimaced, tugging his lip as he considered the matter. 'You are fortunate I don't charge you with attempted murder.' He tapped on the desk, a frustrated look on his face. 'Luckily for you the guards back up your story.' He gave out a vexed sigh. 'Now I'll have to arrange for the fool to be transported to another prison, thanks to you.' He motioned to the guard. 'Take him back to his cell.'

'Wait!' Jacob pulled away as the guard attempted to take his arm. 'I demand to know why Diaz was put into my cell, the man being clearly deranged and a murderer into the bargain?'

Captain Perrault gave him a poisonous stare. 'Are you now questioning my allocation of prisoners?'

'Yes.' The blunt reply took even himself by surprise.

'Damn you!' The captain pushed back his chair and got to his feet, a bilious look on his face. 'You've been a thorn in my side ever since you arrived. Don't think I don't see you plotting with your fellow conspirators all day long!'

'What?' Jacob stared in surprise. 'What the devil are you talking about?'

'Hold your tongue! You are the prisoner here, not me.' Seething at such insolence, the captain gestured to the guard. 'Remove him at once!'

'And give my regards to your lovely wife!' he shouted as Jacob was escorted out.

38

A Dinner Party

SEVEN YEARS AFTER THE deadly riots, Gaston Tremblay Square was once again a place for strollers and lovers, albeit under the vigilant eye of authorities still apprehensive of the public mood. The curfew and martial law had been lifted with dire threats of a swift re-introduction if there were any more acts of rebellion against the public order. Burned shops and businesses had long since re-opened, freshly painted, their wares placed invitingly outside. The designation, 'Special Autonomous Region,' had been stripped from all official references to the city and its surrounding regions—now known on official maps as *La région de la Nouvelle-France.* But despite their seeming acquiescence to the new order, the long memories for which the townspeople were famous, persisted in graffiti scrawls and painted insults aimed at the provincial government and all those who were perceived to have betrayed the city.

The cautious authorities had placed a ban on the raising of all new statues, which, for over two centuries had been the town's way of memori-alising and celebrating episodes and events in its history. Even the official accounts of the city's founding were subject to censorship through the odious practice that was bitterly referred to as 'overwriting'. Thus, school textbooks and the curriculum itself were subtly edited to emphasise the role of Jean Talon and the colonial authorities in establishing the city. Gaston Tremblay was recast as a roving freebooter who took control of the nascent settlement to further his own piratical ends. Bernard Benoit, now officially installed as Administrator—the designation 'Governor' deemed inappro-priate—even went so far as to consider pulling down all statues of the 'buccaneer', only to be dissuaded by fears of reigniting the violence. He did, however, succeed in renaming the central square as *Place Samuel-de-Champlain*, a change furiously resisted by the populace who insisted on calling it by its original name and defacing or tearing down all signs to the contrary. Exhausted by the struggle to regain their cherished autonomy, the population adopted a stance of sullen resentment while going about their daily lives. Thus, the news of another amnesty was greeted with mute passivity, except by the hopeful relatives of those still imprisoned and the imprisoned men themselves.

'I'm being released!' Denis Vachon's face showed his shock at the news.

Jacob exclaimed in surprise. 'What? Have they posted a new list?'

'No.' Denis shook his head, still bewildered. 'A guard came up and said I was to be released within the hour!'

Jacob grasped his friend's hand. 'That's wonderful news, Denis. Yvette will be so happy!'

Denis gazed back at him, his eyes full of concern as he regarded Jacob's disappointed expression which he was doing his best to hide. 'You have heard nothing? I don't understand. Why me, and not you? After all, I at least confessed to banging a few heads in the square, but you're guilty of nothing.'

'Lascelles.' Jacob grimaced with the name.

'But he is dead. He can't accuse you now.'

'No, nor can he be disproved.'

Pierre Guyot, a leading figure in the resistance, approached with a jubilant expression on his face. 'You too?' asked Denis before the other man could open his mouth.

'Yes!' Guyot's voice conveyed his relief. 'And you?' he asked Jacob.

Jacob shook his head, his face glum.

Someone hailed Guyot. 'I'm sorry, truly,' he said as he left.

'Guyot?' Denis whistled in surprise as he glanced after the other man. 'Wasn't he supposed to hang?'

'Then I must reside at the very bottom of the barrel,' said Jacob, his voice bleak.

'But they cannot exclude you! It must be a mistake.'

'You've heard?' Roland Abreu joined them, his face doleful. 'I don't understand it.' He cast a sour glance at the jubilant Guyot. 'Why him and not me?'

'Just what I was saying to Jacob.' Denis scowled. 'What idiot makes these decisions?'

'How many of us are left?' asked Jacob.

Roland sighed. 'Langlois, Béraud ... Caron. I don't know. It can hardly be more than a dozen or so.'

'The other scrapings,' said Jacob

Denis' voice was grim. 'You know who's to blame, don't you?'

Jacob nodded, his face bitter. 'The bastard will do his best to keep me here until I die.'

'Surely, there must be something we can do?' Roland thought for a moment. 'You will bring pressure to bear from outside, right Denis?'

'Of course. And if reason won't prevail ...' Denis's face hardened.

Reclining on his office chair, a pleased Captain Perrault clasped his hands behind his head, recalling the wording of his letter with pride at his success.

The prisoner Wheeler is a special case. We have a sworn witness who testifies to seeing him stab the unfortunate police officer in cold blood. To release him now would inflame the officer's widow and anger the entire police force. In addition, the man has been a provocateur in prison, continually encouraging his fellow prisoners to acts of defiance and violence. He brutally attacked one prisoner, a poor simpleton, injuring him so badly the fellow had to be removed from the prison and sent to hospital. It is my strong recommendation that he be held until such time as he shows sincere penitence for his actions, including an admission of his crimes, and an apology to the widow of the man he so callously murdered.

The recommendation had swayed his superiors, who baulked at the prospect of releasing a known cop-killer and persistent agitator back into the febrile population.

Perrault sighed, filled with an immense gratification when notified that his superiors endorsed the recommendation. *When you leave here, Wheeler, it will be for delivery to your damnable shrew of a wife in a pine box.*

'A PARTY?' HUGO LOOKED up from the newspaper in surprise.

'Well, not a party exactly,' said Josette, 'a dinner, to welcome home Denis and cheer up Isabelle.'

'It might make her feel worse.'

'How?' asked Josette with a frown.

'How? You don't think to see Denis released and not Jacob might upset her?'

'No, I don't think so,' said Josette, in a voice that told him she most certainly didn't agree. 'She will be glad for Denis. It will give her hope that Jacob may soon follow. Besides, it will be good for her—get her out of that dreadful little house. Have you seen how worn-out she looks?'

Hugo sighed and set down the paper. 'I wish she would let us help out with money. It must be difficult relying on what little Louis makes at the post office.'

'And all that darning!' Josette shuddered. 'I don't know how she does it, taking in work like … like a common seamstress.'

'My dear, there is nothing shameful about being a seamstress.'

'With taking in work? After her husband's former position? Really, Hugo.'

'Will she come to the dinner?' He picked up the newspaper again.

'I'll insist! Now I must telephone Yvette. She'll be happy as a lark to have Denis back.'

To her disappointment, Isabelle sent back a regretful note declining the written invitation. Undeterred, Josette called on Marguerite for assistance. 'Tell her she simply must come,' she urged over the telephone. 'Tell her that if she doesn't, I'll send for the police to arrest her and drag her here!'

'You must go, darling, for my sake, if not your own. Josette will positively murder me if you don't.' Marguerite clucked in exasperation as she cajoled the reluctant Isabelle. 'Are you to live like a hermit until Jacob is back home with you? Is that what he would want?' She looked around the small, dingy parlour, unable to supress a shudder.

'What?' Isabelle observed her through narrowed eyes.

'Nothing.'

'Liar! Out with it. Confess, as Sister Genevieve would say.'

Marguerite chuckled. 'And rap me over the knuckles with that horrid stick she carried?'

'Exactly. Don't make me find my stick.'

Marguerite's face sobered. 'It's just that this house .... Why won't you come and live with me?'

'You know why.'

Marguerite nodded, chewing on her lower lip as she observed her sister. *She looks threadbare, the poor thing!*

'What now? Honestly, Marguerite. You are like an open book!'

'Please do come. Dominic and I will pick you up in a cab and see you home afterwards. You need this diversion. Can't you see that?'

'And how is Dominic?'

'Oh!' Marguerite groaned in frustration. 'Like himself.'

'And what does that mean?'

'He gets these strange obsessions. Lately, its over that new building they are putting up across the street. He sits and stares at it all day while grumbling like it's the end of the world. And do you think I can get him to stop complaining about it?' She exhaled a deep sigh. 'When we were first married, he was so ...'

'So what?'

'Attentive! It was as if he found every little thing about me irresistibly charming.'

Isabelle giggled, sounding to Marguerite at that moment like her old self. 'And you suspect that your charms have worn off?'

'I ask him why he doesn't obsess over me as much as he does that silly old building.' Reaching out, she took Isabelle by the wrists. 'You must come!' she wheedled, 'to please your only sister?'

'Alright! If only to stop you pestering me.'

'Promise?'

'Yes.' Isabelle gave a theatrical sigh, 'I promise.'

Marguerite smiled, pleased with the success of her mission. 'I feel we are back in our bedroom with mama calling from downstairs!'

Isabelle made a rueful face. 'It's not like our former home, but we are perfectly suited here.' She stood up. 'More coffee?'

Marguerite watched her sister boil the kettle, worry replacing her former mood. *Perfectly suited? What on earth would mama say?*

A WEEK LATER, ISABELLE put on the one remaining good dress she had not sold and squeezed into a cab with Marguerite and Dominic. No sooner had she taken her seat than Dominic began to complain about the 'dreadful stench' coming from the rotting garbage in the street. 'An absolute disgrace!' he fumed. 'I intend to make a strong complaint to the council first thing on Monday morning.'

Ignoring her husband's outrage, Marguerite leaned forward to touch Isabelle's knee. 'You look divine!'

Upon arrival, they were greeted by a cheerful Josette, who swept Isabelle into her embrace. 'Darling! I'm so glad you came! It wouldn't be the same without you.'

Josette's sister, Claudette, pecked Isabelle on the cheek. 'Dear cousin! It's been such a long time.'

'My turn!' Hugo kissed Isabelle before giving way to a smiling Yvette Vachon, who hugged Isabelle before taking her by the arm to steer her into the parlour. 'Look!'

Denis Vachon stood before the fire, thinner and older looking, his gaunt complexion still sallow from prison.

'Isabelle!' He advanced with outstretched arms.

'Denis!' Her eyes shone with tears as they embraced. 'It's so good to see you again.'

He held her hands as he studied her, his expression sombre. 'I'm only sorry that Jacob isn't here with me. But it can't be much longer, surely.'

She nodded, unable to speak as a sympathetic Yvette leaned in and dabbed at her tears with a perfumed handkerchief.

'Isabelle?'

She turned at the tentative voice to find Camille Couture smiling at her. Camile's husband, Rene, stood alongside his wife, looking out-of-sorts.

'Camille!' She bent her cheek for the other woman to kiss, disconcerted to see how matronly and middle-aged she had become. I suppose I must look the same to her, she thought.

'Marie! I'm so glad you could come!'

Isabelle glanced up at Josette's effusive words to see her taking Marie Villeneuve's coat. Marie wore a dark-coloured blouse and black skirt, her characteristic choice of colour since the execution of her husband. Her hair was drawn back in a severe bun, clasped with a plain ivory broach. She smiled politely in response to Josette's welcome, her features relaxing as she caught sight of Isabelle.

'My dear!' She regarded Isabelle with genuine warmth before embracing and holding her tightly.

Claude Charbonneau and his wife Anna, and the next-door neighbour Charles Mercier and his wife Amélie were also present as were Martin and Danielle Cloutier. The men greeted Isabelle with respect before being brushed aside by their eager wives, who embraced her with unrestrained warmth.

'We're so sorry Jacob isn't with you,' cooed Anna, the sentiment repeated by Amélie.

'Surely, they can't keep him locked up much longer?' said Danielle, echoing Denis Vachon's sentiment.

'Come, everyone, and take your seat.' Josette clapped her hands. 'It's been an age since we were last gathered like this. Sit, friends, and enjoy a glass of wine.'

As the dinner proceeded, Isabelle observed the couples, feeling keenly the absence of Jacob. Further along the table, Marie Villeneuve returned her gaze with unspoken sympathy, her face touched with the sadness that had etched itself into her features since the day she learned of her husband's execution. Isabelle smiled wanly in return.

Her gaze turned to the Coutures, noting with surprise that the husband appeared to be refraining from the wine. Is that why he appears so glum? she asked herself.

Yvette chatted merrily alongside Denis, who stared at his plate, a distant look about him that set Isabelle to wondering. Is he thinking back to the prison … to Jacob? She tried to catch Marguerite's eye amid the bustle of conversation, but her sister seemed lost in an 'air of herself' as their mother scoldingly referred to Marguerite's rare introspective moods.

The dinner conversation touched on the continuing tensions in the city as well as the likely release date of the last of the detainees, including Jacob.

'I'm sure it will be any day now,' said Josette with a consoling glance at Isabelle.

Talk then turned to the administration headed by Bernard Benoit, Claude Charbonneau remarking that the former leader of the Reformist Party had at last, 'got his revenge' on the city, that had scorned him for so long.

'I disagree,' said Charles Mercier as the main course was cleared away and dessert introduced. 'Benoit stands opposite to me politically, but I believe he wants what's best for the city.'

'Josette?' Yvette called out. 'What was that game we played last time? Something about love?'

'Oh, that. I barely remember. It really was an age ago.'

'Do let's play it again!'

A groan went up from Dominic. 'No games, please! I'm too old!'

The protest brought a chuckle from Hugo. 'Aren't we all?'

'Why not?' Josette went to the sideboard and retrieved some paper and pencils. 'Anything to stop us talking about politics.'

'Love is … politics!' called out Claude Charbonneau to laughter. 'There! I've said mine!'

'Does everyone remember the rules?' Josette retook her seat. 'You must write a sentence beginning, 'Love is …' followed by a single word. You have two minutes. Hugo, time please.'

'Wasn't it one minute last time?'

'That was when we were still young,' joked Martin Cloutier.

'And when love was so much simpler,' said Josette, the reply drawing amused laughter, which seemed to surprise her.

'Time, everybody.' Hugo's eyes were on his pocket watch. 'Begin!'

Two minutes later, he snapped the watch shut. 'Down pencils!'

'Yvette, as you suggested the game, you have the honour of going first.'

The beaming Yvette had donned reading glasses. 'Love …' she paused, 'is patience!' She took Denis' hand and kissed it as the others acknowledged the pair with applause.

'Good old Denis!'

'Anna?' said Josette. 'Or Claude—whichever one is still in love.' The *bon mot* drew laughter.

'Then allow me,' said Claude, to more laughter. 'Love,' he paused, 'is forbearance. *Loving* forbearance,' he added hastily at his wife's furrowed brow.

'Camille?'

As Camille picked up the slip of paper, her husband, to everyone's astonishment, including Camille's, placed his hand over hers. 'Please dear, allow me,' he said. She looked on with startled eyes as he turned to the table at large. 'Love,' he said, his gruff voice thick with emotion, 'is forgiveness.' He turned to his wife. 'As you have shown me,' he mumbled. And with that he kissed her rather awkwardly on the cheek.

The other guests were so surprised that they forgot to applaud for a moment. They then clapped heartily as Camille burst into tears.

Josette made eyes at Isabelle as Camille continued to weep, comforted by her penitent husband.

'Marguerite, you're next,' declared Josette. 'Follow that!' she added, drawing nervous laughter.

As eyes turned to her, Marguerite took a breath. 'Love is … compromise.'

Dominic's brow puckered. The applause was uncertain as Marguerite avoided his questioning look.

'Marie?'

Marie Villeneuve hadn't bothered to write her answer. 'Love,' she said, her voice sombre, 'is sorrow.' The response brought muted words of comfort as Marguerite reached out to rub her hand.

'Isabelle?'

'Oh!' Startled, her eyes still on Marie, she answered, 'Love is … acceptance.'

'Acceptance?' Josette's eyes crinkled.

'Can you elaborate?' asked Hugo.

'Not fair! No one else was asked to explain,' objected Marguerite.

'As you say,' he acknowledged, and turned to Josette. 'You, dear wife, get to finish, just as last time, if memory serves, you got to start.'

Josette cleared her throat, her normally ebullient manner absent. 'Love is … sacrifice.'

The reply drew surprised murmurs before a round of hesitant applause. Hugo appeared a little perplexed, but proud nevertheless, as he leaned in to kiss his wife.

As the festive mood returned, the kitchen door opened and the serving maid entered bearing a tray with two bottles of brandy. 'Hugo old chap, where did you hide the cigars!' called out Dominic.

Several toasts were made, René Couture sipping from a glass of water as Camille did the same, her expression tearfully happy as her husband clung tightly to her free hand.

The clock struck nine o'clock, the pleasant-sounding chimes inducing a momentary lull in the conversation. Denis Vachon, who had barely spoken a word all evening, swilled his wine glass. 'Hugo,' he said, his voice loud in the contented pause. 'I must say we were all very surprised by your early release.'

Hugo seemed taken aback by the remark. 'You and me both. I have absolutely no idea why they let me out.'

'After all,' said Marie Villeneuve, joining in. 'You were up there on the platform with Chaban and Joubert. My Serge was hung for the same.'

The other guests sat in silence at this sudden shift in the convivial mood.

'What are you implying?' Josette's face turned pale.

'We just all wondered—and by *we* I mean the other prisoners—why Hugo was so suddenly, and conveniently, released?'

'Conveniently?' Hugo frowned at Denis. 'What do you mean by that?'

Denis returned Hugo's stare with cool deliberation. 'I mean what inspired our notorious Captain Perrault to release you so unexpectedly, in spite of your known role as an organiser?'

'How the devil should I know? He doesn't explain himself to me!'

'Must we talk about this?' pleaded Claudette. 'Can't we just be happy Hugo was released, for whatever reason?'

'That's the point I'm making,' said Denis, his eyes still trained on his host. 'What was the reason?'

'Am I to be subjected to an interrogation at my own table?' Hugo stared angrily at Denis. Next to him, Josette sat with a petrified look on her face.

'Well?' persisted Denis, ignoring his wife as she tugged at his arm.

'Well what? What would you have me say, Denis?'

'I would have you answer the question: Why were you given early release in spite of your role as an organiser?' Denis stared with the question, his gaunt features demanding a reply.

'How dare you accuse my husband!' Josette's voice trembled as if she were on the verge of hysteria.

'I accuse him of nothing, I am simply asking a question. Well, Hugo?'

'Who the devil do you think you are? To dare cast aspersions on my name—and at my own table!' Hugo glared at Denis, who stared back, not a whit chastened by the reprimand.

'Hugo, I'm sure that Denis didn't mean to insult you,' said Andre Petain, in an attempt to soothe the brewing tempest. 'Denis, why spoil a magnificent evening. Will you not apologise to our host?'

'I will not.' Denis' voice was flat. 'I simply asked a question and am still waiting on a reply.'

'Then you may wait until hell freezes over!' Hugo slapped the table, causing the cutlery to jump.

Amid the buzz of recriminations came urgent calls for Denis to apologise or explain his remarks. 'I will not,' he repeated amid persistent calls for him to withdraw the implication.

A hush fell over the table as Hugo rose from his seat, the action drawing a gasp from Josette. 'Denis,' he began, his voice choked with emotion, 'We have been friends for a long time. Therefore, I am willing to forgive the insinuation so long as you withdraw it and, further, publicly apologise for having made it.'

'I have no intention of apologising,' retorted Denis. 'You were released while other men suffered in prison. Why?' The pointed question was aimed like a dagger.

All eyes turned to Hugo, who replied in a strained voice. 'If you will not apologize, you are no longer welcome at this table or in this house.'

The announcement drew a collective intake of breath. Denis stood up, his manner stiffly formal. 'In which case, I take my leave. Come, Yvette.'

Yvette stood to join her husband. 'I am so sorry,' she mumbled, clearly mortified at the turn the supper had taken, and speaking to no one in particular.

'Wait!' Heads turned as Marie Villeneuve stood up, the slow deliberateness adding to the import of her gesture. 'I will come with you, Denis. My coat, if you please,' she said to the open mouthed serving girl. She walked around the table to where Denis stood, refusing to look at Hugo as she passed. The three of them left the room as a stunned silence fell over the other guests.

ISABELLE TOOK A CAB home—the fare paid by Hugo—her head buzzing with thoughts of the party and the surprising turn it had taken. Denis had no right to say that she told herself, glancing out at the darkened streets. An image of Josette's face—white as a ghost—moved her to a sympathetic murmur, 'he should have spoken to Hugo in private if he wanted a reason.'

Back in the house, she made herself a cup of cocoa, still pondering the dramatic incident. Later, her toilet completed, she knelt by the bed to say her customary prayer for Jacob's safe return. The night air had turned cool, and she took a hand-sewn quilt from the cupboard and spread it over the bed cover. Turning down the sheets, she climbed into bed, her mind still dwelling on the supper. '*I am simply asking the question … They hanged my Serge! … Love is sacrifice.*'

She turned on her side, unwilling to give full rein to her suspicion. She tried to put the evening from her mind and go to sleep. But after several frustrating minutes she gave up the attempt and turned on her back to stare up at the ceiling, her mind troubled by a new and haunting doubt: Which is the greater love?

39

A Proposal and a Confession

RENÉ TURGEON, ONLY RECENTLY back on his feet following a bout of pleurisy, came to visit. He followed Isabelle into the parlour, his animated expression indicating he had some news or gossip on his mind. Has he heard about the supper party? she wondered.

Accepting a cup of coffee and a biscuit, the former deputy enquired after her health, listening with barely constrained politeness before turning to the purpose of his visit.

'I have a suggestion, my dear Isabelle. Something for you to consider. It came out of the blue while I was resting in bed. I cannot think why it did not occur to me before!'

'Do tell.' She smiled, glad to see him back in health again, although she noted a certain pallor to his cheeks that concerned her.

He sat forward, resting his hands on the brass crown of the cane as he so often did when imparting information. 'Why not publish Jacob's nursery tales as a book—under his name?' he said, his face glowing with enthusiasm. 'They would be eagerly accepted, I'm certain, and the sales would help greatly with your predicament. What do you think?'

The suggestion took her by surprise. 'But they have already been published—in the *Tribune*.'

'True, but that was twelve years ago—a lifetime in the popular memory! Besides, they were published individually, and anonymously, on newsprint. I am talking about the collected tales preserved in a proper volume with Jacob's name on the cover as author.' He leaned forward even further. 'I firmly believe that publication would be the final push we need to get Jacob released from prison. I do not wish to falsely raise your hopes, but publication of the collected tales might inspire a popular clamour sufficient to convince the authorities to set him free.'

Isabelle caught her breath at the prospect. 'Do you really think so?'

'I cannot promise, but with the pending return to full civilian governance, I imagine that the authorities are keen to put all this unpleasantness behind them and close the book, as it were, on the unrest. If Jacob were publicly celebrated as author of the tales, that would give them the excuse they need to release him. The government would win favour by appearing to bow to popular demand.'

'Then by all means, let us publish!' A thought occurred to her. 'But do you think people—the public—will still care to read them?'

'I should think doubly so! Do you not remember the acclaim when they were first published in the *Tribune*? And if we could somehow entice Jacob to contribute two or three new tales …?' He raised an eyebrow with the possibility.

Isabelle knitted her brow. 'I don't see how. After all, he is in prison.'

'But he is allowed to write letters, is he not?'

'Subject to that dreadful captain censoring them.'

Turgeon nodded. 'I understand. But there are ways,' he said, without elaborating. 'It is entirely up to you, my dear, and Jacob, of course. I had intended visiting him again this week. If you allow me, I would like to raise the possibility?'

She sat still for a moment, feeling a weight slip from her shoulders. 'My dear Monsieur Turgeon, I have every confidence in your judgement. I should be pleased and relieved to entrust the entire task to you.'

He stood up, a delighted look on his face. 'Then I shall arrange everything.' Bending, he kissed her hand. 'Farewell for now! I hope, when I return, to bring positive news.'

THE GUARD LED JACOB out of the cell area into the dimly lit corridor, the distinctive smells of horse manure meeting his nose as he followed.

'Wait!' The guard fumbled at a set of keys hanging from his belt. Unlocking the door, he stood aside to allow Jacob to enter one of the visiting rooms.

René Turgeon rose to his feet as soon as Jacob entered. 'My dear fellow!' He embraced Jacob, ignoring the frown on the guard's face. 'How are you, my friend?'

'Passing well,' answered Jacob, disappointed not to find Isabelle also waiting for him.

'You are certain?' The elderly man furrowed his brow as he took in the drawn features, thin frame, and greying hair of the former general manager of the Ferguson-Selt Automobile Company.

'It's nothing—a headache, that is all.' Jacob sat down. 'How are Isabelle and the children?'

'They are fine. I saw Isabelle but two days ago.'

'She does not want for anything?'

Turgeon tutted, his expression regretful. 'It is no use pretending money isn't tight, but she is a most resourceful woman.'

Jacob grimaced. 'Is the bank still chasing her for repayment of the debt?'

'Ah! There I might have some news,' said Turgeon, eager to take advantage of the opening. In a few brief sentences, he explained his idea, emphasising the possible financial benefits of the proposal, even should Jacob remain in prison. 'Which I doubt,' he concluded, 'once your identity as author of the tales becomes known.'

'You really think so?'

'I do. I don't see how the authorities could maintain this ridiculous charade any longer if your authorship is revealed. I urge you to consider the suggestion.'

Jacob let out a deep breath his pessimism lightening at the possibilities outlined by his friend. 'Then by all means, proceed. And thank you, Monsieur—René, for all your efforts on my behalf. And I do not doubt but that they have been strenuous.'

'One does what one can,' said Turgeon modestly. 'There is something else.' He regarded Jacob with enquiring eyes. 'It would be most useful to include two or three new tales—as an added enticement for both the publisher and potential readers.'

Jacob smiled. 'I have written them already—in my head. To endure the boredom,' he added. He glanced at the guard, who was preoccupied with trimming his nails. 'But how will I get them to you? That brute Perrault reads everything. I doubt he would permit me to pass them on.'

Monsieur Turgeon also glanced at the guard. 'You have access to pen and paper?' he asked, lowering his voice. 'Good. Then write them down, secret them on your person, and bring them with you this time next week. Don't worry,' he said as Jacob motioned with his eyes toward the guard. 'I shall arrange things. They can always use a little extra,' he added, with a conspiratorial smile.

'Time's up!' The guard approached, giving one final glance at his nails. 'Hurry up!' he complained, unhappy with one nail he had cut too close to the quick.

Turgeon rose to his feet. 'Goodbye my friend, until next week. If there's any justice, you will soon be home with your dear wife and children.' Embracing Jacob, he turned to leave, the guard escorting him to the corridor.

'You are new, are you not?' he asked the guard. 'I haven't seen you before.'

'So? What of it?'

'Nothing. Except be kind to my friend.' Turgeon indicated the room behind them. 'He is an innocent man and has many friends to defend him.'

The guard snarled. 'Do you say that as a threat?'

'No, but as a promise ...' Turgeon dug into his coat pocket. 'For your forbearance, friend.' He held up some dollar bills.

The guard scanned the empty corridor before snatching at the proffered bills.

'Then we understand each other?'

The soldier sniffed. 'We do,' he muttered, stuffing the money into his pocket.

Fired with a new sense of hope, Jacob was led back to his cell where he sat on the single chair with a sheet of paper and immediately proceeded to write out the tales he had composed in his head, using the worn mattress as a desk.

In the space of two hours, he had filled several pages. Satisfied with the results, he pulled the cot back from the wall. Kneeling, he carefully inserted the pages in a gap between the timbers. He stood up and moved the cot back into place. He then lay down, his heart beating faster as he contemplated the possibilities should Turgeon be successful in publishing the tales. 'For your sake, dearest,' he murmured, 'for your sake.'

On his next visit, Turgeon was delighted to receive the sheets of closely printed paper Jacob handed to him, the guard ostentatiously turning a blind eye. 'I shall read them as soon as I get home!' he promised. Leaving, he pressed a few dollars into the guard's hand. 'For you, friend, if I may call you such,' he said. 'A small token of my appreciation.'

The ex-deputy was in a buoyant mood as he sat down with a glass of wine in hand, eager to indulge himself in the new tales. In spite of his initial enthusiasm, his reading slowed as he took in the first tale. He stopped to sip the wine, a perplexed look on his face. He read the other two more quickly, his puzzlement giving way to a troubled frown. He laid the pages down, mulling his response, before taking them up to read again as if he might have missed something in the first reading.

'Well? What is your opinion?' he asked Hugo Gagnon the next day. He sipped from a cup of coffee as he awaited a reply.

Hugo set down the first of the tales, a look of bafflement on his face. 'It is different,' he said, still forming a response.

'Different? How so?'

Hugo tapped his fingers on the page. 'It is ... darker.' At Turgeon's encouraging nod, he continued. 'Unlike the earlier tales, this one shows a world full of cruelty, violence, and broken promises. Hardly fit subject matter for children.' He raised his eyes to the former deputy, inviting a reply.

'My sentiments, exactly.' Turgeon scratched his chin, the conundrum he faced sounding in his voice. 'And yet, the truth of the matter is still there, wouldn't you say?'

Hugo shrugged. 'I must confess to being a little disappointed. I do not understand, for example, why the owl chose to release the mouse it had only just caught in its claws?'

Turgeon's face brightened. 'I have thought about that. Surely the answer is that the owl is the voice of conscience inside the anarchy of the barn?'

Hugo considered this. 'I think it one interpretation,' he said carefully. 'However, could it not equally be argued that the owl releases the mouse only to catch and torment it again—as suggested by the final lines?'

'That would be a grim view of humanity,' conceded Turgeon, 'and go against the tolerance and wisdom displayed in the earlier tales. Although hardly surprising,' he added, 'considering what harsh abuses Jacob has had to endure. And the other two?'

Hugo returned to the loose-leaf pages and cleared his throat. 'Toussaint the Cunning Fox,' he read aloud, his brow furrowing as he continued.

Toussaint the fox was notorious for his skill in entering the most tightly guarded chicken coops in order to feast on the delicacies within. One night, however, his confidence got the better of him and he found himself trapped inside a coop by an angry farmer pointing a musket.

'Please sir, don't shoot!' cried the fox, terrified of the large gun.

'And why should I not? You have been stealing my chickens for months!'

'I am but a poor, hungry fox. I promise I will never steal your chickens again.'

'Ha! What does your promise mean to me as I can as easily shoot you as depend on your word? But …' said the farmer, lowering the gun, 'you have a reputation for cunning. If you can answer a question which has beguiled me for years, then I will spare your life.'

'Thank you, kind sir! What is the question? I shall do my best to answer it.'

'The question is this: Which is the greater mystery, life or death?'

Poor Toussaint felt his tail droop with the question. 'That is very hard to answer, sir—but I will give it a try!' he cried as he saw the farmer raise the musket again.

'Well?' demanded the impatient farmer.

Toussaint thought hard, knowing his life depended on the answer. 'Sir,' he began, 'since we come from nothing and return to nothing, why should life prevail knowing that it must end in death? The answer is because we are born ignorant of our ends. And yet, even if we knew what awaited us, surely, we would still choose to be born? The brief knowledge of blue skies, birdsong, love and hope, is all the more precious for knowing that all memory of such delights will be lost in death. In contrast, death itself has nothing to cling on to, nothing to look forward to, nothing to remember or recall. Therefore, life is the greater mystery because it triumphs, however briefly, over nothingness. And even knowing its end we would insist on being born. If there was no life, then there would be no mystery over its end. Therefore, life is a greater mystery than death.'

'Have I answered your question, sir?' He looked hopefully at the farmer.

The farmer looked at him for a long moment before setting down the gun. 'You have, Master Fox. My poor wife lies dead in our bedroom. And you have taught me that rather than mourn her death, I should give thanks for her life. Go. But do not steal my chickens again!'

'Well?' asked Turgeon, an expectant look on his face as Hugo finished reading.

Hugo hesitated. 'Surely, it is too … philosophical, for a child to grasp?'

'And?' Turgeon prodded.

Hugo sighed. 'The church will not like it. It is too …'

'Pagan?' suggested Turgeon.

Hugo looked surprised at the word but nodded. 'In a word. Certainly, the tale lacks the assurance of the blessed afterlife or any mention of God's grace.'

Turgeon nodded. '*Ex nihilo in nihilum*,' he quoted. 'Not much comfort there,' he agreed, 'for the church, or Isabelle or anybody else, for that matter. Treated as philosophy it is acceptable although hardly, as you point out, suitable for young—or pious—minds. See what you make of the third.'

Hugo picked up the remaining sheet. 'The Chicken and the Fox,' he read aloud.

The tale started out in the bright, breezy manner of the earliest fables, but halfway through it took a darker turn, Ferdinand the chicken bitterly questioning a predatory fox on the nature of existence.

'You wish to eat me, but I am no threat to you,' Ferdinand pleaded, appealing to the fox's better nature.

'I do not eat you because you are a threat,' laughed the fox. 'I eat you because I am hungry!' And with that he gobbled down the poor chicken.

And the moral of the tale, dear reader? Foxes and men do what they are predisposed to do, and no amount of pleading will alter the nature of either! For neither prayer nor good-natured optimism can protect the innocent from this implacable truth: foxes will always eat chickens, no matter the fine words or cherished beliefs of the chicken.'

Hugo took off his reading glasses and put them on again before clearing his throat to offer an opinion. 'Could Jacob not alter the moral?' he questioned. 'Make it more suitable for children?'

Turgeon shrugged. 'I asked him as much. His reply was, 'This one is not meant for children. It is written for grown-ups.' I protested. I told him it violated the spirit of the earlier tales and was hardly suitable for inclusion. I pointed out that the weight of the tale presses overmuch on the final lines.'

'And what did Jacob say?'

Turgeon made a rueful face as he recounted Jacob's reply to his objection.

'But is it not true that foxes will eat chickens?

Why, certainly. I did not mean to imply otherwise.

Then chickens would be well advised to bear this truth in mind whenever they encounter a fox, would they not? Instead of trying to argue the fox out of its nature, they would do far better to flee.'

The former deputy gave a worried sigh. 'I fear captivity is taking its toll on Jacob. It is no wonder the tales lack the freshness and optimism of the originals, given what Jacob has gone through. The grave injustice he is suffering would surely colour one's view of the world.'

'But did you ask him why the tales must be so pessimistic?'

'I did indeed. I urged him to think of Isabelle and her feelings.'

'And what did he say to that?'

'He simply said she would understand, which she may, but it would affect her all the same. However, the tales together—what is your opinion?'

'I don't think you should publish them,' advised Hugo. 'They may confuse and alarm innocent minds, especially when compared to the earlier tales.'

Turgeon tugged his chin. 'You are right, of course. It would be a mistake to include them.' He thought for a moment. 'Perhaps they could be published separately, in the *Catholic Tribune*?' He brightened. 'You know, that might be a good idea. We could title them along the lines of 'Letters from Prison', for instance.'

Hugo gave a bleak smile. 'That would certainly invite interest. Will you show them to Isabelle?'

'Only if she asks. I fear they would distress her and lead to alarm over Jacob's state of mind.'

'Which is?'

Turgeon hesitated, as if debating with himself whether or not to reveal a confidence. 'Uncertain,' he said finally. 'I spoke to the prison doctor following my last visit. A good man by the name of Lapointe. He has examined Jacob and could find no obvious cause for the headaches. But he suspects that the bullet fragment still lodged in his head after all these years is the likely cause.'

A look of horror crossed Hugo's face. 'What? He knows about that—the bullet wound?'

'Yes. Jacob must have mentioned it. Why?'

'Nothing.' Hugo gave a heartfelt groan. 'It is just so tragic—on top of everything else.'

'I agree. But that is life, my friend.' Turgeon's expression turned sombre. 'Sometimes, as I get older, I think our sorrows are all that we have.'

Hugo's face was full of anguished self-recrimination as he recounted the conversation to Josette. 'Still, after all these years, my sin comes back to haunt me!' His voice trembling, he looked to her in desperation.

'I should have told him at the time, confessed my action. It would all be behind me now. What a fool I am!'

Josette looked up from the dried flowers she was arranging into a wreath. 'Darling, you did the right thing. You have been a loyal and constant companion to Jacob all these years. He could not have asked for a better friend. Do you not think that repays the debt?'

'Debt?' He stared, his eyes filled with horror. 'Then you *do* think me at fault?—as I am!' His voice rose to a semi-wail. 'And if the doctor is right, I may end up killing him yet!'

'Stop this!' said Josette firmly. 'Torturing yourself won't help Jacob. What happened was an accident. I'm sure even Jacob would agree.'

'You don't think I should confess—tell him?' He gazed at her, his face shadowed with guilt.

'I think you should forgive yourself and not breathe a word. What he doesn't know can't hurt him.' She set aside the wreath. 'Shall we have a glass of brandy before supper?'

He nodded, still pale at his crime. 'Perhaps I should talk to Father Chatelain about it?'

'If it helps. But my advice?'

'Yes?' He looked up, a hopeful spark in his eyes.

'Say a prayer, instead. Or light a candle at mass. Or save it for the confessional—if you think it safe.'

'Good God! Surely you don't believe a priest would betray a sacred confidence?' He looked shocked at the suggestion.

She regarded him, a sad look on her face. 'My dear, he is human. Why not?'

IN LATE AUTUMN, RENÉ Turgeon arrived on Isabelle's doorstep brimming with the news that he had found a publisher for Jacob's nursery tales.

'They promise an edition by the spring!' he declared, happily accepting a cup of coffee and enthusing at the plate of chocolate biscuits.

Sharing his delight, Isabelle poured coffee for herself. 'Who?'

'Pardon?'

'Who will publish them?'

'Oh! The Provencher brothers, on rue Matelot. Are you familiar with the family? They own the Three Rivers publishing house. It is a small, family-owned business that has been operating for half a century. And they are loyal habitants, fierce defenders of old New France.'

'What did they say? Tell me all!' She moved the sugar bowl closer to his cup.

'Let me see …' He added sugar to the coffee, basking in her curiosity. 'I spoke to the older brother, Andre—he is the one responsible for the print list. And my dear Isabelle,' he said, drawing out the words, 'I must tell you he was absolutely delighted to receive the opportunity. Both he and his brother were huge admirers of the tales when originally printed in the *Tribune*. Indeed, Andre confessed that they had often wondered why no one had proposed publishing a collected edition before now.

'I tell you,' he added, his expression varying between cheerfulness and solemnity, 'this can do nothing but good for Jacob. Once the tales are published and the public at last know the identity of the author, the demands for his release will be impossible to ignore.' He sat back in the chair, his eyes twinkling. 'What do you think of that?'

'Jacob will be over the moon. Thank you, my dear Monsieur Turgeon, for all your hard work in achieving this.'

'Hard work? Nonsense! It was a labour of love, I assure you. The tales deserve nothing less.' He dunked a biscuit in the coffee, extracting every morsel of flavour from his success. 'And there is more!' With a teasing smile, he took a bite of the sodden biscuit. 'The brothers intend taking out large notices in both newspapers to announce the release. As well, they will paste posters around the city to declare the event. Why, Andre even mentioned the possibility of advertising on the side of city trams. Can you imagine?'

'Have they set a firm date—for the publication?'

'It is hard to be exact with such things. They promise only by sometime next year.'

Brimming with the news, she shared it with Louis and Marie-Odile at supper. 'Your father will be a published author,' she announced, slicing a loaf of bread. 'Won't that be nice?'

'I thought he already was,' said Louis, busily cutting his food.

'That was the newspaper, silly!' Marie-Odile rolled her eyes at such unworldliness. 'This will be a proper book, just like Madame Bovary.'

Isabelle suspended the knife in surprise. 'You have read that?'

'Oh, mama!' Marie-Odile sighed theatrically. '*Everyone* has read it.'

'I certainly haven't. Have you, Louis?'

'Never heard of it. May I please have another potato?'

'Have you honestly not read it, mama?'

'Certainly not. I have heard that it is scandalous.'

She went to bed that night aching to share the news with Jacob. How proud he will be! It will give him something to look forward to after all these years. The reminder of the unjust nature of his imprisonment soured her optimism. Eight years! Eight years of happiness denied! The injustice was like salt in her mouth. She felt a twinge of jealousy at the thought that Hugo and Josette had enjoyed that time together, raising their children, dining with friends, getting on with life. And all because … If I were another woman … if I were Madame Bovary …

She felt sinful even to consider the prospect. *But that is what life is*, a voice argued. *Life is a marketplace where everything may be bought, sold or traded. Foolish not to accept this. Think of how easily you might have avoided these eight years of wretchedness!*

Her conscience, nourished on stained glass, candles, incense, the crucifix and daily catechism under the eagle eye of Sister Ursuline, rose up in rebellion at such a view, one which struck her as dreary and impoverished.

In Jacob, she had discovered—miraculous given their different backgrounds!—a soul-companion, someone who, despite his resistance to religion, intuitively understood, she was certain, the numinous presence bubbling beneath the material surfaces of life. It was fidelity to the holiness of this presence, to its sacramental nature, that gave her the strength to suffer through the injustice of his absence; to create a satisfying meal from scraps; to scrub the slate floors uncomplainingly; to smile and endure and to love. *'Love is sacrifice.'* Only not the sacrifice she now felt certain Josette had offered up, but sacrifice of a different, finer sort.

Josette's sacrifice had been for earthly love. But there was another, higher sacrifice, one that surrendered to divine love; that resisted the easy way; that yielded, with unwavering faith, to the holy presence infusing all things; a presence that would, in time, enfold Jacob, the children, and herself in its merciful embrace. What were eight years compared to eternal blessedness?

Her fingers closed on the crucifix around her neck, and she said a prayer, beseeching forgiveness for her sins, for her pride, for her preoccupation with worldly matters, for her love for Jacob that, intense as it was, sometimes blinded her to the source of that love. 'Amen,' she murmured, warm tears in her eyes.

The light from a passing cab reflected briefly on the ceiling as she whispered a prayer that Jacob might somehow find a path to God's ineffable grace. 'Shine your face upon him, Lord,' she prayed, her eyelids growing heavy. 'Bless him with dew from Heaven.'

SHE KNELT AND CROSSED herself in the dimly lit confessional. 'Forgive me, Father. It has been one week since my last confession.'

The voice behind the darkened grille intoned a response as she gripped the rosary between her fingers. She had chosen this out-of-the-way church in the suburb of St. Agathe to finally make her confession for the sin that had so tortured her that she had repressed it from conscious thought. But still it broke through in nightmares, in bouts of agonised shame as images popped into her head, and in silent weeping when she sat alone in her boudoir.

'Yes?' The voice prompted.

She bowed her head. 'I did something so that my husband might be released from prison where he was being unjustly held.'

'What did you do, my child?'

She strained her ears. *Did she recognise the voice?* Telling herself to remain calm, she took a deep breath. 'I sacrificed my virtue,' she whispered, overcome with shame.

'In what way?' The voice sounded genuinely puzzled.

'Must I say?' Riven with anxiety, she hissed the words.

There was silence on the other side of the grille. She waited in agonised suspense for the voice to resume.

'And do you repent of your sin?'

'With all my heart!' She burst into tears.

There was a further silence before the voice spoke again. 'Then recite the rosary ten times, donate to the poor box, and pray for absolution. I also will pray for you, my child.'

Her body shook as the voice began the familiar invocation, her lips following along. '*Deinde ego te abslovo a peccatis tuis in nomine Patris, et Filii, et Spiritus Sancti. Amen.*'

'Amen,' she sobbed, experiencing a profound spiritual agony in the darkness—in *her* darkness. The unseen presence behind the grille remained silent as she wept into her handkerchief, inconsolable in her contrition.

40

A Certain Dormouse

I T WAS A LOVELY spring morning in 1929, so lovely that Isabelle almost forgot her cares. She had just finished taking in a dress for madame Chernier when a knock sounded on the door.

'Bright star, arise! Bring on the day!' monsieur Turgeon declaimed cheerily as the door opened. In spite of the mild morning, he was wearing his heavy winter coat, a scarf around his neck, and a fur hat perched on his head. Isabelle laughed, overtaken by fondness for his pink cheeks, twinkling eyes and merry expression. The cab that had delivered him drove away with a toot of its horn, the sound seeming to her to blend somehow with the cheerfulness of the twittering birds and the blue spring sky.

'Forgive me, my dear,' said her visitor, bestowing a kiss on each cheek. "Tis my childhood Latin. It has been sounding in my head ever since I woke up this morning. Over my croissant I thought of nothing save the green pastures and rolling meadows of Virgil and Horace.'

'Is it not strange,' he asked, still pursuing the thought as she helped him off with the heavy coat, 'that the older one gets, the younger the thoughts one thinks? A moment, if you please!' Before she could hang up his coat, he took from the pocket an object wrapped in brown paper and tied with string. 'I come bearing a gift, although not of the Greek sort,' he said, continuing his theme as he held the package.

'You are cryptic this beautiful morning,' she teased, leading him into the parlour. Indeed, the morning was so fine that even the drab room with its musty wallpaper seemed to glow with an unaccustomed freshness.

'Coffee?'

'In a moment, my dear. But first, please sit down!'

Amused, and not a little intrigued by his barely concealed excitement, she sat down as directed.

'I have it! *Res ipsa loquitur*. The thing speaks for itself!' With a triumphant smile, Turgeon flourished the small package before handing it to her.

Confused, she felt the contents of the parcel beneath her fingers. Her eyes widened as the realisation struck her.

'Jacob's book!'

'Indeed, it is!' Her visitor chuckled with anticipation.

Carefully undoing the string and paper, Isabelle exposed the slim volume encased in green leather. 'Goodness!' Thrilled, she stroked the grain cover and the gilt title, "The Collected Fables of Jacob Wheeler." She caressed the words with her fingers, tears filling her eyes.

'Open it!' urged the former deputy, barely able to restrain his pleasure at her response.

She did so, turning to the frontispiece: "Thirty-four original fables by the esteemed author." She murmured with delight at the full-page wood-cut illustration of Jacob's head above an ornate mantlepiece adorned with images of various creatures from the fables. 'Hector the cockerel! Lisette the wise owl … the little dormouse … and Edouard the goat!' She laughed with happiness as she held up the page to share with the beaming Turgeon. She was about to ask the name of the artist when her eye fell on the inscription on the facing page. 'Illustrations by Alois Giroux'?' She looked up in wonderment.

'A surprise!' Turgeon laughed, his face flushed with animation. 'There are more!' He said, urging her on.

Each fable was prefaced by an engraving of the creatures it described. 'Gracious!' she exclaimed, her breath taken at a finely detailed etching of Celeste the duck flapping indignantly at a rival in love.

'Happily, monsieur Provencher spared no expense,' said Turgeon, leaning forward to admire the illustration. 'He is determined that the volume will make the name of his house known far and wide.'

She turned to the first fable, caressing the page with her fingers as she read aloud. 'And so it happened that a certain dormouse …' She was unable to continue, overcome with tears.

Moved at her emotion, Turgeon laid a consoling hand over hers. 'I read the entire volume at a sitting. Such wit! Such wisdom! The foibles of humanity caught as in a lens!'

Isabelle released a deep sigh, her fears for Jacob temporarily forgotten in the splendours of the illustrated volume. 'It is marvellous! Utterly marvellous! Dear Monsieur Turgeon, how shall I ever thank you?'

'Please, dear. I insist you call me René. It is my name, you know!'

She smiled through tears of gratitude. 'I couldn't. It wouldn't seem right. All my life I've known you as Monsieur or Deputy Turgeon. Mama would turn over in her grave! But the book—has Jacob seen it?'

'My dear Isabelle that pleasurable task belongs entirely to you. Jacob gave me authority to approve all aspects of publication on his behalf, so the book will be as much a surprise to him as it is to you. You must bring it along with you on your next visit. If it raises his spirits half as much as it has raised yours, then I could ask for no greater reward. And now, if you don't mind, to more practical matters.' He sat back, his eyes on her. 'The publisher intends a first print run of two thousand copies.'

She gasped at the figure.

'I know,' he said happily. 'A remarkable first print run, but the brothers have great confidence that readers of the newspaper versions will snap it up. And good reviews and word of mouth will do the rest,' they assured me.

'The book will be released in either September or October. I had hoped for an earlier date, but monsieur Provencher tells me they have a backlog of publications to clear. However, he is so confident they will sell he is already planning a second run. Hopefully, you should begin to see royalties within six months of publication.'

Overcome with emotion, she jumped up from the chair and bestowed a kiss on his brow. 'I cannot wait to see Jacob's face!'

AS SOON AS JACOB sat down, Isabelle reached into her bag and handed him the book. 'Monsieur Author!' She laughed at the look of surprise on his face. With wide eyes, and darting the occasional disbelieving glance at Isabelle, he turned the pages, every bit as moved by the handsome volume as she herself had been.

'It is even better than I had hoped!' he exclaimed. He pored over the pages, enchanted to see his little 'nursery tales' in print. His eyes swimming with gratitude, he kissed her hand. 'Thank you, darling!'

'Thank dear monsieur Turgeon! He has spared no effort in bringing it to print.'

'I will, of course. When is he coming to visit?'

She was leaving when a guard approached, an older man with a scarred cheek, whom she had noticed on previous visits. 'The commandant wishes to see you, Madame. He said to tell you he has urgent news to discuss concerning your husband.'

She froze, appalled at the shameless audacity of the man. 'Tell the captain,' she said, trying to control her emotions, 'that he can go fish in the river!'

Sequestered back in his cell, Jacob read the volume from cover to cover, his heart filled with pride. He caressed the volume, felt it in his hand, rubbed the spine, held it to his nose and pressed it against his cheek before opening it again to admire the workmanship. He chuckled with delight at how well Giroux had captured the various creatures and their expressions.

He read through the index, stopping at one point with a puzzled frown. Where were the newest tales?

The omission perplexed and disappointed him for a brief moment, but he could not indulge in the feeling for long, pleased as he was at the result. Perhaps it was right not to include them, he conceded, they are different in tone. And with that, he opened the cover and read through the entire contents again.

IN LATE SEPTEMBER 1929 "The Collected Fables of Jacob Wheeler" was released to popular and critical acclaim. The news soon penetrated the walls of the barracks, eliciting astonishment and congratulations from Jacob's fellow prisoners who stopped to shake his hand and express their surprise at the revelation that one of their own was the mysterious author of the familiar tales.

'I was certain it was a priest!' exclaimed one prisoner in the exercise yard shortly after professing his amazement that Jacob was the anonymous author, 'perhaps even the bishop himself!'

'Why, you dark horse!' said another, coming up to seize his hand. 'I remember my father reading the tales aloud from the *Catholic Tribune* as we all sat around. My father and mother argued for weeks over who the author could be. It almost drove them crazy trying to figure it out. And it was you! All this time!'

The prisoners treated him as a celebrity, flocking around in admiration as he showed his copy. 'Read to us!' insisted Roland, the demand taken up by the other prisoners. Happily acceding to their requests, Jacob read aloud as they listened with attentive faces. 'The duck!' A man shouted after he had finished the tale of the dormouse. 'Give us the duck tale!'

He obliged, reading in a dramatic voice, and finishing to applause. He was surprised to notice three or four of the guards edging closer to listen. No sooner had he finished reading the tale of Celeste, the lovelorn duck, than he was besieged with requests for other favourites.

'Hector the cockerel!' a voice shouted, followed by another voice demanding 'The billy goat and the apples!' After reading both tales he pleaded tiredness and put the volume in his pocket to cries of disappointment. 'I will read again tomorrow,' he promised as his fellow inmates jostled to shake his hand and clap him on the shoulder. Accepting their congratulations, he happened to glance up. Captain Perrault stood at an upper window staring down at the scenes in the yard, an intensely vindictive look on his face.

The guards, too, became aware of the captain's surveillance and at once sprang into action, needlessly harrying and bossing the prisoners under his venomous stare. 'Back to your cells! Hurry up, over there. No talking! Form a line!'

The next morning, Jacob returned to his cell following a turn around the exercise yard—and more backslapping congratulations—to discover the precious volume had disappeared from under his mattress. Alarmed, he set up a hue and cry, thinking a prisoner had made off with it. His commotion attracted the attention of the guards, who cursed him and gave warnings to 'shut his mouth!' When he continued to complain bitterly, Desmarais, the guard whom Turgeon had paid off, took him aside to whisper that the captain had ordered the book be seized and brought to him. 'Doubtless you will be hearing from him—for better or worse,' he cautioned.

And sure enough, shortly after dinner, he was summoned to Perrault's office, Lieutenant Charest appearing at his cell door to escort him.

'So, it's true then—that you are the author of the *Fables*?' Charest asked as he led Jacob through the corridor leading to the captain's office.

'It is,' answered Jacob, curious to note a subtle change in the other man's demeanour.

Perrault was lounging in a chair, his feet up on the desk, the green leather volume in his hand. 'Ah! Wheeler!' He glanced up from reading as Jacob was escorted into the office.

'Sit down. You never let on you were the author,' he said affably , holding up the book. 'You sly old dog!'

Jacob said nothing, on guard for the ever-present malice underlying the deceptive bonhomie. Perrault read aloud from the book, ostentatiously chuckling to himself. 'And so it happened that a certain dormouse, fed up with being cold and hungry for the winter, ventured into the house of a rich man who owned a cat …' He stopped.

'Charest. It's cold in here. See if you can't do something about that fire.'

Surprised by the request on such a warm day, Charest took a moment to respond. 'Right away, sir.' He went to the door and stuck his head outside to call someone.

Perrault read a few more lines. 'Charming! And this?' He pointed to the illustration. 'What do you think, Monsieur Author?' Jacob declined to answer, now certain the affected amiability was a prelude to some other stratagem or turn of mood. At his silence, the captain's cheerful air evaporated. He returned to the volume, reading to himself for a few minutes and ignoring Jacob as if digesting the affront. As he read, turning the pages, his expression became thoughtful and then disapproving.

He glanced up at Jacob before returning to the book, frowning as he read. 'I see now what you're up to,' he said, tossing the volume onto the desk. 'Clever fellow!' A thin sneer formed on his lips as if daring Jacob to deny whatever it was being suggested.

Determined not to rise to the bait, Jacob maintained his composure, averting his gaze from the mocking eyes.

'Do you think you could fool me?' goaded Perrault. 'Charest, this murderous anarchist thinks he can fool the whole world with his clever lies.' He leaned forward. 'Well? Answer—or you'll pay for it!'

Unwilling to risk provoking the captain unnecessarily, Jacob mumbled a reply.

'What's that?' The captain cocked his head, a menacing look on his face 'I asked if I am suspected of some wrongdoing?'

'Wrongdoing?' Perrault huffed with indignation. 'What else do you call corrupting the minds of children?'

'Corrupting minds!' Jacob stared in bewilderment. 'What the devil are you talking about?'

The captain scratched his cheek at the outburst. 'I'm talking about your seditious little tales.'

Jacob glanced at Charest and then back at Perrault, too genuinely perplexed to respond.

'Do not pretend you are ignorant of what I am talking about.' Perrault picked up the book. 'This tale of the farmer and the apples for instance—' he turned to the page, 'is nothing less than a manifesto of lies and propaganda.'

'It's a story about a goat!'

'A very particular kind of goat, wouldn't you agree? A *habitant* goat, perhaps?' Perrault studied Jacob's face for a reaction, 'and a rich, bourgeois landowner? Tell me, Wheeler, are you a revolutionary—like those frightful fellows in Russia?'

Before Jacob could answer, the door opened, and a fellow prisoner entered bearing some logs and kindling in his arms. With a glance at the captain for permission, he knelt down before the grate and began building a fire. Perrault waited a moment before lolling back in the chair to read aloud from the book.

"On a bright spring morning a goat, let us call him Edouard, trotted into the orchard of a wealthy apple grower and began to eat the apples he found

lying on the ground. He was enjoying himself when he heard a dog bark and a man shout. 'You!' The farmer came over to where Edouard stood, a half-eaten apple still clutched in his jaws. 'You are stealing my apples!' The farmer's face was crimson with anger as he confronted Edouard. His dog stood beside him, growling and snarling, and looking as if he might, at any moment, tear Edouard apart.

'I am sorry, sir' said Edouard, dropping the apple from his jaws in fright. 'I did not mean to steal. The apples, after all, were lying on the ground and starting to rot.'

'It doesn't matter where you found them—on the tree or on the ground—they are my apples,' said the angry farmer, 'that do not belong to you, and yet you feast on them as if they were your own!'

The dog snarled menacingly …"

Captain Perrault stopped reading as the prisoner building the fire stood up.

'Will that be all, sir?' the man asked nervously. A fire burned in the grate.

'Yes. Get out!'

As the man left, he locked eyes with Jacob, his frightened look seeming to vindicate Jacob's suspicion of the captain's motives.

"Now, where were we? Ah, yes!' The captain continued reading in an attentive voice as if genuinely curious to see how the tale would unfold.

"Edouard swallowed his fright as he answered the farmer, his voice quavering in the way of goats. 'Sir, I am sincerely sorry for eating your apples. How may I repay you?'

The farmer tugged at his chin as he considered the question. 'You can repay me by wandering through my orchards and picking up every fallen piece of fruit that you find. You will put the fruit in that empty bin. Do you understand?'

'Yes sir. I shall begin at once.' Edouard was about to begin when a thought struck him. 'What will happen to the fallen fruit, sir, once I have collected it and placed it in the bin?'

'They will feed the pigs or be mulched into compost,' said the farmer. 'Not that it is any of your business!'

'Then could I not equally well eat the fallen fruit?' asked Edouard. 'I have some goat friends who are hungry and who will gladly join me in this.'

'Why should I feed you and your lazy goat friends!' the farmer demanded, glowering at Edouard.

'Sir, is it not more charitable to feed a hungry goat than to put to waste all those spoiled apples?'

'Charity!' The farmer bellowed the word as the dog growled. 'Do I look like I am running a charity for goats! Start collecting the rotted fruit or I shall set Bully here on you!' The dog snapped its jaws, foam dripping to the grass.

Edouard bleated with fear. 'Sir, have you never been hungry?' he pleaded. 'If so, you will understand why I ate your apples. Can I not appeal to your good conscience?'

The farmer gave a mocking laugh, but then grew thoughtful. 'I'll give you a chance. If you can answer my riddle, you may eat as many apples as you like. But if you cannot,' his voice turned menacing, 'then you must agree to work for me for the rest of the season collecting fallen fruit. Do you agree?'

Edouard thought hard for a moment. 'Yes,' he said, for he prided himself on solving riddles.

'Good! Then answer me this.' The farmer's eyes gleamed. 'Is it better to be a farmer or a goat?' The riddle caught Edouard by surprise—"

'Me too!' jested Perrault, looking up. 'And Charest, too, I see!'

Jacob glanced at the adjutant, who was following along with the story, an absorbed look on his face. At their combined glances, the soldier coughed and stood up straight.

'It's alright, Charest.' The captain smiled indulgently. 'Let us see what happens to poor Edouard!' His eyes flicked to Jacob for a moment before he began reading again.

"Edouard thought furiously as the farmer, a gloating look on his face, waited for an answer.

'If I say a farmer, he will agree at once,' reasoned Edouard to himself. 'If I say a goat, he will demand to know why the goat is better off than the farmer.' He thought carefully about the riddle under the impatient eye of the farmer and the panting glare of the dog.

'Well?' The farmer demanded. 'What is your answer?'

'The answer, sir,' said Edouard, 'is that the goat is better off being a goat, and the farmer being a farmer.'

'What kind of trickery is this?' demanded the farmer. 'That is no answer at all!'

'Sir, consider our positions. You are the farmer, who owns this wealthy orchard. Surely you are happy with that?'

The farmer scowled, his eyes suspicious. 'Yes, I am. Better be me than you!'

'Exactly. But suppose our positions were reversed, and I was the rich goat that owned the orchard, and you were the hungry farmer eating the apples?'

The farmer considered this. 'I suppose I would rather be the one who wasn't hungry.'

'In other words, the goat?'

The farmer frowned. 'I suppose so, if that were the case—but it isn't!'

'But sir, I am unravelling the riddle,' answered Edouard. 'The answer as to which it is better to be—the farmer or the goat—depends entirely on who is the hungry one or not. Do you not agree? In other words, you are asking whether it is better to be well-fed or starving? And the answer is obvious—it is better to have a full belly than an empty one. That is the true answer to your riddle. Not whether it is better to be a farmer or a goat, but whether it is better to be fed or starving.'

The farmer thought long and hard about Edouard's answer. Finally, he could see no recourse but to give in. 'You win!' he said. 'Eat as many apples as you like!' And with that he whistled the dog and left Edouard to feast happily on the fallen apples.

And the moral of the tale, dear reader? A full belly is better than an empty one. And many seemingly complex and difficult questions in the world can be reduced to this simple truth!"

The captain chuckled without humour and closed the volume. 'Clever Edouard saved his neck!' Getting up, he warmed his hands at the fire. 'You are, of course, familiar with parables,' he asked, his back to Jacob. 'Yes?'

'Yes, I am familiar. But I don't see—'

'Then you will know that parables illustrate a moral, just as your fables do. And the morals your stories make are consistent, I'll give you that.' He turned to face Jacob, rubbing his backside. 'The wealthy are always the enemy of the poor and innocent. Landowners are always rapacious, untrustworthy, willing to allow the virtuous, simple habitant to starve, as with Edouard, as with the dormouse, as with Reynard the fox. Meanwhile, religion is mocked, as in the tale of Hector the cockerel. You are a true follower of Karl Marx.'

'Ridiculous!' In his annoyance the word slipped out despite his vow not to engage in the captain's games. 'You twist and torture the meaning to make a false point. Children do not read such perverse meanings into them.'

'Not at first,' Perrault conceded, as if concerned to appear reasonable and just. 'But through subtle repetition, they ingest the propaganda infecting the so-called simple tales.' He studied Jacob, his manner judicial as though playing the role of magistrate. 'One might say they are corrupted by what they consume, the poison concealed in an agreeable dish.'

Jacob stared, dumbfounded. 'You cannot be serious?'

The captain made a humming sound as if pleased to have not only established his point, but ready to expose all to the attentive Charest. 'If the stories are as innocent as you claim, then why did you deny your authorship? Ah, yes. I know about that!'

Too flummoxed to reply, Jacob sat in silence as the captain crossed his hands behind his back, his face stern as he wrapped up the case. 'Surely, you must have reasoned that the tales were not all that they seemed. That you had, in fact, good reason to hide your identity as their author?'

'Not so,' said Jacob, suddenly weary of the cat-and-mouse fencing. 'May I go? Or do you intend reading back more of my own stories to me?'

He thought he saw a tight smile cross Charest's face. Captain Perrault, too, had glimpsed it. He stiffened. 'Wait!' he barked as Jacob got to his feet. Going back to the desk he picked up the volume and tossed it onto the fire. 'Now get out!'

WITHIN A WEEK OF its release, the entire first edition of the Fables sold out as the printer hastily expanded the second run to 3,000 copies. These, too, sold quickly, the *Catholic Tribune* promptly anointing Jacob the most successful author in New France's history: "A third print run is already underway, with orders coming from booksellers and readers right across the province. Plans are also underway to release an English-language version of the Fables." The newspaper did not hesitate to blow its own horn as "the original publisher of the inspired tales." It ran a separate story on Jacob's exposure as the author, admitting to its own surprise that "a person better known for manufacturing automobiles should be revealed as equally adept at manufacturing such charming creations."

The *Daily Register*, not to be outdone, glossed over the original publication, focussing attention instead, on its 'explosive popularity', and opining on the implications of this celebrity for the jailed author's future:

*It is a matter of considerable embarrassment to the authorities that such
an acclaimed author remains locked up in prison on an unproven and,
many claim, unfounded charge of murder. In spite of fresh demands for his
release, the authorities are strangely reluctant to accede. The government
of Quebec insists on passing the onus to the federal government, which
just as adroitly swats it back again by declaring the affair, 'strictly a provincial matter'. Since when did human rights become a purely provincial
affair? The whole city stands behind monsieur Wheeler in his fight for
justice. A new voice is that of monsieur Bernard Benoit, acting as interim
Administrator. Perhaps sensing a shift in the wind, the latter now declares
his late fidelity to the notions of justice. 'I have long condemned monsieur
Wheeler's arrest as a travesty of justice and do continue to condemn it
in the strongest terms,' he said. 'Progress ought not be at the expense of
justice and the individual's right to a fair trial.' Meanwhile, the entire
country watches and waits.*

A few days after Jacob's confrontation with Perrault, Charest entered
his cell carrying two volumes of the *Fables* in his hand. 'I do not agree
with what the captain did,' he said, his voice respectful. He held out one
of the volumes. 'This is for you, Monsieur, to replace the one burned by
the captain.'

Deeply moved, Jacob accepted the volume. 'Thank you, Lieutenant. It
is very kind of you.'

'I am a great admirer of your tales, Monsieur Wheeler,' said Charest,
using the formal address for the first time. 'I purchased a copy for my daughters as soon as they became available. I should be most appreciative, sir, if
you would sign it and include their names.' He held out the second volume.

Stunned, Jacob stared at the soldier. 'You wish me to sign it?'

'Yes, if you would.' Charest cleared his throat in some embarrassment.
'It would mean a great deal to them, as it would to me.'

'I am happy to oblige.' Reaching up he accepted the pen offered by
Charest. He grimaced as he opened the cover. 'You are certain your daughters will not be corrupted by my little tales?'

Charest glanced around before replying. 'There was only one corrupter
in that office, Monsieur. But do not underestimate the captain, for your own
safety. He is a very dangerous man.'

Jacob nodded. 'I assure you, Lieutenant, I need no convincing of that.
Now, what are the names of your daughters?'

41

A Strange and Fragrant Air

THE WINTER OF 1930 was regarded by older inhabitants of the Quarter as the coldest in living memory. Pipes froze, services were disrupted, and several homeless men were found frozen to death in the street. In an unprecedented step, the Old Town Market was closed for a week as the citizens battled blizzards and snow-filled streets to get to work. Inside number 24, rue Marguerite Bourgeoys, Isabelle kept the fire blazing around the clock, relying on sacks of coal supplied by Hugo, René Turgeon, Denis Vachon, Andre Petain and others.

Seamstress work had all but dried up in the winter freeze, and she was reduced to dependence on the moneys contributed by her children, plus the monthly rental cheques sent by Jules Desjardins. For two weeks she was unable to visit Jacob, tram services having been suspended due to snow and ice on the rails. Inside the draughty house she wore her coat, wool hat, scarf and gloves to keep warm. She made several trips to the corner store to pick up essentials as food supplies gradually diminished due to the severe cold.

One morning, as she struggled against a bitingly cold wind while carrying two bottles of milk, a loaf of bread and a dozen eggs in her basket, she slipped on a patch of ice. Her feet were whisked out from under her, and she fell heavily, striking her head on the snowy sidewalk as the breath left her body.

'Hello! Who are you?' a voice was calling. She opened her eyes, trying to remember where she was. To her surprise, the air was warm and bright. A bearded stranger dressed in buckskin had laid hold of her shoulder.

'Where am I? And who are you?' She opened her eyes, dazed and blinking in the sunlight.

'I found you lying here in the grass, fast asleep. Don't you know that's dangerous? Anyone could have come along and discovered you. An Iroquois buck might have taken a fancy to those pretty locks.'

The stranger helped her sit up. 'Who are you?' she repeated, frightened at his strange appearance.

'Me? I'm Gaston Tremblay. This is our settlement.'

'Gaston Tremblay?' She closed her eyes to clear them but only succeeded in filling them with blue sky, grass, and the bearded man kneeling next to her.

'How are you here?' she asked, greatly confused and thinking she must be dreaming.

'How?' He laughed, showing stained teeth. 'Because I am, that's how! What happened to you?' he asked, noticing some blood on her hair.

'I must have hit my head on the ice.'

'Ice?' Frowning, he examined her head, probing carefully with his fingers. 'You've a fine lump there. It feels like an egg! Can you stand?'

He assisted her to her feet. A sickly feeling rose in her throat, and she moaned, thinking she might faint.

'Steady! Take your time. You've taken quite a knock.'

Leaning on his arm she looked around, perplexed to see thick forest on three sides. On the fourth, just behind her, a broad flowing river sparkled in the sunlight. 'What river is that?' she asked, feeling faint again.

'That? It doesn't have a name. It's just a river.'

'It's the Mercier, I think,' she said.

He looked at her strangely. 'If you say so. I suppose that name is as good as any other. Although I did think of calling it after myself! And why not? After all, I led the families here. It's a fine place for a settlement, don't you think?' He gestured at the surrounding forest. 'Fresh water, lots of firewood, good farming land when its cleared. We even have our own flour mill. And best of all, we are far away from those motherless bastards in Montreal. What is your name, Mademoiselle?' He was looking at her strangely once again.

'Isabelle.' She looked wonderingly at the smooth, unwrinkled skin on her hands and wrists.

'Isabelle who?'

She had to think for a moment. 'Isabelle Tremblay,' she said.

The bearded man frowned. 'Is that a joke?'

'No, I assure you. It was my mother's maiden name. My father's name was Ouellet.'

'Ouellet? We used to have a cook by that name.'

'Then perhaps …' She gasped as another wave of dizziness swept over her and clutched his arm for support.

'Come on,' he said, easily supporting her. 'Let's get you to the healer.'

'Healer? You have a doctor here?'

He laughed. 'Doctor? This is not Montreal! There's a heathen who fixes bones and delivers babies. She's proven herself knowledgeable at curing all kinds of ailments.'

'Delivers babies? You mean a midwife?'

'She answers to that title as well.'

Isabelle stopped in amazement. 'The midwife's here?'

'Perhaps.' He muttered with irritation. 'She comes and goes as she pleases. Maybe she's here, maybe she's back with the Iroquois. Who knows? Come on, this way.'

He assisted her through grass buzzing with summer insects. She leaned heavily on his arm, weak from the blow to her head. They went past a screen of woods toward a group of 20 or 30 log buildings clustered around a large clearing. Pigs and goats grazed on the grass and skinny mongrels wandered back and forth. She heard the sound of hammering from an unseen forge. Men clad in long shirts and breeches with wool stockings turned to stare. Some wore moccasins instead of shoes. One or two were dressed in buckskins like her rescuer. All wore wide-brimmed hats. The women were dressed in stays, lace caps, neckerchiefs, and petticoats covered by an apron. Several half-naked Indians sat cross-legged before an open fire. Trying to ignore the stares, she held her breath as they passed a rack upon which were hung a dozen pungent-smelling pelts with tails attached. 'What are they?'

'Those are beaver hides. There are lots of them around here.'

As they passed through the settlement, they attracted a throng of curious onlookers.

'Who is this, Gaston?' a man asked, approaching to stare at Isabelle. 'And where did she come from?'

'I found her lying in the grass. She's taken a blow to the head.' The statement evoked murmurs of alarm. More men and women appeared, her unusual appearance provoking a flurry of questions.

'How did she get here?'

'Is she alone?'

'Who is she?'

Isabelle shrank back under the frank stares.

'A helpless young woman, can't you see? Now stand aside!'

He escorted her through the onlookers towards a cabin situated before the line of woods. The curious crowd followed, staring suspiciously at Isabelle and peppering Gaston with questions.

'Where did you say she was from?'

'Was she a captive? Will the savages come looking for her?'

'How the devil did she escape?' A thick-set man with a balding head thrust himself into their path.

'Go count your bags of flour, Samuel Benoit!'

The retort drew laughter as well as an affronted glare from the man addressed.

As they approached the cabin, a woman wearing a linen cap stepped out, a hand shading her eyes as she investigated the disturbance.

'Marie!' Gaston crooked an arm in summons.

The woman hurried towards them. 'Merciful Jesus!' She stopped, her eyes wide as she took in Isabelle from head to toe. 'What have we here?' The onlookers fell silent to listen.

'This is Isabelle. She was struck on the head.'

The woman's astonishment turned to an expression of concern.

'What happened, pet? Did you escape from the heathen?'

'I …' Isabelle struggled to recall. 'I don't quite remember.'

'Then don't fuss, dear.' The motherly woman took hold of her other arm. 'Let's get you inside out of the sun. Help me, Gaston.' The woman turned a scolding look on the others. 'Do you not have work to do? Is it a holy day?'

Between them, the woman and Gaston escorted Isabelle to the cabin. She felt nauseous as they assisted her inside and sat her down in a chair.

'Are you not overly warm, miss?' The woman gestured towards Isabelle's scarf, coat and gloves. 'They are curious garments to be wearing on such a warm day.'

'I am …' She struggled to take off the heavy coat.

'Let me help.' The woman helped her off with the coat. 'There, that's better. My, it's a fine, heavy coat.' Her eyes lingered on Isabelle's embroidered blouse and long, winter skirt. 'Fine clothes altogether,' she said, a suspicious look on her face. 'You didn't escape from the heathen, did you?'

'It doesn't matter where she came from. What she needs now is to rest. I'll be back when you're feeling better, Mademoiselle.' Gaston opened the door, surprised to find three or four people still gathered outside, gossiping to each other. They fell silent at his irritable look. 'Have you never seen a young woman before? Go about your business!'

'Shoo! Be off with you!' the woman exclaimed from behind. 'Go gawk at yourselves in the pond.'

She closed the door. 'Don't let them bother you, lamb. It's just that its most unusual to see a young woman alone in these parts. Did you say your name was Isabelle? I am Marie Therese Pepin. My husband is Joseph. He's a farmer—when he's not busy hunting.'

The woman suspended her evident curiosity as she took in Isabelle's feverish pallor and trembling hands. 'But there I go, chatting like an orphan with a new toy. Wait but a wagtail and I'll dish you up some fine stew.'

The log walls of the small, one-room cabin were rough and untreated, the scent of pine mingling with the smells of cooking and woodsmoke. A fire blazed in the stone hearth. An iron pot was suspended above the flames. The woman bent over the pot and stirred the contents with a ladle. She handed Isabelle a wooden bowl, heaped with stew. 'There, get this inside you, pet.'

Isabelle was ravenous and ate hungrily as Marie sat down, a look of unquenchable curiosity on her face. 'I don't know how you came to be lying in the grass—unless that be one of Gaston Tremblay's tall tales! Can you tell me more about where you are from and how you came to be here?'

Isabelle shook her head, her mouth full of the rich stew. 'Pardon.' She looked for something to wipe her mouth on and wiped it with her hand. 'But I really don't remember. I just woke up and found myself here.'

'Blessed Mary!' The woman crossed herself in fright. 'Are you a witch?'

'Witch? Good God, no. There aren't any such people.'

'Oh, there be!' The woman eyed her suspiciously. 'Do you belong to the Church?'

'Yes. I attend twice or three times a week.'

'And can you recite the Lord's prayer?'

'I can. Would you like me to?'

'No. I see by that Cross around your neck that you are no witch. 'Tis said witches and demons cannot bear the feel of a crucifix.'

'The stew is excellent,' said Isabelle, to divert the woman from talk of witchcraft.

'Aye.' Marie beamed at the compliment. 'If it's not immodest to say so. Your garments be indeed strange,' she said, reaching out to run a hand over the coat that seemed to fascinate her. 'Is this from Paris? It looks so fine. And pure wool, I'll be bound.'

'I made it myself.'

'You did?' The woman exclaimed in surprise as she examined the coat. 'We could use a seamstress with such fine skills. But here am I, prattling on while you sit white as a ghost! Why don't you sleep for a while? You look fair worn through.'

Isabelle nodded, surfeited from the meal. 'Perhaps I will. Thank you for the food.'

'Such fine manners! Careful!' Marie took Isabelle's arm as she stood up and led her to a bed against the wall. 'Lie there. You'll be quite safe.'

Isabelle lay down, closing her eyes in exhaustion as the cabin began to spin about her.

She awoke to the sounds of her hostess fussing over a tub filled with water as she washed some clothes. Bright sunlight streamed through the single opening cut into the logs. 'What time is it?' she asked, looking around. She was surprised to find herself lying on a bearskin near the fire.

Marie looked up from the tub. 'It be morning, lamb. You slept right through the day and night. You must have been altogether drained. My husband carried you there as we needed the bed.' She dried her hands on a strip of cloth. 'How is your head?'

Isabelle put a tentative hand to her scalp. 'Better, thank you.' She looked around the small cabin, a sense of strangeness overwhelming her. 'Where am I again?' she asked, thinking perhaps she was still dreaming.

'You be here—in the village. We don't have a name yet, although Gaston would doubtless like to call it after himself.' She chuckled. 'That man and his schemes! Now, come and eat some bread and milk.'

Isabelle ate a small mouthful of bread and took a sip of the milk, grimacing at the earthy taste. 'I am eager to explore your settlement,' she said, wiping her mouth. 'It looks … special.'

'We've been here less than seven years, but made fine progress,' said Marie proudly. 'We be on good terms with the heathen and trade with them for our wants. And there's plenty of deer in the woods and fish in the stream, so we be well placed. But there's not much to see apart from the other houses. Are you sure you feel well enough to go walking?'

'I am. Thank you.' Isabelle got to her feet, pleased that the feeling of dizziness seemed to have passed.

'Then I'll accompany you.' The woman regarded Isabelle's blouse and skirt, a dubious look on her face. 'Mayhap wear a light shawl,' she said. 'It wouldn't do for you to be mistaken for a witch.' She took off her own shawl and handed it to Isabelle. 'Not half so fine as your coat, but good enough. And you'll need a cap, can't have you going out half dressed.' She placed a white linen cap on Isabelle's head, tucking her hair into place before tying the ribbon. 'One more thing,' she said, and picked up a patterned neckerchief, which she placed around Isabelle's shoulders under the shawl, using a pin to secure it to her blouse. 'There. Now you be respectable and won't attract so many stares.'

They set off, walking through the grass towards the other buildings. Now that she felt better, Isabelle's eyes were everywhere at once, taking in the blue sky, the log houses, and the scent of spruce and pine that pervaded the air.

'Everything smells so fresh!'

A great flock of ducks flew overhead, and she shaded her eyes to observe their flight.

They approached a woman digging outside a cabin. The woman straightened up as they drew near, a pitchfork suspended in her hands. 'Who is that with you, Marie Pepin?' The woman observed Isabelle with suspicious eyes.

'A friend!' Marie dragged Isabelle along without stopping.

'What do you mean, a friend? Where did she come from?' The voice followed, sharp and demanding.

'Here and there!' Marie tutted in annoyance. 'Never mind her, pet. That's Agathe Benoit. She has the longest nose in New France.'

'Benoit?' Isabelle looked back at the figure, still gazing after them. 'I think I know her. Or her daughter—or grand-daughter,' she said in confusion.

Her newfound friend laughed merrily. 'I should hardly think so! Her youngest is less than six-years old, if I remember rightly. But she has a cousin,' she added, 'who is a young lady like yourself.'

They continued into the main settlement. The buildings were uniformly constructed of crudely cut logs and wood shutters. Most had small gardens attached as well as chicken coops. Pigs, dogs and the occasional goat wandered freely in the grass clearing. They heard the sound of metal clanging on metal as they neared a forge.

'That be Henri Giroux, the blacksmith,' said her companion. 'Always tinkering with things, like his father before him.'

Isabelle saw a tall rangy-looking fellow bent over an anvil, the hammer momentarily silent as he examined his handiwork. A man seated on a log cleaning a musket touched his forelock as they continued. 'Good afternoon, Madame Pepin—and to your young friend.' He stared at Isabelle as she passed.

'Norman Beaulieu,' said Marie. 'A nice-enough fellow but he takes these strange fits that scare the wits out of his family.'

'Is there someone called Gagnon here?'

'Gagnon? You know him?' Marie looked at her in surprise.

'Just the name.'

'Well, I can tell you there is indeed a family by that name, headed by Pierre Gagnon. He was married just three months ago to Monique Allemande. 'Tis rumoured she was two months with child at the time of the marriage, but I pay no attention to such gossip. And here be our church.' She stopped before a primitive log building topped by a heavy Cross consisting of two logs lashed together. 'Father Roussin agreed to accompany us from Montreal provided we built him a church, which we did. It was the first building we put up.'

'Is that an arrow?' Isabelle shaded her eyes to look up at where a shaft protruded from the cross-piece.

'You have sharp eyes, young Isabelle. An Iroquois war party, not the local ones, attacked us last autumn. We drove them off, but not before one of the devils fired that projectile up there. Father Roussin insisted we leave it in place as proof of God's will to defy the heathen.'

'Father Roussin,' she repeated, determined to remember the name.

They came to a store house, its door open to reveal sacks of provisions inside. A man was taking an inventory, calling out items to a young boy who noted them down in a ledger. 'That's Samuel Benoit,' said her companion 'husband to Agathe. He's a merchant who tagged along in hopes of making a fortune in furs. Pierre Gagnon accused him of cheating people over the price of flour. They had a falling out over it and have been on bad terms ever since.'

Isabelle couldn't help but giggle. 'They still are!'

'What is that you say?' Her companion stared.

'Nothing. Where is Gaston?' She asked, looking around.

'Up to mischief I'll be bound. Hunting or gambling or drinking, or all three. Founder, my arse!'

Isabelle blinked in surprise. 'But he is … I mean was …' She stopped in confusion. 'But did he not found the settlement?'

Marie sniffed. 'He says he did, often enough. More like it were chance or fortune. We were coming down the river in a dozen canoes when one of the heathen guides pointed out this spot. Gaston took it as a sign. "Onangwatgo says this is a good place to settle!" he told everyone when we had pulled ashore. But my Joseph, who understands heathen better than any man, told me that the savage was really pointing out the spot where he once took a most tremendous shit!' She laughed heartily. 'But don't you never say a whisper of that to Gaston! He thinks the fellow was divinely inspired!'

Isabelle chuckled in spite of her mortification. 'Nevertheless, he's a great man,' she said. 'They will put up statues in his honour.'

'Gaston? How do you know this?' The other woman looked at her with the same alarm she had displayed earlier when thinking Isabelle a witch.

'Oh! It's something I dreamed,' said Isabelle, hastily.

Her companion shook his head. 'You are a strange one of that there is no doubt.'

'What is that flower?' asked Isabelle, admiring a tall plant with bright pink flowers.

Marie shook her head. 'The good Lord knows. Everything is so new we haven't had time to name them yet.'

'Gaston said there was an Indian healer, a midwife?' Isabelle remembered.

'Oh! Her! A talkpot. She does gab on.'

'Can you describe her? What does she look like?'

Her companion looked nonplussed. 'Like any other heathen, I suppose.'

'Is she fat?'

Marie chuckled. 'What a question? I suppose one might well say she is on the plump side. Oh, and she has a fresh scar on her cheek.'

'Scar?'

'She claims it were a bear. But I reckon she scratched it while looking for blackberries.'

'And she's not here now?' Isabelle looked around in disappointment.

'Oh, she'll turn up like a bad penny as my husband is fond of saying.'

They walked into the clearing, curious heads turning to observe their progress. A small crowd, including five or six Indians, was gathered around a makeshift stall and appeared to be bargaining with the stall holder.

'What are they doing?'

'Once a week, the people bring eggs or chickens or sundry items to trade with the heathen for skins or furs.'

Overcome once again by a sense of strangeness, Isabelle turned in a half-circle to take in the noise and activity of the settlement. She felt light-headed, her senses assailed by the smells, the inquisitive stares cast her way, the freely wandering livestock, the log buildings, and the fragrant air laden with the scent of pine.

'Are you feeling alright, dear?' Marie was examining her, a concerned look in her eyes.

'Yes. It's just all so—'

'Hello again!' Gaston Tremblay wandered up, a musket slung over his shoulder. 'So, Mademoiselle Tremblay, what do you think of our little habitation?'

'Tremblay!' Marie looked from Gaston to Isabelle. 'Are you related?'

'We are,' Isabelle confirmed proudly. 'Gaston is my great ancestor.'

'The blessed saints preserve us!' Marie crossed herself, a frightened look on her face.

Gaston frowned. 'You should mind how you talk. People will get to thinking you're a witch or touched in the head.'

'But it's true! "I sing the matchless deeds of a hero bold, and chant of a city that shall never be old," she quoted. 'That's written on your tomb.'

'Christ in Heaven!' Marie blessed herself again. She gripped a cross around her neck, her eyes wide with fright.

Tremblay appeared confounded, a look of alarm on his face. 'What is this talk of tombs?' He eyed Isabelle, suddenly suspicious. 'Were you deliberately planted in the grass as a trick by that old fox Jean Talon? Did you come here to spy on his behalf?'

'No!' She looked at Marie, whose rosy face had turned pale. 'I don't even know the man. Forgive me. I get carried away sometimes. It was the knock to my head,' she said, concerned to allay their suspicions. 'It makes me ramble and say foolish things.'

After a pregnant pause, Tremblay nodded slowly. 'That must be it,' he said to Marie. 'She was out cold when I found her.'

'Then you ought watch your tongue, silly girl!' Having scolded her, Marie gave a nervous laugh. 'Such talk will have people thinking you belong in the lunatic asylum.'

'I'm sorry. I promise I'll be more careful from now on.'

'See that you are.' Gaston scratched his chest. 'It's devilish hot,' he said, looking around. 'I could drown a mug of ale.'

'Goodness!' Isabelle put a hand to her brow.

'What is it?' Gaston reached out just in time, catching her as she collapsed into his arms.

'MAMA!' MARIE-ODILE WAS SEATED on the bed, rubbing Isabelle's hand. 'Mama, are you awake? Can you hear me?'

'Gaston?' Isabelle opened her eyes.

'He's not here. You had us so worried! Monsieur Lamont found you lying in the snow. You had hit your head. He and another man carried you home. The doctor has been to examine you. He says you must rest. He gave us some medicine for you. Would you like a spoonful?'

Blinking, Isabelle looked around the dimly lit room, startled to find herself at home. The curtains were drawn shut, but she could see daylight outside.

'I had a dream,' she said. 'I think it was a dream.'

'You were unconscious when they brought you home!' Marie-Odile's face crumpled, and she started to cry. 'I thought you were dead!' She sobbed into a handkerchief as Isabelle sought to comfort her.

'Hush, darling. I'm fine. I have a strong head—like your grandmother!'

'Marie-Odile, you talk too much. Let mama rest,' said Louis, entering the room.

'It's cold!' said Isabelle, wondering where the blue skies and sunshine had gone.

'We sent a message to Aunt Marguerite. She will come as soon as she can.' Marie-Odile dabbed at her eyes. 'I told you not to go out, Mama. Louis and I will fetch whatever you need.'

'Hello!' They heard a voice and the sound of someone climbing the stairs. Marguerite entered, her face flustered as she scolded Isabelle while removing her coat. 'You gave us all such a fright! You had no business being outside in such dreadful weather!' She kissed Isabelle and adjusted the pillow, her eyes moist. 'Such a fright!' she repeated.

Isabelle put up with a procession of worried visitors for the rest of the day, each one expressing concern while she protested her health, insisting it was 'just a little bump'.

Hugo and Josette arrived bearing a potted poinsettia and a big bowl of habitant soup. Josette fussed and oohed, while Hugo, his hair now grey, reproached her for leaving the house unassisted.

'The streets are covered with ice. You should know better.'

'I'm all right,' insisted Isabelle, 'good as new.'

The visit was interrupted by an announcement from Louis that the Vachons were waiting downstairs. Hugo rose immediately, a frown on his face. 'Come, Josette. It is time we were leaving.'

Isabelle heard the couples pass in the downstairs hallway, a brief and stiffly formal greeting the only communication between them. She heard footsteps on the stairs followed by a cautious knock on the door.

'Yvette! Denis. Come in.' She sat upright in the bed. 'Come see the silly woman who knocked her head in the street.'

THE NEXT MORNING, HER daughter came into the room, a smile on her face. 'Mama, look who's here!' She stood aside as an anxious Gaston entered.

'Mama! I came as soon as I could.' Bending, he kissed her brow and sat down on the bed taking her hand in his. 'How are you feeling?'

Smiling, she reached out to stroke his cheek. 'You look just like him!'

'Who? Papa?'

'Where is he?' She looked past him at the door.

'He's still in prison. Don't you remember?' He cast a worried look at his sister.

In the afternoon, René Turgeon came to visit, bearing chocolates and a bottle of wine. 'I bring news,' he said, after enquiring into her health and giving a detailed account of his own tumble the year before.

'I was blessed not to crack my head open!' he recounted, as if still astonished at his good fortune. 'Ever since, I inch sideways down the streets like a timid crab. If it were not for a cab, I would not be able to come today.'

'What is your news?' she reminded him.

'Ah!' He beamed at her. 'I am very pleased to tell you I had a telephone call today, from a friend in the Quebec government.' He waited while she took this in, a slight frown on her face. 'Well,' he continued lightly, 'it seems that the government has ordered a total amnesty for all those remaining detainees, including, of course, Jacob.'

She stared at him, unable to speak, a look of mingled joy and disbelief on her face. 'When?'

The former deputy gave a regretful sigh. 'Saint-Jean-Baptiste Day, I'm told. Some idiot politician decided that releasing the prisoners on the anniversary of the massacre would symbolically close the chapter on the tragedy. Still,' his voice grew more cheerful, 'at least we know he will be released. And Saint-Jean's is only five months away.'

Her lips trembled and she started to cry. 'At last!'

NEWS OF THE LATEST amnesty sparked an outpouring of joy among the prisoners. The guards, too, seemed to relax, knowing that the inmates would soon be set free. Finding out the release date was the question on everybody's lips. Jacob approached Charest with the question, accosting the latter one morning as he crossed the yard.

'Saint-Jean-Baptiste Day, not before.'

'Why then? Why not now?'

'Orders. Don't ask me why.'

'But Perrault—he knows of my wife's ill health?'

'He does. And—' Charest held up a hand. 'I know what you're about to ask. Save your breath. It won't be a minute sooner. I told you, the captain has a long memory for insults.'

'But surely—if I see him? Apologise even …?'

Charest sighed heavily 'You will only disappoint yourself. Better to wait. It is only a few more months.'

'Then I'll appeal directly to the premier.'

To his surprise, Charest shrugged, 'Why not? You are a famous author. That may count in your favour.'

'I need to write a letter—on proper stationery.'

Charest glanced around. 'I'm sure your friend the former deputy would be happy to oblige. Aye, and to post it as well.'

Back in his cell, he immediately began to compose the letter, stopping every now and then as Hugo's account of Isabelle's accident returned to jar him with fresh anxiety.

He finished the letter—composed on assorted scraps of paper—bidding René Turgeon to write a formal letter on his behalf. 'You may attach this note, with my signature on it,' he wrote, and waited with mounting impatience for the next visit day. As he paced up and down the cell, he heard a commotion coming from the exercise yard. A moment later, three or four guards rushed past in that direction. He heard furious shouts and strained to see through the narrow window set in the door.

'What's happening?' called out Roland from the adjoining cell.

'I don't know.'

A new voice from a cell with closer proximity to the yard was pitched with excitement. 'There's a fight in the yard! I think someone attacked a guard!'

A few minutes later, they saw a guard, supported by two of his comrades, helped past the cells. The wounded man's face was ashen, blood streaming from his neck as he limped between his fellow guards. 'What happened to him?' Roland called out.

'Shut your mouth, you!' one of the guards snarled as he passed.

It was the next morning before they learned details of the attack. 'It was the new inmates,' a prisoner revealed. 'I was exercising when I heard a shout. Next moment, two of those scoundrels from the Blocks,' he said, referring to a notoriously crime-ridden part of the city, 'had ganged together and attacked the guard. You know the fellow … Zuchin, the big oaf with the scar under his eye?'

'Is he alright?'

'Who knows? He was bleeding like a stuck pig. His comrades beat the attackers black and blue. They may have killed them both.'

'What's the matter?' Jacob eyed Roland, who was stroking his chin, a worried look on his face.

'Let's hope this doesn't affect the amnesty,' answered Roland.

'Surely, it won't? It wasn't the politicals, it was the criminals who attacked the guard.'

'I wouldn't put anything past that dog, Perrault.'

Two days later, Jacob sat in his cell awaiting his turn to be called to the visitors room, the scribbled notes in his pocket. He leapt up in anticipation as the cell door was unlocked.

'Wait!' The guard rudely pushed him back. 'No visitors today. The captain's orders.'

'But why?' He stared in shock. 'Has something happened?'

The guard muttered as he scanned the cell, his eyes flicking over the few objects on the table. 'Who knows? Perhaps he spilled his coffee or stubbed his toe.' Satisfied that everything was in order, he left, bolting the door behind him.

Jacob heard angry shouts from other cells as the news spread that all visits were cancelled.

'Jacob! Can you hear me?' It was Roland's voice. 'Didn't I warn you? Give that vile pig any excuse!'

Stunned, Jacob sat on the cot, trying to comprehend the decision. Getting to his feet he paced the small cell, his shock giving way to mounting anger. This is deliberate! The vile creature has somehow guessed at my intention. But how could he? Unable to contain his desperation, he banged furiously on the cell door. 'Guard!'

It took the intervention of Demarais before he was granted his demand to make a complaint. The soldier escorted him across the yard and halted outside the door of a small office. 'Tell your deputy friend he owes me!' he hissed before knocking.

'Monsieur Wheeler.' Charest stood up as he entered, a weary look on his face. 'I've been expecting you.'

'But where is Captain Perrault?' asked Jacob, puzzled to see Charest in his place.

'He has gone into the town, no doubt to get drunk and … Anyway, he left me to deal with you. And I must say, Monsieur, before you even ask, he left the strictest instructions.' Charest shook his head in apology. 'And the answer, I'm afraid, is no.'

'No to what?' Jacob could barely restrain his anger.

Charest sighed. 'No, to everything.'

'MAMA, ARE YOU FEELING alright? Can I fetch you something?' Marie-Odile was peering at Isabelle, concern on her face. 'You were mumbling to yourself.'

Her mother was propped up in a chair before a blazing fire. 'I don't remember falling asleep,' she said, wrinkling her brow in puzzlement. The clock, the window curtains, the discoloured wallpaper, and her daughter's face all perplexed her.

'Are you cold? Shall I build the fire?' Marie-Odile rearranged the blanket across her mother's knees.

'There's no need to fuss.'

'And you have had no more headaches?'

'No,' she lied. 'It has been a week, and my head is fine.'

'Did you take the medicine Doctor Soulet left for you? He said you must take it every four hours.'

'Oh, doctors! They fuss over nothing. It was just a little bump on the head. I have more faith in the midwife.'

'Who?'

'The Indian midwife. You don't remember your father and I discussing her?'

'No, I don't. Marie-Odile tutted, concerned that this might be one of the symptoms the doctor had warned her to watch out for.

'You really don't remember?' Her mother looked at her in dismay. 'She warned me of this.'

'Who did? Warned you of what?'

'The midwife. She said people would forget. And something else. Something important.' She furrowed her brow to think before moaning in frustration. 'I can't remember!'

'Mama, please try to nap for a half-hour. You need your rest.'

Isabelle sighed. 'I must ask your father on my next visit. I wish he were here.'

'Don't you remember? He's coming home. They're releasing him.'

'They are? When?'

Marie-Odile stifled a feeling of alarm. Was this another symptom? 'Not yet Mama, but in a few months. The doctor telephoned the prison and asked for father's release to be brought forward on compassionate grounds, but the commandant refused. Monsieur Turgeon was outraged and is writing to the minister in protest.'

It seemed to Marie-Odile that her mother listened without understanding, a fact that increased her alarm.

'What was it she said?' Isabelle had a vexed frown on her face. 'It was when I was in her cabin that time, with your father.'

'Whose cabin? Who are you talking about?' Fighting back tears, Marie-Odile got to her feet. 'Perhaps I should send for Doctor Soulet?'

'I know!' Her mother's face brightened. "Remember not to forget!" Her expression turned doubtful. 'Or perhaps it was 'don't forget to remember." She glanced dubiously at her daughter. 'They mean the same, don't you think?'

'I'm sure they do, Mama. Now you really must get some rest.'

42

Ubi Sunt

ON A DAY OF weak sunshine, Isabelle insisted she felt well enough to attend Mass at the cathedral. Marie-Odile walked on one side, Louis the other, each supporting an arm.

'I'm not an invalid,' she protested, although secretly pleased at the concern they showed. She carried a bouquet of flowers in a small wicker basket. They walked up rue Sainte-Anne under an aisle of budding sugar maples before crossing to rue Mi'kmaq. Midway along the street, Isabelle stopped before a bronze statue raised on a pedestal and read the familiar legend: "Henri Giroux, first blacksmith in New France, a founder of the nascent settlement."

'It doesn't look like him,' she said, gazing up at the statue. 'He didn't have that beard, for one.'

She missed the startled exchange of glances between Louis and Marie-Odile. 'Your father was a sort of founder too,' she announced as they continued. 'After all, they found him in the woods.'

'Mama?' Marie-Odile's voice was hesitant. 'Are you sure you are feeling alright?'

'Quite sure.' Isabelle smiled as she patted her daughter's hand. 'And spring is here at last. Aren't we lucky?'

Following the service, she led the protesting Louis and Marie-Odile around the back of the cathedral to the graveyard. 'You should be home before the fire,' objected Louis. 'You'll catch cold.'

'Just a few minutes,' she said. 'I haven't visited your grandparents in a while.'

They made their way between the crowded headstones and memorial statues in search of the Ouellet family plot. Most of the granite headstones were cracked and discoloured, their inscriptions barely legible. Some leaned at precarious angles, a century and a half of weather and shifting soil contributing to the decay. Some graves also displayed footstones, the inscriptions inviting observers to pause, read and ponder.

Isabelle stopped before a faded headstone overgrown with grass and weeds. 'Marie Charbonneau, Claude's grandmother,' she said. 'Mama never trusted her. She claimed her ears were oddly shaped.'

They had barely continued before she stopped again. 'Fleur Dubois,' she said, crossing herself. 'She was your great aunt. I remember she used to wear a ghastly blue hat she found in a milliner's shop on rue Gaspard. It was quite hideous.'

'Norman Benoit,' she said, pausing before a grave with a stone angel raised above it. 'The Church finally stopped allowing statues because they take up too much space—everyone wanting a bigger one than their neighbour's. But the Benoits bribed the bishop to allow this last one.' She sighed. 'And to think, it all came from flour.' Marie-Odile glanced at Louis, who shrugged.

Isabelle halted before a very old headstone with a crack running down its granite face. 'Marie Therese Pepin! It can't be her, surely? The dates are wrong,' she said, peering at the faded inscription. 'Perhaps it's her granddaughter.'

'Whose granddaughter, Mama?'

'Marie Pepin's! Didn't I just say?'

'I count at least a dozen with the same date of death,' remarked Louis. 'Look, there's another, 1919. Was it the war?'

'The Spanish flu, I expect,' said Isabelle. 'It was dreadful. So many died.'

They continued past a cluster of headstones before Isabelle paused again, a pensive expression on her face. 'Your great-grandparents,' she said. 'They insisted on being interred in the same grave.' She brushed a cobweb from the headstone. 'I barely remember them. I was so young when they died—tragically, in a house fire.' Crossing herself, she said a prayer before moving on to the neighbouring headstones.

'Mama!' she exclaimed. 'And Papa. How I miss you both!' Taking out the flowers from her basket, she knelt and laid a knotted bunch on each grave. 'We've just come from the service,' she said, standing up to explain. 'Mama, you would have liked the sermon. Father Langlois spoke about the old days in New France and about how it used to be before this dreadful business with the government started. Do you remember Charles Dupont, the butcher's son—from avenue Montaigne? Well, he died, poor thing. They say it was a heart attack. His wife found him and had the most dreadful shock. And Papa, they've raised the price of bus tickets again. I know, shocking. I can hear you say it.' Her voice broke and she began to sniffle.

Marie-Odile leaned her head into her mother's neck. 'Don't cry, Mama.'

Louis was silent, contemplating the inscription: "Odile Francine Élise Ouellet (née Tremblay) 1857–1913 Be faithful unto death, and I will give you the crown of life."

'Do you remember your grandmother?' Isabelle asked her daughter.

'Not really. I think I remember her telling me off.'

Isabelle smiled through tears. 'That was mama!' Bowing her head, she stood in silent prayer. Marie-Odile followed her example while Louis, bored, gazed around at the forest of headstones.

'There's no more room,' he said. 'It's full up.'

'Almost.' Isabelle contemplated the overgrown plot that neighboured her parents'. It was littered with sticks and leaves from the windy spring weather. 'This is where I shall lie, and your father beside me.'

'Shall we go? This is morbid.' Marie-Odile fidgeted, uncomfortable with the conversation.

'Why? It's natural. Your grandfather reserved those plots many years ago. He had to outbid René LeBeau as they were the very last plots available. I remember Francine LeBeau was very upset and accused the bishop of favouritism.' She took out a handkerchief to blow her nose. 'The Ouellet name meant something in those days.'

'Mama, please can we go?'

Isabelle exclaimed suddenly and bent to examine the fresh shoots of grass poking through the dirt.

'What is it?' asked Marie-Odile.

'Do you know what that is?' She scuffed the grass with the toe of her shoe.

Her daughter stared at the spot, a frown on her lips. 'Grass? What else?'

'That's grass, but this over here is a plant.' Isabelle indicated with her toe. 'Do you know what it is?'

Marie-Odile stooped to observe. The young plant had small, elongated leaves and reddish-green stems.

'It's fireweed,' Isabelle said before her daughter could hazard a guess. 'And there's more.' She moved to the next headstone. 'And here, too. I never noticed before,' she said wonderingly. 'It's everywhere.'

'So what Mama? It's just a weed.' Marie-Odile glanced at Louis for help, but he was just as perplexed as his sister.

Isabelle was observing her mother's headstone, her face despondent. 'We shall all be forgotten—in a few short years after our deaths.' She spoke softly, as if to herself. 'It's the way of things. Even our headstones won't remember us.' There was a sadness in her voice that made Marie-Odile want to burst into tears.

'How can you say that? I won't forget you. Not ever! Nor will Louis, will you Louis? See! There's no need to upset yourself.'

Her mother extended a gloved hand to stroke her daughter's cheek. 'I know you won't, darling.' Her tone was wistful, her eyes forlorn as the long-ago voice cooed—or crooned, perhaps, in her ear. '*In the end, even love and the memory of love will be forgot.*'

'I HAVE TO GO out and buy some bread and milk. Will you be alright by yourself?'

'Of course! I'm not a child. I may have that nap now.'

Marie-Odile smiled. 'Good. Louis will be home very soon. And I'll be back as quick as I can.'

'Be careful! It's wet outside.' It had rained heavily overnight, the spring storm leaving puddles of water in its wake.

'Don't worry Mama. And stay warm. There's a chill in the air.'

She pretended to be asleep as her daughter put on her hat and coat, coming in once more to check on her. A few moments later she heard the front door close. Waiting another minute just to be sure, she turned back the blanket and got to her feet. She held onto the chair for a moment as a wave of dizziness overtook her. *I must hurry, before Louis gets home.*

She took the number 17 bus to the outskirts of the city. Pleased to be out of the house, she observed her fellow passengers, bundled up against the unseasonable cold, and the passing scenes outside the window. She was as happy as a child taking its first journey unsupervised by an adult.

To her surprise, instead of terminating at the city limits, the bus continued on past the old stone walls and past rows of streets lined with houses. Her hand reached for the bell cord before she put it down again, puzzled at the suburban maze.

'What happened to the woods?' she asked the woman seated next to her. The woman looked at her strangely but didn't answer. Standing up, Isabelle pulled the cord.

'There used to be nothing but woods,' she said, irritable at the woman's disapproving face.

She watched the bus pull away, standing back to avoid being splashed. The sky was grey, and a light drizzle began to fall. She faced around, bewildered by the rows of houses that met her on all sides. Momentarily confused, she set off, following the tarred road. The rain became heavier, and she scolded herself for her carelessness in not bringing an umbrella. She stepped in a puddle of water and tried to prevent herself stepping in with her other foot. Too late! Grumbling at the feel of her cold, sodden shoes and stockings, she continued on up the street. She walked for a quarter hour, unable to find shelter in the rain, her wool hat now soaking wet. *Marie-Odile will be cross with me.*

Undecided whether to turn back, she pressed on as the rain stopped and the sky cleared. Ahead, she spied a woman sweeping water away from her doorstep. 'Good morning,' she said as she approached.

The woman looked up, taking in the elderly woman, her face frail and fatigued-looking. 'Are you alright, Madame? Are you lost?'

'I was looking for the midwife. Have you seen her?'

'Midwife?' Concerned, the woman set aside the broom. *The poor old thing was confused. What would she want with a midwife?*

'There are no midwives around here, dear. Are you sure you have the right address?' *Perhaps she should call her husband or alert monsieur Albert, who had an automobile? He could drive the woman home—if she remembered where home was.*

Isabelle turned this way and that, a distressed look on her face. 'What happened to all the woods?' she asked, her lip trembling.

'There are no woods here, Madame. There haven't been for at least twenty years. And as for this midwife, I've never heard of one around here.'

'She was Indian. She gave me a necklace.'

'Indian?' The woman wanted to chortle but didn't. 'There are no Indians around these parts. Maybe a hundred years ago! Would you like to come in and sit down? Perhaps have a cup of tea? We have a telephone,' she said. 'I could call someone to come and fetch you.'

The woman, who was kindly, reached out for the old lady's arm as she paled and appeared to sway on her feet. 'Come inside, Madame, you must be half-drowned.' Worried for the woman's health she noticed her wet shoes.

'Goodness! Come sit by the fire and dry your feet.'

'I should find the midwife. But there are so many houses.' The elderly woman's face was fretful as she looked around at the residential street.

'Of course there are. This is a housing estate, what did you expect? Come on, come inside.'

FRANTIC WITH WORRY, MARIE-ODILE summoned her uncles and aunts from the public callbox. Louis had taken off to search the surrounding streets, full of remorse for having lingered on the way home. Marie-Odile was standing outside on the footpath, anxiously awaiting Aunt Marguerite, when an automobile approached, slowing as it drew nearer before stopping right in front of the house. And seated in the front, looking worn and frail, was her mother! 'Mama!' Bursting into tears, she ran to open the vehicle door.

In spite of her protests, Isabelle allowed them to put her into bed, Marguerite and her elderly aunts and uncles holding court as they gathered around the bed to express their concern and relief that she was home safe.

'Who were those people, Isabelle? And where were you that they had to drive you home?' Marguerite's voice was agitated as she fussed with the blanket and pillows. She touched Isabelle's hand. 'You are cold. You'll take ill before you know it in this weather. It's a wonder if you haven't caught pneumonia. You need to be more careful,' she scolded.

Isabelle reached out to touch her sister's cheek. 'You look the very image of mama.'

'That's very nice, darling. But where were you? What happened? Marie-Odile was out of her mind with worry. You shouldn't have wandered off like that. Not in your condition.'

'My condition?' Her voice was sharp.

'What she means,' said Désirée soothingly, 'is that you've only just recovered from a severe blow to the head. Don't you remember falling on the ice in winter?'

'Of course I remember! I'm not a mental patient.'

'Of course you aren't, darling,' clucked Marguerite in her mother's voice.

'I was looking for the midwife. But I couldn't find her.'

'Who?' Delphine glanced at her husband, who shook his head.

'The Indian midwife. Don't you remember?'

'Yes, I'm sure we all do. Don't you, sister?'

'Yes, the midwife,' Désirée murmured reassuringly. 'Get some sleep now. You'll feel better in the morning.'

'Everyone's downstairs,' said Hugo, entering the room. He lowered his voice in deference to Isabelle, who seemed to be sleeping. 'Monsieur Turgeon telephoned the prison. He begged the commandant to release Jacob on compassionate grounds, but the villain refused. Can you believe it? Monsieur Turgeon even prevailed on Bernard Benoit to try, but with the same result. The captain insists his hands are tied and that he will not alter prison policy without permission from the authorities in Quebec city.'

'Then let us appeal to the authorities—whoever they are!' cried Josette.

'We tried,' said an exasperated Hugo. 'They referred us back to Captain Perrault.' '

Does Jacob know what is going on?' asked Marguerite.

'I believe he does. The captain said he had personally informed him. Such an odd duck!'

Marie-Odile had re-entered the room. She felt under the covers for her mother's feet. 'Her poor legs are cold. The doctor said it will be a wonder if she doesn't catch pneumonia.' She started to cry.

'Didn't I say?' insisted Delphine.

Isabelle suddenly opened her eyes. 'She warned me' She clutched at Marguerite's wrist. 'Remember not to forget!' A look of confusion crossed her face. 'Or was it, don't forget to remember? I get the two mixed up.' Her head sank back onto the pillow.

'Of course we won't. You rest now.' Delphine glanced at her sister. '*Delirious*,' she mouthed, her eyes filling with tears.

'Come, dearest. Allow her to sleep.' Henri put an arm around his wife, gently steering her away from the bed. Isabelle was already asleep, fatigue written on her face as she snored softly, her lips moving as though speaking to herself.

'Will she be alright?' asked Delphine, her voice frightened. 'Her breathing doesn't sound right. Should we call Doctor Soulet again?'

'I did,' sniffled Marie-Odile, her eyes red from crying. 'He said she needs rest, and to keep her warm. He will call around tomorrow.'

Désirée stroked her sister's wrist. 'Listen to Henri. You need rest yourself, my dear Delphine. None of us are getting any younger.' '

What was she mumbling?'

'Something about an Indian midwife, who knows?

Perhaps she's dreaming. I wish Jacob were here. It's cruel to keep him away.'

CAPTAIN PERRAULT RE-READ THE despatch, his expression furious.

> *Given the reputation of Jacob Wheeler as an author, and given reports*
> *of his wife's ill-health, you are instructed to bring forward his release*
> *date on compassionate grounds.*

He considered the despatch a moment longer as he tapped his fingers on the desk, his mind racing. Picking up a pen he began to draft a reply, stopping several times to cross out words or insert new ones. Finally satisfied, he read over the finished draft:

> *Sir, with all due respect. I must inform you that the prisoner Jacob*
> *Wheeler has lately been involved in several egregious—*

He picked up the pencil again and crossed out the last word, substituting 'blatant' in its stead before continuing, re-reading from the start.

Sir, with all due respect, I must inform you that the prisoner Jacob Wheeler has lately been involved in several blatant breaches of discipline. The guards report him as wilful and boastful, bragging that 'the fools in government will have no option but to release me. I shall make them dance to my tune!' He also instigated the brutal bashing of a prison guard, almost causing the unfortunate man's death. He remarks daily on his ambition to rekindle the fight for independence and asserts that he will use his reputation as an author to inspire his fellow citizens to rebel against the government. If anything, he should be held beyond the release date and given an additional sentence for his mutinous and defiant behaviour. I fear to release him now would be a victory for the insurgents, of whom many remain among the populace at large. I await your further orders once you are in possession of this information.

He sealed the despatch and placed it in a leather bag. Content, he lounged back in the chair. 'Charest!'

WHEN SHE OPENED HER eyes again, the air was warm and pungent with the smell of cooked meats.

'You're awake!' Marie smiled. 'You slept like a newborn babe.'

'I did?' She looked around the small cabin. 'I remember this!'

Marie chuckled. 'Mercy! I should hope so. Here, drink this.' She placed a mug of broth in Isabelle's hand.

Isabelle sipped on the hot broth, still trying to puzzle out her surroundings. 'How did I get here?' she asked.

The other woman shook her head. 'You don't remember waking up in the grass? Or Gaston finding you?'

'I do. But that was before.' Or was it after? she asked herself, confused.

'My husband came home for his breakfast and left again to finish harvesting. He said you looked a right lamb, sleeping so peacefully.'

'My head!' She placed her hand there, remembering.

'Is it still troubling you? Gaston feared you had taken quite a blow.'

'No, it feels much better.' She glanced at her hand, her eyes widening. 'I'm still young!'

Marie laughed in amazement. 'The things you come out with! Of course you are. Did you imagine you would wake up and find yourself old, like me?'

Isabelle yawned and put a hand to her mouth. 'Pardon. I don't know why I'm so tired. I've only just woken up.'

'It will be that knock to the head, I shouldn't wonder. If the midwife were here, she'd mix you up a potion to make it better.'

'The midwife!' Isabelle jumped to her feet, startling the other woman. 'I remember! Do you know her?'

Marie looked at her strangely. 'Why wouldn't I? She's in the village every other day.'

Isabelle chuckled with delight. 'I was looking for her!'

Marie tutted and shook her head. 'When she wants to be found, she'll be found, no doubt. She's a curiosity all to herself. Now sit down and eat some of this pie. And don't you worry yourself. You can sleep tonight by the fire.'

She slept soundly on the hearth that night, her mind marvelling at the absence of sounds to disturb the stillness. Once she awakened and thought she heard a cry, like the shriek of a bird. She listened intently for a moment before slipping back into sleep.

She awoke early and went outside to pass water. Mist hung over the settlement and the surrounding trees. As she crouched, she heard the cry of a cockerel and smiled to herself, remembering the future. '*Your gift is not to forget, as your husband's is not to remember.*' Jacob! She got to her feet, suddenly anxious to return home.

When she re-entered the cabin, Marie was already up and about making breakfast. She turned at Isabelle's entrance. 'There you are! I feared for a moment that you'd run off. Turn that hock over the fire, if you'll oblige.'

She turned the venison on the iron pole suspended above the flames. 'I expect I'll leave after breakfast,' she announced.

Marie gave a look of surprise. 'Leave? And where would you go, pet?'

She thought for a moment. 'I'm not sure,' she confessed.

Following breakfast, she accompanied Marie to the communal well, raising several buckets of water which they carried on shoulder yokes back to the cabin.

'I must do the washing,' said Marie, brushing hair back from her forehead. 'Why don't you go and find Gaston? He might have some counsel for you. Invite him back for dinner, if you like. Here, take my bonnet.' She placed the lace cap on Isabelle's head, tucking in a few stray hairs. 'And my straw hat.' She placed a hat over the cap. Next, she fetched a neckerchief which she pinned to Isabelle's blouse. 'There! You be all set.'

She watched as Isabelle headed out from the cabin. 'Don't go roaming off into the woods! Or talking nonsensical things!'

Isabelle wandered around the settlement in a daze of excitement, her eyes darting everywhere at once as she again drank in the sights and sounds in the fresh, glittering air. She halted in fright as a party of Indians approached. Two of the men carried what appeared to be dead fawns slung around their shoulders. They were naked from the waist up, their brown bodies glistening with sweat. Their heads were shaved except for a coxcomb of hair that stuck up from their crowns, giving them a fearsome appearance. Their eyes, black and unblinking, stared at her as they passed. She recoiled from the rank smells that clung to their bodies. Flies buzzed above the gutted carcases they carried.

'Who are they?' she asked a man who had stopped alongside, leaning on his musket to allow the Indians to pass.

'Who are they?' he repeated, bemused at the question. 'Why, heathen of course. What did you think—honest Christians?'

'I mean, which tribe?'

'Ah! They be Mohawk. Fierce fellows on their day but peaceable enough for the moment.'

She eyed him, intrigued by a certain familiarity about his appearance. 'Pardon, but you look familiar,' she said. 'Is your name Villeneuve by any chance?'

He shook his head. 'No. My name be Charbonneau. Joseph Charbonneau.'

'Charbonneau!' She laughed. 'That's it!'

His face crinkled with puzzlement. 'Pardon me, Mademoiselle, but have we met?'

'Not yet!' She continued on her way, chuckling to herself at the bewildered look on his face.

She found Gaston sitting on a bench with his back against the timber wall of a storehouse. He looked haggard, his unshaven face drawn and pale.

'Pardon,' he said, looking up and shading his eyes against the bright sun. 'I have a head like a beehive this morning.' He grimaced and leaned back so that he was partly in shadow. 'I wondered where you were.'

'You did?' Pleased, she sat down beside him.

They were sitting at one side of the clearing opposite what appeared to be a fortified bunkhouse replete with musket slits. Men and women wandered by, greeting Gaston with familiarity while casting curious looks at her.

'They wonder at your clothes,' explained Gaston. 'Especially the women. They consider you under-dressed, no doubt!'

'Oh!' Embarrassed, she reproached herself at not bringing the shawl as Marie had suggested. 'It's too hot,' she said, marvelling at the women in their stays and long, apron-covered skirts. Some wore straw hats atop lace bonnets like her own.

A particularly pretty young woman caught her eye and she turned to glance after her. 'Marie Benoit,' said Gaston, following her gaze. 'Samuel's niece.'

'Gaston!' A man dressed in buckskin trousers and shirt strode up, a musket under his arm. 'Will you join me for a hunt?'

'Not today, Pierre, my friend. I've a sore head. Maybe tomorrow.'

'Pierre?' She gazed up at the man, who appeared to be in his late twenties. He wore a straw hat, his bearded face beneath the brim browned by the sun.

'This is Pierre Gagnon,' said Gaston, introducing the man. 'A fine hunter—almost as good as me.'

To the discomfort of the stranger and the puzzlement of Gaston, Isabelle laughed with delight. 'Pardon! Pardon!' she giggled, trying to control her outburst. 'You are a hunter?' She coughed to control her embarrassment.

'I am, and I'm glad it gives you such amusement, Mademoiselle,' he said, apparently too flummoxed by her reaction to be insulted.

'This is the young lady I told you about … the one who suffers from a blow to the head,' said Gaston by way of explanation.

'Ah! Then I thank the Lord you are alright,' said Gagnon. 'Blows to the head be nasty things. Well, I'll be off. Goodbye, then.' He raised his hat.

'Goodbye, Pierre.' She had tears in her eyes.

'What's the matter?' asked Gaston.

'It's just that he seems so … familiar.'

He frowned. 'You keep saying that!'

'But it's true!' She looked around the nascent settlement, taking in the blacksmith's forge, the cabins, the livestock grazing on the grass, the men and women going back and forth, the sound of children's' voices, pigs squealing, dogs barking, and the noises of goats and hens. And beyond the clearing she took in the luxuriant forest, the sparkling river, and overhead the vast, shining blueness threaded with wisps of cloud. She breathed out a deep, contented sigh. 'This is how I always pictured it would be.'

'Are you alright?'

'Yes,' she said, inclining her face toward to the sun. 'But I long for Jacob.'

'Who's Jacob?'

The question surprised her. 'Don't you know? He's my husband.'

'Husband?' Gaston grimaced in confusion. 'You're married?'

'Of course!'

'Then where is he?' he asked, his confusion growing by the minute.

'He is in prison. Unjustly accused.'

'Ah!' Gaston nodded in understanding. 'Well, I shouldn't worry over-much if I were you. Once he's released, he'll no doubt come looking for you. Does he know where you are?'

'No,' she fretted. 'I must go and look for him.' But still she sat, feeling suddenly sleepy. 'It's cold,' she said.

'Cold?' Gaston studied, her, his own sore head forgotten as he observed her pale cheeks. 'Why don't you rest?' he said kindly. 'Your husband may just surprise you and turn up suddenly.'

'Do you think so?' She asked, her voice hopeful.

'I'm sure of it.'

She closed her eyes, her head resting against Gaston's shoulder. 'Maybe I will,' she said, yawning. Her body ached with a dull heaviness that made her want to sleep. 'Just until I'm rested, and then I'll go and find Jacob.'

'WHAT DID SHE SAY? She looks like she's sleeping, poor little lamb!' Delphine had rushed over at Marie-Odile's panicked summons. Marguerite was already there, kneeling beside the bed and weeping uncontrollably as she held Isabelle's hand.

'She asked for my father.' Marie-Odile broke into sobs and leaned against her mother's shoulder. Louis was slumped in a chair, crying. They heard feet coming up the stairs. Désirée came into the room, breathless, her aged face showing the strain and exertion of her hurried arrival. Her eyes found Isabelle, lying motionless in the bed, and she uttered a wail of grief. 'My poor darling!' Weeping, she embraced the grieving Marie-Odile.

The house filled as word spread, and more and more concerned friends and relations stopped by. Hugo kept them downstairs, pacifying their anxieties with coffee and wine as Josette sent down word every few minutes.

'I fear it won't be long,' she said, weeping softly in the hallway when Hugo went up again to enquire. They heard a wail from within the bedroom and glanced at each other in alarm before hurrying inside. Delphine was bent over Isabelle, checking for breath. She glanced up as they entered and shook her head

'Mama!' Marie-Odile uttered an anguished cry and laid her head on Isabelle's breast, her body convulsing with grief.

'She's at peace now, darling,' murmured Désirée. Marguerite was still on her knees holding Isabelle's hand, her face numb with despair. Louis rocked back and forth in the chair uttering distraught moans.

Concerned at Marguerite's dazed appearance, Dominic led his wife into Marie-Odile's bedroom where he prevailed upon her to lie down. Hugo and Josette coaxed the distressed Marie-Odile and Louis away from their mother's body and closed the door behind them. Left alone, Delphine and her sister smoothed the bedclothes and arranged Isabelle's hair on the pillow. 'She looks so peaceful! And so like her mother!' Désirée burst into fresh tears, her face wretched with misery. 'She was so young!'

Delphine blew her nose, her eyes puffy from crying. 'It was cruel for her to pass without Jacob.' It was only then she noticed the necklace in Isabelle's hand. Curious, she bent to examine it. 'I haven't seen that before, have you?' To her surprise, the necklace was made up of leather strips decorated with beads and what appeared to be dried animal parts. 'Well, I never!'

'I thought it was a rosary,' said Désirée, blinking through tears. 'Where did it come from?'

'I don't know.' Intrigued by the curious object, Delphine felt it between her fingers. 'I've never seen her wear it,' she said. 'I'm sure I would remember.'

SHOCKED AND UNCOMPREHENDING, JACOB had to be helped to his feet after an upset Hugo left, still murmuring words of condolence. Back in the cell, he collapsed onto the cot and lay there for the remainder of the day, refusing the order to attend supper.

'Leave him be,' said Charest when informed.

He refused food the next day also, stretched out on the cot with an arm over his face. Waiting until Perrault had retired to his quarters, Charest arranged for several of his fellow inmates to be admitted to the cell, one by one, in an attempt to assuage his grief. 'You must eat,' the soldier said, leaving a plate of food on the chair.

He received the sorrowful commiserations of the other prisoners with dazed passivity, grateful when they were shown out of the cell. Then, ignoring the food, he sat on the cot, his face in his hands, tormented at the thought of Isabelle lying cold and composed in a narrow box, all colour and warmth fled from her face. The image was so tortuous that he stuffed the pillow into his mouth to choke his sobs. 'Isabelle, my poor, dear heart!'

His grief was reported to Captain Perrault by the sympathetic Charest.

'He refuses food?'

'He does.' Charest bit his tongue at the captain's malicious delight in the news.

'And his wife is assuredly dead?'

'I believe she has been buried already, Captain.' Charest averted his eyes as his superior officer coughed to smother a snigger.

'Sir. Monsieur Wheeler is taking his wife's death very hard. Would it not be possible—'

'Monsieur Wheeler is it now?' Perrault cocked an eyebrow as Charest mentally cursed himself. 'Perhaps you should be down there comforting him, Charest, along with his other admirers?'

Ignoring the taunt in the captain's voice, Charest stared straight ahead. 'Your orders, sir?'

'My orders are to do nothing. Do you understand? If he wishes to starve himself to death, so be it. Let Nature take its course. Now be off with you. Beg him to read you a fable, perhaps!'

As his adjutant closed the door behind him, Perrault put his booted feet up on the desk, luxuriating in the report. *I promised you that your husband would be returned to you in a box. Well, one box is as good as another!* He ground his teeth at a memory of her shocked face as she repulsed his advances. *Who would want you now, my fine madame? Not even your husband!* Feeling cheerful, he signed the document on his desk with a flourish.

His gratification lasted only until the following day, when he received another despatch in reply to his own.

Your concerns have been noted, Captain. But the situation warrants an immediate release for the prisoner Jacob Wheeler.

In addition, you are ordered to bring forward the release of all the remaining rebels. The minister expects you to comply with these instructions in an expeditious manner.

Enclosed with the despatch was a hand-written note from his superior, Colonel Soubry:

Damn you Perrault! I know your games. If you do not release the prisoners—all of them—within a week, I shall see you stripped of your command and sent to Kativik to rub noses with the eskimos! Damn'd if I won't! You have your orders!

A violent rage gripped Perrault as he read the note a second time. With a loud curse he ripped it to shreds and tossed it on the fire. He paced up and down the office, his mind seething with the injustice of it all. *Me! A decorated veteran. To be addressed in such insulting terms? That fat oaf can barely stand out of his chair and yet he has the gall to threaten me!*

Throwing himself back into the chair, he scribbled a hasty note to a friend in the minister's office. He sealed the note in an envelope and marked the outside 'Personal and Confidential'.

'Well, my dear Colonel,' he muttered, 'let us see who has the most influential friends, and which one of us shall be rubbing noses with the damn'd eskimos!'

OVER THE FOLLOWING DAYS, Jacob tortured himself with self-blame and recrimination. 'I reduced my family to penury and then abandoned them to subsist on charity while rotting inside this stinking prison,' he lamented to Roland, inconsolable in his grief. 'And not a word of recrimination from Isabelle. Not one!'

'It was not your fault, Jacob. You were imprisoned for a crime you didn't commit.'

'No, but I lost our fortune—the house, our savings, and everything else. And my poor wife died in a hovel without me by her side to comfort her.' He pushed his fist into his mouth to choke back a sob.

'That was not your fault, either. Blame it on that vile creature, Perrault.'

'I do!' Giving vent to his grief and anger, Jacob proceeded to castigate Perrault, his bitterness rising to such an extreme that his companion worried for his health.

'I am seriously concerned for him,' admitted Roland, appealing to Charest for assistance. 'He is out of his head with grief. And he blames Perrault for not releasing him to visit his wife in her sickness or to attend her funeral. I fear he intends harm to the man.'

'Then you'd best keep a close eye on him,' warned Charest.

The following morning, the captain made an appearance in the yard accompanied by Charest and another officer. A concerned Roland saw Jacob stiffen and glare as the captain passed within earshot, regaling his subordinates in a loud voice as he boasted of some petty triumph. 'And I said to the fellow—a real mouse, by the by, who'd faint with the shits if he ever had to face a bayonet charge—I said to him, tell your master that the prisoners will be released on Saint-Jean-Baptiste day, and not a minute before!'

Roland glanced anxiously at Jacob. It was then that he noticed the knife in Jacob's hand. 'Good God, man! Where did you get that? Are you mad!' He grabbed Jacob's arm as he made to lunge after the captain

'Let me go!'

'Calm down! This won't help!' Roland struggled to restrain Jacob in a tight bear hug as he fought to free himself and reach Perrault.

The commotion attracted the attention of Charest who turned to observe. He flashed a look of alarm before diverting Perrault by pointing to something across the yard. The trio strolled off in that direction while Roland struggled to restrain the raging Jacob.

Jacob cursed with despair as Perrault disappeared through a door on the opposite side of the yard. 'You should have let me kill him!' He cast a furious stare at Roland.

'You would have killed yourself as well! You have children to consider. Think of what you have to lose!'

Shaken by the violence of his emotions, Jacob allowed Roland to take the knife and escort him back to his cell.

'I didn't even get to attend her funeral!' He stared despairingly before burying his face in his hands with a cry of anguish. 'Isabelle! My poor darling!' Overcome with grief and remorse, he wept a flood of tears as Roland stood helplessly by.

43

Monsieur Author!

O N MAY 25TH, 1930, the *Catholic Tribune* reported that the dozen remaining 'anarchists' as they were officially designated, would be released on the morrow, three weeks ahead of schedule. The report was confirmed by the new commandant, Acting Captain Jean Charest, the former commandant having been transferred to other duties in the far north of the province.

The appointed hour had been trumpeted in the newspapers, both dailies hailing the event and, in particular, the much-anticipated release of the renowned author of the *Fables*. A crowd of several thousand gathered outside the prison gates in joyful expectation ahead of the event. Many held up signs proclaiming the captives as martyrs and heroes. Patriotic airs were sung, including the once forbidden, now tolerated, song that had become the unofficial anthem of New France.

'*At the clear fountain as I was strolling by …*' began a woman's voice, rising up from the crowd. The chorus was chanted by the massed voices in patriotic celebration of their city. Up on the ramparts, a sentry started humming along until silenced by a withering look from his sergeant.

Late in the morning the first of the prisoners was released to emotional outpourings from the joyous crowd. The freed man—looking pale and malnourished by his long ordeal—was greeted by tearful friends and relatives as the crowd cheered. He was quickly followed by another, and then by two more, the prisoners emerging to shouts and applause as they blinked in the warm light of freedom. Soon, all of the remaining prisoners except Jacob had emerged, the delay provoking the impatient throng to chant his name as they demanded his release. A great roar went up as he was observed walking through the gates, his face drawn, his head and beard entirely grey. Thus, nine years after his imprisonment and four weeks after his wife's funeral, Jacob Wheeler, writer, industrialist and political martyr walked free from prison.

Hurrahs! erupted as the delirious crowd surged forward to greet the celebrated author. Hugo, waiting amidst the crush of bodies, was jostled aside as a bewildered Jacob was rudely hoisted up onto boisterous shoulders and carried through the crowd to cries of 'Monsieur Author!' He struggled briefly to be set down, his efforts ignored by the admiring, chanting mass. The cheering mob paraded him through the surrounding streets, the noise attracting hundreds of others who came first to gape and then to join the festive procession. Onlookers lining the pavements held up copies of his book as he was carried past. 'Bravo Monsieur Author!' went up the cry.

Men jostled for the honour of carrying him as he was borne through the Old Town marketplace in scenes reminiscent of a Roman triumph. Stall workers and shoppers alike abandoned their commerce to rush outside and lend their voices to the celebration. Caps were thrown into the air as whistles and applause rang out in the ancient square.

He scarcely realised that the jubilant mob had carried him out of the square and into the park, until his gaze fell upon the bench—looking bare and forlorn in the sunshine—where he had sat with Isabelle. At the sight he wept unashamedly. The crowd, mistaking his tears, sent up shouts of gratitude for his heroic suffering. 'You are a martyr for New France!' was chanted from a thousand fervent throats.

The singing, cheering crowd bore him through the narrow streets of the Old Quarter all the way to rue Marguerite Bourgeoys. People came out of their front doors to stare at the commotion, holding aloft small children to witness the historic event.

Standing on the footpath outside number 24, Jacob's grown-up children and relatives waited eagerly to welcome him home. It was only then that the triumphant mob set him down to be tearfully embraced by his family.

The front door closed behind him as the joyous crowd continued to sing and chant in the street outside. Despite being urged to sit down and rest, he insisted on being shown to the room where Isabelle had died. Observing the impoverished furnishings, the tattered wallpaper, and the narrow bed, he was overcome with emotion. Sobbing Isabelle's name, he sank to his knees by the bed, burying his face in the sheets as his children cried uncontrollably behind him and the noisy acclaim of the crowd rose from the street outside.

THROUGHOUT THE WEEKS AND months that followed, his release, he remained largely a recluse, turning down invitations to supper and repeated requests from both daily newspapers and the radio station for an interview. He endured the seemingly endless visits, the murmured condolences, the flowers, the anxious glances of his children, and the accusations of his own tormented soul as he sat, unmoving in a chair, a dazed look in his eyes. The pendulum clock inherited from Isabelle's mother struck the hour, and he listened to the chime feeling as if his heart might burst from grief. *Time goes on, but not for my Isabelle.*

At night he slept in her bedroom, his sleep disturbed by constant awakenings from dreams of her. At times he imagined he saw her smiling at him in the darkness and sat up, his arms outstretched, imploring her embrace. 'Dearest!' he cried out, waking Louis, who slept downstairs. The youth sat up in bed, his ears straining for sound. He listened for a while before going back to sleep, telling himself he'd imagined the stark cry.

In the cramped second bedroom across the landing, Marie-Odile was awake and listening, knowing the source of, and the reason for, the anguished cry—similar to those she herself had uttered in the days following her mother's death. Turning on her side she wept into the pillow, her hands clasped over her ears.

During the day he kept to himself, grateful that the children, now absorbed in their own adult tasks, left him alone to grieve. Whenever they registered upon his consciousness, it was as remote, yet strangely familiar, persons. Gaston had a fiancée in Montreal, Louis was about to complete his apprenticeship, and Marie-Odile, now a young woman, had a job at the telephone exchange.

'They are grown, and I hardly know them,' he reflected, bitterly regretful of the fact. The knowledge added to the burden of losing Isabelle, making him more reticent and even more reluctant to receive company.

In this he was helped by his protective children who decided to restrict visits from all but close relatives. '*Papa is too much in mourning to receive visitors at present,*' explained Marie-Odile in her careful handwriting as she replied to a request from a family friend. '*He will receive visitors again after this period of mourning.*' As *de facto* housemother she made an exception for René Turgeon, the former deputy now so frail he had to be assisted down from the cab and half-carried into the house.

His eyes moist with tears, Turgeon sat in a chair opposite Jacob. 'Your dear, dear wife had hoped to buy back your former home with the royalties from the book. But alas …' His voice was choked by a sob. 'Such a peerless woman. Surely, she is among the angels.' Dabbing his eyes with a handkerchief, he murmured with sadness. 'Thus, do triumph and tragedy join hands to mock our petty lives.'

He sat gathering himself for a few minutes before speaking again, his face etched with sorrow. 'In spite of unendurable loss, life must go on, Jacob. You have your children to care for and must, however regretfully, look to the future. You have no need to work for a living. The royalties have made you a prosperous man again. Like Job, your fortunes have been restored.' He paused to reflect on the aptness of the comparison. 'Should you wish it, those other fables, the ones you handed me in prison ...' His voice tailed off at the look of utter misery on his friend's face. 'No matter.' He sighed heavily, 'Art must give way to life.'

'Be good to your father. Look after him,' he told Louis and Marie-Odile as he left. He paused and brushed a finger against Marie's cheek. 'You look so like your mother,' he observed with a sad smile, bringing tears to her eyes. With a solemn 'farewell!' he was assisted into the waiting cab.

'Why not visit mama's grave, papa?' Gaston suggested before supper, pitying this father he scarcely knew.

'I will, but not now.'

His son kissed his head and left the room. 'He'll go soon,' Gaston told his concerned siblings waiting at the foot of the stairs.

'When?' asked Louis, his voice anxious.

'When he accepts that mama is not ever coming back,' said Gaston, and blew his nose.

BARELY TEN-YEARS OLD WHEN her father was sent to prison, Marie-Odile was, she admitted to herself, nervous in the presence of this gaunt, stern-faced patriarch whom she remembered chiefly through her mother's stories and the hushed conversations carried on when visitors thought she wasn't listening.

She kept a watchful eye, trying to reconcile the aloof and despairing man with the tales she had insisted her mother read to her each night. She had formed a childish opinion of the absent author, imagining a preternaturally wise, patient and god-like figure whose omniscient pronouncements on the lives he had created she carried with her into dreams and the occasional nightmare. The discordance of that vision with the distant father who took tea by himself and gave short, detached responses to her attempts at communication, disconcerted and troubled her.

'You must be patient with him, darling,' advised her aunt Marguerite when Marie-Odile sought her advice. 'He has suffered a great deal. What do you remember of your life before he was imprisoned?'

'I remember we had a big house and a garden with lots of roses. And papa drove an automobile. And he and mama were so happy.'

Her aunt sighed. 'No doubt he is remembering the same. Give him time, sweetness. He has only just been released. His whole world has turned upside down. Have you talked to your brothers about it?'

When questioned, neither Gaston nor Louis was willing to admit to any discomfort in their father's presence. 'I'm just glad to have him home again,' said Gaston to nods from Louis.

'You don't find him different—moody, even?'

'Of course he's going to be different. We haven't seen him for almost ten years.'

'He's a stranger to me,' Marie-Odile admitted.

'That's because you're comparing him to mama. They are different.'

'I know that! But he avoids everyone, even Uncle Hugo.'

'What do you expect? He's still in mourning for mama.'

In spite of her father's expressed wish for seclusion, she approached him one afternoon, determined to re-establish the filial relationship she dimly recalled before he was so cruelly snatched from her childhood.

'Papa?' In her hand she held a much-thumbed edition of the *Fables*. 'Papa?' He was sitting in his usual position before the fire, his hands linked on his lap in brooding contemplation.

'Oh!' he started. 'Yes? What is it?' His furrowed brow and put-upon tone almost caused her to lose her nerve and abandon her purpose.

'I just wanted to say how much I enjoyed your stories while you were … away. Mama used read them to me each night.' Her voice was shy with apprehension. 'I remember you reading to me as well.'

Slowly, his absorbed expression changed to one of bemusement, as though he was trying to place the young woman standing before him. 'Which one was your favourite?'

'The little dormouse. He was so brave.'

'I thought it was Lisette, the wise owl?'

She wrinkled her nose. 'No, the little dormouse.'

He looked at her for some time before giving the faintest of smiles. 'I wrote that story especially for you.'

'You did? Mama always said I reminded her of the mouse!' Sighing with relief, she advanced into the room.

He smiled again, less distantly this time. 'Come, sit by me. Tell me of your mama and the stories she read to you.'

And thus, she recovered her lost father, reading his own fables to him while he listened with a wistful, pensive air. At times he gave a quizzical frown as she arched an eyebrow to indicate she required a response.

'You remind me of your mother,' he said, his voice breaking. He reached out to touch her cheek, a gesture that thrilled her.

'Not the dormouse?' she teased.

'Him, too.'

'And Celeste the duck?' She waited with eyes wide as he cocked his head in surprise. And then he laughed, a genuine laugh that warmed her through and through. 'Aye, Celeste as well!'

Perhaps refreshed by this degree of restored intimacy, he declared himself at last ready to visit Isabelle's grave. Thus, on a day of blue, resplendent skies he knelt before the fresh, unweathered headstone in the cathedral graveyard. Standing behind him, Marie-Odile admired a plant with pretty pink and purple-coloured flowers growing next to the headstone, chewing her lip as she tried to recall its name.

Her father leaned forward to brush aside the grass where it obscured the inscription. "Isabelle Marie Tremblay Ouellet Wheeler, *1883–1930*. *Beloved wife of Jacob, loving mother to Gaston, Louis and Marie-Odile. At rest in God's loving embrace. Remember not to forget!*"

'Who chose the inscription?' he asked, his voice thick with emotion.

'Mama. She always worried that we would forget.'

'Forget your mother? Never!' He appeared shocked at the notion.

'I don't think she meant forget her,' explained Louis, 'but everything else.'

'Is it a quote from somewhere?' asked Gaston, his voice curious.

His father was silent. 'I don't know,' he admitted after a pause, his face etched with longing and despair. 'Perhaps she took it from a novel or a poem. I don't remember.'

AMIDST HIS ON-GOING GRIEF, the strict routine of prison life with its regulated hours for eating, sleeping and everything in between reached out to structure his day. He rose early and ate breakfast alone, stopping often to stare at his toast or the milky tea, his mind roving back to the shriek of whistles and the harsh commands snapped out by the guards. He read without interest news of the closure of the military barracks. '*The site will be turned into a museum,*' the *Catholic Tribune* reported, '*although a new proposal gaining ground is for it to be turned into housing for the poor.*'

He jumped at sudden sounds, half-expecting a guard to come storming into the room demanding why he wasn't outside. His hand trembled as it reached for the sugar bowl and while stirring the tea. And sudden, splitting headaches that flashed like lightning in his skull reduced him to an ashen wreck until the intense pain subsided. He hid these 'fits', as he came to call them, from Louis and Marie-Odile, getting up to excuse himself on some pretext or other whenever he felt one coming on. Once in his bedroom, he convulsed on the bed, shaking and trembling, his head on fire as he lost all control of his body, his limbs twitching this way and that. Afterwards, he sat on the side of the bed, pale and nauseous.

His fingers strayed to the welt in his skull where his scalp had been sewn so many years before. 'I'm afraid the fragment has moved and is now pressing on the blood vessel.' The prison doctor had softened his voice in sympathy. 'We can't operate, it's far too dangerous. We must just hope that it moves back again or else releases the pressure.'

'And if it doesn't?' Jacob had asked.

'Let us hope that it does.'

'Papa, where are—oh, there you are.' Marie-Odile entered the room. 'Is everything alright? You look pale, like you've seen a ghost.'

'Just a little tired.' He smiled wanly and pressed her hand.

'You would tell me if anything was wrong, wouldn't you?' She peered into his eyes, a worried look on her face.

'I'm fine,' he insisted, squeezing her hand.

'Because if anything should happen to you …. I don't think I could bear it, not so soon after mama.' Her eyes filled with tears.

'Hush, nothing will happen.'

'Promise?'

'I promise.'

She gave a tearful smile, her eyes softening. 'You were mama's true love, her heart and soul. You know that don't you?'

He felt a lump in his throat. 'I do, as she was mine.'

She took a breath. 'Papa, would you come to church with me on Sunday? It would mean so much to mama.'

He gazed at her anxious face and felt, in that moment, an overwhelming love. 'Yes,' he said, his voice gruff with tenderness. The glad light in her eyes—so reminiscent of her mother!—as he said this made him want to weep.

'Thank you!' She kissed his cheek. 'That reminds me, will you write any more of your tales, everyone keeps asking?'

'No. I'm done with writing.' His voice was firm.

'Why? It will give you something to do.'

'I don't think people would like them. They'd be different, for one thing.'

'Is it because of what you've been through? I would understand,' she said, although her hopeful expression suggested she wouldn't.

'They'd just be different,' he tried to explain. 'A different way of seeing, that's all.'

'But I liked the old way! They are how life should be—like stories, where everyone, including the reader, learns a lesson and comes to see the folly of their ways.'

With a wistful smile he traced her nose with his finger. 'Wouldn't that be nice?'

Summer gave way to fall, and his headaches grew worse. At his daughter's urging, he consulted a specialist who examined him before confirming the prognosis of the prison doctor.

'I'm afraid it's not good,' pronounced the specialist, his voice grave as he sat behind the polished desk. 'Any sudden shock or blow to the head could be fatal. You must exercise extreme caution. An operation?' he said, guessing the question on Jacob's lips. 'Far too dangerous. And the truth is we simply don't have the knowledge or skill to undertake such a complex procedure. I'm afraid it's a condition you will just have to live with.'

Live with or die with? wondered Jacob as the doctor showed him out.

In late September, just as he was beginning to accept the finality of Isabelle's death, René Turgeon passed away, the death of his long-time friend and mentor plunging him back into depression.

'What did he die of?' he asked Hugo, who came bearing the sad news.

'Of old age, I suppose. He wasn't sick, except towards the very end, when he complained of fatigue. Your book was at his bedside.'

'It was?' He dwelt on the fact. 'It was entirely thanks to him that it was published at all.'

Hugo nodded, his face sombre. 'He was a great man,' he said. 'New France owes him a debt of gratitude.'

'Will there be a state funeral?'

'No.' Hugo shook his head. 'The offer was made to him while still alive, but he refused.'

'Why? Surely, if anyone in New France deserved such an honour …?'

'That's what I said. But he joked that he wished to fully retire from public life.'

In spite of his dejection, Jacob smiled. 'Where will he be buried?'

'At his family church back in rural Chamblay. He said it was about time he paid a visit home.'

Jacob smiled again, picturing his friend's twinkling eyes as he made the jest.

They sat in silence for a while, sipping wine while lost in remembrance of the scholarly, curious-minded deputy. 'I remember the first time he invited me to visit Government House, do you?' asked Jacob, breaking the silence.

Hugo nodded and smiled. 'I do. I can see him now.'

'Ah! Jacob, Hugo!' The deputy had crooked an arm inviting them to join him where he stood before a small sculpture mounted in an alcove. He was flanked by a particularly obsequious aide.

'A fine bronze, is it not?' The deputy asked as they joined him before the figure, an early piece by Emile Poirier. There's something of the sublime about it, which speaks well of its creator. Was that Aristotle?' He paused to think.

'Plato, sir,' volunteered the toadying aide, 'or one of the Greeks.'

44

Who Are You?

H E SAT BEFORE THE embers of the fire, wrapped in a blanket. It was early morning, and the mid-October weather was chilly with the threat of snow. He had been unable to sleep beyond a few hours and was feeling restless. He made himself a pot of coffee, standing back as the gas ring hissed to flame. While drinking a cup, he scribbled a note to Marie-Odile, the sole other occupant of the house now that Gaston had returned to Montreal and Louis was lodging with a friend. '*Have gone for a walk. Do not worry, am well wrapped.*'

He drew back the curtain from the alcove where the winter coats were hung. He was about to reach for the wool overcoat when his eye was drawn to his old buffalo robe, sheathed in paper. Surprised to find it after all these years, he smiled to himself. She never could bear to throw anything away. He took it down, running his hand over the familiar fleece, now faded and musty smelling. He put it to his nose, remembering the many times he had worn it in his first winter in New France. On an impulse he tore off the paper and tried on the coat, giving a hum of satisfaction at the heavy yet comfortable fit. It was—is—a good coat. It has served me well.

He found his fur-lined gloves on a shelf and tugged them over his fingers. He looked at himself in the hallstand mirror. A lean, grizzled face stared back, the beard and uncombed hair imparting a gaunt aspect to his reflection. *The midwife wouldn't recognise me.* He stared at his reflection, thunderstruck. The midwife! What happened to her? I haven't thought of her in an age.

She saved my life, he reminded himself, troubled at having forgotten her until now. Taking down the worn, Stetson hat, he placed it on his head. Memories of his days in the smoky, claustrophobic cabin came to mind as he peered at his reflection. It's time I gave her a visit—if she's still alive. And with that thought in mind he left the house, carefully closing the door behind him.

THE EARLY-MORNING AIR WAS cold, and he shivered in spite of the warm robe. He took a moment to collect his surroundings before heading off through the market toward the city outskirts.

He walked through the market square, nodding to the delivery drivers and the stall holders as they set up for the day. Some of them stopped to take in the unusual figure in the bulky coat and Stetson hat. His stride increased as his body warmed up. I used to take the bus here—or was it the tram? Mulling the question, he was surprised to find himself at the old stone wall that surrounded the city. I didn't even notice the walk, he told himself, bemused by the fact.

Leaving the walls behind, he followed the tarred road where it led past rows of houses. Despite the cold air, he felt briskly energetic, his spirits raised by the blue October sky. He followed the road for an hour, marvelling at how much the housing estate had grown in his absence.

Spotting a man bent over the engine of an automobile, he hailed the fellow. 'Good morning, friend. Are you familiar with the area?'

The man stopped what he was doing to peer up at him, his eyes suspicious. 'Suppose I am?'

'Pardon. I was merely seeking directions—to the midwife's house. Do you know her? It was somewhere around here, although surrounded by trees at the time.'

'Midwife?' The man's brow furrowed. 'What midwife? I've been here more than ten-years now and I have never heard of such.'

'She was Indian. Fat. She sold lotions and powders and healed people.'

'Indian?' The man took off his cloth cap and scratched his head. 'We ain't got no Indians around here. Are you sure this is the right place?'

'I'm sure. She was well-known as a native healer. She lived here for many years.'

'I sure as Jessy ain't never heard of her.' The man studied Jacob. 'What did you say your name was?'

'Where then are the woods that used to be here?'

'The woods?' The man cogitated on this. 'The nearest woods are way over yonder.' He waved an arm to indicate the distance. 'About two mile, I'd say. There's a bus comes through on the hour if you'd prefer to ride.' He looked up at the sky. 'I reckon we're in for snow today. Best keep warm.'

Jacob's eye was caught by the automobile engine, and he started in recognition. 'I built this!'

'What?' The man frowned.

'This vehicle. My factory produced it. It's an old Roadster, isn't it?'

The man picked at his nose. 'It is. Reliable as anything. You say you built it?'

'Well, my employees. The Ferguson Selt Automobile Company. Ever hear of them?'

The man shook his head. 'Can't say that I have. American?'

'Yes. No, I mean the owners were, but the Roadster was assembled right here, in New France. How old is it?' He leaned over the engine to search for the manufacturing stamp. '1910! Twenty years ago! This was one of our first models.'

'We'll I'll be.' The man scratched his head to digest the fact.

Jacob's gaze lingered on the dented, badly rusted bodywork and faded leather upholstery.

'You can buy her if you want,' said the man. 'I'm thinking of trading her in, anyway.'

'Thank you. But I must be on my way. Good day to you, sir.'

'Wait.' The man made a gurgling noise and spat in the dirt. 'There's a fellow,' he said, wiping his mouth with his sleeve. 'Old Lucien. He's been around here longer than most. If anyone knows of your midwife, it will be him. Over there.' He pointed across the street. 'Corner house with the blue paint.'

'Lucien? And his family name?'

'That's it, Lucien. He don't go by no other.'

'And he won't mind me calling?'

'He don't mind much of nothing these days—'cepting he's got a supply of whisky.'

'Thank you again, friend.'

'Sure enough.' The man watched him go. *Where in the name of Halley did he fetch that coat?*

THE OLD HOUSE WAS badly run-down, the paint weathered and cracked, with large splits in the timbers. An abandoned sofa sat outside in the grass, the stuffing poking through. He knocked on the door, hearing a dog bark inside.

The door opened a crack and a surly face peeped out, the eyes suspicious behind thick-rimmed glasses. 'Get down!' The face disappeared for a moment as the man wrestled with the excited dog. 'What do you want?' he said rudely, appearing again.

'Pardon, sir, for taking your time. But I am looking for someone and was told you might be able to help?'

'Looking for who?'

'An old woman who used to live in these parts. A healer. She was Indian—'

'The midwife?' The face showed astonishment.

'You've heard of her?' Jacob was equally astonished.

The elderly man studied him for some time, distrust on his face. 'You'd better come inside,' he said grudgingly, and pulled open the door.

Seated in a chair with a glass of whisky—which, despite the early hour—the man had insisted he accept, Jacob spread his coat over his lap under the watchful gaze of the dog, a ragged-looking creature with bright eyes and a pink tongue. A fire blazed in the grate. The stale air smelled of tobacco and woodsmoke. The room was full of books, the volumes crammed in tightly next to one another on library shelves. Other books were stacked on the floor in piles. The sparse furniture—two stuffed armchairs and a table piled with yet more books—was dusty and faded with age.

'I haven't heard that name in a very long time.' Lucien sat down opposite Jacob. 'How do you know of her?' His voice was techy as though waiting to find fault with the answer.

'I owe her a debt of gratitude. She saved my life a long time ago, when I first arrived in New France.'

'When you first …' Lucien's eyes widened behind the thick lenses. 'You are the American!'

Jacob stared in surprise. 'Yes. How did you know?'

The elderly man wrapped a bony forefinger and thumb around his jaw and tugged as though it were stuck. He ruminated for a while before clearing his throat. Leaning forward he made a hacking sound and spat into the fire. The dog whined and barked. 'Quiet!' He began to hand-roll a cigarette and lit it before answering in a voice hoarse from the effects of smoking. 'I heard the story from …' He frowned at the dog as he tried to recall. 'A jumpy fellow—always asking about God's plan. What in Purgatory was his name?'

'Gagnon—Hugo Gagnon?'

'Gagnon!' Lucien rumbled the name in his throat. 'Another ghost from the past.' He peered at Jacob through the thick lenses. 'What happened to him?'

'He's alive and well. I saw him not a week ago.' Feeling overly warm, he placed the buffalo coat on the floor. 'Monsieur …'

'Just Lucien.'

'You were saying you recalled the Indian midwife?'

Taking out a dirty strip of cloth, Lucien hacked into it, coughing up thick phlegm which he folded into the cloth before tossing it into the flames. He watched it burn for a moment before continuing. 'I never met her—' he rasped and spat some shreds of tobacco from his lips—'but this Gagnon fellow prattled on about her non-stop. He feared she was a witch and worried for his immortal soul.'

'That sounds like Hugo. But do you know what happened to her?'

Lucien topped up his whisky and lifted the bottle at Jacob, who shook his head. 'God knows. She vanished, like everything else.'

'Oh.' Disappointed, Jacob let out a sigh. 'I suppose she must have died.'

'I didn't say she died, I said she vanished,' corrected Lucien, his voice testy.

'Vanished? I don't understand. 'Where did she go?'

'Where did the woods go? Where did all the birds and the deer go? Even the rabbits. Old Drolet there used to love chasing them in his day.' He looked critically at the dog who cocked its head in return.

Suspecting the man to be half-drunk, Jacob let the question go. 'Thank you for the whisky, friend. I should be getting back to the city. It looks like snow.'

'Wait. Stay awhile. I don't get many visitors. Any, in fact. You're my first in years.' His voice plaintive, Lucien splashed more whisky into Jacob's glass, ignoring Jacob's attempt to cover it with his hand.

'And how is your wife? Madame ...' Lucien frowned as he tried to recall the name.

'Wheeler. Isabelle Ouellet Wheeler. She passed away, I'm afraid.' Downcast with the admission, he sipped on the whisky.

Lucien ruminated on this. 'Loss is the constant companion of age,' he said. 'Age changes us.' He contemplated the dog. 'One time I heartily disliked most people.' He pushed the glasses up on his nose. 'Why beat about the bush?' he muttered. 'The truth is I disliked everyone, myself not least of all.'

'And now?'

'And now?' Lucien stubbed out the cigarette. 'And now, none of it matters. I wonder at how I was.'

'We all do. Age, as you say.'

Lucien began to roll another cigarette. 'Are you a believer?' He looked over his glasses with the question.

'No, I'm afraid not.'

'But your wife was, as I recall?'

'She was,' said Jacob, further downcast at the past tense. 'What?' he said. Lucien was looking at him strangely.

'You are the author! The author of the Fables! I have a copy—over there, on the shelf somewhere.' Lucien gestured to a pile of books.

Jacob nodded in admission, glum that Isabelle wasn't there to observe the conversation.

'I have thought often of your tale of the cockerel.'

'You have?' said Jacob, surprised at the remark.

"It is better to accept life as it is than to pine for some imagined paradise," Lucien quoted. He grimaced at Jacob. 'That line woke me up. It decided me on this.' He gestured to the whisky bottle and tobacco pouch. 'I lost my faith—not that I had much to begin with.' He sucked on the cigarette, hollowing his cheeks. 'The older I get—' he coughed out smoke—'the older I get, the further away I get from God. I hoped it might have been different but—' he licked the end of the cigarette. 'I prayed but he wasn't listening. And he wasn't listening because he wasn't there.' He sipped on the whisky. 'He wasn't there,' he repeated accusingly.

He brooded on this before speaking again. 'I cannot believe in God, and yet I believe in sin. Sin is as real as that bookcase,' he said, nodding toward the heavy oak shelves. 'But grace, God's grace, is nowhere to be found.' He was silent for a few moments, ruminating on this.

'Who are you looking for? Ah, yes! The midwife. I thought at one time that she might have the answers I sought. But to my regret I never got to ask her.' He lapsed into moody silence.

Jacob finished the whisky and thought about announcing his departure for a second time. Before he could open his mouth, his host spoke again, a troubled note in his voice. 'I had doubts, always, severe doubts. I was always in search.' His voice tailed off into gloom.

'In search of what?'

Lucien gave a heavy sigh. 'Forgiveness, repentance … grace—call it what you will. I used to be a priest.' He pushed up his glasses to observe Jacob as if weighing up the effect of his statement. 'Your wife, I recall, was a staunch Catholic, was she not?'

'She was. Her dearest wish was for me to accept the faith. And I let her down. And now she's gone, before I even had the chance to say how sorry I am, about everything.' A familiar bitterness filled him. 'Can you explain that? For I should dearly like to know.'

'I cannot, for I am in search of the same answers myself—if there are any to be had.'

'You are a strange priest!'

Lucien gave a humourless laugh. 'Former priest!' He took another swallow of whisky. 'I sometimes wish I could go back into the past. I imagine things were simpler then and that God was, perhaps, closer.'

'If he exists.'

Lucien eyed him. 'You said you let your wife down?'

'I did.'

'And you would like to be forgiven for that?'

'With all my heart.'

'Then know this: without God there is no forgiveness, and no possibility of forgiveness.' Lucien pushed back the glasses on his nose, fixing Jacob with a questioning stare. 'You have to ask yourself, which is the more frightening: a world with God, or without God? For me, it's the latter. A world with God brings certain punishment for our sins, but also, in time, the hope of forgiveness. And yet, I cannot believe that he exists.'

Lucien drained the whisky, a weary look on his face. 'And a world without God? No punishment, at least not of the divine sort, but also no possibility of forgiveness.' He gave a doleful sigh. 'As you say, a strange priest—for a strange time.' He studied Jacob through the thick lenses. 'But if he did—exist, what would you ask for, in addition to pardon for your sins?'

Jacob thought for a moment. 'Understanding, I suppose.'

'Ah!' The other man's face brightened. 'Understanding of what?'

'Life, death. My life … her's. It will all be over soon, and I should like to know what the point of it was—if it even had a point. I would like,' he continued, musing on the question, 'some revelation, some answer or insight into *why*.' He gave a rueful grimace. 'I seem to myself like a creature in one of my own tales, desperate for some unknown and invisible author to speak up at the end and cast light or meaning on what has happened—a moral or epigraph that would show the point of it all.'

Surprised and a little embarrassed at his own loquaciousness to a stranger, he cleared his throat and yet continued. 'For a moment, just a moment, to understand the meaning of life. And, above all, why someone as good as my Isabelle should have to suffer while evil men prosper.'

'Ah!' Lucien made a dismissive noise. 'The Job question! I should have stayed a farmer, like my father, and his father before him—got married, raised sons and daughters—something to warm my old age.' His face wrinkled in a half-resentful, half-regretful frown.

'Perhaps that is the answer—realising too late the life we ought to have lived.' Jacob thought for a moment. 'Not that it offers any kind of—what did you say—grace? It is simply more punishment.' The notion made him gloomy. 'I must be going.' He stood up.

'I enjoyed our little talk,' said Lucien, his amiable manner different from his surly reception. 'I would be glad to see you should you pass this way again.'

'Who knows? Goodbye, Father.'

'—Lucien. And I hope you receive it—your revelation.'

'Perhaps I already have. That life is pain and sorrow, without purpose.'

Lucien grimaced, his voice coming from behind the door as it closed. 'You will get no argument from me!'

HE WALKED BACK TOWARD the town, feeling increasingly warm inside the heavy robe in spite of the chill air. After a half-hour he stopped and took it off, continuing with it over his arm, swapping arms as he became tired. After walking another hour or so he stopped to look around, realising he had somehow wandered away from the main road and was now lost. Fatigued from all the walking, he stood on an intersection, his panted breaths frosting in the cold air.

'Are you alright, ducks?' called out a woman crossing the street.

'How far is it back to town?'

'Too far to walk! That's where I'm going. There's the bus stop. Why don't you sit down on the bench? You look done in, poor ghost. The bus will be here in a minute. Look! Here it comes now.

GETTING OFF THE BUS at the Boulevard, he heard the cathedral bells toll the hour and turned in that direction. Crossing the square, he suddenly felt cold and put the coat back on again. The early morning blueness had all but disappeared behind a bank of thick grey cloud. Spotting a bench, he sat down to catch his breath. It took him a moment to realise that he was sitting on the same bench where he and Jules Desjardins had sat and talked over thirty years before. Desjardins! Whatever happened to him? He tried to picture the man's face but couldn't, any more than he could picture the midwife's.

The birch trees bordering the square were almost bare of leaves, the branches stark and ghostly in the wintry air. Recovering his breath, he got up and made his way toward the cathedral steps. If someone had stopped him to ask why his steps took him in that direction, he couldn't have said why except, perhaps, to joke that he was following his feet.

Inside the cathedral doors he paused, taking in the hushed air. A few parishioners were kneeling before the altar. Deciding to light a candle in her memory—*after all, she lit so many for me*—he made his way to the side chapel nearest the stained-glass windows. He lit a candle and wondered whether to cross himself. He did so while murmuring her name. Tired from the long walk and feeling a touch lightheaded, he sat down in a pew.

He opened his eyes, surprised that he had fallen asleep. The candle had burned down to half its length. He sat there, breathing in the scent of smoke and incense. The light from the stained-glass windows cast a rainbow pattern across the pews. His eyes dwelt on the depiction of Gaston Tremblay discovering the site of the future settlement. *She loved that scene in particular.*

He heard music coming from the organ loft and looked up but couldn't see the organist. The notes of a song floated through the air as the organist practiced by playing a secular melody. He recognised the tune as that sung by the young woman in the square all those years before. '*I will never forget you …*' Tears came to his eyes as the notes evoked the plaintive words. Isabelle rose up before him as she showed off the window, her youthful face shining with happiness. A profound despair engulfed him at the memory, and he cried out in his agony. A beam of winter sunlight lanced through the stained glass, illuminating the motes in the air and briefly flooding the aisle with light. He wept freely and unashamedly—a new-born penitent, stricken with grief and sorrow as the memory of his beloved wife reached out in a balm of incense, candle wax, music and tinted light. '*I pray that you will one day, Jacob, experience the peace and holiness of God's grace.*' The music stopped and still he wept—for Isabelle, for himself, and for all that was and ever would be.

THE SKY HAD DARKENED considerably when he exited the cathedral. He made his way slowly homewards, knowing that Marie-Odile would be worried. Flakes of snow drifted through the air, and he shivered inside the heavy coat. He turned into Gaston Tremblay Square, intending to cut through it to rue Saint-Joseph. The snow had become heavier, swirling through the gloom. The square was semi-deserted, the few pedestrians hurrying home to supper and a warm fire. Ahead of him, the great bronze bull glowed in the dull light. Of a sudden, he felt a searing pain in his head and stopped, doubling over to catch his breath.

'Jacob!' He turned at the hail. Denis Vachon hurried across the square towards him. He was dressed in a heavy wool coat and a fur hat with ear mufflers. 'Are you alright? You look unwell?' Denis peered from beneath the hat, his face lined with concern,

'I'm alright.' He was unable to prevent another gasp as a blinding pain shot through his head.

'What is it? Shall I call you a cab?' Denis reached out to steady his old friend.

'No. I am on my way home. A cup of cocoa and a warm fire are the best medicine for headaches.'

'Headaches?' Denis frowned, his face changing as he recalled something. 'Your daughter told Yvette that you get these painful headaches.' He scowled. 'Damn that Gagnon!'

'Hugo?' Jacob blinked. 'What does he have to do with my headaches?'

Denis paused, his face sombre. 'It's time you knew.'

'Knew what?'

Denis sighed. 'It was Hugo that shot you all those years ago, in the woods. He kept it from you and made us do the same. Something I have long regretted.'

'What?' He gripped Denis's arm. 'What in God's name are you talking about?'

'It was Hugo's bullet that struck you down—when we found you in the woods.'

He stared, incredulous. '*Hugo* shot me?'

'Not on purpose, of course. He mistook you for a bear in that coat you were wearing—and are wearing now! What a coincidence.'

His mind reeling, he stared at Denis, unable to form thoughts.

'Are you sure I can't hail you a cab?'

'No,' He said his voice dazed, still shocked with the revelation. 'I'd rather walk.'

'I would accompany you,' Denis apologised. 'But I am on my way to pick up Yvette from her sister's. She finds it hard to get about nowadays.'

'I will be fine,' he insisted. 'I am going straight home. Goodbye.' He felt Denis' eyes follow him as he set off through the falling snow.

He made his way across the square, his mind stunned by what he had just learned on this day of astonishments. Rage at the enormity of Hugo's secret—nay, deception—roared like a furnace within him. *How could he lie to me all these years?* He walked blindly, blinking against the swirling snow his heart pounding, his breath coming in shallow pants as he tried to absorb the betrayal. A convoy of brewery wagons pulled by dray horses clopped across the square, their iron hooves ringing against the stone.

A sharp pain knifed through his chest, and he stopped beneath the bull's eyeless gaze, suddenly confused as to his whereabouts. His legs went from beneath him and next moment he was lying on the flagstones, the stones cold and hard against his head.

'Monsieur are you alright?' A bearded man was bent over him. Behind the man more people gathered around, their faces alarmed but curious in the falling snow. The sound of the dray wagons drew closer, the wheels rumbling across the stones and resounding like thunder in his ears. He struggled to breathe, feeling the wet flakes on his cheeks. He tried to speak, but could not, the words coming out in a confused mumble.

'What?' The bearded man inclined his ear. 'Who are you, Monsieur? What is your name?'

The sky—or perhaps it was something inside his eyes—seemed to flash in time to the thunderous noise in his head. And then he experienced a dazzling burst of clarity that freed his tongue to speak. 'My name,' he wheezed, his voice faint as the astonishing light began to fade, 'is Ghost Bear.'

New France concludes the fourth part of *Monuments of Grass*, a five-book series charting the creation story of one man's epic vision and its unfolding over time. The five books in the series are *Exile*, *The Fur Post*, *The Claim*, *New France*, and *Voyages of Discovery*. Print copies can be ordered online through bookstores, libraries, and online retailers such as Amazon. The series is also available in eBook format.